Gordon Thomas was a successful and bestselling writer of non-fiction in the 1970s before turning his pen to fiction. *Poisoned Sky* is his fifth David Morton novel, and the whole series is being developed for the wide screen.

His earlier career as a foreign correspondent specialising in intelligence and terrorism took him on assignments covering the Suez Crisis, the Six Day War, the Iran–Iraq War and the Tiananmen Square massacre.

He now lives in County Wicklow.

D0755204

POISONED SKY

■

GORDON THOMAS

WARNER BOOKS

A *Warner* Book

First published in Great Britain in 1996
by Little, Brown and Company

This edition published by Warner Books in 1996

A CIP catalogue record for this book
is available from the British Library.

ISBN 0 7515 1757 7

Typeset by Solidus (Bristol) Limited
Printed and bound in Great Britain by
Clays Ltd, St Ives plc

Warner Books
A Division of
Little, Brown and Company (UK)
Brettenham House
Lancaster Place
London WC2E 7EN

Special thanks go to Hilary Hale, for editing in the very best sense of the word – no writer could have asked for more; Greenpeace, who provided some of the inspiration and many of the answers; David Jensen, who ensured Air Force One moved from the drawing board of my imagination into a realistic aircraft for tomorrow; Ruth Boswell and Gregory Stewart, who, each in their own unmistakable way, provided a source support during the time of what became known as The Jordan Episode – this book would have been all the poorer if they had not helped to keep it on track; Zvi Spielmann, whose encouragement and friendship were simply invaluable and remain so; Noel Walsh, whose medical skills made so much possible; Dermot O'Leary, for wise counsel and unerring judgement; Sean Carberry, who lent far, far more than his name; John Chapman, an ally in all sorts of ways; Brinsley and Dorothy Hutson, for holding the fort in all sorts of unexpected ways; Al White, for keeping Morton in the frame; Carolyn Dempsey – she made the transition from my almost illegible handwriting to impeccable manuscript, and did so with a cheerful capacity for work that, at times, was awesome.

And to Edith, as always.

POISONED
SKY

ONE

In the safety of the tunnel Bodor pulled up the sleeve of his expensive grey jacket, seeking a vein for the cocaine to do its work. He tried not to hurry, having discovered that the longer he waited, the more pleasurable the effect.

His nose continued to identify smells: the damp, the mould from the mortar and, closer, the more pleasant one of mothballs, a reminder of how long since he'd worn the jacket. Its foreign cut once marked him as one-of-those-allowed-to-travel, a person at the pinnacle of his profession. He'd worn the jacket as an honoured guest of the Old Order in the Kremlin, and later of its successors who had briefly installed themselves in the Moscow White House.

Like so much else they had disappeared, vanished with the same swiftness as the cocaine would streak through his body. As a scientist he knew all its pharmacological pathways, and that this one shot would make him feel powerful again. Able to do anything. Just like the old days.

Then his very name – Sergei Mikhailovich Bodor – had been spoken with the awe befitting one of Soviet Communism's leading scientists: the youngest member of the Academy of Sciences, the holder of so many medals and prizes that he had needed a special room in his dacha to display them.

Now, in this dank and cold tunnel, he'd become a common thief.

The Arranger had said that at this hour there would be no one in the building. But, just in case, wear your best clothes. Russians still respected the way a person dressed.

Mostly, they liked to ape American habits: eat their hamburgers, gulp their soft drinks, wear their flashy clothes. Even the organised criminals called themselves the *mafiya*. He'd rejected the possibility that the Arranger worked for one of those gangs. But he worked for somebody. You could tell that by the way he'd organised matters. In one of the jacket pockets was Bodor's new Swedish passport with its exit visa, stamped customs declaration, a wad of American dollar bills and Kroner travellers cheques, together with an assortment of papers showing he was a resident of Stockholm – a city he had never visited. You needed to be part of a large organisation to arrange all that.

Although the Arranger spoke like a true Muscovite, and his manner suggested someone who had spent his time pushing paper in some obscure government department, it hadn't been in Moscow. He was as certain of that as he was that the Arranger was not a Russian.

Bodor inspected his arm carefully under the tunnel's lighting; the skin was pock-marked with needle tracks. He began to rapidly open and close his fingers to make the veins more prominent, allowing his thoughts to drift . . .

Bodor had started to inject himself after the Third Russian Revolution. People had this stupid habit of telling each other where they were that October night in 1993 when it started. Like those in the West who still insisted they knew what they were doing when the American President, Kennedy, was killed.

Even before the revolution he had not fooled himself he still had a future in Mother Russia. First Gorbachev, then Yeltsin, had weakened her sinews. The new New Order completed the process, leaving her too broken to make use of his latest weapon. You needed another Stalin for that.

The idea had come to him in what he now realised had been the last glorious year of Soviet Communism when he'd visited the United States and experienced a Los Angeles smog. For those two days in his downtown hotel he'd looked out on the result of reckless lack of control over pollution. In half a dozen other American cities he'd seen the same evidence of damage caused by car exhausts and industrial effluent. There had to be a way to exploit this militarily.

On the long flight back to Moscow he had jotted down his first ideas. Six months later they became formulae, based upon the behaviour of ozone in the upper stratosphere. He'd turned the formulae into blueprints. A year later he had a mock-up of an Ozone Layer Bomb. Prototypes were continually improved. Finally, no bigger than a conventional artillery shell, the OLB was shielded by a detection-free casing made from a new kind of plastic his chemists had created. Even its small nuclear trigger was undetectable.

For another year he conducted lab tests on cadavers. What he learned from the dead enabled him to conduct his own field test on the living. Using the unsuspecting crew of a Soviet bomber had needed the personal sanction of the Chief of Air Staff, thankfully a general with old-fashioned priorities. The pilot's last radio message said they were in an electrical storm — the ideal condition to test the OLB.

Nikita Vassiley's post-mortem examination revealed that the crew had all suffered massive haemorrhaging. By then he was himself in the terminal stages of AIDS and obsessed with which one of any of the dozens of infections his condition made him prone to would, in the end, kill him. It turned out to be pneumonia. Looking back, Vassiley's death was a precursor.

In the Kremlin there had developed a sickening mood of appeasement towards the West. Bodor's plea to be allowed to continue his work was coldly rejected. The New Order said it was essential to destroy anything that would threaten its plans. His secret research centre, like so many others, was bulldozed. Gone forever was the five years' work which he was convinced would have turned the balance of power once more in Russia's favour. All that had survived were his earlier blueprints. The hiding place he'd chosen for them would ensure their preservation.

That night he had injected himself for the first time. The cocaine gave him a new clarity. To work for any government again was to risk further disappointment. Political masters had their own agendas: he had been useful only as long as he served their purposes.

The next time he'd injected himself he had seen even more clearly the reality of his betrayal, only this time it had been accompanied by a whispering to be patient, to wait. That somewhere there was somebody who needed him, would know how to appreciate him. After the drug once more lost its effect, the fear that he was going mad touched him like a dark shadow. He read all he could find about cocaine-related experiences and realised this was a normal side-effect.

From then on he planned with meticulous care. He fed the rumour mills of Moscow with hints that he had been working on a revolutionary new weapon. The few details would have been sufficient to arouse curiosity, perhaps even scepticism. He wanted no one to be quite sure how far he had gone, or where he now was. News spread that he had left the country, destination unknown. That he had suffered a breakdown and was in some private hospital, location unknown. That he was dead, burial plot unknown. The mills did the rest, sowing confusion and uncertainty. Exactly what he intended.

In utmost secrecy he returned to the village of his birth far beyond the Urals. And waited. Regular injections reassured him that his patience would be rewarded. Then, as his supply dwindled and the prospect of a trip to Moscow to obtain replenishment daily came closer, the stranger had come to the door. The man had stood in the earth-floored kitchen and said it was good to be here at last. As if it was the most natural thing in the world, he added that people called him the Arranger. His face would have been pleasant if it weren't for his eyes. The two little black pebbles suggested a reptilian quality. But Bodor had immediately sensed he was dealing with someone of substance.

They had talked long into the night and, by dawn, it was clear the chemistry between them worked. They were both loners and contemptuous of the pack. Encouraged, he allowed his own anger at the New Order to boil over. The Arranger listened, his eyes heavy from red wine. Finally he explained how that justifiable rage could be turned into something worthwhile.

In the weeks that followed, they had dined in several of those discreet establishments created by the black market where money could buy anything. Afterwards, a different woman was always provided for him. It was a tribute to the Arranger's careful research that he understood Bodor's sexual requirements.

Yet, when the Arranger's first offer came, he was wary of accepting it too eagerly. In the deep-shadow world he had inhabited for so long, experience had enabled him to avoid all the many pitfalls which could have delayed promotion, sent him to a labour camp or an asylum for the sane into which many a colleague had disappeared. The Arranger returned with another offer. Bodor considered it coolly, and negotiated a further substantial increase. For the merest of moments it seemed as if old age had descended upon the Arranger, as if he could see the future. He had sat there, cradling his plum brandy, his eyes deep alleys of darkness.

'Everyone will be very pleased with your decision. Let me be the first to congratulate you,' the Arranger had said.

It had sounded like a benediction long prepared.

The Arranger had proved his credentials by paying a substantial sum into a new bank account opened for him in

Zurich. Enough to continue financing Bodor's drug habit.

Bodor looked over his shoulder towards the curve in the tunnel. Nothing. Even the rats had been hunted from here; nowadays the starving ate anything. The sound of his leather shoes on the concrete was loud in his ears. When he paused beneath another of the low-wattage bulbs set in the ceiling, there was nothing except the silence.

Reassured, he fished in his pocket for the sheathed needle and loaded syringe. His movements were cast in shadow against the tunnel wall. He looked at his watch. Two forty in the morning. The syringe shook in his hand. It was colder than he'd remembered in this repository for the unclaimed dead.

He and the Arranger had gone over the final plans, taking the Metro out across the Moscow River to the Lenin Hills. The walkways had teemed with *churki*, people of the swamp, as northern Russians invariably referred to those from the south.

The Arranger had delivered a final reminder. 'Make sure your packet is intact. If it has been tampered with, leave at once. If everything is in order, bring the packet with you. After that you will have nothing further to do. From then on everything will be done for you.'

Once more the Arranger had sounded as if what he said was not subject to the whims of fate.

Bodor shivered again. He could not wait any longer. Removing the sheath from the needle, he worked it into a vein and depressed the plunger.

In his mind's eye he could see the cocaine molecules surging through his bloodstream, sweeping over the cholinesterases, the plasma enzymes which were the first line of defence his immune system provided. Desperately trying to separate the invading molecules into tiny

physiological fragments for easier destruction, the cholinesterases would dissipate their own power, become
weakened and succumb. Even as he completed the injection, the molecules were racing into the right side of his
heart, through the lungs, and back into the network of
arterial veins. Already the pharmacological effect of the
drug was ringing all kinds of chemical alarms in his body
as the cocaine surged along the carotid arteries and burst
through the blood–brain barrier. He had ensured the shot
would be sufficiently large for that.

As he crushed the syringe under his shoe, the cocaine
began its pleasurable work. Circuits of nerve cells fell
under its spell. Part of his brain still tried to wage war
against the invaders. But the drug soon vanquished
everything it touched. Each victory created further excitement in his central nervous system. Once more he believed
everything was possible as he strode purposefully down the
tunnel to the elevator used to carry the bodies, and rode up
to the fourth floor.

Emerging into a short corridor, he paused. He began to
breathe deeply, forcing his mind to stop its racing.
Gradually the thoughts and feelings, which a moment ago
had been too swift for him to grasp, came under control.
It was all a matter of calculation. So much; no more. Just
enough to maintain this rapturous feeling.

He checked his watch again. On time. The Arranger
had said it was vital to keep to the timetable. At this
moment he would be driving into Kalnin Prospekt.

Bodor walked slowly down the corridor to the solid steel
door. From a pocket he fished a key, which hadn't left his
possession since his betrayal. He opened the door. The
ceiling strip-lights automatically came on and he blinked
to adjust to the brightness. The room was filled with metal
containers mounted on castors for easy movement, with a

temperature gauge and a number stencilled in red. The container he wanted was numbered 17. Its gauge was set, like all the others, at −190C. At that temperature all biological activity stopped.

He walked to the alcove where the protective clothing was kept. Dressed in a one-piece suit and his face shield secured, he looked like a firefighter about to tackle a chemical blaze. From a pegboard he selected a ratchet key and returned to the container. He inserted the key in the hole on the lid. There was a hiss of a vacuum seal being released and the lid swung silently upwards on canti-levered hinges.

A small cloud of liquid nitrogen engulfed him. When it cleared, he peered inside at the body bag heavily coated in ice on a metal tray. He used a gloved hand to press a button and the bag rose slowly under hydraulic power.

The bag was secured by frozen webbing. On each tie was a push button. He pressed them and the straps snapped open with a sound of breaking ice. He pulled a toggle on the bag, and it slowly unzipped itself.

The body of a naked young woman was visible, pale, the bright blue eyes covered with a film of frost that also encrusted her fair wavy hair. She looked as freshly dead as when he'd last opened her shroud.

From under her buttocks his hand extracted the envelope in its thick plastic covering. When he removed the packet and saw the seal was unbroken, he gave a low chuckle of relief. Placing the packet in his pocket, he returned the bag to its place.

After he had screwed down the lid he fetched one of the cylinders at the far end of the room and attached its nozzle to a valve on the side of the container. There was a sharp hiss as the container's liquid nitrogen was replenished. He returned the cylinder and replaced his protective clothing.

At the door he looked around one more time. There was no trace of his visit. He locked the door and pocketed the key again.

Bodor took the elevator back to the tunnel and reached the building's exit door. He looked at his watch. Two fifty-nine. He opened the door and climbed the stairs to the street. A moment later the Zhiguli turned a corner and pulled up.

'Successful?' asked the Arranger, opening the door for him. He had the soft voice of a lettered man.

'Yes.'

'Excellent.' The Arranger might have been pronouncing on the food at one of the restaurants where they'd dined.

The car drove on down the street.

From the entrance to a run-down pre-revolutionary building, a woman dressed like a *babushka* followed the tail lights with sharp eyes. It had been too dark to identify the driver. But there was no mistaking the passenger.

Sergei Mikhailovich Bodor.

Mischa Kalenkov smiled briefly to herself. She had never quite believed when everybody had said he was either dead, institutionalised or had fled the country. From the West they had come looking for him: the head-hunters with their promise-the-world contracts, the intelligence teams posing as businessmen. The Arabs, the Africans, the Asians. They had all come, and left empty-handed. Sergei Mikhailovich had vanished as if he had never existed. But she had never given up looking. Now here he was, coming out of a house of the dead in the middle of the night, and being driven away in a car which only the very rich or powerful used nowadays.

Where was Sergei Mikhailovich being taken? And by whom? And why? Clearly he was not the driver's prisoner.

Besides, the Federal Counterintelligence Service would have sent a team to arrest someone so important. The Zhiguli smacked of officialdom. Yet whose? Foreign diplomats used imported cars. The *mafiya* settled for Mercedes. But the Zhiguli was a car in which you could travel a long way in comfort. To the borders? There were a lot of those. Almost as many as her unanswered questions.

In the past, the mortuary attendant had contacted her about bodies which he thought to be interesting, none of which turned out to be the case. But she was a patient women and always paid him. This time he had called to say someone was using the place as a safe-deposit. He didn't know who, and he couldn't risk removing the packet from the container.

Since then she had come to keep watch here every night, having decided that whoever had hidden it would come and retrieve the packet after dark. Waiting, she had asked herself one more question: what could be so important to store in such a place?

Gathering herself, Mischa shuffled down the street, hugging her threadbare coat to her body. In her mind she began to compose the message she would sent to David Morton.

TWO

At mid-morning the President of the United States strode on to the lawn of the White House accompanied by a boy. It was a photo-call for television and newspaper photographers. The boy had won a national science competition.

The President was a sizeable man with the watchful look of someone who'd roughed it with life and managed to come out on top; most of his peers agreed he was probably the best living lawyer his profession had lost to politics.

He was fifty-seven years old and a widower these past five years. He had married a college sweetheart who had died in the middle of his first gubernatorial term. She'd gone alone on a fishing trip they had planned for months after he had had to cancel because of an unexpected court case. She had slipped on a rock and been swept away by a river in flood.

Their only son had been killed in the Gulf War.

A popular theory was that he had run for the Presidency partly as therapy for his grief. Certainly there had been a discernible sympathy vote in his landslide victory. Yet unlike his recent predecessors, he had no true, intimate confidant. No one close enough to share the vision he had begun to create in those nights when he could not sleep, when the past intruded. What he had produced was intended to be both a monument to his wife and boy and one that would literally change the world from which they had so cruelly been snatched.

'Mr President! Look this way!' a cameraman called.

The President obliged, shook the boy's hand one last time then, still smiling, walked back into the White House.

Alone in the Oval Office he hunched over his desk, once more studying the single sheet of paper that contained the distillation of months of diplomatic activity and weeks of personal telephone calls.

The paper contained the essentials of a plan for the leaders of the other great industrial nations to join him in spearheading a radical change in global policies towards the environment. This would include halting the devastating destruction of the rain forests, the ruthless resettlement of indigenous populations and all the other ecological threats.

The uniquely frustrating thing about them was that the solutions were obvious. But there was no denying that enacting them would require paradigm shifts in human behaviour – particularly in the field of co-operation between nation states.

When he had first formulated his idea, he had carefully briefed a handful of his most trusted advisors to privately approach the upper echelons of carefully chosen foreign governments for their support. They were initially rebuffed by incredulity, suspicion or arrogance. The French assumed the whole scheme was a cynical PR exercise for the President's domestic ratings, the Italians were distracted by a new corruption scandal, the British were preparing for another round of argument with their European partners. Several heads of state were too involved with their own perilous state of power to listen properly. Everyone advised the Americans that they were declaring open season on the Western leaders for every terrorist group in the world.

After the President learned of the initial reactions to his plan, he had taken personal control of the mission. Gradually, his sincerity and articulate belief in his cause persuaded the majority of those initially approached that they should be seen to be in concert with the President's strategy. While his lieutenants undertook co-ordinating the nightmarishly complicated logistics, the President concentrated on gathering in the remaining reluctant few. Aware that many of his fellow leaders needed to gain personal advantage from attaching themselves to his coat-tails he patiently listened, argued and reasoned, on occasion effectively pleading or losing his temper.

His message to them all was the same. 'What we can achieve between us literally has no precedents in human history. That is our challenge. Our legacy could be that we solved the single most important issue in contemporary human affairs.'

His plan called for them to fly with him around the world in the new presidential airliner. In the seven days they would journey together, they would try and persuade other nations to balance their own ecologies with that of industrial progress. Those of Africa and Asia, for example, would have to reduce their demands for luxury goods until they understood how to cope with the environmentally unfriendly waste those goods created.

Other nations which depended on fishing for their national economy would have to agree strict new limits to preserve the ecology of the sea. Oil-producing nations must put aside a percentage of the profit from each barrel to improve their own environments. The dumping of nuclear waste must be rethought, even if it meant that some countries would have to reduce their dependency on reactor-driven power. During those seven days, these and many other issues would be negotiated. The technology to achieve change was there. He had to make sure that there was also the will to use it.

At last these pleadings and manoeuvres had come to fruition and he was able to give this bold, imaginative plan a name: Operation Earth Saver.

It would begin in exactly three weeks.

Putting aside the paper, he wondered how Ignatius Bailey would respond. More than any government, including his own administration, the single most powerful tycoon in the world possessed the resources to ensure the success or failure of Earth Saver.

Beneath the luminous sky of East Anglia, bulbous shadows drifted over the ground. The fifty balloons were taking part in a race from England to Holland. Among the spectators was an overcoated figure. He had driven from London after arriving on the Moscow flight. Once the last of the balloons had cleared the coast, he called a number on an oil rig out in the North Sea from a pay-phone at the launch site. When the phone was answered, he counted off fifteen seconds under his breath, then hung up. The timed pause was to replace a need to confirm that the balloon he was interested in was safely on its way. From past experience he knew that at this early stage it was important to stress security.

He drove back to Heathrow, arriving in good time for his Munich flight. From there he would take another car journey to a very different sporting venue. The variety of his work was relished by the Arranger.

THREE

Inside the steel-walled chamber David Morton spun the hatch wheel to create a watertight seal. The air smelled faintly of lubricant and something else. All his training on how not to feel claustrophobic in the total darkness could not quite remove the fear. If you didn't feel it, you shouldn't be here. Only a fool told himself he was without a little fear at a moment like this.

Understanding fear was a lesson he had learned early in life, from that day when, still a child, he had seen his family killed in what had turned out to be the last of the Stalinist progroms in Russia. Later, a teenager, he and his younger sister Ruth were among the first the Kremlin had allowed to emigrate to Israel. There, newly qualified as a doctor and working in a children's hospital, Ruth had been killed by a terrorist bomb on the way home. That same year he had joined the Mossad. Five years later he became its Director of Operations. By then he knew more about fear than any man should. A year later, after some very discreet lobbying between Tel Aviv and Washington, he was seconded to the CIA. For another year he provided its agents with the benefit of his own experience, taking them into Iran, Iraq, and later Bosnia. For them, fear had continued to be a daily way of life. Along the way a grateful President of the United States had quietly bestowed on Morton American citizenship. Morton had accepted this was a precursor to the job he now held. To those few he ever allowed close to him, he would sometimes say that his background made him an ideal candidate for any passport that proclaimed him to be a citizen of the world.

His finger pressed the button sealed into the one-piece suit, and the lithium battery activated the thermal imager goggles. Switching to wide-angle gave his surrounds the appearance of a futuristic tomb.

There was something feline about him, a cat's still grey eyes and quick hand movements as he fitted the breathing mask over his nose and mouth. His fair hair and the clean angles of his face were already concealed under the moulded head cover. His clothing had taken Technical Services a year to devise.

Walter – Walter Bitburg, Hammer Force's Administrator – had blenched at the cost. He'd pulled out his pipe, the latest of his many props, and delivered another of his reminders for economy. With Walter there was always a way for him to try and put his axe to your tree.

Hammer Force – only Bitburg and the United Nations accountants called it by its formal title of the Hard Attack Multinational Megaresponsibility Emergency Response Force – had been formed by the United Nations after spectacular failures in a number of global trouble-spots as the first non-political international intelligence-gathering task force with a strike capacity. Morton had been appointed Operations Director because of the universal respect he commanded within all intelligence communities. He'd spelled out his conditions for accepting: his own choice of team and state-of-the-art equipment, together with the unchallenged right to answer to no one on operational details.

Morton's hands continued to check the pouches built into the suit's belt. Each contained one minute's compressed air. He felt to make sure the quick-release toggle hadn't worked loose on the thigh pocket. Inside was the Walther PPK/S with its seven-shot magazine. He wriggled his feet inside the boots, each with a fin at the heel for easier passage through water.

All the time he breathed slowly, the result of great self-discipline and much exercise. He was a man who showed no emotion, who would never be taken by surprise and who expected from everyone what he demanded of himself. And if someone was not part of the answer then they were part of the problem; that helped further to reduce the unexpected.

The rush of water flooding into the chamber still came without warning, surging through the opening where a moment before there was steel plate, driving him back against a wall. Submerged, he somehow managed to remain standing in the ruptured chamber, waiting for the pressure to equalise. Then he swam through the opening and began to propel himself towards the surface. He moved slowly, his passage marked by chains of bubbles escaping through the valve of his mouthpiece. When he glanced up, the imager showed the green becoming lighter. A moment later he gently broke the surface.

The water was choppy and shrouded with mist. He switched the imager to telephoto and scanned the shoreline. To his right there were hot spots. Trees. Beyond, cooler than the vegetation, were larger ones. Buildings.

Morton began to swim towards the shore, frequently pausing, investigating and assessing. Close-in, he lay face down in the water, his body inert like a log. Long ago he'd learned all the rules for survival. There was a simplicity about them, of falling back ultimately on what his own body could provide, which went to the very core of who and what he was.

Touching sand, he moved with swiftness and silence

into the undergrowth. Unfastening his breathing mask, he switched the imager back to wide-angle and removed the pistol from its pocket. Once more he weighed the Walther in his hand, feeling the small spur on the bottom of the magazine. His usual Luger didn't have that. The spur was supposed to make aiming better.

Gun in hand, Morton began to move through the undergrowth. Moving and stopping. Then moving again. Reaching the first building, he scanned it with the thermal-imager. Cold.

The street appeared deserted. But different from the last time. There was a gap where the church had been and the school seemed closer than he remembered it. Or maybe it was a trick of the mist. Further down the street it clung with the density of fog.

He continued to take his time. Everything seemed to recede in his mind as he stood perfectly still, listening and focusing down, absorbing information with his eyes and nose.

They would appear soon. Each time he'd have one chance, no more.

Despite his anticipation, the first one took him by surprise, rising swiftly from behind a dustbin. The figure wore a flak-jacket and balaclava. His hands were coming out of his pockets. Only a split second to decide. The gun suddenly in the man's hands settled matters.

In one smooth, co-ordinated movement Morton crouched, aligned both sights and fired twice. Part of his brain registered that the shots were so close that they sounded like one. The figure spun under the impact of the bullets. He heard the Walther's cartridge cases pinging as they ejected on the ground. By then he was already moving forward, sweeping both sides of the street in a continuous arc, arms straight, gun loosely held.

He'd passed the clinic, marked by a lit red cross, when its door banged open. A second figure, Uzi at the hip, emerged. She wore a blouse and short skirt and matching green high heels. He'd be asked about the colour later. Asked all sorts of questions. He spun and fired three times into her body. The shots once more were almost inseparable.

Five gone. Two to go.

He moved on down the street, half-turning then turning back again, always moving, his breathing quicker now.

Across the street a window slammed upwards. He hurled himself to his left, the kerbside catching his hip. There was a hiss as the last of the pockets of compressed air ruptured.

Still rolling, he brought the gun into the aim, eyes urgently trying through the swirling fog to make out the figure in the window. The pad of the first joint of his index finger began to tighten on the trigger. And stopped. A child's face in the sight.

Morton rose quickly. As he crouched and backed, two more gunmen rose out of manholes. Young, dead faces. Hand guns. He fired twice, catching both in the chest.

Suddenly, overwhelmingly, they came at him from rooftops, doorways.

His arms dropped, still holding the empty Walther in a two-handed grip. Four kills in seven shots. He began to walk down the street, ignoring the silent figures.

From somewhere above the buildings a loudspeaker crackled. 'Same score as last time.'

Big Mike was stingy with praise, a soldier's soldier. He was up in the control room from where the targets were controlled, studying the computer print-out.

'I shouldn't have used three on her, Mike.'

'She had an Uzi. Better be certain than sorry.'

The amplified grunt made Morton smile. 'For the record she was wearing green shoes. And the kid in the window was a girl.'

A moment later Big Mike appeared from one of the doorways at the far end of the street. Even from that distance he looked a small giant, dressed in fatigues and combat boots. People half-joked he slept in them. Every six months all operational personnel came down here to sharpen their skills under his watchful eye.

There was the sound of whirring machinery returning the target silhouettes to their lairs as Morton walked towards him.

He'd found Big Mike at the tail end of the Gulf War and brought him here to this cavernous basement in Hammer Force headquarters. The building had once housed Switzerland's gold reserves. Situated on the north, less fashionable side of Lake Geneva, its two hectares were protected by the most sophisticated electronic perimeter Big Mike could devise. Afterwards Morton had told him he could spend what else was needed. Big Mike took him at his word, on the same theory Catholics like to glorify their churches.

The result was the world's most advanced indoor combat range. The length of a football pitch, it could produce sandstorms, blizzards, a flash flood or a street riot. The chamber from which Morton had emerged was the escape hatch from a Polaris. That it had cost a quarter of a million dollars to buy and install hadn't lost Big Mike a moment's sleep.

'How'd the suit behave?' Big Mike asked.

'It worked fine.'

'Good. I'll put in an order for a dozen. Might as well get the underwater people in Covert Action used to them. And the Walther?'

Morton balanced the gun in one hand. 'For me, it's too light.'

'The Armourer's going to be disappointed. He could have gotten a good deal with his old firm.'

Morton almost smiled. 'Don't let Walter hear that. He's about to start his quarterly economy drive.'

Big Mike looked around proudly. 'You should send him down here. I'd show him what value for money really is.' He pointed to a realistic rockface on the far side of the training area, festooned with pitons and abseil ropes. 'I'd like to put in one of the new ice-makers so that halfway up somebody suddenly finds himself in the Arctic. That's bound to concentrate the mind.'

Morton shook his head. 'Better wait until Walter's balanced his books.'

Big Mike emitted a sound like a wrestler's grunt. 'There's no mileage in cutting back on basics. You know that.'

'For sure. But still hold it for next quarter.'

Above them the blowers in the roof were sucking up the last of the artificial fog when the loudspeaker crackled. 'David, if you're still down there, I need to speak to you.'

The amplification made Danny Nagier's voice sound more gravelly than usual.

Danny had served with Morton longer than anyone else in Hammer Force, in all those places where alleys have no names and death comes in multiple forms. Danny ran Communications.

'You can use my mobile,' Big Mike offered, fishing the phone out of a jacket pocket.

Morton punched Danny's extension number as the instructor continued up the street, checking that the targets were all back in hiding.

'What gives, Danny?'

'Mischa's come up with a sighting of Bodor. She wants a meeting with you in Cracow as soon as possible.'

For a year now rumours had filtered out of Russia that the acknowledged *Wunderkind* of Soviet military science had been working on something special before the system collapsed. Several Western intelligence agencies had tried to find him. All they'd come up with was where Bodor had once worked – now a pile of rubble on the far side of the Urals.

Everyone had said Bodor didn't matter any more: Mother Russia was no longer a player in the Big Stick League.

'Why Cracow?' Danny asked.

'Auschwitz. She makes a pilgrimage once a year.'

Danny had momentarily forgotten. 'She's leaving Moscow on the afternoon train,' he said.

'I'll meet her at the main gate,' Morton said.

Mischa hated flying. But she remained his best field-mouse and continued to work for him for all the right reasons because from the beginning she had understood precisely what he needed from her.

Morton walked slowly to the changing rooms. Though he spent an unusually long time under the steam shower he could not purge the chilly feel that if Bodor was alive, so was his weapon.

FOUR

For a fleeting moment George Manders shook his head, relieved. This wind gusting over the vast open expanse of the Fens of East Anglia would dissipate any residue of the nerve agent.

Beyond the hole in the cyclone fence, five bodies lay on the ground, their faces suffused and contorted. Pringle, the MoD pathologist, had insisted they could not be removed until he'd completed his post-mortem on the sixth body. He was doing so in the tent he'd brought from Porton Down, the Chemical Warfare Establishment.

Tall and wide-shouldered, hair brushed back so smoothly it resembled a grey helmet which curled regally around Manders' expensive collar, his was a face to grace a coin. George Manders was head of E Division, the anti-terrorist unit of MI5.

He continued to face into the wind, looking beyond the corpses, concentrating on the mounds. They looked as if a giant mole had thrown them up. The humps – bunkers – were bigger than he had thought, the height of a bungalow. During the helicopter flight from London he'd read the security specifications: fence reinforced with a high voltage cable; ground sensors linked to a monitoring station; bunkers made from yard-thick reinforced concrete; doors resistant against sufficient Semtex to topple an office block; lock combinations changed every twelve hours.

Yet one of those doors had been opened. Not forced. Just opened.

The soldiers in the monitor station swore they had seen nothing suspicious. By the time they realised there could be a problem, it had taken another couple of minutes to get the back-up squad moving. Three minutes more to reach the burgled bunker and discover that the nuclear trigger mechanisms had been stolen.

Manders now knew each could be fitted to a bomb no larger than the shell that had killed his grandfather in a trench in Flanders. Only with this mechanism, the shell would have wiped out the entire front line. Six triggers were missing.

Who wanted to launch his own version of Armageddon? The person who had daubed 'Greenpeace' on the inside of the bunker door? There were some pretty wild characters nowadays in all the environmental movements. But not *this* wild. And they'd hardly need the triggers to bomb a furrier or a cosmetic company using animals for research.

The Blessed Nancy had chipped in with her pennyworth. His director had delivered herself over the radio as the chopper headed towards Norfolk. 'You will need to take this on board, George. Science and Technology reckon at least one of the thieves had a high degree of expertise. The triggers were anchored to explosive bolts which should have killed everybody who went into the bunker.'

Except that they hadn't.

Had the boys from across the Irish Sea gone freelance now that peace had come to the bogs? Possible. One of the European groups? The new German Red Brigades were peopled with out-of-work Stasi who would know one end of a nuclear trigger from another. The Italians had found room for the best of the Hezbollah bombers now that Beirut was quiet. The French underworld had started to recruit SAS mavericks. The Japanese? The Muslim fundamentalists? Even Africa's new dictators in need of a little extra protection?

The choice was daunting.

The only certainty was that this was terrorism to order. Somebody had sent in a team with a shopping list: six trigger mechanisms. Someone like that would have thought it through from beginning to end.

Manders sighed and turned back to watch the activity. Already the area was taking on an air of permanency. A helicopter pad had been marked out. Army Special Investigation Branch teams were scouring the immediate area. Further out, local police had set up road blocks. You had to go through the motions. The decon squad were stripping off their protective clothing, a further sign that the area was safe. Time to go and see Pringle.

Manders reached the tent, pulled the flap and entered.

A portable autopsy table stood in the centre of the area, lit by two powerful lamps on stands. Between them were trolleys of equipment. The air smelled faintly of blood.

The pathologist was small and tubby and almost completely bald. Pringle looked at the world from behind wire-rimmed glasses with the air of someone who probably was good at dissecting in school. His two assistants towered over him. Tall and thin, both women had eyes devoid of expression.

Pringle waved a rubberised hand. 'Come on over. He's safe enough.'

The soldier lay naked and face upwards on the table, torso cut from neck to crotch and the top of his skull hinged back. The man's brain, along with his lungs, liver, stomach and kidneys, were in large stainless steel basins clipped to one side of the table.

'You find out what killed him?' Manders asked.

'Soman.' The pathologist chuckled. 'Chemical name

methyplinacolyloxyfluorophoshineoxide. Expect you won't want to say that too often.'

Manders smiled, his expression more imperious than friendly. 'Tell me about Soman.'

Pringle turned to one of the assistants. 'Sara, his liver. Could you do the necessary?'

The woman produced a glutinous black-red organ from a basin and placed it on a dissecting board on one of the trolleys.

'You'll need to come a little closer to get a good sniff,' said Pringle.

Manders stepped up to the trolley. The assistant took a scalpel and sliced away a section of liver. She pierced the piece with the tip of the knife and held it towards Manders.

'Slightly fruity, isn't it? A bit like over-ripe peaches. Pleasant enough, if that's the last thing you're going to smell in this world,' Pringle said.

The assistant replaced the slice on the board.

Pringle glanced at the woman. 'All right, you two. Might as well practise your needlework.'

They began at opposite ends to sew the torso's cavity while Pringle continued addressing Manders.

'Soman is something we have to thank the Germans for. They came up with it in the last months of the war. Hitler wanted a nerve agent to stop our push into the Third Reich. His chemists tried it out in Auschwitz. Killed a thousand prisoners in half the time the regular gas did. Poor devils must have thought they were close to some hidden orchard. Thankfully, before it could be mass produced, we'd over-run their chemical plants.'

Manders nodded. 'Who makes the stuff now?'

Behind him the assistants had started to sing softly in harmony.

'It's strictly on the banned list. The Soviets had a stockpile. Probably enough to poison the other half of the world.'

Manders shifted slightly so as not to see one of the assistants shoving the soldier's brain back into its cavity.

'They say they destroyed all the stuff. But how do you prove that?' Pringle asked. He paused to watch the women working at the table before turning back to Manders. 'It's the one thing I could never quite master. A neat double-stitch.' He shrugged. 'If you're looking for a likely supplier, try Baghdad.'

Manders was silent. With the triggers, Saddam could turn Israel into a graveyard. 'Any clue how the stuff was used in this case?' he asked.

'From the state of the victims' lungs, almost certainly an aerosol. Wouldn't have to be big. Soman's invisible. And quick. They'd all be dead by the time they hit the ground.'

'How d'you deliver the stuff without killing yourself first?'

Pringle shrugged. 'I imagine you can pick up protective suits at any half-decent army surplus store.'

The tent flap opened and a soldier stuck his head in. He said to Manders, 'There's a call for you on the chopper radio, sir. It's Downing Street.'

'To be wanted,' said Pringle. 'Even by our illustrious Prime Minister.'

As Manders left, the pathologist began to harmonise in a pleasant baritone with the assistants. But he had noticed the contempt in Pringle's voice at mention of the Prime Minister.

Striding towards the helicopter, Manders saw the search teams working steadily backwards from the fence. Some were using metal detectors. He could sense their lack of enthusiasm; morale had never been lower throughout what remained of the armed services. The cause was the man he was on his way to speak to: the Right Honourable Arnold Bostock, Prime Minister and First Lord of the Treasury.

Arnold Percival Bostock's first act in office had been to scale down all three services to unprecedented levels. Times had changed, he declared in the rich confident tone that was his hallmark. The last of the great regiments had been cannibalised; the navy reduced to a size comfortably able to berth between the Isle of Wight and Portsmouth. The air force was now hardly bigger than that of an African state.

By then the political map of Britain was dramatically changed. It began when a Labour government collapsed after a failure to grasp the nettle of the new-style Marxists once more bedevilling the party. The Conservatives fared no better back in office. Labour returned to power.

During those upheavals Bostock resigned the Tory whip. His speech to the House was measured and magisterial; on both sides of the Dispatch Box there was a clinging to policies long past their sell-by date. The electorate was being poorly served by Members who were self-servers. Then, timing his pause to perfection, he revealed his intention to set up a new party. Ignoring the tumult, he calmly walked out of the chamber — and many predicted it would be the last they would see of him there. But a handful of wealthy, disaffected Conservatives had provided funding for the United Party. Following another Labour collapse, the Tories returned with a modest majority. The United Party had not won a seat. His former colleagues spoke of Bostock in the past tense. When they spoke of him.

Only months back in office, scandal once more engulfed the government. A parliamentary private secretary was discovered to have made a personal fortune from insider dealing in privatised utility shares. A junior minister's body was discovered among the victims of a fire in a Soho hard-porn cinema. Then came the revelation that two senior cabinet ministers had lied to the House over the government's borrowing requirements. A shattered Prime Minister, himself a decent man, having failed to convince the nation that Conservatism held the moral high ground, called another election. Labour returned to govern. But, over a year, its tiny mandate was reduced by death and the failure to hold marginal seats. Labour called yet another election.

United Party candidates were fielded in every constituency. Bostock was everywhere. His stump speeches led the news bulletins. At first his opponents tried to ignore him. Then dismiss him. And finally, when it was too late, to fight him. They only managed to appear even more tired and defeated. The United Party obtained an overall majority of ninety-three seats. There had been nothing like it in British politics.

Touching a populist chord, the new Prime Minister promised to put the Great back into Britain. There was something for everybody. A back-to-Church crusade. A marriage-is-sacred campaign. Early legislation for a ten-year mandatory sentence for anyone convicted of robbery with violence, or rape. Drug-pushers faced a similar fate. Offenders served their sentences in prison ships moored off-shore. His insistence that a little sea-sickness would do them good had, for a while, become a catch-phrase. And a nation increasingly intimidated by decades of violence had said: why not? Everything else had been tried.

But the greatest welcome was for his promise to reduce the country's dependence on nuclear power. It was not only increasingly expensive, but there had been several potentially serious accidents at the plants. Bostock promised to explore the use of wind power and harness the surge of the sea. Exploit the potential of organic waste. Reforest. Use every available form of renewable energy that was harmless.

The environmentalists were ecstatic. There was fervent talk of Britain becoming the new Green Jerusalem. And a ready acceptance to pay for this would mean cuts elsewhere in public expenditure. Beginning with cuts in the armed services, in Britain's NATO commitment, in its contribution to the UN coffers, in overseas aid, in all those areas where previous governments had spent so lavishly.

But the bold environmental vision still largely remained a dream. Only a handful of windmills produced enough power to meet the needs of a small town. There was not a single working scheme to harness tidal energy. Pollution remained rampant. Britain's beaches remained the dirtiest in Europe. Its motor vehicles generated more dangerous hydrocarbons than anywhere outside Russia.

Recently the environmentalists had begun to challenge Bostock publicly.

Manders was still pondering whether some of them could be responsible for the thefts as he climbed into the helicopter to take the call from Downing Street. He picked up the handset and identified himself.

A moment later came the faint click indicating the link was now secure, then the Prime Minister was on the line.

'What's happening down there, Manders?' The scrambler gave a slight echo to the Prime Minister's voice.

Manders told him, speaking in the precise English of the military classes.

'So you have nobody in the frame yet?' There was a sharpness to the words.

'Not yet, Prime Minister, no.'

Overhead the wind whistled through the rotor blades.

'Look, man,' Bostock said at last, using the word 'man' in an old-fashioned, high-born way. 'We can't allow whoever took these devices to run around unchallenged.' The Prime Minister was silent as if waiting for confirmation.

'No, of course not, Prime Minister. But it's early days yet.'

Through the cabin window Manders watched the soldiers moving out across the fields. He felt a small surge of anxiety in his stomach. Could the stolen triggers be the first step towards the unthinkable? A backlash by those who had suffered most under Bostock's cutbacks: a group of soldiers turned terrorists? Absurd, absolutely bloody absurd. This was still Britain, not a banana republic.

'You don't have days, Manders. If it's any help, the Secretary of Defence thinks whoever took the devices intends to export them.'

Manders forced himself to remain polite. 'It's a possibility, certainly.'

By now Bostock would have taken soundings from his Inner Circle. Every Prime Minister had one. 'Then you're going to need some help.'

Manders sensed that Bostock was trying to press agreement from him before he knew what exactly he was being asked to agree to.

'What have you in mind, Prime Minister?'

When Bostock spoke again it was as if he had not much time left. 'Hammer Force. Let them handle things. That's what they're there for. We all think it makes a great deal of sense.'

Manders made no attempt to challenge the idea. This had to be connected with the rumour he'd heard last night in Whitehall: that Bostock was working on something to win back the environmentalists, so he wouldn't want any domestic ruffling of their feathers. And there was bound to be some of that once things got under way. That could draw anger towards Bostock. So better let an outsider take the heat.

'This way, Manders, you don't have to carry the whole burden. If Hammer Force succeed, you'll still get credit, I'll see to that. But let them do the running. You can still play your part. But no need to lead from the front.'

Manders glanced out of the window. A group of searchers were disappearing into a stand of trees. Long ago he had learned that investigations, like battles, are never won, only lost.

In the mountain fastness of Sardinia, in a house which seemed to reach out to the edge of the world, a dark-skinned man, a Sard with thinning black hair that constantly fell over his eyes, causing him to flick his head in a nervous manner, went about the last of his preparations.

Since he had arrived, he had stacked logs beside the fireplace and filled the larder with food. Now he made up the last of three beds. As he worked, he hummed to himself, a contented man who knew his place in the world.

Bedmaking completed, he descended the wooden stairs to the ground floor. There were stains on the flagstones but you couldn't tell what had caused them. Nevertheless, he repositioned the living room's large goatskin rug to hide the marks.

He looked out of the window. The rocks pressed in with an unbearable weight. In the hour he had been there, the wind had risen to rattle the windows and roof tiles. The sound was like the maundering of something evil. It would snow soon.

Closing the front door behind him, he did not bother to lock it. He knew the house was so well concealed that no visitor would stumble across it and no islander would dare come here.

The house existed for one purpose only.

FIVE

On the flight from Warsaw Morton sat next to an old woman wrapped in shawls who continuously fingered her rosary beads with the fervour of someone for whom the rules of life had been laid down before she was born. He thought again how lives, like cardboard, fold so reliably along certain lines.

In his own work a person hid his habits and was vague in conversation about his responsibilities, drawing strength from concealment, taking pride in obscurity. Someone had written that it must be like living permanently inside a confessional. An outsider's description, for sure, and it took no account of the healthy scepticism that went with the job. Or the doubts which whispered at you like conscience. Not that you needed much of that. Intelligence work wasn't a vocation – yet it was often as mysterious as the elements of the eucharist. And, like the priesthood, you developed an understanding which allowed you to sit here in a cramped seat listening to an old women mumbling her rosary.

He saw that the flight attendant, blonde and strong-jawed, was staring at him speculatively. Another of those sexually predatory females who nowadays prowled the aisles of eastern Europe's airlines. They seemed to be inspired by a kind of air piracy, regarding it as another victory to take any male foreigner hostage. Once more she began to patrol, checking that safety belts were fastened for landing, and paused beside Morton's seat.

'You make business in Cracow?' She spoke in German, in a superior, knowing, way.

'No. Holiday.' He lied in English.

'In Cracow? In winter?' She pretended to be appalled, her English the precise intonation of the airline's training school. 'This time of year, there is nothing to see. It is best to stay indoors. To stay warm with a little vodka.'

'This time of year the churches are empty of tourists.' He continued to speak in English.

The old woman looked away quickly, as if the strange language scared her.

'Churches?' echoed the flight attendant, her smile starting to fade. 'You come to Cracow to visit churches?'

Morton lifted his head and his eyes turned full on her. 'Churches. Icons. Altars. Tombs and gravestones,' he recited cheerfully.

'You are serious?' The smile had all but gone.

'Oh yes. Very.'

She looked down the cabin, not quite able to hide the disappointment. 'I don't believe you,' she said, pouting, making one last effort.

'It's true.'

'You are a priest?'

Morton's smile was just enough to make her feel she was right. We are born and we die. And somewhere along the line, some of us learn the art of making someone believe what we want by the merest of gestures.

'Have a good visit, Pater.' She continued her patrolling, her misfired encounter making her brusquely order another passenger to straighten his seat-back.

Morton closed his eyes and continued to place Mischa's message in the context of what he now knew about Bodor.

Psychological Assessment's profile went some way to explaining the man behind the scientist. A personality driven by distrust and endurance. Computer Graphics had displayed their matchless skills. Working with a passport photograph US Immigration had copied when Bodor visited the States, its technicians used their screens to age Bodor to how he could look now: whittling down his face, giving more breadth to his flared nose and sinking a little deeper his eyes which were almost simian. His hair would be touched with an early frost, his skin the texture of alligator.

Lester Finel had fed his computers with all the known rumours about what Bodor was supposed to have been working on. They came down to one. Something to do with controlling atmosphere. Chantal – Chantal Bouquet who ran Foreign Intelligence – summarised the assessments from the CIA, MI6, BND and the French DGSE. No one had produced as much as a sketch of what Bodor might have been developing.

Over the cabin speaker system the flight attendant said they would be landing shortly.

The air inside the arrivals hall smelled sour and damp; it reminded Morton of chilled cabbage-water as he strode across the concourse. Even though he was bare-headed, he was taller than most of the fur-hatted figures.

The strip of carpet in front of the car rental desk was the grey of dead mackerel and spotted with mildew. The clerk was pale, with a moustache like a used toothbrush. He studied Morton with more than resentment, something that went beyond nationality and echoed back across the centuries, some gene-encoded memory of the time the first invaders had swept down out of the steppes.

'Your name?' he demanded.

'Morton.'

The clerk checked a list and looked up. 'You are late. Your plane was due over an hour ago.'

'We were late leaving Warsaw.'

'We do not reserve a car one hour past pick-up time.'
Like many tyrants, the clerk was physically small.

'I'll take what else is available.' It didn't really matter.

'How will you pay?'

'Cash.' Never leave a paper trail.

'You wish extra insurance?'

'No.'

'The roads are dangerous.'

'I'll be fine.' You didn't need death benefit in his
business.

'The car we have is more expensive than the one you
reserved.'

'Fine.'

The clerk stared across the counter, then set about the
paperwork with an urgency, as if he had suddenly seen
something in those eyes which had not been there before.

Thirty minutes later Morton found himself driving the
length of another run-down Cracow street, the windows of
its store fronts and tenements dulled by grime, the
brickwork permanently darkened from the years when the
city ran on coal. Clouds, grey and lifeless as scrap metal,
warned of more snow.

His hands moved in a harmony of gear changes, as if he
had once been a rally driver, as he headed west, passing
through several villages, each so small that, by the time he
reduced speed, he was back in open country again. The
road narrowed and he was forced to slow for farm traffic:
huge men in padded jackets perched high on carts pulled
by massive dray horses emerging from barns whose roofs
sagged as if from centuries of oppression. The grey mantle
broke for a pale sun to appear as he entered a small town.

There was nothing to show as he drove down its main
street that it was branded forever with its own mark of

Cain – as were all the other streets here. Until the end of time this place would be remembered by the name it bore: Auschwitz.

Morton stopped to allow a gaggle of schoolchildren to cross. They looked at his car, suddenly silent and watchful, resenting him as another intruder. He drove past the railway station refurbished with new brick; once it had been the hub of the single most important junction in the Final Solution.

Beyond the town limits he turned on to a lane. The snow was falling as big, heavy flakes, settling on the freezing ground as if somehow by covering it, they could hide for a short time what had happened at the end of the lane. He drove slowly out of respect. Through the gloom appeared brick- and slate-roofed buildings on either side of a central tower with an arched opening. The Gate of Death which led into Auschwitz.

Parking where the lane intersected a rail track, he walked on to the line and scuffed snow from a sleeper. The wood had worn well, despite the years when there had been endless traffic. The iron ties still clamped the sleepers to the rails. For a moment he stood, thinking there was something more subtly evil about this permanent way than all the butchery which had taken place inside the gate.

'David. I'm over here.'

He turned and there, standing inside the arch, was Mischa. Small, buttoned up in a long topcoat that came down below the uppers of her boots, hair concealed beneath a fur cap, she was a woman in her sixties with a thin face and marmoset eyes filled with a bright intelligence.

'Hullo,' he said in Russian, kissing her quickly on both cheeks. 'A good journey?'

'I've had better.' A hardy humour lit her brown eyes.

For a moment they stood looking towards the gate.

'Come,' Mischa said abruptly. 'We can talk as we walk. And I think we should speak English. Many of the guards understand Russian.'

'There are guards here?' he asked in English.

'Poles. They wear black, just like the SS did. Officially they are here to protect the place.'

'Against what?' The surprise remained in his voice.

She looked at him quickly. 'Thieves. They come here with metal detectors at night and they go to the ash pits. Some of the Jews, just before they went into the gas chambers, knew what was going to happen and swallowed their jewels so as not to let them fall into the hands of the Nazis.' She spoke quietly and completely without emotion.

They reached the infamous ramp where Mengele had made his selections: he had been a kind of gatekeeper between the worlds of the dead and the living. Morton had read somewhere they'd come at the rate of a thousand an hour. In two months, in 1944, almost half a million had been gassed, so many that even the usually efficient crematoria could not cope.

Mischa clutched the handle of her travel bag very tightly. The way, Morton thought, she must have clung to someone's hand when her train rolled in here. She stood for a moment longer, as if in private contemplation. When she spoke, it was almost unwillingly. 'You know what I remember most, David? It was the engine whistle. That was the most frightening sound of all.'

Morton said nothing. Long ago he had learned to know when words were needed and when silence was better.

The snow swirled around them as Mischa led the way off the ramp.

They walked in silence past the huts where the victims

had waited, and the crematoria whose ovens still bore the name of the Erfurt manufacturers, and in and out of rooms filled with human hair and artificial human limbs. When they reached a room heaped with suitcases, Mischa spoke again.

'The Nazis said each of us must fill our case with our most treasured possessions. A lot of people filled theirs with gold sovereigns and precious stones. I just brought clothes.'

Her words, measured and toneless, had the inevitability of catharsis. As she was speaking he drew a pace closer as if he wanted to shield her from further pain.

'Does this help you, Mischa, coming here?' Morton asked softly.

She looked up at him. 'Oh, yes. It makes everything I do seem so much more worthwhile.'

As they approached another hut, a guard emerged, stared briefly at them, then tramped away, his boots leaving a trail which the snow immediately began to obliterate. They entered the building. The low-ceilinged room was lined with shelves neatly stacked with empty tins.

'In each tin were enough poison crystals to kill a thousand people, David. I keep on imagining the impatience of the guards who poured the crystals into the gas chambers. As if they were in a hurry to get home and have tea. Play with their children. Behave like anyone else. How could they do that?'

'I think we will both ask that question until the end of our lives. And we will never get a full answer, because there probably isn't one to be fully understood,' Morton said.

He had read numerous attempts to rationalise the psychology of genocide. None had ever begun to convince him, and their ideas took on an additional layer of blasphemy in this room. There was something *banal* about these rusty tins, a reminder that the most ordinary of people can perform the most evil of acts.

After a while Mischa stirred beside him. 'Every time I ask myself, were they *beasts* when they did what they did? Or were they *human beings*?'

Of this he had no doubt. 'What they did was demonic, but they were not demons. That's what makes it so hard to understand; that they were *human*.'

She crossed her arms, as if hugging herself. Once more he knew it was important for her to simply stand here and know she was a living witness to this.

When they went outside, the snow was easing. She brushed flakes off her coat, the reflex action of a woman imposing order on her own emotions.

'So, Bodor,' she said finally.

'Let's start with what you saw in Moscow,' Morton suggested, 'when Bodor came out of the mortuary.'

They began to walk down a roadway lined with a row of crumbling watchtowers. While Mischa spoke, Morton listened without interruption. Then he produced from his pocket a copy of the photograph Computer Graphics had produced.

She studied it for a while. 'It's very close. He's, if anything, a little thinner in the face now.'

'The packet. Anything new on that?'

She shook her head. 'Nothing, David. But you want my guess? That packet could be to do with some weapon Bodor's been working on. Drawings, maybe. Data. That sort of thing.'

'What happened to Bodor's staff?'

Mischa shrugged. 'He'd disappeared, of course, before his research complex was bulldozed, but they were rounded up and taken to one of those holding camps out on the steppes while the New Order decided what to do. Most were released to work on non-military projects. They ended up in hospital labs, doing blood analyses or checking sputum counts. That sort of thing. A few managed to slip out of the country. It's anybody's guess where they went to.'

He asked, with the dispassion of an archaeologist reimagining a long-dead creature from shards of bone, what work they had done for Bodor.

'There's no way of telling. Some were climatologists. There was the usual spectrum of physicists and chemists. Plus a pathologist, Nikita Vassiley, who'd worked with Bodor from the beginning. How he fitted into things is anybody's guess. But having someone of Vassiley's status on the team meant that Bodor had to be working on something very important. Vassiley had worked on the cosmonaut programme.'

'Where is he now?'

'Dead. HIV positive. The matter was hushed up at the time. Nobody wanted to admit how rife the problem was: AIDS was a Western disease. Now, of course, we know differently,' Mischa said bleakly.

'What was Vassiley doing in the space programme?'

'I tried to find out. But all that stuff's gone the way of Bodor's research. At a guess I'd say Vassiley was working on the effects of space on the human system.'

Morton looked down at her, following the logic. From one of the watchtowers a small landslide of snow slid from the roof as he continued to question. 'What about the car you saw? Do we know where it took Bodor?'

'To Moscow Central Station. From there, Bodor took the Red Express to St Petersburg. The night sleeper is booked solid several weeks in advance, so it would have needed

planning and bribery to get him on the train.' She sighed.
'I only managed to reach Sergei Andreya Malenko shortly
before the train arrived.'

Malenko worked as a senior detective with the St
Petersburg Central Investigating Board. He had been the
first recruit Morton had permitted Mischa to make.

'Did he have any luck?'

Once more she hugged herself before answering. 'The
train carries over five hundred passengers. But working
from what I could tell him, Sergei Andreya found a taxi-
driver who had driven someone of Bodor's description to
Zelenorski. That's about fifty kilometres north-west of the
city. It's not much of a place. The driver remembers Bodor
because he paid in hard currency.'

They reached a rusty gate leading into a small wood.
Mischa opened the gate as she continued. 'Zelenorski is
close to the Gulf of Finland. A boat could have picked
Bodor up. It's the way the *mafiya* bring in drugs. They'd
have no problem bringing him out.'

He glanced down at her. 'Do you think they did?'

She considered. 'No. Somehow, Bodor doesn't fit with
the *mafiya*.'

They reached the far side of the wood. Beyond was a
deep trench as wide as a moat, and a small lake, its surface
frozen. Mischa closed her eyes for a moment then, when she
spoke, her voice was once more drained of emotion. 'Do
you remember what the poet Anna Akhmatova wrote,
David? About how the Russian earth loves blood? But this
is Polish soil, and it loves ash.'

For a moment the remark hung there as he sensed her
roaming an inner empyrean landscape before she spoke
again.

'This was one of the burning ditches the guards used
when the crematoria could no longer cope. The bodies were

brought here and stacked like Hindu funeral pyres. The ash was then thrown into the water. That's why there are no fish. Why nothing, not even a single weed, will ever grow here. Nothing can grow in human ash.'

They stared in silence out at the lake where the powdered residue of entire cities of people, of generations, of a whole continent, lay beneath the ice.

'Why?' she asked, touching her forehead. 'Why? I keep asking myself why I was spared and they weren't.'

Morton finally spoke. 'All survivors ask that, Mischa. It's part of the pain of surviving. Without pain there can't be healing.'

Then, very quietly, she replied, 'Thank you for trying to understand.'

'Thank you for showing me this, Mischa.'

For a moment he thought she was about to reach out to him. He did not know what stopped her. Upbringing, perhaps, or maybe for her, other reasons. She simply looked at him.

'This must never be allowed to happen again, David.'

'That's one more reason I need to know what Bodor was up to. Evil didn't end here, Mischa.'

He led the way out through the Gate of Death.

From inside the car came a low, intermittent ringing from his overnight bag on the back seat. He unlocked the bag and removed a small black box with a rectangular screen and two buttons. He pressed one to stop the alarm, then the other. The message from Danny gave brief details about the theft of the nuclear triggers. Morton cleared the screen and placed the box back in the bag.

With Mischa beside him, Morton drove back down the lane, and in a moment the old horror of Auschwitz was lost in the falling snow. He began to wonder what new horror lay ahead and whether some of the answers would be found in a small town on the east coast of Ireland.

Late in the evening, the President continued to prepare the speech he would give to the world leaders when they arrived in Washington. It would set the tone for Operation Earth Saver. He had chosen to work in the oval study – a smaller version of the Oval Office – which adjoined his bedroom. Few outsiders knew the White House had two such circular rooms.

The venue appealed to his sense of history. In this study Franklin Delano Roosevelt had penned his declaration of war against Japan after Pearl Harbor. Here John F. Kennedy threw down the gauntlet against Russia over Cuba. And, he reminded himself ruefully, it was also here that Richard Nixon had written his resignation speech after Watergate.

Would he emerge triumphant like Roosevelt and Kennedy or face the same ignominious fate as Nixon? Certainly what he was proposing was radical, even unheard of. Yet if the United States did not lead by example, what right had he to ask others to follow?

He continued to dictate into the recorder on the side table beside his chintz-patterned armchair.

'The cost of insuring against forecast climatic changes to the United States is estimated at forty billion dollars a year. Huge though the sum is, it still represents less than two per cent of what Americans already spend on insurance. But, as not all Americans can afford that extra, I am going to propose to Congress that the money be found by raising a levy of seventy-five cents a barrel on all petroleum consumed in this country – and that levy should come from oil company profits . . .'

He paused, already seeing the furore in the boardrooms of the oil companies, then continued in the same calm, measured voice, synthesising all he had pondered these past weeks.

'While this country has played its part in ensuring all motor vehicles are fitted with state-of-the-art emission controls, more measures are needed. Therefore I am going to ask Congress to support legislation for new fuel-efficiency levels in all future vehicles. That will reduce our present pollution problem by a further thirty per cent. All vehicles which do not achieve the new level will be subject to an additional tax . . .'

Detroit would fight. So would its lobbyists on the Hill. But he had come too far to back away now from confrontation with a Congress long steeped in the protection of out-moded ideas under the guise of tradition.

He began to formulate his next thought. 'What is at stake is the future of the atmosphere . . . the very air we breathe. What we all presently face is a global problem not faced before . . . a problem that does not have boundaries or frontiers . . .'

He pressed the pause button, his mind returning to an earlier thought. Would Ignatius Bailey agree with him? Would he set aside their past differences and join him in ensuring a new and better future, not just for the United States, but for the entire world? The President was a seasoned enough politician to realise the folly of trying to second-guess Bailey. He had surprised everyone in Washington by not responding to the administration's firm but fair action against a number of Meridian companies operating at the environmentally dubious end of the market.

But the President knew there were still those mornings when he awoke, and other cares of office did not immediately snap for attention, when he wondered whether Bailey was simply biding his time. There was no way of knowing.

Bailey was a law unto himself. That was what made him both so formidable an enemy and so worthwhile an ally for Earth Saver.

Shaking his head almost impatiently, as if the gesture would somehow dislodge the troubled thoughts, the President depressed the button which would allow him to record his next thought.

'... my friends, you will see the full extent of this problem as we travel together on a plane which, I am assured, will be the most environmentally friendly aircraft to fly ...'

SIX

Stepping from the Boeing courtesy car on to the tarmac at the company's world headquarters in Seattle, Edwin Scott Patterson instinctively glanced at the sky. Seven-tenths cumulus. But the overcast should be long gone by midday, and so would he.

The graceful means to do so towered above him. The new flagship of the President of the United States bore the most magical name in aviation: Air Force One. Patterson was her commander.

Even without the badge on the right pocket of his coverall and the silver wings pinned above, he could be a model for any artist needing the classic face of a pilot: hair worn in a tight military cut, deep-tanned features devoid of excess flesh, and the set of the jaw suggesting a special responsibility.

Not even the overcast could diminish the shine on the plane's aluminium skin; it had been burnished with coats of wax to give an additional lustre to the gleaming white body emblazoned on either side with the blue legend *United States of America*. The engine pods were silent, but there was no mistaking the awesome power of each jet. The stabiliser, with its blue trim on the leading edge, had a Stars and Stripes painted the size of a nightclub dance floor. Below the flag were the figures which embodied so much tradition: 26000. Legend was that they were President Kennedy's favourite crap-shoot numbers. More certain, it was he who had first authorised the President's personal aircraft to be called Air Force One.

Patterson began to walk slowly around the perimeter of the parking bay. His duties to the Man – as every crew member informally referred to an incumbent president – included making this inspection before every flight. Though Patterson walked with a relaxed dignity, his eyes missed nothing.

A week ago they had stared out from the cover of *Time*, part of the inevitable publicity surrounding the new plane. The magazine had noted approvingly that Air Force One would remain under the command of someone who was the perfect example of the saying that there are old pilots and bold pilots, but almost never old, bold pilots.

Not so much of the old, he'd thought wryly. At forty-eight he was statistically over-age for a bird colonel, but he had made it clear he would rather resign than not continue commanding Air Force One. The decision, he knew, had marked a further downward spiral in his marriage the night he'd finished telling Bron about his intention and his hope that she would understand his need to go on flying.

The silence between them was like a caught breath.

'You can't do this,' Bron said at last. 'What am I supposed to do? Sit here and wait for your postcards, if I'm lucky, while you gallivant round the world!' Her voice filled the kitchen with an anger he had never heard before

He kept his own voice steady. 'Being the President's pilot is the ultimate ambition of any airman, Bron. Apart from you, it's all I've ever wanted. And it won't be forever. When I do hand over, I'll be able to pick and choose just about any desk job going. Then we'll have all the time together you'll want.' He tried to make a joke. 'You'll probably get tired of having me around the place all the time.'

She seemed to have withdrawn into herself when she spoke

again. 'Have it your own way, then. You always do.'

As he moved towards her, she walked out of the room, not looking back.

Since then her accusations had become more bitter. Those times he would find himself observing her, wondering what it was that consumed Bron, made those intense blue eyes seem driven by some compelling inner dissatisfaction that he realised now must always have been there.

They had met in London, on a weekend pass from his bomber base in Norfolk. It was post-Gulf-War time and an American uniform was a symbol of a just war, commonly won. He'd gone to a party; the usual mish-mash of guests and fast food he'd found in his short time in England. But she had struck him as different from anyone he'd ever met – full of ideas, yet always in motion, driven by restless energy. She'd explained she was an actress; day-time television alternating with stage work. Her voice had an intensity which underscored certain words. She was Welsh, she'd said; Bron was short for Bronwen. Bronwen Jones from a village he couldn't pronounce.

Getting her a drink, she'd surprised him. 'Take me home.'

'To Wales?'

'No, to bed.' She made it sound as if it was the most natural thing for them both to do.

Bron's apartment off the Fulham Road had been somehow more elaborate than he imagined. There were animal skins on the floor, a marble fireplace, a hardwood floor and an expanse of window that framed the rooftops. The furniture was a mixture of Oriental: Indian brass tables, Thai stools, and brightly coloured Burmese prints on the walls. The lights were close to the floor. It looked like a stage set.

Without any preamble, she undressed and led him to the futon in a corner of the living room, and watched while he took off his clothes. For a while they lay entwined, touching, discovering, learning, making noises that were not words, suspended in an absence of time, of everything. Then her stomach and hips began to move in unison, drawing him against her, as if she needed to touch as much of his skin as possible with her own. She adjusted her rhythm to his, signalling every change without words. Suddenly she began to move faster, almost with a desperate ferocity, her mouth shuddering and an animal cry deep in her throat.

Afterwards they lay quietly beside each other. Then they played backgammon and drank wine.

'Tell me about yourself, Edwin.'

He began to talk of his failed first marriage. 'The classic college romance. It lasted a year after we graduated.'

'Children?'

No, thank God.'

She watched him for a long moment. 'Then?'

'Nothing serious. You know, ships that pass in the night.'

'Or in your case, planes.'

'Something like that.'

She rose on her elbow so that she looked down at him. 'Is that what keeps you going? Flying?'

He nodded.

She continued to stare down at him. 'What are you offering in return, then?'

Because he was a little tipsy he gave her a slightly tipsy answer. 'Everything. All I have. All I can give. Just everything.'

'That's quite a deal, Edwin.'

She kissed him and this time there was no longer any urgency about their lovemaking.

A month later he'd arrived to take her for dinner. By then he had his own key to her apartment and, opening the door, he'd found her standing by the living room window, the light behind her.

'Where would you like to go tonight, Bron? There's a new place opened in Chelsea. It's offering authentic Texas beef. One steak'll probably feed both of us.'

She'd waited a moment before answering. 'I'm already feeding two, Edwin.'

He stared at her. 'What are you saying?'

'I'm pregnant.' Her voice was still flat calm.

He looked at her in stunned disbelief. 'Are you absolutely certain?'

'Yes. Very.'

'But I thought . . . it was okay.'

'So did I.'

He squared his shoulders. 'So what do we do?'

She stiffened almost imperceptibly. 'You have to do nothing.'

He was silent. 'That still leaves you, Bron. What about you?' he asked gently.

'I'll do what everyone else does in this situation. Have an abortion.'

'No.' His voice had a deliberate edge. 'I don't want that.'

She almost smiled. 'It's a little late now to raise that, Edwin. And certainly when you were screwing me, I didn't get the feeling you were wondering what the Pope would say!'

'I still don't want you to have an abortion. Let's get married.'

From where he stood, her face held nothing but watchfulness.

'Is that what you really want?' she demanded at last, moving from the window.

'I'd very much like to marry you, Bron.'

She turned and looked out across the rooftops before replying. 'Okay, if that's what you want, then.'

Three weeks later they were married in the base chapel. A month afterwards Bron had taken a trip to London while he was on a training flight back to the States. When he returned, she told him her pregnancy had been terminated.

A tide of blackness had engulfed him. Looking into her face he'd asked why, dammit, why? Suddenly a keening sound came from her and her eyes showed only the whites, and her head began to move to and fro, as if she was issuing some frantic denial. He'd *tried to hold her still, but she'd wriggled and struggled like a fish, and her breathing came in great explosive gasps as if she were holding it until her lungs threatened to burst. They had remained like that for an indeterminable time until she had finally become calm. Then she had looked at him and said, in a totally controlled voice, that she was sorry. He'd closed his eyes and his mind had filled with effort, as he'd found the words to reassure her that everything was going to be all right. He'd wanted to believe that more than anything.*

A month later he was posted to an air base in Germany, to become part of the UN spearhead flying aid into Bosnia. Bron had joined him in officers' quarters.

One morning he'd left her at the kitchen table and had come home to find her still there, holding her coffee cup in both hands, red-eyed from crying. She'd smiled and said she was always weepy at this time of the month. Another time he'd returned from a night flight to find her still wearing the bathrobe she had put on the day before. On that occasion she had screamed at him that she couldn't stand this life. Then, as despair tightened his throat, her tears came again.

'How can I help you, Bron?' he asked gently.

'I'll be okay,' she insisted, suddenly smiling through her tears.

The outbursts had continued to come from some wellspring deep inside her. Her behaviour had bewildered him, the more so because there were times when she was her old self. Perhaps, he'd decided, what she really needed was to resume her career. He'd made enquiries. The base had a theatre company; they would be glad to use her. She could even find work in German television, he told her.

Bron screamed at him. 'How can I act in a bloody language I can't even speak, then? I can't even understand the road signs in German! And if you think I'm going to perform with a bunch of officers' wives, you can bloody well forget that as well!'

She raged on until, exhausted, she had gone to sleep in the guest bedroom for the first time. He spent the rest of the night cocooned in his own misery in their bed.

He had hoped the move to Washington to become the President's pilot would make it easier for Bron. That the pride he took in his job would be shared by her. Instead she had flared, 'The trouble is that you are still a glorified chauffeur for someone who doesn't even invite us to the White House! That's how much he thinks of you, Edwin!'

He tried to explain that even if he was the President's pilot, he did not end up on the Man's guest list – let alone expect his wife to be invited for afternoon coffee with the First Lady. And it was true: he was on constant call. But that was the job. At any given hour of the day or night he had to be ready, at sixty minutes' warning, to fly the Man anywhere.

He hugged her, kissed her and whispered in her ear that he loved her, hearing the tears choking her throat, blinding her eyes, and he was filled with a sadness so painful that it filled his ears and his chest to overflowing.

The pain he felt at that moment was similar to one he had experienced for the first time over Sarajevo. At 44,000 feet his face-mask oxygen pipe had ruptured and he felt nauseous and dizzy. Instinctively, he dived to a lower level and the attack passed. On landing he found blood in his urine.

A Russian doctor attached to the UN Command had drawn blood, analysed his urine and run a battery of stress tests. Afterwards, he explained that porphyria is a very rare condition caused by the breakdown of haemoglobin in the blood. However, the doctor continued, there was no cause for alarm. New steroids, coupled with iron shots, could ward off further attacks and hopefully build up immunity. With a generous supply of medication, he delivered a final reassurance.

'While you must always be careful, the important thing is not to worry about this. Take your medication and don't fly when you are over-tired or have experienced prolonged stress.'

Since then he had flown scores of high-altitude test flights in the new Air Force One. Before each one he swallowed the contents of one of the ampoules the doctor had prescribed. Each trip passed uneventfully. A month ago the medication finally ran out. Next day he had flown another proving flight nine miles above the earth. It also had passed without incident. The immunity the doctor had spoken of must now be in place.

'Fuel's okay, Colonel.' The voice of William Kerr, the flight engineer, brought Patterson back to the present.

With his fat-lidded eyes and a receding hairline that steadily dragged his forehead further back to the top of his freckled scalp, Kerr looked like a small-town garage mechanic. But he'd been the first man Patterson had selected when he had chosen the crew for the new Air Force One. He'd flown with Kerr in the Gulf, then Bosnia. You learned all you needed to know about a man's capability in places like that.

A short time ago Kerr had analysed a gallon of jet fuel siphoned from a tanker. During one of the proving flights he had rejected an entire supply because there was a trace of sediment swilling around the bottom of the bowser.

'Have them start pumping, Bill,' Patterson ordered crisply.

Coveralled crew were checking the fresh fluid in the hydraulics. Checking the tyres for tread wear and pressure. Checking the engine pods to make sure no object had entered. Check and check again was the motto of everyone involved with Air Force One.

Almost twice the size of the venerable jumbo, Air Force One was the first three-deck, super-stretch aircraft capable of circling almost half the globe without refuelling – three hundred and fifty tons of gleaming machinery with exquisite appointments rivalling those of a luxury hotel. A cabin staff of thirty-five ensured the usual high standards of service. Yet the flight deck crew was no larger than for a 747.

As Patterson passed under the tail, a slightly-built man looked up from his clipboard. Sergeant Tom Sutter, the crew chief, knew the checklist by memory but he drummed into his men that you never trusted to memory.

'I figure the waxing's added another seven clicks to her airspeed,' Sutter grinned. A good polish reduced friction and added a few more knots to the clock.

Patterson looked at his watch. Ten twenty. He kept it on Washington time, no matter where he was. He could still be home by mid-afternoon, flying with the jet stream which, at this time of year, swept through the centre of the country. Just time to shower and change into rig-of-the-day before attending the White House briefing. He still had no idea why it had been called. Only that it must be another trip with the Man.

Twelve hundred miles to the south, a 747 freighter climbed into the sky from Ontario Airport in southern California, passed above the Uplands Holiday Inn and headed north for the eleven-hour flight to Rome.

The manifest listed the only item of cargo as a high-altitude balloon and its gondola. The documentation stated it had been sold to a theme park in Italy. The customs agent who signed the paperwork had received another substantial payment to ensure there would be no questions asked.

The 747 belonged to Global Transport, based at Galveston, Texas. The balloon and gondola were built by the Free Flight Corporation of Bakersfield, California. Both were subsidiaries of Meridian International.

The theme park did not exist.

SEVEN

The sixty-seventh floor of the Meridian Building, a pyramid-shaped tower on the outskirts of the town in the mid-west of the United States from which it took its name, was the executive level of the world headquarters of Meridian International. A corner suite was reserved for its President and Chief Executive Officer, Ignatius Bailey.

At this hour, close to three a.m., the suite was in darkness, concealing that from here was ultimately controlled an organisation which, in one form or another, did business with every fifteenth person on earth.

They used its buses, airlines, cruise ships, banks, leisure resorts, theme parks, hotels and conference centres. They watched its television channels and listened to its radio stations. Tens of millions every day read the newspapers and books produced under Meridian's imprints, ate the foods Meridian marketed and drank the wines it bottled, and gratefully accepted the wide range of Meridian-produced hangover cures. They dressed in Meridian designer clothes, and used the latest perfumes and after-shave lotions created by Meridian chemists. They often paid for all this by one or more of the forty-three credit cards Meridian controlled.

The prudent took out life assurance with Meridian brokerages, and every year Meridian estate agents rented or sold homes to several million people around the world; all were routinely advised to join one of Meridian's private health insurance schemes. If they had to go into hospital, there was every chance they would need a Meridian-manufactured item of surgical or diagnostic equipment.

From infant school to graduation, children were taught by Meridian-created educational systems, and played with a variety of Meridian-made sports gear. At an increasingly younger age they learned about safe sex by using one of the wide range of contraceptives produced by Meridian's pharmaceutical companies. By the time they graduated, the adults of tomorrow were already full members of the ever-expanding Meridian consumer family, regular users of products provided by over two thousand corporations and companies Meridian totally owned. A global workforce larger than that of many nations ran them. Meridian's stock was prime-listed on over a thousand exchanges and bourses. Its annual declared profits were greater than those of Shell and Exxon – combined.

Ultimately the decision of how that achievement continued was approved here in the corner suite. Even now, fifteen seconds past three on the clock above the electronic map on one wall, there was an air of muted power about the darkened office.

At twenty seconds past the hour a pinprick of light blinked on the map. The computer gave a hum so faint that even in the silence of the suite it could barely be heard. The transmission time was three seconds, during which thirty-six blocks of numbers were received.

The computer took fourteen seconds to turn the numbers into plain speech, add a prefix number, instruct itself to make no copies and transfer the message to the modem on the partner's desk.

At forty seconds past three, the message light came on in a corner of the screen. It would be three hours before Ignatius Bailey arrived in the suite and knew the stolen nuclear trigger mechanisms had left England.

*

Morton flew back to Geneva via Munich, changing his passport as well as the plane. After the atmosphere of the camp, the Hammer Force headquarters seemed full of life, although it was late in the evening and the corridors were quiet. It would be even more peaceful on the east coast of Ireland, he thought, as he dialled Sharon McCabe's number. Their friendship had survived lengthy periods when there was no contact. They'd first met at another what-shall-we-do-for-Russia conference in London. He'd been impressed by her faultless Russian and had discovered she was the ranking specialist on Soviet science with *Defence Review*. The magazine, then and now, was the leader in its field, read in the right places. She had made it clear she knew who he was and what he did. Over dinner she had said, in that direct way of hers, she could be useful to him – as long as he didn't expect her to compromise the magazine or her contacts. He'd immediately accepted her terms and she had, from time to time, given him background. As his own position in the ever-changing world of daily intrigue altered, so had her information. Often it no more than confirmed what he already knew, but from different sources. More important, she had never misled him, and she had become one of the very few outsiders he completely trusted, even though nowadays her journalism was far removed from the almost dull respectability of *Defence Review*.

The change began when Sharon came to Ireland to recover from a near-marriage, came to this house which had belonged to her dead parents, who had left it to her, together with a sizeable bequest. Two days into her stay, she had gone riding in the Wicklow hills. The horse had bolted and Sharon had broken her neck. She'd spent a year in hospitals in Dublin.

As soon as he could, he'd come to see her. By then she had accepted that the total paralysis below the neck would be permanent. She'd smiled and said the doctor's verdict had settled another matter: she'd been thinking for some time that it was time for a change. She'd had her fill of the Whitehall cocktail circuit, listening to the temporary stewards of government offering a secret in return for a reputation to be discreetly tarnished. She had told him what she was going to do: produce a monthly newsletter for those interested in environmental issues without the spin put on them by others. *Science Watch* was now respected by governments and the various friends-of-the-earth movements.

Now, listening to the ringing tone, Morton imagined her in her home, where several small rooms on the ground floor had been turned into one large space and the walls lined with shelves filled with more books than some public libraries possess. At the far end was a bank of screens mounted on a rack and, against a wall, a couch with a body-hoist and a trolley filled with tubes and bottles.

She would be in a wheelchair close to the fire. Even on a warm day she'd have difficulty keeping warm, the doctor had explained. Her hands would be resting uselessly in her lap, her feet lifeless on the chair's metal footrests. Attached to the chair would be a large tray supporting a computer keyboard and a number of mouthsticks, each with its small plastic ball at one end. A light telephonist's headset would frame the wonderful bone structure of her face.

'David!' She exclaimed, when he announced himself. 'It's good to hear you, though the phone's a poor substitute for seeing you.'

'I'll be over to see you soon, for sure. How's Brin looking after you?'

Brin had looked after Sharon's parents in their declining

years, and had slipped quite naturally into the role of caring for their daughter. When Morton had met him Sharon had referred to him as her Yellow Pages. 'He does all the walking for me, he takes care of all the things I can't do.'

Now she laughed lightly. 'He says he's in love with me, David.'

Morton felt an odd tug in his gut. 'And you? Are you in love with him?'

'My situation puts a certain limit to such feelings.' There was a second of echoing silence on the line. 'Well, David, what's the problem?'

'Bodor.'

'So what's Bodor gone and done?' Sharon asked.

'Disappeared and then re-appeared.' He told her about Mischa's sighting.

Sharon sighed. 'Most people say Bodor's crazy, David. Brilliant, but crazy. In recent years he became ...' She paused. 'That's the point. No one knows what he became. But when he was in the public arena, coming to conferences in the West, he was someone way ahead of his time. I'm surprised the Americans or the Brits didn't try to grab him. But I guess he was just too damn dedicated to the system to be bought. And his political masters certainly treated him with due reverence. He wanted it, he had it. I remember when he went to the States, he flew in the party chairman's private plane. When he came to London or Paris he had a hard currency allowance which made his hosts blink. And he knew how to spend. Clothes, jewellery, women. He bought them all.'

Morton asked what Bodor had been working on.

There was a silence before Sharon resumed. 'High-altitude precipitation and all its spinoffs. Polar surface warming. Cooling above the Equator. He was right at the sharp end, and always ready to push an idea way beyond where it was. That's when people started saying he was crazy. But he just bulldozed on.

'One day he was there, very much still the visible jewel in the Soviet science firmament, the next he was gone. Talk was he had come up with some fantastic new weapon, and that his paymasters had tucked him away in some place safe to develop it. When I joined *Defence Review*, it was still being talked about. When everything began to unravel in Moscow, other rumours came thick and fast. That Bodor was dead. Or finally been locked up in one of their loony bins. Or escaped to any place you care to mention. Then after a while, the rumours stopped.'

'I know,' Morton said.

'I'm going to send some stuff to your modem. Hold on.' He heard the sound of her tapping keyboards, and within seconds text began to unravel on his computer screen.

Morton read the short account of an incident involving a Soviet bomber. It had crashed in central Russia, killing everyone on board. Underneath was a summary of the pathology reports on the crew. They had all died from haemorrhaging according to the doctor who had conducted the autopsies. His name was given as Professor Nikita Vassiley.

'You know Vassiley?' Morton asked.

'Only by reputation. He went into the woodwork about the same time as Bodor.'

He remembered what Mischa had said. 'Think there's a connection?'

'You mean could Bodor be responsible for the plane crashing? Or everyone having their brains burst?' She responded quickly.

'Is that possible?' Morton asked in the same careful voice.

'A few months ago I got a fax from a Russian journalist. He said he'd worked on *Pravda* around the time Bodor and Vassiley went out of circulation. Let me see if I can find it.'

Another document appeared on his screen, written in Cyrillic.

'How's your Russian, David?'

'Probably not as good as yours.'

She laughed. 'I doubt that.'

The message began formally – *'minya zavat Nickolai Nevsky'* – and then explained that its author had been at a conference in Kiev where one of Vassiley's assistants had read a paper.

'Those conferences were strictly for the faithful, David.' Then she added quickly, 'Sorry – I'm telling you something you already know.'

'It's good to be reminded,' Morton said easily. 'Let's see what Nevsky says happened at that conference.'

The assistant's paper had dealt with the effects on the human metabolism caused by sudden climatic changes in the upper stratosphere. According to Nevsky, the pathologist had been frank in admitting that many of the effects were poorly understood.

Morton rubbed his eyes after reading the Russian script. 'Why would Nevsky send you something like this? After all, they've shot people over there for revealing less.'

'Nevsky was probably job-hunting. You'd be surprised how many journalists over there send me stuff. If they get me to publish anything, they see it as a calling card for a job.'

'Did you publish Nevsky's information?'

'No. There wasn't enough to go on. My policy is to resist rushing into print until I can present the whole picture. That way people come to respect something when I do run it.'

'Any idea where Nevsky is now?' Morton asked.

She laughed. 'That information I don't keep. But it's a safe bet that he's not with Bodor. He hates journalists.'

EIGHT

In the flame from his lighter, Bodor saw that the face of Muktar, his guide, was paler, the deeply lined skin sheened with perspiration.

The Kurd's sickness had started after they had left the foothills and begun to climb into the mountains proper of northern Iraq the night before. When they reached the cave he coughed up blood and hardly touched his food, the last of their spicy *piti*.

At this height here was nothing available to make a fire, and they had huddled together, his own fitful sleep broken by long bouts of membrane-ripping coughs which made Bodor's own chest ache just to hear them.

Now the Kurd looked worse than the last time he checked: the old man hadn't moved from his crouched position, the front of his robe stained with mucoid mush. Bodor flicked off the lighter.

'It will pass,' Muktar said feebly.

It was the sickness which afflicted many who spent their lives in these mountains. They called it *gomla*, and it could rack a man's lungs until he was too exhausted to move. These past weeks he had made several trips, so that there had been no proper interval for his body to recuperate. Wiping a dribble of phlegm from his lips, he reminded himself that none of those trips were as lucrative as his fee for this one. Guiding this infidel was worth a thousand American dollars.

The woman he had negotiated with in Baku had

smelled of anise. They had sat in a café filled with whores in the Old City and, sensing there was room to haggle, he'd asked for half the money up front. She had walked to another table and spoken to a man she'd called Salim. He'd shrugged, and the woman had returned and produced from the folds of her dress a wad of dollars, counted out half and handed them over. He had been about to leave when she'd asked if he would like whisky. He'd refused as politely as possible, not wishing to offend someone who would enable him to fulfil his one great ambition. The money would provide his one remaining unmarried daughter with a dowry sufficiently attractive to make a suitor overlook her advancing years.

But none of this he would share with this infidel. While he dressed, looked and behaved like one of the faithful, he had seen the way the man prayed. Though he squatted correctly on his haunches and put his hand to his face, bowed, and put his hand again to his face, there was no pleasure there; and certainly he did not own a Koran, and certainly he could not read it if he did. The infidel recited the suras of the Holy Book with no thought of their true meaning. Now, in the darkness, he could sense his fear.

Bodor gathered his robe about him. If the Kurd died, there was no way he would find his own way out of the mountains. Then, it would only be a matter of time before he, too, succumbed to this merciless landscape. He been seen enough to know there were no margins in these mountains: they could kill him quickly, with a bite from one of the scorpions, or slowly, through blood poisoning by brushing against one of the thorn bushes the Kurd had warned about. Or he could die from thirst, hunger, heat or cold. The choice of death would be the only one available to him.

Ignoring the itch of the coarsely-woven camel-hair robe

against his skin, Bodor crawled over to the suitcase. Inside were his precious blueprints and, wrapped in his suit, the last of several bottles of vodka he had bought in Baku, his last staging post in a long journey.

Immediately the taxi had dropped him in Zelenorski, a car emerged from a side street. The woman had taken him to Vologda. During the drive she had not spoken a word, chain-smoking throughout the journey. At the city's airport she handed him a paper bag. It contained his air ticket for the flight south to Baku, on the Caspian Sea, and a syringe filled with cocaine. He had injected himself in the airport toilet, flushed away the syringe, and once more experienced the familiar excitement from the drug coursing through his body. He marvelled again at the thoroughness of the Arranger.

At Baku, a city as old as the Silk Road, he had been met by a man in the uniform of the local militia who drove him to a house well inside the mediaeval walls. He had been shown to a room and offered coffee. A small man grown large had appeared with a suitcase and had studied him with a sharp intelligence. From the case the man produced a make-up kit.

'Sit down, please,' he said in the broad accent of the region.

Over several hours he transformed Bodor's face, staining it darker, thickening the eyebrows and yellowing his teeth with a paste. Next he gummed in place a tangled beard before showing him how to insert the contact lenses to make his eyes appear dark brown. Satisfied, he asked Bodor to remove his expensive jacket and customised shoes, and took from the suitcase a brightly embroidered winter farwa *and its accompanying outer* aba. *Finally he proffered a sturdy pair of hide boots.*

The man invited Bodor to look in a mirror after he was dressed. He was startled at the change. His appearance was no different from any of the other traders in the streets of Baku. The man inspected him carefully before passing judgement.

'Now that you look like one of the faithful, you must also learn to pray and eat like one. Though you are unlikely to meet anyone else in the mountains, for your guide is skilled in such matters, it is wise to be prepared.' The man glanced sideways. 'But you will surely have discovered that already.'

Once more Bodor had the feeling he was in the hands of an immensely powerful organisation.

From the suitcase his mentor produced a prayer mat and a cassette player. After showing him how to kneel correctly on the mat, the man switched on the tape. The timeless words of the call to prayer had begun to fill the room: Allah Akbar, Allah Akbar . . . God is Great.

For the rest of the night he had practised the ritual responses and learned to eat like a mountain Kurd, dipping his right hand into a variety of pungent-tasting foods and chewing noisily.

At dawn his mentor pronounced himself satisfied. From his pocket he produced a hermetically sealed syringe, a selection of sheathed needles and several ampoules.

'I understand you know when and how to use these,' the man said in a non-judgemental voice, handing them over. 'You may wish to use one now to prepare yourself for the journey through the mountains.'

Under the man's impassive gaze, Bodor injected into an antecubital vein. The feeling of euphoria was like nothing else, but the pleasure had faded by the time Muktar appeared.

His mentor spoke to the Kurd in their own language. The old man had looked at him with barely concealed contempt. On the way out of Baku they had stopped at a tea-room where Bodor had bought bottles of vodka, placing them in the suitcase, among his own clothes and the envelope with the blueprints.

They had flown to Tabriz in Iran. From there they had taken another flight to Rezaiyeh, close to the mountains dividing Kurdistan from Iraq. No one had given him a second glance.

But as they climbed, the Kurd had looked disapprovingly at

the frequent swigs he took during rest periods. Once, when he had
been about to throw away an empty bottle, the old man had taken
it from him and angrily hidden it beneath a cairn of stones.

Removing the last bottle from the suitcase, Bodor crawled
over to Muktar and unscrewed its cap. Guided by the
Kurd's rasping breathing, Bodor brought the bottle to
Muktar's lips.

'Here, drink this, old man. It will help your sickness.'

Muktar shook his head. 'The Prophet says alcohol is a
sin.'

'The Prophet also says it is a sin to die needlessly,' Bodor
said quickly.

'You have read the Koran?' Muktar asked weakly.

'Yes. And it says no man has the right to refuse the
means to live.'

'I do not remember that verse.'

Bodor forced impatience not to show in his voice. 'It is
there.'

He flicked the lighter and held the flame close to
Muktar's face. The Kurd's lips were trembling.

'Drink,' commanded Bodor. 'Then you will be able to
continue. It cannot be much further we have to travel.'

Muktar nodded. 'We shall be there soon. But I cannot
drink alcohol.'

The darkness beyond the mouth of the cave was
becoming lighter. Soon the rocks and scrub would take on
their familiar shapes, as well as the trees with their
branches turned away from the prevailing wind. For them
there was no escape.

'Please, drink, old man,' Bodor coaxed. He brought the
neck of the bottle against the Kurd's lips.

Muktar's lips remained tremblingly closed.

'The Prophet understands,' Bodor urged.

Slowly, almost imperceptibly, Muktar's lips finally parted and he began to drink.

'May Allah forgive me,' he muttered hoarsely.

'Your voice already sounds stronger,' Bodor said. 'Are you ready to move?'

'I will need to pray first.'

'Then be quick.'

'Will you not also pray?' asked Muktar tremblingly, wondering if the Prophet would forgive him for enjoying this strange warm feeling in his body.

'I have done my praying.'

'*Allah akbar*,' mumbled the old man, beginning to pray.

Bodor watched as, beyond the cave's entrance, light bounded across endless miles of peaks and valleys, climbing and dancing into the sky and the world was created anew. When Muktar finished his devotions, they stood together outside the cave and the desolation of this mountain fastness seemed almost redeemed by the dawn of a new day.

Bodor turned to the Kurd. 'You look better.'

Muktar nodded; he felt better. 'Are you a doctor?' he asked in the respectful voice of someone who could never afford one. 'Is that why you inject yourself?'

'Not so many questions, old man,' Bodor said sharply. During the night he had used the last ampoule of cocaine.

Lifting the suitcase, he followed Muktar on up into the mountains which once more swallowed them, effortlessly and utterly. From time to time they stopped to catch their breath.

As they climbed, Muktar felt the pain continue to ease in his lungs. In part he knew this was because this was his country, and the sense of power that gave him was strong, almost as intoxicating as the alcohol the infidel had forced on him. He'd prayed to be forgiven for that lapse, even though he realised the drink had helped. The higher they went, the more he had sensed the infidel's unease; and it was true, the mountains could be very intimidating. Time and again as they picked their way through the rocks, the infidel had asked how much further, in a voice which said, 'Don't leave me alone up here.'

During each halt Muktar studied the sky, allowing his gaze to travel the entire length of the horizon, slowly, then back again at the same pace. They had climbed for a further hour when he once more stopped. There was a strange silence: no wind and the temperature had risen. Though the sky was clear of clouds, it was now an unhealthy colour, reddish-yellow, like the gobs he had coughed.

'We must find a place to shelter,' Muktar said abruptly. He knew what to listen for, what to look for.

'What is it? What is wrong?' Bodor demanded in irritation.

Muktar pointed to where the sky was a darker red. 'A sandstorm is coming, a big one.' The signs were as familiar to him as streets are to a city-dweller.

'We can still continue,' Bodor said impatiently, his eyes quickly scrutinising the sky.

But already Muktar's eyes were like those of a man frantically seeking safety. 'Have you ever been in a sandstorm?' he demanded hoarsely.

'No. But I have seen rainstorms in the Urals sweep whole villages away.'

Muktar bared his teeth. 'Here the entire world disappears. We must shelter.'

Bodor stood with an arm outstretched, a finger pointing stiffly ahead. 'No! We must be close to the meeting place. We will continue!'

Muktar stared at the sky. The darkness was spreading

like a great stain. He turned to the infidel and saw the determined look that had accompanied a voice suddenly strong with menace. 'Very well. We will continue as long as we can.'

They pushed on upwards towards peaks which glowed as if great flames were licking at them. Suddenly an icy shaft of wind whistled from between a pass immediately ahead, its force so great as almost to throw them off their feet.

'We must shelter . . .'

The rest of Muktar's words were lost in the roar of the wind which in the same moment became a gale and, in another second, the full fury of the sandstorm engulfed them, driving them first to their knees, then forcing them flat.

Somehow Bodor held on to the suitcase and, blinded and half-choking, crawled behind Muktar to a rocky outcrop. Faces buried against the granite, they huddled close to each other for protection. Bodor had managed to wedge the case between his body and the rock, gripping the handle with both hands to stop it being whipped from his grasp.

The outcrop acted as a baffle, driving the worst of the storm up over them. Its sound reminded Bodor of a rocket barrage he had once experienced in Afghanistan: the same continuous crackle of discharged electricity intermingled with peals of thunder echoing around the mountains. Then there was only the voracious roaring dance of the great columns of sand, spiralling and then collapsing back into themselves before once more twisting and turning to bind together into a massive single front. It swept down on them with lacerating force. Bushes, pebbles, small boulders all were gathered up as the earth and sky became one unified, blinding, crashing darkness which seemed to have neither beginning nor end.

How long they remained in their positions Muktar had no idea. He could sense rather than see the infidel beside him. A moment earlier he had still been desperately clinging to his suitcase, eyes screwed up, the force of the wind still flattening his cheeks. Now he was no longer there.

The infidel must have panicked and gone to try and find other shelter, but there was none. Normally he would have left someone who was so clearly a lunatic to his own fate; a person like that had no right to live. But, kept alive, this infidel was worth a fortune.

Muktar staggered to his feet and was immediately buffeted and slashed by the storm, his robe almost torn from his body. He dropped to all fours and began to crawl through the maelstrom.

The sand threatened to rip his eyes from their sockets, his teeth out of their roots. He did not know how far or in which direction the infidel had crawled. But in the moment before the storm, he had seen him looking towards a rock pile. It seemed to take a lifetime before Muktar reached it. The infidel was not there. Exhausted, Muktar lay face down on the ground pulling his *farwa* around him to stop the robe ballooning and lifting him into the air.

Once more compressing his lips in a futile attempt to keep out the sand, he resumed crawling, his hands and knees bloodied from the stony ground. Great gouts of sand struck him; pain racked and tore at his muscles, a searing pain that knew no cessation.

Suddenly, to his left, he made out a shape, a darker something within the all-pervading darkness. It was the lunatic infidel, still clinging to his suitcase, only feet from where the rock sheered away into a gorge. The wind had blown away his beard and scoured off most of the stain on his face.

Bodor felt his feet slipping dangerously on the scree, dragging him closer to the edge of the precipice. He dug the heels of his boots more desperately into the shingle to try to get a better grip. But he continued to slip inexorably towards the gorge. He opened his mouth to scream. But the words were whipped away. Then he felt something grip his arm.

Muktar had removed his *ghotra* and used the headscarf to tie him to the infidel. The cloth was strong enough to bear the weight of a man. Once he had secured it to the infidel's wrist, he wedged himself between two boulders, his own body providing a windbreak.

They remained like that while the ceaseless pounding roared on and on, carrying with it a small desert of sand. Then, as suddenly as it started, the storm was over. Silence returned and all around them the mountains were again still and seemingly unchanged by the great fury which had assailed them.

For a while longer they lay, their heads only inches apart, staring into each other's eyes.

'It is all right now,' Muktar said at last, undoing the *ghotra*.

Slowly, painfully, Bodor climbed to his feet, the suitcase handle gripped so tightly his fingers seemed fused to the metal.

'Thank you, old man,' he said moving carefully from the edge of the gorge.

Muktar managed to smile. 'The Prophet says the best life to save is that of a lunatic. Then he may stop being a lunatic!'

He turned and led Bodor on the final stage of the journey, head bent, his feet regularly scuffing aside fresh deposits of sand to confirm their direction. Bodor walked as if in a trance, legs moving by an automatic reflex as if long ago they had crossed the pain barrier. Gradually they descended through the mountains.

Emerging from beneath an overhang, Muktar stopped and pointed. Below was a vast curving wadi, the depression divided by a thick coil of razor wire that snaked away on either side. In places there were gaps in the wire.

'The border with Iraq,' Muktar said.

On the other side of a gap in the wire an army truck was parked. Beside it a khaki-uniformed figure was searching the mountains with binoculars. Suddenly he stopped.

Muktar turned to Bodor and again bared his teeth in a smile. 'He has seen us.'

In silence they continued to pick their way down through the scree under the watchful eyes of the Iraqi. When they reached the wadi, the ground felt as soft as a mattress to Bodor.

The truck drove through the gap. The uniformed figure who jumped from the cab was an officer.

'Welcome to Iraq, Mr Bodor,' he said in faultless Russian.

He reached out and, for the first time since leaving Baku, Bodor allowed the suitcase to pass from his grasp.

Continuing to ignore Muktar, the officer nodded to the truck. 'You will find a clean uniform in the back, Mr Bodor, but you can change later. Right now it is best we go from here before someone becomes curious. The Americans have surveillance teams up here, working with their Kurdish friends.'

Bodor nodded. The Arranger had warned him about that.

Muktar remained a little distance away, wondering when it would be polite for him to take his leave. He had no love of the Iraqis; they could be very arrogant when the mood took them – like the way this one had deliberately ignored him. And the sooner he was back on the other side of the mountain, the sooner he would claim the rest of his money. Already in his mind's eye he could see his daughter's wedding feast, the finest the village would have had for years. And then he would retire and there would be no more attacks of *gomla*. He would live out his life like all the other elders. He stirred; the infidel was saying something to the Iraqi.

Bodor pointed to the officer's sidearm. 'Please give me that.'

When the officer had done so, Bodor turned and pointed the pistol at Muktar and fired twice in quick succession; both shots entered by the forehead and scattered the back of the Kurd's brain over the ground. For a fraction of a moment, Muktar remained standing, his mouth open, as if he had been about to protest that this was no way to be treated by someone whose life he had saved. Then he crumpled to the sand, a pool of blood beginning to ooze around his head. By the time Bodor handed back the gun, the liquid was already absorbed.

The Arranger's last instruction had been to kill the guide. There must be no trail to follow.

As they climbed into the truck, the suitcase between them on the bench seat, the officer spoke again. 'Your gifts have arrived safely.'

Bodor gave a perfunctory nod. Without the nuclear trigger mechanisms he'd asked the Arranger to provide, he would be unable to build the Ozone Layer Bomb.

NINE

Manders had decided to lunch Morton at Simpson's in the Strand. As they followed the head waiter across the crowded floor, Manders gave a little tip of the hand towards a woman dressed in a tweed suit that hid her figure. She smiled before turning back to her table companion, a courtly man in his early sixties, well-groomed, with a weather-beaten face.

When they were safely past, Manders murmured, 'The Blessed Nancy doing her duty by our less-than-esteemed Secretary of Defence. The genius who whispered in our Prime Minister's ear that those mechanisms have been spirited out of the country.'

'Of course,' Morton said equably. If he was going to add something, he never did.

Morton spent the night in his office suite in Geneva and woke at his usual hour of five a.m. Swinging his legs over the side of the cot, he bent down and placed both palms flat on the carpet and pushed downwards, driving the blood through his spine and hamstrings. As he did so, he focused his breathing to empty his mind of everything. Next came his exercises – each one forcing his muscles to their maximum tension to maintain physical balance and control over his body. Finally he began his karate. In that moment the bedroom filled with imaginary opponents. One he disposed of with a flying kick to the throat. Another fell to an elbow strike to the nose. A third collapsed under a head-butt to the jaw. Each strike was done without panting and sweating and

*with the minimum of movement. The real effort was in his mind,
constantly reminding himself that everything he did was to also
maintain him mentally in peak condition. Ten minutes after he
started, he stopped, closing his eyes and breathed deeply through
his nose. Shaved, showered and dressed, he used the bedside phone
to ring Manders in London to say he was coming.*

*At Heathrow a Special Branch officer was waiting on the
tarmac; he drove fast down the motorway. At Northolt an RAF
helicopter took him to Norfolk.*

*One look at the site told him the journey was a waste.
Everything had been restored to normal. He flew to Aldermaston,
Britain's nuclear weapons development centre. It took a while for
the establishment's director to mellow, to admit that, while the
triggers were inserted into the bombs at Aldermaston, they were
built by Nuclear Components in California's Silicon Valley.*

*'Naturally we don't spread that around. You know how
sensitive these things can be with political masters,' the director
said.*

*Leaving Aldermaston, Morton used the chopper's phone to ask
Lester Finel in Geneva to check on Nuclear Components.*

*Manders was waiting on the tarmac back at Northolt. On the
drive into London, Morton listened to his briefing and thanked
him. Then, in the same quiet voice, he added that what had
happened over running the investigation was none of his doing.
Both knew it was the closest Morton would ever come to saying
sorry. Suddenly Manders waved an open hand and smiled and
said there was no problem. No problem at all.*

*Since then Morton was always careful never to allow the
controlled urgency of his own enquiries ever to suggest to anyone
that he was the successor to Manders.*

*From time to time he had slipped away from the Englishman.
From one of those forays he learned about the balloon race from
England to Holland. Another private little voyage of discovery
brought him news of the weather at the time in the North Sea.*

Almost by accident, though not quite, he'd discovered that, although one of the balloons had suffered some sort of mishap, its crew had been rescued. All this he'd passed on to Chantal Bouquet in calls he made to Geneva from various pay-phones.

He hadn't shared any of this information with Manders; it was too early for that. Each time he rejoined him, it was to hear more of the same.

All the usual anti-this and anti-thats had been rounded up and given a sweating. A group of animal rights activists Special Branch had infiltrated were collared before they could raid a lab extracting dog-brain cells to use in cosmetics. A French gang boss was arrested at a magnificent rijstaffel in Manchester's finest Indonesian restaurant as he celebrated with a bunch of SAS veterans he'd just recruited. A Panamanian-registered cargo ship about to leave Liverpool was searched; in a container marked 'Diplomatic Property of the Government of the Republic of Yemen' were half a dozen young girls, all drugged. A raid on a fishmonger's in Glasgow turned up heroin with a street value of ten million pounds. There had been all sorts of successes. But not the one that mattered. Manders had shaken his head in angry frustration. Morton had known then what kind of man he was dealing with, and had adjusted accordingly, including graciously accepting the invitation to lunch at Simpson's.

Once they were seated at the back of the restaurant, Manders gave the tables on the far side a final glance.

'Only a few from Six at their troughs today,' he announced, his eyes slipping back to Morton. 'No doubt on this one they will, as our American cousins say, be waiting to see how the cookie crumbles. Dreadful expression, don't you think?'

Morton smiled his on-loan smile; he had no strong opinion on the way Americans spoke. After handing out menus, the maitre d' hovered with that look which waiters cultivate to imprint an impression on clients before the tipping stage.

'I can recommend the steak-and-kidney pie or the beef from the trolley,' Manders said, still not having looked at the menu. He turned to the waiter. 'And the usual decent bottle of claret to go with it, Hubert.'

'Certainly, Mr Manders.'

The waiter glanced at Morton.

'I'll take the beef. And just a glass of Ballygowan,' Morton said.

'Sparkling or plain, sir?'

'Sparkling. With a twist of lemon.'

When the waiter had padded away, Manders spoke in a low tone. 'It's not Lent, old boy.'

Morton looked as if until then it had not occurred to him. 'It's been Lent for a long time as far as I'm concerned.'

'Oh. I see. Yes, of course.'

'But I'll still enjoy the beef.'

An hour later, Manders had drunk the last of a respectable Burgundy and they were on their coffee. He had also ordered brandy. He balanced his empty glass in one hand as if deciding whether it needed refilling, before putting it down and looking across the table.

'We've still got every air- and sea-port sealed. Ditto all the private flying fields. The boys in blue have conducted so many random searches of the travelling public that the Home Secretary's had over a thousand complaints. Special Branch has turned over the families of those dead soldiers and my own people are putting the other squaddies through a similar hoop. We're squeezing all the usual arms dealers, and running dawn raids on some of the more dubious of our accountants and bankers. Just about anyone who, if the price is right, would handle the triggers. Not even a whisper of a whisper.'

'What about an insider?' Morton asked.

'Some disaffected group of servicemen?' Manders shook his head. 'And we've ruled out all the protest movements, animal liberation, anti-pollution – the lot. We've checked all army surplus clothes stores. Not one sold an NCB suit in months.'

'The nerve agent?' Morton asked, as if he was working from a checklist.

'Porton Down has a few ounces of Soman, for research purposes. It's all still there. So obviously this lot was imported. We're going back through all the manifests at sea- and air-ports for anything that could tie in to the Russians, Iraq or Iran. But nobody's holding their breath. As we both know, they all have a lifetime experience of playing hide and seek.'

Manders was rewarded with an admiring and strangely knowing smile from Morton.

'Can we go back to something you said earlier about the Prime Minister planning something to please the environmentalists,' Morton said.

'Still only a rumour, I'm afraid. But it could be one with legs. This morning I heard the PM has got his Press Secretary to call in CNN. That usually means Bostock's planning to say something for the international stage.'

'Why doesn't he use the BBC?'

Manders smiled sourly. 'He dislikes them intensely. It goes back to the way the Beeb wrongly called his election. He's a great one for rubbing people's noses in their mistakes.'

The Secretary of Defence and the Blessed Nancy were leaving, imperiously making their way out of the room. The waiter was hovering with a bottle. Manders nodded. The waiter poured and withdrew. Manders took a pull of brandy and immediately wiped his mouth with his napkin as if to relieve any guilt.

'How does the Prime Minister get on with your environmentalists?' Morton asked.

Manders took another swallow before he leaned across the table. 'He knows how to keep everyone on his side. But recently the greenfingers brigade have started whingeing that he hasn't lived up to his promises to turn this country into what would be a peasant economy. And he's making lovey-dovey visits to what remains of our industrialists, telling them he wants to see the country return to the days when their factories covered the landscape. Never happen, of course.'

From his smile Morton seemed to think so too.

Late in the afternoon a Jordanian Airlines freightmaster from Rome swept low over the razed, burnt landscape to land at Amman Airport. The air shimmered above the tarmac and the plane seemed to tilt and slide in the throbbing heat. The engines roared halfway down the runway as the thrust was reversed.

The aircraft taxied to a remote corner of the field and remained there. When darkness came with its usual swiftness, a fork-lift and a closed truck drove to the plane. The fork-lift removed two large containers from the hold and loaded them into the truck. Afterwards, a Jordanian customs officer fixed seals to its locks. The truck left the airport by a guarded gate well away from the brightly-lit main buildings and turned east into the desert. In thirty minutes it reached the border crossing into Iraq. Sentries at both check-points waved the driver through. The truck roared on into the night, driving into the desert to deliver the hot air balloon and gondola that had left California the day before.

TEN

A sensor concealed near the wadi where Muktar was murdered had recorded on magnetic tape the two gunshots fired by Bodor. The sensor had been installed by NSA, the National Security Agency, the United States' prime electronic ear to the world.

Following the collapse of the Soviet Union, which saw much of the US intelligence activities restructured, NSA clung to its original brief. From Fort George G. Meade in Maryland, the agency continued to be responsible for all signals intelligence, satellite surveillance and cryptography.

The sensor automatically transferred the tape to a satellite geopositioned over the Black Sea. One of its on-board computers deduced in milliseconds several important details. The shots had been fired 1.5 to 1.7 miles south-south-west of the sensor. The echo level suggested close proximity to high ground. The weapon used was a handgun. This information was transferred to one of the new-breed fast computers at Fort Meade.

The size of a family house and buried deep under the Maryland Hills, the computer was sited close to the runway Air Force One had used for its landing approach to Andrews Air Force base after its flight from Seattle. The computer analysed the data to decide which other computers within the US intelligence community required to see it. Two were selected.

One was a computer at the Defense Intelligence Agency

at Boling Air Force base on the Washington side of the Potomac. Its memory bank decided that the two gunshots warranted no further action on the part of anyone in the agency; the NSA transmission was consigned to LIBFIL, the huge electronic library at Boling.

The second computer was one of seventy-five the Central Intelligence Agency currently used. Its memory recognised an instruction it had received almost a year earlier, after an Agency field officer was caught servicing another sensor, and was summarily executed by gunfire by members of the Da'Irat al Mukhabarat al-Amah, or GID, Iraq's main intelligence organisation. CIA computers were now programmed to be on the alert for any shots fired in the vicinity of any sensor along the Iraqi border.

The computer referred details about the two shots to William Gates, the Director of Operations, who was away when the message arrived in his desk terminal. Details were also fed by satellite link directly into the Hammer Force computer system at its Geneva headquarters. All such information was sent as part of the working relationship between the agencies.

Finally, a copy of the message was sent by secure telefax to the CIA station in Istanbul, which had direct responsibility for the area where the two shots were fired. There the matter might well have rested, but for the fact that the station chief was Ken Adams, and it was springtime in Turkey and he was feeling horny.

The message was waiting for Adams when he arrived in his office at the rear of the United States chancery in downtown Istanbul. Adams was into the foothills of middle age, handsome in a hawkish way, with a barrel chest most men in these parts looked upon with respect.

This was the first communication in a week he had

received from Langley, a further indication that, despite the glamour still associated with the city, it was now, in intelligence terms, the arsewipe of his business. Mata Hari may indeed have plied her trade in the Pesa Palas Hotel down the street, but she wouldn't have picked up any worthwhile titbits nowadays.

He read the message one more time and shook his head. What the hell was going on at Langley that they bothered with something like this? So somebody had fired a couple of shots. So *what*? That Baghdad was about to go on the rampage again? Jesus H. Christ! That was the trouble with those assholes. They'd have you chasing your tail round the clock. It was part of their same arsewipe mentality that had seen him assigned to this post rather than one of the stations his seniority deserved. He'd done Beirut, Kuwait and Sarajevo, and had hoped for London or Paris. Instead they'd given him Istanbul. He knew why: someone like him no longer fitted into the new Langley. He was still hands-on, a veteran of every secret battle since the Cold War was hot. A can-do field agent with an open dislike of over-qualified deskmen. He told them he couldn't change; they'd smiled politely and gone back to their electronic keyboards.

He unlocked the steel shutter covering the wall map. The matching co-ordinates on the flimsy were midway between somewhere and nowhere on the Iraq border. Suddenly he smiled. Baku was the logical place to start. A lousy journey, with a couple of stopovers which would add the best part of half a day's travel time. But he'd crawl on all fours if need be to make sure he wouldn't be here when Betty came back.

Once he finally realised she was the kind of wife who should have married a banker, preferably one with a private fortune, their relationship had been downhill all the way.

Now Betty loathed him and his work equally. A couple of months ago she had packed herself off to ski with friends in Aspen. Until yesterday he hadn't heard from her. She'd called to say she wanted him to send a consulate car to pick her up at Istanbul airport and to make sure she didn't have to go through the lengthy Customs checks.

But the best reason for going to Baku was Madame Lutke. He had met her a year ago; they had dined together, then slept together in her apartment in the Old City. He had never bothered with her first name, only to make sure to use the condoms she thoughtfully laid out on her bedside table. Like him, there was something very basic about Madame Lutke.

In growing good humour, Adams began to plan his journey eastwards. First he sent a coded cable to Langley saying he would be off-station for a week. Then he booked a flight to Baku.

Morton was driven to Heathrow immediately after lunching with Manders, knowing his business in England was almost finished. To complete it he had asked Manders to arrange an office for him at the airport.

The room was on the upper floor of Terminal Three, a windowless box with hessian-covered walls and leather-backed chairs spread evenly around an oval table. On a sideboard was a telephone and a fax machine. The Special Branch officer who'd shown him into the room said it was used for interviewing suspicious passengers.

Morton used the phone to call the British Balloon and Airship Club in Leicester. A helpful voice said it would be a pleasure to provide the names of the balloonists in the race from Norfolk to Holland. The details arrived on the fax machine shortly afterwards. There had been fifty balloons in the race, drawn from nine countries. The names of the competing crews meant nothing to him. Against a Dutch entry was the penned notation: 'did not complete – ditched in sea'. He wrote instructions for what he wanted done and fed the fax back into the machine and sent it to Chantal Bouquet. Moments later the Special Branch officer returned to take him to his flight for Geneva.

ELEVEN

With her long-legged, aggressive stride, her eyes focused ahead, the lights from the TV cameras blurring into one, Zita Marcello knew the media throng pressed around her in the corridor of the courthouse in Garmisch-Partenkirchen, Bavaria, were making one comparison.

Carlo Marcello. The deal-maker who had sold out to Meridian International for a personal profit of a billion dollars and a five-year contract to remain as head of Marcello Enterprises. The corporation continued to fill every household between London and Leipzig with cheap products from the Third World: clothes, furniture, foods, toys, cigarettes and footwear.

Carlo Marcello: invariably dressed in a suit from the pages of *Gentleman's Quarterly*. Every salt-and-pepper hair carefully trimmed as he divided his time between bedroom and boardroom. Always ready with a joke for his corporate partners. Always with the model-of-the-month on his arm.

Carlo Marcello: whose wife was dead these past six years from a self-inflicted gunshot. The only way she could revenge herself for his constant and crushing betrayals had been to place the barrel of the shotgun in her mouth and use her middle toe to pull the trigger.

Carlo Marcello: the man she totally hated and despised for everything he stood for. Had done to her.

Carlo Marcello: her father.

Through the white noise Zita heard familiar questions.

'What do you think your father will feel about what you did?'

'Do you hate him because you have turned your back on society?'

'Are you an anarchist?'

'Will you accept the judge's recommendation that you should see a psychiatrist?'

'Why do you want to change the world?'

'What will you do now?'

She forced herself to continue looking straight ahead, still ignoring them all.

Around Zita the three policemen made a half-hearted attempt to hold back the reporters with microphones, photographers with flashbulbs and the cameramen with minicams on their shoulders, walking backwards to film her progress towards the building's exit.

The youngest of the policemen, Ludwig, the one with the thick neck, and endearing in the childlike way some physically strong men are in the presence of women, gave her a sideways look.

He had done the same the night before when he'd come to her hotel room, saying he had to check her statement. It had been late and she was already in her pyjamas. She'd known, as soon as she had handed the document back, uncorrected, that was not the real reason he was there. She'd gone out on to the bedroom balcony and stooped to rest her forearms on the rail, knowing he was looking at her, had felt the stirring, experienced again the primal yearning in her body. And with it came the familiar images.

From behind her Ludwig asked if she was enjoying the view. She didn't reply and he moved closer, easing down the waistband of her pyjamas until it was around her thighs and ran his fingers gently between her legs. She closed her eyes and in her mind the images grew stronger, dissolving one into another, until once more there was only one: her father's.

She made an awkward movement with her feet to stand more spreadeagled, and felt Ludwig pressing against her buttocks, groaning softly.

She'd ground out a brief command. 'Hurt me.'

Pain made it easier to hate. Ludwig squeezed her waist, the lower edges of his hands digging hard into the firm blades of her hips. She deliberately tensed her flank muscles to increase the pain.

'Hurt me more.' The shame of her command was part of the pain.

She felt him slide inside her, his bull-neck resting on her shoulder, his face looking out over the balcony.

For a moment a nameless emotion swept her body and her hands gripped hard on the balcony rail as she enjoyed what was happening. Then the shame of that made her cry inside. But the tears never reached her eyes. He father had said she must never shed them as, afterwards, he'd stroked her hair and said he truly loved her. And the hatred she felt for him had been rekindled with each of Ludwig's quickening movements.

Here in the corridor she sensed the hostility of his colleagues. They had arrested her after she drifted in her hot air balloon over the peak of the Zugspizte, the mountain backdrop to Germany's winter-sports capital. Close to a hundred thousand spectators in the Olympic Ski Stadium had watched her descent, together with some twenty million television viewers across Europe. Directly above the ski-jump platforms she had released her environmentally harmless but indelible green dye. The ice had turned the colour of an alpine meadow, forcing the European Ski Championships, sponsored by Marcello

Enterprises, to be abandoned. Drifting on across Garmisch-Partenkirchen, expertly avoiding the needle-like spire of the town's Alte Kirche, when she finally landed, Ludwig and his colleagues were waiting. The oldest, a small, wiry man, had probed her endlessly for a motive. She had quoted to him the words of Kant, that only those able to believe themselves to be the final end of creation would understand what motivated her. The policeman had shaken his head, bewildered and angry.

Now, through the babble of questions Zita continued to refuse to answer, she could sense what these reporters were thinking: why had she, born to all the advantages, exchanged them for a life where, once more, she was striding from a court? This time she was poorer by half a million Deutschmarks, her fine. Her balloon had been impounded and the judge had warned that if she flew one again in German airspace, she would have to serve her three-year suspended prison sentence.

Let them write what they liked. She had long stopped explaining that someone had to make a stand against what was being done to Mother Earth. How many of these reporters could even begin to understand her consuming conviction that the only hope was to launch a great greening of the earth, to fight all those who, like her father, took their profits from raping the rain forests and polluting the soil and the seas? When she had tried to explain her views, the judge had cut her off, allowing the prosecutor to mock her. In a score of courts across Europe and North America she had experienced a similar response in the wake of other headline-making protests.

They had begun after that momentous day, four years previously, her twenty-third birthday, when she overflew Everest in a hot air balloon, then landed on the mountain's summit and planted a Greenpeace flag. But she had realised that more militant action was needed to stop those destroying the world. Since then she had launched herself against their factories, their whaling fleets, their logging camps and surface-mining installations. As her protests attracted increasing hostility, Greenpeace withdrew its support. Now she was a protester without any backup.

Though she had learned from painful experience to hide behind an icy exterior, the truth was that, deep inside her, was an unlanced sac of pain: the knowledge that she had suffered so much. The law said she was a criminal, but the law was unforgiving and uncaring – and itself guilty of a far greater crime than she had ever committed. The crime of doing nothing to protect Mother Earth. Somewhere society had lost its way, and she wanted to be no part of those who were responsible. She would go on hurting them until they came to their senses. The more she was punished, the more determinedly she would respond.

A blonde-haired TV reporter slipped between the escort and stood directly in Zita's path. 'Your father says he understands your concerns about the environment, but your methods are not the way to address it.' She had to shout to be heard above the din.

Zita stared at her, a brief smile of wry amusement softening her face. 'That is impossible,' she answered calmly.

'Impossible? Your father has said it,' cried the reporter.

'My father is dead.'

'Dead? What do you mean?' The reporter seemed uncertain how to proceed in the sudden silence.

Zita looked directly into the camera. 'For me he died when he said the first duty of every officer of every company is to feel in his heart, in his very soul, only how to make a bigger profit.'

She resumed striding down the corridor as a fresh

torrent of questions was unleashed.

'Are you as mad as the judge seems to think?' shouted a reporter.

'Do you realise how many people were put out of work by your protest here? How much pleasure you denied others?'

'Will you buy another balloon?'

'Will you fly again?'

'Who will you attack next?'

Approaching the exit door, she gathered her trenchcoat around her. Outside, a crowd was waiting, their presence fuelled in part, she suspected, from her face once more being on most front pages and on every network newscast.

'Do you have transport?' Ludwig asked.

'No, I will walk to the hotel,' Zita replied.

The media pack swept her out of the building on to the courthouse steps. The first murmurs of anger came from the crowd.

Zita continued to ignore the flashbulbs exploding in her face, remaining poised and somehow still in command. Motioning to the policemen to stand aside, she walked towards the crowd, stopping before them. 'If you wish to harm me, I cannot stop you. But ask yourselves this question. Why do you want to hurt me when you are being hurt in so many other ways?'

As she continued to move steadily forward, their ranks sullenly parted.

Behind her the woman TV reporter began to speak into a camera. 'Zita Marcello has done this before ... many times ... faced down a crowd ... cynics say it is all part of her act ... to present herself as a modern-day Joan of Arc ... someone ready to die for her belief. Others say as her stunts become more desperate, she might well end up doing that ... but for most people, like this crowd here, she is an object of resentment . . .'

At that moment a car parked further up the street started. The crowd's anger was growing.

A tomato burst against the back of Zita's coat. The reporters and cameramen hurried forward. The car drew level. The tinted window by the driver's seat rolled down and a pleasant face, unremarkable except for the blackest pair of eyes she had ever looked into, appraised her briefly.

'Please get in. I am not Press. Neither am I from your father,' he said.

She stood stiffly, for the first time uncertain. 'Who are you?'

'That doesn't matter now. Just do what I say.'

Another tomato hit her in the back. The policemen were running forward. The shouts from the crowd were louder, angrier.

'In a moment they will become a mob,' said the driver.

The rear door of the car was open. A piece of over-ripe fruit hit the windscreen.

Zita climbed into the back. She was momentarily astonished to find her luggage from the hotel on the seat. As the door closed, the driver picked up speed to escape a fusillade of rotten fruit.

'We'll lose them soon enough. And by the way, about your luggage. I thought it best to collect it from the hotel as I didn't think you would wish to return there.'

The Arranger had spoken in his native tongue, English with an American accent.

In the driving mirror he smiled at her. After a moment she smiled back.

TWELVE

Morton sat with his back to the room, his head so still above the high-backed chair that he could have been asleep. In the late afternoon the mountains were like the glacis of a mediaeval fortress, rising abruptly out of the foothills. The glass gave a slight distortion to the view. The first thing Johnny Quirke's people in Technical Services had done was to treat all the windows to deflect a bugging device. Only Morton's eyes betrayed his watchfulness as, beyond the window, a pair of hawks wheeled above the icy peaks and deep-set gullies. He had chosen this room in Hammer Force headquarters for its magnificent view of the Alps behind Geneva. They helped him to think.

Returning from London he'd found a message asking him to come to Walter's office.

Bitburg was seated in his grand corner office decorated in rich panelling, every space filled with memorabilia: Walter with this President, that Prime Minister, a First Lady, being received by the Pope, bowing before the Queen. Morton had always felt that this slavish attachment to these symbols served somehow to underline the fact that Walter's own life would never quite measure up to them.

Bitburg leaned forward across an expanse of desk towards which all the room's other furniture was subtly angled.

'I must say, David, it would be immeasurably helpful if you told me where you were going. The first I knew you had been to London was when I received a fax from the Ministry of Defence

*confirming we were now officially in charge of this search for their
missing devices. That means the meter is ticking away against us.
Or rather me. In the end I have to balance the books,' Bitburg
said.*

*The silence between them was more than distance, it was
something wider and deeper.*

'You'll balance them, Walter.' Morton said at last.

'And before London, where were you?' Bitburg asked.

*Morton continued staring at Bitburg, remembering again
what had happened at Auschwitz, each distinct, detachable,
unforgettable moment. Then he spoke, holding nothing back. He
told Walter what Mischa had seen, what Sharon had confirmed,
what Manders had said. He described the site in Norfolk, his visit
to Aldermaston. He even mentioned the balloon race and the
weather in the North Sea. He gave none of what he said a special
emphasis, delivering it almost in a monotone, the way he always
did when the throb of the war drum was still distant.*

*When he had finished, the sun, low, cast a long shadow over
Bitburg's desk. He was toying with a piece of paper, thin bony
fingers rubbing its edges. At last he shrugged, part of some inner
dialogue. To complete, it, he produced his pipe.*

*'Poland, then England,' Bitburg said, sounding like a tour
guide checking an inventory. 'Not much to show for all that
travel, is there?'*

*Bitburg's eyes started to dance, like balls being repeatedly
struck by a billiard cue in his head. What else was going on in
there, going round and round? Walter's way was to keep
everything in separate compartments, each labelled with the
amount of proof it contained. When Walter thought there wasn't
enough, his eyes led a life of their own. They continued to dance
as Morton spoke.*

*'Are we now in the business of measuring returns by
expenditure?'*

'I could think of a worse yardstick, David.'

Bitburg bent across the desk, pipe stem in one hand, his voice dry and precise. 'I certainly think you should treat the Irishwoman's information as background. From what I'm told she no longer has the same access. And Manders doesn't really take you anywhere. That probably was why the baton was passed to us.' He paused, drawing a breath. 'So what we have left is the Russian woman, this Mischa. Any connection, for want of a better word, between Bodor and the theft of those mechanisms is based on what she says. That seems very risky to me, very risky indeed.'

Bitburg began to fill his pipe as Morton continued to watch him expressionlessly.

'And what about this packet Bodor's supposed to have stored in that mortuary, David? She didn't see him leave with it. And even if she had, what does that prove? It could have contained hard currency, drugs, even the family jewels. Bodor could have tucked anything away. But there's absolutely nothing to show they were his work plans — assuming, of course, they exist. This Mischa woman admits that nobody in Moscow's seen them, which strikes me as more than a little unusual. If these plans were that important, somebody would have wanted to hang on to them. And you've read the intelligence summaries. The consensus in Washington, London and just about any other place is that whatever Bodor might have been up to, he's now certainly out of the frame. So what do you have, David? Speculation, pure and simple. No proof, not even a scintilla. You need more than this woman has told you. A great deal more to link Bodor to those trigger mechanisms.'

Bitburg sat back, his eyes steady now, back on home territory.

'What could Bodor do with the triggers? You've admitted yourself his old masters have no need of him any more. And there's nothing to suggest that anybody else has bought him up. And what would they do with him? You have always said that at the end of every act of terrorism lies one key question: what is the real

goal? What could the real goal possibly be here, David? Who's going to hire Bodor to produce something they can't use? Even if there is some connection between those triggers and Bodor, even if he actually makes a weapon – then what?'

In the renewed silence a longcase clock in the corner struck the quarter. Bitburg had been presented with it to mark his fortieth birthday. By then he was long embalmed in his own certainties.

'No, David, until you know a great deal more I must ask you to be extremely judicious in how you commit our resources.'

Morton watched him go through the process of finally lighting up, drawing the flame of a wooden match into the bowl. The smoke wreathed his balding head.

'Are you telling me to hand this back to London?' Morton's voice was dangerously calm.

'That would be the sensible thing to do, David.' Bitburg glanced down at the piece of paper. 'Those triggers come very much under the British defence of the realm and all that. Domestic, not international. We are very much international. And if we start getting caught up in tracking down the likes of our friend Bodor for no good reason, in no time we'll have the Salvation Army asking if we'll open a Missing Persons Bureau!' Bitburg let out a small laugh, and picked up the paper. 'I really think we have to be extremely cautious in what we take on. So, as I say, I've prepared this hand-back memo. Feel free to change anything. But I think I've got the basic thrust about right.'

'Tear it up, Walter. You don't do anything involving my work without first checking with me.'

The only sound in the silence was the paper fluttering back on to the desk. In the light from the window Bitburg's face was suffused with tiny broken blood vessels. When he spoke, it was with effort. 'No offence, David, I was trying to be helpful. Of course, as this is an operational matter, it's your ultimate decision. I only wanted to point out all the ramifications.'

Morton's on-loan smile was iron-hard, coming and going so

fast it might never have touched his lips. He suddenly felt tired — tired and wasted. He pushed back his chair and stood up, needing to end this nonsense. Needing to be with his own people. Needing to do some serious work before they joined him.

In the past hour he had done so.

Morton could see the hawks once more quartering the ground, crossing one just below the other, as if they were following lines of some invisible grid in the mountains. Watching them swoop earthwards, their broad wings taking the thermal, he could sense the certainty of their hunting.

It was the way he had worked since he'd chosen this life. In doing so he had deliberately turned his back on another: marriage, children, a sense of continuity. These were not for him, not that at times he hadn't thought of them. But in the end he realised that the skills he commanded did not extend to those required for domestic harmony. The selectivity with which he approached everything made that impossible: he was focused to such a degree for lengthy periods that domesticity would be impossible with other commitments. Long ago he had decided that the only rules he could live by were his own.

Apart from his desk, with its built-in modem and keyboard, the office was furnished with informally grouped armchairs and state-of-the-art communications equipment. On one wall was a bank of monitors and a 24-hour clock showing the times in various capital cities. The screens enabled him to communicate visually with police and other government agencies in those countries.

The opposite wall was covered with a computerised liquid-crystal-display map of the world. A yellow pinprick glowed in the centre of Norfolk at the site of the MoD site. Form there a pencil-slim red line entered the North Sea stopping at a point equidistant between the English and Dutch coasts. Another pinprick, green, indicated a point north-west of St Petersburg. Radiating from it, like the spokes of an illuminated wheel, ran other lines, all coloured red. These extended north into Finland and Sweden, west to Germany and south to Turkey. The line running eastwards petered out towards the Kazakhstan border with China. A third light, white, glowed brightly at a spot inland from San Francisco's Silicon Valley. From there a flickering blue dotted line extended all the way back to the yellow pinprick in Norfolk.

Morton had created the map from what he had learned in England. It would be the focus point for his assessment briefing.

In a bedroom in the Frankfurt Airport Sheraton Hotel, the Arranger lay beside Zita, watching her sleeping. Both were naked and the bed damp from sex. For him it had been release after months of abstinence. She took him with a passion as though every time would be the last, each time offering him a different position, a different woman.

Once, during the night, he'd returned from the bathroom to find her lying awake, her thighs loose and spread.

'You look marvellous,' he'd said.

She'd looked up at him and dropped a hand, her forefinger extended between her legs, touching her tumescent lips, continuing to make it easy for him.

Now he wondered again whether somewhere along the way she had reached a plateau between expectation and compromise: that she knew she was not intending to change the world, but trying to was a good way to raise a finger to her old man. Studying what he could see of her face not buried in the pillow, he thought she really did look like Carlo Marcello: the strong eyebrows, the straight

Roman nose, her father's uncompromising jaw. And if he was like her in bed, there must be a lot of satisfied women.

Seduction was a part of his work, but it was a long time since sleeping with someone had been such a genuine pleasure. Looking back, he realised it had been in both their minds.

She was silent and watchful as they drove out of Garmisch-Partenkirchen. Once he reached the Munich autobahn, she thanked him for helping her escape from the crowd and the reporters. Still driving north, he explained why he had rescued her. He had rehearsed the offer until it was word perfect. He explained that, in all technical matters, she would have complete control and her fee would be one million American dollars, payable in a currency of her choice; half now, the balance on completion of the assignment. All her expenses would be met.

She told him to stop the car. She joined him in the front passenger seat and asked him to repeat everything. When he had done so, she sat immobile, her strong hands clasped on her lap, the denim skirt stretched across her thighs. Behind the eyes he'd seen the same quick intelligence, weighing the information. Then the questions began.

He'd been prepared for them, matching her technical queries with detailed responses. For almost a month he had studied ballasting and valving, the burning rate of propane at various altitudes, ascent rates, wind drift and much else. What really impressed her, he knew, was his casual reference to a new kind of polyester envelope, heat-welded by a secret technique.

'No bumpy rides,' he smiled.

'And make a great platform,' she added. 'But you're not spending all this money just to test out a platform.'

'That's just part of it.'

'What's the rest?'

By-passing Stuttgart, Heidelberg and Mannheim, he'd gone

on answering her questions. Her clear, clever eyes continued to appraise.

'How d'you know so much about balloons?' she suddenly asked.

'My job.'

'But you don't look like a balloonist.'

He'd shown his amusement. 'They come in all shapes and sizes. Rather like balloons. But no, I'm not a balloonist. Just one of the drawing-board backroom boys.'

'Well, we need them too.' Replacing the appraisal was acceptance. Her questions were now couched in a tone of partnership. What was the storage space in the gondola for the oxygen bottles? What kind of breathing suit? The thickness of the reflection paint on the gondola? Who had made the flight suit? He answered everything.

Finally, as they reached the Darmstadt intersection, she asked one last question. 'And afterwards, the balloon will be mine?'

He'd slowed to avoid a tanker before answering. 'Not only yours, but you will be provided with all the back-up facilities you will need for one year.'

She had looked directly at him. 'Who do you work for?'

But the one thing he had learned in his profession was that if no two liés are the same, the one essential for them all to succeed is that there must be a complicity between the deceiver and the deceived, based on an interlocking of differing needs.

'Let's just say for people who sympathise with your views. For the moment, though, they would prefer to remain in the background. But if you do this, you will find they are generous.'

He'd fished out a plain sealed envelope from his pocket and handed it to her.

Inside she found a bank draft for US$500,000 drawn in her name. She sat in silence for a while, looking at him, yet not seeing him. Her thoughts were elsewhere. Slowly she began to nod. With this, everything was once more possible.

'Would you like to lodge the draft now?' he asked.

He waited in the car while she completed her business in the bank in Frankfurt.

As he parked outside the hotel, Zita reached across and rubbed his thigh and began caressing him. Her eyes were luminous and very much alive.

'I'm trying to make up my mind what you would be like in bed,' she murmured in a different voice.

'Probably as good as you.'

Now, six hours later, he had proved that. And she had taken her pleasure with a wildness he had never expected.

The Arranger closed his eyes.

Zita was awakened by the dawn creeping between the half-closed curtains. She glanced quickly at the piece of paper on her bedside table, almost as if she needed to reassure herself this was not all a dream. But the bank transfer confirmed it all. Not only her fee, but the plan itself was staggering. To be part of this was the one opportunity she had always wanted to concentrate the minds of all the most important leaders in the world. Not one of them, she had been assured, would be physically harmed. And after they had recovered from the shock, and probably anger, world opinion would surely make them understand that all she had done was to bring them to their senses. This one single, dramatic gesture would achieve more in her campaign to save Mother Earth than all she had done before. The prospect once more released the strong sexual urge in her.

She lay for a little while, allowing her sexual excitement to build, then she slid her palms lightly over his body and began to nibble at him gently. The Arranger opened his eyes.

'Time to raise the flag one more time?' she murmured,

her lips on his skin, increasing the tempo, feeling her lips open, only dimly aware that this time the old, disgusting images of her father had not surfaced.

Afterwards the Arranger had told her about the next stage of her journey.

Two hours later, showered and changed into fresh denims, Zita followed the Arranger into the airport's executive jet compound. He walked her to the door of the waiting Lear. After the plane had taken off, he went to the departure concourse. Using a credit card he dialled a number in Los Angeles. An answering machine told him to leave a message. When he had done so, he walked over to the Alitalia desk and collected his prepaid ticket for a flight to Sardinia.

In the Oval Office the President pushed aside the food tray his valet had brought. Nowadays he often lunched alone at his desk to catch up with paperwork that needed settling before he left on a trip. Usually he managed to keep an eye on one of the television network news programmes on the bank of screens across the room. Today he had selected Global News, the brash, thrusting challenger to CNN.

What he had heard a moment before made him shudder inwardly, an emotional rather than a physical tremor. The network's chief Washington correspondent continued to develop an attack, all the more devastating for its crisply persuasive tone, against the administration's environmental policies to date. The broadcast echoed identical editorials that morning in a hundred newspapers. All were owned, like Global News, by Meridian International. The President sat for a moment longer, listening to the on-screen voice saying that, if the administration continued on its present path, the result would see American business and industry plunge back into the doldrums.

Leaning forward, as if he almost knew the President would be watching, the commentator concluded. 'What we need today from Washington, from the Oval Office itself, is a clear signal that this administration, while fully recognising the need for a sensible environmental policy, will also not forget that what once made this nation the envy of the world was the toil of its machines and the power beneath its smoke stacks. What has to be done . . .'

Cursing softly, the President cut the voice off with his zapper. Ignatius Bailey had given his answer. This was his response to Earth Saver. This was Bailey . . .

The President stopped in mid-thought. He hadn't yet sent out the invitation to Bailey! What was behind these attacks was Meridian's belated response to the administration's action against those of its companies which had blatantly disregarded even the minimum of environment safeguards.

The President's good humour was completely restored. If this was all Bailey could come up with, it was liveable with. The first thing he'd learned in this office was that he couldn't afford the vulnerability of being thin-skinned, otherwise he would act to avoid criticism rather than out of conviction. He decided that instead of sending Bailey a written invitation he'd call him personally to show him there was no ill-feeling. Then, once he'd gotten Bailey on board Air Force One, he'd use every trick to convince him who was right.

THIRTEEN

Tommy Nagier was the first to arrive in Morton's office. He glanced at the wall map in a moment of flushed self-consciousness. This was his first assessment briefing, and a sign of a hard-won standing within Hammer Force; the onset of saltiness at his temples was the result of five years in the field.

'You tried out the new wet suit yet?' Morton asked from behind his desk.

Tommy turned from the display. 'Mike put on one of his storm specials. But those fins are great stabilisers in twenty-foot waves.'

Tommy had his father's way of looking at you directly when he spoke. And that fine-boned build and deep-set eyes spoke of a total absence of fear. Danny's boy to the last.

As Tommy settled in an armchair, Anna Cruef arrived. Tall and slim, thighs and legs long, it was easy to see why men found her attractive. But no man in his right senses would try and get a jump on Anna more than he would on a sleeping tigress. She'd studied at Oxford, case-officered for MI5 and lectured at Sandhurst before joining Psychological Assessment. Anna gave a little hand-wave to Morton before turning to the map.

Scrutiny over, she took a seat beside Tommy as Lester Finel walked in, mopping his forehead. A skinny man in his late forties and prematurely grey, Finel wore another of his bold-check jackets and golfer's plaid trousers.

'This building's like a hot-house, Dave.' No one else called Morton that.

The others smiled. Lester kept his computer room at a constant 55 degrees Fahrenheit, insisting that was how to obtain maximum efficiency. No one was going to argue. At Honeywell, he'd virtually rewritten the lexicon on computers in intelligence-gathering. Ignoring the map, he walked over to Morton's desk and handed him a sheet of paper.

Morton studied the details of the shots fired on the Iraqi border.

He tapped his keyboard and on the map a green light appeared south of Baku. 'Anything on Nuclear Components, Lester?'

Finel continued speaking in torn-off sentences. 'Part of Meridian International. Hundred million turnover a year. Used to be twice as much. Probably not sure now where the next war's coming from. A year ago talk was Meridian planned to sell off Nuclear. But they're still there. Meridian's probably keeping them for a rainy day.'

'How'd they get into triggers, Lester?'

'Smart bombs. Nuclear produced the on-board electronics for those through-the-keyhole missiles the Americans used on Baghdad in the Gulf War. Bush said their chips were better than the Japanese.'

'Where'd he say that?'

'Some cookout in Texas. Ignatius Bailey was there. A week later Nuclear was in the Meridian portfolio. Work began on those triggers straight away. Meridian's capital meant it was expense-no-hassle time. The Brits took the first batch. At a million dollars a pop. When their nuclear deterrent programme got mothballed, the MoD put the triggers in cold storage.'

Morton glanced for a moment at the map. 'Nuclear make any other sales?'

'Not so far as I can tell, Dave. Fact, they stopped making triggers about six months ago.'

Morton managed a brief smile. 'Useful to know, Lester.'

As Finel took his seat, the door opened to admit a trio of middle-aged men. They were dressed in the denims favoured by most department heads.

Danny Nagier, Hammer Force's surveillance supremo, was distinguished by an eye-patch. Losing an eye had done nothing to reduce his skills in tracing a bug or hiding a microphone in places no one thought possible. Sean Carberry and Johnny Quirke were Irishmen of similar chunky build. Carberry had been his country's spokesman at the United Nations; few had known that his skills as a fixer were equalled by his marksmanship. Quirke was an outstanding lawyer at the Dublin Bar until he took early retirement to concentrate on his passion for inventions. Morton had recruited them both in the same week: Carberry to run Covert Action, Quirke to take control of the eclectic group of boffins in Technical Services. Both had shown him that they could maintain control in any situation. They'd also passed the hardest of his tests, loyalty. Giving it to their country was one thing. He demanded the loyalty that came from ignoring the book and doing it his way.

Glancing quickly at the wall display, the trio made no comment as they took their seats.

Chantal Bouquet's arrival caused a small stir; she always did when she came into a room. Deeply tanned, she avoided make-up or jewellery, anything to detract from her natural good looks. She knew a good deal more than most women ever get to learn about evil. Morton had appointed her head of Foreign Intelligence after she'd shown what she could do in places like Bosnia and Iran.

After giving the map a careful scrutiny, Chantal turned

to him. 'I can add something to that, David,' she said quietly, glancing down at the clipboard she carried. 'The balloon that ditched came down near one of the oil rigs in the North Sea. The gondola sank, but the rig's rescue launch picked up the crew. As they were Dutch, the oil company's helicopter flew them on to Alkmann.'

'The crew file an accident report?' Morton asked.

Chantal shook her head quickly. 'No need to. The incident happened outside Dutch waters. No one was hurt, and the cops at Alkmann sound like cops everywhere when it comes to unnecessary paperwork.'

'Wouldn't there have to be something for the insurers?'

Chantal checked the clipboard. 'The crew said they'd deal with that.'

'They leave any home addresses?' Morton asked.

'No. The cops didn't bother. But the one I spoke to who'd driven them to the station said they'd caught a train to Amsterdam.'

'Any idea where they went from there?'

'Sardinia. The cop remembered them saying something about that. I checked Schipol. All three caught an afternoon flight to Cagliari. I had Schipol security feed their names through its computers. Nothing known.'

In the silence everyone watched Morton add a new line, yellow, on the light display, linking Schipol Airport with the one at Cagliari.

'And from there, Chantal?' he asked.

She sighed. 'No trace.'

'Do we know who made the balloon?'

Chantal glanced at the clipboard, nodding. 'The Free Flight Corporation. They're based at Barstow, out in the California desert. The company was acquired by Meridian a year ago.'

'Did Meridian keep the staff on?' Morton asked carefully.

'Some. But mostly when it acquires, it puts in its own people.'

'For sure. This race. Who sponsored it?'

'Choc-Lait. A confectionery subsidiary of Marcello Enterprises – also now part of Meridian.'

Morton tapped a key to produce this time a purple light out on the plains between Kansas City and Denver. 'Meridian. World headquarters of Meridian International,' he announced.

'The oil rig's owned by Globoil, another Meridian subsidiary,' Chantal added briskly.

'For sure,' Morton said again.

As Chantal took a seat, the door opened to admit a tall, white-haired, dishevelled, elderly man who looked at Morton quizzically, then raised an eyebrow.

'Thought I'd be early. Clearly not. But better late than never. All here, are we?'

'All here, Prof,' Morton confirmed.

In his cardigan and baggy cords, the Head of Psychological Assessment still looked the donnish figure who had once held the Chair of Psychology at Harvard. Morton had persuaded him to join Hammer Force to see his theories put into practice.

'Pretty display, David,' said the Prof, nodding at the map. 'Can't think I can be very much use to you at this stage.'

'Don't worry, Prof. You'll have your work cut out on this one. We all will.'

After the Prof was seated, Morton came from behind his desk to stand beside the map. For a long moment he remained silent. Then he began to speak in a quiet voice, telling them where he had been, whom he had spoken to, and why they were here. 'In the hands of anyone who has a modicum of knowledge of explosives, those triggers could create havoc. In Bodor's hands the damage could be incalculable,' Morton added.

They continued to listen in rapt silence as he gave them a concise account of Bodor's career. He then detailed the objections raised by scientists in the West to Bodor having achieved anything worthwhile with his research. All this was delivered with the same controlled energy which seemed to be continually saying that the only way to succeed is to keep an open mind.

Pausing only to pick up a pointer, Morton turned back to the map and moved the stick across the British Isles.

'Given that Manders had closed down every exit point, the only way the triggers could have been smuggled out was by balloon. Almost certainly it was the one which went down near the Globoil rig. To arrange that needed organisation way beyond the reach of run-of-the-mill terrorists. And there would have been very substantial funding. Certainly enough to write off half a million dollars for that balloon and to deal with its crew who, even if they didn't know exactly what was going on, would still need to be kept quiet. To pay the supplier of the nerve agent. We are looking at somebody ready to lay out several million dollars, possibly more.

'Somebody with that kind of money would have made sure that, at every stage, there would be a cut-off point. We have to identify those points because they are the ones we could waste time on. The Brits think the Soman could have come from Baghdad. But even knowing that isn't going to bring us any closer to who is behind Bodor and the trigger thefts. The same with the protective clothing the thieves must have used. Manders has had every army surplus store in Britain turned upside down. We could waste even more time doing the same in Europe. My gut feeling is the suits were stolen a long time ago. This whole thing has a long-term feel about it.'

Morton tapped the yellow light marking the position of the burgled site in Norfolk. 'My bet is that the team who went in, killed the patrol and removed the triggers is the same one who crewed the balloon. At that stage it would be important to keep things as tight as possible.'

He used the pointer to follow the line extending into The Wash. 'From the bunker to the coast is no more than a couple of hours by road. It took the best part of an hour for the search to get under way properly. By the time Manders had his people up at the coast, there was no way to recall the balloons.

'But even if the search had immediately included the Continent, it would have made no difference. When that balloon dropped into the sea, the crew transferred the triggers on board the rig. The devices are small and light enough for each man to have easily carried two. They could have passed them off as something to do with the balloon. No one would have suspected anything, so questioning the oil riggers won't get us anywhere.'

Morton began to trace the extended line to Alkmann. 'The same, for sure, applies to the helicopter crew. They also wouldn't have seen anything suspicious. Neither did the Alkmann police. By the time the search finally spread to Holland, our balloonists were well on their way to Sardinia.'

Morton's pointer followed the flight path from Schipol Airport to the Mediterranean. 'It's a direct flight, but they didn't take the triggers with them. They would have shown up on baggage radar. The devices, I am certain, were handed over in Amsterdam.'

He paused, standing there like a human ultimatum, demanding of himself an answer, but never passing on the pressures he was feeling.

He moved the pointer back to Amsterdam. 'Where did

the triggers go from there? Rule out Russia or any of the other republics. From what Mischa said, Bodor would never be able to start up there again. But let's stay with Mischa for a moment. She thinks the packet contained the blueprints for his new weapon. I'll buy that until we know otherwise. But that still doesn't bring us any closer to the answer. What kind of weapon? The best guess is that it is something to do with the stratosphere. But *what*? Anything in space requires a back-up system only few governments can afford. But supposing somebody as powerful as those governments wanted such a weapon?'

'Someone like Meridian International?' Chantal asked softly.

Unexpectedly Morton smiled, the crinkles around his eyes deepening. Then, as quickly as it had appeared, the smile went. 'Why would anyone at Meridian want to have those triggers stolen? And if they did, why not have Nuclear Components run up a handful?' Morton needed confirmation.

Danny was frowning, concentrating. 'Maybe that would take too long for why they are needed.'

The Prof leaned forward and began to nod. 'Questions could be asked in lots of places if Nuclear tooled up again. That sort of thing wouldn't go unnoticed in the Pentagon or by the nuclear energy authorities.'

'Supposing the theft was deliberately meant to have people looking the wrong way?' Tommy suggested.

'You mean that Greenpeace slogan on the outer door?' Anna asked.

'Yes.' Tommy looked at her, half expecting an answer but getting nothing more than a shrug.

'How'd anyone get into that facility in the first place? It must have had max security,' Finel said.

Carberry spoke. 'With the kind of money David says is

behind this, you could build a mock-up of the place and hire another Big Mike to train your thieves.'

Morton continued to patrol the exchanges, allowing them to flow without interruption.

'Where could they build a realistic nuclear bunker?' Lester asked.

'I could name you a hundred places,' Carberry said cheerfully.

'And someone at Meridian secretly funded all this?' asked Tommy doubtfully. 'Surely there'd be all kinds of checks and balances to stop someone doing that?'

'It wouldn't just be any old someone, son,' Danny said. 'And in many ways, because of their size, a conglomerate is easier to steal from. Once you've found a way round the system, it would be easier than robbing a smaller business.'

'Someone who would know how to sign the cheque without anybody knowing where the money was going.' The Prof stirred in his seat. 'It happens more times than you realise, Tommy.'

Tommy grunted, looking at Morton, trying to imagine him adding each tiny dollop of information to some mosaic he would be creating in his mind.

'That still doesn't explain why anyone at Meridian, or anywhere else, would steal those triggers,' Tommy said. 'Or have I missed something, Colonel?'

Morton let his silence speak for him. And the others, who understood so much about him, seemed to understand this too, for when he spoke, it was as if they were now securely in business.

Morton looked at Finel. 'I want you to run a complete check on every one of Meridian's companies. Start with Nuclear Components and Free Flight.'

He turned to Tommy. 'See if you can pick up those

balloonists.' He began to move the pointer eastwards from Sardinia across the Mediterranean. 'If the island was only a staging point, you're looking for familiar boltholes. Beirut, the Bekaa Valley and beyond, Iran and Iraq.'

The Prof once more stirred. 'Awful place, Sardinia's become, Tommy. Filled with two-hundred-pound frautanks from Düsseldorf and Rhine maidens with moustaches.'

Morton waited for the laughter to subside; the Prof could always be counted on to ease the tension. He began to move the pointer along the line towards Kazakhstan as he spoke to Anna.

'My bet is that Bodor went east. But unless something turns up to say otherwise, rule out China. Beijing's trying to mend fences with the West. Having Bodor tinkering with those triggers in their backyard is not going to help that.'

Anna could feel the energy in Morton. She could feel it in all of them – a keenness, a quickness of eyes in exchanged looks. She studied the map a while longer, then smiled at Morton. 'But he's in someone's backyard, right?'

He seemed to smile in return, but suddenly Morton's smile had little to do with what normally passes for humour. He had to get close; close enough to see his man; to walk in his footsteps; to be there in the passenger seat; beside his bed while he slept; dining at the same table; standing in the bathroom. He wanted to be the shaving mirror. *He wanted to be that close to Bodor.*

He used the pointer to tap the light on the Iraqi border. 'Let's keep an open mind about those shots. They happened four days after Mischa saw Bodor in Moscow. So, logically, he could have reached there. But this spot's on one of the recognised smuggling routes out of Asia the Kurds use into both Iran and Iraq. The shots could have been no more than a fallout among them. It happens all the time.'

'Or they could be a diversion to make us think Bodor went that way,' murmured the Prof.

'If he did, we should be looking for him both in Iran and Iraq,' said Tommy.

'Those are the places we would be *expected* to look for him,' Anna said.

Quirke squinted at the map. 'If Bodor did reach there – and it's a big if – he could be on his way to Pakistan or North Korea. Both are in the market for his skills – and have the money to pay for them.'

'If we include them in the frame, that's going to stretch our resources somewhat,' Danny objected.

'Just to cover Pakistan would mean I'd have to use pretty well everyone. Include North Korea, and I'm out of manpower,' Carberry added.

The Prof clasped his hands over his knees. 'The intention could be to run ragged anyone chasing after Bodor, don't you think?'

Tommy continued to listen, beginning to hear a wordless second conversation from the one going on around him.

'For the moment keep North Korea and Pakistan in the frame. But until we know whether Bodor came anywhere near this spot, we also keep an open mind about where we send,' Morton said.

Carberry nodded, satisfied. Beside him, the Prof closed his eyes.

Morton turned to Danny. 'I want you to go to Amsterdam. See if you can find the handover point for those triggers.'

Next it was Carberry's turn. They were going to need a team with the usual backup on a thirty-minute start-up time.

Morton looked at Chantal. 'I want you to cast your

net loose and wide. Tell your people to let anything which swims to the surface continue on its way. We need to give them breathing space so that we hook who really matters.'

He waited for her comments. 'Those fanatical balloon-ists live on their own planet. They'd notice a stranger immediately, or if one of their regular colleagues behaved out of character.'

Morton nodded approval.

Quirke spoke. 'Zita Marcello,' he said. 'Carlo Marcello's daughter. A court in Bavaria whacked her a massive fine for spoiling some ski contest her old man's firm sponsored. She knows that world inside out.'

'See if we can find her, Johnny,' Morton said.

Like a mystery train which has suddenly vanished from the track only to reappear again, the Prof opened his eyes and re-entered the conversation. 'I know something about that child. One of my old colleagues at Harvard had her for a semester. He said she was gifted but totally out of kilter. Most of it was to do with her mother's suicide. Apparently the child had to identify the body, and I gather half the mother's face was missing. And I suppose it didn't help that her father has had more mistresses than an English royal. No wonder she's turned out like she has.'

'See what we've got on her and her father, and I want profiles on the top men at Meridian,' Morton said.

'There's only one: Ignatius Bailey. He runs the set-up like it's his own kingdom. But nothing to show there are any skeletons in his cupboard. The accepted wisdom is that when he makes a move, people tend to find out they've lost a company or two before they can call in their bankers. And he's personally rich enough to impress even Bitburg. He spends his annual bonuses on rare books. Supposed to have a collection the British Museum would kill for. On the social side he's been through a couple of wives and still enjoys sex, but nothing weird. And there's the usual team of muscle in tow when he steps out of his eyrie.'

As Morton looked thoughtfully at the Prof, one of the monitors on the wall began to bleep. On the screen came a message: 'Thirty Seconds to Link.'

It was Bill Gates calling. They both shared an old-fashioned attitude to the job: that in intelligence the best parts are always wholly unpredictable; big, juicy windfalls which drop off trees often without a murmur of wind, coming to earth with the gentlest of thuds; the conversations not recorded; the embellishing of a story with all the finer details of life which even the closest electronic surveillance fails to detect; the inner monologues of the most taciturn individuals and their secret fears; the desire to justify; the need for expiation. This was the world Bill and he knew intimately.

He'd worked with Bill since Hammer Force was created and they were as close as any outsider would ever get to him. They'd last met almost a year earlier when Gates had stopped over in Geneva on his way back to Washington. For a month he'd led a CIA team through the old Soviet republics on a fruitless search for Bodor. Wherever he was, Gates had grunted, he wasn't there now. His own private feeling, he'd told Morton, was that Bodor was dead, another victim of the purges the New Order had conducted with the efficiency of the Stalinist era. With nothing else to go on, Morton hadn't challenged the theory.

Morton went and stood before the screen for the linkup with Langley. A red light on the small camera on top of the monitor signalled that the line was open. The bleeping stopped.

Everyone fell silent, watching the numbers in the corner

of the monitor counting backwards. A pinprick of light appeared in the centre of the screen and grew to a rectangle which began to expand in rapid jumps.

A moment later, Gates came into focus. 'Hullo, David. How are you all keeping?' The satellite bounce gave an echo to his voice.

'The pressure's on, Bill. Bodor's very much back in the frame.'

Gates grunted. 'So I heard. I should have stuck with it. Any idea where he is?'

'Out of Russia, for sure.'

'I've also heard you've drawn the short straw on those triggers. Any connection with Bodor?'

Morton told him there was, summarising all he knew.

'Anything I can do, David?' Gates asked when Morton had finished.

'I'll have a better idea when we've flared out a little more this end.'

'Let's talk some more when you come to Washington, David.'

'That may not be for a while, Bill . . .'

'Wrong there, old friend!' Gates grinned. 'The President wants to see you, asap. The new Air Force One will collect you. It's doing a cabin crew familiarisation flight to Paris overnight and can pick you up in the morning; you'll be in Washington for lunch.'

'Any idea what the President wants?' Morton asked.

'It's his call, David.'

Morton nodded, understanding perfectly. Even Bill could not risk pre-empting the President.

'Those shots on the Iraqi border. Can you tell me anything more?' Morton asked.

Gates grunted. 'I've sent our station chief in Istanbul to check, but I wouldn't hold my breath. Sometimes our computers get a little above themselves.'

Morton heard Finel make a little choking sound as the transmission ended.

FOURTEEN

The blizzard conditions over northern Europe extended all the way to Cagliari. The Arranger heard passengers grumbling about the weather but he felt no such emotion. Feelings got in the way of good procedure.

After clearing airport formalities, he found the jeep in the parking lot. It contained a hand-drawn map, a snowmobile and appropriate clothes for such weather. There was also a long-barrelled handgun fitted with a silencer and a box of bullets.

He studied the map long enough to be able to find the route into the mountains even in darkness. He drove with total singlemindedness, increasingly using the gear shift as he climbed up the granite spine of Sardinia. Eventually he stopped, cut the lights, and sat and waited. Only the sound of the wind broke the silence. Finally, to one side of the jeep he glimpsed movement. A moment later a dark-skinned man tapped at the window, flicking his thinning black hair out of his eyes. He wore a ski outfit.

When the Arranger stepped from the jeep, the Sard spoke. 'They are still there. One always stands guard. There is also a woman. A whore from Cagliari.' His accent was thick, leaning on the vowels.

'How far to the house?'

'Five kilometres. It will be no problem for the snow-mobile.' The Sard continued to speak rapidly, as if anxious to please. 'I will prepare it while you dress.'

While the Sard hauled out the snowmobile, the Arranger donned the white suit that was windproof and insulated. The legs fitted into the heavy boots; ribbed rubber bands at the wrists were overlapped by expedition ski gloves. He adjusted the waterproof turtleneck to the face mask, and zipped the outer collar to the helmet. He loaded the gun with the same care that he did everything, then replaced the box of bullets in the back of the jeep. He wouldn't need more than one chamber.

Behind him the Sard started up the snowmobile, the roar of its engine lost in the wind howl. From the jeep the Arranger removed a set of snowshoes and fitted them into a rack on the back of the snowmobile.

The Sard watched appreciatively, flicking hair from his face. They had told him he was dealing with a professional.

'The locals?' the Arranger demanded. 'They have been taken care of?'

The Sard nodded. 'All of us here live by the *codice barbaricino*. How you say in English, code respect?'

'Code of honour.'

'Yes, yes, code honour. And here we have no *basista*. Spies.'

The Arranger settled himself astride the snowmobile, testing the controls, keeping his weight on the machine. The wind pecked snow against his faceplate.

The Sard pointed towards a track to his right. 'Go two kilometres. Then you reach a stream. It will be frozen now. Beyond, the way forks. Take the left track. Go another two kilometres and you will come to a rock overhang. The house is a hundred metres beyond, no more.'

The Arranger released the brake and the snowmobile began to slice across the ground. A bend came up fast, and he felt the machine sliding from beneath him. He opened the throttle to provide more power and crabbed around the bend. Maintaining speed he slewed over the ice, keeping on course by sheer brute power.

In twenty minutes he reached the stream. He cut the engine and dismounted. Standing on the bank he stamped hard on the surface. It did not yield. He remounted and crossed, taking the left fork, climbing between rock formations. The wind whistled between the crevices with such fury that it threatened to topple him. Huddled down over the control bar, he followed the twisting track, counting off in his mind the distance covered.

One kilometre. The wind was like a beast with invisible claws searching for a grip. A real killer.

He must have covered another half-kilometre. He travelled a further hundred metres before he saw it. Not so much an overhang, but a massive arched formation stretching out over the track. Icicles hung from its roof, like the bars of a portcullis.

The Arranger cut the engine and sat and listened. The wind was like a howling animal screaming at him. He turned the machine to face back down the track, parked and dismounted, stamping his feet to return circulation.

He removed the snowshoes from the rack, laid them on the ground and stepped into the quick-release bindings. He bent and snapped them shut. Then he walked under the archway, ignoring the needle-point ice crystals bouncing off his helmet, feeling only the shape of the gun against his body. Beyond was the house. It would have been difficult to find even in daylight.

The Arranger stood in the mouth of the overhang, watching the light in the window and the figure framed there.

*

Van Kloep, the oldest of the three Dutch balloonists, turned from the window to watch what was happening in the living room. Pieter, his cousin, and Tomas, the navigator, were both being serviced by the woman. For the past two days she had let them use her in every way they liked.

Soon, thought Van Kloep, they could afford to spend the rest of their lives like this, rich beyond their wildest dreams for breaking into that military dump in England and stealing those devices.

For a month they had rehearsed the operation in a training camp near Bilbao; their Stasi instructors had been good; hard and thorough. Afterwards they had flown to Tehran. Kicking their heels around their hotel, working on their tans. After ten days they had flown separately to London. The actual break-in had not posed any problems. It had been a matter of following the lessons of training. In Amsterdam they handed over the devices to a woman who had given them each an envelope containing their air tickets to Sardinia. They had come here to collect their fees for the operation: a quarter-million dollars each. The woman had said the money would be delivered by the courier who would then take them to the boat on which they would travel to Larnaca in Cyprus. From there they would take separate flights to South America.

In the meantime it was time to enjoy himself once more. Abandoning his duty as lookout, Van Kloep joined the others on the floor.

Like a shadow moving through a shadow, the Arranger moved towards the house, gun held loosely by his side, eyes never leaving the window. Twice he stopped to listen. Both times the sound of laughter carried clearly from inside. Quickly peering through the window, he saw the older of the men astride the woman's face. Another was underneath her. The third had his head between her legs.

The Arranger moved to the door and stooped to release the snowshoes. When he stood, his helmet nearly reached the lintel.

For just a second the wind stopped, as if nature was herself holding her breath. Then the howling started again.

The Arranger kicked open the door and stepped inside, gun in hand.

Van Kloep half turned from the woman to see where the sudden cold air was coming from. The gun bucked in the Arranger's hand. The Dutchman tumbled sideways, blood pouring from a neck wound.

The woman screamed.

Moving just enough to align the foresight on the head of the man beneath the woman, the Arranger fired again. The bullet entered Tomas's scalp and exited through his right eye.

The Arranger's next shot caught Pieter in the forehead. The force of the impact drove him back from between the woman's legs. She screamed again.

The Arranger laughed quietly but there was an ugly undertone to the sound. 'Stand up,' he ordered in Italian.

She was aware of him watching her, of his intent black eyes following her as she did so. As she pulled down her skirt, he fired. She collapsed on the others. The Arranger did not give the bodies a second look.

He lowered his gun and produced a piece of paper from his jacket pocket, crumpled it and tossed it into a corner of the living room, then turned and closed the door behind him. In minutes he reached the snowmobile. In less than an hour he was back at the jeep. By dawn he was on the first plane to Rome. By noon he was on another to Baghdad.

By then the Sard had removed the bodies from the house.

An hour after the refuelling stop in Malta, the pilot came into the cabin and asked Zita if she was enjoying the flight, deliberately leaning against her armchair so that his crotch was level with her eyes.

'Anything I can do, just ask.' He looked down at her.

'That could cover a multitude of things.' She looked up at him.

He laughed. 'There's something about you.'

'What's that?' Her eyes flicked briefly to his trousers.

'You want me to tell you?' he asked.

'I think you're already showing me.'

He glanced over his shoulder at the closed cockpit door. Matteus wouldn't leave the controls. He reached down and pulled her to her feet, hoisting her skirt around her hips.

'Wait.' She tugged at his belt, then kept her head pressed to the pilot's chest so that he couldn't see her face, feeling him explore her wetness, allowing her to feel his hardness.

'You ready?' he asked hoarsely.

She lay down in the aisle and he knelt above her, his trousers round his ankles, straddling her thighs. She reached up and squeezed him until a drop of liquid appeared at the tip of his glans. In the end her father hadn't been able to contain himself very long either. With her other hand she parted her lips and tugged the pilot's weight on to her.

FIFTEEN

Rising from his armchair, which like all the furnishings seemed to have been carved out of the past itself, Ignatius Bailey walked swiftly across the rich Tabriz carpet and stood at the panoramic windows of his suite on the executive level of Meridian Towers. His light grey summer suit, maroon tie and polished brogues complimented his spare frame. Men said he was a power dresser. Women remarked that a glance of those dark eyes could reach the depths of their sensuality. Now his eyes were filled with anticipation of a different kind. No matter how many times he witnessed an almost identical sunset, it held an undiminished fascination for him.

The move to the window would also provide an opportunity for the three men he had summoned to reflect on what he had just said. They were the Management Committee of Meridian International, his most trusted aides. To turn back now, he had reminded them, would be to lose everything; there would never be another opportunity like this one. Obtaining the nuclear triggers and the services of Bodor would have been wasted. So would the millions of dollars expended on the Iraq site, but the real loss would be one of opportunity.

Instead, he had urged, they must seize it. Everything was in favour of doing so: the technical reports on the new Air Force One; the details about its chief pilot discovered in a dusty medical file of the United Nations command in Sarajevo; the report on the man's wife; the safe arrival of the balloon and its pilot; the weather forecasts. Disparate pieces had all come together. There really couldn't be a better time.

That was why he had ordered the launch of the media campaign against the administration, the first response to that shattering day when Washington had moved against Meridian corporations violating anti-pollution laws. When sixteen billion dollars had been wiped off Meridian holdings and when, in the aftermath of that Black Monday, he'd called them here and said that while the wolf was not at the door, he was out there in the woods. When he had first outlined what must be done, he had made it sound so sensible, so reasonable, that they had agreed. But then he knew no one better able to produce a solution to a problem.

Always, he had operated through surrogates. He had used them to arrange money transfers to pay for the balloon, to obtain the nerve gas, to hire the break-in squad to steal the triggers, to arrange for murders to be committed in Russia, England and Sardinia. Finding the money for all this had never been a problem. The men in this room had seen to that.

The youngest, at forty, was Ronald J. Sterling, Meridian's chief financial officer; for the moment the angle of the light hid the deadness in Sterling's eyes. Seated beside Sterling was Samuel R. Keller Jr, a pale man in his midfifties with an overbite. He was general counsel at Meridian. The oldest, at sixty, was Elliott Forde, titular chairman of Meridian and its merger chief. Like those of the others, his eyes were fixed on the back of Bailey.

'Any of you want a drink, cigar, you know where they are,' Bailey reminded them, not bothering to turn, his voice deep and thrilling with its Scottish burr. In the window reflection he saw them walk over to the credenza and help themselves from the bottles and the humidifier. He continued to watch what was happening beyond the window. There was one moment of particular magic in the swiftness of the transformation, the moment a mauve blush bathed the banyan. He'd personally positioned the tree in the centre of the vast expanse of Meridian International Plaza, shipping it from India, where he had seen a banyan that covered acres, an entire forest which was at the same time a single living tree. He had chosen the banyan as the logo for Meridian International.

He could hear ice clinking in glasses, matches being struck, followed by the pleasant aroma of cigar smoke. A non-smoker and teetotaller himself, he had never tried to persuade others to follow his example.

Forde was talking to the others. 'The *New York Times* just published an interesting piece about how the destiny of this great country has so often been decided by assassination. Abraham Lincoln's, of course. Then John F. Kennedy's brought Lyndon Johnson into office. And Robert Kennedy's assassination made possible Richard Nixon's election. In each case they were said to be the work of a lone, mad assassin.'

'I saw that article,' Keller acknowledged. 'According to the *Times*, the prevailing wisdom is still that anyone who says political assassinations are the result of conspiratorial activities are themselves considered cranks or crackpots.'

'I don't know about you, but I don't recognise the description,' Sterling said.

Bailey smiled as they continued to discuss the article. Good to have them on the team; good to know they would do everything to help him sustain the greatest commercial empire the world had known.

As far as his eyes could see in the fading light, everything belonged to Meridian. Millions of acres of prime wheatlands stretching to the horizon were only a small part of its agricultural assets. The town itself – more properly a city, with its quarter-million population – was totally owned by Meridian. No doctor or nurse could heal here; no preacher minister; no teacher impart knowledge; no undertaker bury the dead if Meridian International had a mind to say no. From cradle to grave this was the ultimate company town. His town.

The sky was darkening behind the Meridian First National Bank and Trust, a glass-sheathed skyscraper that was the tallest building downtown, its vaults filled with Meridian International's stocks and deposits. On the thruway, on Interstate One, on all the roads, lights were coming on to illuminate the billboards devoted to Meridian products. To the west he could see the brightly-lit tower black of Meridian Memorial, now a major teaching hospital and research centre, thanks to the bequests he had authorised.

Wherever he looked he could see the results of other money well spent: the new Meridian High School; the Meridian College of Fine Arts refurbished with some of the finest modern paintings available. The Meridian International Foundation which every year gave away millions in profits for good works. Beyond the plaza he could see the lights of Le Meridian, the finest French restaurant in town, which kept a permanent table for senior executives.

The dusk cast a shadow across the bell tower of Meridian International College, the trick of the light ageing it in a way the builders had never quite been able to achieve with their fake gothic beams and battlements. The campus was the site of the old stockyards which had employed only a handful of people towards the end. They had been told that no one owed them a job, a reminder that in Meridian's rule book there is nothing so insecure as a secure living.

In the window reflection Bailey saw Keller going back to the drinks cabinet. Sam always like to take his second gin-and-tonic quickly.

The lights of the Meridian Galleria were now blazing under the dome of the old railway station. Home to several floors of delicatessens and boutiques, the Galleria had been an early addition to the Meridian portfolio.

Still not taking his eyes off the view, Bailey called out, 'Elliott, how many Gallerias do we have now?'

Forde answered promptly. 'Four thousand and two between here and Moscow, here and Tokyo, and here and Sydney, Australia. Four thousand and three if you count the one that's going to open in Beijing in an hour, local time. We're doing the same as we did in Red Square. Landing the local Chinese hobnobs by balloon in Tiananmen Square. It always goes down a treat, Ignatius.'

'Sell the Galleria portfolio. It's reached its peak. Get it in play and shoot for three billion, but the bottom line's two-nine. Meantime, push up the rentals five dollars per square foot per unit. It'll give you a little leeway if you have to haggle. Try the Japanese first as an opening strategy,' Bailey said.

In the reflection, Bailey could see Forde writing on a small notepad. He knew that in another company there would have been discussion, questions, perhaps even challenge and dissent. That was not the way at Meridian. His decision was final – always. It was the only thing he had in common with that dangerous fool in the Oval Office who had warned of the dangers of a world of plastic floors and artificial carpets, air conditioning and fluorescent light, one in which windows don't open and background music never stops, days and nights when the sky never stops glowering under its artificial illumination.

It was the nearest the President had come to stating his

opposition to all Meridian International stood for. To all Ignatius Bailey stood for.

That meddler in the White House wanted to turn back the clock. He had come into office promising to end the uninhibited pursuit of gain. But he didn't have to compare last month's profits with this month's, judge his performance against that of another head of state or compete with anybody until his term was up. Meridian was in the competition business, every minute of every day and night. The paradox of success is that what you have today won't keep you there tomorrow. You had to make sure those numbers kept clicking one way. Up. Growth, returns on investment, employee morale all depended on that. On him. Sometimes you had to make tough decisions. But that was why he was here.

Behind him, Keller was swirling the cubes in his glass. 'As we're talking strategy, Ignatius, I think it's time to buy Trans-Aviation.'

'Make sure it's out from under Delaware law first, Sam. That way we avoid all that fiduciary nonsense that could allow some minority shareholder to block the sale,' Bailey said.

'You got a number in mind?'

'Why don't we stay just north of the highest price Trans-Aviation stock has turned?'

'Sounds good to me,' Keller said.

'That means we should get it for no more than one-three bil. Not bad' Sterling added.

'About right,' Bailey acknowledged.

Forde nodded and made another note in his pad.

Bailey continued to watch the banyan's gnarled and twisted branches finally fade into the darkness, and he thought how, not for a moment, could he ever lose sight of his own ultimate responsibility. He was the ultimate arbitrator of how Meridian should go forward. He was the final trustee of Meridian's future. The one man who must ensure that its present course was not deflected until the future arrived.

Turning back into the room, Ignatius Bailey addressed the others. 'When I was a laddie employed by the Coca-Cola Company, I was struck by the motto that is still there in its headquarters: "The world belongs to the discontented." Coca-Cola was warning against complacency. Complacency remains the enemy of any business. Our business. Complacency is our enemy. In the White House today is the leader of the discontented.'

He paused and looked at each of them in turn. Then he resumed. 'He and his supporters will go on screwing up the world. Not just theirs, but ours. You'd better believe it.'

One by one the others nodded. As he had known they would.

When Bailey now spoke his voice was so low the others had to lean forward to hear. 'Those who came before us had to remove Kennedy to preserve what was important. Taking that one life assured the future of millions ... no doubt about it. We owe it to the memory of those men, to all we have inherited from them, to ensure we succeed ... to ensure that in less than three weeks the President of the United States and the other world leaders he has persuaded to support his ruinous crusade will no longer be in a position to do so.'

One by one he silently shook their hands. Their grip, like his, was filled with resolve.

There would be no turning back. The plan would go ahead, driven by the juggernaut resources of Meridian International. In the end, driven by him.

SIXTEEN

Close to midnight a plane descended across the broad arc of Apsheron Peninsula and flew into the city of Baku. Its only passenger in business class was Ken Adams.

An hour later a taxi deposited him at the entrance to the Citadel. The Old City was as busy as at noon, its narrow streets and alleys filled with the accents of Central Asia. Carrying his bag he walked towards the Maiden's Tower, ignoring the pimps and the drug-pushers and savouring the aromas of cooking and coffee.

Madame Lutke's apartment was directly above a café-bar filled with the dark, intense faces of the region. One of the women winked at Adams. He smiled and shook his head. The whore turned and said something to the men at her table. They laughed loudly, especially a man dressed in a sleeveless undershirt, a cigarette drooping from his lip.

Adams vaguely remembered him from last time. Salim. Madame Lutke had introduced him when they'd eaten here, but the man's face had given nothing away. The Kazaks were an odd people: resentful and difficult, like their language. And they rarely laughed. Nice to see Salim breaking the rules.

Entering the building, Adams wrinkled his nose at the stale smell of anise, cheap perfume, sweat and, for those who could pay, imported beer and whisky. He began to climb the brothel's bare treads. Reaching a landing he paused to peer through a window. The view was spectacular: minarets and domes, and, beyond, the riding lights of ships out on the Caspian. He climbed three more flights of stairs to Madame Lutke's apartment. As soon as his finger pressed the bell-push, the door opened and she stood there.

'So. Mick-ee, my friend from Athens comes back to see me. That is good, very good.'

Madame Lutke embraced him and kissed him on both cheeks, then stood back as if to allow him to inspect her, tilting her head to one side, then the other, so that her breasts began a little jig of their own. Beneath her diaphanous robe they were large and firm and the areola around the nipples glistened so redly they might have been varnished.

'You look good,' he said.

She laughed throatily. 'I very bad, Mick-ee. You like me be bad, yes?'

'Every time.'

'You eat?'

'On the plane. But I could do with a drink.'

She turned and led the way into the apartment. The living room was lit by a converted oil lamp which cast shadows on the ruby-red ceiling and the kilms on the floor; he judged the gilt-framed paintings on the walls must be of Baku in mediaeval times. Madame Lutke motioned him to a couch and went to a brass side-table filled with bottles.

His eyes never left her. She must have been a show-stopper once with those legs, even if the years had added poundage to her hips and across the shoulders, the way exotic dancers often go when they quit. But she was still a looker.

She turned, waving a bottle. 'Vodka? How you say in American, it fell off back of Russian truck?'

Adams laughed. 'Then it must be good.'

Madam Lutke poured two generous measures and joined

him on the sofa. 'Chin-chin, Mick-ee.' They were the first words he'd taught her. They clinked glasses and drank.

'So why you come to Baku again?' she asked.

'To see you, of course.'

'Very nice. But I do not think that is all. A man like you must know many womans in Athens. In lots of places.'

'But not like you, Madame Lutke.'

She laughed, delighted to be lied to. 'But also you come for business . . . yes?'

'Not exactly business . . . But yes, I'm looking for someone,' Adams said.

She frowned coquettishly. 'You have another friend here?' Another womans?'

He sipped his drink and shook his head, smiling. 'No. Not a woman. A man. I'm looking for him. Probably a foreigner.'

Madame Lutke tilted her head once more. 'I no understand. What you mean "probably"? You mean, he may not be your friend?'

He drank some more. There was no rush. 'Well . . . not a friend like you. But someone who may be able to help me with a little business.'

'What business you make, Mick-ee?'

He allowed himself a cautious smile, his mind already on the next step. He hadn't expected to get there so soon. But in his work you took it when it came.

'Now you never ask a man what he does for a living,' Adams chided her gently.

Madame Lutke gave a twitch of her head he had not seen her do before. 'Then why you tell me about this foreign mans?' But she was not offended.

He gave himself time to think and the silence seemed to join rather than divide them. 'I don't even know him,' he said. 'Only that he may be dead.'

Her hand went to her mouth. 'Dead?'

'Dead,' he repeated. 'It happens in my business.'

'You smuggler, Mick-ee?'

'Well . . . let's say I do a little importing and exporting.'

'You smuggler,' she said triumphantly. 'What you smuggle, Mick-ee?'

'Not drugs.'

'What you smuggle? Guns?'

He shook his head, as if he couldn't remember.

'Oh, mans, you some damn big mans, Mick-ee,' Madame Lutke murmured admiringly. 'Guns for Kurds – right? This other mans, he smuggle guns too? That why he killed. By the Iraqis, maybe?'

He hadn't mentioned Iraq. But if you were running guns to the Kurds, the Iraqis are the logical people to take you out. 'I don't know who killed him,' he said truthfully, watching her struggling to understand.

'This mans, Mick-ee. You have his name?'

Adams drained his glass, concentrating on the work in hand, unprincipled and uncontrite. 'No. But he may have gone up into the mountains. That's where he could have got shot.'

Madame Lutke stared at him.

'To go to the mountains he would need a guide. Yes?' he asked.

She nodded.

'Then I need to find his guide.'

She pulled a sour face. 'There are many guide mans.'

'I'm looking for one who went up there a few days ago.'

She stared at him and he could see the uncertainty working in her face.

'What you do with him?'

'Talk to him. That's all,' he smiled. 'And give him some money for his time.'

She nodded. 'I ask, Mick-ee. Maybe someone know. How long you stay here?'

'I'd like to be gone before tomorrow night. But I'll be back soon.'

Once more he saw her give that peculiar little twitch of her head. Then she was smiling. 'Okay. Now we have very good times.'

She stood before him, letting him encircle her waist. He placed a palm on either buttock and she followed the pressure, allowing her robe to fall open and jutting her pelvis towards his face. And he knew he would not get much sleep before he went up into the mountains.

The President of the United States awoke in the White House with a headache – caused by the tensions sleep had failed to dissolve.

He had gone to bed after reading the summary of the latest attack by Meridian's newspapers, TV and radio stations. They made grim reading, editorials peppered with words like treachery and the dark thought that his administration was edging down the road to impeachment.

Only Bailey would have authorised the onslaught. But there was still no way he could have learned about Earth Saver, otherwise he surely would have ridiculed it. And yet, mused the President, there had to be something more than just a reaction to sanctions against a bunch of Meridian companies who had overstepped the mark environmentally. The uncertainty of not knowing was compounded by the call he had received when he had finally drifted into a fitful sleep.

It had been five a.m. in London when Sandy Richardson phoned to say that Bostock was appearing on CNN that morning. The ambassador had no idea what the Prime

Minister was going to say, but surely to God he wasn't going to announce the loss of those triggers? That would get the environmentalists on the rampage for all the wrong reasons, and not only in Britain but here too. When news leaked, as it was bound to, that the triggers had come from California, the environmental movement across the country would attack him as fiercely as Bailey was doing. And it wouldn't help the situation if he said the triggers were made by one of Meridian's companies; that would just open up a new can of worms for Bailey to exploit. He glanced at the digital clock on the bedside telephone console and reached for the zapper to turn on the TV in a corner of the bedroom. Three minutes to the CNN bulletin.

The newscaster was running through a round-up of the overnight stock market prices. Hong Kong and Tokyo were down and London had opened quietly. He continued to half-listen, his mind pondering what Bostock might be going to say. For some weeks there had been whispers – no more – that Britain, France and Germany were anxious to end sanctions against Iraq. You didn't have to be skilled in the art of politics to know why. The three most powerful nations in Europe wanted to exploit the potential market a still-devastated Iraq offered. He had considered confronting Bostock, but had held off until he had more hard evidence. Instead he had fumed inwardly at having to deal with such grasping politicians. For America there would be no easing of sanctions until Saddam went. This administration remained firmly committed to the line in the sand his predecessor, George Bush, had drawn.

The stock market prices faded from the screen to be replaced with an exterior shot of No. 10 Downing Street, then the Prime Minister appeared, sitting in his study talking to the network's London bureau chief.

Once more the President admired how Bostock managed to combine charisma and influence. After what must have been an agreed soft-ball question, the Prime Minister was up and running.

'There has been criticism, some of it deserved, much of it ill-informed, about my government's position on environmental issues. So I am taking this opportunity to remind the people not only of this country, but everyone else who is watching, that Britain has long been in the forefront of environmental protection.'

The President let out a loud growl. 'Son of a bitch! The crafty, conniving son of a bitch!'

He should have expected this. Bostock's instinct for an opportunity was as acute as his manipulation of the media was astonishingly deft. He was trying to secure his own role as one of the architects of Operation Earth Saver.

The President watched the Prime Minister lean forward slightly, not to crowd the camera, but enough to lend emphasis to what he was saying.

'A new car *is* built every second. More than half the world's oil consumption *is* used in vehicles. Close to two hundred million tonnes of sulphur and nitrogen oxides *is* rising every year into the atmosphere, destroying lakes and forests and producing serious respiratory diseases in human beings and animals. Over two million barrels of oil *are* dumped into the world's oceans. Every year the irreversible contamination of coastlines *is* growing by some five hundred miles.'

Once more the President cursed forcefully as Bostock claimed Britain was leading the fight against pollution. He should have known that the Prime Minister's volte face over Earth Saver had a hidden agenda, and one which would put Her Majesty's chief representative in pole position.

On the screen the Prime Minister was in full flow. 'A distinguished predecessor of mine, Winston Churchill, said he would fight this country's enemies on the beaches. We will fight *for* the beaches! But we live in a fast-changing world. Yesterday's enemies are today's allies. Here in Europe we have seen the reality of that. Along with much else, Britain, Germany and France help each other to eradicate the scourge of domestic pollution. We would like to do more, in all those countries which can benefit from our pooled skills. In all those countries where we still cannot help because of sanctions, I believe firmly, and so do my European colleagues, that those sanctions must be looked at again.'

Switching off the TV, the President growled once more, 'Son of a bitch!'

SEVENTEEN

After Tommy and Danny Nagier had caught their flights to Cagliari and Amsterdam, Morton sat with Anna in the departure lounge at Geneva Airport reviewing all they knew about Meridian. Now, as she stood up, ready to make her way to the departure gate, Anna's eyes held Morton's for a moment. 'Meridian has absolutely no involvement with Iraq. Fact is, since the Gulf War they've ignored every Baghdad overture to set up shop. But one of their companies does have a plant in Tehran, producing refrigerators. I suppose it could re-tool for anything Bodor might need.'

Morton agreed that was a possibility.

'The mullahs are buying themselves all kinds of lethal stuff through the back door from North Korea. All-in-all they are getting their act together and Bodor could be the kind of top-of-the-bill turn Tehran would go for. But he'd strictly be their very private star.'

Morton said that also made sense. The ayatollahs had gone on secretly funding the IRA while everybody pointed a finger at Syria and Libya. Bodor could be the latest arrow in the Tehran quiver.

After Anna had left to board her flight to Moscow, he continued to think.

The Prof's profiles of Ignatius Bailey and Carlo Marcello were what you'd expect of two of the gods of management. Both were consummate players in the search for a new deal, a greater yield. But nothing even to hint they were dabbling in murky waters. Zita Marcello's profile confirmed her to be a rebel who had gone from one brown-rice-and-rope-sandal cause to another until she'd run out of protest movements. Her anger with the world came through all too clearly. Johnny had still not managed to pick up her trail, while Lester's computer trawl had unearthed nothing suspicious on Free Flight, Globoil or Nuclear Components. Other Meridian companies checked out equally squeaky clean.

The fragments that had brought Morton this far now stubbornly refused to form a pattern. Yet something still nagged. It was like looking at a painting of some creature he had never seen before. The more he thought about it, the more it eluded him.

The sun was rising behind the airport buildings, a gold, gravid disc which appeared for a moment to linger just above the horizon as if trapped there by its own unnatural weight. It began to climb into the sky, its burnishing light doing nothing to clear his thoughts as his flight to Paris was called.

For the next hour Morton gave himself over to the boredom of air travel. Landing at Charles de Gaulle, he watched a flock of crows settle on the grass beside the taxiway. They formed a circle while one bird began to strut back and forth, the others standing with head bowed and wings gathered, like black-gowned students listening to a teacher. Ornithologists called it a crows' parliament, but no one had yet explained why the birds behaved like this. Suddenly a clatter of helicopter rotors drove them back into the air. Wheeling in tight formation, Bible-black against the early morning light, they squawked towards the airport perimeter.

As the chopper crabbed above the grass, Morton saw a figure cradling a machine gun squatting in the open cabin door. In the distance was the towering tail of Air Force One.

Emerging from one of the plexiglass tunnels into the arrivals area, Morton was met by a French security agent. The woman had an earpiece in her left ear. Once he identified himself, she whispered into the mike concealed behind the top button of her blouse. They were the only words she spoke on the drive to where the President's plane was parked.

French paratroopers had formed a cordon. Closer in, Secret Service agents from the White House detail stood guard. The chopper swooped to take a closer look before resuming its patrol.

Stepping from the car, Morton took in the activity around the plane. Already she was alive, her radars probing the sky, her radio in touch with the tower. He glimpsed a white-shirted figure on the flight deck and remembered, as if it was only yesterday, the last time he sat at the controls.

He'd been in the co-pilot's seat of the Hammer Force freighter bringing out the team which had cleaned up a nasty business with an organ transplant clinic in Nicaragua when Bill Andrews, the pilot, had had a heart attack. Bill had slumped over the stick, sending the plane yawing. Morton had brought the 747 down on the runway at Costa Rica. After seeing Bill on the way to recovery in hospital, he'd flown the plane back to Geneva. Since then he had only piloted the simulator next door to Big Mike's training school. But that was enough to keep his full pilot's licence for big jets.

As Morton walked towards the boarding ramp, a figure in uniform came down the steps. Major Ken Locke, Air Force One's co-pilot, was still slim enough to look taller than his five foot eleven inches. Controlled tension had kept his cheek muscles tight, but even a tan which seemed three skins deep could not quite disguise the lines of a lived-in face.

'Welcome, sir,' Locke said, shaking Morton's hand. 'Colonel Patterson, the aircraft commander, is on his final walk-through, but he'll join you immediately afterwards.'

Locke turned and led the way back up the carpeted stairway.

Edwin Patterson had begun his walk round Air Force One under the watchful gaze of crew chief Tom Sutter and Bill Kerr, the flight engineer. With quiet satisfaction he saw that, in contrast to the stained coveralls of the French ground handlers, their uniforms were immaculate. In his own case, Patterson thought wryly, it was no thanks to Bron. In their married life she had still to iron a shirt.

He had been dropping his dirty washing into the base laundry for some months before discovering that Sutter had decided the CO's clothes had no business being washed in the machines used for other ranks. Instead, the crew chief took the garments to a French cleaner near the base, paying for the specialist service with Air Force One matches, cocktail swizzle sticks and the occasional highball glass. Worth cents in themselves, they were collector's items because they bore the presidential seal. Sutter could have been charged with theft. But in everything else the crew chief was scrupulously honest, and a conviction would have automatically meant his transfer out of the outfit – a definite loss to everyone. So Patterson had decided to turn a blind eye. And besides, he'd never worn better pressed clothes.

Bron had accused him of having one of the women cabin crew do his ironing. He'd heard the cool rational part of him telling her the truth, but once more she had stormed out of the room; the dream of happiness he'd hoped would have locked them romantically together forever shattered a little more.

Looking back, he now saw that each day had become its own nightmare; he was unable to do anything but wait for her next outburst. Slowly, gradually, the thought came to him that Bron could be mentally ill. Numbed and shocked by the possibility at first, as he came to accept it old memories took on a new meaning: of Bron's emotions, naked and limitless, spilling out as if they were emerging from some dark, secret corner inside her. The more he thought about it, the more fearful he became. Yet he knew he was still too emotionally involved with Bron as his *wife* to begin to see her as a *patient*. He could handle most things, but he would be lying to himself if he said he could cope with mental illness in anyone, let alone in Bron. The failure was his; there was something in his make-up which made it impossible for him to deal with that kind of situation.

Sutter brought him back to the present, jerking a thumb towards the port side undercarriage assembly. 'We gouged a piece of rubber coming into land,' growled the crew chief.

'Show me.'

Patterson examined the sidewall of one of the huge tyres from where a small piece of rubber had been lost.

'Right, Chief. Put it down for a change when we reach Andrews.'

Patterson resumed his inspection tour, pausing to peer intently at the wings and fuselage, using his pilot's sixth sense to look for something untoward. He found nothing. Reaching the ramp to the main cargo hold, he told Kerr to start pumping fuel. As the flight engineer motioned the bowsers forward, Patterson followed Sutter up the ramp.

The cavernous space was empty. When the President

was on board the hold was filled with baggage and the cartons of White House crested notepaper and envelopes to be used for the thank-you notes to local dignitaries which the President always wrote between stops. Gestures like that, Patterson mused, kept the Man in touch.

But what else would be needed by White House staff on this mission? This past week, in between filing flight plans with aviation authorities around the world for what were still only described as crew familiarisation flights, Patterson had spent long hours working out gross take-off weights and all the other data needed to be fed into the on-board computers before he started up engines for the mission. A few more boxes which somebody on the Man's staff insisted were essential could make a weight difference. And how much baggage would those other leaders have? It was one more matter he would have to settle when he returned to base. Meantime, better to be prepared.

Patterson turned to Sutter. 'You're going to need some extra space, Chief.'

Last night at Andrews before take-off, he had briefed the crew on the mission, reminding them it was still under a presidential oath of secrecy.

Sutter pointed to a bulkhead. 'I can move this back twenty feet. That'll give room for a further three hundred pieces of average-sized baggage.'

'Do it,' Patterson said. He climbed a steel ladder and entered Air Force One's rear cabin through a door beside the cabin crew toilet in the tail.

For a moment he surveyed the area. There were twenty rows of first class seats, two abreast and divided by twin aisles. Each recliner was equipped with a pullout keyboard containing a personal telephone, fax, and a screen on which to view the latest video releases. Stowed in bulkhead racks were current hardback US bestsellers and a selection of magazines and newspapers.

The White House Chief of Staff and his key aides would normally sit here, together with the Secret Service detail. But on the upcoming mission neither Thacker Stimpson nor the presidential bodyguards would be travelling. The Man had insisted that he wanted to keep the trimmings to an absolute minimum.

Top Sergeant Brian Cowan, the senior flight steward, appeared from the midships galley. Dressed in blue waistcoat, white shirt and a dark blue tie relieved by the presidential seal just below the knot, his sharply creased pants fell to burnished shoes. A stocky, sandy-haired man in his early forties, Cowan was unmarried. The other cabin crew joked that Air Force One was his wife and mistress. Only Patterson knew Cowan had supported his crippled mother until her death the year before. Now he was putting a younger sister through medical school.

After testing a recliner to turn it into a comfortable horizontal bed, Patterson turned to Cowan. 'I'm sure our guests would appreciate a little domestic entertainment during the trip. Order their local bestsellers and a selection of their latest videos.'

'No problem, Colonel. I'd also like to be able to offer each leader his favourite daily paper.'

Patterson nodded appreciatively. 'I'll talk to someone in State to see if our embassies can provide copies for us to pick up en route.'

Cowan grinned. 'It shouldn't be a problem, Colonel, when it's for Air Force One. I always like to think we're Silverplate's successor.'

Patterson looked puzzled. 'Say again?'

Cowan's grin broadened. 'Silverplate was the get-any-thing-you-need code word the atomic bomber squadron had when they were getting ready to nuke the Japs back in '45.'

Patterson frowned. He'd forgotten that Cowan was a World War Two buff.

'I don't think our Japanese guests would want to be reminded of that, Cowan. And I think it would be a good idea to refer to them as Japanese, not Japs.'

'Yes, sir. Absolutely right, Colonel.' Something came and went so quickly in the steward's eyes that Patterson almost missed it.

'Your grandfather was killed in the Pacific, isn't that right?' Patterson asked, remembering now what he'd read in the steward's file.

'Yes, sir. Okinawa, 1944. He was giving close cover to the Marines when a Zero got him. My grandpa went straight into a Jap – Japanese – machine-gun post holding up our boys. He got the Purple Heart. Thirty years later my dad was killed when dive-bombing a gook village in Vietnam. They also gave him a Purple Heart.'

'That's quite a family record, Cowan.'

'Yes, Colonel.'

If it had been hurt he'd seen in Cowan's eyes, it was now a fierce pride.

Feeling slightly embarrassed, for he was a man who kept his own private life under careful lock and key, Patterson made the last check in the cabin.

He reached for one of several push buttons cleverly concealed at regular intervals along the length of the cabin's wall panelling. Immediately a lightweight steel shutter, tested to withstand machine-gun fire, dropped in front of the access door to the baggage hold while another blocked the exit forward from the cabin.

The measure was designed to isolate the cabin from the rest of the plane in the highly unlikely event of terrorists managing to get on board. Similar barriers were built into the airframe to block off the flight deck and access to the President's suite. If Cowan or his staff were unable to reach a button in time, there was an override button on the flight deck.

'Everything looks shipshape here,' Patterson said.

'I expect you to find it the same everywhere,' Cowan remarked, pride now in his voice.

Patterson entered a galley. Nodding to the aproned flight attendant, he checked the microwaves and the racks of crockery and drawers of cutlery. Everything was spotless. He turned to the attendant, Carolyn Dempsey, who wore the inverted stripes of an airman first class on her sleeve.

'You run a good kitchen, Dempsey.'

'Thank you, sir. Can I get you a coffee, anything?'

'No, thanks. I've got a way to go yet.' He smiled at her. 'You find this a bit different from your other flying?'

'More interesting, by far. And you never know what to expect.'

'The training school showed you that.'

'It sure did, sir.'

All cabin staff had previous flying experience, but still had to pass the special Air Force One training course. The day he dropped in, he'd watched Dempsey coping with the professional actor whose job it was to test the patience of even the politest flight attendants. First he spilled his coffee on the floor of the mock-up cabin. When she'd mopped up, he'd dropped his drink. To complete his act, he vomited over his jacket. Patterson knew the vomit was cold custard mixed with pea soup. The actor had demanded that Dempsey clean him. She had done so with professional calm.

'You're not likely to get anything like that happen on board here. And if it did, it would be the last time that passenger flew with us.'

Leaving the galley, he walked along a short corridor to the dining salon. Panelled in dark wood, the cabin contained half a dozen circular tables, each sitting five in armchair comfort. Two flight attendants were spreading starched white cloths over the tables, while a third laid out the solid silver cutlery, the finest of china plates and crystal glasses. All bore the presidential seal and had been donated by their manufacturers. Though no firm was supposed to advertise that its items were used on board, Patterson knew it happened all the time.

Beyond the salon was a lounge furnished with armchairs, coffee tables and a sideboard with cups, milk jugs and coffee pots. Each table had its own vase of fresh-cut flowers. Even though the Man was not on board, Patterson insisted that no detail be overlooked. Crossing the lounge, he entered another corridor. The presidential seal was on the door of each VIP bedroom.

He checked each one in turn. All were identical with panelled walls and dark blue carpeting, a queen-sized divan bed, a table with a reading light and radio equipped with an earpiece to avoid disturbing people sleeping in adjoining bedrooms. Behind sliding doors was a airline-type toilet, wash basin and shower. Air Force One carried sufficient water in its storage tanks for a ten-minute shower per cabin. A computer controlled the supply. After checking the fresh soap, clean towels and a range of toilet accessories — all bearing replicas of the presidential seal — Patterson climbed a blue carpeted circular staircase to the second deck and entered the communications shack.

A dozen technicians worked under shadow-free lighting. From here they kept the President in touch with anyone, anywhere, through the link to an NSA satellite reserved for the White House. There were also fax machines, encryptors, decoders and printers. Patterson took aside the communications chief, a signals major.

'Any luck yet with people to handle the extra languages?' Patterson asked.

'I've got somebody from our Tokyo embassy for the Japanese end of things. She acted as interpreter for the President when he was over there,' said the major.

'What about German and French?'

'I went through our records. A couple in the back-up team are fluent in both languages.' For every man on duty here there were three more in reserve at Andrews.

'Keep me posted,' Patterson said. He gave the room a last sweeping look before stepping back into the corridor. He walked to the secretarial bureau. Deserted now, it would be occupied with half a dozen senior secretaries from the White House when the Man was on board. They'd work under the gimlet eyes of Martha Wilson, his personal secretary, typing up on the WPCs anything from drafts of speeches to updating schedules and briefing papers, together with all the other paperwork that keeps the Presidency on course while airborne. Not forgetting those thank-you notes.

He closed the bureau door and went to the last door in the corridor. As he opened it, the lights automatically came on in the largest of the public areas on board Air Force One. The salon's seventy-five armchairs allowed it to double as a conference room and cinema. The same screen could be used to project the latest releases from Hollywood or data about an area the President was about to visit. There was a podium to one side of the screen from which he could address the room, or have someone brief him. Once more satisfied that everything was in order, Patterson climbed the flight of stairs in a corner of the salon.

At the top was a small vestibule. On one side was a short

corridor. On the other a door adorned with a golden eagle and thirteen gold stars. Behind was the President's suite. In a recess was a jump seat for the Secret Service agent who sat there whenever the Man was on board.

Walking down the corridor towards a second unmarked door, Patterson remembered the words of Rear-Admiral Luther Cox, the White House physician.

Leaving the Oval Office after the President's briefing, the elderly physician's face was a study in misgiving. Taking his arm, Cox led Patterson into his own office and came straight to the point.

'Colonel, this trip is going to be no turkey-shoot. A number of those G7 leaders are, if I may put it bluntly, a little past retirement age. So, for that matter, is the President – though I would deny it flatly if you ever even thought I had said that!'

Cox laughed his doctor's laugh before continuing.

'Even I can only guess at the pressures the President faces at times. He told me about this trip before he told anybody else. He wanted reassurance he was physically up to it. And I gave it to him. He is physically in good shape. No doubt about it. I also knew that if I said he shouldn't go, he'd still go. That's what makes him what he is. But this trip is just one more pressure on top of all the others. On a typical day he signs his name to up to six hundred documents – which means he has to read them, decide on them. That's pressure. And there are all the other never-ending problems. Most days there is the makings of at least one crisis only he can diffuse, coming on top of yesterday's so often still unresolved crisis. All this extends the demands on his body and mind. This trip will only add to those pressures.'

Once more Cox laughed softly, but there was little mirth there. 'People see only the upside of things with the presidency. All the trimmings which go with the job – including this fancy new plane of yours. Which brings me to the point. A new plane needs a new approach to the President's medical care. I've told him, and he accepts, that I'm too old to be going around the world with him on this one.'

Patterson waited while the rear-admiral gathered his thoughts.

'People forget that, statistically, a President's life-span is five years below the national average, meaning that the distinction of holding our nation's highest elected office is really a sentence to a reduced life expectancy.

'With the Man there's another problem. I thought he'd gotten over his wife's death on that fishing trip. After all, it is now six years since it happened. But lately he's shown signs it's come back to trouble him. He's not sleeping as well as he used to. For a man who pushes himself to the limit, that's not good. He needs his rest.'

Patterson looked at the doctor. *'Should you be telling me all this, Admiral?'*

Cox sighed. *'Probably not. But I've decided to do something about it. As well as your flight attendants, who are all trained up to paramedic standards, I'm putting on board a doctor. In my view she's the very best in her field. Next to you she'll have the most direct responsibility for the President's safety.'*

As Patterson reached the unmarked door, his pager sounded. It was Locke, announcing that Morton was on board. Patterson knocked on the door, and a woman's voice told him to enter.

EIGHTEEN

United States Navy Surgeon-Commander Helen Curtis turned from a drug cabinet as Patterson entered. Over her uniform Helen wore a doctor's coat, its whiteness emphasising the blackness of her skin. High cheekbones and clear brown eyes gave her the look of being barely out of her teens, not someone in her mid-thirties.

'Not intruding, I hope?' he asked, standing in the door.

'Not at all.' She glanced around the office. 'I'm pretty well sorted out.'

'That was pretty quick.' Patterson closed the door, leaning against it and continuing to appraise her.

She nodded. 'You get used to that in my business, Colonel.'

She had a husky voice, softened by the low cadence of the Deep South. Louisiana, he'd judged, when Rear-Admiral Cox introduced them. They had all come here to inspect the changes made in what had been Air Force One's storage area for laundry. It was now divided into her office and, adjoining it, a small, well-equipped operating room and a one-bed recovery suite. In the time they were together, he'd been aware of being observed through the eyes of a capable doctor. The look was there now.

'Anything I can do for you?' Helen asked. She saw him absorb the question without changing expression. A careful man.

'You're my last stop. I'll be starting engines soon.' He

continued to look around the office. 'I never thought you'd find space for everything.'

'The layout's basically the same whether it's for the President or a naval rating. That's the first thing they teach you at Bethesda.'

Patterson glanced towards the open door of the operating room. 'Let's hope you don't ever have to prove that, Commander.'

'Me too. But that's why I'm here. I'm the Just-In-Case. And not only the President's.' She turned to a small stack of files on the desk. 'I've been reading up on the medical conditions of our other VIP guests.'

Patterson did not bother to hide his surprise. 'Where in the name of God did you get that stuff from?'

'Now that,' Helen answered lightly, 'is what's known as classified information. But between you and me and Admiral Cox, it comes courtesy of the CIA. It's quite amazing what Langley has on computer tape.'

She began to rifle the pages of a file. 'Seems Yoshio Nagoda, Japan's Prime Minister, has a scrotum the size of a bagel. The tumour's benign, but he's had to have his trousers fitted with a special truss. God knows how the boys at Langley discovered that. Maybe they bribed his tailor.'

'Or the truss-maker,' Patterson said drily.

Helen smiled and picked up another file. 'Bill McKenzie, the new man in Ottawa, has Kimmelsteil–Wilson syndrome.'

'And what exactly is *that*?'

She spoke with quiet authority. 'A spin-off from his diabetes. It leads to hypertension and oedema. Kimmelsteil was the German who made the initial discovery. Wilson, an English doctor, came up with the oedema link. In someone of McKenzie's age – he's just sixty – it's something to watch out for.'

The words held a resonance of feeling, reminding Patterson she lived a life outside this room. 'Is it safe for him to fly in that condition?' he asked.

'Oh, sure. As long as he doesn't get too stressed, or run into a sudden atmospheric change. Something like that could give him a problem.' She gave another smile. 'But I guess you've got instruments to warn of anything like that.'

He nodded emphatically. 'We've got instruments that tell instruments what to do.'

She nodded, keeping her tone level. 'In my work I always say it's touch and feel which matters. Once you lose that, all the instruments in the world count for little.'

Patterson smiled. 'Every time. Any instrument's only as good as the hand which holds it.'

He watched her rifle through a new file.

'Arnold Bostock, Britain's Prime Minister, was treated for syphilis at Oxford. He's also a good candidate for a heart attack. High blood pressure. Lousy cholesterol count. The CIA say it's from years of port drinking.'

Patterson didn't bother to hide the incredulousness in his voice. 'You really believe all this stuff is true?'

'Certainly makes for fascinating reading.'

She opened a different file. 'President Pierre Marceau of France. A history of reactive depression. He had a course of electro-shocks when he was in some fancy Paris clinic supposedly for a slimming cure. According to this, he still eats like a horse.'

'The shock treatment work?'

He saw her eyes narrow; he couldn't tell whether it was in contemplation of the question itself, or of why he had asked it.

'It doesn't say. Chances are, not. That kind of treatment is often very much hit-and-miss, largely because no one knows how it's actually supposed to work. Except it usually produces memory loss, anything from forgetting telephone numbers or addresses, to remembering to make really important decisions. Like whether France votes for something at the UN or what to buy for his wife's birthday.'

There was something about him at this moment, she thought, which somehow made him vulnerable, as if he was searching for another answer.

'What other treatments has he had?' he asked quietly.

She glanced at the file. 'Mostly drugs to control his mood swings.'

Once more the image of Bron came and went in his mind. 'Did they work?' he asked.

'It doesn't say.' She smiled suddenly. 'Nice to know Langley's not infallible.'

'Can those drugs produce any side effects?'

'Heavy drinking and fatty foods are out.' Her eyes flicked over a page. 'According to this, for a Frenchman anyway, the President is a moderate drinker. Half a bottle of wine a day. No spirits.'

'What about flying?'

Helen laughed. 'Nowadays a pre-med student can probably create a drug regime that'll keep a psychotic happily balanced ten miles high.'

Patterson leaned back against the door. 'Anything else I should know?'

She nodded at the other files. 'The German Chancellor, Helmut Sturmer, is as strong as the Bavarian boar he enjoys eating. A three-litres-of-beer-a-day man. In comparison the Spanish Prime Minister, Pedro Esplana, is a role model for Weight Watchers.'

'Well, that's a relief, Commander.'

She laughed. 'Wouldn't it be easier to just call me Helen?

Someone might think I was the aircraft commander.'

The throwaway line hung there.

'Any more than it would do for someone to think I could give them an injection.' Patterson nodded. 'Okay. I still call you Doctor in public, but Helen when not. I imagine it was the same for you at Bethesda.'

She stacked the files neatly on her desk as she spoke. 'Not really. The top brass there are pretty stuffy even away from the wards. I guess it comes from Bethesda being the President's official hospital, and all that. What struck me here is how relaxed everyone seems.'

'I'm glad to hear that, Helen. I like to think it's because everyone knows what they have to do.'

Helen once again sensed something unspoken. 'I suspect you're underselling your own role.'

They looked at each other. Her face, he thought, was attractive, despite containing none of the classic lines of beauty. Yet that's what made her attractive. He had not thought of another woman in those terms since Bron.

'So what do I call you? Edwin or Ed?'

'Ed will be fine.'

For a moment there was a look about his face which made Helen want to keep it there and, in that moment, she realised how attractive he still was. Lucky Mrs Patterson, she thought foolishly, whoever she was. If there was one.

'I knew an Ed once,' she said. 'He also was a pilot. Last I heard, he was still soaring for the stars.'

'You never asked more from him?'

'No, it was never the right situation. And by the time I realised I was ready to give more, he was gone,' Helen replied carefully.

'It happens. Too often.'

The last remark, delivered matter-of-factly, held an undertone of regret.

'You married, Ed?'

'Yes. Three years. Last month.'

'Then you're still honeymooning.' She smiled. 'You have to be.'

'I guess.'

For a moment she felt dim-witted, trying to decide how this changed her perception of him. But all she could think was that Ed Patterson had his own very clear idea of himself and had never wanted anyone to tamper with it. Mrs Patterson, whoever you are, you are one lucky lady.

Helen looked at Patterson. 'So how are things going?' she finally asked.

'Is that a professional question directed at me or the plane?' It had been a long time since he had bantered like this with a woman.

'The plane, I assume, is in the best of health,' she replied lightly.

'That I can promise you. She gets more attention than anyone on board. Even the Man doesn't get more pampering.'

'And who pampers you? Decides you're in the best of health?'

'Well, that doesn't arise,' he said quickly. 'And we all get regular check-ups every six months.'

She laughed softly. 'I was only kidding, Ed. You look in positive good health to me. But any time you feel like a consult, it's on the house.'

'I'll remember.' His tone changed as if to signal a switch of mood. 'How come you pulled this job?'

Helen eyed him steadily. 'You mean because I'm a woman, a black, or what?'

'I mean because you look too young to be looking after the Man.'

Helen laughed. 'Don't be fooled by appearances, Ed.

I've had six years of hardship at Bethesda. And three years before that at Memorial, New York. But to answer your question, I did the work-up on the President during his last medical check-up. We seemed to get on fine together. Leastways, that's what he told the Admiral. Ergo: here I am. And as I was saying . . .'

The urgent peep of Patterson's pager stopped her. She watched him stiffen as he held the receiver to his ear. He looked suddenly older and more drawn as he listened.

'Right,' he said, snapping off the pager.

'A problem, Ed?'

'Nothing to worry you about,' he forced a smile. 'But I'd better go take care of it.'

He turned and left the office. How could he begin to tell her Bron had done the unthinkable?

Bodor awoke as the creeping grey marked the start of a new day. His eyes were red-rimmed from lack of sleep and long hours of total concentration these past days, his mind already beginning to fill with what he must do in the long day ahead. It had been like this from the time he had arrived in this vast underground complex.

During the Gulf War the subterranean warren was a reserve headquarters for Saddam Hussein; so buried, he had learned, that the Americans most powerful bombs could never have reached down here. Now, as he watched the first movement out by the perimeter, he recalled the fear it had induced when he first came here.

The Iraqi army officer drove him south for an hour to a military airfield. There he showered and changed out of his Kurdish peasant disguise into the clothes waiting for him. In a jacket pocket he found a loaded syringe and injected himself. As the cocaine raced through his body he suddenly felt as if insects were crawling under his skin. The feeling lasted only a short while before the familiar mood of well-being took over. But in that moment he was badly frightened. The effect of the drug wore off quicker than usual and he decided the narcotic must have been of poor quality. By the time he boarded the helicopter he felt tired, his mouth was dry and he was sweating slightly. He told himself this was the result of the tensions and anxieties of his journey, compounded by that bad coke.

They flew low enough to see the twisted war wreckage in the sands. The Iraqi said they were the remains of American tanks and planes. He had not been fooled: there was enough left of the burnt-out hulks to show their Iraqi markings. Late in the afternoon they landed at an airfield south of Baghdad.

Standing on the tarmac was the Arranger. He was as controlled in his manner as ever, and once more there had been a feeling of some invisible powerful force behind him. This was reinforced by the way he asked no questions about the journey from Moscow: it was as if he already knew everything that had happened.

They drove along a metalled road in a limousine with tinted windows, the type of car which, in Moscow, would have been used only by someone who was a senior member of the New Order. Its one unusual feature was that the partition was opaque, so that the driver could not see them. The divider was bullet-proofed, the Arranger explained, adding that the car had once belonged to Saddam Hussein. After a while the road gave way to a scree track. As the sun began to set, the Arranger ordered the driver to stop. They climbed out of air-conditioned comfort into the furnace-like heat of the desert proper.

To his untutored eye the landscape seemed desolate. But the Arranger pointed out the tracks of desert foxes and, for a while, he seemed absorbed by this barren place, as if it were his natural habitat. When the sky darkened abruptly, until there was left only a pale band of light stretched across the horizon, the

Arranger led the way back into the car.

They arrived at a guard post which appeared deserted until a soldier emerged from the hut. The Arranger said something in Arabic and the soldier saluted before waving them through. An hour later, having passed two more check-points, the car reached a pile of rocks in the sands. Here the track forked. Turning on to the left fork, the limousine drove between dunes which had a stillness he had never before encountered.

The journey continued in a state of heightened awareness, so that he heard the barking of the dogs some time before the animals materialised out of the darkness; they were penned inside a perimeter of razor wire. A gateway swung open to enable the car to cross the perimeter. They travelled a further distance before reaching a huge natural rock formation which formed an arch, completely hiding the mouth of a tunnel. The car reduced speed and entered the opening, its tyres crunching over the rocky ground. Suddenly there were travelling down a smooth incline. Rounding a bend, the ramp became sufficiently wide for two cars to pass. But no vehicle came from the opposite direction. The limo stopped and started, moved on, then stopped again as if it were in a traffic jam. The Arranger explained that the car was being electronically guided.

At the bottom of the ramp a steel shutter rolled up on its hydraulics, then closed behind the car. They were in a brightly lit area. When the engine stopped, there was the sound of a klaxon, followed by a sensation of descending. He realised they were in an elevator and, as far as he could judge, they were going down at something like a hundred feet or so a minute. Two minutes passed, he judged, before the descent stopped. They stepped out into another brightly lit area, a corridor propped like a mine shaft he had once seen in the Urals. There were arrows painted on the walls indicating the way forward. The elevator had begun to ascend, taking the car back to the surface. At the far end of the passage they walked through a steel hatch. Beyond was an escalator which *carried them down to yet another level ending in a long corridor. To its left and right were doors, each bearing a sign which looked familiar. He inspected one, then the others with a sense of growing astonishment. They were identical to the signs on some of the doors of his establishment in Russia.*

'Welcome to your new research centre,' the Arranger said, opening a door. Inside the work area, everything had been done to replicate the facility destroyed on the orders of the New Order in Moscow. There were identical centrifuges, laser-lathes, computer-driven transformers and welding machines. And not only that — but here were the key personnel from his old team.

They, too, looked at him in astonishment. Nodding foolishly at them, he took the Arranger aside and asked how all this had been achieved.

The Arranger smiled enigmatically and replied it had needed a great amount of money and planning to achieve. Once more the feeling of being in the hands of an all-powerful force was overwhelming. He suddenly found the prospect exhilarating. Something that powerful could achieve anything.

Over dinner the Arranger spoke with great conviction, finally explaining why he had been brought here. He was now privy to knowledge no one else in the complex possessed. They shook hands before the Arranger left, gone before the gathering light signalled the start of another day.

On the monitor the dogs had suddenly fallen silent out by the perimeter, the prelude to going about their deadly business. Consumed by hunger, they once again set out to stalk one of their number. First they cornered their victim, creating a circle from which there would be no escape. Then the pack leader launched himself, tearing and snarling, going for the throat and spine. Others joined the assault. It was over in seconds. The slaughter did not bother him any more and he thought how, in his time here, he had also come to accept other parts of his life with equal indifference: the poor food, the cold of the night which made the concrete walls glisten and the heat of the day which, by noon, made a mockery of the air conditioning.

Even his supply of cocaine was restricted. Every morning a sealed packet with a syringe was placed outside his door. Bodor had no idea who put it there. Another packet would be waiting when he returned from work.

Even now he could not quite believe what had been achieved since his arrival. What had taken weeks to build back in Russia was accomplished here in days – sometimes even hours. Only an unrestricted budget could have assembled so secretly and so swiftly all the equipment and men to operate it. Using the blueprints and working shifts around the clock, they had produced the first casings. These had been subjected to a series of tests, to the point of destruction, the results analysed and refinements incorporated in the next generation.

Today, if further tests proved satisfactory, the first of the nuclear triggers would be fitted. Then would follow the first launch trial, under the control of the woman.

They had finally met the night before when she drove out into the desert to inspect the launch site. She had smiled challengingly at him, and he knew then that she could be dangerous. Even her name suggested sensuality: Zita Marcello.

He sighed with irritation. During the night he had thought of her again.

In his office, Ignatius Bailey was winding up his telephone call with Li Chung, the President of the Sterling Group, Hong Kong's largest investment banking firm. 'I hear what you're saying, Mr Li. But the initial mistake was your people's.'

'We didn't do the due intelligence,' came the reedy voice of polite protest from across the Pacific.

'Beside the point. Absolutely beside the point. You brought us this biotech company. We took it into Meridian in good faith. On your recommendation,' Bailey stressed. 'Next thing we have a potential lawsuit on our hands.'

'Hackett and Marshall did due intelligence, Mr Bailey. They're your people.'

'Correction. They are out-of-office counsel. One of a hundred law firms we use. But Hackett and Marshall could only work with what your staff provided. And that turns out to be less than enough.'

A year earlier Sterling had recommended the purchase of a company that had come from nowhere in the medical field, and looked to be going to the top with its claims for a product that could, if not cure, at least prolong the lives of AIDS sufferers. Meridian had agreed to take the company public. Now a Congressional medical watchdog committee had said claims made about the product couldn't be substantiated. A lot of investors were going to lose their money.

The problem had made its way up through Meridian's various echelons before finally reaching the executive floor level. Here it had shuffled through the offices of the management committee, each time collecting another initialled recommendation, until finally ending up on Bailey's modem. Ultimately he was the only one who could decide how to resolve the matter.

'Meridian can't afford to get caught in something like this, Mr Li. Our own Congress people are saying that what that company did came pretty close to fraud. Some of their R & D reports turned out to be phoney as well. There has just got to be a settlement. There's no other choice. We settle now or we face an even bigger mess.'

A throat-clearing came from Hong Kong. 'How much are you going to settle for?' asked an unhappy Mr Li.

Bailey glanced at his modem. On screen was the figure Costing had come up with.

'We're looking at a $150 million payout to investors. Maybe a little more. Add another two million to that for damage-limitation public relations. An expensive mistake for something we took in good faith, Mr Li. But we have to settle. We'll make the payout – and bill you.'

The hiss of breath on the line sounded like static. 'We can't find that money, Mr Bailey.'

Bailey switched gears. 'Yes, you can. Last quarter your billings to us were $90 million. We'll spread the payments over three quarters. Fixed interest. That's the best I can do.'

From Hong Kong came the voice of defeat. 'And then?'

'Until the settlement is in place, I'm going to have to ask you to suspend all dealings for us.'

'But that means we could be down almost three hundred million dollars . . .'

'Mistakes are always expensive. Be glad we have the resources to settle for you now, Mr Li.'

'I am grateful, Mr Bailey. Very much so. And after we settle . . . can we continue as before . . .?'

Bailey gave a short, harsh laugh. 'You mean making more mistakes?'

'No, working together.'

'First we settle, then we talk.'

'I understand.'

'I'll have someone send you a fax confirming our agreement.'

After Bailey hung up he dictated a memo to dispense with Sterling's services once they made the final repayment.

A moment later the soft buzz of a call waiting came from the modem. He spoke directly to the screen. 'Who is it, Susie?'

'The White House, Mr Bailey. They're calling again.'

'Tell them I can't be reached.'

'Can I tell them when you can be contacted?'

'No.'

He turned away from the screen. He already knew why the White House was calling.

NINETEEN

Morton sat on the jump seat in Air Force One's cockpit, listening to the preparations for take-off. Kerr and Top Sergeant Mike Turner, the radio operator, were working through their own check-lists and, a moment ago, after one of the French ground crew radioed that refuelling was complete, Locke had ordered the power-cart on the tarmac to be disconnected. Its line supplied electricity until the plane's own batteries took over. Everything was ready for engines to start. But the pilot's seat remained empty.

If Locke was surprised by Patterson's absence, he gave no sign as he continued to brief Morton on the history of presidential flights.

'It's hard to believe now, but until 1943 no American President had ever flown. It was supposedly too dangerous. Franklin Roosevelt changed all that when he went to see Winston Churchill in Casablanca. For Roosevelt it was either fly – or run the risk of being torpedoed by a U-boat. So he flew from Miami to Trinidad, then across to Dakar in West Africa, and finally north to Casablanca. It must have been some trip. Roosevelt spent most of it near an emergency exit, wearing a life-vest and parachute. The pilot had instructions that if they ditched, his first job was to push the President into the water. The plane was a Boeing 314, a real bone-rattler by all accounts, but Roosevelt loved the experience. He also became the first President since Abraham Lincoln to visit a war zone. The first to visit

Africa. And the first to leave the continental United States in time of war.'

Locke grinned. 'And it set one more precedent still to be broken. The pilot was air force. And since then, the air force has had the responsibility of flying the President. So far we haven't lost one.'

'How do you pick your crews?' Morton asked.

'Not just the crew. Every man and woman in the 89th, that's the President's Wing, is hand-picked. The pay's the same and the hours tough. When you're not flying the Man you practise to do so. Checking out unfamiliar routes and new airports, you're on the go all the time. It's not everyone's idea of a life. But we still turn down one out of every three who apply.'

Turner looked up from his console, smiling. 'I was in a bar when this guy came up and said, "I hear you can work a radio." I said, "Well maybe." Next thing I knew he was trotting out my military record, personal background, pretty well everything I had done since enlisting. The guy turned out to be FBI. He called another guy over who turned out to be the 89th's personnel officer. Seems they'd been checking on me for weeks. Next thing I knew I was up before my CO and asked if I'd like a transfer to the 89th. That was a year ago. I've got three more to go.'

'You still enjoy it?' Morton asked.

'It isn't everyone's cup of coffee. But it satisfies a man's curiosity. I've seen more of the world than most folk do in a lifetime,' Turner replied.

'Correction. More of the world's airports,' Kerr called out at his side-saddle instrument panel with its hundreds of flasher-type lights and switches.

'Last year we visited thirty-one countries,' Locke explained to Morton. 'Most of the time we didn't step beyond the airport perimeter.'

Kerr paused in his checking. 'The one thing I've learned from those trips is that you can't beat home cooking!'

Morton thought air crew were the same the world over, never losing sight of the basics, never taking their eye from what was important. Around him the galaxy of pale lemon and green dials and gauges continued to respond to every touch.

'When your stint is up, can you stay on?' Morton asked Locke.

'It rarely happens. For a start, there's a lot of competition. And most of us feel by the end it's time to move on.'

The co-pilot turned back to his work and the final pre-flight checks continued: emergency-exit lights armed, flight control-hydraulic power and yaw-danger switches operative, anti-ice feeds to the engines clear, cabin-pressurisation mode functioning. The routine of confirmation went its orderly way.

'Colonel's on his way down,' Locke called out. A moment ago through his head-set one of the cabin crew had reported that Patterson had left the upper deck.

'Better strap in,' Locke added. 'The colonel will want to light out as soon as he's here.' Over his shoulder he offered Morton a word of explanation 'We're famous for our fast take-offs. It's something all Presidents like.'

Below on the tarmac the last of the fuel trucks was pulling away.

'We're a little heavier loaded than we were outward bound,' Kerr announced.

'No sweat,' Locke replied. A moment later he swore softly. 'We're showing a fault on the rear baggage door.'

Morton saw a red light flashing on the overhead panel above Locke's seat.

'Try cycling the switch,' Kerr suggested.

Locke reached up and flicked a metal toggle back and

forth repeatedly. The light remained on. As he tried again, the cabin door opened.

Patterson entered, extending a hand to Morton.

'Sorry about not being here to meet you,' said the pilot.

'I can imagine your hands are full,' Morton replied.

'Thanks.' Patterson's eyes continued to scan the banks of instruments.

'Looks as if we have . . .' he began.

The red light went out.

'Problem solved . . .' Locke started to say as Patterson reached for an intercom phone and dialled a digit.

'Chief, we've been showing a red light on the rear baggage door.'

They all heard Sutter's reply. 'Checking right now, Colonel.'

Morton caught the quick look Patterson gave Locke. The unspoken reprimand was clear. Locke should have ordered an immediate physical check on the door.

In the silence Patterson eased his way past Morton into his seat.

Strapping himself in, he hoped he showed no sign of how shaken he had been over what Bron had done.

She had gone to his desk in the den at home and found his list of special telephone numbers. They were all work-related, and among them was the direct-line listing for the console on the President's office desk on Air Force One. The number was shown as being in the Washington area code: all calls made anywhere in the world to and from Air Force One were charged at the local rate, a cost-cutting scheme President Reagan had introduced.

Patterson knew Bron must have chosen the President's number purely by chance. There was a moment to think what would have happened if the Man had been on board, then Bron began accusing him of still being in Washington when he'd told her he was going to Paris. The more he tried to calm her, the angrier she became.

'You listen to me, then! I know what you're doing, you two-timing son of a bitch,' she screamed.

'Bron, I'm just about to take off,' he pleaded. 'I'll be home in a few hours. Then we can talk.'

'Tell me more lies, you mean! Where are you – shacked up in some motel? That's about all you can afford . . .'

'Bron! Please . . .!'

'Don't you bloody well "Bron please" me! I know what you're doing. What all you pilots do . . .'

'Bron, I simply can't talk now. Wait until I get home, then I can explain everything . . .'

She was screaming, 'You'll talk now . . .' when he disconnected the call.

He had sat for a while in the President's day cabin, feeling drained. Finally he'd forced everything else from his mind and gone to the flight deck.

'Colonel, this is Sutter,' came the voice over the cockpit's squawk-box. The crew chief was using a hand-set to communicate from the tarmac. 'Tell me what you're showing – *now*,' Sutter ordered.

'A red,' reported Patterson.

'Okay, stand by. Looks as if the door handle wasn't locked in fully.'

Through the squawk-box came the sound of the large metal door being slammed shut. The light blinked and went out. For good measure, Sutter repeated the procedure. The red light stayed off.

'Problem now solved, crew chief,' Patterson announced.

After Sutter was back on board, Patterson ordered engines to start.

'Starting Two,' repeated Locke.

The inboard engine rumbled and caught. The RPM

needle quivered, then steadied.

'Two is steady,' announced Locke.

'Start One,' Patterson intoned.

'Starting One.'

Morton listened to the familiar ritual, knowing both pilots were communicating with that sixth sense instilled early in their careers. Instinctively he liked Patterson. Nevertheless, something or someone had left him a little on edge. The signs were there in the compressions around his jaw, the way he sat a little too rigid for comfort.

'Start Three and Four,' Patterson told Locke.

'Three and Four starting.'

The last of the turbines stirred into life, whirring softly at first and then building up quickly to a screaming crescendo.

'We have taxi power,' Locke said.

'Let's move out,' Patterson ordered.

Air Force One shuddered under the increased power, then began to move slowly towards the runway.

Zita felt increasingly lost as another pair of steel doors shut. The naked fluorescent lights from the tunnel roof were hard on her eyes. The denim boiler suit, featureless except for her name tag, clung damply to her skin in the heat. Her guide seemed to suffer no such problems as he walked stoically beside her.

Down here everybody wore the same uniform. She'd decided it was to help create the feeling of anonymity. People worked, ate and slept; there was almost no socialising. Living comforts were minimal, probably because the effort of building anything this far beneath the earth must have been formidable. Her own quarters, small enough, were still larger than most people's. They shared cubicles, which reminded her of the police cells she'd occupied from time to time.

After the preliminary inspection of the balloon launch site, she had spent most of the time alone in her quarters. A moment ago, on her way to inspect the minor changes in the gondola she had requested, the guide had received over his bleeper the order to return her to her quarters. As usual, no reason was given for the change of plan.

All this had heightened the tension in her, already fuelled by the realisation that she could breathe, but was this fresh air? I can walk, she told herself, but I cannot go for a walk in the accepted sense. And the only sun she'd seen was on the monitor screen. She had seen Bodor several times, hurrying out of, or going into, some room. Apart from a curt greeting he had ignored her.

'Where are we now?'

'Not far now,' the man said, glancing sideways.

She felt a stirring. As well as the tension, the old familiar demand had returned. The dampness between her legs was no longer only sweat. It was shame.

As if sensing her mood, the escort had increased his stride. Perhaps there was a punishment for anyone down here who had sex.

'What's your name?' she asked, drawing alongside.

'Kunsk.'

She saw his cheekbones flush.

'You are Russian?'

Bodor had warned everyone to stay away from this woman.

'Georgian,' Kunsk finally admitted.

'Kunsk from Georgia,' she repeated.

From somewhere overhead came the sound of machinery. Bodor would be somewhere up there, driving everyone with his incessant demand.

'You like to work for Bodor?' Zita saw him suck in his breath.

'Pliss? Why you ask?' He exhaled like he was blowing out smoke.

She smiled at him. 'It's okay. I'm not going to tell anyone.'

Kunsk was trying to form the musculature of his face into an indifferent expression. 'Pliss. I no understand.'

She made a circle of her finger and thumb and held it in front of her face. 'Yes, you do.' Slowly, deliberately, she began to move the forefinger of her other hand in and out of the circle.

'Yes, you do, Kunsk.' She increased the finger movement. 'Oh yes, you do.'

'You are a crazy woman.' But he was hypnotised by her hands, her eyes almost level with his own, the muscles round her eyes seeming to move in tandem with her finger.

Suddenly she broke the movement and pulled him towards her. 'Find us a place,' she said urgently.

He walked them towards a heavy steel door set into the side of the tunnel, produced a bunch of keys from a pocket, and after several attempts found one that fitted. Beyond was a short flight of stone steps leading upwards. He turned to her. 'Saddam Hussein private place,' Kunsk said, pointing above his head.

Still holding his gaze she reached down, feeling him tremble, feeling the dampness of the cloth on her fingers.

'Nice,' she said, closing the door and leading the way up the steps. At the top was a second door, plated with steel.

'No key,' Kunsk mumbled, watching her opening the buttons on her suit.

'Come, Kunsk. Show me what a Georgian can do,' Zita breathed in his ear.

Dawn in Tabriz came pale and watery as Ken Adams stepped on to the tarmac after the flight from Baku. The weather did nothing to improve his mood.

He had stayed in Baku longer than intended in the hope that Madame Lutke would find the guide. She had left her apartment for a short while, returning with no news but urging him to be patient, and to continue enjoying her company. In the end he decided her promises were only a ploy to keep him in her bed.

The flight north into Iran was bumpy and his stomach felt even more queasy from the body odours of his fellow passengers.

Crossing the tarmac, rucksack over his shoulders, he passed an Iranian air force helicopter. He wondered if it had brought another team of archaeologists to continue excavating the only claim Tabriz had to fame. Fifteen miles outside the town were the ruins of Tell Disbar, a city already three thousand years old when Christ walked on earth. He had driven to the site the last time he came this way. Then, the heat of summer had shimmered over the excavation and the fragments of history were hot to the touch. Now, beyond the ramshackle arrivals hall, Tabriz stood dark, misty and forbidding.

The check-in desk clerk said the flight to Rezaiyeh, from where he would begin the long walk into the mountains, was delayed by five hours. Last time the delay had been a three-hour one. That decided him. Rather than wait here he would hire a car and drive out to the dig. For a while at college archaeology tempted him as a career, and his passion for the past had never quite left him. Was it because his own profession was so similar? Both certainly had much in common. An archaeologist sifted through layers of buried information, separated rubble from dust, ashes from odure, reconstructed shards into vessels, scratchings back to texts, trying to recreate what had happened. Just like his own work.

Twenty minutes later he left Tabriz and was following a route no map-maker would engrave on his plates. The car bucked and rolled continuously, and only his strength held the steering wheel more or less on course. Sometimes the road seemed to fall away under his wheels, and he kept his foot constantly hovering near the brake. Whenever he saw anything resembling human habitation, he pumped the horn. As a foreigner he would automatically be blamed for an accident. And if he was to hurt, let alone kill anything, his life would almost definitely be forfeit.

He passed through a village too small to have a name, the streets deserted, the mosque minaret rising like an accusing finger above the mud-walled houses. Through the windows of a tea-house he glimpsed old men drinking and playing backgammon. Then the empty road again, an evil-coloured brown ribbon stretching into the gloom, his tyres throwing up small furrows of mud in a constant patter.

Another nameless village. Snatches of Oriental music came to him and as quickly faded. Finally the car began to climb, and soon the light improved. A truck swirled past, its horn blaring. The higher he climbed, the more the air held moisture like a cold sponge. Soon there was frost on the ground. He turned on the heater, but that caused the windscreen to fog so he switched it off again.

A watery sun appeared as he finally reached a plateau, a vast space stretching to the mountains. Here all was silence, a place filled with fast-moving shadows from clouds scudding between the patches of blue. Almost a mile away was Tell Disbar with its dark stones, ruined gateways and broken walls. There was no sign of any activity around the dig. In the sunshine there was both a beauty and a mysteriousness about the ruins.

He drove across the stony ground and parked in the lee of what remained of the outer wall. Through one of its gaps he entered the city and the illusion was broken. Inside was a maze of grey mud walls and filthy little streets filled with ancient rubble. Little progress with the excavation seemed to have been made since he was last here. Mounds of disinterred earth stood everywhere, as if a colony of giant moles had been at work.

Standing inside the remains of an arch he tried to imagine what it must have been like three millennia ago. Then, a thriving community had lived here; caravans had come and gone through this archway. Men had probably died defending its access. There had been gardens, trees and bushes; burial places; domed buildings beneath which men and women had loved. Now only vague shapes of walls and doorways remained. Occasionally a stone staircase rose a few faltering steps, then stopped, hinting at what might once have stood here.

He began to walk, pausing from time to time to pick up a fragment of rock, a piece of history. Once more he thought how much his work had in common with archaeology. Buried beneath his feet were the bones of the long dead which could still provide answers as to how the people here had lived. Not just what they ate, but perhaps how they lied and stole to obtain food; even how they betrayed one another. Here, still in some tomb waiting to be discovered, could be the answers to how injustices were righted, wrongdoers punished. He shivered slightly, his feet crunching under the thin covering of ice, his nose wrinkling at the rotten dankness of a past which did not wish to be disinterred.

He reached a trench whose sides were partly collapsed and the anger he'd felt when he'd last come here returned. Permission to excavate anywhere in Iran was slowly given; you had to win the trust and confidence of the mullahs in Tehran. They insisted on the highest standards: like ensuring a trench was properly shored. He knew enough about archaeology to see that whoever was in charge of this dig was incompetent. There was something haphazard about the way the work was being conducted. No proper effort had been made to clear the ground in layers. Yet the evidence was clearly visible to suggest that a properly conducted excavation here would uncover priceless secrets.

All around him the limestone and baked brick formed tantalising outlines of buildings. Had that one, leading to an inner courtyard, been a temple? Were those stumps all that remained of tall columns, the entrance to a public bath-house? And over there, beyond where another trench had collapsed, had that once been the palace of the local caliph? Certainly the ground space between the walls indicated that it had been a far more imposing structure than those surrounding it.

He reached a stairway. Beneath it was an opening. He squatted on his haunches and peered inside. What had this been used for? A storage place for water, or an escape route should the city fall to invaders? All archaeology, he reminded himself, depended on violent death to unravel the past. He picked up a handful of dust. Had it once mingled with blood? Was it the ashes of the dead? Now it only felt lifeless between his fingers. He let the dust fall back to the ground and stood up. Continuing to walk, he thought how every step stirred the deposit of aeons of death and plunder. He climbed a rampart and beyond, over the outer wall, he could see far across the plateau, right to the rim where the mountains began.

He began to think about the mission ahead. Those gunshots, if they turned out to have any importance at all, could be linked to something he'd heard when he was here last year. Beyond these mountains was an altogether more imposing range – the Dead Mountains. Rumour was that the Russians had been doing some experiments up there to do with those splash lasers they'd used to such good effect in Afghanistan. From his pocket he produced a small compass and checked the bearings. Then he jotted down the co-ordinates on a piece of paper. If there was time he would try and take a look. He shoved compass and paper back into his pocket, walked a little further along a walkway, then looked at his watch. It had been two hours since he'd left the airport. It was time to drive back.

Stooping, he picked up another fragment. Bone. He turned it over in his hand. Who had it belonged to? What dreams and tragedies was it once part of? Impulsively, he stuck the piece in his pocket.

He had reached his entry point when he heard the sound of rotors. The helicopter was coming low across the ground, sending dust swirling. He watched it land, coming to rest between him and the car. It was the chopper he had seen at the airport.

As if alerted by a sixth sense, he began to walk quickly towards the car. He had left his rucksack in the boot; inside was the Colt handgun which Langley said was now obsolete.

The dust around the chopper was settling. In the cockpit he glimpsed the pilot; he had a beard and aviator's glasses. The chopper itself looked like a giant insect, black, its rotors idling. The cabin door slid open. A figure stepped onto the ground. Even in his long military greatcoat buttoned up to the neck, and a soldier's beret on his head, there was no mistaking who he was: the Kurd from the bar beneath Madame Lutke's apartment. Salim's hand swung loosely by his side and he was almost smiling. In his right hand he held a pistol.

As if in a dream, Adams watched the gun hand come up, saw the barrel steady, felt his own feet refusing to move, heard something in his brain screaming for him to turn and run. To do *something*.

As he threw himself to one side he felt pain in his chest, a searing, surging pain which spread throughout his body. He would never know how far it travelled.

Salim walked over and turned the body over with his foot. A moment later from inside the cabin a voice called out in Kurdish. 'Can you lift him by yourself?'

'Yes, of course,' Salim said, bending to his task.

Hoisting Adams over his shoulder, Salim carried him back to the helicopter.

A pair of hands reached forward to help pull the body on board.

'Hurry. We have to be in Tehran before dark,' said the Arranger.

TWENTY

At fifty-one thousand feet, an hour into his climb out of Charles de Gaulle, Patterson levelled out Air Force One, keeping her in the centre of the invisible track known as high-altitude jet route W21. The sky was blue-black above, the cloud almost a mile below, obscuring their last landfall, the west coast of Ireland. Patterson could almost see the curvature of the horizon.

Since take-off there had been little small-talk in the cockpit; Patterson disliked it. His eyes scanned the instruments again; everything was normal. He reached down beside his right leg, to the pedestal between him and Locke, and pushed the master throttle lever forward a click. He felt a slight pressure against his seat as the engines notched up another five hundred revolutions per second. Air Force One was at cruising speed.

Bron started to intrude once more into his thoughts. How could he persuade her to see a doctor? He didn't know anything about psychiatrists except that a large number were listed in the Washington telephone directory. Someone who would prescribe her pills? Then he remembered she had an aversion to taking medicine. And certainly no electro-shocks after what Helen had said. Perhaps Bron needed a doctor who would simply listen to her. He didn't know much about psychotherapy except that you went in and spent time on a couch unburdening yourself. You did it for a year, maybe years. The doctor went on listening, making suggestions, redrawing the flight plan of your life. People said it worked. But again, would she agree? So many damned questions to which he didn't have answers.

Air Force One rocked gently and the altitude dial lurched counter-clockwise past two numerals. It was the only indication that the plane had dropped a couple of hundred feet.

'A playful leprechaun,' grinned Locke.

At this time of year there were often air pockets near Ireland.

'Let's show him we don't want to play,' Patterson said.

He pulled gently on the yoke and the artificial horizon returned to level position. Air Force One continued her uneventful way.

Over his shoulder Patterson called to Turner. 'Our passenger still on the phone?'

The radio operator glanced at his panel. 'Yeah. He's working that console hard.'

After take-off Morton had asked if there was somewhere he could use a telephone, and Patterson asked one of the flight attendants to show him to the cubbyhole behind the crew sleeping quarters.

The cubbyhole was known as the One Step from Armageddon – the Step for short. A Marine signals officer who travelled everywhere with the President would go there in a crisis to open a metal suitcase with an intricate combination lock. Inside was an envelope. Sealed with wax and bearing the signature of the Chairman of the Joint Chiefs of Staff, it contained the codes for the President to order a nuclear attack on a number of targets. Moscow and key Russian cities had been removed from the list, but Beijing and other Chinese cities remained. So did Baghdad and Tehran. The bagman would use the Step's secure phone to call the Chairman and verify the codes before the

President gave the launch orders. It was a fail-safe order introduced after President Reagan had once threatened to bomb Moscow.

Patterson glanced at his watch. In five hours fifty minutes they'd be on the ground. Maybe he should just call the first doctor in the phone book? In his headset he heard an Irish voice.

'Air Force One, this is Shannon air traffic control.'

'Air Force One, go ahead, Shannon,' Locke replied.

'We've a big squall two-fifty miles ahead of your present position, and crossing diagonally at rapid speed. An incoming Delta flight reports unable to get on top at forty thousand.'

'Shannon, did your Delta indicate level of turbulence?' Locke asked.

'Affirmative, Air Force One. Moderate to severe at forty thousand. But radar shows it's weaker higher. Do you want to vector?'

'How big a vector?'

'A couple of hundred miles to the south, Air Force One.'

Patterson shook his head. 'We can go higher. The squall should pass well beneath us,' he told Locke.

The vector would add another thirty minutes to their flying time – thirty minutes longer before he could start calling doctors. He felt a twinge in his stomach. Dammit, he must put Bron out of his mind until he reached Andrews.

'Shannon, Air Force One. We'll maintain,' Locke intoned.

'Roger and out, Air Force One,' acknowledged the ground controller.

Patterson set the weather radar to two hundred miles. The scanner line began to revolve slowly as the antenna in the nose of Air Force One searched for the first signs of the weather front.

'Shall I take her up a couple of thousand?' Locke asked.

'Make it four. That should give us ample clearance. And it'll show us what we have in ceiling reserve,' Patterson replied.

Air Force One had never flown so high.

Locke's right hand moved the yoke back and the plane began to climb effortlessly towards its new altitude, sweeping westward at 650 miles an hour.

Everything was routine, Patterson thought, except for this nagging pain in his gut. Damn Bron, she had no business doing this to him.

Inside the Step, Morton sat hunched over the telephone console listening to Lester Finel.

'Meridian has no plans to expand beyond that one plant in Tehran. It's got five plants in Pakistan producing software and domestic electronics. They could be tooled up for military use, but that would take weeks. North Korea? Same as Iraq. Meridian hasn't had anybody near the place.'

'Anywhere else come in the frame?' Morton asked, his voice soft and unhurried, as if he was already half-thinking of something else.

'Meridian's people have been talking to Libya. Gaddaffi wants them to set up a new desalination plant in the desert. Those triggers could be adapted to drive it.'

'And Bodor?'

Finel laughed. He had a distinctive laugh, high-pitched, as if it had been fed through a synthesiser. 'Gaddaffi was one of the first to send a team to head-hunt Bodor in Russia. They left empty-handed. Couldn't find him. Nor the Egyptians, Turks and Indians. He was probably hiding out until he got the deal he wanted.'

'With Meridian?' Morton suggested. But it wasn't really a question.

'Where could they possibly use him? South Africa? Meridian's big down there. To keep the last of the white mavericks in check? Hardly. South America? A number of large Meridian holdings in Venezuela, Brazil, Colombia and Peru. As you know, all potential trouble spots. But again, you don't need a Bodor to come up with something to protect them. And certainly nothing nuclear.'

Morton looked down at a pad in front of him. 'Bodor was into climatology in a big way. Could Gaddaffi use those triggers to change someone's weather? Use that desalination scheme to launch the equivalent of a new Flood on a neighbour? Maybe try and turn Chad into a sea? Or create a permanent drought in Egypt or Morocco? Bodor could do any of that for him.'

A grunt came before Lester's response. 'It's a possibility, certainly.'

'Check them all,' Morton said, hanging up.

These were the times he most enjoyed: putting together fragments of data, testing fact against fact, comparing times and locations, wondering about coincidences and circumstances, creating situations – experiments in his mind, he called them – which were all at the centre of his endeavours.

He called Johnny Quirke. He'd caught him, by the sound of it, lighting a cigar. Johnny had given up cigarette smoking since an insurance broker told him cigars didn't carry a premium penalty.

'Still no sign of Zita Marcello, David. I've run a computer search for all arrivals at airports in Iran, Pakistan and North Korea in the past week. That's close to a million names. And the airlines say business is dropping! But in her case – *nada*. Not even one sounding anything like a Zita Marcello.'

'She could be using a different name and passport, Johnny.'

'In that case I've been wasting my time,' Quirke sighed wearily. 'Except she's a high-profile figure. She'd be instantly recognisable to Customs and Immigration. A phoney name or passport would only draw attention.'

'A private plane?' Morton asked.

Quirke sighed again. 'Airports don't keep records of private flights for more than twenty-four hours. Anyway, few bother filing a passenger list. The rich and famous, or the rich and infamous, don't like to advertise. Also, Meridian has over a hundred private planes on tap. Seems their executives use them like taxis. Any one could have taken Zita Marcello just about anywhere.'

Morton consulted his pad before he spoke. 'I want you to go back through your names and see if you can spot these.'

Morton gave Quirke the names of the three Dutch balloonists, hung up, then called Chantal.

'Anna called an hour ago, David. She's met up with Mischa. But the mortuary attendant is dead. The Moscow police fished his body out of a sewer last night with his testicles shoved down his throat. Mischa says it's the local *mafiya*'s calling card.'

Someone was doing an efficient job of cleaning up; someone whose highest purpose was to leave his complicity hidden and ambiguous.

'Where are Anna and Mischa now?' Morton asked.

'On the night train to St Petersburg, going back over Bodor's route.'

There was a pause. He knew it was another way for Chantal to keep a self-imposed distance which went back to that evening, a year back, when she hinted she was willing to develop their relationship. He had told her he had no time for emotional entanglements. He knew he had been brusque and that she had been hurt. Sensing this, he tried to tell her about Carina, but it was her turn to brush him aside. They'd hardly met socially since then, and only in the company of others. Loving Carina, he'd wanted to tell Chantal, had been like opening a secret drawer from which he'd emerged to give himself in a way he'd never thought possible. Carina's death had closed that door for ever, the more so because of the sudden, senseless, shocking manner of her dying. Carina had been gunned down in the same city as the morgue attendant was murdered.

'Keep everybody looking, Chantal. Bodor and those triggers are out there, for sure.'

For a while afterwards he sat, going through his notes, then dialled a new number. The Prof sounded as if he'd awoken from a deep sleep.

'I've been reviewing the Nuclear Components back-ground,' the Prof said, his voice gaining strength by the word. 'They were taken over when Washington was cracking the whip at Meridian over those pollution violations, and their shares dropped right down the scale. Money had to be tight for even a big spender like Bailey. Yet he still paid over the odds for Nuclear, and cheerfully enough, my market mole tells me.'

Morton was writing while the Prof spoke.

'And, as Lester said, Nuclear's heyday was the Gulf War. But what's really interesting is that before the war Nuclear was working on splash lasers about the same time, it turns out, as friend Bodor was doing the same thing,' continued the Prof.

Intelligence work, Morton thought, is a continuing education in small surprises. 'How far had Bodor gone, Prof?'

'No way of telling, David. I came across the reference purely by chance in one of those old Afghanistan files Walter wanted to toss because they were taking up too much space. I knew they'd come in useful one day. Anyway, there was this note the Russians had tried laser splashing to give their helicopters a better shot at the mujaheddin. They certainly needed help to hit anything in those mountains. But they were still only getting a strike rate of under thirty per cent even with splashing. Horrendously wasteful, given that each pot-shot cost ten thousand dollars – and God only knows what in roubles. Then somebody in Kabul had the bright idea of sending for Bodor. In the six months he was there he upped the strike rate to eighty per cent.'

'How did Bodor achieve that?' Morton asked.

'He inserted a nuclear chip in the laser splasher. The principle, Sean assures me, is simplicity itself, but the small print depends on the kind of engineering science Bodor specialises in.'

Morton made another note. 'This nuclear chip. Could it be similar to the one in those stolen triggers?' Morton asked.

'Sean says it's probably safe to assume so,' the Prof replied.

Morton sat for a moment, pondering all of it. 'How have Nuclear reacted to the thefts?' he asked.

'Publicly, not a word. Not that there's been any publicity. Manders has still managed to keep the lid on. But my own contacts in Washington tell me the Nuclear line is that, once they sold the stuff, it was up to the Brits to keep it safe.' The Prof gave a small laugh. 'With these things, as we both know, it's Pontius Pilate time.'

Morton could sense Air Force One climbing. Beneath his feet there was a faint tremble, as if the aircraft was flying close to turbulence. He shifted in his seat and asked another question. 'Have you had a chance to cast an eye over that balloon company?'

'I was just coming to that, David.' There was a hint of reproof in the Prof's voice. 'Free Flight joined Meridian when the balloon business, if you'll pardon the pun, was literally taking off. Since then more and more companies are appreciating the value of balloons as aerial billboards. But here's the interesting thing. Free Flight hasn't really gone after that guaranteed money-spinner. Last year they built a hundred balloons, and not one's being used for advertising purposes. Instead, the company is concentrating on balloons as platforms. They're building them so they can rise to sixty, seventy thousand feet.'

'What's the purpose?'

'Weather research. You get better atmospheric readings from instruments on a slow-rising balloon than you do from an aircraft or rocket. And these balloons are different from what Free Flight produced before Meridian came along. Until then it was strictly competition stuff. Their balloons regularly won all the worthwhile national championships. Matter of fact, those Dutchmen were using one. They bought it second-hand from a Swiss company. Nothing unusual in that. There's a good market in used balloons.'

'Zita Marcello use a Free Flight balloon?'

'No. She'd been using those made by Euro-Balloon, a British outfit. But they've told Manders they ended their association with her some months back. Seems she was attracting the wrong kind of publicity.'

The Prof had given Morton another lead.

The MI5 switchboard traced Manders to the Registry. He sounded as if he'd just returned from Simpson's.

'It wasn't just the publicity,' Manders said. 'It's the

whole shooting-match of what Zita Marcello is doing to the balloon industry. From what the Euro-Balloon chappie told me, it's pretty conservative. Zita Marcello has gone way over the top and Euro-Balloon is planning to sue her for bringing their product into disrepute.'

'Have they any idea where she is?'

'None. But the chappie I spoke to said she'd once mentioned something about doing mountain ballooning in Afghanistan, of all places. Maybe after what happened at Garmisch, she's gone there.' Manders paused. 'You planning to chase after her?'

'Too early to say,' Morton said, before hanging up. A moment later the phone rang. It was Tommy, calling from Sardinia.

'You made good time, Tommy.'

'Your contact helped, Colonel.'

Morton had given him the name of a senior police officer in Cagliari he had worked with in the past.

'You find the Dutchmen?'

'Yes and no. They were holed up in the mountains. The contact said it's a Mafia safe house and the locals know to stay away. When I arrived, the place was empty.'

Tommy told him about the piece of paper he'd found with flight times from Cagliari to Istanbul and then on to Tehran.

'Leaving that behind was careless on their part, Tommy.'

'This lot are amateurs, Colonel. Once the job was over, their security went out of the window. They'd picked up a prostitute in town here, and took her with them to the house.'

'You talk to this woman?'

'No. Your contact reckons she's gone to the mainland, Naples or Rome, on a spending spree. Apparently she's done that before, after she'd found a good mark. He'll pick her up when she returns.'

'Where are you now?' Morton asked.

'At the airport. Nobody here remembers the Dutchmen, but that's not surprising. At the best of times, this place operates in a shambles. My bet is all three had no trouble passing through unnoticed. There's another flight to Istanbul in a couple of hours, with an onward connection to Tehran. Want me to catch it?'

Morton came to a decision. 'Only as far as Istanbul. If they've gone on to Tehran, then they've gone for good. From Istanbul I want you to go to Baku. Bill Gates' man should be back from the mountains soon.'

From the corridor outside the Step came the sound of hurrying footsteps. Then a voice was calling out for a First Aid box to be brought to the cockpit immediately.

TWENTY-ONE

Patterson's nose-bleed happened without warning. Levelling out Air Force One at fifty-five thousand feet and turning on the auto-pilot, he felt a sudden uncomfortable pressure in his nose. Next moment his shirt front was flecked with blood which also spilled over the instrument panel. Pinching his nose to stanch the flow, he felt a pressure in his chest, accompanied by a stinging feeling in his eyes. The symptoms were those he'd experienced over Bosnia.

Dammit! He remembered what that Russian doctor had said in Sarajevo. *Don't fly when you have experienced undue stress*. Thinking about Bron had brought this on. Knowing, he began to feel better. The smarting in his eyes stopped and the chest pain eased.

Turner said one of the cabin attendants was bringing the First Aid box, and Surgeon-Commander Curtis was on her way. Locke and Kerr both produced handkerchiefs for him to hold to his nose. He took Kerr's.

'Your eyes look pretty bloodshot,' Locke said.

'Specks of dust,' Patterson said crisply.

'You'll be okay, Colonel,' Kerr insisted reassuringly.

'I'm fine.' His voice sounded nasally through the cloth he was pressing to his nose.

While Locke wiped the blood from the instrument panel with his handkerchief, Air Force One trembled momentarily. Patterson glanced at the weather radar; the turbulence was moving away below them. 'Tell Shannon we'd like to step down to where we were.'

As Locke obtained clearance, Dempsey entered the flight deck carrying a First Aid box. Behind her was Morton.

'What happened?' asked Dempsey.

Turner told her. She turned to Patterson. 'Colonel, I'd like to get you back into one of the bedrooms. You feel up to walking there?' she asked.

Patterson frowned. The pain in his chest was gone and his eyes were clearing. He shook his head. 'I don't need to lie down. Just to change my shirt.' He snapped open his harness. As he stood up, Helen Curtis arrived with her doctor's bag, pushing quickly past Morton and Dempsey.

'Hold it, Colonel,' the doctor said brusquely. 'Let me check a few things before you risk doing yourself more damage.' She gave him a professional look. 'What happened to your eyes?'

'Dust. No matter how hard they clean an aircraft, you still get some left behind.'

'Okay.' She reached for his wrist pulse. Next she took out a thermometer from the bag.

She inserted it in his mouth. 'You feel dizzy?'

Patterson shook his head.

'Any nausea?'

A headshake.

'Pain anywhere?' Helen asked.

Another shake of the head.

Helen removed the thermometer. 'Normal. Okay. Tip your head back.' She used a pencil torch to peer inside each nostril. The blood had started to clot.

'Ever had a nose-bleed before?' she asked.

'Only as a kid.'

Helen stepped back. 'Okay. Let's get you to that cabin. I'll do a few more checks and then you can get cleaned up.'

'You really think all this is necessary, Doctor?' he asked, the irritation plain in his voice.

'I do, yes,' Helen said calmly.

Morton wondered about the side effect that produced a slight tremble in the pilot's hand as Patterson passed him.

Sergei Andreya Malenko, the senior detective with St Petersburg's Central Investigating Board, met Mischa and Anna off the Red Express from Moscow, greeting Mischa with a kiss on both cheeks and Anna with a formal handshake. It was like being gripped by a vice, she thought, noticing his eyes had a pupil so much wider than normal that they seemed to absorb immediately everything around him.

'Did you manage to sleep?' he asked.

'We took it in turns,' Mischa said.

He sighed. 'The gas gangs are getting worse. A few nights ago they knocked out a whole compartment of foreigners and robbed them of everything, including their shoes.'

'Good shoes are almost unobtainable,' Mischa said quickly to Anna.

'Like everything else,' Malenko grunted, carrying their bags, the steel cleats on his shoes striking a relentless beat against the concourse concrete. He turned to Mischa.

'As far as anybody is concerned, you are here to show your Swiss colleague something of our police methods. And very appropriate, given our history.' He smiled, displaying a row of uneven teeth. 'Peter the Great built our city on a swamp because there was no shortage of convicted criminals to do the drainage. That's why no Dostoevesky novel is without its axe murder set here.'

They walked out of the station on to Nevsky Prospekt. The pavements were as crowded with people as they were in Moscow but here, Anna thought, they seemed dowdier, or perhaps it was because the buildings were more elegant.

'How have people taken to freedom?' she asked.

Malenko answered without a hint of self-consciousness. 'Better than they took to Communism. For me the big change is that the *mafiya* has taken the place of the Party.'

'It's the same everywhere, Sergei Andreya,' Mischa said.

'Ah, but our crime's different,' Malenko replied, leading them towards the parked Zhiguli. 'In Moscow they steal for food. Here, so they can buy a satellite dish to watch MTV.'

The driver had a slate-grey face and wore wrap-around sunglasses. Malenko said his name was Nikolai. He gave no acknowledgement as Anna and Mischa sat in the back of the car.

'He's dumb,' explained Malenko, settling beside Nikolai. 'And seven-tenths deaf. As part of democracy we employ a percentage of disabled. We have traffic cops with peg legs and a blind woman on the switchboard.'

Anna glanced at Nikolai. 'Doesn't that make it dangerous for him to drive?'

Malenko grinned at her in the mirror. 'Here in Peter *everyone* is a danger when they get behind a wheel. Foreigners say it's like the Monte Carlo rally, only here no one knows the course rules.'

He scribbled something on a pad attached to the dashboard, tore off the paper and handed it to the driver. Nikolai nodded, crumpled the paper and dropped it on the floor. There were dozens of crumpled pieces around his feet. Anna wondered when Nikolai ever cleaned them out.

'Now he takes us to Zelenogorski where Bodor was last seen.' He half-turned in his seat. 'I've had two men up there, Mischa – strictly unofficial. In the bad old days we could go anywhere. Now everybody has to' – he frowned at Anna – 'how do you say, stick to their potato field.'

'Turf,' she corrected, thinking it remarkable how each part of Malenko's policeman's face seemed dedicated to a separate function: the raised eyebrows signalling worldliness; the eyes wide with sincerity and the rubbery mouth covering all the emotional territory in between. When the mouth finished laughing, its owner said, 'Right. Stick to their turf.'

'Where'd you learn your English?' Anna asked.

Malenko tented his fingers to his lips, a new expression making the gesture vaguely like prayer.

'Where most of us learned it,' Mischa said quickly. 'At one of the elite schools of the Party.'

'My father was a commissar,' Malenko said. 'Now he's a cleaner in his old office block – for the same salary.' He raised one eyebrow and then screwed his mouth into a bark of laughter. 'That's democracy, I tell him.'

Nikolai drove down side streets before joining the autoroute heading north. As the Zhiguli picked up speed, the car phone rang. Malenko clamped the handset to his ear, grunting several times before replacing the receiver. He scribbled on the pad, handed the paper to Nikolai and spoke over his shoulder. 'That was one of my investigators. The woman who drove Bodor from Zelenogorski to Vologda has been found.'

'That's a long drive,' Mischa murmured.

'A long drive,' repeated Malenko. 'Six hours in this, even if Nikolai puts his foot down.'

Anna waited a moment. 'Where is the woman now?'

Malenko was watching her in the mirror. 'In the woods beyond Zelenogorski.' He sighed. 'Unhappily, she won't be able to help us. My people are with the local State Prosecutor's people at the scene. She's been murdered.'

'Because of her involvement with Bodor?' asked Mischa.

Malenko shrugged, still watching Anna intently in the mirror, as if comparing what he'd learned to what he knew.

Patterson dunked his head in the bedroom's washbasin. Towelling off, he examined himself critically in the basin mirror. Helen had checked his blood pressure, peered into his eyes and ears with a scope and listened to his chest before pronouncing herself satisfied and leaving. Except for a hint of fatigue around his eyes, he looked in good physical shape. As he put on a clean shirt there was a knock at the door.

'Who is it?'

'I've brought you coffee.'

Morton stepped into the cabin, holding a cup. 'How do you feel?'

Patterson smiled ruefully. 'You'd think I'd had a heart attack, the way our doctor reacted.' He completed dressing, took the cup and drank a little, aware of Morton's eyes watching him.

'You ever done any mountain climbing?' Morton asked, as if the thought had only just occurred to him.

'What?' Patterson blinked, giving Morton a puzzled, contemplative look. 'No. My sport's strictly court stuff. Tennis, squash. Why do you ask?'

Morton leaned back against the door, folding his arms. What set him apart was his way of watching. 'The last time I saw someone with a tremble in his hand after a nose-bleed was a climber. Turned out he had porphyria.'

Morton let the silence hang a moment longer, seeing Patterson glance away, waiting until he looked back at him. It was a trick of his mind, Morton knew, but in that moment Patterson seemed to curl in a shell. Then he held himself straight, as though strengthened by some bitter memory.

'What's that?' Patterson asked.

'It's pretty rare. The medical wisdom is that it's congenital, carried down through the generations. Usually it's caused by physical stress combined with a change in oxygen pressure. Above certain heights you get pockets where that happens. It comes from ozone getting trapped.'

Patterson shrugged. 'Oh, sure. They told us something about various oxygen levels at pilot school. But nothing special.' He squinted at Morton. 'But then, you would know that, being a pilot yourself – and a pretty damned good one from what I heard happened over Costa Rica.'

Morton made a deprecatory little hand movement. 'Going back to porphyria, a lot of people come close to passing out during an attack.'

'Then that rules out pory . . . what did you call it, in my case.'

'Porphyria,' Morton said quietly.

'Right. Porphyria.' Patterson's mouth remained slightly open; it gave him the look of a runner, deep in the thoughts he ran with.

'Victims also get a sudden stabbing pain in the chest which is often followed by a hand tremor. I gather it mimics a heart attack,' Morton continued in the same even voice.

Composed again, Patterson shrugged. 'Then that definitely rules me out. The Surgeon-Commander checked my heart. She said it was as sound as a bell. And that tremble you saw was probably no more than an over-reaction to a somewhat embarrassing little incident. Sorry that my knee-jerk response has given you needless concern.'

Patterson glanced meaningfully towards the cabin door. 'I'd best not delay you. I gather you've been working that phone pretty hard.'

Morton seemed about to frame another question, then thought better of it. 'Glad you're feeling better.' He left the cabin.

Patterson sat on the edge of the bed, picked up the handset and dialled a White House direct line number. The crisp voice of Martha Wilson, the President's secretary, answered.

'Martha, this is Colonel Patterson in Air Force One,' he said formally.

'Don't tell me you're going to be late, Colonel,' she began. 'The President's on a tight schedule.'

'Don't worry. We're right on the button for touch-down,' Patterson replied.

'That's good news, Colonel. Things here are falling a little behind.'

He could sense she was about to hang up. 'Martha.'

'Yes, Colonel.'

'Why does the President want to see Morton?'

There was a moment's hesitation before she answered. 'He's going to be in charge of security on Air Force One for the President's trip. Now, if you'll excuse me, I've got to go . . .'

After she had hung up he drank some more coffee. He was over-reacting to what Morton had said. If there had been any trace of his porphyria, Helen would have spotted it. Bron's call was the cause of all that had happened. He should have spent a little more time on the phone, even told her he was going to find her a doctor. He felt a sudden pressure in his bladder. Dammit! Stress always made him have to go to the bathroom.

Patterson walked over to the commode. 'Oh, sweet Jesus,' he whispered aloud. 'Not *again*.'

There was blood in his urine.

*

Nikolai drove the Zhiguli along the forest track at high speed. From time to time Anna had glimpses of a vast expanse of water through the trees.

'The Gulf of Finland,' Mischa said. 'A long way from Vologda.'

Malenko half-turned in his seat. 'The question is: from Vologda, where did he go?'

Nikolai parked before a semicircle of other Zhigulis and a battered Mercedes. Malenko climbed out to open Mischa's door, then hurried round to do the same for Anna. Nikolai settled behind the wheel, whistling tonelessly between his teeth.

Two men detached themselves from the group around the Mercedes and walked over. Malenko introduced Vitali and Eugene, his assistants. Both detectives were young and thick-set, dressed in sweat-shirts and jeans and trainers. They were as respectful of Malenko as if he was their father.

Malenko nodded towards the Mercedes. 'Who's in charge?'

'Stalin,' Vitali murmured.

Malenko turned to Mischa and Anna. 'Stalin, what we call the local prosecutor, is Colonel Joseph Ivanovich Gori.'

Mischa offered Anna a further explanation. 'Gori is where the real Stalin's family came from. Ivanovich means son of Ivan.'

'Our Stalin's a son of a bitch,' Malenko growled. 'But I'm not in the mood for him today.'

Anna could see on the far side of the Mercedes a short, fat figure in a military uniform with red tabs on the jacket lapels. He looked to be in his late fifties, with a face as lumpy as rice pudding.

'So tell me why you think the woman drove Bodor to

Vologda,' Malenko asked Vitali.

Vitali lit a cigarette before replying. 'Stalin's people found a stub of a Vologda airport restaurant ticket in the dash compartment. It was dated the same day as the taxi-driver drove Bodor out to Zelenogorski. I called the airport. They remembered her because she paid for the meal in hard currency. They have a record.'

Malenko nodded, following the logic. He turned to Anna. 'Another aspect of our democracy is better book-keeping. Any restaurant or hotel which takes hard currency must enter it in a book. Most don't. But clearly the airport restaurant still runs by the rules.'

'Just like the old days,' murmured Eugene.

Malenko glanced sharply at him. 'Sometimes I have a feeling you miss them, Eugene.'

'Only the days off, Sergei Andreya,' Eugene replied, unabashed.

Anna turned to Vitali. 'That ticket still doesn't really prove she drove Bodor there.'

'There is more,' Vitali said in a wounded tone.

'I thought so,' sighed Malenko. He glanced towards the Mercedes. 'Well, be quick. Stalin's probably wondering if we're plotting here to take this case from him.'

'I wouldn't recommend that, Sergei Andreya,' Eugene said, puffing a cigarette.

'Why?' Mischa asked.

Eugene coughed smoke. 'Twenty-four hours after a murder most of the worthwhile clues have gone – which means it's harder to find out what happened in the twenty-four hours before she died. The time either side of death is vital . . .'

'Thank you, Eugene,' interrupted Malenko. 'I'm sure the same rule applies in Moscow or anywhere.' He turned to Vitali. 'What else do you have?'

Screwing up his eyes as if the sunlight hurt them, Vitali spoke. 'After the woman paid for dinner, one of the waiters followed her. Claims he was curious about where else she would spend her hard money. He sounds a real little spy. Most airports have them.'

'Get on with it,' Malenko said heavily.

'At once, Sergei Andreya.' Vitali turned to Anna. 'The waiter followed her to the airport departure lounge. All catering staff have permission to go there to sell sandwiches and drinks . . .'

'Vitali!' growled Malenko.

The detective spoke more hurriedly. 'The waiter said she was obviously keeping watch on a man who fits Bodor's description. No doubt on that. I checked our records.'

'Good. So it was Bodor,' interjected Malenko.

'Did the waiter say which flight Bodor boarded?' Mischa asked.

Vitali opened his eyes. 'There were two. One to Kuybyshev. That's in the Volga region. The other went to Baku.'

'Did you check the passenger lists?' asked Anna.

Malenko smiled faintly. 'There are no such things here. People just get on and fly. Some don't even have tickets. They just pay the pilot in cash.'

He led them over to the group around the Mercedes. Anna counted a dozen men, several in militia uniforms. Stalin came from the far side of the car and greeted Malenko coolly.

'Who are these?' he asked in Russian, glancing at Anna and Mischa.

'Official visitors. One from Moscow, the other foreign,' Malenko's tone grew flatter, quieter.

Stalin grunted and paid no further attention to Mischa or Anna.

Malenko peered pointedly into the car. 'Where is the body?'

Stalin's eyes were lifeless as nailheads. 'I've left her where she was found until you came.'

Stalin led the way to the back of the car. He flicked a finger and a militiaman lifted the lid of the boot. Inside was the body of a woman. Over her woollen shirt she wore dungarees tucked into calf-length hide boots. Her hands were tied with wire behind her back and she had been shot through a cloth covering her mouth. In life she would have been no more than forty, but the pale waxy skin added another ten years to her age. There was a smell of petrol. Malenko stepped back.

'What happened – somebody disturb them before they could burn her?' he asked.

Stalin was silent. 'The exit wounds went through the petrol tank. There was only a drop in it,' he finally said. 'Her killers probably siphoned off the rest. Very common in these parts.'

'She known?' Malenko asked, still watching Stalin.

Stalin gave a sour smile. 'A *mafiya* courier. Mostly drugs. She probably got greedy. We've had two like it this year already.'

Vitali lit a fresh cigarette.

'How long has she been here?' Mischa asked politely.

Stalin gave her a hard look, as if he was about to be challenged. 'The pathologist says four, five days. He can't be certain – any more than your people would be in Moscow. She could have been here for weeks, except a hunter chanced to come by.'

Malenko looked speculatively about him, as if searching for the route that had brought the hunter here. 'He touch anything?'

Stalin turned his mouth into a tight, thin slit of

triumph. 'Fingerprints says he rummaged around inside the car, then opened the boot. Looking for something to steal, no doubt. Luckily he had the sense to call us when he found her. We're holding him as a material witness. You want to talk to him?'

Malenko looked past Stalin. 'No point. It's your case.'

Waiting until they reached his car, he turned to Mischa and Anna. 'Would you like me to drive you to Vologda?'

'That would be nice, Sergei Andreya,' Mischa said. She turned to Anna. 'And afterwards, where do you plan to go?'

'Baku,' Anna said decisively.

TWENTY-TWO

In the Step, Morton heard Patterson announce over the paging system that Air Force One had begun its descent into the Washington area. Morton was reassured to hear the pilot sounding his usual confident self. Thinking about it, he realised he could be wrong about the cause of Patterson's nose-bleed. While a concentration of ozone affected everyone differently – even the permitted level of 0.1 part per million would be a problem for some people – probably the nose-bleed had a simpler explanation, which would also account for the pilot's embarrassment over his momentary hand tremble.

Morton was about to return to the flight deck when the Step's phone rang. Danny was calling from central police headquarters in Amsterdam. 'We could have something, thanks to Piet and his boys,' he said, through the slight warbling of the microwave link regularly changing frequencies to avoid being intercepted.

'What's Piet got?' Morton asked, settling back in his chair.

Piet van Nuys was Amsterdam's police commissioner.

'He sent his best ID sketcher over to the police at Alkmann. He came back with likenesses of those balloonists that brought an immediate response from Piet's new Cray mainframe. All three have form. The oldest, Markus van Kloep, did a year for attacking a prostitute. The others, Pieter Noorde and Tomas Vandel, served the same for drug-trafficking.'

Morton made a note as Danny continued.

'Once the computer produced their court convictions, we were up and running. Their military records showed they'd all been in the Dutch Special Services. As well as the usual stuff, they'd been trained to deal with terrorists who take over a high-security facility. Looks like the old story of gamekeepers turned poachers.' There was feeling in his words, something deeper than anger.

'What happened when they came out of prison?' asked Morton.

'They drifted around Amsterdam for a while, then suddenly they were gone. It turns out to Spain. I called Interpol. Lutyens was on the desk. He must really have burned up the wire to Madrid because in no time the Spanish were back with the news that our three had flown into Bilbao. ETA country.'

Morton knew there were still training camps operated by the Basque terrorist independence movement in the Bilbao area.

'Our three spent a month in Spain, then flew to Tehran. Piet's mainframe supremo called Lester Finel. They got on like a couple who'd found true love. In no time they'd linked up their Crays and burrowed into the Iran Air system. And there were our three. They'd been booked on separate flights to London, arriving the day before the balloon race. Manders is trying to find out where they stayed, but I wouldn't hold my breath. He says most of the balloonists camped out on the launch site.'

'What about Meridian?' Morton asked. 'Any links there?'

'They have four subsidiaries in Holland. One's a chain of hotels. They never stayed or worked in any of them. The other two outfits are suppliers to the tourist industry. Knick-knacks, novelties, junk foods. Their employee records also don't list them. The fourth outfit's called Near Orient Care, and supplies state-of-the-art surgical equipment for a dozen countries between Egypt and Pakistan. Nothing in their employment records, and when we accessed their shipment manifests we got long lists of what you'd expect. I asked Piet's people to check the airline shipping manifests. Everything matched, except one. The morning after our three went to Sardinia, a KLM freighter flew to Tehran. On board, according to the manifest, were six isotopes listed for use in the Ayatollah Khomenei Hospital in Tehran. But the corresponding Near Orient manifest didn't list them. Those isotopes could be the missing triggers.'

Morton sat for a long moment, his head angled slightly, feeling an old tug in his gut. Euro-Balloon had suggested that Zita Marcello could be in Afghanistan. Free Flight was in the business of manufacturing high-altitude balloons. Bodor's weapon was somehow connected to the stratosphere. Bodor could provide the mullahs with the means of a pre-emptive attack against Baghdad. But he would need a platform for his weapon, and somebody capable of piloting it into position. Zita Marcello could be in Iran instead of Afghanistan. And Meridian? No matter which way he cut the pack in his mind, their card never came face up.

'Danny,' Morton said at last, 'This is what I want you to do.' He then spoke for a further fifteen minutes without interruption.

In the Oval Office the President of the United States was speaking intently on the phone to the chief of Meridian.

'Mr Bailey, I happen to think it would benefit us both if you would come on this trip,' he said, completing a detailed briefing on Operation Earth Saver. He had deliberately avoided mention of Meridian's continuing and ever more virulent media campaign.

He spun his chair and gazed out of the windows. For days Washington had been without a breeze, leaving the atmosphere hazy with industrial pollution. To that, he sensed, could now be added wasted breath and oxidised hopes after talking to Bailey. Not that Bailey had spoken a word of disagreement or argument. Only this dead silence.

Thacker Stimpson mouthed: 'Keep cool. You're the Man.' The Chief of Staff was listening on an extension on the opposite side of the desk.

The President nodded and forced his voice to remain light. 'Several of your companies played their part in outfitting Air Force One. It would be a pleasure to show you how everything came together.'

Stimpson grimaced. *Wrong tack.*

'That's very kind of you, Mr President' Bailey said flatly, 'and I surely appreciate your taking the time to make this call and to share with me your, your ...' he deliberately paused as if finding it hard to choose the right word, 'your vision, yes, that's the only word for it – a vision – which you and your fellow leaders are embarking upon. Operation Earth Saver, Mr President, I must admit, does have a certain ring to it.' This time the pause was accompanied by a soft, mirthless chuckle. 'And, of course, also the debatable assumption that our planet is indeed in need of saving.'

'It is. And Earth Saver is the first step, Mr Bailey. Everything else will flow from it,' the President said steadily. Out on the lawn a Secret Service agent strolled past, waving to somebody out of view.

'That, of course, remains to be seen, Mr President.'

Once more came the soulless chuckle Bailey knew

people found so unnerving; it went with his silences, designed to allow someone to reflect upon the futility of their actions.

'It will require determination to change things. That's why I called you, Mr Bailey.'

'I appreciate the compliment, Mr President, I surely do. But as I recall, you are not lacking in determination yourself. I still remember the way you gave teeth to the Economic Crimes Commission. A lot of people felt your heat.'

'That was a long time ago, Mr Bailey.' His role as legal counsel to the Commission had given him a rare opportunity to probe deeply into the darker corners of financial corruption. But none of Meridian's companies had been involved.

'I wasn't against what you did at the ECC, Mr President, quite the opposite. The tree needed shaking. That was good for business. Good for Meridian too, because we picked up a number of those companies whose managements you worked over. We turned them into what they now are, well run, profit-making divisions. But the ECC was good for you as well. As I recall, it was your stepping stone into politics.' Another soft chuckle. 'I guess grilling all those crooked business folk must have taught you a lot about how to handle folk up on the Hill. I take it that the right folk in Congress know about this ... Operation Earth Saver?'

'Not yet,' said the President, his words measured and toneless. 'You're among the first to know, Mr Bailey, because I want to give you time to think how you could help.'

'That's very flattering, Mr President.' Bailey's tone was dismissive.

In the new silence, Thack shifted in his chair, shaking

his head. He'd said Bailey could be like a rogue elephant, suddenly trampling everywhere: that having him on board Air Force One would mean having to be head keeper and ringmaster, and collector of any shit Bailey felt like dropping. But the risk was worth it. Winning over Bailey was as important as persuading a Third World country to mend its ecological ways, or convincing an industrial nation to change its environmental policies. Despite its current editorial diatribes, Bailey could still use Meridian as a mighty driving force to propel Earth Saver.

'Mr President, let me be frank with you. My colleagues and I have closely followed your policies since coming into office. We had hoped that, with your background, and your understanding of the business community, you would be the President we had long waited for. Not another Clinton, but somebody who would understand the realities of our world. Sadly, Mr President, this has not turned out to be the case.'

The President's voice was tight. 'Mr Bailey, if you are referring to the moves I had to make over reckless anti-pollution . . .'

'Mr President, I am not specifically thinking of that, though what you did hurt Meridian badly. I'm talking about the overview. *Your* view of the world as seen from Washington. You've now given that view a name. This Operation Earth Saver. Again, let me be frank with you. A lot of people, myself included, will not be easily convinced what you propose is not only workable, but the best way to resolve matters. I'm not denying there aren't problems. There are. But to think they can be solved by changing the environment is, if I may say so, wishful thinking. People are people. If you look back through history, pollution has always been there. The Egyptians had it. So did the Romans. The Middle Ages in Europe were some of the most polluted in history. So was the Industrial Revolution. But everyone knew and accepted that there had to be a price to pay for new-found prosperity.'

Bailey paused to emphasise his following words. 'Mr President, you start telling folk' – Bailey spoke the word as if describing a separate species – 'they can't make a living because it's messing up somebody else's environment and you'll have a revolution on your hands. Folk just won't stand for it.'

'If it's sold to them properly, they will,' the President cut in sharply. 'You're in the selling business just as much as I am. Between us we can change opinion.'

'Mr President, this is *your* hunt. But some jungles are really dangerous and some animals don't die easily.'

The President gave a short laugh. 'You have a way of making a point that can sound like a threat.'

'Only stating a fact, Mr President.'

'Where I sit, Mr Bailey, a fact is usually someone's interpretation of someone else's observation,' said the President.

Thack made a swift cutting motion with a finger across his throat. The President shook his head. He wasn't going to give up trying to make this arrogant son of a bitch at least understand.

'Mr Bailey, every day close to the equivalent of the population of a town like your own dies as the result of one ecological disaster or another. *Every day*, Mr Bailey. *Every day* of *every* week in *every* month. And the only certainty is that this will continue. We owe it to the dying, and all those who will follow, to stop that. And to begin to stop it *now*.'

'Mr President, that's a noble thought. But I'm old-fashioned enough to believe that your Operation Earth Saver will simply open the way for the mob to go on the rampage and grab what they can. You give them free medication and, when they get better, they steal the drug cupboard. That's human nature. You try and tell them to stop smoking, eat healthier, cut down their drinking, and they'll use that as an excuse to try and drive you out of business. They'll see it as some sort of new and dangerous political creed. Consumer communism if you like. That's the way folk will see it. And nothing's going to change them.'

In the renewed silence, the President glanced at the small framed plaque on the desk top. Grace had given it to him when he'd entered public life, the day after their tenth wedding anniversary. The plaque read: *Oh God, Thy sea is so great and my boat is so small*. No one, not even Bailey, was going to capsize it.

'There are no political boundaries to the problems of pollution, Mr Bailey. The Russians are as keen to solve it as we are. And the same goes for the Chinese and everybody else.' The President paused as if gathering strength, then the quiet words continued. 'Just take one example. For two million years the peoples who live by the oceans have been sustained by its bounty. In the past hundred years this harmony has been broken by the actions of others very distant from their shores. There are, of course, some governments who still say we need more scientific proof. To them, to you, to everyone, I say the proof is here outside my window. Even on a good day the pollution is often intolerable. As it is outside the windows of untold millions. Individually, they have little or no voice. But collectively they are crying out for a just and equitable economic order built upon a new global environmental policy. If we don't listen to their cry, then there will indeed be a revolution – not because of change, but because there has been no change.'

Across the desk Thack was nodding vigorously. The President looked past him out of the window. Think about each detail, he told himself, one sentence at a time.

'We – government, the business community, everybody – can begin by drawing up a new balance sheet. Just as some companies now have separate watch committees for social policy and ethics and publish their reports, so it must become commonplace for every company to publish a separate environmental account with its annual financial report. ICI in Britain already does it. It explains exactly what it has done to safeguard the environment from which it takes its benefits. ICI sees it as good business. And I bet it impresses their stockholders no end.'

'Mr President, the one thing I've learned in business is that just about the only thing which impresses shareholders is profit. You can give them all the reports you like and if the bottom line's in the red, they'll have you out before you can ask for a show of hands. That's the reality of my world, Mr President.'

'Mr Bailey, I'm not suggesting a dip in your profits, or anyone else's. A healthy economy is a prerequisite for ecological responsibility. You've only got to look at Russia to see that. If it cleaned up its pollution, the country would be in far better financial shape. And there are new profits to be made in helping them do so, in helping everyone do so. Let me give you one example. The environmental cleaning business in this country alone is currently worth annually around $80 billion. Worldwide it tops the $300 billion mark. They're not my figures, but the World Bank's. Whichever way you cut them, there has to be a lot of profit there. And all from improving environmental standards and creating a full energy-accounting system. It's always been part of the American reality to make money where others fear to tread. I'd be the first to cheer if Meridian led the way in a global clean-up!'

Bailey was silent for a moment, the silence like an intake of breath. When he spoke his voice was cold and remote. 'Let me offer you some rebuttal evidence. The other day I called in one of the managers of a plant we've bought in the old East Germany. I was curious to know how come his men were achieving better productivity than their colleagues were in West Germany. You know what he said? "Work used to be a place where you went, and something you did. The pollution was awful, but we got paid the same whether we did anything about it or not." And now? I asked him. "Now," he said, "it's all about performance. You perform better, your pay is bigger. And the pollution's got no worse. No better, but no worse. We can live with that." And he's right, Mr President. For him, for everyone in the Meridian family, the bottom line is that people are used to living with what they're used to, and living happily as long as their pay-packets are full.'

The President adjusted his spectacles; during the past year his long-sightedness had become markedly more noticeable. Luther, as usual, had been reassuring. It was no more, the White House doctor said, than the inevitable sign of approaching old age.

'You're a dinosaur, Mr Bailey. You really are.'

'I'll take that as a compliment, Mr President.' Another mirthless chuckle. 'Here, in the competitive world, we are governed by certain realities, the most important is making sure you survive. If this Operation Earth Saver ever became a reality, it would mean higher prices for our customers. They're the ones who ultimately would have to pay for your global spring cleaning. And it wouldn't even be a one-off spring clean. From what you have said, it would have to be an ongoing process. Day in, day out, with no time limit. And while we would be trying to do what you want, everyone else would be stabbing us in the back. The bottom line for us, if I were to follow your argument to its logical conclusion, would be eventually to place Meridian in bankruptcy!'

When he now spoke, the President's voice had the edge of suppressed emotion. 'Thank you, Mr Bailey. You have made your position perfectly clear. Under the circumstances I think you are wise to decline my invitation. There really would be no space on Air Force One for somebody with such a blinkered outlook. Good-bye, Mr Bailey.'

The President hung up. He looked at Stimpson.

'You need a drink,' said the Chief of Staff, rising from his chair.

'Make it a large one, Thack, I need something to wash the taste out of my mouth.'

He accepted the whiskey tumbler Stimpson brought and sipped, allowing the alcohol to soothe his anger. When he spoke there was only resignation in his voice.

'It always was going to be a long shot, Thack, but the only question is: what will Bailey do now?'

In the sterile comfort of his office, Ignatius Bailey had swiftly turned his attention to another call. Japan's new government couldn't resist what he'd offered. Five nuclear power stations on a ten-year deferred loan.

On the flight deck, Patterson glanced over the instrument panel as Air Force One continued its steady descent into the restricted airspace around Andrews Air Force base.

'Morton still on the phone?' Patterson asked over his shoulder.

'Yeah,' acknowledged Turner.

Patterson grunted.

'Gear down,' Locke reported. A moment later, 'and locked.'

The plane rocked slightly under the impact of thermal activity, great bubbles of air rising swiftly from the ground.

'Switching to ILS,' Locke announced.

An Instrument Landing System approach was not necessary given the excellent visibility, but on Air Force One it was a standard procedure. The pilots would monitor the landing visually, allowing the instruments to do the work, right up to touch-down.

'I have the runway in sight,' reported Patterson.

A moment later Locke announced, 'One thousand feet. Crossing outer marker.'

Away to his left, Patterson could see the first familiar clump of buildings inside the Andrews Air Force base perimeter.

'Forty degrees flap,' intoned Locke.

Air Force One continued to sink towards the ground.

'Flaring out.'

The plane levelled off, twenty feet above the runway stretching ahead for over two miles. The wheels touched and there was a screech of scorching tread before they found a grip.

Both pilots were now at the controls.

'Reverse thrust,' ordered Patterson.

Locke threw the thrust lever forward and raised the wings' spoilers to kill any lift the plane might still have remaining in its forward motion.

'Brakes,' Patterson ordered.

Tyres squealed as Air Force One thundered down the runway, steadily losing speed. By the time it reached the primary turn-off, the plane was moving slowly enough for Locke to guide the nose-wheel along a white marker line.

'Home sweet home,' Locke said.

If only, thought Patterson. His mind once more began

to think about the phone calls he must make to find Bron a doctor.

In the Step, Morton thought about what Gates had told him on the phone as Air Force One came in to land. Adams was dead, his body dumped outside the Swiss embassy in Tehran.

TWENTY-THREE

Halfway across the bridge over the wide Potomac Valley, a sign announced that this was now Washington, District of Columbia, and beware of the radar.

'Last year the city collected a couple of million bucks in fines,' Gates growled. They were the first words he'd spoken since briefing Morton about Adams as they drove out of Andrews.

Morton had listened without interrupting. Now he looked one more time at the copy of the fax the Swiss embassy had sent from Tehran. It contained a detailed medical report on Adam's injuries, together with a list of items found on his body. His injuries included a gunshot wound to the chest and others consistent with someone who had fallen from a considerable height. An ID card was in the name of Michael B. Latway, managing director of Croxis Importers and Exporters of Solinake Street, Athens. Bill had explained that Croxis was an Agency front. A billfold, each dollar meticulously listed, and an airline ticket in the name of the same Michael B. Latway, completed what Morton would have expected to find on an agent in the field.

It was the piece of paper found in Adams' trouser pocket which was surprising. It seemed to have been torn from a lined exercise book and appeared to be a map reference, with a crude drawing of a hot air balloon. Underneath was something which had been obliterated by a felt pen.

Gates slowed to take a long deceptive curve before he

spoke. 'The Swiss were able to read through the scratch-out mark enough to make out the word "Bodor". The word's block-lettered, something Adams had a habit of using, and they've compared it to a note of his we faxed over to them, and it seems pretty close.'

Morton glanced one more time at the paper. 'Adams have a habit of making notes like this, Bill?'

Gates grunted. 'He was an old-timer. He came from a school where tradecraft still included a course in opening mail. He'd never used a computer in his life, so, yes, it would be par for him.'

'He have a contact in Baku?'

Gates smiled thinly. 'Our embassy security people in Istanbul went through his office and turned up the name of some woman – a Madame Lutke. According to our computers, there's a Helena Lutke who ran a KGB whorehouse in the Old City. She's gone freelance now and caters for anybody with hard currency.'

With a trace of weariness, as if his worst expectations had been confirmed, Morton nodded. They drove a little while in silence before he spoke again, his voice once more deliberate, uninflected. 'There isn't a building high enough in Tehran for Adams to fall from to get those injuries, Bill. My bet is he was tossed from a chopper. The mullahs' secret service used to do that to spies in the Iraqi War. Old habits are hard to change.'

'I called the Swiss embassy security chief. He says Adams' clothes had traces of sand.'

'Which means he was dropped someplace out in the desert, and his body brought into the city. But that doesn't explain why they left his ID and that piece of paper.' Morton carefully folded the fax and put it in his pocket.

'Adams could have jumped them. He was as strong as a bull. Once he'd got going, he could have created havoc in a chopper. Someone could have panicked, shot him and dumped him as quickly as possible.'

They drove some more in silence. Morton looked out of the windows. The Potomac was slate beneath grey skies; there were a few sailboats and a steamer filled with tourists. He thought he preferred Lake Geneva. 'Anything on the paper?' he asked, turning back to Gates.

Gates' lips formed something halfway between a smile and a grimace. 'Nothing. Our cartographers say the problem is that as a reference it doesn't make any real sense. Of course it could be in a shorthand that only Adams understood.'

'The balloon shape's clear enough,' Morton said.

The strange semi-smile remained on Gates' lips. 'But what's it mean, David?'

Morton told him. By the time he had finished they were turning on to Pennsylvania Avenue and heading towards the White House.

Gates groaned. 'We'd need a small army to find Bodor and this Marcello woman in those mountains in Iran, David.'

Zita stood beside Bodor on a steel walkway overlooking an area the size of a tennis court which appeared to be an amalgam of workshop and laboratory. White-coated technicians moved among bench workers. The air was filled with the arc of welders' torches and the high-speed whine of machinery. An area at the far end was isolated behind a canvas screen.

She watched a technician put on a breathing head-set and go behind the screen. Its presence reinforced a feeling that once more she was not privy to what was going on. This only increased the unease she felt, but some distant part of her brain warned she must not show it to Bodor.

Instead, she focused on a monitor suspended from the roof; the screen was linked to one of the surveillance cameras positioned among the sand dunes.

Against the setting sun the birds were wheeling before swooping to land among the dogs. The carrion birds began to pick at bones, and the animals, normally so savage, ignored them, as if there existed a relationship she would never understand. The thought further increased the tug in her gut.

The feeling had been there since Bodor had collected her from her quarters, something he had never done before. Standing in the door he had studied her, and she felt naked under his searching gaze that became a stare. It was a moment before she'd realised her fists were clenched, another before she opened them. She had stood stiffly, unsure when his examination was over, anxiety catching hold like a bush fire inside her and rushing to her cheeks. Had Bodor found out about Kunsk? How he had continued to open the door and lead her up the staircase? Had someone reported missing a mouldy mattress on which they'd lain, not bothering to undress fully?

If Bodor suspected any of that, he'd given no sign. They had walked in silence through the maze of corridors, passing through several steel doors, each of which Bodor opened with a key, before finally climbing a steel staircase to reach this walkway.

On the monitor the birds were fighting among themselves for the last of the spoils. Soon they would be gone, as if it was imperative they reached their roosts before the deep black of the desert night. A moment earlier she had sensed Bodor looking at her and forced herself not to return his gaze. What was he thinking? Still wondering about her and Kunsk? What it would be like with him and her? Was there somewhere deep inside Bodor a need to possess her?

He would not be the first man to think like that. One had even proposed marriage in the hope of doing so. But the thought of a relationship terrified her: it would be like being chained to her father for life. Her instinct told her that Bodor wouldn't want a relationship. He'd just want her. Maybe if she let him, this fear would go. Once more she breathed in deeply. She felt calmer, stronger, listening to him, his back half to her, issuing orders in Russian into a palm-sized telephone.

He pocketed the phone and turned to her. 'Watch.' He pointed down across the floor.

The screen was rising slowly, like a stage curtain. Behind was a huge glass dome. Inside lay a naked man, face up and strapped to a surgical trolley. For the moment his face was obscured by what looked like the camera of an x-ray machine moving slowly above him. The technician who had gone behind the screen stood before a console, monitoring what was happening.

'What is this?' she asked, turning to him, her voice almost a whisper.

He deliberately ignored her, keeping his eyes trained on the dome, feeling her sudden tangible fear as if it was something he could reach out and touch, like the sexuality she normally exuded. He'd known what she was the moment he'd set eyes on her: a bitch on permanent heat. She'd come to him last night while he'd slept, hovering at his bedside, naked, displaying and flaunting herself, using a hand to part her lips, the other reaching under the sheet for him. He'd still been groaning when he awoke, soaked in sweat, reaching out for her. But the bitch had gone. To Kunsk, no doubt.

But, in her eagerness to satisfy herself, she had forgotten that every part of the complex was under surveillance. A camera concealed in an air-duct had secretly filmed them.

Continuing to ignore Zita, Bodor watched the climometer continuing its slow traverse. Until now he'd used it only on the Kurds from the holding pen. But the Kurds were undernourished and often suffered from severe chest ailments. They had all died before they received anywhere near the maximum exposure to ozone. In their last telephone conversation, he'd told the Arranger he needed healthier subjects. The Arranger suggested he select some of his own men.

'Bodor,' Zita said softly, 'What is that machine doing?'

The climometer's movement was beginning to expose the man's face.

'It replicates the elements in the upper atmosphere,' Bodor said.

Zita's words escaped in twos and threes. 'But isn't that . . . dangerous? I mean, shouldn't that man be . . . wearing some kind of protective mask, like the technician?'

'That is not the purpose of the test,' Bodor said, his tone unnaturally calm.

'Then what is the purpose?'

Something in Bodor's face made her turn back to look at the dome. The man's face was almost fully exposed.

'You recognize him?' Bodor asked.

She nodded, feeling a new tug of fear. 'It's my escort.'

'Kunsk.' Bodor smiled – a smile as bleak as an Arctic wind. 'Your escort, Kunsk.'

'Why is he here? What is happening to him?' she asked, looking away from the dome.

'Are you concerned for him?' His voice was low, but harsh enough to hurt her ears.

She managed a shrug. 'I hardly know him.'

'Then you need not be concerned with what's going to happen to him.'

'What does that mean?'

'Wait. Be patient. I think you will find it instructive,' he said softly.

'Unless this has any bearing on my own work . . .'

'Just watch!' He had wielded his voice like a lash.

Zita turned and gripped the safety rail, watching the climometer creeping back down over Kunsk's body. He still showed no reaction. Beside her Bodor was sounding as if this was a lecture he'd given many times.

'Kunsk has been given a sedative. Not that he is presently feeling any pain. The climometer releases a controlled amount of hydrocarbons equal to those found in ozone levels at between eighty and one hundred thousand feet above ground level in this region, at this time of year, given a number of other atmospheric conditions which the climometer replicates.'

'The exposure will kill him,' Zita said in a strangled voice. Out of the corner of her eye, she saw Bodor glance at her once more. 'But why, why . . .?' she asked helplessly.

He gripped her elbow hard with one hand, using the other to point to another part of the work area. 'Look there! By the electron furnace!'

A coveralled man removed a casing no bigger than an artillery shell from inside the furnace, and carried it over to a row of pressure chambers. He inserted the casing in a chamber, spun the door-valve shut and reset the dials.

'What's happening?' Zita asked, in spite of Bodor's grip, glancing towards the dome. The technician was adjusting a control on the console. Kunsk lay as inert as before.

Bodor ignored her, intent on the man who was once more opening the chamber. Using a pair of tongs he removed the casing. Bodor grunted and reached for his phone.

The casing was crushed almost beyond recognition.

Beside him Zita suddenly screamed. Blood was running from Kunsk's ears and nose. As she watched, it began to dribble from a corner of his mouth.

Zita screamed again as Kunsk's face imploded.

Bodor began to speak into the phone, ignoring Zita.

Late in the evening, the Prime Minister sat in his study at the rear of No. 10, trying to immerse himself in the official red boxes, which were an integral part of his working life. Each box contained the minutiae of that day's Whitehall output requiring his ultimate approval.

Reading the boxes at the end of his own long day was a time-consuming business, the more so as he had no natural aptitude for paperwork. The public crescendos of life were more to his liking; he well understood that exposure, especially on television, was a powerful source of political strength. You had to be seen, and speak to the masses in a language they understood, not depend on the dry words of the civil servant who had drafted in his minister's name the paper he had just reached for.

The Prime Minister wrinkled his nose, a sign of his irritation. The document was a summary of the arguments for a new motorway which would bisect another swath of southern England. He skim-read, frowning increasingly. Michael Belton, the Transport Minister, had paid no attention to the unholy row the proposed motorway route had already generated. The entire environmental spectrum of protest was threatening to lie down before the bull-dozers. Reaching for a pen, the Prime Minister wrote in the space left blank for his comments that he wanted the route referred back to the planners.

The Prime Minister knew his irritation was furthered by the vote in the House the government had almost lost that afternoon because of a couple of inept speeches from the

Front Bench. Poor performances by Matthew Spooner at Heritage, and Judy Dawson, the Health Minister, reinforced his feeling that the time was coming for a reshuffle. He'd start mapping out the changes after he'd finished the boxes. But he'd hold off making an announcement until he returned from the forthcoming trip with the President.

On top of the box from Mark Duggan, who soldiered on manfully as Foreign Secretary despite his heart condition, was a note that Sandy Richardson, the American ambassador, had telephoned to say the President had watched the CNN broadcast with great interest. Bostock smiled thinly. Washington was trying to regain the high ground.

He turned from the boxes and looked out of the window. Despite his distaste at having to spend a week mostly in the confines of a plane, a form of travel he disliked, the undoubted political gain would be considerable. It would place him centre stage with the electorate, win him the approval of the environmentalists, yet at the same time, with a bit of luck, he would keep the business community on side. And not just his, but those of Germany and France. He'd promised Sturmer and Marceau that he'd tackle the President head-on over Iraq. He'd cajole, reason, argue – do all the things he knew best.

There was a knock on the door. He frowned. The standing instruction was never to disturb him when doing the boxes unless there was a matter of the utmost importance.

'Enter!' he snapped.

The Director of MI5 stood in the doorway; behind her hovered a flustered Downing Street secretary.

'Nancy?' The Prime Minister half rose in his seat.

The Director glanced at the boxes while she spoke. 'I'm sorry to butt in, Prime Minister, but this couldn't wait.'

Bostock nodded and settled back in his chair, still

frowning, but suddenly pleased that her intervention would take him away from the tedious work of reading and initialling. He motioned her to an armchair, dismissed the secretary with a nod, waited until the door was closed, then turned expectantly to the Director.

'Well, what do you have? Another scandal brewing? Hopefully not,' he murmured, coming from behind the desk to sit in an armchair opposite the Blessed Nancy.

'The Japanese government's about to fall, Prime Minister,' she said crisply.

'I won't shed any tears over that.' His frown deepened. 'But there's nothing in from GCHQ or Six. And certainly nothing about a crisis in Tokyo came up at this morning's JIC.'

'The information has just come to hand,' she replied cautiously.

'May I ask the source?'

She gazed at him with veiled eyes. He had never been able to reach her fully. She had a stillness he still found unsettling.

'A telephone intercept,' she finally said. 'The Japanese ambassador received a call from the Foreign Ministry in Tokyo with the news. You remember, you personally authorised the tap after that business at the last World Climate Conference.'

The Prime Minister nodded, the lines on his forehead small furrows. At the conference in London the ambassador, clearly acting on instructions, had briefed selected journalists that the British government had commissioned, and suppressed, a report that large areas of the United Kingdom coastline would have to be abandoned by the middle of the next century if the present rise in sea-levels continued.

The purpose of the briefing quickly became cynically

plain: the Japanese wanted an excuse to transfer a sub-stantial portion of their investment in Britain to con-tinental Europe. Bostock remembered how he had been forced to admit to the House that a plan did indeed exist for what his spin doctors suggested he call 'a managed retreat' from parts of the coastline; rather than squander billions on sea defences, he had added, the land would not simply be abandoned but would become marine theme parks. Despite an excellently crafted script, it had not been his finest hour at the Dispatch Box.

Bostock snapped out of his reverie. 'So why is Nagoda's government going? Someone at last find out he's on the take?'

The Blessed Nancy picked at a fold of her dress, like a smoker without a cigarette. 'That too, Prime Minister. He was about to do a deal for a new range of nuclear reactors to power, among other cities, Hiroshima and Nagasaki.'

Slowly, the Prime Minister shook his head.

'Nagoda's cut was going to be even larger than the Saudis give on a deal. Somewhere between ten and twelve million dollars,' the Director added.

'Who was going to offer that kind of kickback, Nancy?'

'Meridian International. Their CEO, Bailey, conducted all the negotiations personally.'

Bostock looked up sharply. 'He's a reputation for keeping everything close to his chest. But from what I've read, twelve million would be small change for Bailey. He'd also make very sure any kickback, if it did surface, would look legitimate. There'd be the usual raft of surrogate shelf companies and letterhead-only directors for the money to rub against on the way to Nagoda. So how come it was traced to him?'

The Blessed Nancy did not seem to like the question. 'Nagoda was working through his daughter.'

Bostock frowned. 'So? I assume she'd have known how to keep things under wraps. What's her part in all this?'

'She runs a consultancy specialising in the energy area. One of her clients, incidentally, happens to be Nuclear Components . . .'

'The outfit that made those damned nuclear triggers?' The frown became a scowl. 'This gets more incestuous all the time. Now don't tell me that . . .'

'There's no connection between the thefts and Nagoda going, Prime Minister,' the Blessed Nancy said quickly.

'So tell me why he's going.'

She waited, silent, for a moment. 'His daughter was all set to stash the first tranche of Meridian commission into a Swiss bank account when her husband, of all people, blew the whistle.'

'Good God! Why? I thought the Japanese were big on family loyalties.'

'No one seems to have had even an inkling that Nagoda's son-in-law was a dyed-in-the-wool environmentalist. Anyway, when he got wind of what Bailey and Nagoda were cooking up, he went to the Opposition with chapter and verse. He only had one condition. There was to be no public scandal. He wasn't interested in having Nagoda disembowel himself, or see the country's honour further damaged.'

'How very Japanese, Nancy.'

'Very. When the Opposition party leader put the evidence to Nagoda, it was agreed he would resign on ill health. The spin doctors recommended an unsuspected cancer. Curable, as long as Nagoda didn't have to continue facing the stress of office.'

'Even more Japanese.'

The Blessed Nancy smiled.

'Who's going to take Nagoda's place.'

'The bet money's on Japan's man in London.'

'Holy Christ!'

'It could be an advantage, Prime Minister,' the Blessed Nancy said carefully.

Their eyes met. 'We now have quite a file on His Excellency. He has some unusual sexual peccadillos.'

'I see.' In the soft light, Bostock's eyes seemed clear and comprehending.

'It means, of course, that the Japanese won't be represented on Air Force One. Even if they rush the election, there won't be a new Prime Minister for at least a month.'

Once more their eyes met. 'One less to work on, Nancy,' murmured the Prime Minister. 'Is the President likely to know – suspect – any of the background to Nagoda's resignation?'

'Probably not. Since the Bush years there has been a steady decline in American ground intelligence in Japan. The sort of deal that Nagoda was doing with Bailey doesn't get picked up from outer space by a sat. Same with the ambassador. To catch him in his full finery, you need a bug in his bedroom.'

Bostock thought the laughter in her eyes seemed friendly. He stood up. 'Let me know how things develop.'

As they reached the door, he regarded her with the detachment of a priest who has learned that the benediction he would give is pointless.

'I assume that Manders has come up with nothing on the whereabouts of those triggers?'

'Not a thing, Prime Minister.'

'And Morton?'

'He seems to be in pursuit of the mullahs.'

'Ah yes . . . the mullahs. Well, well . . . Exactly what you said he'd do, Nancy.'

She gave a quick, funny little smile.

'Good night, Nancy,' the Prime Minister said softly, closing the door.

TWENTY-FOUR

Beyond the windows of the Oval Office, the last flag limped down its pole into a Marine's arms, marking the end of another official day in the White House. The men grouped in armchairs before the President's desk gave no outward sign of its passing. Like him, they had sat in rapt silence while Morton spoke.

He had begun after the President explained why he wanted Hammer Force to take charge of security for Operation Earth Saver; how, even with the sudden resignation of Japan's Prime Minister on health grounds, there would still be a need to find space on Air Force One for over a hundred bodyguards. Thacker Stimpson had murmured about not forgetting their private arsenals: at the last G7 summit half a ton of imported weaponry had been on the security manifest on top of what the host country provided. The President had asked Morton how many seats he would require. Morton said one would be sufficient – for himself. A surprised murmur had come from Barney Oldman, Director of the FBI. Before discussion could start, the President asked Morton to brief them on the security aspects of Earth Saver.

Now, an hour later, in the glow of the soft lighting, their faces reflected reactions to what he'd said. The President's look was one of tension; Secretary of State Clifford Palmer had abandoned his fingernail study to sit bolt upright, making him even more aloof; in Stimpson's eyes was a watchfulness; in those of Rear-Admiral Robert

Stanway, who ran NSA, speculation; Oldman registered a new, unhappy expression: Gates' eyes contained confirmation that he knew to be true what the others had been told.

The first audible response came from the deep-tanned man seated in the middle of the semi-circle of armchairs. The sound of Blake Faraday, the Vice-President, clearing his throat was loud. He turned his well-bred face to Morton, seated on his left. 'Even if this Russian – Bodor – is holed up with his nuclear triggers and that crazy, Zita Marcello, in those mountains, it won't make a heap of difference. Air Force One won't be entering Iranian airspace . . .'

'You're wrong there, Blake,' interjected the President, reaching for a paper on his desk. 'This morning Ayatollah Muzran finally responded. He's sent a fax saying he and the Revolutionary Council have no objection to receiving me in Tehran.'

'Terrific,' said the Vice-President unenthusiastically. He looked to his left. 'What's your take on this, Cliff?'

Palmer glanced at his fingernails before he spoke. 'Muzran will want us to blame his pollution problems on Baghdad and the Israelis,' he predicted. 'Then for good measure, expect us to offer a credit-free loan for his country to go nuclear powered.'

The Vice-President shifted in his chair, frowning, as if pondering a complex thought. 'Why not tell Muzran his invite's come too late? At the same time you can invite him here. It would be good for him to come out of his isolation, and it signals to Baghdad that we know how to make friends on its doorstep. It would also keep in check those Israelis who seem to think they can be as militant as they like as long as they can call on our Patriots to look after them.'

'That's an interesting perception of the region's politics.' Stimpson's voice held the barest trace of irony.

Glancing over his spectacles at Faraday, the President's irritation was plain.

'If I start cancelling out now, the whole purpose of Earth Saver is defeated, Blake. Iran, just as much as everybody else over there, needs to have the message spelled out that if we all don't work together, then the entire region will become a permanent cesspit – a dumping ground for many of the more useless products the industrialised world still foists on them.' He leaned forward. 'But I don't want to get side-tracked. Right now I want to hear your views on what we've heard from Mr Morton.'

In the silence the President looked around the semi-circle, his eyes stopping at Oldman. 'Barney?'

'Well now, if this was a domestic problem involving a visit to one of our more ethnic ghetto states, I'd have advance teams on the ground, Mr President.'

'You ever think of putting anyone into Iran, their security people will throw a collective fit,' Gates said without changing expression.

'My very point, Bill. Neither your people nor mine can go snooping without invitation.' The Director's tone was dry, and the careful way he sat so that there wasn't a crease in his suit – even Oldman's moustache seemed dry-cleaned – made Morton momentarily wonder about the relationship between obsessive neatness and inner tension.

'How about Hammer Force?' the President asked Morton. 'Could your people do a spot of minesweeping?'

Morton shook his head. 'The timetable's too short. That kind of surveillance needs to have been set up weeks ago.'

'That was not possible,' the President replied crisply.

'Jesus!' snapped the Vice-President, turning to the President. 'If you won't cancel Tehran, why not let Muzran know the score? That we know he's got Bodor tucked away some place in his mountains and that he'd better make damn good sure he keeps him there out of your way!'

The President shook his head. 'That would just make Muzran mad as hell.'

'But still, suppose he is directly involved in all this?' the Vice-President had spoken quickly.

The President glanced over at Morton. 'Is he?'

'Nothing points to that, Mr President,' Morton said.

For the first time Palmer turned to Morton. 'Is there any reason you know of why the President couldn't meet Muzran somewhere in the south of his country? That way Air Force One could have full cover from our navy in the Gulf.'

The President sighed. 'This is supposed to be a peace-making mission, the industrial nations extending a helping hand to the rest of the world, Cliff. I show up with what looks like an invasion task force on my heels and I lose all credibility. The whole ethos of Earth Saver is trust. We have to persuade people to trust us. We must trust them.'

Oldman touched a finger to the handkerchief in his breast pocket before he spoke. 'Mr President, why not have Bobby divert one of his satellites to grid-search those Iranian mountains? That way we'd find out what Bodor is up to. And the Marcello woman's balloon should be easy to spot.'

'Wouldn't work, Barney,' Rear-Admiral Stanway said crisply. 'There's so much military junk up there that it would take months for our computers to decipher. The chances of spotting that balloon with a sat are zilch. Hamas proved that when they launched those balloon-bomb attacks against Tel Aviv from Gaza. Because the bombs were in plastic cases and the balloons made from poly-thene, they slipped right through the Israeli radar.'

Stanway turned to the President. 'The best I could do, sir, would be to move the sat we have over Baghdad to cover the Tehran region. That would give us an even-stevens chance of spotting anything in your path. The probability is that any attack would be designed to catch Air Force One as she comes in to land or take off.'

The President raised an eyebrow at Morton.

'What's the effective range of your sat, Admiral?' Morton asked Stanway.

'It's one of the new breed of Halos. It gives us a fifty-mile sweep even on a cloudy day.'

'This time of year you get sandstorms up there,' Gates said. 'Real blowers. You can't see more than a few yards.'

'Assuming the threat is this Marcello woman and her balloon, then she's not going to get off the ground in such a storm,' reported Stanway.

Faraday's tone was suddenly aggressive. 'Mr Morton has yet to explain how she would use her balloon to attack Air Force One. Perhaps he would like to tell us.'

Morton gave an apologetic shrug. 'I don't know – I don't even know if she is going to do that, at least when Air Force One is airborne. The balloon could be just as easily used to launch an attack when the plane's on the ground.'

'Jesus,' said the Vice-President, looking startled. 'You're giving yourself a lot of latitude.'

Morton ignored the interjection.

Once more the President raised an eyebrow. 'A ground attack seems to go against your theory that Bodor is involved – given that his speciality is high-altitude weaponry.'

Morton nodded as if something had just occurred to him. 'Why not leave the Baghdad sat in place and bring in another one to cover Tehran?'

Stanway's response was less stubborn than wounded. 'Mr Morton, the days have gone when I could jimmy-up a sat just like that. Now I have to go through an oversight committee and make a case . . .'

'I can short-circuit that, Bobby,' the President said quickly.

'Thank you, Mr President,' Stanway acknowledged. 'But in this case that wouldn't help. If I don't move the Baghdad sat, the nearest available one is over North Korea. For the reasons I outlined at the last National Security meeting, North Korea remains a problem and I would be loath to move our Halo from there. Anyway, to re-orbit it for Tehran would take maybe three to four days. The new Halos have a lot of advantages, but speed isn't one of them.'

The President consulted another piece of paper on his desk. 'In four days time Air Force One will be flying out of Beijing and heading for the Middle East.' He looked up at Gates, removing his glasses as he spoke. 'What's the latest on Saddam?'

'He's gone quiet, Mr President. But that last purge of his generals has left him with almost no real command structure.'

Listening, Morton watched the President's face as he paused for a moment before turning to the Secretary of State.

'Cliff?' the President prompted.

The Secretary once more considered his nails before he spoke. 'Saddam's hoping the Syrians will use their new relationship with Tel Aviv to persuade it that, in return for having to make only a modified withdrawal from the Golan Heights, Israel will give up supporting sanctions against Iraq.'

'You think that's possible?' Faraday asked doubtfully.

'When I was in Israel they were still hell-bent on starving Saddam out.'

'That was three months ago, Blake. Right now, things get out of date in three days over there,' Palmer said.

Once more the Vice-President shifted in his seat. 'Maybe we should lean on the Israelis a little over Iraq,' he suggested.

The President frowned. 'Saddam's entirely responsible for his people's plight, Blake, and they know and accept that. They're ready to go on putting up with sanctions if at the end of the day their army finally takes the plunge and turns on him.' He glanced at Morton. 'Let's hear from you, Mr Morton.'

'I'd move the Baghdad satellite,' Morton said.

The President nodded. 'I agree.' He turned to Rear-Admiral Stanway. 'Once I'm clear of Iran airspace, you can re-orbit it back over Baghdad.'

Faraday spoke directly to the President. 'After what we've been told by Mr Morton, shouldn't there be some kind of surveillance mounted on Meridian? If not on all their companies, then at least its headquarters? If Bobby can't get a satellite in place overhead, shouldn't Barney's people move in?'

The President's frown deepened. 'If Bailey had even a whiff that anybody from this administration was sniffing around, his media pitbulls would tear me apart even faster than the *Post* and *Times* devoured Nixon. Nobody, and I mean nobody, is to go near Meridian.'

The room was silent. When the President next spoke, it was to Morton, and as if they were alone. 'Are you absolutely certain that Meridian is somehow directly involved with Bodor and those triggers? I've listened to all you have already said most carefully and I know something about Bailey's methods. But that said, it still seems incredible he could threaten my mission.'

Watching the President's face, Morton recalled he had liked him instinctively. Part of it, he decided, was the man's clear-eyed intelligence: he gave the impression of an inner balance in which no hidden angers or ambitions stopped him from being fair. The other part was a driving sense of commitment, fuelled by an innate decency.

'I'm not certain, in a lawyer's sense. No.' said Morton quietly.

The President's expression changed but slightly. 'But with something like this, surely Bailey would have to be involved?'

'Logically, yes. Of course.'

Thacker Stimpson broke the new silence. 'Maybe that's why Bailey refused your invitation.'

'That's still a big assumption, Thack,' the President said tensely.

Stimpson seemed poised to ask another question, then did not. It was left to Palmer to do so.

'Mr President, there's a real danger here that, despite all Mr Morton has said, we are chasing shadows. Bailey is undoubtedly Machiavellian, but you are right to say it's still a mighty big leap to assume he wants to do harm — let alone kill you. Just how would he do that? Or have this creature Bodor do it for him? Mr Morton does not know — and had the honesty to tell us that. If he doesn't know for certain, and neither does Mr Gates here, or indeed Bobby or Barney, I think we should be very careful.' He paused to glance quickly along the row of armchairs. 'I remember from my days as a young deskman in the Nixon administration how quickly paranoia can take hold. This adminstration has been blessedly free of that.'

'Thank you for that, Cliff,' the President said quietly.

Barney Oldman fingered the handkerchief in his breast

pocket. 'Mr President,' the FBI Director began, 'Mr Palmer has made a good point, several of them. Given that you have ruled out surveillance on Meridian, there's not a heap I can do. If there had been more time, I could have had our Moscow bureau try and pick up Bodor's trail . . .'

'Chances are you wouldn't get any closer than I managed,' Gates growled. 'Those working Bodor will be taking damned good care to keep him out of harm's way. That's one reason why I think they hid him away in those mountains in Iran. Right now, until Bodor or the Marcello woman make their move, we have to sit tight.'

In the renewed silence the President turned back to the window. He knew they were deciding in their minds what they would do if they were him. But they weren't. While he could still substitute another country for Iran, it would send the wrong signals to start chopping and changing at this late stage. Besides, Air Force One had some of the most sophisticated on-board equipment to warn of any threat. An attack on the ground might be more of a problem. But from the beginning he had always accepted that he couldn't live his presidency in a cocoon.

The President turned back to face them. 'Gentlemen,' he said firmly, 'whatever the potential threat from any quarter, it cannot be allowed to interfere in any way with this mission. It goes forward exactly as planned.'

In the four hours since Patterson had parked Air Force One in its own hangar at Andrews Air Force base, he had conducted a full on-board debriefing.

While he monitored the flight-deck checks – between them Locke, Kerr and Turner satisfied him on some hundred items – crew chief Sutter and chief flight steward Cowan were doing the same with their staff. The missing piece of rubber lost from a port side wheel when landing in Paris, the state of the flowers on the lounge tables — 'drooping, suggest we use a new florist,' Cowan had written — were noted, together with a slow-filling toilet cistern, a lack of pressure to one of the galley taps and a need to make over the bedroom Patterson had used.

While their reports were being completed, he'd gone to the crew toilet and this time found his urine free of any trace of blood. Reassured, he'd walked through the aircraft, mentally noting a seat cushion which required replacing, a window shade that had worked loose, a faulty hinge on an overhead bin.

He found them all listed on the reports Cowan and Sutter brought to the flight deck. After he'd read and initialled them, he told both department heads to remind their staff that the sixty-minute rule was in force. No crew member could go more than an hour's travelling distance from the base, and before leaving, each must have packed their personal flight bags for a seven-day mission. Under the rule no one was allowed to drink alcohol, and even a minor ailment had to be reported to the base hospital to obtain medical clearance to fly.

A similar reminder was delivered by the signals major to the communications staff after he had completed an equipment report that everything had functioned perfectly. He attached to the report a print-out of the telephone calls made and received by Air Force One during the flight. He had just brought the documentation to the flight deck.

Patterson was alone, reading the last of the cockpit reports. Locke, he noted, had written against the light that had signalled a fault with the rear baggage door: 'Crew chief needs to tighten up check procedures.'

'Any problems?' Patterson asked, as the major handed over his report.

'None, Colonel.'

Patterson glanced at the print-out. Listed after the long list of calls Morton had made was his own to the White House and Bron's. Base communications who would routinely check the print-out might wonder why the President's direct line number had been called when the Man was not on board. He looked up at the major.

'Those calls by Morton don't have to be listed. They've got the same exemption as the Man's. I'll hang on to this and give it to Morton.'

The major nodded. 'I'll make a new print-out listing only the other two.'

Patterson managed to smile. 'No need. The incoming one to the Man's number was to remind me to make my call at a certain time.'

Folding the print-out, Patterson slipped it into his pocket, initialled the equipment report and handed it back to the major. Alone again, he used the telephone in the armrest to dial his home number. There was no reply. Bron must have gone to an afternoon movie. He replaced the phone and became aware that on the catwalk that ran round the inside of the hangar, a guard was watching him.

Twenty-four hours a day a sniper was posted on the catwalk ready to deal with any intruder who managed to get past the other guards outside the hangar. The guard was speaking into the mike clipped to his collar. He'd be reporting that the aircraft commander was still on board. Patterson pointed at his watch and raised a spread of fingers to indicate how long he'd be. The guard waved in acknowledgement.

'Practising semaphore?' Helen Curtis asked from the doorway.

Patterson turned to her. 'I wondered where you'd gotten to.'

'Sorry I've been so long, Ed. Filling out a check-list is

something they didn't teach at med school – or Bethesda for that matter.'

She handed him her report. The first few pages were an inventory of drugs and medical equipment. The last page – Procedures Performed on Flight – was blank.

He glanced at her quizzically. 'You figured my nose-bleed was nothing, after all?'

She smiled at him. 'How do you feel now, Ed?'

'Not a bother.'

'Then there's no need for me to file anything.' She leaned against a bulkhead. 'You know what would happen if I did report it? You'd have to undergo a full medical at Bethesda.'

'You're kidding!'

'Never been more serious.' Helen searched his face. 'It's in the new rule book the Admiral gave me. Any member of the flight deck who displays any symptom that could impinge upon his ability to perform his duty has to be fully medically investigated.'

'So why aren't you turning me in?' he asked lightly.

'Partly medical judgement. I could find nothing to suggest that your nose-bleed was anything but a nose-bleed. And partly because if I did send you up to Bethesda, it would mean your missing this mission.'

He glanced down at the blank pages and initialled the space left for his signature. 'Thanks, Helen.'

'No sweat.' She looked around the flight deck. 'You about finished here?'

'Pretty well.'

'Are you hungry?'

He looked at her, surprised. 'What?'

'Hungry. Food. I didn't eat during the flight and I'd settle for an early dinner,' she said.

Feeling awkward, he looked at his watch. 'I've still got

a stack of paperwork to do back in the office.'

She moved away from the bulkhead. 'Maybe soon.' She smiled at him. 'It wouldn't be a problem for you, would it?'

Once more he had the sense that Helen was silently examining him, that beneath her cool, detached surface was a woman in touch with her own emotions. He gave her a level look. 'You mean, would my wife mind?'

She was startled at the sudden intensity she saw in his face. 'You could bring her along as well, if you like.'

He shook his head. 'She's not a great socialiser.'

Helen saw that his sadness had once more come close to the surface before being swiftly returned to some inner sanctum.

'I imagine your job's like mine, Ed. A real bitch when it comes to living a normal life.' Her voice grew softer yet. 'You should try and make time for your wife.'

Patterson found he could not speak; his few seconds of confusion seemed infinite.

'That may be a little late,' he began quietly at last. 'Bron – that's her name – says if someone asked either of us to get in touch with our feelings, we'd probably need a map.' He stopped, forcing a smile. 'I'm sorry. I don't want this to get personal. I have a firm rule that private life stops at the ramp.'

'It may not always be a good rule, Ed.'

He looked at her frowning. 'You're a very perceptive woman, Helen, but my life isn't your problem.'

'It may be your wife's,' Helen said quietly.

'But don't try and get involved in this, please. I'm asking you not to.'

'I'm already involved, Ed.'

He spoke more sharply. 'How? How do you make that out?'

'Your nose-bleed. It could, after all, just be due to stress.'

'What are you saying, Doctor? That you'll ground me? Send me to Bethesda after all?' His voice was filled with a sudden cold anger. 'What is this? Some kind of mind-game you're playing? Showing me that you have the final say?'

Helen gazed at him for a moment. 'No. I just want to help.'

In the silence he felt not only exposed but chastened. 'I'm sorry. I shouldn't have blown off like that,' he said at last.

'No apology needed.'

They looked at each other silently for another long moment before she continued, 'I didn't mean to intrude. God knows, I value space myself. I really didn't mean to come in here . . .'

'No, no. It's okay. I appreciate your wanting to help. But, like I said, it's probably too late. She probably needs . . .' He stopped; he couldn't bring himself to say she needed a psychiatrist.

'Maybe I could talk to her, Ed. A woman's viewpoint on this job could be a help in making her understand what kind of pressures are on you.' She smiled at him. 'I've done it before, you know. There was a surgeon who was driving himself into the ground because he thought that was the only way to please his wife. When I spoke to her, it turned out to be the last thing she wanted. Once they'd struck a happy balance, things were fine. Maybe I could help Bron do that.'

'It wouldn't work. Besides,' he added as if this closed the subject, 'she's an actress, used to putting on a performance. She'd make you believe that the only thing she wants is for me to give up flying.'

'And would you?' Helen asked steadily.

'No.' His voice was emphatic. 'I've thought about it. But each time I knew it would destroy me to do so. Flying is my life.' As if he had said too much, he began to gather his paperwork into his flight bag.

'If you change your mind about my seeing Bron, let me know, Ed.' She turned to leave.

'I'll remember that,' Patterson said. 'And remember, the sixty-minute rule applies to you as well.'

'I plan to stay on base,' Helen said.

He waited until he saw her sign out at the guard desk by the hangar door, then followed.

Emerging from the main aircraft cabin door on to the ramp, Patterson felt water strike his hat; the hangar was so high that on moist days condensation dropped, rain-like from the roof. Overhead lighting gave Air Force One a gleam to her aluminium skin, against which mechanics were beginning to position their inspection gantries. Under Sutter's watchful eyes, a maintenance crew had rmeoved the damaged tyre and were fitting a new one.

At the door, Patterson initialled the Movement Book and walked the short distance to the administration building. A sign proclaimed that this was the headquarters of the 89th Military Airlift Wing, Special Missions – the official title of the President's air fleet. His sergeant had laid out his messages on his desk in what she'd decided was descending importance. It took him an hour to return the calls.

State had sent over a list of food preferences for the President's guests. He spent twenty minutes discussing them on the phone with Cowan, whose office was over in the flight kitchen.

The Pentagon had called with the name of the new bagman – a black Marine who had distinguished himself in Bosnia; his selection was a reminder of how many of the peacetime armed forces were non-white. He passed the Marine's name on to the 89th's adjutant.

Another call was to the unit's personnel officer. It was time to repaint the enlisted ranks' quarters, and some of the women wanted a hand in the redecorating. No problem, he told the personnel officer: giving them the choice of colour and curtain fabric would help to ensure the highest morale of any air force unit.

A call to Security revealed that they had failed to pass a maintenance man — not because he had even a small skeleton in his cupboard but simply because they'd spotted an administrative mistake in his air force records: the mechanic was two months short of the minimum requirement of three years in his particular speciality before he was eligible to join the 89th. He told Security to ask the man to apply again in a couple of months.

At the bottom of the message pile were the usual invites to address luncheon clubs and a couple of high schools. He'd deal with these after the mission. Same with the manufacturer who wanted to come calling with a new sample of floor covering for Air Force One. The man's request was a further reminder of how far-reaching were the demands made on his own time.

It was late afternoon when he finally was able to reach for the telephone directory and begin to dial the listings for psychiatrists. Each time there was either no reply or a service came on the line to give the doctor's office hours, usually ten till four. He glanced at the wall clock. It was a little after four fifteen. Washington kept company town hours. By now the psychiatrists, like most other people, would probably be on their way home. He called Bron once more. There was still no reply. She must have stopped off some place for something to eat.

He stood up and stretched, feeling the tiredness grip his body in all the familiar places: across his shoulders, in his calf muscles and, above all, in his lower back. As he reached for his flight bag the fax machine in the corner came to life. He walked over and watched the message emerge on White House stationery, with the mandatory 'Secret' stamped across the top. The message was addressed to him and commendably short.

'Subject: Flight Readiness. The Presidential aircraft and crew are hereby placed on alert for the mission some time within the next forty-eight hours.' It was signed as usual by Thacker Stimpson, Chief of Staff.

He sighed. There would just be time to go home to see Bron before he'd have to return here. One of the many things she complained about was that for the two days before a mission he had to remain on the base.

TWENTY-FIVE

Dressed in a black one-piece flight suit tucked into fleece-lined boots, Zita continued her careful inspection of the balloon envelope spread out on the desert sand.

Despite all that had happened since she'd run screaming from the catwalk, unable any longer to watch what was happening to Kunsk, she managed to concentrate. Her life depended on this inspection, she had told Bodor. He'd looked at her for a moment, then said that not only her life, but his as well. It was the first indication he'd given that he intended to accompany her on the ascent.

He was over by the truck, among the huddle of men who had brought the balloon and gondola to the launch site. In the darkness she could sense their impatience for her to finish. Despite their heavy coats, it would be cold standing there doing nothing, forbidden by her to smoke in case a spark ignited the envelope. She knew the chance of that happening was small, but it was another way to establish her authority, to show that out here *she* was the law, something even Bodor had to acknowledge.

It had produced a feeling in her that was like an ancient, primitive force. She had never known anything like this. She could feel it now as she crouched to examine the seal between two more panels and, in that moment, she not only neither hated nor feared Bodor, but also felt something about men for the first time that could not be explained in terms of what her father had done to her. It was something she could not express or rationalise, only know that here in the desert night she had finally found out who she was and what drove her: it was something she would never be able to explain to anyone else.

But it would answer so much that had puzzled her about herself: why she could at times feel vulnerable, and at others unfeeling. Some of it, she knew, was bound up with her deliberate transgressions; this need to challenge, often for the sake of doing so. But she also now realised it was nothing to do with vindicating herself: she would not change anything even if she could.

With a new purpose she continued her careful examination: checking the calendering, the heat-sealing process which lapped the edge of one panel over another; tugging at the webbing tapes, each with a break-strength of a ton, which helped to secure the envelope to the gondola. She ran her fingers over the lock-stitching on the fabric closest to the burner, and did the same to the felled-seam stitching on the rip-stoppers. Next she minutely examined the skirt around the base of the envelope and the tapering cylinder of fire-proofed fabric that shielded the burner flame from the side gusts of wind. On the burner she checked the hoses and tested the valves.

Satisfied, she moved to the gondola, pulling hard on the shackles of the rigging wires which passed down through the roof and basket-weave walls and beneath the reinforced floor, so that it would remain securely suspended beneath the envelope even if the webbing tapes snapped. She stepped into the gondola. In the cramped space were wooden bench seats facing each other and a trapdoor in the floor that could be raised by a ring bolt. On one wall was the instrument panel. The needles of the altimeter and variometer, which would indicate the rate of climb and descent, twitched when she rapped their glass dials with a finger. Securely strapped in place were the oxygen cylinders that would be used to

replenish air in the breathing sets needed for the final part of
the ascent. Beside them were the fuel tanks, linked to the
burner with copper pipes. There was sufficient propane in
the tanks to allow the balloon to reach 40,000 feet, then
make a controlled descent.

Checks completed, she looked at her watch. There were
still thirty minutes to go before the launch. She sat on the
floor, her back against a seat, listening to the sound of feet
stamping against the cold from over by the truck, and
closed her eyes.

Bodor continued to wait patiently, wondering again
how it was that the Arranger had been able to predict her
responses so accurately from the time she had run from the
catwalk.

*For a moment he had wanted to stop her, make her stay with him
to follow the final destruction of Kunsk's body inside the dome.
Like some lab specimen, Kunsk had literally come apart as his
organs haemorrhaged and ruptured, causing his ribcage to emerge
through his skin.*

*Though Bodor had seen this happen before, many times, the
sight never failed to thrill him. There was something truly
inspiring in being able to harness the forces of nature to such
devastating effect.*

*He heard her clatter down the steps from the catwalk and run,
still screaming, through a corridor, the sound abruptly ending
when an air-locked door opened and closed behind her. As he
turned back to watch the remains of Kunsk being wheeled away
on a trolley to the autopsy room, he remembered the Arranger had
said it was important at this stage that there must be no attempt
to calm her or in any way reduce the impact on her mind of what
she had seen. Hers was the kind of personality, the Arranger had
continued, which would see Kunsk's fate as a powerful reminder
of what she must expect if she failed; she would make the*

connection without the need to speak of it.

For the next twenty-four hours she had been left strictly alone in her quarters, her only contact the kitchen staff who brought her food. At first she hardly ate, but the last tray had not so much as a scrap left. Her mood had also changed: tears had given way to sullenness and then her familiar arrogance. The Arranger had also predicted this.

Meantime, work had continued to solve the problems with the Ozone Layer Bomb casing. Several more were tested to destruction and adjustments made to the thickness of the metal. Finally, close to dawn, a casing emerged intact from its chamber firings. Five more were made to the same specifications and fitted with their nuclear triggers, then stored in a bunker on the far side of the complex.

At noon the Arranger telephoned again. After listening to the progress report, he said the test launch must go ahead that night, adding that the American satellite positioned over Baghdad would have moved by then.

It was the first Bodor had heard about the satellite, and his mind filled with questions. Could it have already detected the surface activity around the complex? Had the two trucks filled with meteorological equipment and parked a couple of miles downrange from the launch site been spotted? Or the weather balloons launched into the upper stratosphere? Had the launch pad itself been filmed? The dogs out by a perimeter fence that appeared to surround nothing but sand? Had the satellite spotted the faint brush-like tracks made by the squad who, before dawn, used palm fronds to sweep away the tyremarks of the night traffic? Had the coming and going of the vehicles been detected? But he knew better than to ask any of those questions – especially the one which intrigued him the most: how did the Arranger know of the satellite's presence and that it had now been moved?

At dusk Bodor had supervised the loading of the balloon and the gondola on to a truck which was then parked at the top of the exit ramp. A bomb had been stowed on board between sandbags to stop it from moving. Then, carrying her flight suit, he had gone to Zita's quarters.

She was at her desk, her back towards him, reading a magazine. He remained in the doorway when she stood to face him.

'Have you come to apologise?' she asked coldly.

'There's nothing to apologise for,' he replied calmly. 'You over-reacted.'

'What did you expect me to do?' she demanded, reaching for a cigarette. 'Stand there and cheer while that poor bastard literally spilled his guts?'

He watched her light up, striking the match like a man; he admired women who knew how to smoke.

'It was necessary,' he finally said. 'What we learned will help with the test flight.'

There was a pause while she considered what she'd been told. 'That's pure bullshit!'

He looked at her impassively. The Arranger had said he must not get into a debate about anything, and that he should switch the conversation abruptly from one topic to another.

'Did you enjoy yourself with Kunsk?' he asked softly.

Her cheekbones flushed with colour. 'What the hell are you talking about?'

'The videos are very explicit.'

The colour deepened on Zita's cheekbones. 'You bastard! Is that how you get your jollies?'

Bodor frowned. 'I do not know the word.'

She smiled obscenely, cupping her hand around the cigarette and demonstrating. 'You understand this, don't you, Bodor?'

This was exactly the sort of situation the Arranger had warned him about. Don't let her use her sex, he had said. It's the one potent weapon she has.

'Enough!' Bodor ordered.

She put the cigarette to her mouth and dragged deeply, sucking in her cheeks.

'Sit down and listen,' he said more sharply.

She blew out a billow of smoke. 'You know, Bodor, there are times when I think your mother never brought you up properly. Gentlemen always say please to ladies.'

He waited for a crushing reply to spring to his lips. It did not come. He walked over and stood close to her, staring at her for what seemed a long time. Then he abruptly thrust the flight suit at her, and returned to stand at the door, as if he needed to keep a distance to maintain control.

'So what do you want to tell me?' Zita asked, finally sitting down.

Bodor watched her suck in another lungful of smoke, then he began to repeat exactly what the Arranger had told him to say. Don't leave any room for her to interrupt or challenge, the Arranger had warned, and above all give the impression that she has been told everything.

Twice while he was speaking she had lit a fresh cigarette, flicking the ash to the floor, the only other movement she made.

Listening, she compared everything with what the Arranger had told her on the car journey to Frankfurt. Bodor was filling in the gaps. And he was certainly right about one thing: what was going to happen would concentrate the minds of those leaders; for them it would be a dramatic demonstration of the folly of policies that continued to destroy Mother Earth.

When he had finished, she continued to stare back at him.

'I have one question,' she began. 'No one will be killed?'

The Arranger had predicted this would be the first matter she would ask about.

'No,' Bodor replied. 'They will experience some discomfort. No more.'

'And the plane?'

'The demonstration will not affect the plane,' Bodor said truthfully.

To his surprise, she began to whistle.

'What is this?' he asked heavily.

'The tune? "Que sera sera." "Whatever will be, will be,"' she replied. 'I always whistle it before a flight.'

Shaking his head, he'd left her alone, not knowing how to respond to her mocking smile.

He could sense it was there now as she emerged from the gondola.

Walking towards the truck, Zita glanced professionally at the sky. There was no moon but the stars were bright between the clouds. As long as they remained like scraps of cotton wool, there should be no problem. That would come with daylight, when the wisps would merge to form fair-weather cumulus, creating thermals capable of carrying the balloon at express-elevator speed to heights where oxygen-starvation and cold would swiftly kill them in spite of protective clothing and breathing sets.

Far to the west the predicted electrical storm was producing its lightning display. It reminded her of fireworks on New Year's Eve at home. Bodor had said the storm would provide the ideal cover for the test launch.

She watched him detach himself from the group to join her. His flight suit was bulkier because of the breathing set strapped to his chest. Shaped like a life-vest, it was filled with compressed air that would be supplied through a rubber hose when plugged into a socket in his dome-shaped helmet. He carried a second helmet in one hand, in the other her breathing set.

'Everything in order?' he asked, handing her the equipment. She could hear the tension in his voice.

'All set.' She felt new energy.

He turned to the man beside the truck and spoke in Russian. They separated to go to the balloon or the back of the truck.

She was starting to move towards the balloon when he stopped her.

'They know what to do,' he said, his tension still there. 'Let's test the intercom.'

She looked at him for a moment, her raised eyebrows making her face seem longer, her expression more intent. Then she shrugged. Waiting until he'd pulled down the vizor of his helmet and lock its sealing clips, she did the same. He reached forward and took a lead attached to a small box strapped to his waist and plugged its socket into a matching box on her belt. Immediately the sound of his breathing was loud in her ears.

'Can you hear me?' Bodor asked.

'Perfectly,' she replied, lifting her vizor.

'Test your breathing set,' he said curtly.

Zita hesitated. Part of Bodor seemed ashamed at some secret foolishness. But she did as he'd asked. The flow of oxygen was unimpeded. She switched off the set and gave him a sideways look. 'You ever flown a balloon at night, Bodor?

He hesitated. 'No.'

'Nervous?'

'No.' She was needling him. The Arranger had also warned him about that.

Zita smiled. 'I am. Every time.'

The first sliver of anger pierced Bodor's voice. 'Don't patronise me.'

She deliberately turned her back to watch the technicians flapping cold air into the base of the envelope. In the dark they looked like huge birds as they waved their arms to drive air through the opening. Already the cloth was starting to undulate gently from the air trapped inside its folds.

From the back of the truck men were carefully man-handling the bomb and its launcher. It was the first time she had seen the contraption. In silence they followed the men to the balloon.

The envelope was now filled with sufficient cold air to create a continuous wavelike movement inside the fabric. Two of the ground crew gripped the restraining line, while another pair were standing on either side of the envelope's mouth, holding it open. The others, the strongest-looking, gripped poles they'd fitted into hooks in the gondola's base, ready to restrain it from dragging or lifting out of control once the envelope was fully inflated.

Inside the gondola, a crew man stood beneath the burner. He ordered the men around the mouth to step back. When they did, he ignited the burner to send a long tongue of flame shooting into the envelope.

The moment always reminded Zita of a story-book dragon breathing fire into a cave. The puff created a seal around the mouth to stop the air in the envelope from escaping. The man began to fire further short, controlled bursts. Slowly, almost magically, the envelope assumed its balloon shape, the fabric, breathing, rising and expanding. The gondola gently lifted off the ground.

'One metre – no more!' Bodor yelled.

The men grunted and braced themselves as the gondola continued to rise.

'More heat!' Zita shouted. The top of the envelope had started to deflate slightly, causing a loss of lift.

Another burst of flame once more lit up the inside of the envelope.

'High enough! Hold it there!' Bodor shouted.

The men splayed their feet to stop the gondola from

rising. Bodor crouched to judge the gap between the sand and its base.

'Now!' He motioned forward the men with the bomb and launcher. Zita followed. She watched them squat beneath the gondola and fit the inverted metal triangle to bolts in the case of the gondola. On each upright of the triangle was a cylinder, each with a nozzle. Next they fitted a metal cone into the apex of the triangle and connected the nozzles to valves in the cone. They moved aside to allow Bodor to check their work. After he had finished, the bomb was slowly inserted into the cone and held in place by springs. It hung like a bulbous pendulum, its fins only inches above the sand.

Bodor motioned Zita to kneel beside him as he explained.

'Because the latest forecast at the launch height predicts a higher wind speed, three extra balloons have been fitted into the cone.' He pointed to the cylinders. 'There's enough helium to handle the extra inflation. Otherwise everything works as before.' He indicated the bolts. 'These are pressurised to release simultaneously at the launch height of 40,000 feet.' He touched the fins of the bomb. 'Once in free fall, the inertial navigation in here will allow the bomb to fall vertically for precisely 500 feet. At that point three things will happen in sequence. The helium will be transferred into the cone and inflate the balloons. When they are inflated, the springs will automatically detach and the frame will fall away. The balloons will then carry the bomb to its detonation point. This is set at 80,000 feet.'

When they emerged from beneath the gondola, the crew man was standing in the door. He extended a hand to help them into the cabin. Zita was the first to pull herself on board. Bodor quickly followed. The man jumped to the ground as the others unhooked their poles. The gondola began to rise rapidly as Bodor closed the door.

Zita positioned herself beneath the burner and fired a tongue of flame into the envelope, again briefly lighting its inside. In moments the balloon rose a further hundred feet; three more bursts and the altimeter showed they were 1,000 feet above the ground. There was no sensation of climbing, no motion of any kind because they were travelling at wind speed, making the relative air movement zero.

Zita motioned to a bench seat. 'It's going to be a slow climb from now on.'

For the next hour the only sound came from the burner being regularly fired as they rose to 10,000 feet. Zita said it was time to put on their breathing suits. Afterwards, when the variometer's needle climbed too quickly, she vented air through an opening in the envelope's side. Whenever the gondola started to sink, she gave another blast on the burner, sending them once more climbing steadily.

They reached 20,000 feet without incident. Fifteen minutes latter they had passed the 25,000 mark on the altimeter. Both of them adjusted the thermostats on their suits to remain comfortably warm.

'How much longer?' Bodor asked, tension once more giving an edge to his words.

'Forty minutes,' she replied promptly, her eyes on the instrument panel. For a while they had been climbing at a steady 500 feet a minute, a smooth, silent ascent which exhilarated her. She felt his glance. 'There's nothing to be frightened of.' The words slipped from her mouth before she had time to censor them.

He did not answer, yet he did not avoid her reassurance. Then he laughed, not very pleasantly, and sat well back, his arms folded comfortably across his breathing set, his head tilted slightly to one side, staring out of one of the gondola's portholes.

The electrical storm was spread out above them; there was no thunder, only this dazzling latticework of intermittent lightning. She was like a child trying to unsettle him, he thought, while in truth she seemed scared herself, her face behind the vizor expressionless and pale as she stood before the instrument panel, hands resting on the burner controls.

At 30,000 feet, Zita switched to a new tank of propane and sent another controlled burst of flame into the envelope. Afterwards the darkness was, if anything, more intense.

'Ten minutes to go,' she said, as a fork of lightning zigged and zagged behind the gondola.

'There will be a slight lurch, no more as the launcher is detached,' he explained.

'I'll burn to get us well clear . . .' she began.

Suddenly the gondola lurched so violently that Zita lost her grip on the burner controls and Bodor was sent sprawling against her legs. The gondola tilted alarmingly. From above came the loud whip-crack of one of the webbing tapes snapping.

'We've hit a thermal,' Zita shouted, struggling to her feet. As she reached up towards the burner's blast valve, the gondola plunged with sickening speed, forcing her back down on to the floor. From the basket-weave wall to her right came a tearing sound as one of the rigging wires snaked out into the darkness.

Bodor's scream drowned the sound of rushing wind in her helmet. She made another grab at the blast valve and failed, once more sprawling back on to the floor.

The balloon skittered sideways across the sky, caught in

the full turbulence of the thermal.

Bodor was crouched on all fours on the floor, vomiting inside his helmet. As she moved to pull him to his feet, the balloon resumed climbing, shooting up even faster than before. From the envelope came a rushing sound of air being forced out. She knew that in moments the envelope could collapse, plunging them both to their deaths. She grabbed a fuel pipe and somehow pulled herself up.

There was another ripping sound as a second webbing strap began to flap furiously in the air.

Zita reached the blast valve and fired a burst into the envelope. The gondola dropped with the same terrifying speed it had climbed.

Behind her Bodor crashed into a wall, winding himself against the fuel pipes. But that was not the reason he was having trouble breathing. Some of the vomit must have blocked his air pipe. He could feel pressure in his head. Suddenly it eased as the oxygen pressure in his headset increased. Zita had opened the valve. He waved a hand towards her. She could hear him breathing deeply.

As the downward plunge slowed, Zita fired again. The balloon began to climb, but this time, she detected, less rapidly. They must be close to the outer edge of the thermal. Suddenly the gondola was rushing sideways through the night once more, as though driven by some huge invisible force.

Tilting the burner's angle control to its maximum to counteract wind deflection, Zita sent another tongue of flame roaring up inside the envelope. The sideways rush eased, slowed by the sheer volume of reheated air inside the envelope.

The altimeter showed they were again ascending, but more slowly. From under her feet came a snapping sound. Another rigging wire must have snaked free. The gondola seemed to sag slightly before righting itself. She looked over her shoulder. Bodor was crouching above the trap-door, pulling at the ring bolt.

Another wrenching sound came from beneath the gondola, and at once the rate of ascent increased.

Bodor had lifted the trap and was peering down through the hole. He began to scream.

The launcher had gone.

Crouching beside him, Zita stared into the night. The balloon had stopped its rapid ascent and was drifting, free now of the thermal.

'Look!' Zita shouted.

A cluster of white blobs had suddenly appeared far below.

'Balloons!' Bodor yelled.

'The wind must have sheared off the bolts,' Zita said.

As they watched, the cluster rose slowly towards them. A fork of lightning illuminated the bomb suspended beneath the balloon.

'Shall we try and retrieve it?' Zita asked.

Bodor shook his head. 'That would be too dangerous. The detonator may have been activated.'

'I'll put as much distance between us as possible,' Zita said, getting to her feet.

Bodor's words stopped her. 'No point. If the bomb goes off, we'd still be killed by the air pressure.'

'But I thought you said it wouldn't kill anyone . . .'

'It'll be different for those on the plane,' he said quickly. 'They'll have sufficient protection. We have nothing but a layer of basket weave.'

In silence they watched the cluster continue to rise slowly towards them. Then, still several hundred feet below the gondola, the cluster stopped climbing and began to drift away into the night.

'What's happening?' Zita asked.

'There's not enough helium to provide full lifting power. Probably the supply line was damaged.' Bodor turned to her. 'Can you follow them?'

'We've already got structural damage. This whole thing could come apart around us. The only way we're going is down,' she said emphatically.

Leaving Bodor still crouched over the trapdoor, Zita stood up and used the vent-line to expel air slowly from the envelope. In moments the gondola began to descend.

Bodor continued to watch as, lit by sporadic flashes of lightning, the balloon cluster drifted eastwards. Unless something happened, by dawn the bomb would be in Iranian airspace.

Morton glanced up as Gates entered from an adjoining office. They'd come straight back to Langley from the White House. On the way Morton had told Gates what he wanted. Now, several hours later, the CIA's Director of Operations had arrived with another bundle of files.

'This is the lot,' Gates said, dumping the folders beside the stack already on Morton's desk.

Each file contained the air force records of every serving member of the 89th, and Morton had already separated those of the flight crew from the others.

'What are you looking for, David?' Gates asked. 'These guys have been checked out by the best in the business.'

'Then this shouldn't take long,' Morton said equably, turning back to a folder.

TWENTY-SIX

Before Patterson left Andrews Air Force base, air traffic control had called to say that the first of the G7 leaders, the Italian Prime Minister, Silvio Briscini, had landed. The others were expected within the hour, arriving in time for the private dinner the President was hosting for them in the White House that night.

Now, halfway home, the White House switchboard called Patterson on his car phone. 'Just a routine check,' the operator said politely. It was a further reminder that in the count-down to the mission he must remain in constant telephone contact.

That was something else Bron had complained about; that his life was dictated by some voice at the end of a phone. The calls could come at most inopportune times, like when Bron had wriggled from underneath him when the bedside phone rang. He'd been told to stand down a mission. By the time he'd made the other essential calls that always followed such an order, Bron had turned her back on him and was asleep. He'd learned she used denial of sex as a weapon with which to punish him.

He came off the freeway, crossed a couple of roads, drove another half-mile, then turned into the tree-lined avenue where he'd rented a house that backed on to a college campus. It was a good deal more expensive than anything near the base, but Bron had insisted she didn't want to live with a background of aero engines.

Parking in the driveway, the twinge of pain in his

stomach was a constant reminder that he was still no clearer on how he was going to broach the matter of her seeking medical help. A feeling of near-relief came when he saw her car wasn't in the garage. As usual, she'd left the garage door open. When he'd told her that even in this secluded suburb there was always the risk of an opportunist thief, she'd yelled that they should live in a safer area. From that had once more sprung a litany of familiar accusations on an abiding theme of hers: that he had never looked after her properly.

He went through the garage into the kitchen. Only the faint hum of the fridge disturbed the silence. He knew it would be filled with the fast foods she'd become addicted to. Apart from the microwave, she hardly used the range of expensive equipment she'd insisted on buying.

Walking from the kitchen, he saw lights burning in every room. Bron had never learned about economy. She'd said leaving the lights on when she went out was the only way to make the place bearable enough to return to. When he'd gently reminded her that she had chosen the furnishings which had eaten deep into his savings, she had rounded on him furiously. What did he expect her to do — pay for everything herself? Or, now that she wasn't working, did she have to account to him for every penny? Most women, she'd railed, had a clothes allowance: they could entertain, live their own lives, take their own vacations, go on regular shopping sprees. But not her! She was totally dependent on him. And what kind of life did she have . . . had he given her? Dumped her in this suburb where she knew nobody. And didn't want to know them! *He* came and went at all hours. He had *his* life. But what did *she* have? Nothing! Not a damned thing! Morning, noon and night: all were the same bloody boring routine.

Suddenly she'd burst into tears and he'd held her in

his arms, telling her he would do anything to help, and she'd cried and shaken until finally she'd stopped crying, only occasional residual sobs making her body shiver involuntarily. He'd made her herb tea and helped her into bed. She'd slept for a full twelve hours and, when she'd awoken, she'd never mentioned what had happened. But the lights had remained burning brightly throughout the house.

Entering the dining area, he paused as he often did to study the portrait hanging over the mock fireplace. The artist had understood that the sum of Bron was greater than her parts: that she had good, wide-set eyes but her nose and chin were too angular; that her hair was a shade of blonde which somehow did not immediately flatter her face, and yet the colour seemed to catch her personality. With his brush strokes, the artist had conveyed her vivaciousness, and just a hint of lust. For the sitting she had chosen a dress made from Indian prayer-shawls and round her neck she wore a heavy piece of tangled, tortured metal, a product of a jewellery-making period when she had not been acting.

Early in their marriage she'd told him the portrait had been commissioned by a former lover. The knowledge somehow made him feel even closer to her and he'd loved her more than he'd imagined he could love anyone. The painting, he'd told himself, bound them together, and was a visible reminder that whatever had occurred in her past, he was immensely fortunate in being chosen by her as a husband. Then one day she had accused him of being jealous of the portrait.

They had finished an almost silent dinner and she'd gone to the kitchen to fetch coffee. Returning, she found him studying the portrait.

'Why do you keep looking at it, Ed?'

He turned and smiled at her. 'I see something new every time.'

She dumped the cups on the coffee table and stood directly in front of him. The storm signals were back in her eyes. 'I'll tell you what you see, Ed. You see me as I used to be. Happy! And you can't stand that, Ed. You bloody well can't stand it, then!'

'You're wrong there, Bron. But I'm sorry you are unhappy again. If only you'd talk about it . . .'

'What's there to talk about, then?' She turned to the portrait. 'Look at me there. Full of life. That was when I had a life.' She glanced around the room. 'Now I'm a bloody domestic in some backwater! That's what I've become. An unpaid duster and polisher. You think any woman would be happy with that, Ed? Then think again! I hate this life. I hate this country. I hate what I've become. Every minute of it!'

Bron ran from the room. Upstairs he heard the bedroom door slam. He knew better than to follow her. Instead he sat in his armchair beside the fireplace and thought about what she had said. She'd refused to employ a maid, insisting she could not trust one. She had refused to join any of the base social clubs, saying they would bore her to tears, and she had refused to return to acting on the grounds she would not lower her standards to the level of local TV. Everything he suggested she had rejected.

He glanced at the portrait. She was right. She did look different there. But she was wrong about his reaction to the painting. He certainly wasn't jealous of it – or, for that matter, of her past. He had never been someone who believed it was necessary to exorcise previous lovers; neither had he been plagued by those dark, destroying thoughts that some people carry with them from adolescence to the grave. He loved her. That was all that mattered.

That night he lay in bed, unable to sleep. Beside him Bron snored lightly. Finally he drifted off, still at a loss as to what he could do to change things.

Some time before dawn he woke to find her staring off into the dark bedroom.

'What a funny pair we are,' she said quietly.

'Why funny?'

'Don't you think we're funny? I went to sleep hating you. Now I feel quite different.'

She reached for his hand, sliding her fingers across his palm and folding them into his. His body responded, remembering past pleasures, the feel of her skin against his, the taste of her lips.

'I can't help the way I am,' she said.

'Can't you?'

She gave him a defensive look. 'It's just that sometimes I feel like I'm being driven into a corner . . . then I feel trapped.'

'I don't want you to feel trapped.'

Quick as a stage actress, her voice conveyed a mystified hurt. 'Why do you bring out these feelings in me then, Ed?'

He felt the numb helpless feeling come over him again. He could think of nothing to say.

'I never was like this, you know.' Her voice became accusatory. 'I used to really enjoy my life. Don't you want me to do that again, Ed? Be happy?'

'Of course I do, Bron.' He put his arm round her shoulder and held her close.

She glanced sideways at him. 'You always think I'm trying to manipulate you, don't you? Wear you down. That's what you think, don't you, then?'

He smiled at her. 'Sometimes it seems like that.'

Her eyes narrowed. 'There's a name for that, Ed. Paranoia.'

'I don't think I'm paranoic, Bron.'

She was watching him with an odd, superior smile. 'Do you think I am, then?'

'Of course not.' He gently kissed her forehead. 'I just wish we didn't always quarrel.'

She was silent for a moment. 'But you always start it, Ed.'

'I don't mean to.'

She shook her head. 'But you do. That's the whole thing. You do. If you didn't, I'd not get angry.'

It was a familiar moment, he knew, where Bron promised peace in return for his surrender. He looked at his bedside clock. It was time to get up. He had a proving flight that morning to worry about, he reminded himself.

'Can we talk about this tonight, Bron? We'll have dinner at that Italian bistro you liked last time. I'll book a booth and we'll be able to talk without interruption. That will be good.'

She moved away from him. 'You're always putting things on the back burner. I tell you what you can do to make me happy and you move away!' Her voice was suddenly louder. 'Well, two can play at that!'

'Please, Bron, let's not start again . . .'

'Off you go to that bloody airplane of yours!' She pushed him towards the edge of the bed with surprising force.

He stood for a moment looking down at her. 'I love you, Bron.'

She had ignored him and turned on the TV.

Now he realised he hadn't understood her or himself very well, understood then that the drives and impulses bubbling inside her were as complex as his own total inability to cope with them. Knowing did not make them any easier to deal with.

The nagging pain continued to torment him as he turned away from the portrait and walked across the living room to the den.

He stood in the doorway, part of him still seeing the room as it had been: the walls of books, the desk over by the window and the couch from which he half-watched the sport on the TV in the corner. Then the evidence of the madness which had gripped her took over.

The den looked like the aftermath of a catastrophe.

Everything that could be upended had been: books swept away from their shelves, photographs tipped from the walls, his collection of albums and CDs scattered over the carpet, the TV toppled off its stand. Seeing what she had done was like peeking into some dark secret corner of her mind. And in this moment he realised he would never be able to understand her, only that he was truly frightened of her: afraid of her fury and distorted feelings, afraid of the darkest, deepest levels of her mind which had allowed her to do this.

He picked his way over the floor to the desk. She had swept everything from its surface: his computer, a brass clock he'd bought in Rio to commemorate his first flight as aircraft commander, a jar of sweets he liked to chew when writing, a bowl filled with paperclips, a tray for bills; Bron had swept them all on to the floor.

She'd forced the desk lock with a paper-knife and rifled the draws, trying to find something that did not exist, the evidence that he was having an affair. All she'd found was the address book listing those high-security numbers, including the one for the President's console on Air Force One. He kept the book at the back of the bottom drawer. It wasn't there. He checked the floor. She hadn't thrown it out. He leaned against the desk, the stabbing feeling in his stomach like a raw wound. Supposing she had taken the book so that she could check out the other numbers? That would produce a security panic which would bring an end to his career. With those few phone calls she could ground him.

The pain in his stomach was like a knife being twisted. He closed his eyes, taking short, sharp breaths. Gradually the vicious stabbing became more bearable. And with the easing of the pain came something else; the realisation that the anger he had repressed for so long about her behaviour had finally taken full hold of him and, even if he could push it away, he felt no desire to do so.

He turned from the desk, this time not bothering to sidestep the debris on the floor as he walked from the den.

Upstairs, lights burned in the bedrooms, even in the spare one Bron used for storage. Nothing seemed to have been touched since he had last looked in there; everything was labelled in cardboard boxes as if Bron was waiting for the removers.

Their bedroom appeared, as usual, as if no one slept in it. Bron insisted all their personal items must be kept in drawers or cupboards, so he was mildly surprised to see the book he had just finished reading, a biography of F. Scott Fitzgerald, still on his bedside table.

Like him, Fitzgerald had also endured a tortuous, complicated relationship with his wife. Yet, according to his biographer, Fitzgerald actually helped to destroy his wife by subtly undermining her worth. Had he, even unwittingly, done that to Bron? Ultimately Fitzgerald had abandoned his wife and yet remained haunted by her, still looking for what she once symbolised to him: mystery and glamour and love. Was he like Fitzgerald? Certainly the idea of mental illness terrified them both.

Fitzgerald had worked out his fear by writing *Tender is the Night*, turning himself into a psychiatrist in the novel who took care of his fictionalised wife, Nicole, helping her to regain her sanity. Then, in a final bitter-sweet twist, Fitzgerald had arranged for Nicole to have an affair with another man – enabling him finally to cut himself free from her.

Yet for him, the thought of letting Bron go was unthinkable. Despite the feelings of anger she had un-leashed in him, he still loved her truly and deeply. When she came home he would try to make her understand that, while what she had done was very very wrong, he still wanted to help her. Then he would introduce her need to see a doctor.

Feeling more resolved and his anger abating, he undressed and walked into the bathroom and showered. He put on a clean uniform and bundled up his soiled clothes for the base laundry.

Halfway down the stairs he heard the doorbell chime. Bron must have forgotten her key. He dumped the laundry in the hall and opened the door.

Helen Curtis stood there. 'Ed, I'm sorry to bust in on you like this,' she began.

He felt suddenly confused. Why was she holding the address book Bron had taken?

'Where did you get this?' he asked, his eyes suddenly alert.

'Can I come in?' Patterson's gaze was level, unfathomable.

'Did Bron give this to you?' He reached out and took the book from her hand, then turned and led the way into the house.

Helen carefully closed the door behind them and, for a moment, they stood silently facing each other in the hall.

'Would you like some coffee?' he asked.

She thought he was like someone not wanting to hear bad news. 'Maybe later,' she said. 'I need to talk to you about Bron.'

He felt a small surge of anger. 'What about her? I thought we'd agreed that was off-limits.'

'She's in hospital.'

For the first time Helen saw the panic in his face as he made his mental calculations.

'What? What the hell are you talking about? Has Bron been in an accident?' The words came in a rush, the questions edgy, guarded.

'Not exactly.' Helen's voice and gaze were steady now.

His eyes narrowed. 'Then what exactly?' His voice held a hint of pain.

For a moment Helen was silent. When she spoke, her words seemed to Patterson like a link between one part of Bron's life and another.

'Bron's tried to kill herself.'

Morton put aside the last of the crew files. He had read non-stop for several hours and his concentration had been total. Nothing had caught his eye. Bill had been right: every member of the presidential flight lived up to the 89th's motto: *Expecto Credo* – Trust One Who Has Experience.

Their backgrounds had all been probed by the FBI; each agent's report counter-signed by another who had checked it out.

He'd been mildly surprised to see that Patterson had married again only quite recently, he had the homely look of a man well into wedlock.

As an actress his second wife had, by all accounts, been going nowhere in her profession. The FBI's London office had discovered that, as a teenager, following the death of her mother, Bronwen Jones was hospitalised for a short while for depression. There had been no recurrence of her illness. Her life before marrying Patterson had followed a not unexpected path; several affairs which, with one exception, had been short-lived. The exception had been her year-long relationship with Harvey Cameron, the English industrialist, who was the first to back Bostock in forming his United Party. Cameron had signalled the end of the affair the way he always did – giving the future Mrs Patterson a portrait of herself. A month later she had met Patterson. According to the FBI, they lived a quiet life away from the base. There was no evidence of drinking, debts or any other problems. He seemed to live for flying and was popular with his men. She seemed to have adjusted to being a Service wife.

Morton flicked back through Patterson's file to the medical section. The man was in his forty-first year and, according to his last medical report, still in prime physical and mental condition. That nose-bleed could have happened to anyone.

As he closed the file, Gates stuck his head around the door. 'I've just had Bob Stanway on the phone, David. One of his sensors on the Iraq–Iran border has picked up something interesting. Stanway's having it put up on my screen.'

Gates' office was large and airy and three of its walls were covered with maps. The fourth was a window offering an unbroken view of the Washington skyline. A modem's screen was glowing.

'Here we go,' Gates murmured, pressing a button on the keyboard. On screen came a wavy line. 'It's the print-out of the bang which initially alerted the sensor, David. The sound is the level of a gunshot. But the sensor decided it didn't match any of the shots it's trained to recognise. So it signalled a sat to train its cameras on the area during its next orbit. The sat's nothing like as good as a Halo for resolution.'

Gates paused, his eyes still on the screen. 'But what it snapped was . . . this.'

Morton watched as, on screen, appeared an image of a cluster of what looked like inflated condoms. Suspended from them was a cylinder.

'The bang the sensor heard was one of the balloons bursting,' Gates said.

Morton leaned towards the screen, then straightened. 'It's a bomb,' he said.

'That's pretty good,' Gates remarked. 'But not any old bomb, Stanway says.'

Morton glanced quickly at Gates before turning back to the screen.

'When the camera recognised the shape as a potential weapon, David, it automatically alerted the sat's on-board computer. On its next pass, the sat sent down an electronic probe and came up with these.'

Gates pointed to the screen. Beneath the cluster-bomb image appeared a line of spiky lines, similar to those emitted by a heart-beat monitor.

'What are they?' Morton asked.

Gates gave a thin smile. 'Radioactive traces. They're coming from inside the casing, specifically from the tail section.'

They both stood silent for a moment, staring at the screen.

'Where you'd expect to find a nuclear trigger,' Morton said.

'But it's a long way from Norfolk, England, David.'

Morton gave Gates another swift look.

'Stanway's analysts had quite a job separating these traces from the emissions of an electrical storm, David. They only managed to because the bomb passed directly through the sat's footprint. If it hadn't, there would have been no way for the traces to be identified. Right now it's the season over there for those storms, so it's a perfect time for Bodor to launch his bomb.'

Morton turned back to the screen. 'When was this recorded, Bill?'

'In real time, about forty minutes ago. It would be dawn over there. The sun's heat could have exploded the balloon . . .'

'That sensor. Which side of the border is it on?'

'The Iranian side. It's actually about a mile inside,' Gates replied.

'How high was that balloon when the sensor picked up the bang?' Morton asked, a rhythm to his questions.

'A couple of thousand feet.'

'Wind direction?'

'Not known. At this time of year there's a lot of eddying up there.'

Morton peered closely at the screen again, then turned back to Gates. 'That burst balloon appears to be on the rising side of the sun.'

Gates nodded. 'So it could have been launched from just inside the border?'

Morton looked from Gates to the screen. 'Or drifted across from Iraq,' he said in a hollow voice.

Gates looked momentarily chastened, then smiled tightly. 'Stanway's people anticipated you there, David. They had their sat check ten miles back inside the Iraqi border. They didn't find even a tyre-mark to point to a launch vehicle.'

'And on the Iranian side?' Morton asked.

'Have a look.' Gates pressed a key. The image on screen changed, to reveal what appeared to be criss-crossing scars.

'These were filmed a couple of miles down track from where the balloon bomb was spotted. Truck-tracks. The best of heavy duty wheels that Detroit supplies to the mullah's army. My bet is the trucks were there either to launch the bomb or to retrieve it,' Gates said. 'It could be a trial run for the real thing.'

'Did the sat camera track the balloon?'

Gates sounded nettled for a moment. 'No. Stanway says the sat's not programmed for that kind of surveillance. It's not like a Halo.'

Morton's face showed nothing.

'The last shot we have is this,' Gates continued, pressing a key.

On screen the balloons could be seen in the upper right-hand corner, already halfway out of the frame.

'Now you see them,' Gates murmured, touching another key, 'now you don't.' The image had vanished from the screen.

Morton turned from the modem. 'How far is that last sighting from the first one?'

'Stanway's programmers estimate about five miles.'

Morton reflected. 'How do they repair the sensor if it goes on the blink?'

Gates shrugged. 'That area's pretty remote. So they simply drop a replacement by parachute from a high-flying aircraft.'

Morton looked at the maps. 'How far's that sensor from Baku, Bill?'

'You thinking of Anna and Tommy?' Gates sounded faintly disappointed, as if that were a problem. 'By plane? A couple of hours. Except there's no way for them to fly there. By road it would take them three, four days, depending on the weather, and if they could find their way through the mountains.'

Morton walked over to the desk, picked up a phone and dialled. When he was connected, he told Chantal what he wanted.

As he spoke, Gates looked at him startled.

The President waited while the butler circulated through the magnificent drawing room overlooking the White House gardens. He had brought the six leaders of the industrialised nations here after dinner, during which he had delivered his speech about what America would do to implement Operation Earth Saver. As far as he could judge, the speech was well received. But now, in the more informal after-dinner atmosphere, he wanted to reinforce other truths.

Several of the men were standing at the windows looking out across the White House gardens, where the sprinkler system was cascading water through the floodlights.

The President joined Silvio Briscini, the Italian Prime Minister. 'Now you know how we keep our lawns so green, Silvio,' the President said, taking his cup from the salver the butler offered. 'But it's ironic to think that over seventy per cent of the world's population is actually threatened by water. They live on coastal plains and are increasingly in danger from rising sea levels.'

Others had drifted over: Bill McKenzie, Canada's new Premier, a big, honest-looking man; President Marceau of France who wore his clothes like the regalia of royalty; and Pedro Esplana, the window reflection showing the impeccable cut of his suit. They, too, listened attentively as the President continued.

'The other great irony is that the rest of the world faces a threat from drought. It's spreading out of Africa and India into the Middle East and southern Europe.'

'El Niño,' murmured Esplana.

The President nodded. 'Right. The El Niño effect is not new. But its pattern is. A few years ago we would see it appear every few years, when there were unusually warm conditions in the eastern Pacific. But now the effect is spreading and becoming more intense.'

'We have it in Italy already,' Briscini said, his voice sombre. 'We have the worst crop losses in memory.'

'France too,' Marceau added. 'We are doing our best to cope. But what can anybody do against nature?'

'Don't be so defeatist, Pierre,' the President said gently.

'If we don't all do something now, it will certainly be too late. And the longer we delay, the more extreme our action will have to be.'

'What kind of action do you anticipate?' asked Arnold Bostock, who had joined the group.

'I think we need to see the whole global picture for ourselves before we decide,' suggested the President. He didn't want to get side-tracked into one area.

'As you know, our first stop is Australia,' he continued as Chancellor Sturmer came over. 'Right now that country has its worst losses from forest fires in its history. It's the same in my own state of California. And in your country too, Bill,' the President said, turning to McKenzie. 'And in a dozen other countries, from Siberia to Zimbabwe.'

He turned and led them over to armchairs. When they had settled, the butler refilled their cups and left the room.

After he closed the door, the President resumed. 'At the same time we are facing another threat: ice melt. Glaciers are literally melting almost everywhere in the world at an unprecedented rate. In the sub-Arctic the sea-ice is disappearing at a hundred square kilometres a month. In the Alaskan Arctic the tundra has become a prime source for carbon dioxide entering the atmosphere. This is because of abnormal warming.'

He paused, giving time for his words to sink in. The reflection from the artificial coals in the fireplace was cosy, casting a glow over the well-fed faces.

'We all live in countries where diseases such as malaria, tuberculosis and leprosy have long been a thing of the past. But, in the case of my own country, they're not. Increases in temperature are creating ideal mosquito-breeding conditions that have seen a return of those diseases.'

He paused and looked at Bostock. 'One of your

predecessors said that global warming could lead to a substantial increase in brown rat populations after recent mild winters.'

'We're doing something about that. There's a whole new range of poisons being used,' Bostock said quickly.

'The problem with those poisons, Arnold, is that they will simply spread the very toxic effects we need to eliminate.'

The President looked around the seated men. 'But Arnold is right in one respect. Action *must* be taken. We *must* provide the political leadership that will promote energy efficiency and conservation measures. We *must* use less energy. We *must* find more renewable energy. We *must* no longer favour policies which only intensify the problems of climatic changes. We *must* find alternative options to reduce our addictive reliance on fossil fuels. We *must* find new mass transport systems that are far less polluting. And we *must* keep all this before us as we go forth on this historic mission. We *must* never forget we have the capacity – the power – to change things.'

TWENTY-SEVEN

Helen's words were like a tattoo hammering in Patterson's head as he drove behind her through the streets of Washington. It was now a full hour since she had told him Bron had taken an overdose of tranquillisers. In a calm, factual voice she had described how Bron had sat in the movie theatre for a couple of hours before one of the staff realised there was something wrong. By the time an ambulance arrived, she was already unconscious. At Memorial Hospital one of the doctors had searched her bag, trying to find an ID.

'He found your address book, recognised your name and called me,' Helen said. 'We'd been students together and keep in touch. I stopped by Memorial on the way over here. He'd just washed out Bron's stomach.'

Patterson felt her words were coming from across some blurred chasm as he sat slumped in his armchair, listening to her explain how she had retrieved the address book, knowing it was a sensitive document, and then driven out to see him. He had watched her face. 'Why?' he asked softly. 'Why did Bron do this? Just tell me that much.'

'What made Bron do this is for later, Ed.' She'd spoken with a cool precision, clinical, but not unpleasant. 'Are you okay?'

He nodded.

'To fly?' Her eyes and voice were cautious.

'Of course.' He gave the perfunctory smile of someone who appreciated there could have been a problem.

'Sometimes,' he added quietly, 'work's the best place to go.' He felt she was trying to read his mind.

'All right.'

'I assume as you are not here officially, that you don't have to report this, Helen?'

She expelled a short breath. 'The way I see it, my responsibility doesn't extend to dependants. No, I shan't report this.'

'Thank you.' He felt more tension easing from him than he had known was there.

In the silence he'd gathered his thoughts. 'What about the hospital ... I wouldn't want this to get out ...' His voice trailed off.

'Memorial's good at keeping everything low key. They know who she is, of course, and who you are. But I've told my doctor friend to batten down the hatches.'

For a moment Patterson was silent, then he sat straighter, looking her in the face. 'You're building up quite a stack of favours I owe you.' He paused, then asked softly, 'Is Bron going to be okay?' Once more the words seemed to take him inwards.

Reflectively, Helen glanced at Bron's portrait before answering. 'Let's just hope that stomach wash was in time.'

Patterson seemed to swallow, then stood up. 'Let's go and see her.'

Helen's voice was still clear and cool. 'I suggest you change out of uniform. Those wings and badges are pretty distinctive. No point in attracting attention.'

He glanced at her uniform. She still wore her surgeon-commander's rig.

'I have a doctor's coat in my car,' she'd explained quickly. 'And they're used to seeing Bethesda people over at Memorial.'

He'd gone upstairs and changed into sports jacket and slacks and transferred his uniform to a hanger, which he'd take with him. When he returned she'd once more searched his face.

'You okay to drive?' she'd asked.

'I'm fine.'

Helen led the way out of the house. Before leaving, he turned off the lights.

Now, forty minutes later, as he followed her tail lights, his hands were shaking so badly he could barely hold the steering wheel. He still couldn't fully comprehend what Bron had done.

Attempting suicide was as alien to him as some of the customs in countries to which he'd flown. Why had she tried to kill herself? How had she obtained those tablets? How long had she been taking them? Had she obtained them from a doctor? But which doctor? Officially, she was supposed to attend the base medical officer. For a moment he felt tempted to speak to him, but that could only provoke dangerous questions. And, if Bron was attending a doctor, it wouldn't be an air force one. Yet if she hadn't gone to a doctor, how had she obtained the tablets? The thought of Bron scouring the streets of Washington like a junkie in search of a fix was even more impossible to grasp. He felt himself losing ground, asking questions he could not even begin to answer.

Wearing her doctor's coat, Helen led the way from Memorial's parking lot into the emergency area. It was filled with people, each intent on his own misery, seated on plastic bucket seats clamped to the floor. The last time he'd seen so many injured had been in Bosnia.

'Welcome to hell,' Helen murmured. 'Working here's a little like trying to direct traffic without ever knowing when the rush hour is about to start.'

He followed her past treatment cubicles and side-stepped a man handcuffed to a stretcher being guarded by two policemen.

From the ceiling intercom came a sudden urgent voice: 'Dr White to ER Four.' The voice continued to repeat the message. A moment later they flattened themselves against a wall as, pushing a red-painted trolley down the corridor, came a stampede of nurses and doctors. After they had passed, Helen explained that Dr White was Memorial's code for Acute Traumatic Resuscitation. The trolley contained the means to deal with a heart attack. Patterson glanced over his shoulder to see the group disappear into a cubicle.

Passing an open door marked 'Paramedics', he paused. Inside the room were several ambulance crews on a meal break.

'I'd like to thank them for what they did, Helen,' Patterson said.

Helen hesitated, then stuck her head into the room. 'Which of you guys brought in that case from the movie house?' she asked.

A paramedic looked up from the remains of a burger. 'Who wants to know?'

'I'm Dr Curtis.' She indicated Patterson. 'And this is the patient's husband.'

The paramedic frowned. 'He wants medical details, he should check with the station.'

The room had fallen silent.

'I just wanted to thank you,' Patterson said.

The paramedic looked surprised. 'Thanks.' He gave a small shrug and turned back to his food.

'You're probably the first person who's ever thanked him,' Helen said as they passed a suture room where a man was almost lost to view behind a scrum of white-coated figures. In the next room a doctor was bending over a woman. Checking her name on his chart, he began to shout, 'Mary! Wake up, Mary!'

Patterson could still hear his call as they reached the nurses' station. It was staffed by a fat, silver-haired nurse. She looked up from a file. 'Yes?'

'Where's Dr Monroe?' Helen asked.

'And you are Doctor . . .?'

'Curtis, from Bethesda. I was here a couple of hours ago.'

The nurse sighed. 'Not my shift.' She picked up a phone and dialled. Moments later a slim, red-haired man in a white coat came striding down the corridor.

Helen introduced Dr Monroe to Patterson. 'Can I see my wife?' Patterson asked.

Dr Monroe hesitated. 'Sure. But I'd like to talk to you first.'

He led the way into an office behind the nurses' station. There was barely room for them in the glass-walled cubicle.

Dr Monroe folded his arms and looked intently at Patterson. 'Have you any idea why she did this, Colonel?'

'I suppose everything just built up.'

Monroe gave him a long speculative gaze. 'Does she have a doctor I can call?'

'Not that I know of.' Patterson paused. 'But I was trying to get her to see a psychiatrist.'

There was a slight change in Monroe's eyes. 'What sort of problem was your wife having that made you decide on that course of action, Colonel?'

'Nothing that would lead her to take her life. She wasn't happy . . . about a lot of things. Mostly her life.'

'Any special aspect?'

For a long moment Patterson simply stared at Monroe.

'My work,' he said finally. 'She hates me flying. She says it takes me away too much.'

'Anything else?' Monroe asked. 'Usually there's a bundle of reasons why someone does what your wife did.'

Patterson began to feel a wordless second conversation beneath the probing.

Helen turned to the doctor. 'Brian, I don't think this is necessary just now,' she said firmly.

Monroe nodded. 'You're probably right. The long term is going to be somebody else's problem.' He turned to Patterson. 'I can recommend a private place, if that'd be any help.'

Patterson felt something shudder inside him. The thought that Bron would have to spend some time in hospital had never occurred to him. 'Thanks. Can I see her now?' he asked.

'She's still in a coma.' Monroe's voice was gentle now.

Patterson could not shake the sense of unreality; increasingly he seemed to have entered a world utterly alien to him. 'What does that mean?'

Monroe laughed quickly. 'Good question, Colonel. Coma's basically a state of deep unconsciousness. In a way it can be a help. Because of the sudden discharge of toxins into your wife's system, her body defences have decided that the best way to deal with those poisons is to shut off her conscious awareness of the world. That way her defences can devote their whole attention to healing.'

'How long will her coma last?' Patterson asked.

Monroe glanced through the glass. The nurse was absorbed in her paperwork. He turned back to Patterson. 'Some people remain in a coma for years. But I'm optimistic that in your wife's case she will come out of it fairly soon. Her kidneys are doing a good job of eliminating those toxins.'

Patterson looked at him: the slender frame, the curly hair, the confident air. 'Could her kidneys fail?'

The doctor gave an apologetic shrug. 'There's always that possibility, Colonel. It's a bit like engine failure in your business.'

Patterson glanced over at Helen. 'I can still fly on half-power,' he said.

Monroe gave another little laugh. 'Same with your wife. She can still function on one kidney.'

'What about an artificial kidney machine?' Patterson asked.

'We don't have one. The nearest is up at Bethesda.'

'Then let's move her up there.' Patterson spoke decisively.

'That's not a good idea, Ed,' Helen said. 'There's probably more risk in doing that than in letting Bron's system fight for itself.'

'Your wife's physically strong, Colonel,' Monroe explained. 'If it came to the crunch, I'd pull out all the tubes and let her fight off the poisons without any help. That's what happened in the old days.'

Helen looked at Patterson. 'It's true, Ed. The first thing they teach you at med school is that the body is a great self-healer.'

Patterson turned back to Monroe. 'When she wakes up . . . what will she be like?'

The doctor breathed out slowly. 'You mean, will there be permanent damage? Physically, she should make a complete recovery. But mentally, I can't say. She took an enormous number of pills. To do that she'd have to be very determined to kill herself. Determination can be a good thing, but in a situation like this it can also be a highly destructive force. Only time will tell if your wife's determination can be re-focused.' He ran his fingers through his hair. Behind him, the nurse was talking on the phone. 'Let's go and see your wife.' He led the way up the corridor to Bron's room.

'We'll wait here,' Helen said, motioning for Patterson to enter.

Standing in the door, all he could see was the mass of wires, tubes and equipment surrounding Bron's bed. She lay flat, the front of her dress stained with blood and mucus. She looked rigid and strangely unreal, her face a death-mask image of his wife. He felt overcome by a terrible sense of sadness. Why had she done this? How could she hate herself so much? Or had she done this because she hated him?

As he walked towards the bed, she stirred, turning her face towards him, though her eyes remained closed. He reached out his hand to touch her, then stopped in mid-air.

'Let her know you're here,' Monroe called from the doorway. 'That's important.'

Reaching down, he ran a finger gently through the hair matted against her forehead, then bent closer to her face. 'Bron, it's me.'

There was no response. He turned and looked questioningly at Dr Monroe and Helen.

'Keep trying, Ed,' Helen urged.

He didn't know how long he stood there, trying to coax a response from Bron without success. Finally he turned away, defeated.

'You can try again later, Colonel,' Monroe said, the disappointment in his voice plain.

As they stepped back into the corridor, the nurse at the station was holding up the phone towards them. 'Dr Curtis, call for you.'

She'd left her name with the hospital switchboard and

also told the duty officer at Andrews where she'd be. She took the phone, listened for a moment, then beckoned to Patterson.

'It's the Man's switchboard,' she said quietly. 'They've been calling you at home and on your car phone. When they couldn't raise you, they started calling the crew to see if someone knew where you were.'

Patterson took the phone from her and identified himself.

'Hold for Mr Stimpson, Colonel,' said the White House operator.

A moment later the Chief of Staff came on the line. 'Colonel, is this a secure line?'

'Yes, sir.'

There was a momentary pause. 'Okay. This is to tell you to prepare to roll at Zulu, 0800 hours.'

'Understood, sir.'

After Stimpson had hung up, Patterson looked at his watch. He had ten hours left to try and rouse Bron from her coma before Air Force One took off.

In the past hour, a map of the Persian Gulf region on Gates' office wall had been regularly added to by Morton each time he received a telephone call. They came from Danny who was using a secure satellite link from the US Air Force base deep in the Nafud, one of Saudi Arabia's three vast deserts. Danny had been flown there from Amsterdam in a NATO supersonic bomber. During the time he had been in the air, Chantal had carried out the instructions Morton had given her.

Since dusk a relay of Stealth bombers had flown northwards from the base into Iraq. At regular intervals each aircraft had released a cluster of fuel drums attached to parachutes. The containers, like the chutes, were made from materials impossible for radar to detect. Suspended from a line beneath each batch was a barrel-shaped device which, upon impact, expanded into a high-speed battery-operated rotor drill known as a mole, which dug a hole. When its work was completed, the mole wound in the line and pulled the sand down over the drums and itself. Only if someone stumbled directly upon a cache could it be discovered. Attached to each mole was an electronic device designed to home in on a matching signal from the air.

Morton had marked each drop-point with a red flag on the map. A line of them now extended across hundreds of miles of desert before crossing the highway which linked the Gulf port town of Bazra with Baghdad. Avoiding the marshlands, the line gently curved to follow, and then cross, the course of the Euphrates, before heading north towards the Dead Mountains of Iran.

Once more the phone rang.

'They've just dropped five miles south of Ground Zero,' Danny reported.

Ground Zero was the name Morton had given to the area where the balloon bomb had disappeared inside the Iranian border.

'What's the status of Anna and Tommy?' Morton asked.

'They landed at Kuwait International forty minutes ago. They should with me inside the hour, David.'

Anna and Tommy had flown from Baku to Karachi, and then the dog-leg back to Kuwait on commercial flights.

'Start-up still on schedule?' Morton asked.

'They'll be on their way thirty minutes after touch-down,' Danny confirmed. 'That'll give them a full six hours before sunrise.' He hung up.

Morton pinned a flag on Ground Zero. For a long time he studied the map, then pulled from his pocket the message the Swiss embassy in Tehran had sent about

Adams. 'Bill,' he called over his shoulder. 'Take a look at this.'

Gates watched as Morton held a copy of the sheet of paper found on Adams' body up against the map, close to Ground Zero. Morton then moved the paper slowly northwards. Close to the foothills of the Dead Mountains he stopped.

'Well, I'll be damned . . .' Gates said.

The mystery of the map reference Adams had scrawled on the paper had been solved. It matched the area around the foothills.

'Adams was trying to tell us that Bodor and the Marcello woman are in there somewhere,' Gates said. 'They must have come down from those mountains, tested their bomb and then disappeared back into hiding.'

Morton said nothing as he continued to study the map.

Ignatius Bailey watched his butler serve the brandies, going first to Elliott Forde, then to Samuel Keller, before pouring another identical measure for Ronald Sterling. Moving with the same gravity, the butler completed the post-dinner ritual by offering each guest a cigar from an antique humidor, expertly snipping the tip with a silver cutter and striking a fresh match each time to light the cigars.

They had spent the earlier part of the evening discussing what to do about Carlo Marcello. He was still working with old assumptions. He still behaved as if he were *running* an organisation, not *part* of one, increasingly refusing to accept that the criteria for all decisions were now decided elsewhere. Above all, he seemed utterly unable to understand that an organisation which talks together, grows together. Marcello opted for monologues which always ended with the reminder that his profits were up. He didn't seem to understand that more was needed.

All three had been careful not to suggest what should be done; they all knew it had been Bailey's own decision to absorb Marcello into Meridian. Bailey had given no indication what action should be taken. They also knew that was his way at this stage.

The butler glanced questioningly at Bailey, who quickly moved his hand over the top of the half-filled glass on the side table; he'd had his fill of iced tea during dinner.

During the meal he had been called away to a pre-arranged telephone call. His caller had confirmed that the Halo satellite over Baghdad had developed a computer malfunction halfway on its track eastwards to Tehran. NSA estimated it would take forty-eight hours to repair the fault. The brief call had been made from a Washington pay-phone to an automatic switchboard in San Francisco, which rerouted it to Bailey. He had then made two calls, one to activate a taped message which closed down the switchboard, the other authorising a further $250,000 to be transferred to his caller's bank account in the Cayman Islands. He had returned to the dinner table in time to join the others as the butler served the dessert.

Now, with a slight nod which somehow embraced all four tuxedo-suited men, the butler padded towards the door, closing it behind him.

Allowing the others to enjoy the taste of fine cognac and tobacco, Bailey walked to one of the windows which provided an unbroken view across the wheatplains of Meridian. It was one of the reasons he had chosen this site for his mansion; he never wanted to be more than a glance away from all he had created. He had invited the others to dinner because he wanted them to hear how well he would continue to protect those interests.

He glanced at the clock to the right of the window:

there were still five minutes to go before he received his next report. Like the other furnishings, the longcase clock spoke of great taste, selectivity and expense. The hidden costs of protecting the library from eavesdroppers were even greater. Behind the silk wallpaper were sheets of lead which, together with a sub-floor of titanium chippings, provided the most effective barrier against even the most sophisticated listening probes. The library's defences were completed by electronic sensors on each window able to detect and deflect any bugging device.

Behind Bailey, the others had returned to a topic raised over dinner.

'I still think it was a little risky paying off that Kurd in dollars,' Keller said. 'That amount of hard currency could attract attention in a place like Baku.'

Sterling sighed. 'Nowadays dollars are all that those people will accept.'

'The Kurd was expensive,' Forde remarked.

'Not if you consider that he took care of both Adams and that whorehouse madam,' Sterling replied.

In the window reflection Bailey saw Forde's face become momentarily obscured behind a haze of cigar smoke.

Sterling sipped brandy before continuing. 'Anyway, the Kurd's fee is really academic. The Arranger made sure he's gone to wherever Kurds go to in their appointed place in the sky.'

'The usual precautions were taken, I assume?' Keller asked.

'Of course,' Sterling said, mildly irritated. 'In both cases, their hands were tied behind their backs and they were each killed with a bullet fired into the base of their skulls. The classic Chinese way. There was just enough evidence left on their bodies to make it clear the Kurd and the woman had been playing footsie with the North

Koreans. Beijing would never tolerate that.'

Forde nodded and the cigar paused in front of his lips.

They watched Bailey stride to a wall of books with a screen inset. This was linked to one of the five communications satellites Meridian owned and which provided a secure global communications network.

One satellite was now exclusively reserved for the Arranger. Without Bailey having to do anything, the screen began to pulse. The mush of static cleared and the Arranger's face appeared on screen, his coal-black eyes staring out unblinkingly. There was no background to reveal where he was.

Bailey spoke without preamble to the screen. 'Did Bodor or the woman suspect anything?'

The Arranger leaned forward. 'No. As I predicted, they blamed the weather. They had a rough landing anyway and the gondola was knocked about quite a bit, so there would have been no way for them to tell that the securing bolts for the launcher had been weakened.'

The others sensed the pride in the Arranger's voice.

'Your technician did well,' Bailey acknowledged. It had been the Arranger's idea to use the first test flight deliberately to create a diversion without telling Bodor. It would also further help to focus attention on Iran as the launch site.

'Will the gondola be repaired in time?' Bailey asked.

'It's already been up two more times. Bodor's like a dervish, driving everyone . . .'

'Why twice?' Bailey interjected.

On screen there was a momentary hesitation, as if the Arranger were arranging the facts. When he spoke, his voice was expressionless. 'Both tests failed. Each time the bomb reached its detonation height, it did not go off. Bodor is convinced the triggers were faulty.'

Bailey looked at the screen. 'What about the other three?'

The Arranger nodded briskly, as if he appreciated Bailey's directness and would be equally direct. 'He's stripped down two. Both have identical malfunctions . . .'

'Can they be fixed?'

The others could see the muscles of Bailey's jaw continue to constrict.

The Arranger spoke matter-of-factly. 'Not in time. Even if the equipment were flown in today, it would still be too late. Bodor says he'd need a week, maybe longer. But he doesn't want to strip down the last trigger in case it's working perfectly.'

'Is that possible?'

'He says, yes.' The Arranger's voice was still crisp. 'The triggers are very sensitive. If this one is okay, tampering could actually cause it to malfunction. Bodor insists it's best to leave well alone; he wants to save the trigger for the real thing.'

There was silence, almost a full minute without any sound breaking the tension.

'It seems there's no alternative,' Bailey said. His jaw movement had stopped. 'We'll stay with Bodor's plan.'

'The schedule remains as before?' the Arranger asked.

'Yes. The plane will be there in three days.'

The Arranger nodded. 'The forecast is for electrical storms to be rather more frequent than usual at this time of year.'

Bailey's expression had not changed. 'Good. When he launches, make sure Bodor goes up.'

'That won't be a problem. He already doesn't trust the woman.'

Bailey turned away, and the screen went blank. 'It's out of our hands,' he said flatly to the others. 'Except for one thing.'

He walked across to a credenza and picked up a telephone. Moments after he dialled, a voice answered. 'The White House. How may I help you?'

'This is Ignatius Bailey. I need to speak to the President.'

There was a short pause before the operator was back on the line. 'The President's already retired for the night, Mr Bailey.'

'He'll want to hear what I have to say,' Bailey said in a voice which had cowed even the most protective of other people's servants.

'One moment, please,' said the operator.

After another pause there was a click on the line.

'May I ask what this is about, Mr Bailey?' Thacker Stimpson asked curtly.

'Just do as I say, Mr Stimpson. I wouldn't be calling if this wasn't important.'

There was another click on the line, followed by a lengthening silence. Behind Bailey, the others were tense and watchful. Then from across the room came the familiar voice over the telephone, irritation coming through the sleep.

'Mr Bailey, I don't take kindly to being disturbed at this hour. I have an early start – and so would you, if you'd been coming along,' the President said.

'I've decided I'd like to be represented on Air Force One,' Bailey said calmly.

This time the silence was shorter.

'Represented? What exactly does that mean?' demanded the President.

'I'd like to have a senior member of Meridian International join Air Force One at the first available point. In every way he will be representing me.'

In the renewed silence the others leaned forward, living from word to word.

'Where is this person now?' the President asked.

'Australia. He's on vacation.' Bailey sounded almost amused. 'But I'm sure he would be willing to exchange the pleasures of his yacht for the comforts of Air Force One.'

Another silence.

'Australia's at the end of our first leg,' the President finally said. 'Who is this person, Mr Bailey?'

'Carlo Marcello,' Bailey replied.

Walking back to Bron's room from the hospital coffee shop, Patterson tried to think of their good times together, those moments when they had seemed bound to each other for ever. Then the painful memories, each one a signpost on the journey which had brought Bron here, threatened to swamp him. He was glad he was alone. He felt close to tears.

Helen had returned to Andrews. He had called the base to say he would be there by midnight. He knew if there was an emergency, she would know where to reach him.

Entering Bron's room, he found Dr Monroe at her bedside, checking the equipment. The pinging and clicking of the machines was confirmation that all was not lost.

'There's no change,' Monroe said. 'Just keep talking to her. It'll help her strain towards consciousness.'

He turned to Bron. 'Mrs Patterson, your husband is here. If you can hear me, just open your eyes or move your head. Can you do that?'

There was no response.

For a moment they both looked down at Bron, then Monroe left.

'I'm back,' Patterson murmured, his finger barely brushing her cheek, as if he was afraid even such contact would cause her pain. 'It's me,' he whispered, bending his head close to her face. 'Bron, can you hear me?'

Bron gave no response.

He straightened and pulled a chair up to the bed and sat down. Once more he felt his emotions being pulled all ways. He could feel himself trying to create pillars of hope, then just as quickly they tumbled down. He tried to concentrate harder, separating himself from the world outside this room: shutting out the voice on the intercom with its continuous demands and requests, the rush of feet and trolleys, the sudden cries of pain.

'I'll always be here for you, Bron,' he said. 'I want you always to remember that.'

Once more he searched her face, looking for a sign that she'd understood, thinking of the fragile bond between them, wondering how he could use it to reach her.

'Bron, when you're better, we'll go away and sort things out,' he said.

It was like talking to a statue, yet he also knew he was still connected to Bron by that bond, and that he continued to suffer under the pain of his love for her – and his hatred of the poison that drained out of her body through a catheter into a plastic container beneath her bed.

Twice already a nurse had come in and replaced the container with an empty one. Each time she had addressed Bron in a loud voice, saying the same thing. 'Mrs Patterson! We're not going to let you go! You hear that, Mrs Patterson? We want you to help us fight!'

Now, having waited at the bedside studying her watch for what seemed an age, the nurse looked across the bed at Patterson. 'As long as her kidneys and lungs remain clean, there's little more we can do,' she said.

After she had left, he looked down at Bron. With her eyes closed, her breath whistling slowly through her parted lips, she appeared no different from when he'd arrived.

He glanced at his watch: eleven p.m. Even at this time

of night he would still need a full hour to reach the base.

He bent one last time and whispered in her ear, 'Bron, I love you. Truly. Always remember that.'

In the silence the sound of the machines was loud.

He straightened and walked from the room, not looking back, not able to trust himself to do so.

TWENTY-EIGHT

Skimming above the desert, the Apache helicopter crossed the Iraqi border, only a swirl of dust marking its passage through the deep black of the night. Even to a nomad, the dust would appear like another of those eddies which blew across the ground. Coated with the same paint as used on Stealth bombers, the Apache was undetectable to even the most sophisticated of radars.

Nevertheless, Tommy switched to silent mode so that the rotor blades made almost no sound.

From the co-pilot's seat behind him, Anna spoke quickly into her throat mike. 'Five minutes to the next refuelling.'

Tommy acknowledged with a nod of his helmet. From now on intercom conversation would be kept to the minimum.

Frigid air suddenly gushed around Anna. The flapper valve on the heating control was wide open. Using a gloved finger, she poked sand out of the vent to close the valve and the cockpit returned to its comfortable temperature.

Tommy scanned the horizon through his night vision goggles, feeling his adrenalin building nicely. He glanced at the information display unit, positioned to minimise eye movement when manoeuvring against an enemy. A red light was flashing. They were locked in to the homing device attached to the fuel drums.

Once more he swept the ground ahead through the goggles. The head-set's protruding lenses amplified the ambient starlight to give the dark landscape a crepuscular definition. He saw it now: a hazy splotch to his right: the sand dunes behind which the bomber had dropped its cluster of drums. With languid deliberation, Tommy swung the Apache in a lazy turn, dropping almost to the desert floor to mask their destination further.

In her head-set Anna continued monitoring Iraqi radio traffic. Somewhere to the north an anti-aircraft gun battery was reporting to its headquarters that there was no activity in its sector. A moment later the crew of a radar unit radioed similar confirmation. On a screen Anna saw that the unit was somewhere to the south and close to the border with Kuwait.

Tommy counted down, even though the blip on the cockpit video screen indicated to within a few feet the remaining distance to touch-down. On an infrared screen the dunes glowed faintly from the radiation of the sun's heat absorbed the previous day.

Anna's instruments indicated that fuel flow, oil pressure and hydraulics were responding normally. The only sound was the steady mush of electronic noise which would be detected only if they flew directly through a radar cone.

The red light stopped flashing and the Apache landed.

Anna remained on board, ready to use the chopper's heavy armaments should an Iraqi patrol appear. Tommy ran the short distance to the buried drums, guided by a sensor in his hands. When its signal remained constant, he dropped to his knees and began scrabbling in the sand until his hands encountered a plastic pipe. He tugged until several feet appeared, then unscrewed the cap at one end. He put the pipe to his mouth and sucked quickly to break the air bubble inside. Jet fuel spurted into his mouth. He spat it out, then, pulling the pipe behind him, he ran back to the Apache and shoved the pipe into its fuel tank.

Inside the cockpit Anna constantly swept the area with her night vision goggles. Wherever she looked all was flat and lifeless, the only sound the fuel rushing into the tank.

Tommy could see his breath. With his flying suit no longer plugged into the cockpit's heating system, he felt cold. When the tank was full he replaced the cap and fed the pipe back into the sand. In the buried barrels was still sufficient fuel for the return journey.

Moments later the Apache lifted, its downwash creating a small sandstorm. By the time the dust settled, they were heading away from the distant shimmer of the Gulf on their left.

Two figures urged their camels across the river bed that marked the boundary between Iran and Iraq at this point. The water beneath the feet was only a trickle. But soon, with the rain, they knew it would become a torrent which would sweep them both all the way south to the Gulf. Behind them, the rain would be falling as snow over the Dead Mountains.

Alim, the lead man, like his son Sala, wore a coarse cloak held in place by straps across his chest and thighs. Their heads were covered with a sheep's wool *hupta*, the hat which marked them both as members of the Sarami, the oldest of the Islamic Sufi sects, whose fanaticism was equalled by their code of honour that a deal, once made, was honoured, no matter what the personal cost.

Although their clothing offered small protection against the driving rain, to turn back now would be unthinkable. There was a delivery to make and the balance of their handsome fee to collect from the stranger.

Once more Alim turned in his saddle. Though he could hardly see Sala, the boy seemed worse now, his cough more pronounced. At dusk the previous day they had left behind his second son, Heka, who had been unable to continue, again because of his coughing. This developed soon after they had recovered the bomb suspended beneath the balloons which had fallen from the sky more or less where the stranger predicted. They had buried the balloons and secured the bomb to Heka's camel saddle.

He had been angry when Heka, curious as ever, had removed an already damaged plate at the base of the casing, then couldn't replace it. The boy had brought his face close to the opening and peered inside. His coughing started soon afterwards. By dusk blood was dribbling out of his mouth and small blisters had started to appear on his skin. They had promised to collect Heka on the return journey and take him to the *soma*; the sect's doctor would surely have something to treat this strange illness.

For several hours they hid with the animals in a cave, watching the Iranian soldiers searching for the weapon. When they failed and had left in their trucks, Alim had set out on their journey to Iraq, the bomb transferred to Sala's camel.

Their family had travelled this route as smugglers for centuries. But never before had he been asked to smuggle a weapon as unusual as this one. Alim wondered whether that was why the stranger, who had already paid over good money, had promised double when he received the bomb at the agreed point in the Iraqi desert? But the reason did not really concern Alim: a job was a job.

On the Apache's radar, Tommy picked out a metal road along which tiny blips moved. He swore under his breath. Judging by their speed, the blips were army trucks. He put the chopper into hover mode, waiting until the trucks disappeared from the screen. Then at full power he crossed the carriageway, climbing slightly to avoid power lines.

Beyond the road he dropped down until the edges of the rotors were whirling barely above the ground.

They reached the next refuelling point without incident. Ten minutes later they were once more airborne. After two more touchdowns they passed over the first foothills, forcing the Apache to climb.

They had covered five hundred ground miles and away to their left the sky was a rosy tint. Tommy checked the map on his knee. The glow was the Iranian port of Basra. He glanced at the instrument panel: it confirmed they were on track and on time.

Passing well clear of a desert oasis he headed towards the Euphrates, crossed the river without incident and once more landed to refuel. As he headed north, the foothills became higher so that he was able to fly between them through the wadis. After another hour's flying there appeared on the radar, extending the width of the screen, a towering mass: the granite of the Dead Mountains, their jagged peaks rising without symmetry or beauty, as though God had started to form them and then moved on to create something more worthwhile.

At the pre-mission briefing, the US air force intelligence officer had been blunt: the only way to fly beyond the mountains was to climb or take the Cave Route. Tommy had spent almost an hour on the phone to Washington discussing the matter with Morton, who had once flown the Cave Route. The important thing, the colonel had said, was not to lose your nerve: once committed, there was no turning back.

Sweeping above another wadi, Tommy bored on towards the mountains.

The rain had stopped but the ground was mud and slush. From time to time the camels ground old bottles and cans under their feet. Alim knew in this vast empty expanse the slightest sound would travel hundreds of yards. But he was banking on the Iraqis not patrolling this far east.

Behind him, Sala coughed again.

'Are you all right?'

'*El hamda l'illah*,' Sala croaked. 'Praise God it will not get worse.'

'A little further and we can rest again,' Alim promised.

Since leaving the river and crossing the border they had made two unscheduled stops because of Sala's condition. They travelled now for another hour before they reached the lip of a wadi. At the bottom was the derelict building which provided a staging post along the smuggling route.

Alim helped Sala off the camel and into the building. In a corner of one room was the sack of tinned food and bottles of water he had left there from the last journey. He used his knife to open a tin and scooped some of the fish into his mouth with his fingers. He extended the tin to Sala.

'I do not feel like eating,' Sala said after coughing. Here in the building the sound was more pronounced. Alim ran his hand over his son's face, touching the blisters and wondering what could have burned the skin of both his sons.

'You stay here and rest,' he ordered. 'I shall continue alone. It isn't far from here.'

Sala nodded gratefully and huddled on the ground.

Alim placed the sack and a bottle close to Sala, then went outside to transfer the bomb from his son's camel to his own. Climbing into the saddle he coaxed the beast to its feet and, at a brisk trot, headed away from the building. Soon the sound of Sala's coughing faded. He could feel the fins of the bomb pressing against his stomach.

*

Tommy checked the map and crabbed the chopper a little to his right, enabling it to pass between two towering pillars of rock. Beyond lay an inhospitable area of uninhabited gullies and deep fissures.

The colonel had said the first King of Babylon had gone mad in this wilderness and that the armies of the Philistines, Phoenicians and Romans all perished here. He could believe it. He could feel the ground radiating its threat through his goggles.

For the first time he felt it was safe to break intercom silence. 'Anna, you're looking for a gully which leads up from a scree slope. The opening's going to be about five hundred feet from ground level.'

She placed her head firmly against the radar scope hood to check their present position against the co-ordinates fed into the navigational system before take-off. She began to call out instructions.

'Left towards that spill of boulders.'

Tommy crabbed the Apache towards the mound.

'Right, right . . . two hundred feet . . . up five.'

The helicopter skirted the boulders, climbing fifty feet as it did so.

'More left,' Anna called out.

Tommy did as ordered.

'Reduce speed . . . cliff face coming up.'

Through Tommy's goggles the mountains were close enough to block out the sky.

'Reduce speed more . . .'

'Sixty knots,' Tommy called out.

'Good, good. Go left,' Anna ordered calmly.

The Apache began to traverse the rockface.

'Up one hundred . . .'

The helicopter climbed.

'Hold it.'

The Apache hovered.

'Up another fifty.'

They rose parallel with the rockface.

'Left, left . . .'

Tommy saw the scree, a mass of boulders and shingle that flowed on down to the broken ground.

'Slow climb,' Anna ordered.

The Apache drifted up the scree.

'I see it!' Tommy said.

Ahead, the scree stopped at a break in the rockface. The opening looked to be no more than a hundred feet across. The colonel had said the clearance for the Apache would be tight.

Gingerly Tommy edged the helicopter closer to the gorge and altered the pitch so that the helicopter hovered before the mouth. 'Switching to sensors,' he said.

From now on the helicopter's progress would be monitored by the two black boxes on either side of the fuselage. They had been personally fitted by Danny at the Saudi base, one of several additions to the Apache he had made.

'Echo-sounder on,' Anna confirmed.

The Apache entered the gorge. The only sounds were the constant pinging of the echo returning from the rock and the steady swish-swish of the rotors.

'Left ten feet,' Anna called out. The digital computer screen showed that the clearance on the right-hand side was too close to the gorge wall.

Tommy instantly corrected the adjustment and edged the helicopter deeper between the rock mass on either side.

'Up fifteen,' Anna called out. The sensors had spotted an outcrop.

The helicopter climbed above it.

'Straight for ninety feet. Then the first bend,' Anna said.

On the computer screen a three-dimensional view of what lay ahead guided her.

The engine's reverberation dislodged loose rocks and shale, sending small avalanches sliding down to the floor of the gorge. If even a small rock hit the rotors, they would plunge after them, thought Tommy.

The pinging changed pitch as it came back from beyond the bend. Tommy edged the helicopter around the corner and his feeling of imprisonment grew.

'One hundred and thirty to the next turn,' Anna called out.

Eyes glued to the foot counter on his instrument panel, Tommy guided them forward, once more edging them around the next bend.

'Two hundred feet,' Anna called out. 'Then down forty.'

It took Tommy three minutes to complete the first part of the manoeuvre.

'Good, good,' Anna breathed. 'Now for the fun part.'

Slowly and steadily the Apache began to descend.

'The cave mouth should be coming up on your left ... now,' Anna whispered.

Tommy felt dwarfed by the immensity of the rock on all sides. He saw it then: the roof of the cave.

'It's reading as fifty deep by eighty wide,' Anna said.

Twelve-foot clearance all round. It would be like trying to manoeuvre the chopper in a living room.

'I'll square her up,' Tommy said. He carefully positioned the helicopter so that it was in the centre of the cave mouth.

'Anything on the screen?' he asked.

'Still checking,' Anna replied. A moment ago she had sent an electronic probe – another of Danny's additions – into the cave. Now the signal came back. There was no obstruction.

'Switch on infrared,' Anna said.

The mouth of the cave was bathed in a red glow that appeared to writhe as if it had a life of its own.

'Welcome to Disney World,' Tommy murmured.

Even though the colonel had warned him, he had not expected this. From the mouth of the tunnel small creatures clung in a writhing, heaving mass. Bats. As the Apache edged towards them, the cockpit began to fill with an almost overpowering stench. Inside the cave the pinging of the sensors sent the bats swooping and diving in a demented frenzy.

'Down five,' Anna said.

The helicopter dropped a little lower towards the floor of the cave, where the hairless young were deposited, creating a carpet of blind flesh between the heaps of droppings.

'Full mush,' Anna said.

The Apache's formidable array of electronics began to send out a relentless screen of signals to repel the tens of thousands of creatures already hurling themselves against the helicopter. The air was filled with continuous unearthly screams. The windscreen streamed with blood as the bats hurled themselves against the shatter-proof Perspex.

'Twenty foot in. Eighty to go,' Anna called out. She felt her skin creep. On either side millions of bat skulls and carcasses were deposited on every ledge, rock and cranny.

'They're retreating,' Tommy reported.

All around him the bats were withdrawing, carrying their young with them. The glare of their eyes was like millions of tiny glowing coals. The Apache moved deeper into the cave. The smell of putrefaction was greater.

Anna bit hard on her tongue. The walls on either side appeared to be moving. These had to be the tarantulas

David had warned about. The bloated, black-bodied spiders moved in serried ranks, their long jointed legs clicking against each other, mandibles probing the air. They were devouring pieces of bat flesh that fell from the helicopter.

'Forty to go,' Anna called out.

Tommy swore loudly. The bats being minced by the rotors were clocking the sensors. He increased pitch. The pinging resumed.

The bats continued crashing against the Apache, their nightmarish screaming if anything louder.

'Right five,' Anna called out urgently.

Tommy moved the yoke a fraction. The Apache lurched and began to drop. The rotors must be clogging. He increased the pitch.

'Twenty feet to exit,' Anna said.

Tommy peered ahead. If anything the air seemed thicker with bats. 'Let's go,' he said, moving to full power.

The Apache cut a huge swath through the bats and emerged from the cave. They flew another quarter of a mile down the gorge before it opened at a rubble-strewn plain. The Stealth bomber had established their latest fuel dump at the far end.

'I'll say one thing . . .' Tommy began.

'Me, too,' Anna said.

'That we sure as hell don't go back that way,' they chorused.

Alim had started to cough shortly after the wind returned, blowing with new strength, whipping sand against his face, leaving his mind a cold blur, making it difficult to think.

Taking the hillocks he had just passed as another navigational point, there were another three hours to travel before he met the stranger. But increasingly he wondered if he would arrive on time: the intervals between having to stop and recover from a fresh bout of coughing were becoming shorter. The last time he'd stopped he had run a finger over his face; his skin was covered with blisters. He had broken one and tasted the liquid. Blood.

Now, a moment ago, his coughing was so violent that he'd almost fallen out of the saddle, only avoiding doing so by grabbing at the bomb's fins.

Head bent low on his chest, body leaning against the casing, Alim guided the camel through the darkness.

Twenty-three thousand miles above the beast and its burden, the Halo satellite that had become immobilised on its journey from Baghdad to Tehran still functioned in one respect: its intelligence-collecting system remained fully operational.

For hours its cutting-edge technology had continuously photographed the same wide swath of Iraqi desert, but because its sensors were programmed to transmit only specific data – such as troop movements or the heat from a Scud warming up – they did not process the repeated view of the terrain.

However, when the camel and its rider entered the Halo's footprint, the full focus of the satellite's imaging system was brought to bear. Receptors scooped up the many billions of energy particles radiated by the man and camel through body-heat loss, and fed them continuously through the visible and invisible bands of an on-board spectrometer to create 'pictures'. These were then fed first into a photomultiscope tube which converted them into infrared images which were transmitted to a scanner, digitised, encrypted and analysed. A second scanner then focused only on those parts which it was tasked to study.

Ignoring the camel and its rider, this scanner concentrated on the inanimate object on the beast's back, identifying it as one which matched one of seven million stored in its memory. The scanner produced a digital-code print-out and sent this on the long journey through space which ended in a large windowless two-storey concrete structure at Fort Belvoir, an NSA establishment on the outskirts of Washington. The code was automatically converted into high-resolution pictures and displayed on one of several banks of screens. Sensors attached to them recognised the importance of the images by giving them the prefix MU – Most Urgent.

The pictures then began their journey through the electronic network of the US intelligence community. The first stopping-point was the desk modem of Rear-Admiral Stanway.

He was reading a report when a bell in the modem signalled their arrival. After scrutinising the photographs for a few moments, Stanway punched a button on his phone with one hand and with the other tapped a key on his board.

'Mr Gates,' Stanway said into the phone. 'Have a look at what's coming on to your screen. And tell Morton.'

On Tommy's cockpit radar the ground beneath the Apache looked like a moonscape, all craters and vehicle tracks. It could have been an old Scud missile site or the scene of a battle in the Gulf War.

Eyes glued to an oscilloscope, Anna murmured in his headset, 'Still no traces. It's weird.'

A full hour had passed since she had located the balloons on the screen: despite being concealed under the scree, they'd given off gamma particles which had shown up on the scope as wavy lines. Tommy had landed and they'd put on protective clothing and respirators. They'd placed the balloons in a bag lined with activated charcoal to stop the particles escaping, and stowed it in a compartment behind the cockpit.

Then they resumed their search for Bodor's bomb. So far the Apache had quartered the ground without success, heading deeper into Iran before turning back.

'Why would the Iranians leave those balloons behind?' Tommy asked as he edged the helicopter towards a massive rockface pitted with caves. 'And those traces must have come from the bomb. So it must be leaking. Yet it's vanished into thin air.'

'We have to be looking in the wrong place,' Anna said.

Tommy grunted. 'Where do we begin to look for the right place?'

'We are!' Anna interjected. 'I'm getting a reading. It's coming from over there . . . on our left . . . from one of those caves . . .'

Tommy drifted the Apache closer to the rockface. Behind him Anna's gloved hands worked in continuous fluid motion, adjusting the oscilloscope's sweep and setting up the thermal imager. 'You're right on the button,' she called out.

Tommy put the Apache into hover mode directly in front of a jagged opening in the rockface.

'Probing now,' Anna said.

The infrared imager began to search inside the cave, tracing its shape on a screen before her. The roof of the cave was the height of a house, rising to a funnel which disappeared inside the rock. The walls were granite, smooth from aeons of wind which had blown dust against them and then sucked it out. The floor was dotted with small boulders and pieces of shale.

'We definitely have something,' Anna murmured. Faint

lines had begun to appear on the screen. 'The reading's too low for it to be the bomb. But it must have been here.'

'Maybe they kept it here while they prepared for the launch,' Tommy said.

'It's a good three miles from where we found the balloons,' Anna reminded him, her eyes still watching the screen. An outline had appeared in one corner. She adjusted the probe setting for close-up. What appeared to be a bundle of rags filled the screen. She spoke quickly into her throat mike. 'Tommy, I think there's someone in there.'

She heard Tommy flick a switch, then saw the armament panel light up as he brought the Apache's machine guns to bear on the cave mouth.

'Don't shoot!' Anna said urgently. 'Back us off. Then we'll go take a look.'

Tommy moved the yoke to a new setting to reverse the Apache before setting it down on a patch of shale some hundred feet back from the cave. Then, once more dressed in protective clothing and respirators, Tommy carrying an Uzi, Anna a palm-sized detector and a flashlight, they returned to the cave, pausing in the entrance while she swept the detector back and forth.

'It's safe to go in. The reading's barely registering,' she said.

Tommy switched the machine gun to automatic fire, and they entered. The only sound was their steady breathing through the respirators. A few yards inside, Anna pointed to her right. Tommy nodded and swung the Uzi in that direction.

Anna switched on the torch and its powerful beam caught the Arab full in the face. Tommy lowered the gun. 'Holy Christ! What did that to him?' he whispered.

The Arab's face was a mass of huge blood blisters, many of which had burst. They covered his eyes, grew out of his mouth and hung like obscene pendants from his ear-lobes. He'd torn at his rough cloak to get at those on his chest, leaving the skin a bloodied mess.

'He can't have been dead too long,' Anna said, sweeping the light over his body with almost exaggerated care. 'There's no sign of rigor.'

Tommy looked at her quizzically. 'Think those emissions did this?'

Anna stepped closer, then crouched to bring the beam level with the body slumped against a wall of the cave. She slowly moved the detector up and down in front of the corpse.

Tommy watched her, silent.

Without haste she finished her check, straightened, and stepped forward and used a gloved hand to feel the Arab's arms and beneath his armpits.

'Radiation didn't kill him,' Anna pronounced. 'There are no nodules or inflammation of the lymph glands.' She stepped back.

'So what did?' Tommy asked.

'Ideally I'd like to take body samples. But by the time we got them back to base, they'd be useless,' Anna said. 'But I'm pretty sure he's been exposed to an overdose of ozone.'

Tommy looked at her, startled. 'What, *here*?'

'Not necessarily. It could have happened up in the mountains. Even a small pocket would have been sufficient. A few lungfuls of high concentration would have done this.'

Tommy glanced towards the mouth of the cave as he spoke. 'Maybe Bodor and the others ran into the same pocket. They could all be out there somewhere as dead as dodos.'

Anna swept the light over the floor of the cave. It was

scuffed and recently trodden. 'Camels,' she said. 'Judging by the foot-marks, there were at least three in here.'

'Wouldn't they have been affected by the ozone?'

'No,' Anna replied crisply. 'Their immune system protects them.'

Tommy nodded; Anna knew her field. He looked at the dead Arab. 'If we find those camels, we find the bomb – maybe,' he said.

Anna was already moving towards the exit, holding the detector in front of her. Outside she began to walk steadily across the ground, followed by Tommy. 'I'm still getting a reading,' she said. 'It's a lot weaker than in the cave, but somebody carried that bomb towards the gap in those rocks.'

They reached the narrow passage cut into the rock.

'The traces are stronger here,' Anna said, as they entered the gap. 'It's probably because the emissions are bouncing off the rocks on either side.'

From beyond the defile came the sound of rushing water. When they emerged from the passage, they saw below them a river in full flood.

'There's no way they could have crossed that,' Tommy said.

Anna went to the edge of the water, then began to walk a short distance up and down the bank before returning to Tommy. 'They crossed, right enough. There's no trace on either side.' Anna looked towards the mountains, then at the swirling water. 'This could be caused by snow. They could have crossed before it started to flow.'

Tommy stared across the river, then turned to Anna. 'That's Iraq on the other side. Why would the Iranians want to take that bomb over there.'

'Supposing they weren't Iranians, or at least not regular army? Maybe Kurds or smugglers? Somebody who saw a quick way of making a few dollars by selling the bomb to the Iraqis,' Anna said.

Tommy looked at her sceptically. 'A leaking bomb . . .?'

'But what if they didn't know the bomb was leaking?'

'Why don't we go and find them?'

Behind the vizor of her protective hood he saw Anna smile. 'I thought you'd never ask, Tommy.'

Twenty minutes later, its tanks topped up, the Apache crossed the river into Iraq. Eyes once more glued to the oscilloscope, Anna guided Tommy.

He had felt a similar excitement the first time he lifted a Royal Hong Kong Police helicopter off its Kowloon pad. Perfect tear-gas weather, the patrol leader remarked when they flew in search of another Triad junk running drugs from the New Territories. They'd returned to base without a shot being fired. His time in Hong Kong had mostly been like that, a promise of action almost never fulfilled. Not like today.

He adjusted his night vision goggles. Nothing except mile after mile of unbroken desert. He glanced at the instrument panel: the clock showed it was just after midnight. The border now lay well behind them.

Anna bent close to her screen. 'Some sort of building three miles ahead. The traces are leading right there.'

'I have it visual,' Tommy confirmed. Through his goggles the building looked like a nomad's shack. He toggled the yoke, once more bringing him to a level of pure perfect concentration, a single totally-focused eye, aware of everything, missing nothing.

Anna saw the armament panel was once more alive.

A mile from the hut Tommy put the Apache into a lazy curve, carrying it beyond the shack. Nothing, not even a tyre-mark, broke the ground. Twice more he slowly circled the hut while Anna used the imager.

'Looks like we have another body in there,' she said softly.

Minutes later after they had landed, they stood over the corpse of Sala, his skin covered with the same terrible blisters as those on his brother, Heka, back in the cave.

Tommy prodded the sack with the barrel of his Uzi, exposing the tins of food and bottles of water. 'Why didn't the last one take this stuff with him?' he asked.

'Maybe he didn't need to.' Anna paused. 'Maybe he wasn't going far enough for him to need to carry supplies.'

Leaving the body exactly as they found it, they hurried back to the Apache.

The wind had risen, sending sand sighing across the ground, reducing visibility. The helicopter headed still deeper into Iraq, flying over an endless expanse of sand and hillocks, the downwash of the rotors adding to the swirl of sand.

'I'm picking up body heat about a mile ahead,' Anna reported.

Tommy eased back the yoke and the Apache drifted forward.

'I see it,' he called out; it looked like another bundle of rags on the ground. The landscape was a black-and-white negative through his goggles. The bundle was in a small wadi. He passed over its rim and collapsed the Apache the last couple of feet on to the sand. He remained at the controls while Anna ran forward, detector in hand. He saw her go into her familiar crouch, straighten, then return.

When she spoke, the alertness in her voice suggested some deeper tension. 'It's our third Arab. Blisters every-where,' Anna said. 'The bomb must contain an ozone concentrate that the nuclear trigger's designed to spread. Like you said, find the camel and we have it,' Anna said.

Tommy swept the area through his goggles as if he

might suddenly see them. 'Do we go on looking, Anna?'

He heard her sigh through the intercom. 'No point. We've got to get back across the border before an Iraqi patrol picks us up. The sooner we get back to Saudi and report what we know, the better. Meanwhile, if any Iraqis find that bomb, they'll soon be very dead Iraqis.'

The Halo's camera continued to film the solitary camel and its lethal casing. The images were sent to Fort Belvoir, whence they were transmitted first to Admiral Stanway's office and then on to the screen on Gates' desk.

Only when the camel finally moved out of the satellite's footprint and the images ceased did Morton turn from the screen and walk over to the map on which he'd earlier fixed the flags indicating the fuel drops. He took several more emblems from a box.

'Give me the sat's co-ordinates,' he asked Gates.

As Gates called them out, Morton used the flags to create a new line on the map which led from the Iranian border into Iraq. He tapped the last flag he'd pinned, then moved his finger across the map, as if to continue the line, before stopping. He turned to Gates. 'If our camel keeps heading the way he's going, he'll end up in Babylon.'

'Have I missed something? I don't quite see the significance . . .'

Morton's smile came and went. 'Do you remember during the Gulf War how Schwarzkopf's pilots tried to knock out Saddam's reserve headquarters? Even their smart bomb couldn't dent the roof. The camel's heading directly for that HQ.'

TWENTY-NINE

From the windows of Ignatius Bailey's executive floor suite, a dawn-lit haze gave Meridian the appearance of a mirage. Only the tower of First National Bank rose above the mist. Down on the freeways traffic was still light.

It was six a.m. and Bailey had already been in his office for a full hour. He had always done his most secret work at this time. In these past sixty minutes he had severed all links with those he had used to implement his plans. Working from his modem, he had accessed their most secure data banks to remove anything incriminating. Details of money transfers which had, anyway, gone through a dozen and more laundering processes, were silently removed. Similarly, all the essential minutiae needed to support such an intricate operation were excised.

A few moments earlier, at the press of his modem key, an accident had occurred almost two thousand miles away. On one of the arterial roads leading out of Washington, two men in a Saab heard a high-pitched tone over the car phone. It was the signal they had been waiting for these past five days. Every morning they had followed the Chevrolet Caprice as it drove out of a government complex behind Sallmudet University. There was nothing to show that the chain-link fence protected the NSA facility which controlled the movement of all intelligence-gathering satellites.

Both men worked for a local drug baron. They had been

told that the Chevvy's driver was a heroin distributor who had cheated on his payments. Once the signal came, they were to move. As the Saab drew alongside the Chevvy, the passenger rolled down the window and emptied the contents of a pump-action shotgun into the Chevvy driver, killing him instantly.

Moments after he had pressed the modem key, Bailey did so again, this time to empty a bank account in the Cayman Islands. For safety's sake, he consigned the money to limbo. There could be no possible reason for the police to conclude anything except that the killing was a case of mistaken identity. What other reason could anyone have for killing a technician who specialised in moving Halo satellites from one orbit to another?

A light blinked on the modem. The first thing Bailey had done when he had arrived was to instruct its computer to locate a telephone number in the Pacific. He settled in his chair and tapped a key to activate the satellite telephone link. 'Carlo? Is that you?'

There was a short delay caused by the bounce of the satellite hook-up. Then came the familiar rasp. '*Si*. Who is this?' demanded Carlo Marcello.

'Ignatius. How is that yacht of yours? Your communications seem to be ten-ten.'

'It's midnight here. You call just to tell me my telephone works?'

In spite of himself, Bailey smiled. 'I thought you kept late hours, Carlo.'

'Not on vacation. Then I sleep plenty.'

Who with this time, Bailey wondered. He leaned forward slightly in his chair. 'Sorry to break into your beauty slumber, Carlo, but this is important.'

'So tell me. Then I can go back to sleep.'

'I'm afraid you won't have time for that.'

'Why? What happened?'

Bailey could sense Marcello was fully awake now. 'Where exactly are you right now, Carlo . . .'

'I told you. In bed.'

'No, no. I mean your location.'

Marcello cleared his throat. 'About a hundred miles off Sydney. I should be there in six hours, maybe a little sooner.'

Bailey smiled, 'Perfect.'

'Why? You have a crisis with some company there you want me to fix?'

'No, nothing like that. But I have a plane for you to catch.'

'What? Where to?' Marcello sounded worried.

'Round the world. It's Air Force One . . . the President's new one.'

'*Si. Si.* I read about it. I could have bought a fleet of yachts for the cost. So why you want me to make this trip, Ignatius?'

Bailey told him. Afterwards there was a lengthy silence. 'You still there?' he finally asked.

'Of course.'

'Carlo, this is very important. You're going to be my point man on this junket.'

'Okay. For anyone else, I say no. I need my vacation. But for you, I'll do it,' Marcello said expansively. 'When it comes to the next board meeting, you remember what I did.'

'I'll remember, Carlo.'

Bailey settled back in his chair. 'Tell me, how is that daughter of yours?'

'What? Why do you ask?' The worry was back in Marcello's voice. 'What's she done now?'

'Nothing, as far as I know. I haven't seen her on the news at all recently.'

'Thank God,' Marcello said fervently. 'Maybe she's come to her senses.'

'The problems of parenthood, Carlo ... I'm glad I'll never have to face them,' Bailey said softly.

Shortly after he ended the call, the modem's message light blinked. He punched a key and onscreen came the words: 'Air Force One airborne on schedule.'

Zita's arm came round the shower curtain, clutching a glove cloth. 'Scrub my back.'

Bodor took the cloth and pulled aside the curtain. Her face was tilted up towards the shower nozzle. He began to move the rough side of the cloth in small circles across her shoulders, working slowly downwards until he reached her buttocks. He began to rub harder, drawing the blood to the surface. Even now, all these hours later, he could not quite believe this was happening.

Zita could sense Bodor's iron control after he'd stripped down the remaining nuclear triggers when they had returned to the complex after the last unsuccessful test flight.

The way he calmly went about his own work had been in marked contrast to how he'd driven others with almost manic fury to repair the gondola and the balloon rigging and prepare for further test launches. On both ascents he had shown no fear, despite the electrical storms continuing to crackle around them. The actual launches had gone perfectly. A cluster of balloons, each with its bomb suspended beneath it, had risen to the appointed detonation height. But each time he'd announced a trigger had failed, she'd not bothered to hide her disappointment. Yet he remained totally calm. The last time they'd landed and she'd expressed concern over what continued to happen, he'd smiled, a quick, perfunctory smile, reminding her of a doctor who sympathises with your illness but treats you as just another case.

There were depths to Bodor she had not suspected. While he'd worked on the triggers she had stood very close to him and the more he tried to avoid her, the more aroused she'd become. Once when he'd reached for a tool, his hand had brushed against her hard nipples and she'd felt the dampness between her legs, and he'd looked at her, his silent hunger more intense for the fact she'd sensed his feelings.

He had abruptly left her and gone to his room: she knew he made his calls to the Arranger from there. She'd returned to her own quarters, stripped out of her flight suit and flopped on the bed in her bra and panties.

The long night of test flights had left a tension in her she knew only sex could extinguish. She'd arched her back and, for a moment, considered satisfying herself, as in the past she had done in dangerous places. When she was driving on the freeway. In a restaurant, using only her muscles. Once, in an act of blasphemy against her father's lip-service faith, in a church in Milan. But the secret, impulsive desire had lost its appeal for her.

So much had happened. So many changes of mood and her own perspective on herself and the world around her, that trying to make sense of them finally made her sleepy.

She'd awoken to find Bodor standing over her bed, staring down at her. He still wore his flight suit.

'What do you want?' she asked, sitting up, leaning on one arm and crossing her legs, feeling the tension running through her body and with it now the uneasy combination of pleasure and danger.

'There will be more tests,' he said.

'Okay.' She shrugged. 'It's your decision.'

Watching her eyes moving across his face, he could sense her uncertainty. 'We have two days before the plane arrives. Until then you can relax.'

'That'll be nice.' Her voice was tight.

'You can stay here, if you wish. I can arrange for you to go out at night.'

She had told him it was important for her to maintain her night vision.

'An hour above will be enough,' she said. 'What will you do?'

'I shall also try and relax.'

'Do you find that difficult to do?' she asked, smiling.

'It depends.'

'On what?'

'What does that mean?'

'Why are you always so suspicious, Bodor?'

He continued to look down at her. She still had perfect breasts and the body of a teenager. Even from here he could sense her heat.

'You look like you haven't seen a woman stripped off before, Bodor.'

He hesitated, not sure how to answer her, what tone to take. 'Not a woman like you,' he finally said.

She moved her feet to make room on the bed. He sat down beside her.

Zita placed her hand lightly on his arm. 'You are a surprising man, Bodor.'

'And you are a surprising woman.'

'Then at least we have that much in common.' She smiled. 'You must be warm in that suit.'

Her eyes were still intently watching him. He hadn't realised until now how long her lashes were.

'It's okay,' she said, brushing a wisp of hair from her face. 'I bet you've been told to stay away from me by our friend, the Arranger. Except he's not such a friend, is he, doing that?'

'What are you saying?' He shifted on the bed.

Zita sat up, her face close to him, her lips half-parted. 'He doesn't like to share me. Does that give you a problem?'

He remembered what the Arranger had said at the end of their last short conversation. 'Enjoy yourself with her. You deserve it.'

'No,' he said slowly. 'That doesn't give me a problem.'

'Good.' She leaned upwards and kissed him lightly on the neck.

Her lips felt warm on his skin, reminding him of how long he had been without a woman.

She gave him an amused glance. 'Still worrying about our friend?'

'No.'

She reached up and pulled him to her, kissing him fully on the lips. 'Let's get out of that suit – now,' she said, pressing her body against his, her hands feeling for his zipper, then helping him to shrug off the suit and boots.

He sprawled on the bed for a moment, feeling her tongue exploring his mouth, driving him to respond. Her breath was hot on his body as her mouth slid over his, her hands tugging at his shorts.

'Where have you been all my life?' she moaned with new intensity, kissing him again, forcing herself on top of him, pinioning him with one leg. He felt himself beginning to slide off the bed and she used her other leg to drag him back.

'You're not going anywhere,' she breathed. 'Not until I say so.'

Suddenly he felt a burst of anger, a male resentment that she was in control, dominating him. He pulled away and slapped her across the face.

She smiled at him, a knowing, victorious smile. 'You want to hurt me, hurt me,' she said hoarsely. Her hands and mouth were once more exploring him, her body pushing him back down on to the bed, straddling him with her legs, her breasts swinging freely in his face. The only sound was her panting and moaning. The heat from her body was beginning to make him feel clammy, squeezing everything else out of him. Then her soft crying as she guided him into her . . .

It had been dawn when she'd finally left the bed and gone to shower.

Bodor lathered his hands and moved them over Zita's body, beginning with the nape of her neck and collarbone, then moving on to her shoulders. She took his hands in hers, leading him with a slow motion up her ribcage, allowing his fingers to lift her breasts and then let them slide soapily through his hands.

Her nipples were once more hard under his touch, her body beginning to squirm and writhe. He reached behind her and slid his hands from her waist to the tops of her buttocks, then back, so that he almost lost his balance.

She clung to him, nodding her head. *Yes.* Then his fingers were inside her. For a moment he was surprised. She was not at all wet.

Her arms went round his neck: water cascaded from her head on to his body. She bit the bottom of his earlobe and she sensed his change. His fingers moved faster, repeatedly, and she gave a little hop so as to stand flat-footed, the better to take the pressure.

He felt the hardness of her teeth against his skin and felt her nails making new welts down his back.

And they stayed like that, locked together, the shower cascading over them.

What a pity, Bodor thought, that this can't last for ever.

But the Arranger had been explicit about what he wanted done.

In the sitting room of the guest suite of the British embassy in Washington, Prime Minister Bostock opened the first of two hand-delivered letters which had been awaiting his return from the President's dinner of welcome. He read it carefully, blinked with satisfaction, then opened the second envelope and did the same.

Both Helmut Sturmer, the German Chancellor, and Pierre Marceau, the President of France, had confirmed that they still completely supported what all three of them had come to refer to among themselves as the Saddam Option.

To preserve its secrecy, Bostock fed both letters into a shredder concealed inside a bow-fronted cabinet.

THIRTY

Air Force One headed out across the Pacific at close to the speed of sound.

Moments after they left Hawaiian airspace Patterson heard Mike Turner acknowledge the on-station signal from another of the US warships stationed along their route to Australia. Together with aircraft positioned on carriers over international waters, Air Force One would never be more than a few minutes from a means of rescue. Over territorial airspace its safety in an emergency was in the hands of local services.

Several countries had still to file their rescue codes before Air Force One left Andrews. Among these were Burma, Pakistan, Afghanistan, Iran, Iraq and Israel. As the plane passed over the Rockies, the Pentagon had radioed Turner details of those of Pakistan and Burma. Crossing the coast south of San Francisco, the radio operator received those of Afghanistan and Israel. He fed the codes into one of the on-board computers.

Behind him Patterson heard Turner give another acknowledgement, then call out: 'The Aussies are up and running.'

A moment ago Perth air traffic control had radioed that the first Australian Air Force long-range rescue aircraft were already patrolling over their territorial waters.

'Have the Pentagon put more pressure on Tehran and Baghdad, Mike,' Patterson ordered. 'We need their codes inputted before we leave Beijing.' He punched a button on his armrest phone. 'How's it going back there, Cowan?' Patterson asked when the senior flight steward responded over the phone in his pantry.

'No problems, Colonel. They all enjoyed their organic lunch – especially our French guest. The Man was really pleased.'

At the President's request, the food served on board was free of all preservatives and chemicals. He'd said it was another way of reminding everyone of the purpose of Operation Earth Saver.

'Chancellor Sturmer get enough to eat?' Patterson asked.

'He had double helpings of dumplings. I didn't tell him they were made from soya protein.'

Patterson chuckled. 'What's next on the agenda?'

'Right now, it's a rest period. Señor Esplana, the Spanish Prime Minister, is working out on his exercise bike in his cabin. Prime Minister Bostock's in the lounge going through the London newspapers we picked up just before departure. He'll have another pile waiting when we get to Sydney. The RAF are flying them out specially. Mr. McKenzie, the Canadian Premier, is enjoying an after-lunch brandy with the Italian Prime Minister, Silvio Briscini.'

'The translator doing her job?'

'Perfectly. She's switching from one language to another just like she used to do at the UN,' Cowan said. 'At present the other translators are on a break in the rear cabin having lunch with the major and some of his communications people.'

'Where's the Man?'

'In his suite. When I took his coffee up he was working on the speech he's going to give this afternoon. Dr Curtis was with him, checking blood pressure. He wasn't too pleased, but she was quite firm and said she'd be doing so three times a day. He was still grumbling at her when I left. But you know the Man. Sometimes he can be more show than bite. Actually, I think he quite likes the attention – especially from someone as pretty as our doctor.'

'Don't let her hear you say that, Cowan. On this plane she is a doctor first and last,' Patterson reminded him. He had one other question. 'Where's Morton?'

'Still in the Step. I served him a snack lunch which he barely touched. When I cleared away, he was working the phone as hard as ever.'

Patterson barely suppressed a sigh. Morton had been in the cubbyhole since shortly after take-off, which meant he still couldn't make a private call to the hospital. The last time he'd checked from his office at Andrews, a nurse had said there had been no change in Bron's condition.

'Anybody want coffee up there?' Cowan said.

'Make it four, Cowan.' Coffee was a flight deck stand-by.

'On its way, Colonel.'

Minutes later Turner reported that Morton had finally left the Step.

Patterson turned to Locke. 'Take over. Nature calls.' Slipping out of his harness, he left the cockpit.

Bailey watched the text unfolding on his desk modem of the editorial he had dictated and which would appear in all Meridian International's newspapers, and be read over the TV and radio stations it controlled.

Headed 'An Unnecessary Journey', the powerful attack on Operation Earth Saver concluded: 'The mission of Air Force One is rooted firmly in the realms of science fiction. Indeed, it could serve as the plot for a remake of that classic film, *The Day the Earth Caught Fire*. For those of us who watch late night movies on TV, the image of the Earth spinning toward the Sun and a fiery demise is gripping enough – but far removed from reality. We know that when the world leaders in the movie urge their scientists to arrange nuclear explosions to veer the Earth away from destruction, we are looking at fantasy.

'Today, that word can be aptly applied to what the President of the United States has undertaken. He believes his mission can save a doomed world. There is no evidence to show that the world is doomed – let alone that he can save it. Indeed, his policies have proven quite the opposite. He may well soon find that the electorate are less comfortable with his attitude than the comforts he enjoys on board his new plane. The pity is that he has not realised that at the height Air Force One now flies, it is very easy to lose touch with reality.'

Bailey pressed a button on the modem's keyboard to approve publication, and turned to a second screen now positioned on his desk.

The VDU was filled with an outline map of the world. Superimposed on the map was a tiny replica of Air Force One. The model was presently just south of Fiji. A digital clock on top of the display unit showed there were six hours flying time left before Air Force One reached Sydney, where Carlo Marcello would board.

Bailey picked up a computer print-out on the desk. It gave the latest profit figures for Marcello Enterprises; four per cent up on the previous month's, a most satisfying increase. Beneath the balance sheet was a list of the corporation's shareholders. Carlo Marcello currently held ninety per cent of the holding capital and the balance was divided between six family members. Against a single percentage point for Zita Marcello was the word 'suspended'. Marcello represented all their interests on the Meridian board, but Bailey was certain that none of them was aware of the last item on the print-out. It was a copy of a legal declaration that, in the event of his death, Carlo Marcello's holding would be automatically transferred to Bailey. The arrangement had formed part of the deal which gave Marcello a billion dollars for selling his corporation to Meridian.

Neatly folding the paper, Bailey thrust it into a pocket of his bathrobe and glanced at the clock above the electronic wall map. Four a.m. On the map only a pinprick of light glowed at a point in the Iraqi desert midway between Baghdad and the border with Iran. Satisfied that there was nothing more for him to do at the moment, Bailey pulled the robe about him and walked back to the bedroom suite adjoining his office.

From now on he would work and sleep on the executive floor until the pinprick of light went out.

In a corner of Air Force One's lounge, President Pierre Marceau bent his head closer to hear what Chancellor Helmut Sturmer was saying to Prime Minister Arnold Bostock.

Passing through the lounge on his way to the flight deck, Morton caught Bostock's response.

'Everything will be fine. You mark my words. I've already asked to see him after dinner. Just the two of us. I always find you get better results that way.'

Morton briefly wondered whom the Prime Minister was going to try and charm.

The wind whistled across the wadi, bending the tufts of desert grass before it and driving needle-point sand crystals, like sandpaper grit, against the Arranger's face. He looked one more time at his watch: it was the hour when the Bedouin faithful in their camp half a mile away to his right would begin to recite their first prayers of the day.

Already the bark of their dogs carried faintly on the wind. But until the sun was high in the sky, the dogs would not come and explore. Behaviour patterns were one of the first things you learned in desert survival.

It had been close to midnight when he'd parked the Range Rover in a recess cut into the side of the wadi which the old Arab had told him about after they'd agreed the deal. Since then the Arranger had laid spreadeagled just beneath the east-facing edge of the wadi, staring out across the landscape, watching for the first sign of the Arab and his two sons to appear from the direction of Iran.

They should have been here two hours ago, one hour at the latest. He had chosen them partly because of their reputation for punctuality, and already paid them well in excess of the current market price for smuggling, because he wanted to be certain the job was done properly.

The Arranger glanced at his wrist compass. The smugglers should emerge between the camp and the wadi. To the untutored eye, the trail they would have followed was invisible. To the Arranger, it was as clear as a well-signposted highway: the tiny rumplings of sand were caused by minute creatures burrowing between the footfalls of passing camels up and down the trail. As the light strengthened, the rock and scrub vegetation gave a ragged edge to the track.

Resisting the temptation to search the terrain with his powerful binoculars in case they gave off a reflection in the dawn light, his eyes scanned the landscape, inch by inch, travelling as far back along the trail as he could see, then searching the ground on either side for signs of recent traffic. There was none.

Once more he patiently extended the area of scrutiny, his eyes seeking beyond the patch of scrub, stiff as coral, on one side of the trail, then moving back to a rock outcrop a good hundred yards on the other. Camels rarely strayed off a known path through the desert. But none had passed this way in the darkness: there were no droppings, no insect activity that turds always attracted.

Then, over the low, snuffling sound of the wind, he heard a new sound from behind the outcrop: the jingle of a harness. A moment later the camel came into sight. The beast walked slowly, picking its way lightly on slender legs. The animal's eyes were soft brown bulges in its long brown face and the body fur was patchy.

All this the Arranger saw in the same instant that he realised the camel was riderless. What a moment ago he'd thought could have been the Arab bent low over his saddle, seeking protection against the wind, was the bomb casing.

The Arranger looked towards the camp. The light was sufficiently strong for him to make out the individual tents. No more than two families. The women had lit the first fires and the smell of cooking borne on the wind reminded him of his hunger. He had deliberately not eaten so as to reduce the chance of an animal picking up his scent.

Hefting the sub-machine gun, he walked towards the camel. The animal had stopped to nibble at a patch of scrub. It paused to look at him incuriously, then resumed eating.

The Arranger circled the camel, his breathing slow but shallow. He came to a stop opposite the saddle, standing several feet back. Apart from the scarcely perceptible rise and fall of his chest, there was no movement about him. His eyes were riveted on the missing plate in the tail of the casing.

He cursed softly under his breath, then turned on his heels and walked quickly back towards the wadi. As he reached the Range Rover, he heard shouting from the camp. He turned and hunkered down just below the lip of the wadi. Slowly raising his head he saw that children, followed by adults, were running towards the camel. They were laughing and shouting in their excitement. He watched them circle the beast. Then one of the men grabbed its lead rein and, with the others surrounding the animal, they drove it back towards their camp, pointing at the bomb casing and shouting even louder.

Waiting until they were safely back among their tents before starting up the Range Rover, the Arranger drove out across the desert. After he had travelled some distance, he parked beside a clump of boulders and used the vehicle's powerful satellite telephone.

'Bodor,' he said when he made the connection, 'you'll have to make do with the casing you have. This one's already killed my couriers and probably more shortly. If nothing else, it shows it works.'

The stationary Halo's receptors were powerful enough simultaneously to vacuum up a million separate telephone conversations within its footprint. Though the rocks from where the Arranger had made his call were normally outside its range, the footprint allowed a degree of spillage in open spaces like the desert.

The receptors silently garnered the few words, faint and mushy though they were. On board the satellite they were fed through an electronic wash to remove the mush and then into an enhancer to improve the quality.

Nevertheless, until an hour ago, the Halo would merely have stored the laundered words on a tape that gave the time they were recorded, together with the location. The tape would then have been transmitted as part of the next transfer to Fort Belvoir, still an hour away.

One word on the tape changed that: Bodor. At Morton's request, his name had been added to the Halo's priority lexicon, an electronic dictionary on which could be stored several million key items.

Recognising 'Bodor' as having a double-helix priority — the most urgent of all NSA classifications — the lexicon ordered the tape to bypass the on-board storage tank and be transferred at once.

Immediately after it arrived and was copied, the tape was routed by a secure land line to Hammer Force headquarters in Geneva.

On the third floor, work began at once behind a heavily-padded door marked 'Voice Analysis'.

On Air Force One, Morton sat cross-legged on the floor of the Step, his back straight against the seat of the chair, and built himself an oasis of quietness; a vacuum. He breathed as if he were asleep, and his mouth sagged. Following a pre-determined routine, he allowed his limbs to become insubstantial: first his neck and shoulders, then his hips and ribcage, followed by his thighs, calves and ankles. Finally, he could feel only the thickness of his tongue, a soft, sleek weight in his mouth that seemed to restrict air to his throat, causing his pulse rate to drop. His mind emptied until he felt incapable of thought. For a while he remained suspended between oblivion and eternity. Then, just as gradually, he began to think again. Possibilities became that much clearer, and he became comfortable with the idea that things which, on the surface seemed unlikely to be true, should be treated as the truth.

Once more he began to think about Sergei Mikhailo-vich Bodor and Ignatius Bailey: and no longer about what the connection between them was, but who that link could be.

After an hour he began to breathe more rapidly and rotate his head, checking his pulse rate until it returned to normal. Then, fully refreshed as if after a long sleep, he stood up and telephoned Humpty Dumpty who, with his bald head and wrinkled forehead, resembled the nursery-rhyme character. The nickname had followed him from MIT where he had held the post of Professor of Synthesised Speech, and who now ran Voice Analysis.

In a perfectly modulated voice he told Morton that work had begun to identify the man who had spoken to Bodor.

'Humpty,' Morton said, 'remember those voice tapes of that group of Stasi killers who were offering themselves as freelancers to that South African?'

'The one with a Pretoria accent? What was his name again? De Berke? No ... de Brug ... That's it, Johannes de Brug,' Humpty Dumpty said.

'That's him. Whatever became of him?'

'I don't know. But I can try and find out.'

'Do that, will you. You still got his voice tape?'

'I can't be sure. When Bitburg said we couldn't have more floor space I had to have a clean out. But I'll have a look.'

Morton had one further order. 'If you find it, run it against that tape from NSA.'

Bodor and Zita ate sitting in armchairs in her quarters, balancing trays on their knees. For the past twenty-four hours they had done nothing but eat, have sex, shower and sleep. Zita hadn't bothered to dress; she was wearing his robe, her damp hair held in a ponytail by a rubber band.

'Terrific,' she said through a mouthful of fish. 'Just right. How do you get such fresh fish?'

'Part of the service.' Bodor leaned from his chair to pour wine into their glasses.

He seemed completely relaxed. Then why, she wondered, did she feel a little afraid of him again?

THIRTY-ONE

From the back of the flight deck Morton watched the pair of escorting Australian Air Force rescue planes turn back. A moment later he heard Turner acknowledge the on-station signal from USS *Houston* that they were now over international waters as Air Force One headed north back up the Pacific.

Apart from the sound of air rushing past at more than six hundred miles an hour, the radio operator's voice was the only thing to break the silence.

Morton suspected that the flight crew were reflecting, like him, on what had happened as Air Force One began the descent into Sydney. He had been on the flight deck when a red warning light began to flash.

'Air condition system failure,' Locke said calmly and clearly.

Even as he switched off the light, the first icy rush of unfiltered air was making its way through the miles of pipes and ducts hidden behind wall panelling and ceiling cladding.

'Switching to back-up,' Patterson confirmed. He punched a button on a console. The on-board computer responsible for regulating air temperature would do the rest.

A second red light came on.

'I'm showing a computer malfunction,' Kerr reported.

'Switching to over-ride,' Patterson announced.

Morton watched him swiftly punch more buttons to isolate the faulty computer and activate its back-up.

The light went out.

Patterson's eyes scanned his instrument panel. The internal tem-
perature reading was once more normal.

'Think anybody noticed back there?' *he asked.*

'Doubt it,' *Locke reassured him.*

'I did,' *said crew chief Sutter. He'd arrived on the flight deck*
a moment ago.

'With your ears, you'd hear a sigh inside a coffin!' *Turner*
grinned.

Sutter ignored the remark and addressed Patterson. 'The
computer's fail-safe switch probably tripped. Once we're down, I
can confirm and reset it in a few minutes. The air conditioning's
something else, judging from the sound I heard; the problem could
be somewhere in the actual pipework. How long are we going to
be on the ground?'

'We're staying overnight,' *Patterson said.*

Sutter grunted. 'Should give us enough time. I'll want everyone
off the plane and to shut down completely.'

'You'll have to finish what you're doing, with at least a couple
of hours spare for me to get everything ship-shape for departure,'
Patterson said.

Sutter grinned. 'I'll do my best.'

'You'll do better than that, Chief,' *Patterson said firmly.*

After the President and his guests were driven away for the
first of their Ecological Summits – this one held in the Sydney
Opera House and attended by leaders from countries around the
Pacific Rim – Sutter and his men crawled all over the plane.

The fault was eventually traced to a space behind Helen
Curtis' workplace. During its conversion into a surgery, someone
had failed to reconnect properly one of the valves which controlled
the inflow of air. The valve had finally worked loose, creating the
knock-on effect which had tripped the fail-safe switch on the
computer. The switch had been quickly reset but the work to replace
the valve involved carefully taking down part of the ceiling on the
upper deck and working in the crawl-space above.

Before turning in for the night, Patterson called Memorial Hospital from air traffic control, where he had gone to check the weather for the next day. Dr Monroe said there was still no change; for the first time Patterson detected concern in his voice.

Returning to the plane he met Helen strolling inside the security cordon around Air Force One. When he told her the news, she offered to call Monroe herself the next day. He smiled gratefully.

Very early the following morning, Patterson informed Thacker Stimpson that he would like to conduct a test flight to check the air conditioning system. The Chief of Staff vetoed the idea.

'You even think of doing a test flight,' Stimpson said grimly, 'and the media rat pack will have a field day!' To reinforce the point, he produced a sheaf of hostile press stories which had been faxed to him from the White House Press Office. Patterson reluctantly agreed to a compromise. The repaired system could be tested on the ground.

Air Force One's doors were closed, the engines run up to taxi power and the air conditioning switched on under Sutter's supervision. The crew chief finally said he was satisfied.

Shortly before take-off there was another incident, triggered by Cowan. The chief steward had gone into Sydney to obtain fresh vegetables and fish from the markets. The supplies arrived in good time but, with departure approaching, there was no sign of Cowan.

The President and his guests were boarding by the front ramp when the chief steward was driven on to the tarmac in a police car. He bolted up the rear steps clutching a flight bag and called the cockpit to explain his difficulty in finding spices he needed to flavour the food of some of his guests. Patterson grunted an acceptance of the explanation, privately pleased at the lengths the steward would go to please their passengers.

The sixty-four Pacific Rim delegates who had attended the Opera House meeting were to accompany the President and the other leaders of the industrialised nations on the next leg of Operation Earth Saver, so that discussions could continue on how best to deal with a variety of regional ecological problems.

Sutter had supervised the loading of their baggage into the hold. That completed, he double-checked the door which had caused a problem in Paris, and was about to climb the ladder into the rear cabin when Cowan came down into the hold clutching the flight bag.

Explaining that there was no space in the galley refrigerators, Cowan said he'd like to store the spices in the hold until he needed them; the chilly atmosphere would ensure their freshness. Though it was strictly against regulations, Sutter allowed him to do so.

And certainly, the crew chief had decided, his decision did not require him to report it to Morton, who had asked to be informed of any deviation in procedure.

Now, four hours into the flight out of Sydney, on-board routine continued.

Morton heard the telephone chime in Patterson's armrest.

'Aircraft commander,' Patterson said formally into the mouthpiece.

'Anybody ready to eat up there?' Cowan asked. 'There's steak, fish, pasta or vegetarian.'

For safety reasons, no members of the flight deck crew ate the same meal so as to reduce any chance, unlikely though it was, of food poisoning. As aircraft commander, Patterson had first choice.

'I'll wait a while,' he said. 'The steak will be fine, just plain.'

Locke ordered pasta, Turner Pacific bass and Kerr a vegetarian dish.

'Mr Morton planning to eat up there with you?' Cowan asked.

Patterson relayed the question and Morton shook his

head. 'I'm going to listen to the President's address,' he said.

Replacing the phone, Patterson grinned. 'I hear the Man ruffled a few feathers with his last one.'

He said that Dempsey had told him that while she had helped serve morning coffee in the conference room, the President had delivered a devastating attack on Saddam Hussein's destruction of the marshlands of southern Iraq, calling it the worst ecological disaster of its kind. By all accounts the Man had displayed his customary grasp of his brief to paint a grim and graphic picture of a whole region being turned into a desert, with catastrophic consequences for its indigenous people and wildlife.

'Those marshes happen to be one of the most important wetlands in the world,' Turner said. 'There's over a hundred rare species of bird there, including the Dalmatian pelican and the pygmy cormorant.'

Kerr looked at the radio operator in astonishment. 'How'd you know all this, Mike?'

Turner shrugged. 'I read a lot.'

'Only birds I read about are in *Playboy*,' joked Kerr.

After the laughter subsided, Patterson glanced at Locke. 'Our Italian industrialist seems to be keeping very much to himself. I gather from Cowan he just eats, makes notes and sleeps.'

'Maybe he doesn't like travelling in the back,' Locke said.

When Carlo Marcello had boarded in Sydney he had been shown to a seat in the rear cabin.

'He's got the same leg-room as everyone else,' Patterson replied. 'Anyway, I'm not sure exactly why he's here. Any idea, Mr Morton?'

Morton was saved from answering by the arrival of the first of the tray meals.

As he left the flight deck, Morton heard Patterson tell Turner to remind the Pentagon that the emergency rescue codes for Iraq and Iran were still not in. Once more there was an underpinning tension he'd first heard in Patterson's voice in Paris.

Elsewhere, the orderly routine of the President's flight continued.

In the communications shack, the signals major watched his operators sampling radio traffic from around the Pacific Rim. Voices from Singapore and Hong Kong were joined by others from Vietnam, the Koreas and Japan. One technician had already established a link with their next landing point, Beijing International Airport.

Chefs were preparing lunch in the galley. Next door Carolyn Dempsey helped a steward select wines from the well-stocked liquor pantry.

In the secretarial bureau, Martha Wilson and her White House staff steadily worked through the list of thank-you notes to people in Sydney. The letters would all be signed by the President, placed in a diplomatic bag and flown back from Beijing to Sydney by a State Department courier who would post them.

Helen Curtis was dealing with a flight attendant who had pulled a back muscle after moving the Spanish Prime Minister's exercise bicycle while cleaning his bedroom. Helen had given the attendant a muscle relaxant injection and a course of pain-killing tablets, together with a note confining her to light duties during the rest of the flight. Shortly afterwards, her phone rang.

'Dr Curtis, this is the chief steward,' Cowan began formally.

'What can I do for you, Mr Cowan?'

'Explain to me what exactly are light duties.'

Helen laughed politely. 'Anything that doesn't put a strain on her back.'

'This whole job's a strain on everyone's back,' Cowan said tersely.

'She can fetch and carry but absolutely no lifting or bending.'

'So what can I do with her?' Cowan demanded. 'With a full complement I need every hand.'

Helen sighed. 'Why not confine her to the dining room and spread her other duties among the rest of your staff?'

'Terrific,' Cowan growled, hanging up.

Morton wandered back through the plane. As he passed the galley, Carolyn Dempsey glanced up.

'Can I get you a drink, Mr Morton?'

'Thanks. Same as before.' He drank only lime juice when flying. Glass in hand, he strolled into the rear cabin. Its only occupant was Carlo Marcello.

The industrialist was dressed casually but expensively in designer jeans and a lambswool sweater. He had tilted back his chair and, mask covering his eyes, was fast asleep.

Morton watched him for a moment, then made his way up to the conference room. He took one of the few remaining empty armchairs as the President rose and walked to the podium. He stood smiling at the room for a moment longer. Then abruptly, in a voice deliberately devoid of emotion, he began to speak.

'Listen to this. If you've ever wondered what governments are for . . . then listen to this.'

He pressed a button on the podium console. Instantly the room was filled with a weak rasping sound. Several of the audience looked at each other; frowning, surprised, embarrassed.

'I'll save you guessing,' the President said. 'It's a child. A little girl in fact. Seven years old. And she's fighting to breathe. There are tens of millions like her. Some younger, many older. You'll find them in your country and mine. Between them they speak all the languages on earth. But they have one thing in common. They have been denied the right to breathe!'

He hurled the words into the room, pleased at the stir they created.

'Each one of them has been denied by us the right to breathe. And not just us. But by all those who govern and rule. We – they – all of us share a collective responsibility for the future of this child. She – and all those who suffer with her – have entrusted their fate to our hands.'

He punched another button on the console and the harsh breathing sound stopped.

Not even a movement now broke the silence of the room. Morton had seen nothing like it since, as a boy, he'd listened to President Kennedy capture an audience.

'The biggest single cause of such breathing attacks is air pollution, and two major causes of air pollution are our present system of power stations and road transport. So what should we do? Uninvent the petrol engine? Close down the freeways? Turn the power stations into industrial theme parks?'

The President paused and looked into individual faces, never dwelling on one long enough to make someone feel he was being singled out. He moved to his next point without breaking the fluency of his argument.

'Petrol engines and power stations have brought us freedom from drudgery and they've saved lives. But they also cost lives. Globally, road accident figures increase all the time. And so do deaths from air pollution. The only other certainty is this. The solution to these and all environmental problems will be found only in that very same place that created them: the human brain.'

Morton saw Prime Minister Bostock now sat upright while around him others were nodding. Chancellor Sturmer was stroking his chins. Prime Minister Esplana was whispering to President Marceau of France.

Waiting for them to finish, the imposing figure at the podium continued.

'Sooner or later, properly inspired, someone will find a cleaner, safer way to power cars and generate electricity. Which is one more reason why I say to each and all of you: your country's most precious resource is its people. In their brains and their inventiveness there lie untapped and unimaginable resources. Do not squander them. Use your people. Educate them. Train them. Encourage them. Then the sound of a little girl fighting for her breath need never again be the price people have to pay for something called progress. Let's all promise each other we'll start making a difference to the world our children live in. Let us each make that promise now!'

A wave of applause swept the room as the President stepped back from the lectern.

For a moment Morton let it sweep around him. Then he, too, was on his feet with the others, clapping. He hadn't done that for a long, long time and he was glad he was doing so now because it was good to be in the presence of such an innately decent man as the President.

In the pre-dawn the Arranger watched the two Stasi teams go about their deadly business. Each commando had been picked because he could take a man on a journey of pain from which he would never quite recover. One moment they were still as vultures, the next moving over the sand at silent speed, wielding their knives like butchers working on carcasses. Except that these were still alive – the last of the Kurds from the complex's holding pen.

Now that Bodor had no further need of them, the tribesmen and women provided perfect practice fodder. When the last dreadful scream had died, the commandos began to fade back into their rocky lair. The Arranger was satisfied they were the best; that they would do the job whatever the difficulties.

He turned and walked across the sand towards the ramp which led down into the complex.

In her office Helen listened a moment longer on the phone link-up to Memorial Hospital.

Dr Monroe had just said there still was no change in Bron's condition; she was still in a coma. The fear now was that she could slip deeper into her unconscious sleep. Both knew that with something as complicated and unknown as a coma there was no real way to anticipate its course.

'I'll call you again in three hours, Brian, when we get to Beijing.'

'Sounds more fun than working up in Emergency, Helen.'

'But not as exciting.' The truth was that after the frenetic pace of Bethesda, she was longing for something to challenge her fully. Here, in the roof of Air Force One, she felt cut off.

'When her husband called me from Sydney, he sounded very much in control. I guess that goes with the job,' Monroe said.

'I guess.' She hoped the uncertainty in her voice did not show.

Inside a control room on the third floor of the NSA facility in the suburbs of Washington, Hernandez, the operative who had replaced the murdered technician, stared in astonishment at his video display unit. A moment ago one of the engineers had telephoned to report that the Halo stranded close to the Iraq–Iran border was once more operational.

On his screen Hernandez saw the Halo had begun to move – but not towards Tehran. The satellite was heading slowly back over Iraq. He grabbed a phone and dialled the engineer.

'It's back to the drawing-board for you guys,' Hernandez said.

'I already know it,' sighed the engineer. 'And there's not a damned thing to be done until she gets back to her original start point. That's one of the drawbacks with a Halo. It has to work through the original programme.'

'How long will that take?'

There was a pause while the engineer calculated. 'From where it is now? Eleven hours forty minutes, an hour to reprogramme, then thirty-four hours to Tehran.'

Hernandez, whose security clearance allowed him to know such matters, realised that the satellite would now arrive over the Iranian capital only long after Air Force One had departed.

He dialled the watch commander in his booth at the far end of the room and told him what had happened. The watch commander relayed the news to Rear-Admiral Stanway's office. From there it was phoned to Gates in Langley. He called Morton on Air Force One.

'Make sure that NSA keep a close eye on that Halo. Maybe, Bill, we could just get lucky,' Morton said.

THIRTY-TWO

In his on-board office directly above the flight deck, the President watched Arnold Bostock consume another petit four. There was, he thought again, indeed something about the Prime Minister which suggested an animal, quick and furtive, a fox perhaps.

After lunch he'd invited Bostock here for the private meeting he'd requested. After they had settled in armchairs and Cowan had served coffee and closed the door behind him, the Prime Minister came directly to the point. 'Some of us who are travelling all the way with you feel we should give Tehran a miss.'

'Why is that?' The President kept his voice steady.

Bostock dusted crumbs into his mouth before continuing. 'Well, for a start, nothing you, or anyone, can say to the mullahs will make them change their attitudes. Believe me, on my side of the pond, we've had a lot of experience in dealing with them. Intransigence is too soft a word to describe their attitude.'

'If we don't try and change it, we'll never know if they are capable of change, Arnold.'

'A few of us have put our heads together on this one and the consensus is that even if we go to Tehran and then give Baghdad a miss, that will only exacerbate the situation.'

'Would you care to develop that a little?' asked the President quietly.

The Prime Minister smiled quickly. 'I don't want to gainsay your own efforts . . .'

'No, no, please. I'd like to hear what you have to say.'

Bostock nodded, as if gathering his thoughts. He'd agreed with Sturmer and Marceau that the best approach would be to focus on the threat Iran posed to the United States.

'Now that Iran has recovered from its eight-year war with Iraq, it offers an ever-growing menace to your country and its allies. The military threat comes from terrorism. My intelligence people tell me that Tehran now has an unprecedented capability in that area. The economic threat arises from its ability to manipulate the price of oil. The political threat comes from Iran's subversion of countries friendly to yours.'

'Apart from oil, that could apply equally to Iraq,' the President observed.

'Indeed, indeed. But Iraq is largely still a spent force. Signs of economic decline are everywhere. Because of this we cannot continue to regard Iraq as the natural counter-balance to dissuade the mullahs from any expansionist schemes. What would happen should Iran decide to take advantage of Iraq's increasing vulnerability and launch an all-out invasion into, say, southern Iraq? The danger for us all would be obvious. The whole region would be destabilised.'

Bostock leaned forward in his chair, cup in hand. 'Let me be frank with you. Much more than Iraq, Iran is on a collision course with the rest of the world. But it won't come with direct confrontation. Not yet anyway. The Iranians are smarter than that. Instead of head-on attacks against us, they will choose feints and indirection. Instead of boasting about their capabilities, they will quietly continue to plot against us – you. Saddam is an open book compared to the mullahs. Some of us feel, to continue the analogy, that we've spent too long turning the wrong pages.'

The President smiled briefly. 'An interesting thought.' There was a measure of truth in what Bostock had said. 'As you know, I still haven't heard from Baghdad,' the President said. 'By the way, who are these "some of us" you mentioned?'

The Prime Minister waved a hand quickly. 'Oh, Sturmer and Marceau. We all think you should call Saddam directly. It's the kind of gesture he would take to. And, if I may say so, it wouldn't do you any harm either. This trip is getting, from what I've read in the London papers, some heavy stick. I expect it's the same with your media. If you could get Saddam to sign up for this crusade of yours, it might just tilt the balance. Some of us think it's now time he was allowed in from the cold, or' – the Prime Minister laughed – 'in his case the heat of the desert.'

The President said nothing.

The Prime Minister drained his cup before he continued. 'There's a mood in Britain and Europe that the Gulf War is now very much in the past. And the one thing it didn't do was to teach the Kuwaitis humility. They're still as arrogant as ever. At times you can't actually blame Saddam for getting mad at them. And, as I say, he's very much one for the grand gesture. A call from you to him could work wonders.'

The President looked at the Prime Minister for a further long moment. When he spoke there was a steely edge not there before. 'Calling Saddam would send the wrong signal. Not just to him but to the Iranians and the Israelis . . . everybody in the region. They'd see me as a supplicant. And that I'm not – to anybody. What I'm offering is a partnership. Operation Earth Saver is ultimately all about that. Working together for a common cause. Trying to make this world a better place for us all to live in today, and our children to live in tomorrow.'

Bostock poured himself more coffee. 'Then why not include the Iraqis?'

'Saddam doesn't want to be included. It has just taken the Pentagon two weeks even to get Baghdad to give us their rescue codes should we have a problem in their airspace.'

'That's just their bureaucracy. You get used to that,' Bostock said quickly.

'I'm sure,' the President said with studied irony.

Bostock peered at him over the rim of his cup. 'Saddam could still be persuaded.'

The President had wondered when it would come to this.

Before leaving Washington, Thack had shown him the report Sandy Richardson had somehow managed to charm out of that strange Englishwoman he had introduced to him at an embassy party in Washington several years ago. At the time Sandy was enjoying a swift, intense affair with her which, by all accounts, both realised could not last. Before matters could become difficult, the woman had been posted back to London, her tenure as embassy security officer seemingly good enough for her to have skipped a few rungs up the promotion ladder. When he'd appointed Sandy as ambassador to the Court of St James, he'd casually mentioned that Nancy Roberts was now head of MI5.

The report itself was a masterpiece of Bostock at his most perfidious. For almost a year he had encouraged some of his industrialists to join forces with their German and French counterparts to provide Iraq discreetly with the materials to rebuild its depleted military resources – just as their predecessors had done before the Gulf War. Bostock called it the Saddam Option.

Abruptly the President rose to his feet and walked over to his desk. From a drawer he produced a document and turned to Bostock. 'Is this how you and your friends intend to persuade Saddam?'

The President thrust a copy of the Saddam Option into Bostock's hand.

The Prime Minister glanced at it, riffling through the pages, to his own signature at the end. 'Where did you get this?' he demanded, his voice blustering.

The President smiled thinly. 'You can keep it. I've got plenty more copies, Arnold. And I'll have no problem making sure they get into the right hands. The media, for a start. Your Opposition. And the environmentalists you've been trying to cultivate. Think what they'll make of it. You name it, and I'll have a copy there in no time.'

'Are you threatening me?'

'Threatening you?' The President shrugged. 'That's a funny choice of words for someone who is hell-bent on giving Saddam a chance to threaten his neighbours once more – just so you and your friends can increase their holdings . . .'

'What the hell are you . . .'

'It's all there, Arnold,' said the President coldly. 'How you and Marceau and Sturmer were going to line your pockets through surrogates. The good thing about people like you is that you always leave a paper trail.'

Bostock sat back in his chair. 'So what are you going to do?' he demanded in a voice that could not quite hide its anxiety behind its rage.

'Nothing,' the President said contemptuously. 'To do anything would be to dirty my own hands. If you want to go to Baghdad to settle your miserable deal, don't do it in my time!' He walked to the door and opened it. 'Go and tell your friends exactly what I've said. And if you all want to get off at Beijing, that's also fine by me.'

*

Ignatius Bailey awoke like a combat veteran, instantly alert, his eyes taking in the flashing light on his bedside console, his ears listening to the voice on the tape.

'Before midnight.'

Bailey smiled. As usual the Arranger had used a synthesiser to disguise his voice.

He erased the tape and settled back in his bed.

The final countdown had begun.

The sing-song accent of the Chinese air traffic controller at Hong Kong's new airport ordered Air Force One to switch to the radio beacon at Guangdong, the next sector.

'Roger,' Locke acknowledged into his lip microphone, pressing a switch to reset a transmitter.

Beside him Patterson stared out at the sky. The sun was near its zenith. Below it the South China Sea seemed bathed in a pale aquamarine light, like watered silk. The colour was another reminder of Bron. On a trip to Bangkok he'd brought her back several blouses in that shade. She hadn't worn one of them.

Now, on the pretext of stretching his legs, he slipped upstairs to the surgery.

Helen was standing at her office's porthole window. She turned as he knocked and entered. 'It's beautiful,' she said. 'I never thought nature could be so beautiful. The clouds are like moving pictures, each one so different.' Her voice was like a salve, warm and comforting, and going straight to the core of his pain.

'My wife used to say that.'

'I called Dr Monroe. There's no change,' she said quietly.

Behind his aviator sunglasses he felt his eyes stinging and when he spoke his mouth seemed stuffed with wadding. 'Is he worried?'

'He'd hoped she would have shown signs of coming out of her coma by now.'

'And he's worried she could sink deeper?' he pressed.

Helen didn't answer for a moment. 'No one can predict that,' she finally said.

'But it's a real possibility.'

'Yes. It's a possibility.'

She wanted to reach for him, her eyes huge with sadness and compassion. But she knew, instinctively, that would be a mistake. If she had any chance of helping him, she had to do so by his rules. He had made it clear that emotion had no place in his work-day. He prided himself on running a tight, dispassionate ship where everyone, including himself, was expected to cover up that most painful and elusive truth, the reality of their own nature. Yet she wanted him to know that he was not alone.

Helen leaned against the edge of her desk. 'Right now what's happening to Bron is a lottery. To some extent it depends on her physical powers and her subconscious ability to marshal them. Dr Monroe – no one – can be sure how well she can do so. Everyone's different.'

'So what you are saying is that . . .'

'I know how painful it is to be in this situation,' Helen cut in. 'I have an elder sister who tried to kill herself.'

'Really,' Patterson allowed himself a moment of wryness. 'Is that supposed to make me feel better?'

There was silence in the office. Patterson was conscious of having spoken out of turn. 'Sorry,' he said. 'That wasn't called for. But everything seems such a mess. What happened to your sister?'

Helen waited a moment to allow them both to settle. 'Beth was in a coma for almost a month. One morning she woke up, just like that.'

'Was she okay?'

'Her doctors said not.' Helen's voice was hurried, as if she was half-thinking of something else. 'They diagnosed her as a schizophrenic. Only when I became a doctor did I realise the diagnosis was inaccurate. My sister had really only been crying for help. When she got it, she eventually became well again.'

'Do you think Bron is schizophrenic?'

'Not a chance,' Helen said, then held Patterson's eyes and said it again. 'Not a chance; that's a promise.'

He nodded. 'Bron wasn't sick when I married her. She was fine.'

She looked at him. 'So, by implication, you're blaming yourself?'

'It's hard not to.'

'What Bron did is nothing to do with you, as such, Ed. She chose the suicide option as her solution. We'll never know if she really meant to go through with it because she herself will never really be able to tell us. The mind is very protective of things like that.'

'That doesn't really make it any easier for me to live with.'

She straightened and stepped away from the desk. 'Ed, if you want to go on a guilt trip, no one can stop you. But save it until we are all back at Andrews.'

'Are you once more suggesting I can't do my job, doctor?' he asked stiffly.

'What I'm saying is that you are under a degree of strain right now. That's understandable. But you need to get a grip on it. Otherwise, I will have to take this further. Remember, my first duty is to the Man and his safety.'

What she had said was perfectly true, of course. He forced a smile. 'Don't worry about the Man. I'll get him home safely.'

As he turned to leave, Helen stopped him. 'I'm no

psychiatrist, Ed, but one of the first things I learned in my work is that no one can really change anyone else's life. At the bottom of everything, people are still only left with themselves.'

'I can't buy that,' he said, his voice still taut.

Helen shook her head, slowly, as if expressing regret. 'Of course you can't, Ed. But I'm only telling you something you really already know. It's buried back there some place in your subconscious. That all the fluff of life, the drive for money, material success or that impossible to define thing called happiness is just a kind of smokescreen, a way for people to hide the truth from themselves.'

She paused, too clever and too experienced not to give him a chance to say something. When he did not, she continued. 'Bron's in hospital and you're suffering badly. But you have to face the truth that whatever happens to her, you – Ed Patterson – will still be stuck with whoever you are. Think about that.'

He had done little else since he had returned to the flight deck. But the more he thought, the more the pain nagged in his gut, mocking his resolve to shake off his guilt over Bron.

In the Step, Morton had set up a conference call linking him to Danny in the American Air Force base in the Saudi desert and Gates in his office at Langley.

His eyes were almost closed and he sat perfectly still, as if some alchemy in his body had converted tension and uncertainty into a powerful resolve as he ran through in his mind what needed to be done. Then he began to give orders.

'Danny, I'm sending you Sean and his shooters. So you'll need two more Apaches and enough Chinooks for Sean's people. Tommy and Anna will fly the lead Apache, you the number two spot and Sean as point-man. Big Mike will be in charge of the shooters. You'll need to be on stand-by from the time Air Force One enters Iranian airspace. But no one moves until I say so.'

Next he addressed Gates. 'I want a constant feedback from that Halo, Bill. Images and sound. An update every half-hour, and sooner if the operator spots anything. Tell him he's also looking for a camel with a shell casing on his back heading towards Babylon.'

Gates chuckled. 'There shouldn't be too many of those around.'

'When the Halo gets close enough, I want it to take a long look at that old underground headquarters of Saddam.'

'That could be a problem, David. Stanway's people say the sat's track swings north before it reaches there. From the co-ordinates I have here that would put the HQ either outside or at the very edge of the footprint.'

'Let me have those co-ordinates,' Morton said. After writing, he pinched the bridge of his nose; he felt like someone who had run a long race which had left his mind and muscles aching with effort, as he calculated. 'Tell them we're looking for indications, not hard-core definitions, so they can elevate the camera speed to maximum, Bill.'

That would give the cameras an additional ten-mile radius. At the outer edge the images would probably be shadowy, but hopefully Stanway's analysts could make sense of them.

'When does the sat reach there?' Morton asked.

'Six hours,' Gates replied.

Morton nodded. It would be a close call. He glanced at the pad before him on which he'd noted something Danny had said. 'Have those Iranians up on the border increased in numbers, Danny?'

'The Kuwaitis say yes. But at the best of times they tend to exaggerate. The feeling among the American intelligence people here is that it's no more than the mullahs going ya-boo to Baghdad. Certainly a couple of thousand troops wouldn't get very far if they crossed the border.'

Morton made another note as he spoke. 'And we don't know if the Iraqis are showing signs of going ya-boo back?'

'None that I can tell. There's nothing on Baghdad Radio. And if the Iraqis were moving troops up to the border, then the obvious route would have taken them across the Halo's footprint.'

Morton jotted one more time. Those Iranians were close to where Bodor's bomb had originally been spotted; they could simply be mounting another search for the weapon.

Over the Step's paging system Patterson announced that they would be landing in Beijing in thirty minutes as Morton gave Danny a final order. 'Set up a new fuel-supply line to where Tommy turned back inside Iran. Make sure the Stealths leave enough at that point to fly on another hundred miles.'

Danny had said that Tommy's turn-back point had been equidistant from Babylon and the Iraqi border with Iran.

Immediately after Morton ended the call he began another one with Humpty Dumpty, Lester Finel and the Prof in Geneva.

The head of Voice Analysis offered an apology. 'There's no tape of de Brug's voice. It must have been junked in the clean-out.'

In his mind's eye Morton could see Humpty Dumpty, his huge bald dome of a head nodding as he spoke, sitting at his large workbench covered with all kinds of sound equipment, while around him his staff played tapes at various speeds and voice pitches.

'We've identified the voice on the Halo tape as of South African extraction. The tonal quality puts your man somewhere between thirty and forty. The way he pronounced "Bodor" suggests he could be a linguist,' Humpty Dumpty said.

There was a diffident cough, then the Prof was speaking. 'My own view is that whether this is de Brug or not, his voice strongly suggests someone who has virtually eliminated any capacity for normal human feelings. All that deadness. Wouldn't you agree, Humpty?'

'Oh, absolutely. And it's a tone which certainly suggests a person who totally believes that what he does is not only not wrong, but is absolutely right.'

Morton heard a succession of cracks on the line. That would be the Prof pulling each of his long delicate fingers. A pianist's fingers on the hands of a Freudian with a killer's touch.

'The tonal quality reminds me a little of the late and unlamented Dr Gustav Romer,' the Prof said. 'Both share the same innate sense of evil in their voices.'

Romer had been a Stasi immunologist who had run a clinic specialising in transplanting stolen human organs until Morton had stopped him.

'Psychologically, de Brug is a loner. All the normal joys of life would be turned inside out in his mind. Sexually, he'd be at the extreme end of the deviant scale. Emotionally, he'd be on a par with a corpse.' The Prof sighed. 'Not a nice man, David, not at all nice.'

'How would someone like that end up working for Bailey?' Morton asked.

'I can answer that, Dave,' Lester said. 'Assuming it is de Brug.'

'Let's assume that.'

'Okay. De Brug was deputy director of security at

Globoil when Meridian took it over. Our computers found his name on an old staff list. After the takeover, de Brug was transferred to Meridian's headquarters. A year ago he went out west as director of security for Nuclear Components. The latest company records show he resigned six months ago.'

'Any idea where he went?' Morton asked.

'Now that's the interesting thing, Dave. We began to run random immigration checks out of the USA. Into Europe, the Far East, South America and South Africa. We could only look at passports which, for some reason or other, an immigration officer had electronically copied. And there, at Heathrow, a day before the balloon race, was de Brug's. He'd come in on the Moscow flight. The Brits routinely pull a number of passports from those flights. And he's shown as leaving for Munich. So we checked the German records. There's a pretty good liaison system within the EU now, so a flagged passport gets quickly circulated. And, right enough, there again was de Brug. It had been copied as he left Frankfurt.'

'Let us guess. On a flight to Sardinia.'

'Hey, Dave! You know this already,' Finel protested.

Morton smiled quickly. 'Where'd he go from Sardinia?'

'Rome. Then Istanbul. Then anywhere. Apart from Israel. Immigration records in that part of the world are still in the bead-counting age.'

'But then he turns up in the Iraqi desert using a sat phone,' says Humpty Dumpty.

'Calling Bodor,' added Morton. 'The question is, was it long-distance or local?'

As Air Force One continued its leisurely descent into Beijing, Cowan made his way down into the luggage hold to retrieve the flight bag. The chief steward returned with it to his cubby-hole office behind the galley and carefully placed it in the small refrigerator which Morton, in his earlier thorough search of the crew's working spaces, had checked.

THIRTY-THREE

Lying on her bed, Zita ticked off the seconds in her mind: each number must be counted in a steady rhythm, like a heartbeat. Indoor time, she had decided, went slowly, not like in the gondola. Here a minute could seem like an eternity.

It was still only an hour since a bleeper in Bodor's flight jacket had gone off, its shrill, demanding sound tearing through the remnants of his sleep.

Throughout the early morning hours they had coupled repeatedly and his unshaven chin against her skin had increasingly felt like sandpaper. Yet even at the height of their passion she noticed his expression was flat, and afterwards, when he lay with his head on his arm, watching her through those deep black, heavy-lidded eyes and she had smiled at him, his smile in return had never quite reached his eyes. Then she once more felt a little frightened. Yet, when he entered her again, the intense pleasure he produced ran through her like electricity and her every limb tingled, and the more she cried out, the harder he had driven himself into her with an intensity she had never experienced with any other man.

She had read somewhere that sexual responses are more individual than fingerprints; if this was so, then she was certain they had perfectly matching prints. Their coupling had been a communion of bodies and minds, producing in her a sense of wonder. Afterwards when they showered, their bodies had once more pressed together and she'd closed her eyes as though she was at the end of some journey.

Yet, at the sound of the bleeper, he'd dressed quickly, not bothering to wash off the musk of her body and, in that moment, had once more become withdrawn: cold and distant, giving no reason for his change of behaviour.

After he left, she lay flat on her back, naked, savouring the last aftermath of sex, the damp sheet rumpled across her legs, and began to count.

She reached the end of another minute. For a moment she listened to distant sounds: the hum of a generator, footsteps, the opening and closing of a metal door. Familiar sounds.

She saw that someone had realigned one of the cameras so that the screen was filled with the wind-blown luminosity of the sky. Once more an electrical storm was raging across the heavens, the lightning moving in no discernible pattern, without sound. It was a scene of beauty and power, of nature at its best.

Suddenly she could not wait to be up there.

Zita started to count again, her eyes on the screen.

Morton strapped himself into the seat beside Carlo Marcello as Air Force One drifted down through pillows of cloud towards a Chinese landscape of subtle colours.

'Enjoying your flight, Mr Marcello?'

The industrialist shrugged. 'A plane is a plane. I prefer boats.'

Morton smiled briefly. Marcello glanced around the rear cabin as flight attendants collected glasses and cups from the leaders of the Pacific Rim countries.

'Which country do you represent?' Marcello asked. He had the air of a man who had chaired too many meetings.

'I'm with the United Nations.' Morton made his tone businesslike.

'And what do you do, Mr . . .?'

'Morton,' said Morton. 'I'm looking after security on the trip.'

Marcello looked at him, the expression on his face one of mild curiosity. 'For all these people, one man . . .?' The industrialist shook his head. 'Surely the President of the United States has bodyguards with him?'

'He is anxious not to appear different from anyone else on board.'

'But he is,' said Marcello with sudden emphasis. 'I listened to him at the Opera House. He is an idealist.'

A lock of hair fell over Marcello's forehead and he pushed it back with a quick flick of the hand, the gesture oddly boyish.

'You think his ideas are unworkable?'

Marcello gave a little shrug.

'The President also said it was a question of balance, Mr Marcello. And, if you remember, he was the first to admit there is nothing more difficult to plan, more doubtful of success, nor more dangerous to manage, than the creation of a new system,' Morton told him.

'He is correct there. And some of what he says is good. Until he described them, I had not thought of some of the problems being a problem. But too many changes too quickly could be equally harmful.'

'He feels the world can't afford to wait, Mr Marcello.'

They sat in silence, one that was neither embarrassed nor companionable. Each man had fallen, for a while, into his own thoughts.

Marcello glanced around the cabin. 'What can these people achieve? Do they think they can change a century of bad habits among their people? I hear them blaming the industrialised nations. But we do not make them smoke more, consume more. We only meet their demands for a better lifestyle.'

'That sounds like an Ignatius Bailey speech. It's people like him the President needs to convince. Maybe you can do that?'

Marcello lit a cigarette and looked at Morton through the smoke. 'I am here to listen. I shall keep an open mind until I have heard everything. But naturally, like you, I have formed certain impressions.'

He sucked at the cigarette, then rotated it between thumb and first two fingers.

'Do you like working for Bailey?' Morton asked.

'I do not work *for* him. I work *with* him,' Marcello replied shortly.

Morton allowed his smile to come and go. 'I have the impression your daughter doesn't quite grasp the distinction, Mr Marcello.'

Something came and went in Marcello's eyes. 'Why would you mention my daughter?'

'She seems a remarkable young woman.'

Marcello appeared not to have heard. He waved a hand as if to indicate a world beyond the cabin. 'I am a wealthy man, Mr Morton. Recently I have become wealthier through my association with Mr Bailey. It is no secret that at times we do not agree. The newspapers write of it. But they make it worse than it is. And in the end it does not matter. Marcello Enterprises remains the jewel in the Meridian crown. Last year we made more profits than any other company in the group. That is what ultimately matters.'

Once more Marcello flicked the lock of hair back into place before continuing.

'I had hoped for my daughter to take over Marcello

Enterprises. She has the ability. A good financial brain. The necessary ruthlessness. She has all the qualities to build on my success. She does not need to be sensitive to what we produce. It is not necessary even to please people or gain their admiration, only their respect. To do that all she should have to do is to make sure we continue to produce and sell.'

He paused and sighed. 'But what does she do? Try and destroy all I have created. Why? Because she wants a different world. Not even one where her values and mine can exist together. But one where only hers matter.'

Marcello looked up, frowning. A flight attendant was standing beside Morton's seat.

'The President wants to see you, sir,' Carolyn Dempsey said.

Morton followed her back up the aisle as Patterson announced over the speaker system that they would shortly be landing in Beijing.

Wreathed in cigarette smoke, Carlo Marcello sat lost in thought.

Morton found the President sat behind his desk, coat draped across the back of his chair, shirt sleeve rolled up, his eyes watching Helen to see if she displayed any concern. She removed the blood pressure cuff and smiled reassurance. 'Still perfectly normal, Mr President.'

'You should have been here a few minutes ago,' the President grunted.

'I'll see you after Beijing,' she said. Carrying her equipment, she left the office.

After she'd closed the door the President told Morton that the Secretary of State had called to say that the mullahs had suddenly cancelled their invitation. No reason was given. Palmer was working through the Swiss embassy in Tehran to try and get Muzran to reconsider – but the

Secretary wasn't holding his breath.

The President squinted at Morton, 'What do you think Muzran is up to?'

'He may have underestimated the response to your visit. Because you're also going to Israel, his fundamentalists would see that as virtually an act of war,' Morton replied.

The President's face was a study in sudden misgiving. 'Whatever's behind this, it's left quite a hole in the Middle East part of Earth Saver.'

'Any response from Baghdad?' Morton asked.

The President's brow furrowed into a deeper frown. 'No. At least not directly.'

He looked at Morton for a long hard moment, then told him about Arnold Bostock's visit.

In the NSA facility in Washington Hernandez had been monitoring the progress of the Halo above the Iraqi desert for five long hours. He had seen nothing, and heard nothing but the faint hiss of static from the feeder link at the satellite ground station high in the Atlas Mountains of Morocco. Suddenly a number of blurred shapes appeared on his screen. He tapped instructions on his keyboard and they became high-definition images.

Hernandez called the watch commander. Then he pressed a tab to produce a hard copy of the images from the laser printer beside the screen. In all he made fifteen prints. Each one showed a slightly different angle of a desert encampment. As Hernandez began to arrange them on a viewing frame on the wall, the commander joined him. They peered intently at the prints, rather like doctors studying X-rays.

'Why are they sleeping out in the open, Hernandez?' asked the commander, pointing to the figures sprawled around the tents. 'It's the middle of the night there.

Has to be cold as hell frozen over.'

'Let's find out,' said Hernandez. He turned back to the keyboard and typed in further instructions.

On to the screen came a close-up of a figure. The man's heavy winter clothing almost covered his face.

The commander squinted at it. 'He's not sleeping. He's dead.'

In moments all the faces had been scrutinised. 'What the hell caused those blisters?' Hernandez asked.

'It could be some kind of poisoning. Maybe nerve gas,' said the commander, reaching for the desk phone.

Beyond the windows of Ignatius Bailey's office, the weather had suddenly turned bitter. A steel-grey sky pressed down and, on the plaza, skaters in leg-warmers and ear muffs made patterns on the ice around the banyan tree. He watched a flurry of snow borne by the wind pass his window so that, for a moment, it seemed suspended before his eyes, then turned back to his desk.

The model of Air Force One had landed in Beijing on the VDU. On the electronic wall map the light blinked steadily in the Iraqi desert.

Bailey pressed a tab on his desk modem keyboard, instantly converting its screen into a television receiver.

The strident music of the CNN network was followed by the voice of an anchorman in Atlanta saying they were shortly going over live to the Great Hall of the People in Beijing to join the President on the latest stage of his global tour.

Bailey settled back in his well-padded armchair.

Inside the Great Hall Morton watched from the side of a stage almost large enough to park Air Force One on, as the President walked quickly to a podium festooned with microphones. Below, news crews recorded the moment.

At the back of the stage, flanked by China's Supreme Leader and members of the Politburo, the other leaders of the industrialised world sat on massive carved thrones. Morton saw that Sturmer, Marceau and Bostock's applause had stopped before the President reached the lectern.

Morton thought it was fortunate for America, perhaps for the whole world, that the President was a man for whom the vexations of office allowed him to retain a sense of perspective. A lesser man would have felt sorry for himself at the behaviour of those three.

Morton's own already favourable impression of the President had been reinforced. Here was a man who would see off any challenge to his own admirable code of ethics.

Now, waiting for the packed hall to become completely silent, the President spoke. 'We are on the edge of a new millennium, one which offers us all two choices. We can either help to end the ravages of a century of industrial-era pollution by producing a new technology to serve humanity. Or we can continue to increase the numbers of people who sink below the poverty line while the rich get richer by controlling the price of gasoline at the pump and food in the shops. And above all, by raping the environment and polluting the very air we breathe. This we must stop – and stop it now. Not tomorrow. *Now!*'

He paused to allow the first thunderous wave of applause to come and go.

'Thirty years ago people used to say they were living in the second industrial revolution. They were properly impressed at the speed and profundity of the changes around them. Man had gone to the moon. There was talk of colonising outer space. But only if you lived in an already established industrial nation. For the rest of the world – for the peoples of China, India, Africa and Latin

America – there was no revolution. They were still on the wrong side of the greatest divide in human history – the great gap between the Haves and the Have-Nots.

'That has now changed. Look around you. In China today there are as many fax machines and cellular phones as in the United States. In India there are more people than ever before plugged into the Internet and the world communications grid. They work on their PCs and export software and high-tech products. In many ways they are not distinguishable from their counterparts in the older industrial nations.'

He quickly waved for silence when the applause started.

'All this is to be welcomed. But with it comes responsibilities. The very technologies which have made all this possible have also opened up a new environment and created new dangers. Let me give you an example . . .'

At Beijing International Airport, inside a high-security perimeter, the crew of Air Force One had gathered to watch the President on the screen in the upper deck salon.

'. . .One of my predecessors was seriously tempted to go along with a proposal to build a barrier across the Baring Strait. The intention was to warm the Arctic Ocean, and use powerful atomic-powered pumps to speed the water northwards. American industrialists, the very ones who helped to produce that second industrial revolution, regarded the plan as the apogee of their creation. They argued a beguiling case of being able to produce hydro-electricity which would turn Alaska and the frozen north of Canada into a fertile land. Where there had been permafrost and snow, cattle would graze on pasture. Where there had been icebergs, wheat would grow. Where there had been tundra, the fruits of the loom would flourish. It sounded a wonderful idea – until the ecologists pointed out that the project would have raised water levels a good seven feet – the height of a very tall man – all the way along the coast of California to Japan. Parts of Hawaii would have disappeared for ever. So would many of the Pacific islands, the Philippines and Hong Kong.

As the President sipped water on screen, throughout the salon came gasps.

'Lenin had roughly the same idea,' Turner said to Kerr. 'He wanted to create a warm-water port for the Russian navy, so he had the idea of turning Siberia into a great lake. When Stalin saw the plan, he had a new idea. Turn the place into the gulag.'

Kerr smiled and turned to where Patterson had been seated. The chair was now empty.

'The Colonel's gone again,' Kerr murmured. 'Maybe he needs a stitch in his bladder.'

Turner shrugged and turned back to the screen.

Bailey had the feeling the President was facing him across the desk as he spoke directly into the camera.

'It is the duty of each one of us on this platform to ensure measures are taken to address the issues posed by ecological changes. Some of those, alas, cannot now be stopped. The best we can do is to slow them down. Others can be checked – if we act now. One way to do that is to ensure that developing nations are assisted, not inhibited, in improving their economies and living conditions for their peoples.'

Bailey saw the President glance to where Carlo Marcello sat among the Pacific Rim leaders.

'The great corporations of the world must use a more significant portion of their profits to help those countries. And not just by investing in machinery and factories which will ultimately only earn them more profit. But by ensuring a protected ecological balance in those countries where they make their profit.'

Bailey pursed his lips in a rictus smile.

'At the same time the developing world – even the poorest of the African countries – must adjust to economic reality. They must no longer be seduced by large and powerful foreign conglomerates. They must no longer allow ecologically devastating projects which destroy their rain forests, silt up their rivers, leave their land arid and worthless. Those nations must insist, and the United States will support them, that any industrialist who wants to work their land must guarantee to do so with energy-efficient conservation methods. If not, they should be refused the right of entry. If they are already there and refuse to change, they should be asked to leave.'

A new wave of applause came from the screen, cut short as Bailey reached forward and switched off the set.

In his pantry Chief Steward Cowan locked the door before removing the flight bag from the refrigerator and checking the contents. Satisfied, he closed up the bag and placed it back in the cooler compartment.

The man who had carefully packed the contents in Sydney had said they could quickly become unstable if exposed to heat.

Morton watched the President grip the lectern more tightly as he came to the end of his address.

'Many of you have already expressed your support for the measures I have already outlined in Washington and Sydney. It has helped to make the criticism from other quarters easier to bear.' The President paused, and smiled ruefully. 'If nothing else, I have learned that in no field is hypocrisy more shameless than in that of trying to make this a cleaner, safer, better world for us all to live in. There are still too many countries who pump their products into every corner of the world market, yet jealously guard their own markets – especially against those products which are not only better but more environmentally friendly.

'My own country must share the blame here. Today the United States has some four thousand tariffs and quotas on everything from sweaters to sneakers, from ice cream to orange juice. I intend to ask our Congress to cut these to the very minimum. I shall look to other industrial nations to do the same. It will be another step to avoid the inescapable truth we must all face. The Earth is slowly dying, and what was once impossible to contemplate – the end of life itself – is becoming ever more a reality. The terrible truth is that we human beings are increasingly becoming the greatest single threat to our planet. That threat can still be averted. I ask each one of you, wherever you are, to join me in averting it.'

This time the President allowed the applause to roll on.

Patterson put down the telephone in the Step and stood for a moment, almost physically bowed under with despair. Dr Monroe had just said there was still no change in Bron's condition.

Once more he felt an urgent need to relieve himself. When he had done so in the crew toilet, he saw that his urine was again tinged with blood.

THIRTY-FOUR

Bodor knew something was wrong; the symptoms shouldn't have returned this soon. Something was once more crumbling inside him, creating a division between body and spirit, in which his mind was disowning the body in which it felt trapped; a part of him craving, another urging him to resist. His mouth tasted sour, his breath putrid.

'You need another fix,' the Arranger said from across the room, managing to hide the disgust and contempt he felt, his voice conveying only that he knew and accepted the solution.

'It's the tension,' whispered Bodor, shifting on his bed, trying to get comfortable. 'The last few hours are always the longest, de Brug.' He knew his name now, knew that he wasn't Russian. But that was all. Except that since de Brug had arrived in the complex, he was like a man walking through a landscape of gravestones under a glowering sky.

'There's not long to go now. A shot will make the time pass more pleasantly for you,' said de Brug dispassionately.

Bodor thought: he has this way of looking through me as though I do not exist. 'You should try it, de Brug,' he suggested. Now that he knew his name he used it whenever he could, as if it would somehow help to establish a bond.

De Brug smiled briefly. 'There are other pleasures in life.'

An hour earlier he'd watched Bodor inject himself, quickly and surreptitiously, turning away as he did so, his hand shaking a little as if he were ashamed.

Afterwards they had completed the changes on the gondola and supervised the launch crew loading it on to the truck, together with the envelope and bomb. The truck was then parked at the foot of the ramp. With nothing further to do, they had both come here to Bodor's living quarters to wait until it was time to be driven to the site.

De Brug rose from the chair and went over to the desk. From a drawer he removed one of the sealed sachets, each containing a syringe loaded with cocaine. There were half a dozen left in the drawer; Bodor hadn't taken a fix now for some days. What was he trying to do? Go through the motions of normal living? Too late for that. You could see that on his face: the skin was loose and sallow, the lines around his mouth more deeply etched.

'Here,' de Brug said, lobbing the sachet to Bodor.

Bodor caught it clumsily, feeling his tension give way to relief. What did de Brug know about the pressures he had worked under these past weeks? Every successive day had become too short, the nights even shorter. He had driven everyone hard, but none more so than himself. Time and again he had forced himself on with the reminder that there was so much to do.

And now, when it was almost all over, de Brug had arrived, no doubt to claim the credit. For a moment a sudden rage once more gripped him, and in that moment he wanted to lash out at de Brug. But that look in his eyes stopped him. Instead he began to tear the sachet open.

De Brug turned to study the monitor; watching the sky, listening to Bodor's little grunt of satisfaction as he pierced the skin of his arm with the needle.

*

Air Force One had reached its cruising height and was heading west through the darkness across China when the communications major rang the galley. The call was taken by Carolyn Dempsey.

'Where's the chief steward?' the major asked her.

'He's supervising snacks and nightcaps, sir.'

'Fetch him.'

Moments later, after hearing what the major said, Cowan returned to the dining salon.

With the Pacific Rim leaders left behind in Beijing to discuss their role in Operation Earth Saver within the framework of China's emerging status as the next superpower, the salon had been re-arranged so that the President and the other leaders of the industrialised nations sat at a table in the centre.

Morton was seated at a table near the door, which had also been assigned to Carlo Marcello. A short time ago a flight attendant had taken a large whisky and water to the rear cabin where Marcello was busy writing. Morton wondered how much of what had happened in Beijing had impressed Marcello.

After the President's address in the Great Hall, the Supreme Leader had paid a fulsome tribute. During the reception and banquet which followed, the Pacific Rim leaders all but mobbed the President in their enthusiasm. So reluctant were they to let him go, they had followed him out to the airport to wave off Air Force One in the velvet darkness.

'I don't know about any of you, but I have never had an experience like that,' the President was now saying. 'It makes me realise that this job is not always a constant hike over an endless treadmill.'

'Time will tell,' Bostock murmured.

The President glanced across the table. 'Sometimes,

Arnold, you have to take people at face value.'

'Never a very good policy in politics,' said Chancellor Sturmer, forking a potato into his mouth.

President Marceau sipped his armagnac and said nothing as the President addressed the table.

'There'll still be scope for all our people to take a fair profit from the region without ruining its natural resources.'

Britain's Prime Minister smiled thinly. 'I'm glad to hear you say that,' Bostock said. 'For a moment, listening to you in the Great Hall, I had the distinct feeling you felt we were on the *Titanic*, and the only question was whether we go down in first class or steerage. Personally, I'd prefer my country to go down in first.'

The President kept his voice calm. 'As I recall it, Arnold, your country, against all expectations at the time, played a key role in abolishing the slave trade. My one great hope is that at the end of this trip you will realise that, just as with slavery, things have to change.'

Morton saw the President pause as Cowan whispered in his ear, then, smiling pleasantly, rise and excuse himself.

Passing Morton's table, the President murmured, 'Would you come with me, please?'

The President did not speak until they reached his office and he'd motioned Morton to an armchair before turning off a flashing light on his telephone console.

'Sorry to keep you, Cliff,' apologised the President, settling in his own chair. 'We were having a post-prandial drink.' He adjusted a dial on the console. 'I've got you on the speaker, as Mr Morton's with me. I want him to hear what you have to say.'

The Secretary of State's dry, reedy voice filled the office. 'There are problems with Iran and Iraq,' Palmer began. 'A little while ago one of Bobby Stanway's operatives in charge of that Halo spotted a bunch of very dead Arabs out in the Iraqi desert. Bobby ordered a full eyeball search of the area. He is now certain they all died from exposure to radiation.'

'Jesus Christ!' said the President.

'It gets worse. Baghdad Radio has just put out a story that Iran had launched a nuclear tactical weapon strike that was supposed to hit Baghdad but fell short. The Iranians are claiming Iraq has done exactly the same to them. They say they've found a dead shepherd on their side of the border who has all the signs of exposure to radioactivity, and they're saying they expect to turn up more victims soon. Tehran Radio has started to remind its listeners what Saddam did to the Kurds a few years back.'

'I remember that,' whispered the President. At the height of the Iran–Iraq war, Iraqi planes had dropped nerve gas on a Kurdish community inside Iran; five thousand men, women and children had died instantly.

'Do you think either side is really crazy enough to have begun trying to nuke the other, Cliff?' asked the President.

The Secretary's sigh carried all the way from Washington. 'Who knows? When it comes down to the wire there's nothing to choose between them.'

'What are the Israelis saying?' the President asked.

'I just spoke to Tel Aviv. They say there's been no evidence of a nuclear explosion on either side,' Palmer replied.

'So what the hell is going on, Cliff?'

'Right now both are at the posturing stage,' Palmer continued. 'Tehran's yelling that Saddam had those Arabs killed to give him the excuse to attack Iran. The more militant of the mullahs are calling for the promised new holy war against Iraq to begin.'

'Oh, Christ,' said the President. 'That's all we need.'

'What's Muzran saying?' Morton asked.

'That's the damnedest thing,' Palmer replied. 'On this – nothing. Either he doesn't believe Iraq is behind it or, if it is, he doesn't think the time is right to launch a *jihad*.'

'Let's hope you're right,' the President said fervently. 'He changed his mind about my visit?'

'No. Only he says you're absolutely free to use Iranian airspace.'

'We'll thank him for that,' said the President drily.

'What about Baghdad?' Morton asked.

'The same,' Palmer replied. 'No visit. But no problem in flying through.'

The President looked at Morton. 'What do you make of it?' He leaned back in his chair. It creaked loudly in the silence.

'They're not going to start anything until we're out of the way,' Morton predicted.

'You're sure of that?' the President asked.

Morton could sense the uncertainty that gripped the President and, in that moment, he could feel the cold rising in the small of his own back, like ice melting upwards. If he was wrong, the consequences for the President could be catastrophic.

'I could arrange for you to have an escort of our fighter bombers as you pass over Iran and Iraq,' Palmer said.

'I've told you, Cliff, I don't want to appear like an invasion force,' the President replied with a hint of irritation. 'Something like that would be a propaganda gift for the fundamentalists. One of the key points of this mission is that I'm doing it without those kinds of trappings.'

'If I may say so, you're putting a lot of faith in a couple of people I wouldn't trust to give you the right time of day,' Palmer said. 'Don't you agree, Mr Morton?'

'Muzran and Saddam are both pawns,' Morton said firmly. 'They're being used to provide a diversion for Bodor.'

From Washington came Palmer's grunt. 'Geographically that gives him a great deal of space in which to pick his spot.'

'Possibly not,' Morton replied.

'Can you be more specific?' demanded the Secretary of State.

'I'd prefer not to,' Morton said calmly. They'd know soon enough.

'Bailey?' asked the President tightly. 'Is he behind this?'

Morton gave a small hard smile. 'I still don't know that, sir.'

'You have Marcello on board,' interjected Palmer. 'Why not put pressure on him, Mr Morton, to see what he knows?'

Morton shook his head firmly. 'I don't think Marcello figures in Bailey's calculations, at least not in the way we would expect. He's probably just another pawn.'

'You seem to have a lot of pawns, Mr Morton,' Palmer snapped.

Morton looked at the telephone console. Had he found answers or only added more questions? The only certainty was that the pot was close to boiling over. And he was holding it. And must continue doing so. That was why he was here.

The President was staring at him across the desk. 'What do you recommend, Mr Morton?'

'That everything remains as at present, sir.' Even as he spoke, Morton could not be sure he had made the correct decision.

THIRTY-FIVE

Stepping out of the shower and towelling herself as she walked back into the bedroom, Zita saw that the view on the monitor had changed back to its familiar desert scape.

After a while, when she'd grown bored with counting off the minutes, she had thought some more about Bodor. He surrounded himself with silence, creating a wall of things left in the air: whenever she pushed against it, he had withdrawn behind the barrier. She had never met anyone like that before. Even when she had felt enclosed by his bodily warmth, there was a distance between them; when he ran his fingers over her skin, there had been something remote about them. And afterwards, when she had wanted to talk, he'd said they should sleep. It was as though talking would have created a gap in his composure, to have enabled her to find a way through that wall.

Zita walked over to the bed where she had laid out the flight suit and the clothes she would wear beneath it. She put on the first set of thermal underwear, tucking the longjohns into heavy woollen socks. She next donned a second layer, a one-piece garment made from heavy cotton. Next she zipped herself into the flight suit and tugged on her boots.

She wriggled her toes and bent and stretched her body to make sure there were no constraints. Satisfied, she looked at the clock, and frowned at the slow passage of time.

Out of the corner of her eye, on the monitor she saw a

flash of lightning out by the perimeter fence, and one of the dogs suddenly collapse. Despite the warmth of her flight suit, she shivered.

Continuing to consume three thousand pounds of jet fuel an hour, Air Force One left China's airspace and entered Pakistan to the south of Amritsar. The snow-capped peaks of the Himalayas fell behind as Cowan called Patterson to say the President and his guests had turned in for the night.

Patterson had ordered the aircraft rigged for night flying. Cabin lights were doused and the air conditioning turned down. The chief steward said he would remain on duty, ready to answer any call bell, while his staff joined crew chief Sutter and his team in the upper deck salon for a few hours' sleep in the pullman chairs. Helen had called down that if anyone needed her she could also be found there.

Patterson turned to Locke. 'I'll go and take a leak, then snatch an hour's shut-eye.' Once more he felt a burning sensation in his bladder.

'I'll holler if anything comes up,' Locke said, his hand gently resting on one of the levers which helped keep them on course and on schedule. The plane was on autopilot, needing only monitoring of the instruments and controls.

In the crew toilet Patterson saw that his urine was still stained with blood and the slight tremble was back in his hand. He gripped the edge of the washbowl and took a deep breath to calm himself, to try and ease the pain in his gut. What the hell was causing it? Maybe it was an ulcer. He sat down on the toilet and closed his eyes, trying to relax. After a while the pain began to ease. He stood up and splashed cold water on his face, patting the skin dry with a hand towel, then he looked in the mirror. Apart from a little paleness, he looked fine. He glanced at his watch. Late afternoon in Washington, time to call Dr Monroe again. He walked the few yards to the Step and stopped outside the door. From inside he could hear Morton's voice.

Who the hell was he talking to now? The guy never stopped working on the phone.

Through his night glasses de Brug watched the Stasi commandos on the other side of the perimeter fence going about their business. They rose and fell like phantoms, seeming uncannily able to judge the interval between each shaft of lightning for them to kill more dogs. The shot carcasses littered the sand. When the last animal was dead, the first phase of the operation would be completed.

Replacing his glasses in their case, de Brug turned and walked back towards the ramp leading down into the complex, once more running through the next stage in his mind.

A moment earlier Gates had told Morton that the Halo had finally spotted the camel out in the desert. The beast was dead.

'The close-ups show he'd gotten caught up in his guide rein and must have choked to death, David.'

In his mind's eye Morton could see Gates, sprawled in his easy chair, receiver cradled under his chin, staring out over the Langley parkland.

'What about the casing, Bill?'

'No sign. It probably fell off someplace.'

Morton glanced towards the door. Once more there was the sound of someone in the corridor. He waited until it had passed. 'What's the life of one of those nuclear triggers?'

Gates glanced at his desktop computer screen. 'Manders says that once exposed to air, five to six hours.'

Morton made another note on his pad. 'So the one in that casing could be spent by now?'

'Right on,' Gates replied.

Morton almost smiled. Bill had a habit of sometimes using phrases which had passed their shelf life. 'How close is the Halo to that underground complex?'

'It'll start tasking in three more hours.'

Morton glanced at the calculations he'd made on the pad before him. 'We'll be just crossing into Iraq about then, Bill.'

Gates knew better than to ask a follow-up question.

Ignatius Bailey watched the model of Air Force One enter Afghanistan airspace south of Kabul. He estimated that its present course and speed placed it less than three hours' flying time from the light on the electronic wall map.

Zita heard footsteps coming down the corridor as she continued to watch the screen. She'd seen more dogs on the ground out by the perimeter fence.

From the doorway a voice called out, 'All set?'

She whirled, too stunned for the moment to speak. When she did, it was as if she still couldn't quite believe her eyes. 'What are you doing here?' she finally managed to ask.

'I've come to wish you a good flight,' Johannes de Brug said.

Carlo Marcello lifted the telephone out of the arm of his seat and dialled.

'Mr Bailey's office,' an efficient voice said moments later.

'*Si*. This is Carlo Marcello. I wish to speak to him.'

'One moment, please, Mr Marcello.'

Marcello looked around the darkened rear cabin he now had to himself with the departure of the Pacific Rim leaders.

'Carlo,' the familiar voice suddenly said, 'where are you?'

'I don't know. Everyone is asleep. Anyway, the President doesn't like announcements. He says they distract,' Marcello replied.

Bailey chuckled. 'So you're still on Air Force One?'

'*Si*.'

'How's it going?'

'For the President, very good. Everywhere he goes he seems to make new friends. He is not like I thought he would be. He is very informal and friendly.'

Play it the way he'll expect you to, Bailey reminded himself. He'd guessed Carlo would be impressed, just as Marcello would expect him to react in character.

'Be careful he doesn't win you over, Carlo. He's good at that. But that's not why you're there, to be soft-soaped.'

Marcello seemed unaware of Bailey's lurking anger. '*Si, si*. Of course. But sometimes we can learn and profit at the same time . . .'

'Not from that dreamer!' Bailey snapped, his pretence gone. 'He's living in another world. He doesn't realise the goal posts have changed. He still thinks the game is all about old dreams. The real dream is what we're building with Meridian. What he's trying to achieve is a nightmare!'

Bailey stopped. Carlo's call could be monitored.

'When do I see your first report?' Bailey demanded, his anger once more sheathed.

'I'll fax it to you when we arrive in Tel Aviv,' Marcello promised.

'Enjoy your trip, Carlo.'

Bailey broke the connection, turned back to watch the progress of the airplane model on the video display unit.

On the flight deck Turner acknowledged the guttural voice of the Afghanistan air traffic controller at Farah announcing that in five minutes he should switch to the beacon at Birjand, inside Iran.

'What's the weather update?' Locke called out.

'Clear over Iran,' replied Turner. 'But the electrical storms are still bad over Iraq.'

'Can we go round them?'

'No. They're running right down from Syria to the Gulf,' the radio operator replied. 'They seem to be worse around fifty thousand feet.'

Locke spoke to Kerr. 'See if we have enough fuel reserve to climb above them.'

The engineer began to calculate.

In the Step, Morton clasped the phone hard against his ear as he spoke. 'Read it to me.'

Chantal had just told him she'd picked up a piece of information from Sharon McCabe.

'*Science Watch* has learned that Sergei Mikhailovich Bodor, the former Soviet climatologist who was widely reported to be dead, is in fact alive and believed to be working on the creation of a revolutionary new weapon. While hard details are at this stage very few, it is reasonable to speculate that, given Bodor's background in military-related science, the weapon could be intended to affect certain weather conditions. Such a weapon could therefore have a number of effects on climatic warming. For example, it could affect the displacement of the jet stream, the rainfall patterns and even increase global temperature . . .'

Chantal stopped. 'There's some more technical analysis, but that's the gist of it.'

'It's enough, Chantal,' Morton said. 'More than enough.'

He told her why everything had fallen in place except where and when Bodor would strike.

THIRTY-SIX

The bouncing of the truck over the ground forced Zita once more to grab hold of the crewman who sat beside her on the wooden bench.

Another fork of lightning briefly lit the second truck as it emerged from behind a dune. It was carrying the gondola, the balloon and the bomb. She glimpsed Bodor's face behind the wheel. His eyes, staring back at her through the windscreen, seemed to be sunk deep in his cheekbones.

During the departure preparations he had seemed to be deliberately avoiding her. She wondered whether it was because of the Arranger's presence. He had stood to one side, carefully watching everything that was happening. When she had tried to help load the gondola, he had stopped her. Again, when she moved to board Bodor's truck, he had politely asked her to travel with him.

He sat opposite her now, arms folded, his coal-black eyes fixed on her. He had not spoken since they had boarded the truck.

Driving out through the perimeter fence, she saw that all but one of the guard dogs had gone. She'd spotted its body hidden behind a boulder, half its head missing.

Earlier, when she had asked, the Arranger had said that now the work was finished here, the dogs had been returned to the security firm which provided them.

She wondered why he had lied to her.

*

'Tehran air traffic control,' Turner intoned. 'This is Air Force One. Do you copy?'

'Ten-ten,' confirmed a voice in his headset.

'I have a question for . . .' the radio operator looked at the sheet of paper which had come down to him from the President's suite, 'His Holiness, the Grand Ayatollah Muzran, the Glorious Upholder of the Faith.'

'What is the message?' demanded the voice.

'It is from the President of the United States on board this aircraft,' Turner continued. 'I will read it to you.' He glanced at the paper on which the President had written and began to read aloud.

'"Greetings to His Holiness the Grand Ayatollah and his Revolutionary Council. It is my earnest hope that you will reconsider . . ."'

'Wait! Not so fast,' interrupted the voice.

Turner paused until he was told to continue. He spoke slowly and distinctly. '". . . reconsider your decision not to meet with me. I believe we have much of common interest to discuss. You would be most welcome to do so on board this aircraft if you will permit it to land." That is the message.'

'Wait on this channel,' the voice ordered. 'But do not deviate from your present course.' There was a click and the connection was broken.

Locke glanced at the instrument panel. They were ninety miles east of Tehran.

'His Glorious Upholder etc. etc. has fifteen minutes to make up his mind. I'd better get the driver back in his seat,' Locke said, punching a number on his headset.

Moments later Patterson arrived on the flight deck. Strapping himself in, he listened without interruption as Turner read back the message. 'Do we have enough fuel to orbit Tehran while Muzran makes up his mind?' he asked Kerr.

'No more than fifteen minutes, Colonel. I'd have stretched it to thirty, but Lockie thinks we should climb to reach max ceiling over Iraq to avoid electrical storms. That will pretty well eat up our reserves.'

Patterson glanced at Locke.

'The storms are mostly at the fifty thou mark. I've provisionally indicated we go to fifty-five to get above them. Subject to your approval.'

Patterson nodded. 'Good thinking, Lockie. We may even try for higher.'

Locke began to study a flight sector map for Tehran's Mehrahad airport. 'It's a westerly approach. We'll come straight in to the city,' he announced. 'The nearest diversion is Shiraz, five-five-nine miles to the south.'

'I flew in there once,' Kerr said. 'It's a grade A dump. They don't even have a follow-me truck. Only a kid on a moped.'

The voice was back in Turner's headset. 'You will continue on your course. The Grand Ayatollah has left instructions that he is not to be awoken until it is time to pray.'

Air Force One bored on through the night. As it passed over the ancient Iranian city of Isfahan, it started to climb slowly.

Above the curvature of the horizon, the first flashes of lightning were visible over Iraq.

Hernandez cursed quietly. The Halo's cameras had stopped transmitting. He picked up the phone and dialled the engineer.

'You've elevated past fail-safe,' the engineer explained. 'Rack back a couple of notches, then wait fifteen minutes for the new focus to settle. You should be okay then.'

Hernandez tapped in a command on his keyboard. In another part of the building a computer the size of a house began to do the rest.

Each rack-back it authorised represented a shrinkage of one mile in the size of the Halo's footprint.

Alone in the back of the parked truck, Bodor felt the cocaine shoot in a concentrated bolus into his arm. He pressed down more quickly on the plunger, shivering in the chill wind which blew into the truck. To inject himself, he'd had to half undress out of his flight suit.

After de Brug had left his room, Bodor had removed the remaining sachets from his desk and slipped them inside the suit. When this was over, the first thing he would do would be to shoot up in comfort.

Plucking out the needle, he tossed the syringe on to the floor and dressed, feeling the familiar responses of the cocaine streaking through his body as the pleasure centres of his brain responded and neurotransmitters began their self-fulfilling excitation.

He closed his eyes as thoughts rushed through his mind too swiftly to vocalise, too unco-ordinated to form a sequence. These first moments of pleasure were always like this. But gradually one thought coalesced: de Brug was trying to steal from him the proper credit he deserved for all he had created. That had happened before, in Russia – the very reason that had driven him to find solace and relief in the magical properties of cocaine. Racing through his mind now was the refrain: don't let it happen again. You are the genius who made it all possible. Never forget that.

He sat on the bench seat, forcing himself to breathe slowly, allowing the lethargy he'd felt driving out to the launch site to continue to be replaced once more with new-found energy. He felt powerful again. He could do anything. No one could tell him what to do. The Ozone Layer Bomb was his – not de Brug's. Yet that was why de Brug was here. To take credit.

He wanted to assure the inner voice he knew all this. But his mouth could not form the words. Yet somehow that inner voice had found a way to speak his name.

Bodor opened his eyes.

'We are ready to launch,' de Brug said once more, leaning over the tailboard into the truck.

'I know what you want,' Bodor screamed, standing up, crushing the syringe under his foot. De Brug didn't answer. 'Without me you are nothing! I made the bombs! The OLB is mine!'

Standing at the tailboard, Bodor glared at de Brug.

The launch crew, busy around the balloon, looked towards the truck.

'Answer me! Answer me, do you hear? *Answer* me!' Bodor screamed again.

Effortlessly, with only the minimum of movement, de Brug reached up and pulled Bodor to the ground. 'Bodor, don't be a fool. No one wants to steal anything from you,' he said calmly.

Bodor continued to scream. 'You've been planning this from the very beginning, de Brug!'

'Be careful, Bodor. Be very careful what you say.'

'Why are you doing this to me? Why? I trusted you!'

'Bodor – shut up. *Now*!'

As if to block out the words, Bodor put his hands over his ears. De Brug reached forward and pulled them away. 'Get hold of yourself, Bodor.' De Brug gripped him firmly by the arm and asked, 'Have you taken another shot?'

Bodor tried to break free. With only a slight movement, de Brug squeezed until the man winced.

'Take your hands off me, de Brug,' Bodor gasped. 'It's none of your business.'

'I'll let that pass,' de Brug replied.

Bodor stepped back, cursing silently. The cocaine had done this, unleashing a frightening neurological storm in his brain, something it had never done before. Thankfully it was raging with less intensity. He could begin to think again. Maybe he was wrong about de Brug, but he needed someone to focus the fury still in his mind.

He glanced to where Zita was checking the support wires on the balloon. Behind him, de Brug was speaking in the same soft voice. 'If you have reason to suspect anyone, it's her.'

Bodor turned back to de Brug. 'Why? She has done everything asked of her.'

'Of course,' de Brug cut in. 'That's what made her so good at what else she does. Think back at the way she slept with Kunsk. You know why she did that, Bodor? To try and pump him for information. The same reason she slept with you. With anyone she can learn something from . . .'

'I told her nothing,' Bodor said savagely.

'Naturally not.' De Brug smiled placatingly. 'But it's second nature for her to use her body.'

Bodor felt uneasy. 'What does she want this information for? She's only a balloonist.'

De Brug looked at him for a moment, as if debating whether to say more. When he spoke his voice was low and confiding. 'Her father is Carlo Marcello. He made his fortune by stealing the ideas of others. His daughter is the same.'

'How do you know?'

De Brug smiled quickly. 'It's my business to know these matters. That is why I am here. That is why you must do everything I have asked you to do.'

Bodor nodded slowly. De Brug was right. Nothing must come between him and the credit he deserved.

'Everything will work out perfectly,' de Brug continued, putting his arm round Bodor's shoulders, as if to reassure him further. 'Believe you me, the last thing the people I work for would do is to take anything away from what you have personally achieved. That I promise you.'

Bodor looked at him, suddenly curious. 'You have never told me who these people are.'

De Brug laughed softly. 'You must contain your curiosity a little longer. But I can tell you this. They are so pleased with what you have done already, and will continue to do, that they have decided to give you a special bonus. It will make all your dreams come true. That I can also promise you.'

De Brug began to walk with Bodor over to where the gondola was already off the ground and being held in check by the pole-men. Inside the gondola they could see Zita directing a tongue of flame from the burner into the envelope.

Suspended beneath the gondola was the Ozone Layer Bomb.

Air Force One continued her climb. Ahead, through the cockpit plexiglass windshield, rose the peaks of the Dead Mountains. Beyond was the border with Iraq.

'Colonel, I'm getting a reading again,' Kerr called out. On the panel before him the on-board geiger counter had already recorded radioactive emissions as they'd passed over the inland sea south of Isfahan.

'Same level?' Patterson asked.

'Yes.'

'Log it, and let someone else worry.' Patterson knew the only way of discovering whether the emissions were from nuclear waste or part of Iran's new atomic arsenal, widely believed to have been provided by the Islamic republics in the former Soviet Union, was when the print-out was analysed at Andrews.

Anything suspicious would eventually end up on the desk of one of the United Nations inspection teams. These were created after the Minsk Agreement under which the Soviet republics, anxious to show the world that they were politically mature, had promised to allow control over all nuclear weapons to remain with Moscow. In reality the Muslim republics had refused to do so. And from within their own turbulent borders no one knew how many nuclear weapons had found their way secretly into Iran.

'Identify yourself,' a voice suddenly demanded in Turner's headphones.

'This is Air Force One of the United States Air Force en route to Tel Aviv,' Turner intoned. 'Who are you?'

'This is Borojurd military air traffic control. You are above your flight plan as filed.'

Patterson half turned in his seat. 'I'll take it,' he told Turner.

He began to speak into his lip mike. 'This is the aircraft commander, Air Force One. My apologies for diverting from the plan. We are climbing to avoid electrical storms on our track over Iraq. Request permission to continue to do so.'

From a transponder came the rapidly fading voice of the Iranian controller. 'Permission granted. May the Merciful Allah guide you through the sky.'

'Allah is Great,' Patterson replied in his gravest voice. '*El-Bukra-e-Mish-Mish.*'

After Patterson clicked off the mike, Locke looked at him in wonder. 'Where'd you learn that?'

Patterson grinned. 'Listening to an ethnic radio station in Washington.'

For the first time since leaving Beijing, the pain had eased in his gut.

Ignatius Bailey watched the model pass over the Dead Mountains. The Iraqi border was less than ten minutes' flying time away.

'Can you patch me through to him?' Morton asked in the Step.

Gates had just told him what the Halo operative was seeing on his screen.

'Can do,' Gates said.

There was a series of clicks on the line, then Morton heard a new voice.

'This is Sergeant Hernandez, sir. How can I assist you?'

'Tell me what's on your screen right now.'

Hernandez continued to speak in the same emotionless voice. 'The commandos are bringing another bunch of people up the ramp from inside the complex. They are being marched out into the desert, close to where they shot the last group.'

'Can you see their faces?' Morton asked. He had to be sure.

'I can look up their nostrils,' Hernandez said proudly.

'Okay. What about the prisoners?'

'They're not Iraqis. More Russian features. If they spoke, we'd know for certain.'

'And the commandos?'

'The sensors say definitely German. From the accents, Prussian, some Silesians. If there was more time we could probably tell which cities they come from.'

Morton smiled non-committally. He didn't need that kind of detail. 'How many have they brought up so far, Sergeant?'

Hernandez replied at once. 'The body count so far is

sixty-three. There's seventeen in the present group. Oh, sweet Jesus – you should see this. One of the prisoners has made a run for it . . . he's zigzagging like a quarter back . . . going like a bat out of hell . . . oh, sweet Jesus!'

Over the phone Morton heard the echo of rifle shots, then Hernandez sigh, a little louder than the hiss of filtered air circulating through the Step. A moment later the sound of a volley reached him.

'They've just shot the rest of the group,' Hernandez confirmed. 'It's a massacre down there. What the hell's going on?'

It was clean-up time.

'Sergeant, can you get your camera to focus on the entrance to the complex?' he asked.

'No problem. What am I looking for?'

'Tyre-tracks.'

'Okay. It'll take about thirty seconds to refocus. With the next generation we'll do it in milliseconds.' There was silence on the line. Then Hernandez was back. 'I have them. Two heavy trucks. Judging by the spread of the sand, I'd say they were fully loaded. With a bit of jiggling, I could probably get you the tyre make.'

The operative, Morton thought, had the confidence of all those who worked at the other shrines of mechanical intelligence he'd visited. They forgot it always needed human ingenuity to create that intelligence.

'That won't be necessary, Sergeant. Can you follow the tracks?'

'No problem. Just give me a mo.'

This time the silence was shorter.

'Here we go. Both trucks went out by the perimeter. By the way, the sand down there looks pretty scuffed and the sensors are identifying patches of blood. I can get an analysis . . .'

'Thanks. But there's no need to.' They would have killed the guard dogs.

'Both trucks swung left out into the desert. They seem to have been going quite fast ... Oh, damn!' Hernandez stopped.

'What's happened?' Morton asked.

'Picture's gone. Camera's on the blink.'

'Call Mr Gates when it's working again,' Morton said before he strode from the Step to the flight deck.

THIRTY-SEVEN

The balloon ascended steadily under the canopy of the electrical storm. Since lift-off Zita and Bodor had spoken only to check on, and confirm, progress.

She preferred it this way; it allowed her to concentrate only on the work in hand. For the moment Bodor, as a man, did not exist; he was simply here to do his job. Later, when all this was finally over, she would ask him the questions that for now she had pushed into the background.

A moment earlier he'd raised the thermostat on his flight suit. But he still felt cold; he always did when the effects of the cocaine wore off, leaving him dull and spent. He could feel the sachets rubbing against his skin, a reminder that he would need another shot soon. But there was no way he could inject himself here. He tried to numb his mind to such thoughts, leaving only this unpleasant ache in his body.

The altimeter passed through the 30,000 mark. The launch would be at 40,000 feet.

'How long?' Bodor asked one more time.

'Twenty minutes.'

He made a mental calculation. 'Then you need to increase the ascent rate by a hundred feet a minute.'

Zita positioned herself beneath the burner and fired a tongue of flame into the envelope. She glanced at Bodor on the bench seat. 'You want to put on your parachute now?'

she asked, not quite able to hide the mocking tone in her voice.

After he had clambered on board, one of the ground crew had tossed a couple of parachutes into the gondola. Bodor had grabbed one while she kicked the other into a corner. She had never used a parachute: either you had faith in your balloon or you stayed on the ground.

'Have you ever made a jump?' she asked.

'Yes.' It had been part of his training as a Soviet military scientist.

'Did they teach you to jump from 40,000 feet?' she pressed.

'It is the same as from this height.'

She looked at him through her vizor. Inside his helmet he was pale, his eyes lifeless. There was something definitely wrong with him. But there was nothing she could do for him, except offer reassurance.

'You won't need to jump. I'll get you down like before,' she promised.

He sat back on the bench, clutching the parachute. De Brug had said it was the latest kind; he would need only seconds to clip it on the hooks sewn on to his flight suit.

Zita switched to a new tank of propane before sending another controlled burst of flame into the envelope as they passed through 31,000 feet. Nine to go. Eighteen minutes.

Above them the electrical storm stretched all the way back towards Iran.

With its contrails trailing behind in the sub-zero atmosphere at 56,000 feet, Air Force One bored on into Iraqi airspace.

On the flight deck the crew sat in stunned silence. Morton had just told them what could be about to happen.

He had told them everything, his voice uninflected, yet unsparing of himself or anyone else.

'What do I tell the President?' Patterson asked in a strangled voice.

'At this point? Nothing. There's nothing he can do.'

Patterson thought for a moment. 'I can declare an emergency – and turn back to Tehran,' he said. The pain in his gut had returned, like a raging, living thing.

'You'd still be refused permission to land. The mullahs are on their own agenda – and it doesn't include letting you in,' Morton said firmly. 'Call Baghdad. Tell them we have to make an immediate course change. That we're low on fuel reserve. Whatever you feel will make them agree. Then head for the base in the Saudi desert. The important thing is not to give anyone a hint we suspect anything. Let's just try and sneak out of trouble.'

'But we don't even know for certain where this balloon and its bomb is,' Patterson said.

Morton turned away from him. It was a gesture, not of dismissal, but of thought. Around him, the others sat waiting, still figures in the diffused light. 'If I'm wrong, I'll take full responsibility. Right now I'd like a headset'.

Turner silently handed Morton one. In moments, using the facilities of the communications shack, Morton was patched through to Danny at the Saudi base and, on the far side of the world, to Hernandez in Washington.

As Patterson began calling Baghdad, Morton listened without interruption while the Halo operative brought him up to date.

'Any new activity around the site, Sergeant?' Morton asked.

'Negative, sir,' Hernandez replied.

After the satellite's cameras restarted, the trucks had been spotted, together with bodies scattered around on the sand. It looked like another massacre, Hernandez had said.

It looked like de Brug hadn't lost his touch, Morton had thought.

Shortly afterwards the Halo had picked up a Range Rover heading east towards the Euphrates.

'Where are those commandos, Sergeant,' Morton asked.

'Also heading for the river. Maybe they have a boat waiting,' Hernandez suggested.

'You hear that, Danny? Get one of the Stealths to take a look.'

'Will do, David.'

'And move everyone up to the Saudi border,' Morton added. In his mind the terrible inevitability of a chain reaction had begun.

Patterson began to intone once more. 'This is Air Force One to Baghdad air traffic control. Request immediate permission to change course due to fuel shortage . . .'

He received no acknowledgement.

On the screen Ignatius Bailey watched the model creep slowly into Iraq, heading towards the unblinking light in the desert. Nothing broke the silence of the office except the wind swirling the snow against the windows. Bailey shivered. Not from the cold. In anticipation.

Air Force One was now at 58,000 feet and still climbing up into the electrical storm.

In the galley Cowan was supervising breakfast preparations. In the bedrooms, the leaders of the industrial nations were beginning their ablutions. In his pullman seat Carlo Marcello still slept. In his office the President was studying his briefing paper for the stopover in Tel Aviv. The Syrians and Palestinians would be sending delegates. He would have hard things to say to them all.

He was interrupted by a knock on his door and the arrival of Helen carrying her blood-pressure gauge.

'Good morning, Mr President. How did you sleep?'

'Like a log.'

'Good. Now let's see how your reading is this morning.'

She completed her check and smiled her approval. Gathering up her equipment, she gave him another smile. 'Enjoy your breakfast, Mr President.'

'Ay-ay, Commander,' the President acknowledged with mock nautical graveness.

She left, pleased at his mood. Carolyn Dempsey was waiting outside with the President's breakfast tray.

Impulsively Helen lifted one of the silver plate covers. Beneath was a cooked breakfast. She shook her head. 'And I thought I was making progress with him.'

Zita broke the silence in the gondola.

'Thirty-seven thousand feet.'

Bodor knelt on the floor and lifted the trap door, then clipped the parachute to his flight suit as icy air rushed into the gondola.

Below him the Ozone Layer Bomb swung from the launcher.

'Baghdad. This is Air Force One,' Patterson said one more time into his lip mike. 'Request permission to switch course now. Our present height is 59,000 feet. Our radars show no other movements in the vicinity.'

There was no response. Patterson felt the pain sear through his whole body. The windshield reflection accentuated the hollows of his face.

Morton was speaking in a quiet, urgent voice. 'Any sign of that balloon yet, Sergeant?'

'No, sir,' Hernandez reported.

'Danny, have the Stealths picked up anything?'

'Those Iranian troops are still on the border. But they don't look threatening. One of the bombers has done a sweep up the Euphrates. There's a lot of traffic, but nothing obvious.'

'Keep looking, everyone,' Morton said into his headset, expelling one short breath.

He peered out into the sky as Air Force One began to bank to the south. Had he chosen the right direction? Supposing the balloon was still in its path? And no one had been able to tell him the effective range of a nuclear trigger on a bomb launched from it.

Bodor watched the launcher fall away, heard the shriek of the casing through the air, saw the cluster of balloons emerge and felt the gondola begin to climb more rapidly as it was freed of the weight of the bomb. As he continued to watch, the cluster drew level with the gondola, then climbed rapidly towards the bomb's detonation height of 80,000 feet. It would reach that point in exactly twelve minutes.

'Close that trap,' Zita called to him. 'It's acting like a funnel. It's already sucked us up another thousand feet.'

Bodor's mouth twitched, then he seemed to steel himself. He watched the altimeter climb towards the 42,000 mark.

'Christ's sake, hurry up, Bodor, and batten down that hatch.'

He turned towards her and laughed.

Zita blinked, still watching him. 'Bodor, what the hell's so funny?' she asked.

'You.'

She saw something in his eyes which had not been there before, a little rolling movement.

'Me? What's the matter with you, Bodor? You crazy or something? Now close that damned trap and don't act so damn crazy!'

Bodor's gaze rose to Zita's. 'You're the crazy one. You and your father. Thinking you could cheat me!' There was something far more terrible than anger in his laugh. A madness.

'*What!* My father? What has he to do with any of this?' The fears she had pushed to the back of her mind raced to the surface. 'Are you involved with my father? *Are you?*'

Bodor laughed even louder. 'You think I'm a fool? I know what you've been planning!'

Behind the vizor she saw his eyes were wild.

'Bodor, I don't know what the hell you are talking about. But just let me get us down, and we can settle all this.'

For a moment the skin around his eyes seemed to tighten. Then Bodor grabbed her parachute and dropped it through the hole into space.

'Bodor!'

But he'd already plunged through the trap, counting off in his head until it was time to pull the rip-cord.

Above him the gondola was rushing upwards at ever increasing speed, the rush of the wind through the trap drowning Zita's screams of terror.

On the flight deck Morton glanced at Kerr's instrument panel. 'Keep your geiger counter running,' he said. The counter would be the only way to differentiate between the electrical storm's discharges and the controlled explosion the nuclear trigger could produce. Except that no one knew how controlled. A trigger had never before been used in this way.

'We're at sixty thousand,' Locke called out. 'She's starting to drop off.'

Air Force One was 5,000 feet above its previous best altitude. The thin air could barely support its weight.

Morton spoke to Patterson. 'We have two options. We try and stay at this height. Or we do a fast-order descent. Both have their risks because we don't know at what height the bomb will be detonated.'

Patterson felt as if his life was in suspension. Was it fatigue or fear? He had felt like this that time over Bosnia. That time he had been lucky. Maybe his luck would still hold. His mouth opened, closed, and then he asked, 'Maybe it doesn't matter? At our speed we could be out of range already?'

The others were looking at Morton. In that moment he had a memory of a surrealist film he'd once seen. Two hours of absurd dialogue which had ended in shocking violence.

'We stay at this height,' Morton said.

Tumbling through space, at the count of sixty in his head, Bodor tugged hard on the toggle to release the parachute. The toggle came away in his hand.

The taste of betrayal co-mingled with abject fear in his mouth. Then, there was nothing.

Using all her strength Zita managed to close the flap on the trap door. The terrible rush of air stopped. She looked at the altimeter. Forty-five thousand feet. She had never been this high. Was that why she had this pressure in her head, as if it was filling with a black liquid?

Half-crawling, she reached the row of compressed cylinders strapped to one wall and managed to attach her air line to a nozzle. She turned on the valve. There was a hissing in her headset. The blackness started to lift. Then the hiss stopped. The cylinder was empty. She frantically uncoupled the lead and connected it to the next one. This time there was not even a hiss. The other bottles were also empty. Bodor had done this. Bodor and the Arranger, the small voice in her head told her.

She sat on the floor. A moment earlier the first grey of a new day had crept into the gondola. Now it was fading, becoming dimmer with each gasp for breath which hurt her chest as she inhaled. The black chaos was now in her ears, swimming behind her eyes. Above her she thought she could see a single star, a small point of light, brighter than the rest.

She could hear her lungs gurgling as the grey dawn faded even further back into a darkness in which only that one star still glittered, expanding like the pieces of a diamond which has shattered.

Around her the gondola began to break up, and above her the envelope was burning.

As she began to fall, the ache of effort for each breath was no more.

THIRTY-EIGHT

Turner's shout rang through the flight deck. 'Emissions! Reading's high enough for a small nuke!'

Simultaneously in Morton's headset, Danny was speaking urgently. 'A Stealth reports a burning object eighty miles north of where he has you on radar.'

'What's the object's height?' Morton rasped.

'It was first seen at forty-four. It's now dropping.'

Hernandez' voice broke in. 'The Halo's just spotted small falling objects in the same area. They could either be parts of the balloon or bodies.'

'Stay off the air until I call you, Sergeant,' Morton ordered. He turned to Turner. 'Can you try and pinpoint the detonation height?'

'The computer's already working on it,' the radio operator said, his eyes fixed on the instrument console. He turned to Morton. 'Around the eighty thousand mark. Emissions are rippling. Blast wave spreading.'

Simultaneously:

The shock wave ripped off the rear baggage-hold door that had caused the problem in Paris. It disappeared. Air entered the hold and, in a millisecond, swept all the baggage out into space. The access ladder leading to the next deck resisted, then was dragged from its mooring. The air mass burst through the door, ripping it from its hinges and entered the rear cabin. All this happened in seconds.

During the first of them, startled by the thunderous

hammering, Carlo Marcello had unbuckled his safety belt and was standing in the aisle, preparing to make his way forward. The wind embraced him in its icy grip and then, as if finding the warmth of the cabin not to its liking, retreated, sucking Marcello down into the hold and out through the opening left by the cargo door.

A millisecond later, an on-board computer − having wrongly identified the wind as the onset of a terrorist attack and assuming the cabin crew were already over-powered − ordered the protective steel doors lowered to isolate the cabin.

Its passage blocked, the wind howled its fury around the empty hold.

Air Force One, despite its battering, was still only lightly wounded. It would take more than the loss of the door to destroy the airframe's integrity.

But the wind would not give up easily.

Rising from the spine-jarring crash which had thrown her to the floor in her office, Helen heard the sound of rushing air above her head. A portion of the ceiling had come away, exposing a maze of pipes. Further back, over the operating room, she glimpsed grey sky.

The shock wave had discovered a weakness which no one realised had been there following the conversion work to create the on-board surgery. Now it continued to peel back slivers of the outer skin of Air Force One, increasing the means for the wind to find its way inside. The wind continued to advance, searching for what it sensed must be there. It found it in the new valves and pipework Sutter had fitted in Sydney. Part of the welding had not yet fully hardened. The impact of the shock wave had worked it free around a valve, allowing the wind to find its way deeper into the plane, to spread its lethal, invisible breath.

Helen, with a cool detachment, realised what she must

do. From a cupboard she removed two breathing masks and ran to the President's suite.

On the flight deck, alarms were ringing and flashing. Air Force One continued to bounce violently. The radio altimeter blared. A new shudder, so powerful that Locke could barely keep his feet on the rudder pedals, rocked the plane.

He continued to repeat into his lip mike. 'This is Air Force One declaring a full emergency. I repeat, full emergency.'

Patterson continued to stare out of the windshield, as if suddenly absorbed by the electrical storm.

Sutter's voice came over a loudspeaker. 'Someone use the override to raise the security shutters. I need to check the status of the baggage-hold door. It's showing open on my board.'

As Locke's hand moved to a switch, Morton stopped him. 'If it's blown, raising those shutters will create a vortex that'll tear us apart.'

'There could be people back there,' Locke said in a tight voice.

'Not any more,' Morton replied grimly.

Patterson said nothing.

A calm voice filled Morton's headset. 'This is Stealth wing leader. Closing on you to inspect damage.'

'Roger,' Morton acknowledged.

'Shock wave's passing, Colonel,' Locke said.

Patterson ignored him.

'Sweet Mother of Jesus!' Kerr was staring at the handkerchief he'd just taken from his mouth. It was flecked with fresh blood. He looked at Turner in disbelief.

The radio operator could barely see through his smarting eyes.

'Turn off the air system, Locke!' Morton said urgently. 'Ozone's found its way on board.'

Locke instantly flicked a switch.

The vacuum the shock wave created in its wake had filled with ozone which had descended from a deep layer in the upper atmosphere. Not moving with quite the same speed as the wave, it had taken a while longer for the ozone to reach Air Force One and begin to envelop the plane in its silent, invisible and deadly embrace, simultaneously entering the plane through the opening in the hold and the smaller ones in the upper fuselage.

'Full emergency descent,' Morton said.

Locke glanced quickly at Patterson.

'Colonel. All set . . .'

'Where are your back-up masks?' Morton demanded.

'On the shelf behind you,' Locke said.

The sibilant sound of air flow in the cockpit had died.

Morton put on a mask and thrust the others at Locke, Turner and Kerr. Each one had its own built-in air bottle. Leaning forward, Morton held a mask to Patterson's face.

'It'll help your porphyria,' he said. His voice was dead quiet.

Patterson ignored him.

Morton called to Locke. 'Start your descent.'

In the flash of lightning that seared through the flight deck, Morton saw the hesitation still in Locke's eyes, saw him glance quickly at Patterson.

'He's not fit to fly. Start your descent.'

'Colonel . . .?'

'Do it *now*,' Morton grated. He understood Locke's dilemma. But this was no time for the rule book.

'As you were!' Patterson's command came in a gasping voice. 'I'm still in command.'

Outside, the engines were labouring. Locke was exerting all his muscle power to hold the yoke.

'Dammit – dive! And that's my order!' Morton rasped.

As Locke reached for the dual controls, Patterson thrust the mask aside and grabbed at his yoke. He began to pull back on the throttles to send Air Force One climbing even higher.

'Christ, Colonel!' Locke screamed. 'What the hell are you doing?'

Patterson ignored him. He began to pull harder on the yoke.

Locke thrust his set of throttles forward.

Air Force One began to shudder under the contra-commands.

Morton grabbed Patterson's wrist. It was like trying to grip a bar of greased steel. The skin was soaked in cold sweat. Patterson broke the hold and lunged at the throttle levers again.

Stepping back, Morton raised his hand and struck Patterson a controlled blow on the side of the neck. The aircraft commander slumped in his seat, his hands dropping from the levers.

'Jesus . . .' Kerr began.

'Give me a hand,' Morton cut in. 'He's had a bad attack of oxygen starvation on top of his porphyria.'

Morton dragged the unconscious Patterson out of his seat and Kerr helped to lay him down on the floor at the back of the flight deck.

Morton fixed the mask over Patterson's face. 'Keep him oxygenated,' he ordered. 'And Kerr, get the doctor here fast.' He locked himself into the aircraft commander's seat and turned to Locke.

The co-pilot flicked a switch and activated the paging system.

'Attention, everyone. We are about to make an emergency descent. Buckle up and wait for further instructions.'

'Okay, Mr Morton. Let's see what this bird can do.'

In tandem they moved the controls forward. The nose tilted down, then they were straining against their harnesses as the angle of descent increased.

'Air Force One. This is Stealth wing leader,' came the calm voice in Morton's headset. 'I'm out on your port side. You've lost a door and some skin off the upper fuselage. Otherwise, I see no other structural damage.'

'Roger,' Morton acknowledged.

'Is that Colonel Patterson?' asked the voice.

'The aircraft commander's injured. Mr Morton has taken his place,' Locke explained.

'Understood. Can you give the status of the President and his passengers?' the voice asked calmly.

'Right now we've got our hands completely full,' Morton said tersely.

'Understood.'

A moment later Helen called from the back of the flight deck. 'The President's fine.'

She'd left his suite at his own insistence. Strapped in his seat, mask to his face, he had waved her on her way, saying her presence down on the flight deck was more important.

Coming down, she'd felt the air becoming appreciably colder. From further back in the plane had come the sound of breaking crockery, shouts and cries. Mask held to her mouth, doctor's bag in her other hand, she'd reached the flight deck.

One glance at Patterson, and she called to Morton. 'What's happened?'

'He's got porphyria. I had to hit him.'

She nodded, understanding, wondering how Patterson had managed to cover up his condition. And how much of what had happened here could be laid at his wife's door? Moments before this emergency Dr Monroe had said that Bron had regained consciousness. She and Patterson would now have all the time in the world to sort out their problems, Helen thought. There'd be one less: if she had anything to do with it, Patterson would never fly again, not even as a passenger. Kneeling, she began to examine him.

'Stealth. This is Morton. The President is unharmed.'

There was no response. Beside him, Locke was straining to hold the yoke as the altimeter dropped through 55,000 feet.

'Stealth, come in,' Turner said more urgently. 'Do you read me?'

He tried again, keying his microphone.

Air Force One's rev counters were on the red mark.

'Christ, I hope she'll stand the strain,' Locke said. 'She's not rated for this kind of drop.'

'She'll hold.' Morton tried to sound more certain than he felt.

'Stealth. Do you read me?' Turner asked one more time.

He glanced out of the window. Through the lightning he glimpsed the Stealth way out on his port side. Why didn't she answer?

'Stealth. Come in. The President is unharmed,' Locke reported.

Air Force One was dropping through 50,000 feet when the communications shack major came on the internal loudspeaker.

'We're in bad shape up here. We've lost all power supplies, including back-up. And I've a couple of men down. Bleeding from the mouth.'

'Tell everyone to mask up,' Morton spat out. The ozone must be spreading fast.

Locke reached for the toggle that would release emergency oxygen masks built into the back of each seat throughout the plane.

'My radio's gone, too,' Turner confirmed.

Morton remembered that the actual transmitters and power supplies for both the shack and flight deck were housed at the far end of the baggage hold, hidden behind a partition screen. With the hold door gone, the wind must have ripped the partition aside and smashed the equipment.

Now, as it continued to plunge through the sky, Air Force One was like someone without his ears.

In the next moment it lost its eyes.

'Radars have also gone,' Locke called. 'The storm must have knocked them out as well.'

'We'll manage.' Morton's mouth was dry and his heart thumped as he gripped the controls.

Kerr called out from his station. 'Lockie, we're burning up sixty-seventy kilograms of fuel a minute.'

'How much flying time do we have left?'

'Less than two hours.'

'How far to the Saudi base?' Morton asked.

'The same.'

'So we'll be okay. How's Patterson?'

'He's coming round,' Helen replied.

'Can you keep him sedated?'

'No problem.' She took a pre-loaded syringe, braced herself on the floor and injected Patterson in his arm.

'Poor bastard,' Kerr murmured. 'What a way to end your career.'

Helen glanced up at him, then looked away.

'Forty thousand,' Locke announced.

The headlong plunge continued. Over the loudspeaker came a frightened sobbing. Everyone on the flight deck tried to ignore it.

*

Chief Steward Cowan sat on the floor of his pantry with tears in his eyes.

Scattered on the floor around him were the spilt contents of his flight bag. Jars had been filled with slivers of deer antler for treating flatulence and lizard scales for curing apoplexy, vials of snake oil for blood pressure and night sweats, powdered tigerhorn for hypertension, ginseng jelly for baldness and frog essence to treat constipation.

His sister had given him a complete shopping list to collect for her in Sydney which, she had told him, was now the main centre for the traditional Chinese medicine she intended to follow when she qualified as a doctor.

He had spent a month's salary buying the items she had requested. When the shock wave struck the plane, the refrigerator door had flown open, toppling the bag on to the floor and smashing the contents.

Holding an oxygen mask to his face, Cowan began to scoop with his other hand the now useless potions back into the bag.

As he did so, Locke announced over the paging system that Air Force One was now at 30,000 feet.

'Twenty-five thousand,' Locke called out. 'Brakes.' As his hand moved to the control which would slow their descent, he began to cough.

Morton reached across and yanked Locke's mask. His lips were rimmed with blood.

'Take her, Mr Morton,' Locke whispered, before slumping in his seat.

Morton instantly knew what had happened. The air supply in Locke's bottle was exhausted. He'd been breathing contaminated air.

'Another mask,' he called over his shoulder.

'There aren't any,' Kerr replied.

'Take mine,' Helen said, stepping forward. 'I'll share Patterson's.'

Morton didn't hesitate. 'Do it.' Right now he needed to keep Locke alive more than anyone on the flight deck.

Helen fitted the mask over Locke's face.

The altimeter whirled through 20,000 feet.

The breakfast service had just started in the dining salon when the shock wave had struck.

Carolyn Dempsey saw that the three leaders who had made it to the table continued to react differently.

The eyes of Britain's Prime Minister were filled with panic behind his mask.

Chancellor Sturmer had lumbered to his feet immediately the flight deck had ordered face masks to be put on, and returned from his cabin with breathing sets which were not Air Force One issue. He had distributed these to his companions and told them to remain calm.

Since then, President Marceau had remained silent.

Now he turned to the Prime Minister and spoke in surprisingly good English. 'You were wrong, Arnold, and Helmut and I were wrong to agree with you. We do not need Iraq. And what our host is trying to achieve is truly worthwhile. If I survive this, I shall give him the full support of France.'

The President of France turned and looked at the Chancellor of Germany.

'*Ja.* I agree. But first we must survive,' said Sturmer with Teutonic pragmatism.

Ignatius Bailey stared with mounting disbelief at the screen on his desk. The tiny model of Air Force One had been moving steadily towards the pinprick of light in the

Iraqi desert displayed on the electronic map. A couple of minutes ago the light had gone out.

But now the model was once more moving, this time away from the site of the nuclear trigger explosion, moving with increasing speed towards the Arabian desert.

The silence in the office was suddenly broken by the president and chief executive officer of Meridian International cursing with a profanity that was all the more frightening for being so unexpected.

Then, his initial fury spent, Bailey tapped a key on his modem to transmit a pre-recorded signal to the bridge of a boat sailing up the Euphrates.

Completely calm again, he next telephoned Thacker Stimpson in the White House.

'Mr Stimpson, one of Meridian International's communications satellites in the Indian Ocean has just picked up something which I felt you should know about immediately . . .'

For the next few minutes, as he knew he would, Bailey had the undivided attention of the Chief of Staff.

On the flight deck Helen rose from her kneeling position beside Patterson and called to Morton. 'I'd like to move him to a more comfortable place.'

Morton told Kerr and Turner to help her. Between them they carried the sedated aircraft commander to the first of the bedrooms. From the pile of London newspapers, Helen guessed it must be Bostock's. The crewmen laid Patterson on the bed and hurried back to the flight deck.

As Helen began to examine him, Patterson began to mumble. She bent close to listen, then squeezed his hand. 'Bron's going to be fine, Ed,' she said.

Through the starlight scope which amplified the smallest amount of natural light, de Brug watched the Stasi commandos emerge from the trucks and move, guns at the ready, to the bank of the Euphrates.

He climbed back into his Range Rover and drove down to meet them. The commandos barely glanced at him. Their work was done. Soon they would be on their way back to their base deep in the mountains of Iran. The mullahs hired them out as a self-contained mercenary force in return for hard currency.

Once more de Brug used the scope to peer down the waterway for a sight of the boat to take them all down to the Gulf and safety. He saw it now, about half a mile downriver, its freeboard low in the choppy waters. As he watched, the water at the stern began to foam as the boat made a ponderous turn and headed back down river, gathering speed.

De Brug ran to the Range Rover's cab and dialled on the satellite telephone the number the boat's captain had given him. It did not answer. He dialled another number. A service-disconnected signal filled his ear. He put down the receiver and stared through the windshield at the sky.

The terrible truth he had forced to the back of his mind as he drove across the desert and spotted the contrails plunging high to the south could not now be denied. He had failed. But Bailey would do more than withdraw the rescue boat and disconnect his phone. Bailey would demand the ultimate sacrifice. His life.

Suddenly de Brug's lips drew back in a feral grin. While he lived and breathed, he would remain as dangerous and threatening as the contagion he had almost succeeded in launching against Air Force One.

He walked back to the commandos, preparing in his mind what he wanted them to do.

THIRTY-NINE

Slowly, agonisingly slowly, Morton continued to apply the air brakes, all the time pulling back on the yoke. Reluctantly at first, then as if it wanted to respond to such gentle but firm handling, Air Force One answered the controls with growing certainty. The angle of its plunge earthwards eased and the plane's nose rose, almost inch by inch. The altimeter began to fall more slowly: 17,000, 16,000, 15,500 . . . 15,000 . . . 14,750 . . .

Away to the east the horizon had started to lighten. To the north the Polaris star was disappearing, and with it went the electrical storm, moving away towards Syria.

Closer, just beyond either wingtip, rode a Stealth bomber. The one on the port side began to bank and Morton followed.

Beside him Locke was once more breathing normally. He looked at the instrument panel and then at Morton. 'Thanks,' the co-pilot said. 'I never thought I'd actually be glad for the taste of compressed air.' He placed his hands on the controls and, over his shoulder, called to Kerr. 'Where are we?'

The flight engineer glanced up from the chart he was studying. 'Close to the Saudi border, probably a little north of . . .'

Turner interrupted. 'Our friend out on the right is trying to tell us something.'

The bomber on the starboard side was dipping its wings, then began to drop away towards the ground.

'It's a follow-me,' Locke explained.

Below, the long purple shadows of dawn were lifting over the land.

'There. At ten o'clock,' Locke announced.

'I have it,' Morton acknowledged.

Ahead, in the middle of the vast expanse of Arabia's northern desert, were the lights of a runway. Strips like this one had been built by the Americans in the run-up to the Gulf War. In the gathering daylight he could make out, close to the runway, shapes too small to be fixed-wing aircraft. Danny's Apaches and Chinooks.

Coming out of the south, flying low, were the unmistakable bulky forms of two C-130 transport planes. They were heading for the runway.

'Here comes the cavalry,' Locke said, the strain lifting from his voice.

Morton knew Washington would have organised the rescue planes. One of them was on its final approach. The other had begun to orbit, the first rays of the sun tipping its bulbous nose.

'He'll want us to watch while he goes in, so we can spot any snags. That way the Man and his guests don't go bumps-a-daisy. At their age, some of them are probably brittle enough as it is.'

'Thanks for that, Major Locke,' came the dry, familiar voice of the President from the back of the flight deck.

He had arrived there a moment earlier after inspecting the situation elsewhere on board.

Sturmer had offered him a breathing set but he'd politely refused, preferring to use the mask Helen had provided. The Chancellor, along with his other guests and the cabin crew, had escaped with nothing worse than bruising; all those who had begun to show signs of being affected by the ozone had quickly recovered as soon as Air

Force One reached a lower height. He'd reassured them the worst was over, though he had told no one of what he suspected had caused the plane to plunge.

The only tragedy appeared to be Carlo Marcello. Attempts to contact the industrialist in the rear cabin had elicited no response. Sutter had explained that it would be too dangerous to raise the security doors because of the baggage-hold door. Unspoken in the crew chief's words, the President had sensed, was the certainty that Marcello had been sucked to his death through the opening. The thought had left him with mixed feelings. Part of him was deeply saddened at the loss of even one life. Though he had barely spoken to Marcello, he had planned to try and persuade him to get Meridian International to put its full weight behind Earth Saver. Yet after what had happened, he realised that if Morton was right, then Meridian was implicated in nearly killing everyone on board.

Only the strength of the plane and the skills of its crew, the President reminded himself as he came on to the flight deck, had averted disaster.

'All I'm asking,' the President continued, a smile in his voice, 'is that you go on taking good care of our brittle old bones. But you all did a fine job. Congratulations.'

'They're mostly due to Mr Morton,' Locke said.

The President turned to Morton, not quite managing to hide his surprise. 'I hadn't expected to see you sitting there. Where's Colonel Patterson?'

Morton told him, told him everything that had happened before and during the shock wave triggered by the nuclear explosion. The President listened intently, his face darkening. When he spoke, his voice was sombre. 'All that will have to wait for later. Right now I just want to say one thing.' He glanced around the cockpit. 'As far as I'm concerned, what happened to Colonel Patterson doesn't go beyond here. I'll make sure the air force takes good care of him. While flying a desk won't be as exciting as sitting where you are, Mr Morton, he'll be able to pass on his great experience to others.'

Murmurs of agreement came from the crew.

'Now if you'll excuse me, gentlemen, I'll go and strap in. Keep up the good work, Mr Morton. It may be a while before you get to sit in that seat again,' the President said.

'For sure,' Morton murmured.

As the President left, Air Force One descended through six thousand feet.

Morton and Locke watched the second C-130 start its final approach, flare out and begin to roll to the end of the runway. Both bombers had pulled away, climbing to join the other Stealths riding shotgun overhead.

The sun was high enough to melt the frost on the ground; soon the soft white caul would be gone. In places, thick coils of rusting barbed wire snaked away on either side, marking the frontier at this point with Iraq.

'Ready to take her in?' Morton asked quietly.

Locke shook his head. 'I'll fly right seat for you.' It was the ultimate tribute he could pay.

After a moment Morton spoke again. 'Commencing descent.'

Locke's eyes watched the instruments, his hands resting lightly on the yoke. It was a new feeling, the way the plane responded to this new pair of hands on the controls. There were moves Morton made which the colonel would not have. But Locke could not fault the man in the command seat.

Morton watched the C-130 complete its roll-out, the reverse thrust of its engines throwing up a small sand-storm.

Out of the whirling sand rose two Apaches, climbing swiftly towards Air Force One.

Locke brought the pager microphone to his mouth. 'We shall be landing shortly at God-Knows-Where. Please remain seated until the engines are switched off.'

'And thank you for flying Air Force One,' Kerr said.

'Not funny,' grunted Turner.

Some people have a delayed stress reaction, Morton thought. But he wouldn't have put Turner down as one. He eased off the throttles and called for the initial approach flaps to be lowered.

The Apaches were on station on either side. Danny was at the controls of one, with Sean Carberry behind him; Tommy flew the other, with Anna in the back seat.

Morton acknowledged their waves.

'Three thousand feet,' Locke intoned.

Morton could feel the cushion of air created by the ground thermals nuzzling beneath the wings. He shook his head to clear the fatigue and scanned his instruments again. They were blurred. He looked out of the windshield. The sun was directly in his eyes. He rubbed them with the back of his hand.

Locke peered ahead, narrowing his eyes to try and make a better judgement. 'We're probably about eight miles from the outer marker lights. But it's only a best guess without radars.'

On either side both helicopters suddenly dropped beneath, then rose and dropped again.

'We're too high,' Morton said. But with the radars gone there was no way of telling by how much.

'Well, I'll be damned,' Locke said admiringly.

Anna was holding a large card against her side window. On it was scrawled, 'Down 500.'

Morton throttled back. The whine of the engines changed pitch as Air Force One descended another five hundred feet.

Carberry was holding up a card. On it was an arrow pointing forward and the figure '6'.

Morton waved. He had his replacement for the lost radars.

'Gears down,' he ordered.

Locke pushed the lever. 'Jesus H. Christ!' he was almost shouting. 'Right-hand wheels are jammed!'

Morton made a decision before he had time to think about it. He pushed the throttle forward and Air Force One began to climb again.

Both Apaches were beneath him, their crews inspecting the undercarriage.

Air Force One passed over the runway and Morton banked as gently as he could, climbing back to three thousand feet, holding the yoke in one hand and the throttles in the other as he continued his left-hand circle.

The only other movement on the flight deck was Turner wiping the cold sweat from his forehead. 'Can't it be racked down manually?' he asked.

'The winder cable must have snapped back in the hold,' Locke said tersely.

'So what do we do?' Turner demanded.

'We wait,' Morton said quietly. 'We wait until we know what the Apaches have seen.'

A tense silence settled over the flight deck.

It seemed an eternity before first Danny's, then Tommy's helicopter appeared on either side.

Anna was displaying a new card on which she had written: 'Port gear 2/3 down.'

Morton waved. Beside him Locke was making rapid calculations on a pad.

Ahead, nomads on camels were pointing at the plane. The sun cast Air Force One's shadow on the sands, over the Bedouins. The camels bolted clumsily as it passed.

Locke turned to Morton. 'It could hold, at least long enough for the start of the roll-out.'

'Let's go and do it,' Morton replied. He raised a hand to Anna and lowered it slowly and steadily.

A moment later she had a new placard to display: 'Good luck.'

Morton began to line up for a final approach. The plane shuddered slightly as the sun heated the sand, creating increasingly more powerful thermal action. The rising bubbles of air would be the least of his problems.

'Two thousand feet,' Locke intoned.

Carberry was holding up an arrow card with the number '3'.

A mile later the Apaches pulled away. There was nothing more they could do.

'Crossing outer marker,' Locke announced. The rack of lights flashed past beneath them.

'Forty degree flap,' Morton ordered.

Locke activated the flap levers.

The tail was heavy because the loss of the baggage-hold door had affected the trim.

Air Force One started to buck. Both Morton and Locke fought the controls. The plane began to yaw. Morton advanced the starboard thrust by a fraction. The yawing stopped.

'Flaring out,' he said.

Air Force One levelled off, twenty feet above the runway. It looked impossibly short in length. The first of the parked Chinooks and a C-130 rushed past.

The wheels touched. A great judder gripped the plane. It began to spin to the right as the damaged set of wheels sought a purchase on the runway.

'Reverse thrust!' Morton shouted.

Locke threw the thrust lever forward and raised the wing spoilers.

Air Force One continued to cant to one side, like some once proud creature brought to its knees as it hurtled down the runway.

'Still holding!' Locke yelled.

'Brakes!' Morton shouted.

The plane gave another huge shudder as tyre rubber burned with white smoke. One of the tandem wheels burst with explosive force, sending strips of burning rubber careering back down the runway.

There was nothing Morton and Locke could do now, but hold on to their yokes. And hope.

The computerised wheel-braking system alternately applied and released pressure on the wheel brakes. Two of the tyres on the partly lowered undercarriage blew out. But the crippled housing held.

Air Force One rolled on. It began to bounce less violently. Finally, of its own volition, it stopped its madcap rush to destruction, coming to a halt with a final bump.

'Thank God that's over,' Locke said fervently.

Morton smiled. It wasn't finished yet.

FORTY

An hour after landing Air Force One, Morton was in the air again, heading north back into Iraq. He had taken Anna's seat in Tommy's Apache. Behind came Danny's Apache and the Chinooks.

They had taken off as soon as the last C-130 had departed, carrying the President and his guests who were being flown to Riyadh, where the king was waiting to offer them traditional Saudi hospitality. Patterson and the crew of Air Force One had flown out on the other transport plane to the US base south of the Saudi capital.

Air Force One was being guarded by a detachment of Saudi soldiers who had arrived on one of the C-130s. They would remain there until the repair crew, already on its way, arrived from Andrews Air Force base. After an inspection of the damage, Tommy Sutter said it would be weeks before Air Force One flew again. The crew chief's verdict put an end to any future role the plane might have had in Operation Earth Saver.

Before he left, the President had sat with Morton in the cockpit of one of the Chinooks and listened over a slightly crackling radio line to the White House while Thacker Stimpson briefed them about his call from Ignatius Bailey.

'The fella claims one of their communications satellites picked up radio traffic from a unit in Iraq heading for the Euphrates. The language was German. The intent was to attack you, Mr President. Bailey had few other details. Except he had been shocked — his word — to learn that the unit was under the command of an employee he'd dismissed some months back, a fella by the name of Johannes de Brug. Ever heard of him, Mr Morton?' the Chief of Staff had asked.

'For sure,' Morton said. He had then said what should be done. Afterwards the President was silent for long seconds.

'Very well. Do it, Mr Morton.'

They'd shaken hands and the President had left the helicopter.

Morton had made one more call, to Hernandez. The sergeant had confirmed that the commandos and de Brug were now entrenched in an old desert fort near the bank of the Euphrates. The Halo had picked up no radio traffic from them.

Now, an hour later, the helicopter force headed towards the fort, flying in a line, no more than a few rotor discs separating one chopper from the next. The formation crossed into Iraq without incident. Ninety minutes later they passed to the east of the holy city of An Najat.

'Thirty minutes to target,' Tommy announced.

From the walkway of the fort, de Brug once more swept the sky to the south with his sight. They would come from there, with the sun behind them. He did not know when. But they would come. That would be Bailey's way. Always working through others. But Bailey had underestimated him.

An hour earlier he had driven a little way from the fort, parking the Range Rover in the lee of a sand dune. Then he had spoken into a cassette recorder for some time, setting out everything as he knew the facts to be. Leaving the tape on the seat, he had walked back to the fort.

The commando leader, a captain, had looked at him

impassively. He was neither concerned nor interested in the behaviour of this civilian, or in his reassurances that once they discovered the boat had turned back, the mullahs would send another one. He expected no less. His paymasters knew how to protect an asset.

The captain rose from where he had been dozing and strolled out into the courtyard. De Brug was descending the steps from the walkway. 'I'm going down to the river to see if a boat is there. I'll take one of the trucks. My Land Rover ran out of petrol,' he said.

While the captain had been indifferent to what the civilian did, he was also bored. 'I'll come with you.'

Something came and went in de Brug's eyes. 'What's the matter? Think I won't come back?' His tone was light and mocking.

'Then I come and find you. Then I kill you,' the captain said seriously.

They drove in silence the three miles to the river. De Brug parked near a mud quay jutting into the Euphrates. Below them the river curved, obscuring the view downstream.

'We'll get a better look from the jetty,' de Brug said.

Together they walked its length. Wind was blowing dust clouds from the opposite shore, obscuring the view.

'Here, use my sight.' De Brug proffered the scope.

The captain began to quarter the water downriver. 'I see nothing,' he called out.

'It doesn't matter,' de Brug replied.

The captain was still turning when the first bullet caught him in the head. The second entered a fraction to its right. De Brug pocketed the gun and stepped forward. Picking up the sight, he kicked the body into the water. He watched it drift into a bed of reeds and slowly sink.

He moved from the jetty and up along the river bank,

his eyes searching the reeds. Half-hidden in a clump he found the *gafa* attached to its pole. Shaped like a large laundry basket and made from reeds coated with bitumen, the craft seemed fragile. But for thousands of years the fishermen of the Euphrates had used *gafas* like this one.

He climbed into the basket, allowing it to sink low in the water. Then, standing erect, he took the *gafa*'s pole and pushed off. Using the pole both as a rudder and a means of propulsion, he began to move downriver.

Morton watched the Apache's shadow skimming over the ground. Behind him the other helicopters hugged the terrain, keeping low to fly under Iraqi radar. There had been little time for the pilots to familiarise themselves with the terrain, but they had absolute faith in their computers.

Flying in their straight-arrow formation, they swooped just above the sand like big birds of prey, banking around, or rising just above, any obstructions. Their path was marked only by a quickly-settling trail of sand. Ahead lay another dune. At its base was a vehicle.

'Any Range Rover out here can't be up to any good, Colonel,' Tommy said into his lip mike. 'Shall I take it out?'

On either side of the cockpit were mounted clusters of Hellfire rockets.

'Leave it,' Morton ordered crisply. Sometimes Tommy could be a little too eager.

The Apache skimmed past the Range Rover. Straight ahead was the fort.

The Chinooks sank to the ground while the two Apaches pressed home the attack. The first salvo of laser-guided Hellfires crashed into the fort's outer fortifications of ancient brick and earth. The choppers banked and fired another salvo. Each rocket leaped from its rail in a shower of sparks and launched itself with the speed of Mach One into the billowing smoke and flame. What remained of the fort vanished in another explosive cloud. Bodies rose high into the air in movements which, if they resembled anything, were those of fractured jackknives.

From the Chinooks, Big Mike and his men were racing towards the scene.

'I guess they won't be needed,' Tommy said.

Nothing moved except the flames. If it had been no contest, Morton thought, it was because he wasn't in one.

The *gafa* was drifting with increasing speed and de Brug was having difficulty navigating. Time and again the pole failed to touch the river bed.

A moment ago he'd heard explosions. Now a cloud of smoke was rising like a funeral pyre from the direction of the fort.

Tommy eased the Apache on to the sand only yards from the Range Rover.

Morton went over and inspected the vehicle to make sure it was not booby-trapped. Satisfied, he opened the driver's door. He saw the tape on the seat and the cassette recorder under the dash. He considered and rejected the possibility that it could be a bomb as too obvious. He closed the door, inserted the tape in the recorder and sat for a while, listening, his face expressionless. When he had heard enough, he switched off the machine, extracted the tape and placed it in his pocket. He walked quickly back to the Apache.

'We're going to do a little fishing,' he told Tommy.

The *gafa* bobbed and swayed and water splashed over the

sides. The river was widening all the time and the pole was completely useless as a rudder or oar. The craft began to spin like a bobbin, making de Brug feel increasingly nauseous. And the wind seemed to have risen, creating increasingly stormy conditions.

He looked up.

The Apache hovered above him.

'It's over, de Brug. I have your tape. We're going to use our rotors to wash you into the bank,' Morton yelled down at him.

In the *gafa* de Brug's hands moved with quick, short movements, producing the gun, then firing at the Apache.

Tommy effortlessly lifted the Apache out of range.

De Brug continued to fire until he heard the click of a spent magazine. As he feverishly reloaded, out of the corner of his eye he saw the helicopter sweeping down on him. He crouched and aimed and began to fire again.

Morton held back for a split second, then hit the switch to release the last Hellfire.

A blinding flash enveloped the *gafa*. When the smoke had cleared, nothing disturbed the surface of the water.

'Let's go home,' said Tommy quietly.

Not quite, Morton thought.

From his office window, Ignatius Bailey watched the helicopter descending slowly on to the plaza. The snow had gone and it was a gloriously sunny day.

His mood almost matched the weather, despite the fact that this morning in Washington, two days after he had returned from Saudi Arabia, the President had announced that, at the request of the other leaders of the industrialised nations, he would continue with Operation Earth Saver. Britain's Prime Minister had offered to provide a Concorde to complete the mission.

The helicopter, Bailey saw, had parked close to the banyan tree and a solitary figure was walking purposefully into the building.

That would be the President's emissary. Bailey turned back to his desk, lowering himself into his chair.

An hour ago the fool in the White House had telephoned to say he was sending his personal envoy to discuss with him the information he had given Stimpson which, the President explained, had permitted the Iraqis to deal with a group of stateless mercenaries who had attempted to foment trouble with the West. While Baghdad still had much fence-building to do, the President had continued, it had been a start. And in the light of Iraq's firm action, Tehran had been persuaded to cool its bellicosity towards its neighbour. Again, it may only be a small step, the President had said, but it was another one in the right direction.

Listening, Bailey had silently congratulated himself. Despite what had happened, he had saved Meridian. And sooner rather than later there would be a new opportunity to deal with that fool and his friends. Of that he was certain.

There was a knock.

'Come,' said Bailey, composing himself to intimidate this envoy. The door opened.

Morton stood there.

'Hullo, Mr Bailey,' Morton said pleasantly, walking over to the desk. From his pocket he produced the thoroughly incriminating tape de Brug had left in the desert. 'You've got some listening to do. And then you're going to spend the rest of your life where nobody's going to listen to you, for sure.'

Warner Books now offers an exciting range of quality titles by both established and new authors. All of the books in this series are available from:

Little, Brown and Company (UK),
P.O. Box 11,
Falmouth,
Cornwall TR10 9EN.

Alternatively you may fax your order to the above address.
Fax No: 01326 317444
Telephone No: 01326 317200
E-mail: books@barni.avel.co.uk

Payments can be made as follows: cheque, postal order (payable to Little, Brown and Company) or by credit cards, Visa/Access. Do not send cash or currency. UK customers and B.F.P.O. please allow £1.00 for postage and packing for the first book, plus 50p for the second book, plus 30p for each additional book up to a maximum charge of £3.00 (7 books plus).

Overseas customers including Ireland, please allow £2.00 for the first book plus £1.00 for the second book, plus 50p for each additional book.

NAME (Block Letters) ....

....

ADDRESS ....

....

....

☐ I enclose my remittance for ....
☐ I wish to pay by Access/Visa Card

Number ☐☐☐☐☐☐☐☐☐☐☐☐☐☐☐☐☐

Card Expiry Date ☐☐☐☐

The Cat Who Brought Down The House

Lilian Jackson Braun

headline

First published in Great Britain in 2003
by HEADLINE BOOK PUBLISHING

First published in paperback in 2003
by HEADLINE BOOK PUBLISHING

5

ISBN 978-0-7553-0525-4

Printed and bound in Great Britain by
Clays Ltd, St Ives plc

Paper and cover board used by Headline are natural, recyclable products made from wood grown in sustainable forests. The manufacturing processes conform to the environmental regulations of the county or origin.

HEADLINE BOOK PUBLISHING
A division of Hodder Headline
338 Euston Road
LONDON NW1 3BH

www.headline.co.uk
www.hodderheadline.com

Dedicated to Earl Bettinger,
The Husband Who . . .

One

Who was Thelma Thackeray?

It was April first, and it sounded like an April Fool's joke.

Had anyone by that name ever lived in Moose County, 400 miles north of everywhere?

Yet, there it was, in black and white – in the newsbite column of the *Moose County Something*:

RETURN OF THE NATIVE

Thelma Thackeray, 82, a native of Moose County, has retired after a 55-year career in Hollywood, CA, and is returning to her native soil. 'I'm coming home to die,' she said cheerfully, 'but not right away. First I want to have some fun.'

It was followed by less startling items: The sheriff had purchased a stop-stick to aid deputies in high-speed car chases . . . The Downtown Beautiful committee had decided on hot-pink petunias for the flower boxes on Main Street . . . The sow that escaped from a truck on Sandpit Road had been discovered in the basement of the Black Creek Elementary School.

Immediately the lead item was being discussed all over town, via the grapevine. In coffeehouses, on street corners, and over backyard fences the news was spread: 'A Hollywood star is coming to live in Pickax!'

Jim Qwilleran, columnist for the newspaper, was working at home when his phone started ringing. 'Who was Thelma Thackeray? . . . Was she really a movie star? . . . Did the press know more than they were telling?'

'It sounds like a hoax,' he told them. He remembered the April Fool's prank that his fellow staffers had played on the *Lockmaster Ledger* a year ago. They phoned a tip that a Triple Crown winner was being retired to a stud farm in Lockmaster under terms of absolute secrecy. Reporters at the *Ledger* had spent a week trying to confirm it.

Nevertheless, Qwilleran's curiosity was aroused. He phoned Junior Goodwinter, the young managing editor, and said sternly, 'What was the source of the Thelma Thackeray newsbite?'

'She phoned our night desk herself – from California. Why do you ask? Do you have a problem with that?'

'I certainly do! The name sounds phony! And her remark about dying and having fun is too glib for a person of her apparent age.'

'So what are you telling me, Qwill?'

'I'm telling you it's a practical joke played by those guys in Lockmaster in retaliation for the horse hoax. Have you been getting any reader reaction?'

'Sure have! Our phones have been ringing off the hook! And – hey, Qwill! Maybe there really is a Thelma Thackeray!'

'Want to bet?' Qwilleran grumbled as he hung up.

Qwilleran had a sudden urge for a piece of Lois Inchpot's apple pie, and he walked to the shabby downtown eatery where one could always find comfort food at comfortable prices – and the latest gossip. Lois herself was a buxom, bossy, hardworking woman who had the undying loyalty of her customers. They took up a collection when she needed a new coffeemaker and volunteered their services when the lunchroom walls needed painting.

When Qwilleran arrived, the place was empty, chairs were upended on tables, and Lois was sweeping up before dinner. 'Too early for dinner! Too late for coffee!' she bellowed.

'Where's your busboy, Lois?'

Her son, Lenny, usually helped her prepare for dinner.

'Job hunting! He finished two years at MCCC, and he'd really like to go to one of them universities Down Below, but they're too expensive. So he's job hunting.'

Qwilleran said, 'Tell Lenny to apply to the K Fund for a scholarship. I'll vouch for him.' The young man had faced personal tragedy, a frame-up, and betrayal of trust – with pluck and perseverance.

With a sudden change of heart she said, 'What kind of pie do you want?'

'Apple,' he said, 'and give me that broom and I'll finish sweeping while you brew the coffee.'

The middle-aged man pushing the broom and righting the chairs would have been recognized anywhere in three counties as James Mackintosh Qwilleran. He had a pepper-and-salt moustache of magnificent proportions, and his photo appeared at the head of the 'Qwill Pen' column every Tuesday and Friday. He had been a highly regarded journalist in major cities around the country; then he inherited the vast Klingenschoen fortune based in Moose County and he relocated in the north country. Furthermore, for reasons of his own, he had turned the inheritance over to a philanthropic institution. The Klingenschoen Foundation, popularly called the K Fund, was masterminded by experts in Chicago, where Qwilleran was recognized as the richest man in the northeast central United States. Around Pickax he was Mr Q.

Eventually Lois returned from the kitchen, carrying two orders of apple pie and a coffee server; forks, napkins, and mugs were in her apron pockets. They sat in a booth near the kitchen pass-through, so she could shout reminders to the woman who cooked dinner. Lois herself

4

would wait on tables, take the money, and serve as moderator of the free-for-all talk show carried on among the tables.

'Well, Mr Q,' she began, 'you missed a good chinfest this afternoon. Everybody's excited about the movie star comin' to town. Do you think she'll come in here to eat?'

Still suspecting a Lockmaster trick, he replied evasively, 'Just because she's lived in Hollywood for fifty years, it doesn't make her a movie star. She could be a bookkeeper or policewoman or bank president.'

Whatever she is, he thought, she must be loaded – to buy a house on Pleasant Street.

Lois shouted at the pass-through, 'Effie! Don't forget to thaw the cranberry sauce! ... Funny thing, though, Mr Q – nobody remembers a Thackeray family in these parts.'

Facetiously he said, 'It would be interesting to know if she's related to William Makepeace Thackeray.'

'Don't know anybody of that name. Who is he?'

'A writer, but he hasn't done anything recently.'

She yelled, 'And, Effie! Throw some garlic powder in the mashed potatoes!'

Qwilleran said, 'Sounds delicious. I'd like to take a turkey dinner home in a box.'

Lois yelled, 'Effie! Fix a box for Mr Q – and put in some dark meat for his kitties.'

'By the way,' he said, 'what's all the action in the next block? All those trucks coming and going.'

'They're movin' out!' she said. 'Good riddance! It don't make sense to have a place like that downtown.'

He waited for his 'box' and walked to the corner of Church and Pine streets, where large cartons were being loaded into trucks and carted away. According to the logos on the cartons they were refrigerators, washers and dryers, kitchen ranges, and television sets.

He said to the man directing the loading, 'Either you're moving out, or you've sold a lot of appliances this week.'

'We got a new building on Sandpit Road – steel barn with real loading dock. Plenty of room for trucks.'

The edifice they were vacating was a huge stone hulk, wedged between storefronts of more recent vintage. That meant it was more than a century old, dating back to the days when the county's quarries were going full blast and Pickax was being built as the City of Stone. It was the first time he had scrutinized it. There were no windows in the side walls, and the front entrance had been boarded up. Qwilleran crossed the street and appreciated the design for the first time: Four columns were part of the architecture, topped by a pediment and the simple words inscribed in the stone: OPERA HOUSE.

Then he realized that the smaller buildings on either side had been vacated also. Something was happening in downtown Pickax!

Qwilleran went home to his converted apple barn, which was as old as the opera house. It occupied a wooded area on the outskirts of town – octagonal, forty feet high, with fieldstone foundation and weathered wood shingles for siding. As he drove into the barnyard two alert cats were watching excitedly in the kitchen window. They were sleek Siamese with pale fawn bodies and seal-brown masks and ears, long slender legs, and whiplike tails. And they had startlingly blue eyes.

Yum Yum was a flirtatious little female who purred, rubbed ankles, and gazed at Qwilleran beseechingly with violet-tinged eyes. She knew how to get what she wanted; she was all cat ... Koko was a cat-and-a-half. Besides being long, lithe, and muscular, he had the bluest of blue eyes, brimming with intelligence and something beyond that – an uncanny intuition. There were times when the cat knew the answers before Qwilleran had even thought of the questions. Kao K'o Kung was his real name.

When Qwilleran walked into the barn, Yum Yum was excited about the turkey, but Koko was excited about the answering machine; there was a message waiting.

A woman's voice said, 'Qwill, I'm leaving the library early and going to the dinner meeting of the bird club. It's all about chickadees tonight. I'll call you when I get home and we can talk about Thelma Thackeray. *A bientôt.*'

She left no name, and none was needed. Polly Duncan was the chief woman in his life. She was his own age and shared his interest in literature, being director of the

7

Pickax public library. It was her musical voice that had first attracted him. Even now, when she talked, he felt a frisson of pleasure that almost overshadowed what she was saying.

Qwilleran thanked Koko for drawing his attention to the message and asked Yum Yum if she had found any treasures in the wastebasket. Talking to cats, he believed, raised their consciousness.

The dark meat of turkey was minced and arranged on two plates under the kitchen table, where they gobbled it up with rapture. Afterwards it took them a long time to wash up. The tastier the treat, the longer the ablutions, Qwilleran had observed.

Then he announced loudly, 'Gazebo Express now leaving for all points east!' Yum Yum and Koko jumped into a canvas tote bag that had been purchased from the Pickax public library. It was the right size for ten books or two cats who are good friends.

The octagonal gazebo stood in the bird garden, screened on all eight sides. In the evening there were birds and small four-legged creatures to amuse the Siamese, and when darkness fell there were night noises and night smells. Qwilleran stayed with them for a while, then went indoors to do some more work on the 'Qwill Pen' column.

From time to time he received phone calls from friends who wanted to talk about the Hollywood celebrity: from Wetherby Goode, the WPKX meteorologist; from Celia Robinson O'Dell, his favorite caterer; from Susan

Exbridge, antique dealer; the Lanspeaks, owners of the department store.

At one point he was interrupted by a phone call from Lisa Compton, wife of the school superintendent.

'Lyle and I were wondering if you know what's going into the old opera house?'

'No, I know only what's coming out. Maybe they're going to bring Mark Twain back. He hasn't been here since 1895.'

'I know,' Lisa said. 'And my grandmother was still raving about him sixty years later. She loved his moustache – just like yours, Qwill. His wit and humor brought down the house! Her favorite was the one about cross-breeding man with the cat: *It would improve the man but be deleterious to the cat.*

'She told me that carriages used to draw up to the entrance of the hall, and women in furs and jewels would step out, assisted by men in opera cloaks and tall hats. Can you imagine that – in Pickax, Qwill?'

'That was over a hundred years ago,' Qwilleran said. 'Things change.'

'So true! Before World War One the economy had collapsed. Pickax was almost a ghost town, and the opera hall was boarded up. In the Twenties it was a movie theatre for a few years. During World War Two the government took it over – all very hush-hush and heavily guarded. They removed the rows of seats and leveled the raked floor, my family told me.'

Qwilleran said, 'The old building has had a checkered career.'

9

'Yes, since then it's been a roller rink, a dance hall, a health club, and finally a storage warehouse. Who knows what's next?'

'If you get any clues, let me know,' he said.

'I'll do that . . . How are the kitties, Qwill?'

'Fine. How's Lyle?'

'Grouchy. He's crossing swords with the school board again.'

Qwilleran was treating himself to a dish of ice cream when Polly phoned. 'How was your meeting?' he asked. 'What did you have for dinner?'

'Robin-O'Dell catered some meat pies. Food always suffers in the transportation, you know, but they were acceptable.'

'Did you learn anything about chickadees that you didn't already know?'

She wailed in exasperation. 'There was more discussion about that Thackeray woman than about birds! . . . There was one thing that I found rather amusing, though. The realty agent who sold her the house was there; he and his wife are avid birders. At first he was reluctant to talk – professional confidentiality, you know – but after a few glasses of wine he relaxed. He said she bought it sight unseen, after they sent photos and specifications . . . They lined up Mavis Adams to check legal details and Fran Brodie to handle the redecorating. In fact, Fran flew to California for a conference.'

Qwilleran asked, 'Did he say why she needs such a large house?'

'He claimed not to know. But it would be interesting to talk to Fran, wouldn't it?'

Feigning a lack of interest, he mumbled something and reminded Polly that they were dining with the Rikers the next night. 'I've made a reservation at the Mackintosh Inn. We'll meet here at the barn at six o'clock.'

'I'm looking forward to it,' she said. '*A bientôt.*'

'*A bientôt.*'

Before bringing in the Siamese from the gazebo, Qwilleran flicked the single switch that lighted the entire interior of the barn with uplights and down-lights. A ramp spiraled dramatically around the inside walls, connecting the three balconies. In the center of the main floor stood a giant white fireplace cube with white stacks rising to the cupola.

The Siamese were waiting, torn between the enchantment of the night and the prospect of a bedtime snack. As soon as they were indoors, they jumped out of the tote bag and raced up the ramp – Koko chasing Yum Yum all the way to the top. Then she turned and chased him down again. Qwilleran clocked them: thirty-seven seconds for the entire course.

Then the three of them piled into the big reading chair and listened to a recording of *Carmen*. It was the cats' favorite. Qwilleran liked anything by Bizet. Wouldn't it be sensational, he thought, if the old opera house started bringing in opera companies! But not impossible. Anything could happen in Pickax, 400 miles north of everywhere.

Two

Just before waking on Wednesday, Qwilleran dreamed about the old opera house. The elite of Pickax were arriving in horse-drawn carriages. Every seat in the house was taken with opera-lovers excited about hearing *Tristan and Isolde*. Then he opened his eyes! The Siamese were performing a Wagnerian duet outside his door.

Qwilleran leaped out of bed. 'You demons!' he scolded. They ran down the ramp, and he took the short cut to the kitchen via a circular staircase.

He prepared the cats' breakfast absently, having two questions on his mind – both of more interest than chopped chicken livers. Who was Thelma Thackeray? he asked himself. And what was about to happen to the opera house? After a career as a warehouse for household

13

appliances, the old building had nowhere to go but up. Suppose the K Fund were to restore it to its former glamour! Would anyone attend concerts and lectures in this age of TV and videos?

He prepared super-strength coffee in his automated brewer and thawed a breakfast roll. Then he made phone calls.

First he called Amanda's Studio of Interior Design, hoping Fran Brodie would be in-house, but she was still in California, working with the client, and Amanda was at City Hall, doing the duties of a mayor. Qwilleran left his name, and the new assistant said, 'Oh! You're Mr Q! I live in Lockmaster, but I read your column in the *Something* and it's neat – really neat!'

Next he phoned the official county historian to inquire about the Thackeray family. Homer Tibbitt was ninety-eight, and he lived with his wife, Rhoda, at Ittibittiwassee Estates, a retirement residence out in the country. They were virtually newlyweds. Neither had been married before, and theirs was considered the romance of the century.

Rhoda answered the phone in her sweet trembling voice and turned it over to Homer, whose vocal delivery was reedy and high-pitched, but vigorous. 'The only thing I know about the Thackeray family is that Milo was a bootlegger in the Thirties. Thornton Haggis would have all that information. He read a paper at a meeting of the historical society – all about our fair county during Prohibition.'

14

So Qwilleran phoned the Thornton Haggis residence. Thorn, as he liked to be called, was a fourth-generation stonecutter, now retired from the family's monument works. He had a degree in art history from a university Down Below and now gave liberally of his time to the local art community. His wife told Qwilleran to call the Art Center; Thorn was helping to hang a new exhibition.

Sure enough, the volunteer was up on a ladder when Qwilleran phoned. 'I can tell you a thing or two about Moose County's boozy history. Where are you, Qwill? At the barn? The job here will be finished in a half hour, and I'll drive up there. Brew some of that lethal coffee you like!'

It was generally assumed that Thornton would take over the unpaid job of county historian when, if ever, Homer retired. The records of the monument works went back to 1850, when tombstones were chiseled with name, the vital statistics, cause of death, and names of survivors and family pets. Also, examples of wit and humor were chipped into the stone at modest price-per-letter.

Qwilleran's visitor had a rampant shock of snow-white hair visible a block away. The Siamese always became unusually frisky when he appeared. 'Is that a compliment?' he asked. 'Or do they suspect me of something?'

Qwilleran suggested, 'They associate your last name with something good to eat. Cats have a clever way of putting two and two together.'

15

'I drove around by the library and picked up the paper I wrote for the local history collection. It's the one I read at the meeting of the Old Timers Club. It made some of them cry.'

'Good! Let's go out to the gazebo with some refreshments, and you can read it to me. I'll take a box of tissues.'

It was a pleasantly warm day – and an hour when the wild creatures were not too noisy. What looked like red wine on the refreshment tray was actually Squunk water from a local mineral spring, with a slug of cranberry juice. Thorn smacked his lips. 'You could bottle this stuff and sell it!'

Qwilleran turned on his tape recorder, and the following was later transcribed for *Short & Tall Tales*, a collection of local legends.

MILO THE POTATO FARMER

Milo Thackeray and my grandfather were good friends. They played checkers and went hunting together – varmints and deer. Hunting was not a sport in those days. For many struggling families it was a way to put food on the table. Hard times had come to Moose County in the early twentieth century. Yet this had been the richest county in the state when natural resources were being exploited.

Then the ten mines closed, leaving entire villages without hope of work; the forests were lumbered out; there was no market for quarry stone; the ship-building industry went elsewhere when steam-boats replaced tall-masted schooners. Thousands of persons fled Down Below, hoping to find work in factories, and those who remained had little money to spend on potatoes and tombstones. Milo was a potato farmer, and Gramps was a stonecutter.

It had been a year of tragedy for the potato farmer. His eldest son was one of the first casualties of World War One; two younger children died in the influenza epidemic; and now his wife died while giving birth to twins, Thelma and Thurston. They were his salvation! Gramps was there when Milo swore an oath to give them a better life than he had known. A sister-in-law came in to care for them, and eventually Milo married her. Eventually, too, his life took a strange turn.

In 1919 the Volstead Act went into effect, and thirsty citizens provided a large market for illegal beverages. Somehow, Milo learned he could make hard liquor from potatoes. Gramps helped him build a distillery, and it worked! Customers came to the farm in Model T cars and horse-drawn wagons. Unfortunately for the jubilant farmer, revenue agents also came. They smashed the still and poured the liquor on the ground. (Even to this day the belief persists that the act accounts for the superior flavor of Moose County potatoes.)

Milo was undaunted! His twins were growing fast, and he had sworn an oath.

Across the lake, a hundred miles away, was Canada, famous for good whiskey. On the shore of Moose County there were scores of commercial fishermen who were getting only a penny a pound for their catch. Milo organized a fleet of rumrunners to bring the whiskey over under cover of darkness. Soon a steady stream of Model T trucks was coming north to haul it away, camouflaged in many ingenious ways.

The poor potato farmer became the rich bootlegger.

Transactions were made in cash, and Gramps held the lantern while Milo buried the money in the backyard.

Every weekend Milo took his family and their young friends to Lockmaster for a picnic and moving picture show. The back of the truck was filled with kids sitting on disguised cases of contraband. Milo never attended the show, and the seats were never there for the return trip.

There was no such entertainment in Moose County. The twins begged their father to open a picture show in Pickax.

Prohibition ended in 1933, but the potato farmer was in a position to indulge his twins. He bought the old opera house, long boarded up, and made it the Pickax Movie Palace. He financed their chosen careers.

Besides their sex, the twins were very different.

18

Thurston was slight of build and more sensitive; he loved dogs and horses and wanted to be a veterinarian. Milo sent him to Cornell, where he earned his D.V.M. degree.

Thelma was taller, huskier, and bolder; she wanted to be 'in pictures.' Milo sent her to Hollywood with her stepmother as chaperone. He never saw either of the women again.

Thelma obtained bit parts in two B films and decided she would prefer the food business, playing the leading role as hostess in her own restaurant. Milo first financed a snack shop (the Thackeray Snackery) and then a fine restaurant called simply Thelma's. She did very well. When Milo died he left his fortune to Thurston, to establish the Thackeray Animal Clinic in Lockmaster, and to Thelma, to realize her dream of a private dinner club for connoisseurs of old movies.

Milo was buried in the Hilltop Cemetery, with Gramps as the sole mourner. And Gramps chiseled the headstone the way his friend wanted it: MILO THE POTATO FARMER.

'Good story!' Qwilleran said as he turned off the tape recorder. 'Is Thelma's twin still living?'

'No, Dr Thurston was killed in an accident a year or so ago. There was a rumor that it was murder, but no charges were brought. The gossips said that a group of horse breeders had been trying to buy the Thackeray Clinic but

Thurston wouldn't sell. Right after his death they bought it from the estate and changed the name. I don't read the *Lockmaster Ledger*, so I don't know any details. But the idea of murder didn't make sense to me.'

'Well, anyway, the twin sister is returning to her hometown for some "fun," according to an item in the *Something.*'

'My wife told me about it. Am I supposed to get excited about it? Sounds to me as if she's been out in the sun too long!'

Qwilleran, although feigning a lack of interest, was beginning to have a nagging curiosity about Thelma Thackeray, and he looked forward to Fran Brodie's return from California.

The Siamese knew something was about to happen – something important, not alarming. Their dinner was served early; the nut bowls on the coffee table were filled; glasses and bottles appeared on the serving bar. The cats watched the preparations, forgoing their usual postprandial meditation in a sunny spot.

Qwilleran was proud of his bartending skills, and he always served his guests with a fillip of formality. Now he had acquired a round silver tray with the merest suggestion of a fluted rim – just enough to keep it from looking like a hubcap. (He disliked anything ornate.) There were modern trays in aluminum, chrome, and stainless steel, and he had served drinks on them all, but silver had *soul*. Even the Siamese felt it. They jumped on the bar and looked at their reflections in its highly polished surface. It had been a gift from two of his favorite young people!

At six o'clock Polly Duncan was the first to drive into the barnyard, having come directly from the library. 'You have a new tray! It's quite lovely. I like the piecrust rim. Is it antique? Where did you find it?'

'It was a kind of thank-you from the Bambas. I recommended Lori and Nick when the K Fund was looking for a couple to run the Nutcracker Inn. Let me read you the inscription.'

It was: *For Qwill with the compliments of the Nutcracker Inn, where all the nuts go.*

Another vehicle pulled up to the kitchen door. The Rikers had come directly from the newspaper office. Mildred was the food editor; Arch was editor in chief and Qwilleran's lifelong friend. The two men had grown up together in Chicago and were secure enough in their friendship to taunt each other at the slightest provocation.

Mildred noticed the new tray on the bar. 'It's charming! Where did you find it?'

'It was a gift. Glad you approve.'

'It's not very old,' said Arch, who considered himself an authority on antiques. 'And it's only silver plate.'

'It will do,' Qwilleran said, 'until you give me an eighteenth-century sterling tray for my birthday, which happens to be next month, in case you've forgotten.'

When drinks were served and they moved to the deep-cushioned sofas around the fireplace, Arch proposed a toast: 'To all who slave in the workplace from nine to five – and to those who only do two columns a week.'

There was a quick retort from the author of the 'Qwill Pen' column: 'If I didn't write my thousand words every Tuesday and Friday, your circulation would drop fifty percent. By the way, do you have any news in tomorrow's newspaper?'

'Yes,' Mildred said. 'Good news on the food page! Derek Cuttlebrink's girlfriend and her two brothers in Chicago have purchased the Old Stone Mill, and it will have a new name, a new chef, and a new menu . . . *And* Derek will be the manager!'

The other three all talked at once. 'Wonderful news! . . . It's about time! . . . There's nothing like having a Chicago heiress for a girlfriend . . . I wonder if he'll stop growing now . . . I remember him when he was only a six-foot-four busboy and his ambition was to be a cop . . . The boy's got charisma! . . . Wait till his groupies hear the news! . . . What will the new restaurant be called?'

'The Grist Mill. That was its original purpose. The farmers brought their wheat and corn to be ground into flour.'

Arch said, 'I hope they get rid of the phony mill wheel! The millstream dried up fifty years ago, they say, and turning the wheel electrically was a harebrained idea! The mechanical creaking and rumbling and groaning gave the diners indigestion . . . It drove me crazy!'

'That's not hard to do,' Qwilleran observed.

The Siamese had not been in evidence during the conversation, and Mildred asked, 'Where's sweet little Yum Yum?'

She was under the sofa, advancing stealthily on Arch's shoelaces.

'Where's King Koko?' he asked.

Koko heard his name and appeared from nowhere, walking stiffly on his long, elegant legs. When he had everyone's attention, he looked haughtily from one to another, then turned and left the room.

'How's that for a royal put-down?' the editor remarked.

The party was in a jovial mood when they left for dinner.

Three

The depressing old Pickax Hotel was now the upscale
Mackintosh Inn – with a life-size portrait of Anne
Mackintosh Qwilleran in the lobby, a new interior
masterminded by Fran Brodie, and Mackintosh tartan
seats in the main dining room. It was now called the
Mackintosh Room, and a new chef had made it the finest
restaurant in town.

The new maître d', being only five-foot-ten, lacked the
panache of the six-foot-eight Derek Cuttlebrink, but he
knew to seat Qwilleran's party at the best table.

They were a jovial foursome – middle-aged and
comfortable with their lives and with each other. Yet,
each had a history that could be told: Jim Qwilleran, after
a failed marriage, had succumbed to alcoholism until a

miracle got him back on track. Polly Duncan, widowed tragically at twenty-five, had never remarried. Mildred Hanstable Riker, stunned by a disastrous family situation, had survived with her warm heart and generous spirit intact. Arch Riker, after raising a family, had heard his first wife announce, 'I'd rather be a single antique *dealer* than a married antique *collector*.'

When they were seated and the menus were presented, Arch said, 'I'd like a big steak.'

His wife said sweetly, 'Hon, you can have a big steak when you go to Tipsy's Tavern. Chef Wingo offers you a chance to expand your gustatory horizons. I think you'd like the garlic-and-black-pepper-marinated strip loin with caramelized onions and merlot-vinegar reduction.'

Arch looked at the others helplessly. 'What's Qwill having?'

His friend said, 'Grilled venison tenderloin with smoked bacon, braised cabbage strudel, and Bing cherry demi-glaze.'

Both women were having the seafood Napoleon with carrot gaufrettes and lemon buerre blanc sauce.

The first course was a butternut squash puree served in soup plates with a garnish of fresh blueberries.

Polly remarked, 'Do I recognize Mildred's influence?'

'I told Wingo that blueberries are legendary in Moose County.'

Qwilleran was alerted. He was collecting local legends for his book to be titled *Short & Tall Tales*. 'Is it one for the book, Mildred? I'd like to tape it.'

'Wonderful!' she said. 'Bring your recorder to the opening of the stitchery exhibition on Sunday.'

'What kind of stitchery?' Polly asked.

'Quilting. But not the kind of traditional bed quilts that I used to make. These are wall hangings, large and small, pictorial and geometric. We're calling it Touchy-Feely Art, and I'll tell you why. A number of years ago I was visiting an art museum in Chicago and trying to examine the brushwork on a certain painting. The security guard tapped me on the shoulder and said, "Stand back eighteen inches. Breathing on the paintings is prohibited." Well! The artwork we're showing on Sunday can be touched as well as breathed on. Even if you don't touch the wall hangings, you get a snuggly feeling just by looking at them.'

'Interesting!' Qwilleran said, as he considered the ramifications of Touchy-Feely Art. 'You'd better post signs WASH YOUR HANDS.'

Then the entrees were served, and they talked about food for a while. The server had placed a small plate of lemon wedges in the middle of the table.

'What are those for?' Arch asked.

Mildred explained, 'Chef Wingo believes a few drops of lemon add piquancy to any dish, hon.'

'Qwill and I used to use it for invisible ink in secret correspondence . . . Remember that, Qwill?'

'Was it fourth grade?'

'I think it was fifth. Miss Getz was the teacher.'

Polly said to Mildred, 'Here we go again!' The two

couples could never get together without another anecdote about rascally boyhood pranks. 'Tell us about Miss Getz and the secret correspondence,' she said coyly.

'Arch and I passed slips of blank paper back and forth in class, and she knew we were up to no good, but she never discovered the secret writing.'

'The way it works,' Arch explained, 'you dip a cotton swab-stick in lemon juice and write on plain white paper. The writing isn't visible until you hold it up to a hot lamp bulb. But not too close.'

Polly inquired, 'Dare I ask what kind of messages you exchanged in the fourth grade?'

'Fifth,' Arch corrected her. 'There's a big difference.'

Qwilleran smoothed his moustache, as he did when trying to recollect. 'Well . . . there was a girl in our class called Pauline Pringle who had a bad case of acne. One day Arch slipped me a bit of paper. When I got it home and over a hot lightbulb, I laughed so hard – my mother thought I was having convulsions. It said: *Pauline Pimple likes you a lot.*'

Arch chuckled at the memory. The two women remained cool.

'The next day,' Qwilleran went on, 'I sent him a message about the teacher. Her face would get very red once in a while, and she'd mop her brow with a handkerchief. The message was: *Miss Getz sweats.*'

The women groaned. Polly was not attuned to schoolboy humor; and Mildred, having taught school for thirty years, empathized with the long-suffering Miss Getz. She said, 'All you two miscreants deserve for dessert is lemon sorbet.'

All four ordered Chef Wingo's famous blueberry cobbler, however. Arch wanted a dollop of ice cream on his; Polly asked for a smidgen of yogurt; Mildred thought she would like 'just a tad' of whipped cream. The host took his neat.

But he asked, 'Should I know what a tad is?'

'Halfway between a smidgen and a wee bit,' Mildred informed him.

As they lingered over coffee, they discussed the Pickax Sesquicentennial celebration scheduled for the following year. Arch had attended the first meeting of the planning committee.

'I hate to tell you this,' he said, 'but they elected Hixie Rice as general chairman.'

'Oh, no!' Mildred said.

'Oh, dear!' Polly muttered.

The promotion director of the *Moose County Something* was a clever idea-person with boundless energy and enthusiasm – and a record of disasters, through no fault of her own. There had been the Ice Festival that thawed out, the Mark Twain Festival canceled because of a murder, the cat contest that ended in a riot (of cat owners, not contestants), and more. The city was still wondering what to do with fifteen thousand polar-bear lapel buttons ordered for the Ice Festival.

Yet, Hixie always bounced back, entranced people with

her optimism and creativity, and found herself elected to chair another fiasco.

The next day was a workday, so the party broke up early. For Qwilleran the evening was not over, however. At home he put a sheet of blank white paper in an envelope and addressed it to Arch, chuckling as he visualized his old friend's reaction. Though suspicious, his old friend would be unable to resist heating it over a lightbulb, and when he found it blank, Arch would lie awake all night plotting revenge.

The next day Qwilleran walked downtown to buy a *New York Times* and stopped at the design studio, a good place to get a cup of coffee and the latest news. Fran was back in town, he learned, but was taking a day off.

Her assistant was trying hard to be her boss's clone — in dress, manner, and hairstyle. But she was more talkative. Her name was Lucinda Holmes. She had a boyfriend named Dr Watson, she said with a giggle. He was a vet at the Whinny Hills Animal Clinic. They took care of her thoroughbred gelding and two English foxhounds. She loved riding to hounds. The clinic used to be the Thackeray clinic. It had changed a lot. It was very sad. Dr Thackeray was killed in an accident. There were rumors that it was suicide, or even murder.

Qwilleran asked, 'Was he related to Fran's client?'

'He was her twin brother. She's a very interesting person. Fran took me out there on her first trip. We had to measure everything in the house. It's all being moved

29

here, and floor plans have to be established before the moving men get here.'

'So you're from Lockmaster! What brought you to Pickax?'

'I studied design at the Harrington School in Chicago and worked in Lockmaster for a while, but I wasn't learning anything. With Fran I learn how to present ideas to clients, how to listen to their own ideas, how to change their minds without offending them—'

A bell tinkled on the front door. Qwilleran drained his coffee cup and left Lucinda to practice her new skills on a client.

Back at the barn a red light was flashing on the answering machine, although Koko paid no attention to it. He had a way of screening calls and making a catly fuss when he deemed one important.

This one was from Fran Brodie, speaking in a throatily teasing way: 'If you'll invite me over for a drink, I'll tell you all about Thelma Thackeray, but don't invite me to dinner; I'm dining with Dutch at the Palomino Paddock. I hope you know how to mix a margarita. Just phone and leave a message: yes or no.'

Qwilleran huffed into his moustache. Of course he could mix a margarita – or anything else in the book. He had earned his way through college by tending bar.

He said to Yum Yum: 'Guess who's coming over for a drink!' The fur on her neck was standing on end; she had recognized the voice on the machine.

Four

The Qwilleran System of Weights and Measures was the topic of his next 'Qwill Pen' column. He wrote:

> How far is it to the nearest gas station? 'Just a hop, skip, and a jump.'
>
> Where is the motel? 'Down the road a piece.'
>
> Would you like more coffee? 'Just a splash.'
>
> How about a drink of Scotch? 'A wee dram.'
>
> How much hot sauce did you put in this soup? 'Not much. Just a kachug.'
>
> How much longer do I have to wait to see the doctor? 'He'll be with you in a jiffy.'
>
> How fast can you sew a button on? 'In two shakes of a lamb's tail.'

How much do you love me? 'A whole bunch!'

When Qwilleran filed his copy with the managing editor, he said, 'I owe you one, Junior; there really is a Thelma Thackeray. I'll take you to lunch at Rennie's.'

'Super! I'm hungry! ... Sit down. Be with you in a sec.' The editor rushed from the office with proof sheets.

While pondering the difference between a sec and a jiffy, Qwilleran noticed a proof of the editorial page, with a letter from a reader who aired her views, forcefully and entertainingly.

TO THE EDITOR – My family attended the last open meeting of the county Board of Commissioners, so that my daughters could see how government works. The issue being addressed was the important one of zoning. May I respectfully inquire what language our esteemed board members were speaking? It sounded like Jabberwocky in *Through the Looking-Glass* – ' 'Twas brillig, and the slithy toves did gyre and gimble in the wabe.' We were not alone. Others in the audience, equally bewildered, gathered on the courthouse steps after the meeting and proposed a message to our elected officials: 'All mimsy were the borogoves.'

Mavis Adams
HBB&A

Junior returned, ready for a free lunch at his friend's expense, and they went to Rennie's coffee shop at the Mackintosh Inn. It was named for Charles Rennie Mackintosh and inspired by one of his tearooms in Glasgow: tables lacquered in bright blue and bright green, chairs with unusually high backs, napkins striped in black and white.

They ordered French dip sandwiches with fries and a Caesar salad.

Qwilleran asked, 'Is there any news that's not fit to print?'

'We're all waiting for Thelma Thackeray. Would you like to interview her?'

'No thanks. It sounds like a story for Jill Handley.'

The editor said, 'We want to run a profile in depth. It will be good to have in the obit file. She's getting on in years.'

'So are we all – except you, Junior. You still look like a summer intern.'

'You don't have to rub it in, just because you're buying lunch.'

'Have you heard what's going into the old opera house?'

'Someone said it's a new county jail.'

'I was hoping for the world's largest emporium of used books. I miss Eddington's old place.'

Junior said, 'It's got to be an operation that requires a lot of parking space. They've torn down the storefront on both sides, and the lots are being paved.'

'The plot thickens,' Qwilleran said. 'Shall we have dessert? The chocolate pecan pie sounds good.'

They ordered the pie, and Junior said, 'Are you still reading to your cats?'

'Absolutely! It sharpens their intellect. Since advocating it in my column, I've received scores of letters from readers, reporting striking results.'

'Let's not overdo it,' Junior warned. 'The felines could take over the local government.'

'Not a bad idea! We can start by packing the town council.'

When the pie was served, they fell into a blissful silence for a while until Junior asked, 'What are you reading to the cats now? Plato and Schopenhauer?'

'Noel Coward's biography. I sing some of the Coward songs. Koko likes the one about mad dogs and Englishmen.'

The young editor never knew whether to take Qwilleran seriously or go along with the gag, so he concentrated on eating his pie.

Qwilleran had said 'yes' to Fran Brodie's cavalier proposal and hoped he would not regret it. As four o'clock approached, he set up the work bar with tequila, lime, salt, the silver tray, and so forth. Yum Yum huddled apprehensively nearby. He told her, 'Fran Brodie is coming for a drink. What do you want me to put in it?' She scampered away.

Fran was the picture of glamour – with her

chic clothing, model's figure, artful grooming, and perfect legs. They were always enhanced by high-heeled strappy sandals, weather permitting. But the sophisticated designer and the sweet little female cat had been feuding from the beginning. Yum Yum was possessive about Qwilleran, and Fran came on strong, attracted by his large moustache, or large fortune, or both.

When he first arrived in Pickax, he gave her a key to his apartment to use in his absence. She came in with her installer to rearrange the furniture and hang the window blinds. Or she came alone to accessorize the rooms with framed prints, pillows, candles, and the like. She thought them important, and her client let her have her way.

The only accessory he owned was the very old Mackintosh crest in wrought iron, said to come from a Scottish castle. It was leaning against the wall in the hallway, and she thought it would do nicely as camouflage for an ugly old radiator. While rolling it into the living room like a hoop, she accidentally rolled the fifty-pound artifact over her sandaled foot. She claimed that Yum Yum had darted out from nowhere and made her do it. A few weeks in a surgical boot cooled her ardor for the Klingenschoen heir. He had never liked sexually aggressive women anyway, preferring to do the pursuing himself. Whether or not Yum Yum had caused the accident was a moot point, but Fran was forever paranoid about female cats.

Her first words, when she arrived for her margarita, were 'Where is she?'

'They're both in the gazebo,' he said.

'You have a new silver tray! It's not what I would have chosen for this environment, but it's nice – not good, but nice.'

She was looking stunning in a periwinkle silk suit and new hair color, and high-heeled strappy shoes – all chosen, no doubt, for her dinner date with . . . 'Dutch.'

Qwilleran said, 'You're looking spiffy, in spite of your arduous trip . . . Let's sit in the living room.'

She sank into one of the deep-cushioned sofas and looked critically at the fireplace cube. Its face – above and on both sides of the fireplace – was covered with adjustable bookshelves. 'Do you really need to have those shelves on this side of the cube?' she asked.

'I'm running out of wall space,' he said as he raised his glass. 'Cheers!'

'Cheers! . . . What are you drinking?'

'The new Qwilleran cocktail . . . Recipe is being patented.'

His guest still stared at the wall of books. 'Is it a good idea to have books above a fireplace? I should think the heat would be bad for the bindings. If you could possibly remove them, I could get you a large sculptural wall accent—'

'Too bad I gave the Mackintosh crest to the inn,' he said, slyly.

Fran changed the subject abruptly. 'You met my new assistant yesterday. Did she tell you anything?'

'Yes, she seems to be interested in dogs and horses.'

'I mean, did she tell you anything about Thelma Thackeray?'

'She simply said she was interesting.'

'She's that, all right,' Fran agreed. 'And a good client! She knows what she likes, is open to suggestions, makes quick decisions, and doesn't change her mind. She's been in the business world for almost fifty years, and it shows! Also, she wants the very best and is willing to pay for it.' The margarita was working its spell. Fran was less edgy; she was willing to talk.

'What kind of career did she have in California?'

'She started with a sandwich shop, then a good restaurant, and then a private dinner club. It's her strong personality, I think, that has made her a success. Friends and customers gave her a smashing farewell party.'

'Why did she decide to come back to Moose County – of all places?'

'Her only living relative is here, and you know how it is: People tend to get sentimental about family as they grow older.'

Fran held out her glass for a refill and kicked off her shoes. 'You really know how to mix margaritas, Qwill!'

He served another drink. 'When does Madame Thackeray arrive?'

'It's all orchestrated. She left before the movers arrived, and she'll arrive after they've delivered. Everything will be unpacked at this end.'

'How much staff does she have?'

'Secretary, housekeeper, and driver,' Fran said slyly, waiting for a reaction. Then she added, 'They're all the same person – more of a companion – a woman half her age, who's really devoted to Thelma.'

Qwilleran said, 'I could use one of those when I'm her age. How old is she?'

'Eighty-two, but she certainly doesn't look it!'

'Face-lift?' he inquired.

'That's another terrific thing about Thelma. She eats right, exercises, and gives herself a daily face-lift with the electromagnetic rays from her fingertips . . . Perhaps I shouldn't be telling all this – to the media.'

'One question,' Qwilleran said. 'Why did she choose to buy property on Pleasant Street?'

'She remembered it from her childhood, when her father – who was a potato farmer – used to drive the family into town in his Model T – to see movies. As an extra treat he also drove up and down Pleasant Street. To those kids it was like Grimms' fairy tales. They were like huge gingerbread houses decorated with white frosting in fancy scrolls. So when she called a realtor here and learned that one of the storybook houses was listed for sale, she flipped!

'Do you know Mavis Adams, the attorney?' she asked abruptly.

'I know she's the new "A" in HBB&A. We've met briefly.'

'The realtor recommended her to handle legal details of the property transfer. Also, Thelma will have to file a new will in this state . . . Mavis thinks the residents of Pleasant Street should give a reception to welcome Thelma.'

'Friendly idea,' Qwilleran said. 'Since half the families on the street are Scottish, you could hold it at the Scottish lodge hall.'

Fran gave him a sly glance. 'We hoped you'd let us use your barn.'

'Hmmm,' he mused. 'That's something to think about!'

'Think fast. It's to be a week from Sunday. Robin-O'Dell will do the catering, and Burgess Campbell will take care of expenses. The Scots will be in Highland attire, which makes for a gala mood.'

'Well . . . since you're working on a short deadline . . . I'll say yes.' Qwilleran liked any excuse to wear his Highland kit.

'Everyone will be delighted, and Thelma will be terribly impressed.' Fran was putting on her shoes.

'Before you leave, let me bring in Yum Yum,' Qwilleran said. 'You two rational females should bury the hatchet.'

'No, no! She'll nip my nylons even if she doesn't break my foot!'

He accompanied her to the barnyard and noted that she was driving a new car – a luxury model. The Thackeray assignment must have been lucrative.

Before stepping into the car, she hesitated and then said, 'As a favor to me, Qwill, would you let me supply an artwork to hang over your fireplace, replacing the bookshelves, just temporarily? Thelma knows I did the interior of the barn, and I want it to look its best.'

'I'll take it under advisement,' he said gravely. He felt about his books the way parents feel about their children.

When he brought them in from the gazebo and watched Koko gobbling his dinner and Yum Yum nibbling daintily, he thought, How could this sweet little creature be accused of nipping nylons?

Later, he asked Polly on the phone, 'Does Catta ever nip women's nylons?'

'No. Why do you ask?'

'I've heard that some female cats have a nylon fetish.'

He was careful not to mention Fran's visit. Polly disliked her flip manner and such gaucheries as kicking off her shoes when offered a second drink. Polly called the gesture 'just too cute.'

So Qwilleran told her only that the pleasant people on Pleasant Street wanted to borrow the barn for a reception welcoming Thelma. 'It'll be a week from Sunday. Highland dress is suggested, since half the residents are Scots.'

'Lovely!' she said. 'Am I invited? I'll wear my clan sash, pinned on the shoulder with a cairngorm.'

'You're not only invited; you're in charge of background music – preferably light classics that make people feel good but aren't too boringly familiar.'

'I have just the thing! The piano pieces of Sibelius. They'll be thrilling on your stereo system.'

Then he told her he was thinking of removing the books over the fireplace and replacing them with artwork.

She approved. 'I've always thought that was a risky place for book bindings. The heat could dry them out, you know. You might find a suitable wall hanging at the Art Center Sunday.'

Having Polly in accord with his two forthcoming projects, he tackled the preparations with a modicum of enthusiasm.

Qwilleran was inept at household maintenance chores. He worked with words and believed that carpenters should work with hammers, plumbers with wrenches, and painters with brushes. Whenever he had attempted a simple do-it-yourself project, the Siamese sensed the gravity of the occasion and watched with apprehension. He said to them, 'Keep your toes crossed and if I fall off the ladder, call 911.'

The job called for removing the books, the shelving, the brackets that held the shelves, and the metal strips that supported the brackets, leaving several large screw-holes in the wall. He seemed to remember that such holes could be filled with toothpaste, but the wall was white, and his current toothpaste was green. The obvious solution was to buy a wall hanging large enough to cover the blemishes. It would require an artwork at least five feet wide and three feet high.

THE CAT WHO BROUGHT DOWN THE HOUSE

Five

In the late nineteenth century the octagonal apple barn had presided over one of the strip farms of the period – almost a half mile long, but narrow. A wagon trail ran its length. Now it was a single-lane country road, seldom used for vehicular traffic. Qwilleran used it to walk from the barn to his rural mailbox and newspaper sleeve on the back road and to the Art Center at the far end.

On Sunday Qwilleran and Polly walked down the lane to the Touchy-Feely Exhibition – he with a tape measure in his pocket.

On the way down, she asked, 'Did I tell you that the library has had a run on novels by William Makepeace Thackeray?'

His acerbic reply: 'Only Moose County could put two

and two together and get seventeen . . . Did you find out anything about his middle name?'

'Not a clue! . . . I had an uncle Makemoney – at least, that's what I called him. He was always talking about making money! My father, who was very precise about language, said you can earn money, invest money, inherit money, save money, and lose money but you cannot make money. You would have liked my father, Qwill, and he would have approved of you.'

'My loss,' he murmured.

The skeletons of blighted apple trees had been replaced by a garden that attracted birds, another designed for butterflies, and reforestation with hardwoods and evergreens.

The Art Center at the end of the lane resembled a rustic residence, and that was what it was originally intended to be. Now it was a complex of exhibition halls, studios, and classrooms. The new show featured stitchery inspired by great artists. There were sunflowers (Van Gogh), apples (Cézanne), super-flowers (O'Keeffe), trompe l'oeil (Harnett), and so forth.

For himself he found an abstraction inspired by Feininger – an explosion of color, leading the eye into the distance. And it was the right size! A 'sold' sticker was affixed. According to gallery policy, purchased artworks had to remain in the exhibition until the end of the month. He consulted the manager about the forthcoming reception.

'No problem! We'll notify the artist, and she'll be

flattered to have her work on display in your fabulous barn.'

Mildred Riker was there, ready to recount the blueberry legend of Moose County, and they went into a vacant studio to do the taping.

'Arch kids me about throwing a handful of blueberries into everything,' she said, 'but they're part of Moose County's history.'

On the desk was a metal scoop about ten inches wide, with about thirty metal prongs. Qwilleran said, 'What's that? It would be good for policing a cat's commode.'

Stifling a giggle, Mildred said, 'That's a blueberry rake used in harvesting.'

He turned on the recorder, and the following tale was later transcribed:

THE INCREDIBLE
MOOSE COUNTY BLUEBERRIES

Long before we knew about antioxidants and bioflavonoids, blueberries were doing their thing; Mother Nature had made them good-for-you as well as good-to-eat. In the seventeenth century French explorers reported that native Americans used wild blueberries as food and medicine.

In the nineteenth century my great-grandfather, Elias King, came to Moose County from Maine to work as a lumberjack and save up to buy a farm. His diary is preserved in the historical collection at the public library.

He wrote that the woods were full of wild blueberries, called bilberries. The lumberjacks ate them by the handful. They were like candy – after the lumber-camp diet of beans and salt pork.

Eventually he had saved enough to buy farmland at the north edge of what is now Pickax. The land was well endowed with wild blueberries – lowgrowing shrubs that crept across the property as if they owned it.

When my grandfather, Matthew King, inherited the farm, he claimed that blueberries occupied more acreage than did corn and potatoes. He said, 'Wild blueberries can't be cultivated, but they can't be killed, either.' So he gave the berries away to anyone who cared to pick them. Grandma King said she lay awake nights, thinking of ways to use them in family meals: a handful of blueberries here, a handful of blueberries there. The perfect blueberry pie recipe that she masterminded is in my security box at the bank.

By the time my father inherited the property, the family was involved in producing, packaging, marketing, and shipping blueberry products. He was jocularly called the Blueberry King, and friends launched a frivolous campaign to change the name of the area to Blueberry County. Their slogan: 'When was the last time you saw a Moose?'

Finally my brothers and I were bequeathed the blueberry empire, but we were interested in careers of our own. We sold out to the large Toodle family, who developed the property in various ways, including a supermarket with extensive parking and loading facilities. They carry excellent produce from all parts of the country. Included are the large cultivated berries that I put in muffins, pancakes, soups, salads, stews, and Grandma King's blueberry pie. Considering my blueberry heritage, it seems ironic that I now buy the berries in eight-ounce boxes ... No matter. There is a postscript to the tale.

The supermarket has had constant trouble with the parking lot. Asphalt buckled. Concrete cracked. One day Grandma Toodle showed me the latest damage. Shrubs were pushing up in the wide cracks.

'What do you think they are?' she asked.

'I know what they are!' I said. 'Nothing can stop the incredible Moose County blueberries.'

Qwilleran turned off the recorder and said, 'Mildred, millions of people wouldn't believe that blueberries could wreck a parking lot ... but I do!'

On Monday morning Koko was huddled over his plate, concentrating on his food, when he suddenly turned his head to the side and listened for a few seconds before returning his attention to the business at hand. Moments later, he turned again, and the telephone rang.

It was a welcome call from Thornton Haggis, the Art

Center's volunteer man-of-all-work. He said, 'Mildred told me yesterday that you bought a wall hanging and it's okay to take it before the show ends. I could drive it up there and hang it for you right now.'

Qwilleran said, 'Best news I've had since Amanda was elected mayor. I have a stepladder. What else do you need?'

'Nothing. I have all the tools and know all the tricks for hanging textiles.'

'Then come along. I'll start the coffeemaker.'

The Siamese were excited when they saw the stepladder come out of the broom closet, and saw a car moving up the lane that seldom knew traffic, and saw a white-haired man approaching the barn with a big roll of something under his arm.

'Where do we hang it?' were Thornton's first words.

'Above the fireplace, covering the holes.'

'It won't cover! It's a vertical.'

'Just hang it horizontally.'

The expert unrolled the hanging on the floor and studied it from all angles. 'Why not?' was his decision. 'But we won't tell the artist.'

After the deed was done and the result admired, the men sat at the snack bar for coffee and some sweet rolls from the freezer.

'Terrific rolls! Where'd you get them?' Thornton asked.

'From a woman in Fishport who sells home-bakes.'

'I know her. She and her husband reported a missing

47

person last summer and got all that unfavorable publicity. A shame! Nice folks, the Hawleys. He's a commercial fisherman, semi-retired.'

Thornton knew everyone in the county, past and present.

They talked about the Sesquicentennial and the Haggis Monument Works, purveyor of gravestones for a century and a half.

'My forebears chiseled some outlandish inscriptions in the early days, and I photograph them whenever I find them.'

'You should write a book,' Qwilleran suggested. 'I'm sure the K Fund would publish it. I'll buy the first copy.'

'Do you think the restored opera house has anything to do with the Sesquicentennial, Qwill? I have a hunch it's going to be the big event of the celebration, and that's why they're being so secretive.'

If so, Qwilleran thought, and if it was Hixie's idea, something dire will happen! Not wanting to be a doom-sayer, he changed the subject casually after a brief pause: 'Where do you get your hair cut, Thorn?'

'When my wife lets me get it cut, I go to Bob the Barber, which isn't very often; she likes the Zulu look.'

Bob the Barber did business in a curious old building on Main Street. It was set back a few feet from its neighbors, and steps led down from the sidewalk to a small patio at basement level. Here there was a park bench, a potted tree, and an old revolving barber pole.

One could look through a large window and see how many customers were waiting.

Qwilleran said, 'You don't often see a barber pole anymore, especially one that revolves. I've often wondered about the significance of the spiral red-and-white pole.'

Thornton was a history buff and the right one to ask. He said, 'In the Middle Ages there were barber-surgeons who did bloodletting with leeches. They hung bandages on a pole outside their shop to advertise the services. The colors on the barber pole that evolved were red for blood, white for bandages, blue for veins.'

'Sorry I asked,' Qwilleran said.

A haircut was on his schedule for Monday, a day that was usually not busy. When he walked down the steps to the barbershop, he discovered that other customers had the same idea. Through the large window he could see both barber chairs occupied and several customers waiting in the row of folding chairs against the wall. A man in overalls, a feed cap, and field boots was leaving the shop. He said, 'Can't wait . . . too slow. Young Bob broke his thumb.'

'Cutting hair?' Qwilleran asked.

He could see Old Bob working at the first chair and Young Bob, with a splint on his left hand, at the second chair.

'Playin' softball,' the farmer said. 'He can wiggle his fingers some, but . . . too slow . . . too slow. Ain't got time.'

Among those who had time to wait were an agricultural agent, a storekeeper, and a lecturer at the community college. Burgess Campbell, blind from birth, was accompanied by his guide dog, Alexander.

The two men played their usual charade.

Qwilleran said, 'Professor Moriarty! Are you here for a haircut or a bloodletting?'

'My friend Sherlock!' he replied. 'Did you bring your violin?'

'Shouldn't you be in the lecture hall, professor?'

'Not until one o'clock. When are you going to audit one of my lectures?'

'What's this week's topic?'

'Geopolitical Machinations in the Nineteenth Century.'

'I'll wait till next week,' Qwilleran said.

Old Bob whipped the sheet off his customer and said, 'Either of you two jokers ready to be clipped?'

Qwilleran said to Burgess, 'You go first. I want to look at the bulletin board.'

'All I need is a trim. You can have the chair in . . . *two shakes of a lamb's tail*.' His emphasis on the last phrase was a pointed reference to the 'Qwill Pen.'

There was a wall of cork near the entrance, where customers were welcome to post their business cards: Bill's Bump Shop, Main Street Flowers, Tipsy's Tavern, and the like. But interspersed with the legitimate cards were computer printouts that local wags contributed:

TRAFFIC TICKETS FIXED — CHEAP

FALSE IDS — WHILE U WAIT

TAX-EVASION SERVICE — TOP-QUALITY ADVICE

Qwilleran asked the head barber, 'Do the police ever raid this joint?'

'When Andy Brodie comes in for a clip, he heads straight for the board and laughs his head off,' said Old Bob.

After Qwilleran's session in the barber chair, he found Burgess and Alexander waiting for him on the patio.

'Got a minute to sit down, Qwill? I want to thank you for letting us have the reception in your barn.'

'My pleasure. But you've never visited the barn, and — as the host of the occasion — you should drop in and get the lay of the land.'

'Good idea! I can have a student driver take me over there any afternoon after three o'clock.'

'I assume you refer to an MCCC student who drives — and not a kid who's learning to operate a vehicle.'

Burgess laughed heartily . . . and an appointment was made.

Six

Qwilleran had mixed feelings about Pleasant Street. Residents included some of his best friends, important in the community and known for intelligence and taste. They lived in large houses set well apart on one-acre lots – frame houses – painted white and lavished with white jigsaw ornamentation.

To Qwilleran, with his eye for contemporary, they looked like a collection of wedding cakes! Yet, the street had been photographed often and featured in national magazines as a fine example of Carpenter Gothic.

They had been built by the Campbells in the nineteenth century, and while the residents owned their dwellings, Burgess Campbell owned the land. That fact gave him a baronial interest in the neighborhood and the well-being of its occupants.

Now, Qwilleran felt it behooved him to take a closer look at Pleasant Street. He would bike, pedaling his vintage British Silverlight. With his slick red-and-yellow bike suit, yellow bubble helmet, sun goggles, and oversize moustache, he had been known to stop traffic on Main Street. (On one occasion a car back-ended another at a traffic light.) So he approached Pleasant Street via the back road.

It was a cul-de-sac, with a landscaped island at the end for a turnaround. The five houses on each side had broad lawns, and the serenity of the scene was enhanced by the fact that there was no curb-parking. Each dwelling had a side-drive with garage and visitor parking in the rear. There was a Wednesday-morning quiet: children at school, adults at work or doing errands or volunteer work. Others would be pursuing their hobbies. A contralto could be heard doing vocal exercises. The distant whine of a table saw meant that the woodworker was making a Shaker table.

Qwilleran biked twice up and down the street then stopped at the entrance to appraise the whole. No two houses were alike, yet they all had a vertical silhouette. There were tall narrow windows and doors, steeply pitched roofs over a third floor. Some had turrets. All had a wealth of ornamentation along roof lines, balcony railings, atop doors and windows.

Before leaving the scene he braked his bike and

scanned the streetscape through squinted eyes. He was reluctant to admit that it had a kind of enchantment, like an illustrated edition of a book of fairy tales. Its residents included businessmen, two doctors, a college lecturer, an attorney, a professional astrologer, a musician, and an artist! Perhaps Burgess could explain the lure of Pleasant Street.

Qwilleran had time to take a quick shower, drop some crunchies into the plate on the kitchen floor, and wolf down a ham sandwich before his appointment with Burgess. Then, a few minutes before three o'clock, Koko rushed to the kitchen window. He sensed that a car was turning off Main Street, crossing the theatre parking lot, and meandering through the woods to the barn.

Qwilleran went out to meet it and saw the two front doors fly open. A dog jumped out the passenger door, followed by a man in lecture-hall tweeds. The driver, in jeans and T-shirt, emerged with an expression of rapt wonder.

'Hey, man! That's some kinda barn!!'

Burgess said, 'Qwill, this is Henry Ennis, chauffeur par excellence. Hank, you can pick me up at four o'clock.'

'Make it four-thirty,' Qwilleran suggested.

The driver said, 'If you want me earlier, call the library. I'll be studying there.'

As he drove away, Burgess explained, 'Hank is a scholarship student from Sawdust City. I reserve my second floor as a hostel for MCCC students without cars, who can't go home every night.'

Burgess employed students part-time to read aloud – from research material, the *New York Times*, and student papers for grading.

Qwilleran said, 'Okay! The tour starts here ... On Sunday night parking will have to be here in the barnyard, and space is limited. So guests should be instructed to car-pool.'

Burgess made a note of it on a small recorder.

'Actually, this is the kitchen door, so someone will have to direct them around the barn to the front entrance. It's a stone path, so women will find it kind to their high heels. I'm assuming it will be a dressy occasion ... I suggest that guests assemble in the bird garden before going indoors. There are stone benches and flowering shrubs, and I think we can get Andy Brodie to play the bagpipe for a half hour.'

They went indoors, and Qwilleran conducted them through the large foyer, where the receiving line would be stationed ... through the dining room, where Robin-O'Dell would have the refreshment table set up ... past the snack bar with its four stools for guests who like to sit and lean on their elbows ... through the library with its comfortable seating ... and into the living room with its large sofas.

Burgess asked, 'Where are the cats? I can tell they're here – by the way Alexander is breathing.'

Qwilleran said, 'They're on the rafters, which are forty

feet overhead. They're watching every move we make.'

When all the decisions were made, and all the notes were recorded, they sat at the snack bar for cold drinks, and another story was taped for *Short & Tall Tales*.

HOW PLEASANT STREET GOT ITS NAME

In the nineteenth century my ancestors were shipbuilders in Scotland – in the famous river Clyde at Glasgow. When opportunity beckoned from the New World, my great-grandfather, Angus, came here with a team of ships' carpenters considered the best anywhere. They started a shipyard at Purple Point, where they built four-masted wooden schooners, using Moose County's hundred-and-twenty-foot pine trees as masts. These were the 'tall ships' that brought goods and supplies to the settlers and shipped out cargoes of coal, lumber, and stone.

Then came the New Technology! The wireless telegraph was in; the Pony Express was out. Railroads and steamboats were in; four-masted schooners were out. In his diary Angus said it was like a knife in the heart to see a tall ship stripped down to make a barge for towing coal. There was no work for his carpenters to do, and their fine skills were wasted.

Then a 'still small voice' told him to build houses! It was the voice of his wife, Anne, a canny Scots-woman. She said, 'John, build houses as romantic as the tall ships – and as fine!'

She was right! The New Technology had produced a class of young upwardly mobile achievers who wanted the good life. Not for them the stodgy stone mansions built by conspicuously rich mining tycoons and lumber barons! They wanted something romantic!

So Angus bought acreage at the south edge of Pickax and built ten fine houses, all on one-acre plots. Although no two were alike, their massing followed the elongated vertical architecture called Gothic Revival, and the abundance of scroll trim was the last word in Carpenter Gothic.

And here is something not generally known: The vertical board-and-batten siding was painted in the colors that delighted young Victorians: honey, cocoa, rust, jade, or periwinkle; against this background, the white scroll trim had a lacy look.

Today we paint them all-white, giving rise to the 'wedding cake' sobriquet.

When the time came to put up sign boards, Angus was at a loss for a street name. He said, 'I don't want anything personal like Campbell or Glasgow . . . or anything sobersides or high-sounding . . . just something pleasant.'

And Great-Grandma Anne said with sweet feminine logic: 'Call it Pleasant Street.'

'And folks have lived there happily ever after,' Qwilleran said as he turned off the recorder. 'I don't even know who my grandparents were, so I'm envious of a fourth-generation native.'

'I wanted to make it five generations,' Burgess said, 'but it didn't work out. I grew up with the girl next door and we were good friends. I always thought we'd marry some day, but she went away to college and never came back. Now she has three kids that should have been mine. But her parents still treat me like a son-in-law. And I treat students who lodge with me on the second floor with fatherly concern.'

Qwilleran said, 'They're very lucky! I hope they all turn out to be a credit to you . . . and how do you feel about the people who own the houses on your land?'

'We work together to keep Pleasant Street pleasant, solve problems, and so forth.'

'Has the California contingent arrived?' Qwilleran asked casually.

'They're due this afternoon,' Burgess said. 'My housekeeper, Mrs Richards, periodically goes over with coffee and cookies -- in the guise of neighborliness but actually because she and I are burning with curiosity. The moving van arrived Monday. Since then, Fran's helpers have worked around the clock, unpacking and getting everything settled. The house looks as if they had lived there for weeks!'

'One question,' Qwilleran asked. 'Do you know anything about the Thackeray family?'

'I certainly do!' was the prompt answer. 'Thelma's father was a potato farmer who struck oil – as the saying goes – during Prohibition. Her brother was a veterinarian who believed in holistic medicine, and the Thackeray Clinic was one of the finest in this part of the country. I took Alexander to him for regular checkups. Dr Thurston's love of animals was such that they looked forward to visiting him. He was healthy and an outdoorsman and should have lived another ten years at least, but he fell to his death while hiking alone on the rim of the Black Creek Gorge. Tragic! The pity of it is: There are nasty rumors in circulation – which I prefer not to repeat.'

A horn sounded in the barnyard, and Qwilleran walked with his visitors to the car. 'One question, Burgess. Fran said the reception was for adults only—'

'Ah, yes! There'll be a party at the Adams house for the six kids in the neighborhood, ages seven to ten. Mavis's two teen daughters will supervise. They're accustomed to working with youngsters. They tell me there'll be games with prizes, movies – such as Disney's *Lady and the Tramp* and/or *The Incredible Journey*. Music will be Sixties-style. Refreshment – four kinds of pizza and make-it-yourself sundaes . . . The Adams girls are very well organized and very responsible . . . And I forgot – favors to take home. Chocolate brownies.'

Qwilleran said, 'Sounds better than the champagne reception.'

Alexander gently nudged Burgess toward the passenger door of the car, and they drove away.

* * *

The next evening Qwilleran and Polly would be dining at the newly named, newly decorated Grist Mill. She always dressed carefully for such occasions and had phoned the restaurant to inquire about the color scheme. It was jade green. So she would wear her dusty rose suit.

She reported this vital information to Qwilleran during their nightly phone-chat.

By a strange coincidence he was writing a think piece on green for his next 'Qwill Pen' column. He boasted that he could take any noun or adjective and write a thousand words about it. Now the word was *green*. First . . . he made notes:

- It's the fourth color in the spectrum: red, orange, yellow, GREEN, blue, violet. Why is it more talked about than other colors?
- In big-city phone directories there are hundreds of Greens – and a few Greenes.
- Yet, there has never been a President Green in the White House.
- Why is blue more popular in clothing and the home? How do you feel about green jeans?
- Why does Santa wear red instead of green?
- Why do crazy kids dye their hair green?
- Green trees fight pollution. Green veggies are good for you.
- Green rhymes with mean. Monsters are green eyed. Nobody likes to be called a greenhorn. 'It's not easy being green,' according to the song.

- We have green alligators, green snakes, and green grasshoppers. Why no animals with green fur?

'Yow!' came an indignant comment. It was a reminder that it was eleven o'clock and time for a bedtime snack.

Seven

In dressing for dinner at the Grist Mill, Qwilleran had chosen light olive-green slacks and a lighter olive-green shirt to wear with his tan blazer, and he had gone to Scottie's Men's Store for a deeper olive-green tie with a tan motif. His interest in coordination amazed Arch Riker, who had known him in his earlier, or 'slob,' period. Now Qwilleran had Polly to please, a host of admirers to impress, and a little money to spend.

Driving to the Grist Mill, they talked about the new animal-welfare project being launched in Moose County. The attorney, Mavis Adams, was spearheading it. It was being called the Kit Kat Agenda.

Polly said, 'Its thrust is to stop the euthanasia of

unwanted kittens. They're going to stage a show to raise funds.'

'Mavis writes clever letters to the editor,' he said.

'She lives on Pleasant Street.'

'I wonder how Thelma will fit into the neighborhood?'

Polly said, 'Guess who came into my office today? Thelma Thackeray's assistant! She took out library cards for both of them and then came to my office to introduce herself and make an offer. She was conservatively dressed, soft-spoken, very nice – fortyish, I guess – and obviously devoted to her boss.'

'What was the offer?'

'Well, Thelma has a collection of autographed photos of old movie stars that she'll lend us for an exhibit. I assured her that we have a locked case for such exhibits. Clark Gable, Mae West, John Wayne, Joan Crawford, etc. – isn't that exciting?'

'If you say so,' he said.

'There's even a signed print of a photo that appeared on the cover of *Time* magazine: Hedda Hopper wearing a hat made of a typewriter, a microphone, and a script.'

Before Qwilleran could react, they arrived at the Grist Mill. 'You must tell me more later,' he said.

It was the same ancient stone mill with cavernous interior and exposed timbers, but color had been added: jade green table linens and carpet in a darker shade of jade green. And the rough stone wall was hung with farm implements of the nineteenth century.

They were greeted in the lobby by Elizabeth Hart, one

of the three owners, wearing a silk coolie suit in jade green. Towering over the maître d's station was the six-foot-eight Derek Cuttlebrink. He showed them to a choice table – under a murderous-looking scythe.

Qwilleran said, 'I hope that thing is securely attached to the wall.'

Polly said, 'You have a fortune invested in antique farm equipment!'

In a lowered voice Derek said, 'Don't let on that I told you, but Liz got them from Hollywood – props from a movie.' Then he added, 'One dry sherry and one Qwilleran cocktail?'

The tables were filling rapidly with guests excited about the restaurant's opening. The menu was new and appetizing. Polly ordered three small courses: mushroom bisque, deviled crab en coquille, and a Cobb salad. Qwilleran ordered minestrone, oysters Rockefeller, and the surf-and-turf special, and no salad. Polly said, 'If Mildred were here, she'd make you eat some leafy greens.'

Suddenly a hush fell on the room. Everyone looked toward the entrance. 'What happened?' asked Qwilleran, who had his back to the door.

The young woman serving them exclaimed, 'It's HER!' and she rushed to the kitchen.

Polly, facing the scene of the action, said, 'Party of three . . . Thelma has a commanding appearance . . . One is the assistant who came to my office . . . There's a man with them . . . Everyone's gawking.'

The hush gave way to an excited babble of voices.

'Thelma,' she went on, 'is wearing a pearl gray suit and small matching hat and jeweled lapel pin . . . She's doing the ordering. They're having champagne . . . The man is about forty. Looks like one of those "snappy dressers" from Lockmaster . . . Is he her only living relative?'

Qwilleran said, 'I believe the house she bought is the one you inherited – one of the best on Pleasant Street.'

'Yes. I was terribly tempted to keep it and live there. I'm glad you talked me out of it, dear. It would have been too much property to care for, considering the demands of my job . . . But the people who live on Pleasant Street are so congenial! I think there's something psychological about the name of the street. The Campbells have always kept title to the land, and the neighborhood is like a dukedom. Did you know that Burgess is affectionately called "Duke" by the residents?'

Polly ordered a small sorbet for dessert and watched without envy as Qwilleran consumed a large serving of cinnamon bread pudding with butterscotch sauce.

Thelma's party was still there when they left. In the lobby Polly excused herself, and Qwilleran sauntered to the maître d's desk. 'Derek, are your responsibilities here going to interfere with your folksinging and theatre club productions?'

'Liz says we can work something out. I'm gonna be in the Kit Kat Revue.'

'Sounds like a nightclub in an old musical comedy.'

'It's a fund-raiser for an animal welfare project, and I

wondered if you could write some lyrics about unwanted kittens. Sort of a tearjerker.'

It was the kind of challenge he relished. He said, 'You mean . . . something like . . . "Frankie and Johnny were kittens . . . Lordy! How they could cry! . . . They sat in a cage for adoption . . . But people just passed 'em by . . . We done 'em wrong . . . We done 'em wrong!" '

'Super! Could you write a couple of more verses, Qwill?'

'I guess so. But if you let anyone know I'm writing your lyrics, you'll be singing without an Adam's apple!'

At that moment Polly joined them, and Derek said, 'Enjoy your dinner, Mrs Duncan? I was just telling Mr Q that our chef trained in Singapore.'

'Oh, really!' she said. 'Elizabeth said he was from New Jersey.'

'Well . . . His basic training was in Singapore,' Derek said with the aplomb of one who is a frequent fibber.

On the way home Polly said, 'I asked Elizabeth about the lapel pin Thelma was wearing. She said it's a parrot pavéd with emeralds and rubies, with a diamond eye, and she was also wearing a matching bracelet. Even Elizabeth was impressed!'

Qwilleran asked, 'Do you know anything about the Kit Kat Revue?'

'Only that it's a fund-raiser for Mavis Adams's new animal rescue project. She'll be at the reception Sunday. I wonder what Thelma will wear? All those kilts and sashes will be strong competition.'

Qwilleran said, 'Fran Brodie will advise her. Fran is making herself indispensable.'

'I suppose the man at Thelma's table was her nephew. He was quite good-looking and he was being terribly charming,' Polly reported.

'As the only living relative of a rich octogenarian, it behooves him to be terribly charming.'

'Oh, Quill! You're being so cynical!'

Cynical or not, he found his moustache bristling – even more so when a motorcycle messenger delivered an envelope Friday morning. A computer-printed invitation: 'Please join us in honoring our California friends at a light repast directly after the reception – in the ballroom of the Mackintosh Inn. Southwest cuisine.' It was signed by Richard Thackeray with no RSVP requested. It was assumed, innocently or haughtily, that everyone would be eager to attend.

The handwriting on the envelope was Fran's. So was the wording of the invitation, although the idea must have been Richard's. A supper riding piggyback on a reception would not occur to Fran. Qwilleran knew her well enough for that. She was humoring Richard – for whatever reason. (He could think of several.)

Nevertheless, he phoned Polly at the library to report the invitation. 'It means you'll be getting home two or three hours later than expected. You might like to clear it with Brutus and Catta.'

'Oh! Didn't I tell you? I have an automatic feeder with

a timer, and it works very well. Wetherby Goode saw the item in a catalogue and bought one for each of us.' The WPKX meteorologist (real name Joe Bunker) was a neighbor of Polly's and had a cat named Jet Stream. 'Why don't you order one, Qwill? I'll get the phone number for you.'

'Thanks, but I doubt whether Koko would approve. It might work for Yum Yum, but Koko likes to know the hand that feeds him.'

Next, Qwilleran finished 'All About Green' and walked downtown to file his copy before deadline. Junior Goodwinter gave it an editor's quick scan and said, 'You always boast, Qwill, that you can write a thousand words about nothing, and – by golly! – you've finally proved it!'

With equal mockery Qwilleran retorted, 'What have you got on the front page today – if anything?'

'Thelma and her parrots,' the managing editor replied. 'Great photo by Bushy, but the text sounds like a press release. It'll be handy to have in the obit file; that's the best I can say for it. You should have written it, Qwill.'

'I always thought Jill was a good writer.'

'Yeah, but she's accustomed to interviewing locals. She allowed herself to be buffaloed by a celebrity. I had a professor in J school who hammered it into our skulls: *Don't be a respecter of persons!*'

'Not bad advice,' Qwilleran agreed.

'On my first assignment I was supposed to interview a Very Important Person. The ignoramus sidestepped my questions and read a prepared speech – until I said,

"Excuse me, sir, may I ask a simple question?" He listened to it and said coldly, "You should know the answer to that one." I said respectfully, "Yes, sir, but I want to know if you do." Wow! Was I taking a chance, but it worked, and I got a good interview.'

Qwilleran nodded with understanding. Junior had a handicap – an appearance of eternal youth. He looked like a high-school sophomore when he was in college, and now – as managing editor of a newspaper and father of two – he still looked fifteen.

When Qwilleran arrived home, Koko let him know there was a message on the answering machine: 'This is Celia, Chief. We're catering your party on Sunday. Okay if I run over this afternoon to check the facilities and see what has to be done?'

Koko recognized the voice, despite the electronic distortion. It was the woman who brought them meat loaf. He hopped on and off the desk in excitement.

Qwilleran phoned her and left his own message: 'Come on over anytime. The cats have missed you.'

Celia Robinson had rented his carriage-house apartment at one time. She was a fun-loving grandmother who had lived in a Florida retirement complex but decided she preferred snowball fights to shuffleboard. She cooked, did volunteer work, and made everyone happy with her merry laughter.

She happened to be an avid reader of spy and detective fiction, and Qwilleran happened to have an interest in criminal investigation. When suspicions made his moustache bristle, as they often did, he had a compulsion to search for clues, discreetly. What could be more discreet than a secret agent who looked like someone's grandma and laughed a lot? Celia called him 'Chief,' and he called her 'Double-O-Thirteen-and-a-Half.'

Then she married the amiable, white-haired Pat O'Dell and moved into his large house on Pleasant Street.

'Faith, an' it's my big kitchen she married me for, I'm thinking,' he often said in his rich brogue.

Pat had a janitorial service, and together they started Robin-O'Dell Catering.

Celia interpreted the invitation to 'come on over anytime' as 'right away' and she arrived in 'two shakes of a lamb's tail.'

'Do you have time for a glass of fruit juice?' Qwilleran asked, inviting her to sit at the snack bar.

'Oh, you have some new bar stools!' she exclaimed. 'Very comfy . . . Where are the kitties?'

'Looking at you from the top of the refrigerator.'

Celia groped in her large handbag and they jumped to the floor with two thumps, Yum Yum landing like a feather and Koko landing like a muscular male.

Qwilleran gave them a few crumbles of meat loaf and told them, 'This is just the appetizer. The main course will be served at five-thirty.'

'Are you enjoying your new career?' he asked her now.

'I love it! But I miss those secret missions, Chief.'

70

'You could still do a little snooping, if you had time, and if Pat wouldn't object.'

'He'd never know,' she said with a wink. 'Do you have any suspicions, Chief?'

'No. Only a nagging curiosity. Who bought the old opera house, and what are they doing with it, and why the secrecy? If I start making inquiries, the gossips will have a field day!'

'I could ask questions. Where would I go?'

'To the courthouse and find out who bought the building. To the City Hall and find out if they've issued any permits for remodeling. It might be a clue to the mystery . . . No hurry, Celia.'

'I could do it on Tuesday. Monday we're doing a birthday luncheon in Purple Point. Would anyone mind if Pat and I didn't attend Richard Thackeray's supper? We have to clear away here and go home and get started on the luncheon. How should I explain?'

'There was no RSVP on the invitation,' Qwilleran said, 'so you don't need to explain. Just do what you have to do. If anyone asks, I'll invent something.'

'You're good at that!' she said in admiration. 'I think of you every time I buy fruit and vegetables at Toodle's Market.' At the recollection she was so overcome with mirth that she choked on her cranberry juice.

'Take it easy!' he said.

In the past, when she uncovered evidence that required the utmost secrecy, there was a clandestine meeting at the market, in the produce department – two casual

71

foodshoppers discussing the price of cucumbers or ripeness of melons, as strangers do. Then she would whisper some amazing revelation too hot to put in writing or entrust to a telephone that might be bugged. The serio-comic charade delighted Celia, who would be forever young. She and Pat still had snowball fights, according to their amused neighbors.

Qwilleran asked her, 'How much champagne has been ordered for the reception?'

'Duke has ordered two cases and wants it perfectly chilled, so we're bringing our portable plug-in cooler with temperature control. And the stemware we're renting is glass and not the plastic kind which Duke calls an abomination. He's lending us his grandmother's banquet cloth and ordering a flower arrangement for the table. Since everyone's going to the supper afterwards, the cocktail snacks will be bite-size, and Duke wants the very best cheese!!'

When Celia had left, Qwilleran walked down the lane to pick up his daily paper from the newspaper sleeve. He took it to the Art Center porch and sat on the bench there, being impatient to read the Thackeray profile.

There was a three-column photo of Thelma conversing with two parrots and the headline read: THELMA AND FRIENDS COME HOME TO ROOST. Only when she spoke of her five parrots did she wax sentimental. 'There were six birds, but Chico passed away. I still have his cage and the cover with his name embroidered on it.'

There was plenty of opportunity for name-dropping, and drop them she did. Film celebrities and political figures had come to her dinner club.

She boasted that her twin brother had been a doctor of veterinary medicine. And a boast about her father caused Qwilleran to do a double take. He read it a second time:

'Pop was a hardworking potato farmer, struggling to make a living – until he had a brilliant idea for putting potatoes to a new use. It made him rich! He could send my brother to college and he set me up in business in Hollywood. He invented the low-calorie potato chip!'

At that moment the front door of the Art Center opened, and Thornton Haggis came out, saying, 'No loitering permitted!'

'Thorn! Did you see today's paper?' Qwilleran waved the front page at him.

'What happened? Have they found a cure for the common hangover?'

'Sit down and listen!' Qwilleran read the entire profile of the bootlegger's daughter.

'What!' Thornton yelped. 'Did she actually say that about potato chips? Does she believe that? Is that what Milo told her? Or did she invent it for Moose County readers?'

'You ask her!' Qwilleran said.

Eight

By Saturday morning Qwilleran had decided that Thelma's potato chip bombshell was a private joke of hers. She had inherited the Moose County penchant for leg-pulling. Only old-timers would appreciate the potato chip quip. That is, old-timers and history buffs.

He phoned Thornton at home to compare theories, and Mrs Haggis answered. 'He's out getting his hair cut, Qwill.'

'Hair cut!'

'Yes, isn't it a crime? Where has anyone ever seen such a beautiful mop of white hair? But he threatened to dye it green, so I said okay, reluctantly.'

'Well, tell him I called. Nothing important.'

It was important enough, however, for Qwilleran to

call Homer Tibbitt at Ittibittiwassee Estates. He was the only old-timer old enough to remember much about Prohibition.

Rhoda answered in the hushed voice that meant her husband was having one of his many naps.

'Don't disturb him. Did you read about Thelma in yesterday's paper?'

'We did indeed! I read it aloud, and Homer said she was just pulling a fast one . . . Homer says she was a great one for spoofing.'

'That's what I wanted to know. When's his birthday?'

'A week from today, and he says he doesn't want any birthday candles or media coverage.'

'He's a dreamer, Rhoda. The TV crews will be up here from Down Below to film the event.' Qwilleran was careful not to mention that he was writing a birthday song, and arrangements had been made for a serenade by Derek Cuttlebrink with his guitar.

On Sunday morning, a light rain freshened the foliage around Qwilleran's apple barn. In the afternoon a soft sunlight made everything sparkle. By five o'clock the gentlest of gentle breezes was wafting about the bird garden, where the guests were to assemble and Brodie was to pipe a few Scottish tunes.

Qwilleran said, 'Whoever is in charge of the local weather decided to show those California dudes a thing or two.' He wore his kilt in the red-and-green Mackintosh tartan, together with a green blazer, green knee socks with red flashers, a calfskin sporran, and, of course, a dagger in the sock.

Polly wore a white silk shirtwaist dress with a shoulder sash in the Robertson tartan, that being the Duncan clan connection.

The Siamese had been given an early dinner and dispatched to the gazebo in the canvas tote bag.

The Robin-O'Dell team had set up in the hospitality center with Burgess Campbell's grandmother's Madeira banquet cloth, an arrangement of red carnations and white daisies, an array of sparkling champagne glasses, and trays of tiny canapés, puffs, tartlets, and tasty morsels on toothpicks.

First, Police Chief Brodie arrived, driving up the lane from the back street – the better to get away after piping his stint. He was resplendent in the Brodie clan kilt and shoulder plaid and his bagpiper's feather 'bonnet,' a good eighteen inches tall.

As the carloads of guests started to arrive, Pat O'Dell was in the barnyard, showing them where to park and steering them to the bird garden. Burgess Campbell and Alexander were in the first carload to arrive – with the Bethunes, his surrogate in-laws. They were all in Highland attire, except the guide dog. There were the MacWhannells and the Camerons, the Ogilvies and MacLeods, all in clan tartans. Mavis Adams and the Morghans, who were not Scots, said they felt like illegal aliens.

The guests strolled around the garden, commented on

the plantings, visited the butterfly puddle, and found the gazebo. They looked at the Siamese as if they were creatures in a zoo and the Siamese looked at them in the same way.

Then Pat O'Dell came around the side of the barn and signaled to Qwilleran by jerking his thumb twice over his shoulder, meaning 'They're here!' Qwilleran caught Brodie's eye and tapped his wristwatch, and the bagpiper plunged into the attention-getting solemnity of 'Scotland the Brave.'

What happened in the next few minutes is best described in Qwilleran's own words. He later wrote in his personal journal:

Sunday, April 13 – Standing in the foyer in a formal receiving line was the Royal Family: Queen Thelma, Prince Richard, and the lady-in-waiting. The queen was wearing lavish jewels – and one of her 'artistic' hats. Richard lived up to his reputation as a snappy dresser by wearing a Nehru jacket and two-tone shoes.

One by one the guests moved through the line, with introductions made by Fran, who was unusually vivacious. I was the last to be presented to Thelma.

I grasped her hand in both of mine and said warmly, 'I've got to talk to you about *that hat*!'

Sounding like Mae West she said, 'And I've got to talk to you, Ducky . . . about that . . . *moustache*!' Her facial expression was pleasant, composed, and a trifle arch. 'And this is my nephew, Richard Thackeray. Richard, this is the celebrated Mr Q.'

He had a good handshake and exuberant personality. 'Call me Dick. I know all about you, Mr Q.'

'Don't tell anyone,' I said.

His voice had a distinct quality – velvety, with an underlying resonance. Later Thelma would tell me that it gave her goose bumps; it was her brother's voice, which four-footed creatures found magnetic, soothing, and even healing.

Janice was the last in the receiving line, her shyness at odds with a kind of eagerness. I couldn't help wondering about her role in the household that had just moved into Pleasant Street.

With the introductions made and everyone holding a glass of champagne, it was time for a toast to the new neighbors. And Burgess did the honors with éclat. Everyone responded noisily and at length. Then Thelma made an acceptance speech, which brought cheers and whistles. I looked at the guide dog to see what he thought of the brouhaha. Alexander, as usual, was completely unflappable.

The group scattered, some clustering around Thelma, others sampling the cocktail snacks or walking up the ramp to be thrilled by the view from the top. Fran escorted Thelma on a tour of the main floor, pointing out decorative features. At one point Fran hissed into my ear, 'What's that thing above the fireplace? I told you I could lend you an artwork for the occasion – something more suitable!'

Thelma's chief concern was the lack of television receivers. 'Where's your TV?' she demanded, sounding like Bette Davis. 'Above the fireplace you could have a fifty-inch screen – the rectangular style for showing movies . . . And with these big, comfortable sofas you'd have a perfect setup for movie parties. I have a large collection of old films that I could lend you.'

Dick viewed the recumbent bicycle leaning against a stone wall in the foyer and asked me, 'Do you really ride this? How does it feel to pedal with your feet up?'

'When you get used to it, there are many advantages,' I told him. 'If you'd like to try it, you're welcome to borrow it.'

Thelma's assistant was standing alone at the bookshelves that filled much of the wall space on three sides of the fireplace cube. When I approached, she asked, 'Have you read all of these?' It was the question I had heard many times from a nonreader.

'Some of them twice, or oftener. If you see a title you'd like to borrow, feel free . . . but if you don't return it, the sheriff will be at your door with a search dog.'

The mild jest fell flat. 'I don't have time to read books,' Janice said. 'I read aloud to Thelma –

newspapers, that is, and magazine articles . . . Where are the kitties?'

I felt she was changing the subject to avoid personal matters. I may have been wrong. I said, 'They're in the gazebo. They don't like large parties. Do you like cats? You might drive Thelma over some afternoon.'

'Oh, Thelma doesn't like cats – not at all!' Janice looked about anxiously and said, 'Excuse me. I think she wants me.'

I felt I was right; Janice was employed to drive the car, cook, and read aloud . . . not to reveal personal details that might reflect on the Thackeray image.

The champagne flowed, guests circulated, and neighbors conversed like long-lost friends.

At one point Polly said to Qwilleran, 'I've been listening to talk about the Kit Kat Agenda, and it sounds like a splendid idea! It's the local name for a national movement. Volunteers provide foster homes for unwanted kittens and their mothers, while other volunteers act as adoption agents, matching up the kittens with permanent homes. Burgess, Mavis, and the Bethunes are providing foster care, and Hannah MacLeod is an adoption agent.'

Qwilleran said, 'But who can tell me about the logistics of foster care?'

'Ask Mavis.'

Qwilleran caught up with her at the snack table. 'Try one of these delicious cheese puffs,' she said.

'I've already had three,' he said. 'Tell me something about foster care. Where do the temporary cat-families spend their time? Where do they eat and sleep?'

'One needs a spare room for that purpose,' Mavis explained. 'People go in to talk to them and play with them and introduce them to sociable activity. A kitten that is socialized has more personality and makes a better pet than a poor little thing cooped up in a cage.'

'I see the point,' he said.

'You should talk to Hannah MacLeod, one of our adoption agents. She's lived here all her life and knows everyone, so she's very successful in finding permanent homes.'

Hannah Hawley, a fine contralto, had recently married 'Uncle Louie' MacLeod, director of the Mooseland Choral Group, and they were in the process of adopting an eight-year-old boy.

'How's Danny?' Qwilleran asked the couple.

'He's such a bright, personable child,' Hannah said. 'He loves to go with me when I take prospects to the foster homes to pick out a kitten – or two. Usually two. It's hard to resist a handful of squirming fur looking at you with big eyes and mistaking your finger for something else.'

Qwilleran said, 'I suppose there's an adoption fee?'

'A modest one, considering that it includes all shots and neutering. To help cover expenses and publicize Kit Kat, we're going to stage a Kit Kat Revue.'

Uncle Louie looked at Qwilleran hopefully. 'Do you sing or dance?'

'I might be able to write a skit,' he replied.

It was nearing seven o'clock, and Qwilleran had talked to everyone but the Bethunes. He found them in the foyer, admiring a long narrow console table. Proudly he told them it was handcrafted, custom ordered by Fran Brodie, and remarkable for the hand-carved dovetailing in the drawers.

'I know,' said Doug Bethune. 'I'm the one who made the table.'

'Shame on you. Why didn't you sign it?' Qwilleran scolded. 'A century from now a signed Bethune masterpiece will fetch a couple of million at auction, the way prices are going.'

Bonnie said to her husband, 'Buy the table back, Doug. Our descendants may need the money to pay the rent!'

'How's Winston?' Qwilleran asked. The Bethunes had adopted the late Eddington Smith's big cat after the bookstore was destroyed.

'He's fine. He hangs out in the library but likes to visit our kitten colony, considering himself a kind of godfather. We have five kittens, but they're all spoken for.'

When the guests left for the next festivities — at the Mackintosh Inn — Polly and Qwilleran were the last to leave, and he said to Pat and Celia, who were clearing away the refreshments, 'Good show! Let's do it again sometime . . . I've brought the cats in from the gazebo, and Koko is upset about something. Give him some cheese; he'll calm down.'

Celia said, 'He's mad because he wasn't invited.'

Qwilleran thought, He's mad because someone was invited who doesn't have his approval.

Koko was prowling about the barn, sniffing diligently, even snarling and spitting in certain areas for reasons of his own. He was a smart cat, but his actions were not always comprehensible.

Then Qwilleran and Polly drove to the inn.

She said, 'The reception was a huge success, and several people commented on the Sibelius numbers, including Thelma. She sounds like Tallulah Bankhead one minute and Katharine Hepburn the next. What do you think about the Kit Kat idea, Qwill?'

'I'm all in favor.'

'As Mavis said, it's heartwarming to know that previously unwanted kittens will have a chance to give years of companionship to families and live-alones.'

'What did you think about Dick?'

'He's charming! I asked if he thought Thelma would speak to our bird club, and he said she doesn't do formal speeches but he could arrange for a question-and-answer session at the club. He would transport two or three parrots in their cages. He's most cooperative! Thelma's lucky to have him.'

Qwilleran huffed into his moustache. 'Is he living with them?'

'No. He lives in Lockmaster but has use of the guest room on Pleasant Street.'

At the Mackintosh Inn, supper was being served in the ballroom on the lower level. A horseshoe table was set with twenty places and a full complement of candles and flowers. The lights in the chandeliers were turned low. And a trio was playing romantic Hispanic music: accordion, violin, and guitar.

Qwilleran muttered, 'They didn't find those guys in Moose County!'

'Probably from Lockmaster,' Polly ventured.

There were place cards, and Qwilleran found himself between Thelma and Dick.

Thelma explained, 'Perhaps you wondered about "California cuisine." That's what I served in my dinner club – a nouvelle approach, with accents on vegetables and fruits and seafood in dishes created with originality. I always considered James Beard to be my guru. He was from the West Coast, you know. I have twenty-two of his cookbooks.'

The music stopped suddenly. Dick said a few words of welcome, and then Thelma surprised everyone by asking a blessing. The music resumed, and servers rolled in carts of lobster and mango in a lemon sauce. This was followed by ramekins of oxtail ravioli, sauced with tomato, basil, and capers. Conversation that was lively at the reception was positively exuberant under the spell of California cuisine.

At one point Dick said to Qwilleran, 'What did your barn look like before you bought it?'

'I didn't buy it; I inherited it – a drive-through apple barn with nothing inside but lofts and ladders – plus bats, rats, and wild cats. An architect from Down Below had the vision and determination to make it what it is.'

'And a hefty commission, I'll bet. It must have cost you a fortune!'

Qwilleran huffed into his moustache.

Undaunted, Dick went on. 'It's a lot of cubic space for one man. If you'd ever feel like recouping your investment, I know a developer who could convert it into an apartment complex.'

'A possibility, though not in the foreseeable future,' Qwilleran replied stiffly.

Throughout the repast Qwilleran had shown a genuine interest in Thelma's parrots. There were five: Esmeralda, Pedro, Lolita, Carlotta, and Navarro. All were Amazons, noted for their intelligence and conversational ability.

'Come and meet them, Ducky!' was Thelma's enthusiastic invitation. 'Come for breakfast tomorrow. Janice will make waffles with fruit sauce. Not too early.' A time was set: 10 A.M.

As Qwilleran drove Polly home to Indian Village, he asked, 'What did you think of Thelma's hat?' (It had a stiff two-inch brim and puffy crown of layered patches of satin, velvet, damask, and tweed – like leaves, in various shades of green, with a green chiffon sash ending in a handmade green rose.)

Polly said, 'Only someone with her good posture and authoritative manner could wear it.'

He was on the verge of mentioning his breakfast invitation, but a tremor on his upper lip stopped him. He stroked his moustache with a heavy hand as he returned to the barn from Indian Village.

When Qwilleran arrived home, Yum Yum rubbed against his ankles warmly but Koko was on the fireplace cube, pointedly aloof and obviously disapproving of something. A note from Celia, left on the kitchen counter, explained it:

'Chief – after you left, Koko acted very strange – prowling and bristling his fur and spitting at everything. I think he smelled the dog. I talked to him and gave him a treat, and he calmed down.'

Qwilleran thought, Alexander had been here before, but Koko observed him from the rafters far overhead . . . this time a strange presence was invading his territory in his absence.

He sat down at his typewriter to sum up successes of the evening.

Sunday, April 13 – Well, it's over! Thelma has been adequately welcomed, toasted, and admired – wild hat and all. As usual in such gatherings there is always a gadfly with a tiny camera who flits around taking candid shots of guests eating, yawning, kissing someone else's spouse, or whatever. What do they do with the prints? Are they ever developed? Is there any film in the camera?

Thelma's assistant was the candid-nut tonight, but her shots were all of Thelma. Are the prints catalogued and filed? Or kept in a barrel? They must have thousands of them if . . .

His typing was interrupted by an imperative howl from Koko. The cats' bedtime ritual had been neglected. There was supposed to be a session of reading aloud, followed by a snack and then lights-out.

'Tyrants!' Qwilleran muttered as he followed Koko to the bookshelves. The cat hopped nimbly to an upper shelf and shoved down a leather-bound book. Qwilleran caught it before it reached the floor. (He had been an acclaimed shortstop in college baseball. Who would think that his fielding skill would be put to use in such a mundane manner?) *C'est la vie*, he thought.

Koko's choice was *A Child's Garden of Verses*, and Qwilleran was not in the mood for Robert Louis Stevenson's poetry. 'Try again!' he said.

Down came another R.L.S. winner: *The Strange Case of Dr Jekyll and Mr Hyde*. It was vetoed again. 'Sorry, but it's not your style.'

The three of them finally settled down with the same author's *Travels with a Donkey* until the phone rang.

A woman's hushed and horrified voice said, 'Qwill,

this is Janice. Don't come tomorrow! Something terrible has happened!'

'Something wrong with Thelma?' he said quickly.

'No. But I can't talk about it. Just don't come tomorrow . . .' and she added in alarm, 'Please, don't say anything about this to anyone!'

A few hours after this enigmatic phone call, Qwilleran was asleep in his suite on the first balcony, and the Siamese were supposed to be asleep on the third balcony. He always left their door open (for a number of reasons) and always closed his own. Rudely he was awakened by a bloodcurdling howl outside his door! He knew it well; it was Koko's death howl! The cat had an uncanny way of knowing the moment of a wrongful death. The clock on the night table said it was 3:15 A.M. Immediately it brought to mind the 'something terrible' that had happened on Pleasant Street following the party.

But what could he do? Call the police and say that his cat was howling?

Koko had done what he considered his duty and had returned to his balcony. After an hour of puzzling thought and aimless speculation, Qwilleran, too, went to sleep.

Nine

On Monday morning Qwilleran was listening to the weather prediction on WPKX while preparing the cats' breakfast. It was something choice, left over from the reception, that Celia saved for them. The Siamese watched intently.

Not bothering to turn the radio off, Qwilleran heard newsbites from the two counties to the south. From Lockmaster: A new president had been appointed for the Academy of Arts . . . The date had been set for the annual flower show . . . A local chess player had won a tournament in Milwaukee. From Bixby: A drug bust in Bixton had jailed four men and three women . . . A couple had been killed in a motorcycle accident on Highway 12 . . . An unidentified male was found shot to death at the wheel of a rented van.

At that moment a bloodcurdling howl came from Koko's throat. Once again, it was Koko's death howl. But why was the cat concerned about an unidentified driver of a delivery van in Bixby County . . . unless . . . it had something to do with Janice's cryptic phone call of the night before. There had been horror and fear in her voice. Qwilleran devised an oblique way of investigating.

First, he called Burgess Campbell and congratulated him on a successful party. 'Has Pleasant Street recovered from the excitement? Did anyone consume too much champagne or oxtail ravioli?'

'I didn't hear any ambulance sirens,' the Duke replied. 'And let me say that everyone thanks you for opening your fabulous barn for the occasion.'

'My pleasure,' Qwilleran said.

'There were some scatterbrained suggestions from the Thackerays,' Burgess went on. 'Thelma thought the barn would make a wonderful restaurant – with kitchen and bar on the main floor and dining on the open balconies and waiters whizzing up and down the ramp on roller skates . . . And Dick visualized it as a twelve-unit apartment complex, if you wanted to install elevators and a whole lot of plumbing . . . The odd thing is, Qwill, that you can't guess whether they're kidding or being serious.'

'Very true, Burgess. I always suspect women who wear crazy hats and men who wear two-tone shoes.'

* * *

Next, Qwilleran phoned Amanda's Studio of Interior Design and was not surprised to hear that Fran Brodie was taking a week off. He called her in Indian Village.

'Qwill, I'm beat!' she groaned. 'No one knows how hard I've worked for that woman – and her inflated ego!'

'You did a heroic job.'

'And now she has another design project she wants me to handle. I'm going to sic her on Amanda. That'll be the battle of the century. Thelma Thackeray versus Amanda Goodwinter!'

'What is Thelma's new design project?'

'She's not telling.'

'Could it be connected with the old opera house?'

'More likely a restaurant, featuring California cuisine.'

'Well, anyway, Fran, you've done admirable work, and I'll make you a margarita whenever you say.'

Qwilleran continued, 'That was a lot of partying for a woman of Thelma's age. Have you heard how she is this morning?'

'No, but she was still going strong when I dropped them off at the curb. She invited me in for a nightcap, but I declined and Janice reminded Thelma that she was leaving in the morning for a couple of days in Lockmaster. For someone over eighty, Thelma has a lot of energy. She doesn't drink, she eats right, and she retires at ten P.M. . . . Maybe I should try it!'

The conversation was all very interesting, but it offered no clue to the 'terrible' thing that had happened at the Thackeray house. The O'Dells lived across the street, and

Pat was known for his powers of observation, while Celia was always a secret agent at heart. But the O'Dells would be on their way to Purple Point with chicken pot pies and blueberry muffins for a birthday luncheon.

Qwilleran left a message on their answering machine under the alias of Ronald Frobnitz. Celia waited until Pat was out of the house before returning the call.

'What's up, Chief?' she asked briskly.

'Did anything unusual happen on Pleasant Street last night?'

'Well, it was quiet and dark until everyone started coming home. Then the street was filled with headlights, and people laughing and shouting good-night, and kids leaving their pizza party. It had quieted down when Fran Brodie brought the Thackeray party home and dropped them at the curb. Just as they were turning the indoor lights on, I thought I heard a scream. Pat heard it, too, but said it was the parrots. How'm I doin', Chief?'

'If you get tired of the catering business, you can always get a job with the CIA.'

'Oh, I remembered something else. Before everyone came home from the party, Pat saw a delivery van drive around the back of the Thackeray house – then leave a few minutes later. We decided it was some kind of fabulous welcome gift that made Thelma scream when she came home.'

Qwilleran huffed into his moustache and thought, How does that explain the panic in Janice's voice . . . and the reference to something terrible . . . and the urgent plea not to tell anyone?

'Tomorrow morning, Chief, I'll get that information you want from downtown.'

'You can phone it. It's not classified.'

'But I want to deliver some chicken pot pies and blueberry muffins, if you think you can use them.'

Gravely he said, 'I imagine I can devise an appropriate way . . . to dispose of them.'

Celia's hoot of delight pierced his eardrum as she hung up.

He had been working on his Tuesday column and now he needed a stretch, so he walked to the public library for the book containing Homer's favorite poem. The parking lot was nearly filled, and the main room was crowded with men and women of all ages. They had seen the announcement in Friday's paper: 'Autographed photographs of old movie stars from the Thelma Thackeray collection – on temporary exhibition.'

Eight-by-tens in individual easel-back frames filled the shelves in two showcases: Claudette Colbert, Ronald Colman, Groucho Marx, Joan Crawford, Fred Astaire, Humphrey Bogart, Esther Williams, Edward G. Robinson, and more. An occasional comment interrupted the awed silence of the onlookers.

Man: 'I'm gonna come back when there ain't such a crowd.'

Another man: 'Valuable collection! One assumes they're insured.'

Woman: 'My mother used to rave about Ronald Colman.'

Child: 'Mommy! Where're the kitties?'

Qwilleran, before leaving the building, stroked the two library cats and dropped coins into the jar that provided for their material needs. 'Handsome Mac! Gentle Katie!' he said, wondering if anyone ever read a little Dickens or Hemingway to them.

The Siamese were waiting for him with stretched necks and pointed ears: They knew he had been fraternizing with the library cats.

'Read! Read!' he announced, letting them sniff the library book. It was well thumbed, and the binding had been repaired twice by the late Eddington Smith, according to notations inside the back cover. Before taping 'Lasca' for Homer's birthday, he would do a practice reading for Koko and Yum Yum.

'Lasca' was written by Frank Desprez. Scene: Texas, down by the Rio Grande. Story: A lonely cowboy hangs around bars, maundering over his lost love, remembering how they rode the range on their gray mustangs. One day, without warning, the weather changed, alarming a herd of steers, goading them into a stampede that trampled everything in its path. When the dust cleared Lasca was dead, but her impulsive act of heroism had saved her lover's life. All was now still on the range, but for a lone coyote, the gray squirrels, a black snake gliding through the grass, a buzzard circling overhead.

Qwilleran paused. It had been more than a hundred lines of galloping rhythm and deep emotion. Yum Yum was breathing hoarsely; Koko uttered a soft yowl.

It was the moment when Rhoda Tibbitt always dried her eyes, and Homer always blew his nose.

The Siamese were sequestered in the gazebo while Qwilleran recorded the poem.

On Tuesday morning Celia marched importantly into the apple barn and reported, 'The opera house property has been held by a bank trust for years and years – no new owner . . . and no permits for remodeling have been issued or even requested.'

Qwilleran said wryly, 'Perhaps the bank is going to rent the space to traveling burlesque shows. The theatre seats were removed long ago, but customers could be told to bring their own floor cushions.'

'Oh, Chief!' she protested with her ever-ready laugh. 'But I drove by to see what was going on, and there was a van in the parking lot with ladders on top, and it was marked BIXBY PAINT AND DECORATING. Pat says everything is cheaper in Bixby County – goods and services and gasoline. We buy our fresh food at Toodle's Market, but once a week he drives to Bixby to fill up the tank and buy staples.'

'Just what I wanted to know, Celia. Have you time for coffee or fruit juice?'

She flopped onto one of the bar stools. 'I know you don't go for gossip, Chief, but I've collected some basic intelligence . . .'

'Let's hear it.'

'During the party, Thelma's assistant hung around the dining room, and we found we have a lot in common: Both of us have farm backgrounds and both of us are involved in food preparation. Janice is from North Dakota.'

'How did she gravitate to Hollywood and the Thackeray household?'

'That's a Cinderella story. She was ten when her mother died, and her father married a woman with three young children. For the next several years, Janice had to help with the kids and the cooking. She had no time for hobbies or sports and felt like dropping out of school and running away from home, but her Aunt Patty made her a deal. If Janice would stay and get her diploma, her aunt would lend her the money to move to a big city and find work in an office. She had taken a commercial course in school.

'Actually she was more interested in cooking than typing and thought Hollywood would have a lot of restaurants as well as glamour.

'Thelma hired her as a dishwasher and Janice worked her way up to assistant chef.'

'Did she tell you all this at the party?'

'Well, no . . . She came to the house yesterday morning and asked if she could do anything to help with the luncheon. I took her along in place of Pat; Thelma's out of town. I feel sorry for that young woman. She doesn't have a life of her own. For example, she loves cats but Thelma hates them.'

Qwilleran said, 'Too bad she didn't get a chance to meet Koko and Yum Yum Sunday night. Would she like to drive over here while her boss is away? She can come anytime but should phone first.'

'That's very kind of you, Chief.'

He shrugged modestly. Actually, he saw an opportunity to satisfy his curiosity about the canceled breakfast date, but he said, 'The cats enjoy meeting a new admirer who will blubber over them. They're only human.'

His quips always delighted her, and she asked, 'Where are the little dears? I have to say good-bye before I go home.' She searched in her big floppy handbag.

'Are you looking for your car keys – or for a possible stowaway, Celia?'

Yum Yum was in the kitchen, batting and chasing a small shiny toy, while Koko peered down from the top of the refrigerator as if amazed by her kittenish antics.

Qwilleran explained, 'One of my fans Down Below – an older woman who can no longer see to sew – sent me her sterling silver thimble for the cats to play with. She's the tenth-grade teacher who inspired my writing career. Relatives of hers in Lockmaster send her clippings of my column now and then. I polish the thimble once a week – and hide it in different drawers, but Yum Yum always finds it, and her famous paw can open any drawer that isn't padlocked.'

* * *

Janice phoned in the late afternoon and arrived soon after in an emerald green coupé.

Qwilleran went out to the barnyard to greet her. 'Did you bring this from California?'

'We towed it behind our van full of parrots,' she explained.

She was wearing blue denim pants and shirt and wore her dark hair tied back in a ponytail. Other times, it had been knotted close to her head.

He said, 'I told the cats you were coming, and they had a good washup. They're waiting for you in the gazebo.'

There they were, sitting tall on their haunches, with expectancy in every whisker.

'Aren't they beautiful!' she cried. 'Those blue eyes!'

'The one with an imperial air is Kao K'o Kung. Yum Yum likes to be picked up and hugged, but Koko is too macho for lap-sitting.'

With his usual perversity, however, Koko was the first to jump on the visitor's lap when she sat down.

'I've never seen Siamese except in pictures,' she said. 'When I lived on a farm, we had nothing but barn cats.'

'That's what these are. Barn cats.'

For the first time he heard her laugh. 'I wish I'd brought my camera.'

'It wouldn't do any good, Janice. They don't cooperate. Koko considers it an invasion of privacy, and naughty Yum Yum poses only for tail shots.' This brought another laugh. 'Are you interested in photography?'

98

'Mostly for practical purposes. I've photographed everything in the house for an insurance inventory, and I take a snap of what Thelma wears whenever she appears in public. Just so she won't duplicate, you know.'

'Smart idea. May I offer you a glass of white wine? I've chilled a nice white Zinfandel.' At the party he had noted that neither she nor Thelma had been drinking champagne, and he had wondered if it might be a Thackeray house rule. Now he would find out.

After a brief pause she said, 'Yes, I believe I'd like a glass of wine.'

For himself he mixed what was becoming known around the county as the 'Q cocktail.' Cranberry juice and Squunk water.

There was more conversation about the cats, and Janice hand-fed them a few Kabibbles, saying, 'I love the feel of a cat's rough, wet tongue and little, sharp teeth!'

'Do you know about the Kit Kat Agenda?'

'Oh, yes, and I'd love to have kittens . . . but we can't. They have a kitten colony next door, and Duke says I can go over anytime to play with them. It's good for their morale. The housekeeper said the back door is always open; I can just walk in. She's very nice. Everybody's nice around here. They told us it was neighborly to leave the back door unlocked. Thelma thought it was too folksy, but . . . when in Rome, do as the Romans do.'

Janice suddenly stopped chattering and looked preoccupied.

Qwilleran said, 'Duke lectures on American history at

the college, and you might like to audit one of his lectures. They're never dry; he has a sense of humor.'

'I'd like that, but it would depend on Thelma's schedule.'

'How long have you been with her?'

'Ever since high school. I wanted to work in a restaurant, and she hired me as a dishwasher. That's a general kitchen helper, you know, and I worked my way up to assistant chef at her private dinner club.' She was chattering again – nervously, Qwilleran thought. 'It was a luxurious club, with a high-ceilinged dining room and crystal chandeliers. Then there was a lounge where you could have cocktails and see old movies on a large screen. In the dining room Thelma moved about the tables, wearing one of her fabulous hats and kidding with the customers, calling them "Ducky" and swearing in Portuguese, which she learned from the parrots. Everyone loved Thelma and hated to see her retire. She sold the club and kept me on as a secretary, housekeeper, and driver. She's strict – but nice.' With a fond smile, Janice added, 'She's always quoting things she learned from her pop: *Don't count your chickens before they're hatched . . . Time is money . . . Try to kill two birds with one stone.*'

Qwilleran said, 'No wonder she was a success in business . . . May I refresh your drink, Janice?' And casually he added, 'It's hard to imagine such a vital personage retiring from the workplace.'

'Well, her twin brother died and Dick, her nephew, asked her to come back east.'

She paused long enough to make him suspect jealousy between the longtime, hardworking assistant and the charming Johnny-come-lately who was the only living relative. But then she said, 'Well, Dick is the kind of person that everyone likes. He cheers her up. But she also treats him like a strict parent.' Janice giggled apologetically. 'Thelma was born to be boss! Oh, I almost forgot, Thelma would like you to come for waffles Thursday morning at ten o'clock. You can meet the parrots.'

Qwilleran jumped up. 'I just had a good idea! I happen to have some chicken pot pies and blueberry muffins. We could warm them up and have a picnic supper out there in the gazebo!'

They went indoors, and Janice was privileged to feed the cats while Qwilleran warmed the picnic fare. He also steered the conversation away from the Thackerays.

During the meal he talked about the classes at the Art Center, the clubs that one might join, and the possibilities for volunteer work. 'You might like to donate some time to the animal shelter, Janice, and Thelma might find a cause that she could support with her presence.'

He felt he was on thin ice, but that's what he wanted.

Janice put down her fork and looked at him with desperate indecision. 'There's something I shouldn't talk about . . .'

'Then don't.'

'But I want to, and Celia says you're the only one in Moose County that you can trust not to blab . . . Thelma isn't really retired; she's working on a business deal. That's all I can say.'

'More power to her!'

'She wanted to go to Lockmaster today to see her brother's grave and the scene of his fatal accident. I don't know why. You'd think it would just upset her.'

'It's called closure.' He lifted the wine bottle. 'Shall I?'

'I'd better not. I'm driving.'

'If the worse comes to the worst, I can tow your car home behind my SUV.'

The comment brought laughter. She was laughing easily. 'Wouldn't Pleasant Street have a picnic with that scene! They don't miss a thing.'

Suddenly serious, he said, 'That's why your mysterious cancellation Sunday night worried me. You said something terrible had happened, and your neighbors heard screams.'

For a moment she was frozen in an attitude of indecision, her eyes darting left and right.

He waited patiently but with encouragement.

'When we got home,' she said hesitantly, 'the parrots were gone! . . . Kidnapped! And there was a ransom note.'

'Did you notify the police?'

'We were afraid to. There were threats – what would happen if we did. So horrible I can't repeat them. Thelma was sick to her stomach.'

'Ghastly experience,' he said, remembering his gut-wrenching horror when Yum Yum was snatched.

'We had to do what they wanted. Fortunately Dick was there, and he brought them back by daybreak, but he's afraid to talk about it. We've ordered new locks on all the doors and a burglar alarm that rings in the police station . . . For God's sake, don't let Thelma know I told you all this!'

As he accompanied Janice to her car, he asked, 'Are you sure you want to drive? I could drive your car and walk home.'

'No, no! I'm perfectly all right. Thanks for everything, and we'll see you Thursday morning.'

After Janice had driven away, Qwilleran brought the Siamese indoors, and the three of them sprawled in the big chair for a little reading. The cats always enjoyed the sound of his voice and Yum Yum – that little rascal – had discovered the vibration in his rib cage when he was staging a good show.

When Qwilleran closed the book his listeners went on to other activities, and he began to brainstorm:

Who were the kidnappers who made off with five talkative Amazons without detection? No doubt they were readers of the *Moose County Something*. They knew how Thelma treasured her pets. They knew that all of Pleasant Street would be celebrating her arrival at a gala party somewhere else. What was their ransom demand? Large bundles of cash would not be readily available on a Sunday night. Did they want jewels? The parrot pin and matching bracelet had created a stir at the Grist Mill; had Thelma been flaunting her rubies, emeralds, and diamonds at other good restaurants in Moose County and Lockmaster? Whatever the ransom demand, the victims were warned not to notify the police.

And what about Dick? He took a great risk . . . As the saying goes, 'Three may keep a secret if two of them are dead.' I wouldn't want to be in Dick Thackeray's shoes at this moment!

Ten

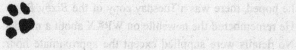

Qwilleran had a strong desire to talk with the photographer who had been assigned to the Thackeray story – called the 'parrot story' in the photo lab. John Bushland freelanced for the newspaper but also had his own commercial studio in Pickax, and Qwilleran found him there, early Wednesday morning. Bushy had become a workaholic since his divorce.

'Just wanted to compliment you on the parrot shots, Bushy. What did you think of the old gal?'

'She's a character! You could write a book about her, Qwill.'

'I'm invited to meet the parrots tomorrow, and I thought I might pick your brain. How about lunch at Rennie's? I'll buy.'

'Well, I've got a lot of printing to do – on deadline. How about picking up some deli sandwiches at Toodle's and bringing them here. I'll make coffee.'

Meanwhile, Qwilleran had errands to do. He returned the book of poems to the public library and was on the way out of the building when his curiosity detoured him into the small room devoted to magazines and newspapers. As he hoped, there was a Tuesday copy of the *Bixby Bugle*. He remembered the newsbite on WPKX about a murder. No details were supplied except the approximate hour: 3:15 A.M. That happened to be the exact time of Koko's bloodcurdling howl. The headline read: MURDER ON SOUTH SIDE. He scanned it for facts.

Sheriff's deputies, responding to a call early Monday morning, found a van driver slumped over his steering wheel. He had been shot in the head. The victim was carrying falsified ID cards, and the tags on the vehicle were stolen.

The call came in at 3:15 A.M., from the occupant of a mobile home on a country lane south of Bixton.

She said, 'My cat woke me up, snarling and growling. The moon was full, and you know how cats are! But there was something else bothering him. Tony is just a plain old tomcat, but he sniffs out trouble like a watchdog.

'So, I looked out the window and saw two vans parked under some trees. They were tail-to-tail, and two men were moving stuff from one van to the other. They were big square boxes, big enough to hold TVs.

'The taillights of the loaded van turned on, and the next thing I knew, I heard a gunshot. I know a gunshot when I hear one. And the loaded van took off in a hurry. That's when I called 911.'

Police are investigating. It is thought that the incident is linked with the recent burglary in a television store.

Qwilleran could not help chuckling. He was no admirer of the reporting in the *Bixby Bugle*, but here was a dry piece of police news that had been turned into a human-interest story, complete with a hero-cat who sniffed out foul play. Tony would make a good partner for Koko. If they could locate a third talented feline in Lockmaster, they would have a tri-county crime-detection network.

Such were his whimsical thoughts at the moment, but he had sandwiches to buy and other matters to discuss at the photo studio, and a tape to deliver.

The question occurred to him: How could Koko know – and why would he care – about the murder of a shady character ninety miles away? There were no answers; Qwilleran had stopped trying to find answers.

Next he drove to Ittibittiwassee Estates, the retirement complex masquerading as a Swiss resort hotel. Using the house phone, he called upstairs and said in a brisk voice, 'Mrs Tibbitt, there is a gentleman here who says he has a package for you and wants to hand it to you personally. He has a large moustache and looks suspect. Do you want us to call the police? It could be a bomb.'

With her hand muffling her hysterical laughter, she said, 'I'll be right down. Tell him not to go away.'

Soon, a white-haired woman, looking gaily youthful, stepped off the elevator. After all, Rhoda was only eighty-eight; her husband would be ninety-nine on Saturday.

'Thank you so much, Qwill. What did you think of the poem?'

'Recording it was an enjoyable challenge, and the cats liked it, especially the stampede and the part about the coyote and the black snake. What is the program for Saturday?'

'At eleven A.M. Derek will sing a birthday song written expressly for Homer – that boy is so talented! – and there'll be city and county dignitaries and media coverage. No birthday cake! Homer says he doesn't want to squander his last breath on blowing out candles.'

'By the way, Rhoda, you used to teach in Lockmaster, didn't you?'

'Yes. That's where I met Homer. He was principal of my school.'

'Did you know of a Dr Thackeray, veterinarian?'

'Oh, yes! He was a wonderful man – used to come to the school and talk to the younger grades about the proper care of pets. He was killed in a tragic accident. He loved the outdoors and was hiking when he slipped on wet rocks and fell into a ravine.'

* * *

Qwilleran stroked his moustache repeatedly when he thought of Dr Thackeray; he wanted to ask more questions. He stopped at the design studio, knowing that Fran's assistant would be minding the shop.

Lucinda Holmes greeted him, brimming with her usual hospitality, but before she could suggest coffee, he said, 'No coffee today, thanks. Just answer a question. Do you take your animals to the Thackeray Clinic?'

'It's the Whinny Hills Clinic now. Some new people bought it after Dr Thurston's tragic death. That's where my boyfriend works.'

'You mean . . . Dr Watson?'

'You remembered!' she said with an appreciative laugh. In a lowered voice she added, 'He's not too happy. His new bosses promised to maintain Dr Thurston's standards, and they even have his photo in the lobby, but it's only to please his former clients – and his son.'

'Do you know Dick Thackeray?'

'I met him once at a party. All I remember is his wonderful smile. But they say he cracked up after his father's death and had to go away for a while. It was thought to be suicide, you know, and that must have been especially painful.'

'Was the doctor hiking alone?'

'Yes, and when he didn't return, his son notified the police. It took the rescue squad seven hours to find him. Very sad. So I don't know . . .'

'Too bad,' Qwilleran murmured.

* * *

John Bushland liked the nickname of 'Bushy'; it made his baldness a joke instead of a calamity. He and Qwilleran had been friends ever since being shipwrecked on a deserted island – only a dozen miles offshore from Mooseville but cold and wet and unforgettable.

On this occasion they got together over corned-beef sandwiches and cream of asparagus soup. 'I've just heard, Bushy, that your portrait of Thurston Thackeray hangs in the lobby of the Whinny Hills Clinic.'

'Yeah, he sat for a formal portrait when I had my photo studio in Lockmaster. He was a good subject – patient, composed, cooperative.'

'Do you visualize him as a suicide?'

'Nah! I never bought that rumor. Somebody was trying to make a scandal out of a sad mishap. People can be rotten.'

'Well, the reason I called,' Qwilleran said, 'is because Thelma has invited me over to see her parrots tomorrow. What's your take on that?'

'I dunno. She's hard to figure. Secretive, and yet avid for publicity. Mad about her parrots but turned-off about any other animals . . . I liked her assistant, Janice – very helpful and down-to-earth.'

'Did you meet Thelma's nephew?'

'Nope. That would be Doc Thurston's son.'

'What's his line of work?'

'Financial management, whatever that means. Investments, I suppose. When I lived in Lockmaster, the joke was that Dick had inherited his father's love of horses, and that's why he spent so much time at the racetrack.'

'Have you put your boat in the water as yet?'

'Last weekend. Would you like to go for a cruise to Three Tree Island?' It was said slyly.

'Bad joke,' Qwilleran muttered. 'I'd rather cut my wrists.'

'I'm taking Jill Handley and her husband for a cruise Sunday. She met Janice when we were doing the parrot story and suggested it would be friendly to invite her out on the boat. Janice is new in town and doesn't know anybody.'

'I'm sure Janice would like it,' Qwilleran said, 'but she doesn't have any regular days off . . . However . . . I might be able to pull strings. I'll phone you tomorrow afternoon.'

On the way home from lunch Qwilleran suddenly realized that he had done nothing about Friday's column, nor did he have the ghost of an idea. He had allowed his work-pattern to be disrupted by a kidnapping, an unexplained death, work on an abandoned building, and an elderly woman's idiosyncrasies.

On such occasions he had a game he played with Koko. The cat liked to push books off the shelf, then peer over the edge to see how they landed. Qwilleran, having failed to discourage the practice, devised a way to put it to good use. He would give the signal, and Koko would dislodge a book. Then Qwilleran was required by the rules to base a 'Qwill Pen' column on that title. There was something about the imperative of the game that stimulated creative juices. It sounded silly, but it worked.

Now, Koko was on the shelf, peering over the edge with satisfaction at a slender book in a worn cover, one of the last to come from the used-book store in its final days. Qwilleran took the book, along with the cats and the cordless phone, to the gazebo. It was a book of proverbs, and he was fingering it and searching for inspiration when the phone rang.

Fran Brodie was calling to say, 'I'd like to collect that margarita you promised me.'

'When!' Qwilleran asked sharply.

'Now!' she replied crisply.

'Where are you?'

'In your backyard.'

When he went to the barnyard to meet her, she added apologetically, 'I hope I'm not interrupting your work.'

'That's all right. I'm sure you won't stay long.'

'Touché!'

'Come indoors.'

She perched on a bar stool while he prepared her favorite cocktail. 'I'm here,' she said, 'because I heard you're going to visit the parrots tomorrow.'

'Do you think I should have a psittacosis shot? Who told you?'

'Dwight.' She referred to their mutual friend, who was handling public relations for Thelma. 'If you're planning to do a Thackeray story, Dwight thinks you should avoid mentioning the interior design. And so do I!'

It was an unusual request from the designer who had just received an enormous commission.

They took their drinks into the living room, where Fran saw the wall hanging over the fireplace. 'I see it's still there,' she said with a sniff.

He ignored the remark. 'So, what's the problem at Thelma's house? I'm invited for a waffle breakfast and a social call on Pedro, Lolita, and company. If I write anything, it'll be a legend for *Short & Tall Tales*. What are you trying to tell me about the decorating — excuse me. The interior design.'

'Have you been in any other houses on Pleasant Street?'

'Two or three.'

'Then you know they all have wallpaper, stained woodwork, draperies, and Oriental rugs on hardwood floors. Thelma shocked us by wanting stark white walls, white-painted woodwork, white mini-blinds, and — worst of all! — wall-to-wall white vinyl cemented to the beautiful oak floors. What could we do? It's her house! Amanda believes in letting the customers have what they want. Her modern furniture looks perfect with that background . . . but not on Pleasant Street!'

'Sticky wicket!' Qwilleran said.

'I know you like contemporary, Qwill, in all its forms, so you'll probably like it. But both Dwight and I feel that it would not be to anyone's advantage to have the interior published. So concentrate on the parrots, her collection of designer hats, her waffles, and her infatuation with old movies.'

'Hmmm,' he mused as he picked up her empty glass. 'Shall I try it again? Maybe I'll get it right.'

She jumped to her feet. 'No, thanks. We're having a family get-together tonight. I have to be there – and sober.'

As Qwilleran watched her drive away, he speculated that there was no family get-together. Fran wanted to avoid answering questions about Thelma's secret business enterprise. He was certain now that it involved the old opera house. Earlier in the day he had driven past the site and stopped to watch moving vans unloading large cardboard cartons. Each had the manufacturer's name and large letters spelling out ONE CHAIR or ONE TABLE.

Qwilleran went directly to the phone and called Dwight Somers.

He was still in his office. 'Qwill! It's been a long time! Are you staying out of trouble?'

'Yes and it's boring. Are you free for dinner? We could go to Onoosh's and plot something illegal.'

Dwight Somers had the kind of face that looks better with a beard – stronger, wiser. He had come to Moose County from Down Below – to handle public relations for XYZ Enterprises. Disagreeing with the management over the development of an offshore island, Dwight resigned and joined a P.R. agency in Lockmaster. Their company policy was: no beards. Too bad. Devoid of whiskers he looked clean-cut, honest, and younger, but not strong or wise. He eventually left to start his own P.R. firm in Pickax. He called it Somers & Beard, Incorporated.

'Now you look like Dwight Somers!' Qwilleran told him when they met at the Mediterranean café. They sat in a booth for privacy. There were beaded curtains in the windows, hammered brass tops on the tables, and spanakopita on the menu.

Politely, Qwilleran asked about Indian Village (where Dwight had an apartment) and about Hixie Rice (with whom he was seen everywhere).

Dwight asked politely about the Siamese.

'I hear you're handling public relations for Thelma Thackeray. How is she to work with?'

'I talk to her like a big brother. I tell her that people have a tendency to be critical, jealous, and antagonistic when a local son or daughter returns with money, fame, and glamour. My job is to let these people know what a friendly, generous person she is. We've lined up donations to all local charities and fifteen churches – the latter in memory of her dear "Pop." She's no public speaker, but she'll appear at social events and answer questions about parrots, old movies, and hats as an art form.'

'I understand,' Qwilleran said, 'that you want me to avoid mention of the interior design.' As a journalist he should resent being told by a P.R. man what to write . . . but this was a small town, and there was more than Thelma's public image to be considered.

'Fran and I have discussed it. Stark white décor is high style in some parts of the U.S. and abroad, but the concept is far-out for Moose County. Nothing would be gained by shocking the gossips and turning off the general public.

Meanwhile we can accentuate the positive by concentrating on the parrots.'

Qwilleran said, 'And waffles, and art hats, and old movies. I'm no expert on interior design, anyway, although I know what I like, and I like most contemporary stuff. You could help me, Dwight, by telling me about her new business venture, which seems to be a deep dark secret. Has she bought the old opera house?'

'It's been in her family for seventy-five years. It's been rented for everything from government purposes in wartime to appliance storage in peacetime.'

'Is she opening a restaurant? I've seen tables and chairs being delivered.'

Dwight lowered his voice. 'It's to be a film club, cabaret style . . . with the latest and best in projection equipment and sound system and screen . . . for viewing old movies exclusively.'

After dinner, Qwilleran shut himself up in his office on the balcony and went to work on the Friday column. The question was: How to make it interesting to the readers? The answer was: Make them think. Keep them guessing . . . Give them something to talk about. He wrote:

WHO SAID THIS?

Three may keep a secret if two of them are dead. You have three guesses. Here are some clues:

He was a philosopher, publisher, scientist, diplomat, mathematician, postmaster general, signer of

116

the Declaration of Independence, vegetarian, and genius. He invented the idea of daylight saving time long before it was adopted. And he invented the incredible glass harmonica. In case you have not yet guessed . . . you'll find his portrait on the hundred-dollar bill.

This Renaissance Man of eighteenth-century America also found time to write collections of wit and wisdom and publish them over a period of twenty-five years under the pen name of Richard Sanders. (They became known as *Poor Richard's Almanac*.) Included are sayings that everyone knows, like *Make haste slowly* and *Time is money*. Some have a trace of cynicism: *Where there is marriage without love, there will be love without marriage*.

Qwilleran ended his column with a quiz, challenging his readers to test their worldly wisdom. He informed them that the answers would be in his 'Qwill Pen' column on Tuesday.

Pleased with his work, he had a large dish of ice cream, then walked three times around the barn with a flashlight, thinking . . .

The next day would start with waffles at Number Five Pleasant Street and a get-acquainted session with the parrots. Would they be nervous after being snatched by strangers in the middle of the night? How much would Thelma want to say about her Lockmaster trip? Did Dick take her to dinner at the five-star Palomino Paddock? Who picked up the check?

He could think of many questions to ask, but they were all out-of-bounds: Do you think the kidnappers followed you from California? If not, did they learn about the much-loved parrots from Friday's newspaper? Did the interview reveal that all the neighbors would be away, feting the newcomer? What was the ransom demand? How could anyone scrape up a large amount of cash on a Sunday night? Do kidnappers now accept checks or credit cards? (Bad joke.) So was it Thelma's jewels they wanted? How did they know she had ten-thousand-dollar lapel pins and fifteen-thousand-dollar bracelets?

Eleven

On the morning of the waffle breakfast Qwilleran tuned in the WPKX weathercast, knowing he would hear nonsense as well as reasonably accurate predictions. His friend Wetherby Goode was more entertainer than meteorologist, but that was what the good folk of Moose County wanted. He always had a few lines of poetry, song, or nursery rhyme to fit the weather.

At least once a week he dedicated a forecast to someone in the news, such as Lenny Inchpot when he won the bicycle road race and Amanda Goodwinter when she was elected mayor.

On Thursday he dedicated his predictions to 'Thelma Thackeray, who grew up here and has returned to God's country after a long career someplace in California . . .

Thelma, you may have forgotten that we have interesting weather here. This morning is sunny with temperatures in the upper seventies, but if you go out, take a jacket and umbrella, because there will be light rain and a chill breeze – that is, if you don't want to catch cold. But if you do get the sniffles, drink some hot lemonade and put a goose-grease plaster on your chest.'

Then he sang a few lines about 'raindrops falling on my head' accompanying himself on the studio piano.

If Thelma happened to be listening, she would scream with laughter at the mention of goose grease. Old-timers in Moose County, reminiscing about the 'bad old days,' always guffawed over the hot, scratching, smelly horrors of a goose-grease plaster.

To Qwilleran's recollection he had eaten waffles only once in his life, and it behooved him to educate himself. A phone call to the public library launched a volunteer on a spirited search.

Thanks to her efforts, he learned that waffles have been around since Ancient Greece . . . that the first waffle iron in the United States was patented in 1890 . . . that waffle irons were the most popular wedding gift in the first quarter of the twentieth century . . . that there was at least one waffle iron in every respectable attic in Moose County.

As the time came to leave for breakfast, the cats watched him with anxious blue eyes, as if they expected never to see him again. 'Would you like to send your regards to Pedro and Lolita?' he asked.

Pleasant Street was quiet – ten gargantuan wedding cakes waiting for a wedding. The most flamboyant was Number Five. The front door, called the carriage entrance, was on the side, and Janice was waiting for him in her cook's apron and floppy hat.

'Good morning,' she said. 'Isn't it a lovely day?'

He handed her the bunch of carnations in green tissue that he had picked up on the way over. His instinct had told him to choose brilliant red.

'Thelma will love them!' Janice said. 'She's running a little late. Shall I bring you coffee while you're waiting?'

The wait gave him a chance to appraise the decorating. He thought it had elegance and joie de vivre. The whiteness of it all reminded him of a white-on-white artwork he had won in a raffle at the Art Center. Against the totally white background, however, exciting things were happening: A sofa and chairs with ebony frames in contemporary mission style had square-cut seats and back cushions in steel gray silk. Cool! he thought. They were accented with puffy down-filled toss pillows in parrot colors: vivid green, brilliant red, and chrome yellow. Tables were stainless steel with plate-glass tops. Handmade art rugs, large and small, defined the areas. Wall art consisted of large contemporary paintings and tapestries that stayed on the wall instead of jumping out at the viewer.

He was attracted to a pair of tall, narrow etageres in

the foyer – stainless-steel frames, each with five plate-glass shelves graduated in width. The frames flared upward, so that the shelf space at the top was wider than the shelf space at the bottom. It was a concept that gave grace and lightness to the design. The Moose County approach, Qwilleran thought, would be: straight-up-and-down like a ladder.

The shelves were filled with an astounding collection of tropical birds in brilliantly glazed porcelain. As Qwilleran examined them, he became aware of a strong presence: Thelma was descending the stairs with one braceleted hand grasping the handrail and the other braceleted hand extended in welcome. She was wearing a simple caftan in brilliant yellow that accentuated the silvery gray of her hair – a short-crop with bangs.

Qwilleran said, 'Your home, Thelma, has an air of elegance plus a certain joie de vivre!'

'Bless you, Ducky! You talk just like you write! And you look even handsomer than you did at the party! . . . Follow me! Waffles will be served in the breakfast room. I hope you like them as much as we do!'

In the breakfast room Qwilleran was served crisp, buttery waffles flavored with toasted pecans and topped with an apple-date sauce. He declared they were the best he had ever tasted in his life. (His previous experience had been in a fast-food place in New Jersey.) 'What do the parrots have for breakfast?' he asked, to nudge the conversation in another direction.

'Standard parrot feed,' Thelma said, 'plus treats like

safflower seeds, apples, bananas, celery, and raw peanuts. They love chocolates and marshmallows, but we don't want them to get fat.'

Janice said, 'Dick gave Lolita a chocolate-covered caramel, and her beak got all gummed up. It was funny to watch her struggle, but she liked it and wanted more.'

'I don't approve of Dick's cute tricks, and I've told him so!' his aunt said sternly.

Twice, in asides to each other, the two women had referred to a 'Mr Simmons.'

'Who is Mr Simmons?' Qwilleran asked. 'Your probation officer?'

Janice squealed in glee; Thelma murmured her amusement and said, 'He's a retired police detective who worked for me at the dinner club. He was a security guard in dinner jacket and black tie, and he felt it his responsibility to protect my personal safety.'

'He had a crush on Thelma,' Janice said mischievously.

'When I sold the club and retired, he became a friend of the family, coming to dinner once a week and keeping an eye on everything. He adored Janice's cooking. When he learned we were moving east, he insisted on giving me a small handgun and showing me how to use it, being concerned about two women crossing the continent alone. He is a dear, sweet man.'

Qwilleran said, 'I hope no one ever calls me a dear, sweet man.'

'Don't worry, Ducky; they won't,' Thelma retorted.

That was what he liked about her – her edge.

Qwilleran had avoided asking obvious questions about the parrots, since the answers had been in Friday's feature story, which he should have read. Actually he had given it a quick scan, so he played it safe. 'How was your sightseeing in Lockmaster, Thelma?'

'The horse country is pretty . . . and the restaurants are quite good . . . though not as good as mine, Ducky!' she said with a confidential wink. Then she said soberly, 'What I really went to see was my brother's grave. I told Dick to leave me alone for a few minutes and I visited with dear Bud . . . and said a little prayer . . . Then I wanted to see the gorge where he and Sally used to hike, and where he had his accident. Dick stayed at the car – he said it was too gruesome. But I thought it was beautiful. There was a trestle bridge in the distance that looked as if it was made of toothpicks, and while I watched, a little toy train roared across it. There was a river far down below.'

'The Black Creek,' Qwilleran said.

'When Pop used to bring us to Lockmaster for a picture show, we never saw anything like the gorge. He'd hitch up the wagon, and my stepmom would make pasties, and we'd have a picnic lunch. Tickets to the picture show were a nickel, so that was twenty cents for four. Pop didn't often splurge.'

'Do you remember the first movie you ever saw?'

'How could I forget? It was *Ben Hur* with all those chariot races! Silent, of course . . . then *The Circus* with Charlie Chaplin. How we loved the little tramp! . . . The first picture with sound was *The Jazz Singer* and that's when I decided I wanted to be *in pictures*, as they said then. By that time we weren't so poor and could go oftener.'

Qwilleran asked, 'When did movies come to Pickax?'

'Bud and I turned twelve, and Pop gave us the Pickax Movie Palace for a birthday present. It had been the old opera house – closed for ages – and he said he got it cheap. That's when we started seeing Garbo, John Barrymore, Gable, and the Marx Brothers. We saw *Duck Soup* three times. When I saw *The Gay Divorcee* with Ginger Rogers and Fred Astaire, that's when I knew I had to go to Hollywood.'

Janice had the waffle iron at the table, and Qwilleran was indulging himself.

'Shall we take our coffee into the aviary?' Thelma suggested.

All the houses on Pleasant Street had been designed with a front parlor and a back parlor, the latter being the family room in contemporary parlance. At Number Five it was called the aviary, however. Half of the space was behind chain-link fencing reaching to the ceiling. The other half was comfortably furnished with wicker tables and chairs and indoor trees in brass-bound tubs.

Inside the giant cage all was aflutter with color and life as parrots teetered on perches, showed off on trapezes, or climbed the chain-link, using their feet and strong beaks. One powerful beak was chewing on a tree branch. At the same time there was chattering, whooping, conversing in two languages, and noisy flapping of wings.

In the background were six single-occupancy cages, five of them with doors open and night-covers rolled back. A cover with the embroidered name CHICO stood alone.

'Who's Chico?' Qwilleran asked. 'Is he in the doghouse?'

'Our dear Chico died three years ago,' Thelma said. 'We keep his cage as a memorial to a very remarkable bird.'

Qwilleran said, 'I must say they're an engaging crew!' He could imagine how tormented Thelma must have been when they were stolen.

They sat in the wicker chairs with their coffee, and Qwilleran said, 'In Friday's paper you were quoted as saying that Amazons are unusually intelligent and talkative, and that yours hold conversations in English and Portuguese. How do birds, no matter how intelligent, learn human speech?'

'They mimic the people they live with, including babies, cats, dogs, and voices on television,' Thelma said. 'Pedro used to live with a professor in Ohio and has a working vocabulary of two hundred words. He also likes to talk politics. That's Pedro, chewing on a tree branch.'

'Powerful beak,' Qwilleran said. 'I wouldn't want to meet him in a dark alley.'

'He's called a Blue Front. Others are: Yellow Nape and Red Lore – all are wonderfully colorful when they fan their tails and fluff their nape feathers.'

Qwilleran said, 'The one with a white circle around the eye seems especially alert and listening to everything we say.'

'That's Esmeralda. She lived with a musical family and has a large repertory of patriotic songs, popular tunes, and operatic arias. Unfortunately she doesn't know anything all the way through. Carlotta can recite the Greek alphabet but only as far as kappa . . . Navarro does a perfect wolf-whistle . . . They pick up whatever they hear . . . The two sitting with beaks together like a couple of gossips are Lolita and Carlotta. They keep looking at your moustache, Qwill – trying to figure out how to steal it. Amazons are very mischievous, you know.'

Qwilleran stood up. 'The situation is getting dangerous! In the interests of sartorial safety, I must leave.'

She responded with her soft little laugh – a musical 'hmmm hmmm hmmm.'

Then soberly he said as they walked to the door, 'Have you ever seen the grave of your father, Thelma?'

'I don't even know its location!'

'I do. It's a beautiful site. I'd like to drive you there Sunday afternoon. And we could have dinner at the Boulder House Inn overlooking the lake.'

'Bless you!' she cried.

As he was leaving, he asked casually, 'Okay to write a "Qwill Pen" column on the Amazons? If so, I'll have to come back and take notes.'

He was aware of Janice's petrified stare, but he concentrated on Thelma's reaction. She caught her breath and paused slightly before saying, with equal nonchalance, 'The cocky little devils have had all the publicity they deserve. Thanks, but no thanks.'

'Too bad,' Qwilleran said, 'I was looking forward to having some dialogue with Pedro on politics.'

'Yes, he has some opinions,' Thelma said, 'but they're not always printable.'

On the way home he pulled off the road and phoned Bushy, leaving a message on his answering device: 'Go ahead and invite Janice for a boat ride. I'm taking Thelma sightseeing Sunday afternoon.'

It was not long before Thelma called the barn:

'Qwill, that photographer who took pictures of the parrots has invited Janice for a boat ride Sunday, with a picnic lunch on an island. The reporter who was here and her husband are invited, too. I'd like Janice to meet some people of her own age, but I'm wondering if it's entirely – safe.'

Was she worried about a seaworthy craft? A competent pilot? Decent weather? Or what?

He said, 'John Bushland comes from a long line of lake navigators and grew up at the pilot wheel. And Jill Handley's husband owns the health food store downtown, so you know the lunch will be safe, too.'

That evening, when Qwilleran and Polly had their usual phone-chat, he said, 'Would you mind if I took another woman to dinner on Sunday?' He waited for her to splutter a question and then explained. 'Thelma has never seen her father's grave at Hilltop Cemetery and I thought it would be a kind gesture if I took her there and then to the Boulder House for Sunday dinner.'

'Why Boulder House?' she asked more or less curtly.

'It's picturesque and historic.' Actually, he saw it as a chance to tease the potato chip heiress.

Toward the end of the evening, when it was still too early for lights-out, he sprawled in his lounge chair with his feet on the ottoman and thought about the next 'Qwill Pen' column – and the next – and the next. A columnist's job, he liked to say, is 95 percent 'think' and 5 percent 'ink.' Koko was staring at him. One could never tell whether he was beaming a message about food or a lofty idea for the 'Qwill Pen.' Qwilleran agreed with Christopher Smart, the poet who maintained that staring at one's cat will fertilize the mind.

What transpired on this occasion may have been the cat's idea or his own; no one was keeping score. The fact was that Qwilleran's mind drifted to Tony, the Bixby tomcat . . . and the two vans . . . and the large boxes thought to contain stolen TV sets . . . Could they have been parrot cages, shrouded with custom-tailored night covers? If so, the person who drove away from the scene fast could have been Dick, the hero of the abduction incident. In that case, it was Dick who killed the kidnapper. And if so, did he recover the ransom from the dead man's possession?

But then he thought: The rescuer of the parrots could

129

have been a go-between, an unscrupulous lout, paid for his services. That being the case, did the go-between pocket the ransom after delivering the birds and killing the poor clod behind the steering wheel? How many of the devils collaborated on the plot?

And then he thought: Was Dick one of the collaborators?

The idea was abhorrent, although – as Shakespeare observed – one can smile and smile and be a villain.

'Yow!' was Koko's strident announcement. After all, it was five minutes after the time for their bedtime snack.

The days that followed were unusually busy for Qwilleran, and there was no time for frivolous conjectures about the kidnapping. Indeed, he had to admit that the large, square objects mentioned in the *Bixby Bugle* might have been stolen television sets, as the police said.

Twelve

When Qwilleran handed in his copy for Friday's paper, Junior scanned it and said, 'We'd better alert the bank to get some hundred-dollar bills out of the vault. People around here think that nothing over a twenty is negotiable.'

Qwilleran commented, 'That was a nice piece on the Kit Kat Agenda in yesterday's paper.'

'Yeah, Mavis Adams makes a good interview. She has all the facts, and she's articulate. She's an attorney, you know, although she doesn't look like one.'

'What is a woman attorney supposed to look like, Junior? After all, you don't look like a managing editor.'

Ignoring the barb, Junior said, 'Wait till you see the big ad on page five—'

He was interrupted by the breezy arrival of Hixie

131

Rice. 'Hi, you guys! What's new and exciting?'

'Old proverbs,' Qwilleran replied. 'Just to test your cultural literacy, see if you can finish this one. *Three comforts of old age are . . .*'

Neither she nor the managing editor could fill in the blanks.

'I'm ending my column with a quiz. Readers will be given the three or four opening words of several proverbs. If they can't complete them, the answers will be in my Tuesday column.'

'So what are the three comforts of old age?' they wanted to know.

'You'll have to wait until Tuesday.'

Hixie objected. 'That's too long a wait. Readers will lose interest. I have a better idea. Bury the answers in today's paper – in the want ads, real estate listings, or wherever.'

Junior, always under Hixie's spell, seconded the motion, and Qwilleran was outvoted. Reluctantly he handed over the answers, and Junior rushed them off to the production department.

Qwilleran asked Hixie, 'And how are the plans progressing for the Sesquicentennial?'

With her usual enthusiasm she said, 'The committee has tons of ideas! And we have a whole year to work on it! It's going to be the biggest little Sesquicentennial in North America!'

'More power to you!' he said.

* * *

Qwilleran's next chore was to take Polly's long shopping list to Toodle's Market, and in the paper goods aisle his loaded cart collided with that of a Pleasant Street resident. 'Sorry,' he said. 'I have insurance, in case I've broken your eggs, or curdled your coffee cream.'

It was Jeffa, the new wife of Whannell MacWhannell. 'Qwill! Isn't that a large load of groceries for a bachelor and two cats?'

'They're Polly's,' he explained. 'I do her shopping while she's at work, and then I get invited to dinner.'

'Smooth! I never had an arrangement like that when I was in the workplace . . . By the way, that was an excellent feature on the Kit Kat Agenda in your paper.'

'Are you involved?'

'Mac has okayed a kitten colony as long as they have their own room and don't run all over the house getting in his shoes and pants legs. There's a meeting Tuesday night to plan the Kit Kat Revue. I hope you'll be there.'

When Qwilleran returned to the barn, Yum Yum greeted him with affectionate ankle-rubbing, but Koko was sitting stiffly and defiantly on one of the bookshelves.

Qwilleran thought, That rascal! He's knocked it down again, just to be funny.

The book on the floor was not *Poor Richard's Almanac* but another old book from the late Eddington Smith's store: a historical novel by Winston Churchill. And that raised a question:

Eddington had named his cat Winston Churchill – a

dignified gray longhair with plumed tail and an impressive intellect. The bookseller attributed the latter to the cat's literary environment. Now it occurred to Qwilleran that Winston had been named for an American author – not a British statesman! The book on the floor was a historical novel about the American Revolution published in the late nineteenth century. Titled *Richard Carvel*, it was by the most popular author of historical novels of his time.

At two o'clock, Qwilleran walked down the lane to pick up his newspaper. Eager to read the ad on page five, he sat on the bench at the front door of the Art Center.

The ad announced the opening of Thelma's Film Club in the old opera house featuring old movies from the Golden Age of Hollywood . . . for members only . . . cabaret style. Beer and wine at the evening show and a full bar at the late-night show. There was a phone number to call for further information. It was a Lockmaster exchange.

As Qwilleran was marshaling the questions he wanted to ask, the front door of the Art Center was flung open, and Thornton Haggis shouted, 'Hey, Qwill! What kind of tricks are you playing on your long-suffering readers?' He was waving a copy of the *Something*. 'I've been through this whole paper, line by line, and I can't find a single reference for your readers about old sayings!'

'Oh-oh! Let me use your phone,' Qwilleran said.

In the office he got Junior on the phone. 'What happened!'

134

The managing editor groaned. 'It was all set up for the business page! And it disappeared! Don't ask me how. Our phone has been ringing nonstop. Hixie's doing a recorded message: *If you wish the answers to the "Qwill Pen" quiz, please press one*. Then the nine sayings are read ... There's always something, isn't there, Qwill?'

Another of Hixie's ideas had gone awry. Qwilleran began to fear for the Sesquicentennial.

When he arrived at the barn, Qwilleran phoned the *Moose County Something* and 'pressed one' as instructed. A voice said, 'We apologize for the computer error that omitted the answers to the proverb quiz in the "Qwill Pen" column. The correct answers are ...'

1. Three comforts of old age are an old wife, an old dog, and ready money.
2. A cat in gloves catches no mice.
3. An empty bag can never stand upright.
4. Eat to live and not live to eat.
5. A used key is always bright.
6. He that lives on hope dies of starvation.
7. There never was a good war or a bad peace.
8. Blame-all and praise-all are two blockheads.
9. Keep your eyes wide open before marriage and half shut afterwards.

When Qwilleran arrived at Polly's condo for dinner, he

used his own key to let himself in and was met by Brutus with a challenging stare.

He said to the cat, 'Do you want to see my driver's license or social security card? Or will my press card do?'

'Come in! Come in!' Polly called from the kitchen, 'and tell me what went wrong at the *Something* today? The library was swamped with calls!'

'What did they want?'

'The answers to your quiz – that should have been in the paper and weren't. We looked up the sayings in *Bartlett*, and the clerks have been reading them off to callers.'

He said, 'You always have everything under control, Polly. Shall we have dinner on the deck? The temperature is perfect; there's no wind.'

'Any bugs?'

'Too early.'

The first course was a grapefruit compote with blueberries and he said, 'I don't remember any grapefruit on your shopping list today.'

'Wait till you hear the story! . . . One of our volunteers received a shipment of grapefruit from an orchard in Florida – with birthday greetings from someone called Miranda. She doesn't know anyone by that name, and her birthday is in November. She phoned the orchard. They didn't seem concerned – just blamed computer error and told her to enjoy them . . . Well, she's a widow, living alone, so she brought them to the library.'

'It seems to me,' Qwilleran said, 'that the computers make more errors than humans ever did.'

'And human errors seemed more understandable and forgivable.'

'I must say it's the best grapefruit I ever tasted. Welcome to the Brave New World of Computer Errors.'

The main course was a casserole combining several recent leftovers, and Qwilleran congratulated her on creating a flavor hitherto unknown to the human palate, even though it looked like a dog dinner. 'It beggars description,' he said. 'I hope there are seconds.' They consumed it in a silence of rapture or stoicism.

'And now are you ready for the salad, dear?'

'As ready as I'll ever be!'

Talking to take his mind off the spinach, endive, kale, and arugula, he asked, 'Did you see the ad for Thelma's Film Club? I phoned the number and got a recorded message, of course. Memberships are fifty dollars for the evening show; a hundred for the late-night show – good for a year. Admission tickets are five dollars. Members may buy tickets for guests. The speaker identified himself as Dick Thackeray, manager, but he added that Thelma Thackeray will host the evening shows.'

Polly wondered if the idea would go over in Moose County.

'It'll draw from Lockmaster and Bixby Counties

chiefly, I'd guess. But there's no doubt it will benefit Pickax restaurants.'

Dessert was frozen yogurt with a choice of three toppings. Qwilleran had all three.

'Any news in your exciting life, Qwill?'

He had to consider awhile. 'Yum Yum threw up her breakfast . . . Koko staged a three-alarm yowling fit to let me know one of the faucets was dripping . . .'

'How were Thelma's waffles?'

'Good, but rich. You wouldn't have approved . . . The parrots were amusing and strikingly beautiful.'

'What was Thelma wearing?'

'A long yellow garment and two armfuls of bracelets – just gold hoops as thin as wire, but lots of them.'

'They're called bangle bracelets,' Polly said. 'Incidentally, I ran into Fran Brodie at the hair salon today, and she said that Thelma has decided jeweled pins and necklaces and bracelets are too flashy for Moose County. She's put them in her bank vault. She'll just wear her tiny diamond ear-studs and diamond-studded sunglasses and bangle bracelets.'

Qwilleran huffed into his moustache and wondered, Are they in her bank vault? . . . or on the way to California with the kidnappers?

He was thinking of his theory – that the ransom demand had been for jewels, not cash. Did the kidnappers follow her here from California? Did she give them everything except diamond ear-studs and bangle bracelets? What jewelry would she wear to visit

Pop's grave and have dinner at the Boulder House Inn?

He helped Polly remove the dinner appurtenances from the deck, and then they made plans for the following evening: dinner at Tipsy's Tavern and then an opera on stereo at home. Polly suggested *La Traviata*.

'Are you going to Homer's birthday celebration in the morning, Qwill?'

'Just as an observer,' he said.

Qwilleran described the birthday celebration in his personal journal.

Saturday, April 19 – The lobby of the Ittibittiwassee Estates was trimmed with colorful balloons and crowded with city and county officials, local and state media, and Derek Cuttlebrink with his guitar. Residents were restrained behind roping. Everyone was facing the elevator door.

When it opened, out rolled Homer in a wheelchair pushed by his young wife. He was wearing a gold paper crown tilted at a rakish angle. One could tell by the expression on his furrowed face that neither the crown nor the cameras nor the balloons were his own idea. Sorry, Homer; when you become a civic treasure, you give up certain individual rights. When the prolonged applause began to subside, Derek strummed a few chords and sang in a nasal voice to the tune of George M. Cohan's 'You're a Grand Old Flag':

He's a grand old guy with a spark in his eye
And as bright as the Fourth of July!
And they say that he's
Got both his knees
And still takes his brandy with rye.
Now he's ninety-nine
And he's feeling fine
And he still takes the curves in high!
We'll all be here
Again next year
To cheer Homer the grand old guy!

They weren't the best lyrics I'd ever written, but
Derek made them sound good. As the applause
reached a crescendo, the elevator doors opened, the
wheelchair rolled back into the car, the door closed,
and the green light signaled UP.

Thirteen

The Siamese knew when Qwilleran was getting dressed to go out. They hung around, as only cats can do, waiting, waiting – for a farewell morsel of mozzarella.

He said to them, 'I'm taking "Ducky" for a drive around the county. Sorry you're not invited. She has an aversion to cats.' He could understand an allergy to cat hair, but anyone who simply hated cats was suspect.

At Number Five Pleasant Street he was greeted by Thelma, looking handsome in a lime-green jacket of soft leather and a white leather car-cap. A T-shirt in narrow stripes of multi-green and white had a jaunty look. Her slacks, sandals, and satchel-type handbag were white. She was ready to go.

'I forgot to tell you,' he said. 'We have to walk up a

gravel path at Hilltop. Do you have something more practical for walking?'

'No sooner said than done! I'll go up and change, and you say hello to the Amazons while you're waiting.'

He could hear them. It sounded like a cocktail party out of control, but the chattering and whooping stopped when he appeared, except for a saucy remark: 'Pretty fellow! Pretty fellow!'

'Skip the compliments,' Qwilleran said. 'Let's hear some intelligent conversation.'

There followed a chorus of non sequiturs: 'What time is it? . . . Yankee Doodle came to town . . . Yoo Hoo – Yoo Hoo . . . Pretty fellow!'

'They like you,' said Thelma, returning in white oxfords with crepe soles. 'They don't like everybody.'

'I'm flattered,' he said.

She hopped nimbly into Qwilleran's SUV.

'Before we push off,' he said, 'let me congratulate you on the Film Club and wish you success. It will be good for the community, but isn't it an ambitious venture for you?'

'My nephew will do the work and take the responsibility, but the club is in my name, and I'll supervise.'

Qwilleran was accustomed to hearing the problems of individuals old and young. They confided in him because he was a good listener and had a sympathetic mien and knew how to say the right thing.

Now he said, 'If there's anything I can do, I'll be only too glad to help.'

With that they headed north to Hilltop – past the medical center, community college, K Theatre for stage productions, Toodle's Supermarket, curling club in a Swiss chalet, and Ittibittiwassee Estates. They were all new in recent years. 'But I remember Lanspeak Department Store,' she said. 'That's where I went to buy my Easter hat. Hats were always important to me. I don't know why.'

'It was your royal instinct. You were born to wear a crown. It shows in your posture, your bearing, your attitude.'

'You say the most adorable things, Ducky! I would have loved to be the gossip columnist Hedda Hopper, and be famous for my hats. She had a hundred of them, you know, and she was photographed for the cover of *Time* magazine, wearing a hat composed of a typewriter, a microphone, and a radio script.'

'It's interesting that you both happened to have alliterative names.'

'Furthermore,' he said, 'let me say in all sincerity that I think Thelma and Thurston are beautiful names for twins whose surname is Thackeray. Who made the choice?'

'My mother, before we were born. If she had a girl, she wanted her to be Thelma; if she had a boy, he was to be Thurston. In the family, though, we were just Bud and Sis. My father was Pop . . . Did you have brothers and sisters, Qwill?'

'No, and my father died before I was born . . . Were you ever married?'

143

'Only once. I kicked him out after six months. He was a gambler, and I had no intention of financing his hobby. Since then I've managed very well on my own. As the saying goes: *A woman without a man is like a fish without a bicycle.*'

They drove in silence for a while. Then she said, 'Beautiful country.' Thelma was relaxed and losing her professional veneer.

'How long did it take you to drive from California?'

'It's about two thousand miles, and we could have made it comfortably in five days; but we didn't want to stress the Amazons, and we didn't want to arrive before the moving van, so we took it slowly, stopping at cabins instead of motels. That way we could take the brood indoors and uncover their cages, and they wouldn't bother anyone. They were good travelers, and Janice is an excellent driver.'

After another few minutes of comfortable silence, Qwilleran said, 'We're coming to Hilltop – ahead on the left.'

The Hilltop Cemetery was in the Hummocks – a ridge running north and south with burial grounds on the summit. The gravestones could be seen silhouetted against the western sky.

Qwilleran said, 'Through a member of the genealogy club I was able to check the location of your father's grave. There are five paths leading to the summit. Taking the nearest and walking along the crest produces a mood of healing serenity, they say.'

They found the monument to 'Milo the Potato Farmer,' and Qwilleran wandered away while Thelma had her few moments alone with 'Pop.'

As they continued toward the shore, Qwilleran said, 'Lower your window, Thelma, and sniff the lake air – a hundred miles of water between here and Canada. The Boulder House was originally the summer home of a quarry owner.'

The architectural curiosity loomed on a cliff above a sandy beach, looking more like a fortress than a pleasant place for Sunday dinner, and the innkeeper was straight out of a medieval woodcut: short, roly-poly, and leather aproned, but he was jovial, and regular customers affectionately called him 'Mine Host.'

Before dinner they had a drink on the parapet, a stone veranda over the edge of the cliff, but Thelma said, 'I'm not supposed to imbibe, Ducky. Doctor's orders. And at my age I have to be a very good girl.'

He recommended a Q cocktail and was explaining about Squunk water when a large, furry animal waddled up to them in a friendly fashion.

'What's that?' she cried in alarm.

'That's Rocky, the resident cat. What you see is mostly fur; he's a longhair, but if you don't want him around, just shoo him away.'

When Rocky had retired to the other end of the parapet, Qwilleran told how the craggy design of the building enabled Rocky to climb up the exterior wall like an Alpine goat and peer in the windows at sleeping guests.

Thelma shuddered visibly.

The dining room was equally rough-hewn and the floor was a flat slab of prehistoric rock on which the structure had been built. There was an immense fireplace, screened for the summer.

'In cold weather,' Qwilleran said, 'guests gather around the fireplace after dinner, and Mine Host tells ghost stories and other hair-raising tales. The menu is not sophisticated, but everything's good.'

They had a simple Chateaubriand, a twice-baked potato, and what Qwilleran called the inevitable broccoli. After the blueberry cobbler and while they were lingering over coffee, the innkeeper inquired if they had enjoyed the meal.

Qwilleran said, 'Ms Thackeray, this is Silas Dingwall, great-grandson of the man who was responsible for this Eighth Wonder of the World.'

'How did he do it?' she exclaimed. 'And why?'

'If you'd like to come to my office,' said the innkeeper, 'it would be my pleasure to serve you an after-dinner drink and tell you the whole story.'

They agreed, and Thelma whispered, 'Isn't he a character!'

Qwilleran thought, It takes one to know one!

In the office he asked permission to tape the innkeeper's tale, and the following account was recorded:

In the late nineteenth century, when Moose County was booming, the lumber barons built huge summer palaces along the shore here. There was more money than taste in those days – maybe today, too. At any rate, the lumbermen tried to outdo each other, each palace being larger or more spectacular than its neighbors.

My ancestors were in the quarry business and were considered in a lower class than the big boys who were exploiting the mines and forests. But my great-grandfather had a sense of humor, and he and my dad and uncles thought up a crazy idea. They hauled huge boulders to the site and piled them up to make a habitation. It took teams of draft horses and musclemen to do it, and the result has been a tourist attraction ever since.

Then in 1912 the economy collapsed, and people fled the area. The few who remained all but starved until . . . Prohibition went into effect, and a new industry was born. Rumrunners smuggled Canadian whiskey into Moose County, stealthily by night, and bootleggers devised crafty ways to distribute it Down Below. The nerve center of the major operation was a network of subterranean chambers under this building, reached by a tunnel from the beach.

During Silas's tale, Qwilleran watched Thelma for a flickering of eyelids or moistening of lips or any other

147

reflex signifying that she knew about Pop's involvement. There was not even a change in her breathing, and she said coolly, 'It would make a good movie ... with a mysterious tapping in the cellar ... and the ghost of a revenue agent trapped by a high tide surging into the tunnel.'

Entering into the spirit of the scenario, Qwilleran said, 'The lakes don't have tides, but it would be a storm-tossed surf with thunder and lightning and some wild passages from Tchaikovsky. Boris Karloff could play the ghost!'

He thought, Maybe she didn't make it 'in pictures,' but she can play a role. Or does she really believe the potato chip story?

Before the day was over, there were more unanswered questions.

They returned to Pickax via the lakeshore, stopping now and then to enjoy the view: sailboats on the horizon ... cabin cruisers going nowhere fast ... fishing boats purposefully anchored.

Thelma said, 'The lake didn't play any part in our life when we were growing up. We didn't even know it was there.'

'What was it like – being a twin? Was there a lot of togetherness?'

'Well, we had different interests, but we were always together in spirit. Each of us had to know where the other was at all times. Although twins, we had very different personalities. Bud was skinny and sensitive; I was husky and tough. Once I bloodied the nose of a bully who was tormenting Bud in the schoolyard. The teacher bawled me out, but I told her I was proud of it and would do it again. After he went east to college and I went west, we kept in touch. I was so proud of him. He was a doctor and had his own animal clinic. He had such a wonderful, caring way with his patients – mostly horses and dogs – and their owners, too. One woman, whose Doberman was not responding to treatment, said she'd like to consult a psychic who diagnosed animals' disorders – by phone! Instead of scoffing at the idea, Bud told her to go ahead and tell him the psychic's diagnosis. He said he might learn something . . . but I'm telling you more than you really want to know.'

'On the contrary! I'm sincerely interested. Do you know that your brother's portrait still hangs in the lobby of the clinic he founded? It's a strong countenance. I wish I might have met him. John Bushland took the photo, and he's famous for catching the real person. He'll have the negative. I can get you an eight-by-ten.'

'Bless you! Bud used to write me the most beautiful letters, Qwill, and I've saved them, thinking they'd make a heartwarming book for animal lovers. What do you think?'

'I'd have to see them, but I'd be glad to give you an opinion.'

'Bud's last letter was so beautiful!' She removed her sunglasses and dabbed her eyes with a tissue.

Then she said, 'I'm afraid Dickie Bird is not the man his father was. That's why I'm here. The Film Club, I hope, will give him a challenge and a responsibility.'

'Very commendable,' Qwilleran murmured, although he considered 'Dickie Bird' as a pet name for a male child unsuitable; it would warp a man for life.

He could feel a mood of tension in the seat beside him. He asked, 'Are you getting good response to your ad about the Film Club? Moose County has never had such a facility.'

Thelma brightened. 'Dick reports hundreds of phone calls, and he's selling Gold Memberships for the evening show and Green Memberships for the late show – on credit cards.'

'Who's selecting the old movies?'

'That's one responsibility I reserve for myself. I'd be glad to include your requests.'

He had never been a film fan, but he remembered *A Tale of Two Cities* and Dickens was one of his favorite storytellers.

When he mentioned the title, Thelma said with enthusiasm, 'That's one of my favorites, too! I still choke up when I hear Ronald Colman's last line!'

'Is Dwight Somers doing a good job of P.R. for you?'

'He's one of the best I've ever worked with. Such a pleasant young man. I adore men with beards! And moustaches, too!' she added with a playful nudge.

Qwilleran felt a tremor on his upper lip – not because

of the saucy compliment but by a feeling that Dickie Bird smiled too much.

Back on Pleasant Street Qwilleran escorted her to her door but declined a cup of tea, saying he had to go home and feed the cats.

He felt he had done his good-turn-of-the-day, or even of-the-week. Thelma had visited Pop's grave; Janice had been free to go for a cruise. A ploy to bring the potato chip heiress out of the closet had failed, but it was only a journalist's nagging curiosity about something that was none of his business. He admitted it. But Thelma had enjoyed the sightseeing and the Boulder House legend. And she had learned that she could say 'shoo' to Rocky and he would oblige. It might be the first step in curing Thelma's ailurophobia.

On arriving at the barn Qwilleran felt the need for a dish of ice cream and some music. He played a Verdi opera that Polly had recently given him on the barn's magnificent stereo system.

All three of them listened. It was one of the things they could do together as a family. The cats huddled in one comfortable chair, sophisticated enough to take the booming bassos and high-pitched coloraturas without flinching, although their ears twitched once in a while, and occasionally they went to the kitchen for a drink of water.

Fourteen

Qwilleran was leaving to have lunch with Wetherby, the wacky weatherman, and the Siamese were watching as if they knew where he was going. He asked them, 'Do you have any message to send to your friend Jet Stream?'

Yum Yum sneezed softly, and Koko felt a sudden urge to scratch his right ear. Why was it always the right?

Wetherby was a native of Lockmaster County who had grown up in the town of Horseradish and had the mindset and social flair and snappy wardrobe of south-of-the-border types – everything except the two-tone shoes, Qwilleran had observed.

Being the first to arrive at Onoosh's Café, he stood outside to enjoy the pleasant April breeze.

Then, who should come along but Wetherby in black-and-white shoes!

'What happened?' Qwilleran asked in mock sympathy. 'Oh! Excuse me. I thought you had an accident and your feet were bandaged.'

Unruffled, Wetherby said, 'You should get some two-tones, Qwill. They're very big right now.'

'My feet are big enough in ordinary shoes, Joe. Shall we go in?'

They sat in a booth and ordered baba ghanouj as an appetizer. (No one had told Qwilleran it was made of eggplant.)

'How's our friend Jet Stream?' he asked.

'He's a good cat. We're buddies,' Wetherby said, 'but I spend a fortune on cat litter. The vet says the old boy has a case of "Gullivarian hydraulics" – nothing serious. But he's aptly named. How are your two brats?'

'They stay busy – Yum Yum rifling wastebaskets, and Koko prowling the bookshelves, sniffing the glue in the bindings. Lately he wants me to read from *Poor Richard's Almanac* all the time, but I get tired of his wit and wisdom.'

'Like what?'

'*A man without a wife is only half a man.*'

'Propaganda!' Wetherby objected.

'Prejudiced, to say the least! So I've decided to publish a compendium of wit and wisdom, to be called *Cool Koko's Almanac* with catly sayings.'

'Do you happen to remember a couple of examples?'

'*A cat without a tail is better than a politician without a head . . . A cat can look at a king, but he doesn't have to lick his boots . . . Hear no evil, see no evil, speak no evil, but be sure your claws are sharp . . .* But enough of that! What's happening in Indian Village?'

In the winter, when the barn was hard to heat, Qwilleran moved his household to a condo unit next door to Wetherby. It was a good address, but the developer had skimped on construction. Floors bounced; walls between units were thin. Now the K Fund owned Indian Village and improvements were being made. It meant soundproofing the wall between Qwilleran's foyer and Wetherby's living room.

'Amazing what they can do without making a mess,' the weatherman said. 'They surround the work area with plastic sheeting, then drill holes in the wall and blow in the insulation; cover the holes; paint over them. Neat operation. I thought our studs would be two-by-fours, but luckily they're two-by-sixes, so they could blow in more insulation.'

'Is it effective?'

'Since you and your operatic cats aren't in residence – and the unit on the other side of me is for sale – I can't tell. But others in the Village are pleased – even fussbudgets like Amanda Goodwinter! She's mellowed somewhat since being elected mayor. I think it's because her P.R. adviser made her get a cat to improve her image.'

Amanda had long been the crotchety owner of a successful design studio and a cantankerous member of the town council. No matter how much she spent on clothes and grooming, she always looked like a scarecrow. When it came to getting a cat, her friends expected her to adopt a scruffy orange tom with half a tail and one chewed ear. Instead she acquired a glamorous longhair whom she named Quincy, after an early president of the United States.

'Speaking of cats,' Qwilleran said, 'are you involved in the Kit Kat Revue?'

'Yeah . . . They asked me to emcee.'

Qwilleran said, 'I'd better brush up my tap dancing and do a brother-and-sister act with Mayor Goodwinter.' Actually he hoped to do a reading of some of T. S. Eliot's madcap verses in *Old Possum's Book of Practical Cats*. He often read them to the Siamese. Yum Yum liked the one about Mungojerrie and Rumpelteazer, who prowled about the house stealing things; she could identify. Koko seemed to feel a kinship with Rum Tum Tugger. *For he will do as he do do and there's no doing anything about it.*

After lunch Qwilleran was walking past the library when he noticed Thelma's green coupé in the parking lot. He went into the building and was surprised to see Janice and one of the volunteers dismantling the exhibit of movie star photographs.

'What's happening?' he asked.

'Oh! It's you!' Janice said. 'What a nice surprise! Thelma said everyone has seen the photos and it's time to show some different ones. She's had a new sign made.'

It read: EXHIBIT COURTESY OF THELMA'S FILM CLUB.

He said, 'I'll buy you a cup of coffee when you've finished the job. Don't hurry.'

While waiting, he browsed, said a few words to Mac and Katie, put a dollar in their jar, and bantered with the young clerks at the circulation desk.

'Mrs Duncan is attending a business luncheon,' one said. 'She didn't say what time she'd be back.'

They found their boss's low-key romance with the famous Mr Q to be of extreme interest and they would no doubt find it momentous when he left the building with the new woman from Hollywood, who was younger than Mrs Duncan but not as nice-looking.

He and Janice walked the short distance to Lois's Luncheonette as he explained the cultural significance of the shabby, noisy, friendly eatery; and when they arrived, a political argument was in progress among the customers, with Lois herself refereeing as she walked about swinging the coffee server.

The voices hushed as Mr Q entered with a strange woman. 'Come in!' Lois called out. 'Sit anywhere! All the tables are clean. Two pieces of apple pie left in the kitchen.'

Janice whispered, 'Thelma wouldn't care for this place, but I love it!'

'What is Thelma doing this afternoon?' he asked casually.

'Meditating in her Pyramid. She has one made of

156

copper, which concentrates the electronized energy more efficiently. It will do her good. She was upset after an argument with Dick this morning.'

'Has he been giving Lolita chocolate caramels again?'

Janice hesitated. 'Maybe I shouldn't talk about this, but I worry about her and it helps if I can get another opinion. She's been so good to Dick, and he's so ungrateful.'

'You're quite right to be concerned, Janice. Do you know what they were arguing about?'

'Employees for the Film Club. They'll need people to take tickets, run the projector, serve drinks, and clear away between shows. Dick wants to bring in people he knows – from Bixby. Thelma insists on hiring local help – for several good reasons.'

'She's entirely right.'

'Well, Dick stormed out of the house and slammed the door, so I guess Thelma used her Big Stick. She always talks about carrying a Big Stick to get her own way.'

Qwilleran said, 'One wonders why Dick was so determined to hire Bixby Bums, as they're called in Moose County.' (He thought he knew.)

Changing the subject Qwilleran asked, 'How was the boat ride yesterday?'

'Wonderful! The *Viewfinder* is a beautiful cruiser. The Handleys were nice. And the lunch was good. Bushy is a lot of fun. He told stories about his ancestors, who were commercial fishermen, and about UFOs, and about the terrible shipwrecks before the government built the lighthouse.'

'And what is the response to the ad for Thelma's Film Club?'

'Very good! Dick is selling both Gold and Green Memberships.'

'Has the opening date been decided?' Qwilleran asked casually.

'Not definitely. Thelma wants it to coincide with a triple-high on her BioRhythm chart.'

He nodded sagely. 'A wise approach!'

'And guess who's coming for opening night?'

He thought, It can't be Mr Simmons! Or can it?

'Mr Simmons!' she announced.

'As a friend of the family or a security guard?'

'Just a friend, although Thelma says he has a suspicious eye that roves around and frisks everyone visually.' Janice said this with much amusement.

'Is there anything I can do to help during his stay? Pick him up at the airport?'

'Thelma says he'd be very interested in seeing your barn. She told him about it.'

'That could be arranged,' Qwilleran said genially.

'And Bushy has offered to take us out on the *Viewfinder*.'

Janice was far different from the shy guest she had been at the reception. Had Thelma decided it was now 'all right' to talk openly with Mr Q? His sympathetic listening always attracted confidences.

Janice was saying, 'Bushy is going to do a portrait of Thelma like the one he did of her brother. And she's commissioned him to do still lifes of each of her twenty-four hats – to be made into a book. A woman in California is going to write the text. You haven't seen the hats, have you? I have some snapshots that I took . . .' She rummaged in her handbag.

Qwilleran looked at them and thought, More art than hat! 'Interesting,' he said.

'Fran Brodie said we should offer them to the Art Center for an exhibit.'

Qwilleran said, 'There's a gallery opening in Mooseville that would get better traffic and a more sophisticated audience. Tourists come up from Down Below and summer people come over from Grand Island on their yachts. I suggest you show these snapshots to Elizabeth Hart. She's co-owner of the Grist Mill restaurant and founder of Elizabeth's Magic, a boutique in Mooseville. Tell her I said it will get statewide publicity.'

Qwilleran was not prepared for the weary 'hello' he heard when he phoned Polly for their evening chat.

'Polly! Are you all right?' he asked in alarm.

'I don't know. I'm at sixes and sevens. I had my quarterly luncheon with my friend Shirley – the Lockmaster librarian, you know. It was her turn to drive up here. We went to Onoosh's, which isn't busy on Mondays, and had a booth for privacy. We met to discuss library problems and solutions.

'We compared notes and personal feelings and came to the conclusion that libraries aren't as much fun as they used to be, twenty years ago. Libraries, we said, used to be all about books! And people who read! Now it's all about audios and videos and computers and people in a hurry. What used to be serenely open floor space is now cluttered with everything except books. Even the volunteers find it less attractive work, and stop reporting on schedule.

'The public flocks in to see movie stars' photos, but no one shows up for a book program. Shirley's quitting! Her son owns the bookstore in Lockmaster, and she's going to work there. I planned to continue, but can I stand another five years of frustration? And if I leave, what will I DO? I could teach adults to read . . . or do you have any suggestions, Qwill?'

Qwilleran said calmly, 'If the K Fund opened a bookstore in Pickax, Polly, would you manage it?'

'What! You don't mean it!' she cried.

'It's a crime for a community of this size to have no bookstore! You could have book reviews, discussion groups, and readings from the classics . . . a busload could come in from Ittibittiwassee Estates.'

Polly said, 'I think I'm going to faint!'

Qwilleran said, 'Before you pass out, let me thank you for the opera recording!'

Fifteen

Qwilleran was serious about the bookstore. There would be long meetings with G. Allen Barter, attorney for the K Fund, and trips to Chicago for Polly's decisions: whether to build a new store on Book Alley or adapt the premises of the old *Pickax Picayune*. Meanwhile there would be the Kit Kat Revue to produce . . . . and Thelma's Film Club to launch, and another Tuesday deadline for the 'Qwill Pen.'

Qwilleran was polishing his thousand words on *Cool Koko's Almanac* when Thornton Haggis phoned. 'I have some interesting news for you, Qwill. Are you free?'

'I'm on deadline. Why don't you come up at two o'clock? Bring my mail and newspaper, and we'll have some refreshments. Will your news keep?'

'It's kept for a century. Another few hours won't hurt. It's something I heard at the genealogical society last night.'

That lessened the newsman's anticipation somewhat but he said, 'I can hardly wait!'

After two o'clock his friend Thorn trudged up the lane from the Art Center, and Qwilleran met him with a pitcher of sangria. They discussed the weather, the future of Thelma's Film Club, and the price of gasoline. Then Qwilleran asked about the G.S., as the ten-syllable organization was popularly called.

'Well ... a couple of years ago they started an inventory of lost cemeteries.'

'How does a cemetery get lost?'

'Starting about 1850, people were buried in backyards and along roadsides and in tiny churchyards. There is no trace of them today, but a group of G.S. members who call themselves grave-finders have searched county records and found hundreds of names and scores of old cemetery locations. Most of the little churches have been destroyed, but they found one small log church about the size of a one-car garage but with a proud little steeple. A stone wall surrounds a small graveyard with headstones no bigger than a concrete block – but with names and dates. The oldest is 1918. But it's completely overgrown. In fact, it's now part of a Klingenschoen Conservancy. The G.S. is getting permission to clear it out as a historic site. But here's the surprise! Three Thackerays are buried there, and they're pretty sure that

Milo and some other farmers built the church.'

'Hmmm,' Qwilleran mused. 'It would make a good story for the *Something* if handled right. Does the G.S. have any plans?'

'Since the last of the Moose County Thackerays has returned, they thought some kind of dedication ceremony might be in order. You know her; do you think she'd go for that?'

'She likes publicity, if it's favorable. She's hired a P.R. consultant. I could sound her out.'

'We won't release the news of the Thackeray graves until we hear from you, Qwill.'

Qwilleran had promised to take Thelma to lunch at the Nutcracker Inn; he could combine it with a sightseeing drive around the county, including the Old Log Church. After Thornton's visit, he phoned her, and before he could extend his invitation, she cried, 'Bless you, Ducky, for sending us to that talented Elizabeth Hart! She came down this morning to see our hats, and she said she'll be thrilled to exhibit them!'

'I want to hear all about it! Suppose I pick you up at eleven tomorrow morning – for lunch and sightseeing.'

'What kind of shoes shall I wear?' was her prompt reply.

He hung up with the satisfaction of 'mission accomplished.'

Before the day was over, he would have a harder task.

* * *

The Kit Kat system of foster care for kittens, which was new to Moose County, had been quietly succeeding, and now it was time to go public with a fund-raising Kit Kat Revue. The question was: When and where? A problem-solving session at the MacLeod residence on Pleasant Street was scheduled for Tuesday evening. Qwilleran walked over there at seven-thirty as several neighbors were converging on the site, and a carload drove in from Indian Village. Hannah MacLeod greeted everyone at the door, while Uncle Louie MacLeod sat at the baby grand and played numbers from the musical *Cats*.

The house had been occupied by three generations of musical MacLeods and was filled with family heirlooms and family portraits of opera singers, violinists, and pianists.

The newest member of the family – the recently adopted Danny – escorted guests to the adjoining family room with the official zeal of an eight-year-old. He brought extra chairs from the dining room, asked if anyone wanted a drink of bottled water, and answered questions about the kitten colonies.

'They have to stay with their mother for eight weeks . . . She feeds them and shows them how to take a bath . . . She picks them up by the back of the neck and drops them in their sandbox. She teaches them how to play.'

When the last guest had arrived – Burgess Campbell with Alexander – Uncle Louie played a few chords of 'God Bless America' and Danny said, 'Everybody stand up and sing!'

The meeting was chaired by Mavis Adams, instigator of the local foster-care program and promoter of the fund-raising revue. She introduced two special guests. Hixie Rice was promotion director at the *Moose County Something*, which would underwrite expenses of the revue as a public service. Dwight Somers was the public-relations consultant who would advise the Kit Kat Revue committee pro bono.

Mavis said, 'We have our program material well in hand, but we can't decide on staging or the price of tickets until we know the when-and-where of the revue.'

Burgess Campbell spoke up. 'May I say that this county has plenty of affluent individuals who will support a good cause if the event has an element of novelty and exclusivity. Fifty persons paid three hundred dollars a ticket for a black-tie cheese-tasting . . . chiefly because it was held at Qwill's barn. The renovated opera house would be a similar drawing card while it's hot news.'

Uncle Louie asked, 'Would the old gal let us borrow it for one night? She's said to hate cats. What does Somers & Beard have to say about this?'

'She's highly sensitive about her image,' the P.R. man said. 'In a county of ten thousand cat-fanciers I'd advise against the ailurophobe label. But since I'm working for her, I can't be a special pleader for the Kit Kat Revue. You'll have to request the use of the opera house. Then, if she asks my opinion – which she will – I'll endorse it.'

165

Wetherby said, 'Qwill's in solid with Thelma. I move that we appoint him special pleader.'

'Seconded!'

'All in favor?'

Every hand was raised.

Uncle Louie asked, 'Has anyone seen the hall?'

'It seats about a hundred cabaret-style, at small round tables,' Dwight said. 'There's a stage, with a full-size movie screen for a backdrop. There's a bar for serving beverages. Plenty of space backstage.'

Someone asked, 'Does anyone know how they've decorated the interior of the opera house?'

Only Dwight had seen it. 'Everything's a grayish purple like an ophthalmologist's waiting room – not too dark, not too light. The tables are small and round and pedestal-type. The chairs swivel and roll on casters and are quite comfortably upholstered.'

There was excited babble in the room, and Mavis rapped for attention, and asked Uncle Louie for an update on the program.

He said, 'Besides musical numbers and humorous readings, there will be performances by the creative dance club at the school and the tumbling team wearing cat costumes with tails. The kids visited several foster-care colonies to get ideas about kittens at play.'

Then Hixie Rice asked to have the floor. 'I would like to suggest a rousing finale for the program: a procession across the stage of prominent citizens with their cats! The mayor, the superintendent of schools, the director of the public library, newspaper personalities, and our esteemed meteorologist, of course.' There were cheers, and Wetherby took a bow.

Hixie went on. 'I know where I can order rhinestone-studded harnesses and leashes – overnight delivery – for marching across the stage.'

A commanding voice said, 'May I say a few words?'

All heads turned to listen. Qwilleran was not only *who he was*, but the 'Qwill Pen' column had made him an authority on feline eccentricities. He said, 'A cat may walk on a leash in a park, stopping to sniff an unidentified object or to chase a blowing leaf. But will he walk in a straight line – from stage-left to stage-right – in front of a hundred strangers?'

All heads turned to Hixie. 'If they won't walk, they can be carried or wheeled in some kind of conveyance. Also, there is a safe herbal sedation that's used in the theatre when a cat plays a role in a play – Pywacket in *Bell, Book and Candle*, for example. It produces serenity.'

'In the actors or the cat?' Wetherby asked.

Mavis said, 'We can cross that bridge when we come to it.'

And Uncle Louie said, 'Everything depends on whether Qwill can twist Thelma's arm.'

'Hear! Hear!' everyone shouted, and the meeting was adjourned.

Back at the barn, Koko was doing his grasshopper act.

'Were your ears burning?' Qwilleran asked. 'How are

you going to feel about a rhinestone-studded harness?'

But no. The cat was announcing a message on the answering machine – from Bushy.

'Would you like to earn a little extra money Thursday morning? Call me back.'

Qwilleran phoned him. 'Doing what?'

'Photographer's assistant. No experience necessary. Easy work. Low pay. I'm shooting all twenty-four of Thelma's hats, and it would speed matters if someone held the lights.'

'Don't you have light stands?'

'Frankly,' Bushy said, 'the two gals will be hanging around and wanting to talk, and you can shoo them away diplomatically.'

'Okay, but give my remuneration to charity. I don't want to report it to the IRS.'

'I'll pick you up Thursday morning.'

Qwilleran liked the idea. He had promised Thelma lunch at the Nutcracker Inn; news about the Old Log Church suggested a nostalgic trip to her distant past; and helping Bushy shoot the hats would be another point in his favor before 'popping the question.'

Sixteen

When Qwilleran called for Thelma on Wednesday morning, Janice came to the door and said, 'Come in. She's all ready. She's just saying good-bye to the Amazons. Do you say good-bye to your cats?' she asked.

'Always,' said Qwilleran.

Thelma arrived in such a flurry of enthusiasm and anticipation that Qwilleran was aware only that she was wearing something lavender and bangle bracelets and diamond ear-studs and crepe-soled shoes.

She hopped into the SUV with the pep of a twenty-year-old and asked, 'Are we going anywhere near Toodle's Market?'

'In Moose County everything is near everything else. Why do you ask?'

'Janice buys our groceries there and raves about it. Also, the woman who runs it is called Grandma Toodle, and she says she knows me from grade school.'

'Then that will be our first stop.'

They found Grandma Toodle in the produce department sniffing pineapples critically. She looked up and flung her arms wide. 'Thelma! I saw your picture in the paper! Do you remember me? Emma Springer! You called me your little sister.'

'You were so tiny! I had to look after you. You had beautiful long curls, and when the boys pulled them, I chased them with a big stick.'

'And now you're famous, Thelma!'

'I still carry a "big stick"!'

Qwilleran wandered away and inspected the broccoli until the hysterical reunion ended.

Thelma bought a fresh pineapple, explaining that it contained an enzyme that would cure what ails you. Qwilleran bought some eating apples, and they joined the lineup at the checkout counter. There was a wait, as usual, while a customer searched for her credit card and the cashier had to find out today's price of bananas. In front of Thelma a boy of about ten years waited patiently as his mother complained about the holdup; he was eating candy out of a paper bag.

Suddenly he turned to Thelma and said, 'Would you like a jelly bean?' He offered the bag to the customer with diamond ear-studs and bangle bracelets.

'Thank you, Ducky!' she said. 'Do you have any black ones?'

'Yep, but you have to dig for 'em.'

Thelma reached into the bag just as the boy's mother said, 'Don't eat all that candy, Jason. You'll spoil your dinner.' And the line moved up a few inches.

'Nice young boy,' Thelma remarked as they left the market.

'Did you find a black one?' he asked.

'After he'd been digging around with his grubby hands? I took one for Lolita. She doesn't care what color it is.'

As they drove away, her musings rambled. 'Just imagine! – little Emma Springer marrying big Buck Toodle! We all went to a two-room school! Eight grades with one teacher and a potbellied stove!'

Qwilleran asked, 'Did you write secret messages to each other with lemon juice?'

'Are you kidding, Ducky? I never saw a lemon until I moved to California! . . . The Toodles had a crossroads grocery, with everything from turnips to kerosene. We had to walk a mile to spend a penny on candy. We walked everywhere, except in blizzards. We'd put on our Sunday best and walk to church and arrive covered with dust . . . I liked going to church because I could wear a hat . . . Always loved headgear. I paraded around the house with pots and pans on my head. I made hats out of cornflake boxes.'

'Do you remember the name of your church?'

'No, but it was built of huge logs. Pop helped to build it. He said it would last forever.'

'He may have been right. The forest grew up around it, but it's being cleared out, and a friend told me how to find it. It has a little graveyard with a stone wall around it.'

Farther on, an arrow pointed to THE OLD LOG CHURCH, and their vehicle bounced down a narrow rutted road through deep woods.

At a jog in the road Thelma cried, 'That's it! That's it!' She jumped out of the car and knew exactly where to find the three Thackeray graves.

Qwilleran waited until her emotions were played out, then said, 'They're planning a dedication ceremony. Would you represent the Thackeray family?'

'Bless you! I'd be honored!'

Back on the pavement they jabbered all the way to the Nutcracker Inn.

He said, 'I've bought a Gold Card Membership.'

'You shouldn't have, Ducky. You can see a show anytime as my guest.'

'But I wanted to be a member. How will we know what's being shown?'

'Members get a newsletter every two months.' She mentioned productions like *The African Queen* . . . *The Godfather* . . . *My Fair Lady* . . . *Close Encounters of the Third Kind*. And then, 'I've been wondering, Qwill, how you handle the housecleaning in your huge barn.'

'Three young men with vacuums and other cleaning

equipment come in on a regular schedule, plus an older woman who does dusting and polishing and is very fussy . . . By the way, I'm helping Bushy shoot your hats tomorrow morning.'

'Glad you told me! We'll have waffles.'

'Not this time. It's strictly a work session. But we'll take a rain check . . . Did the hats make the cross-country trip without damage?'

'Well, each hat has its own sturdy hatbox, and the moving company built four wooden crates that would be a tight fit for six boxes. They were painted THIS SIDE UP in big letters. Perfect!'

The Nutcracker Inn was an old Victorian mansion with a turret and black walnut woodwork, purchased by the K Fund and converted into a stylish resort. Peanuts were supplied for feeding the squirrels that enlivened the extensive grounds, and bread was available for feeding the ducks that paddled about the Black Creek. Qwilleran's old friend, innkeeper Lori Bamba, gave Thelma the kind of effusive welcome she liked. The sleek black Nicodemus, the resident cat, looked on, knowing when and when not to be friendly. Qwilleran noted that Thelma took him in stride.

Their table was reserved in the conservatory, but first they had Q cocktails on the deck, where they could watch the squirrel ballet.

Qwilleran asked, 'What did you think about the black cat?'

'He has wicked eyes,' she replied noncommittally.

'But a sweet disposition. In fact, guests who are lonesome for their pets can arrange for him to stay overnight with them. In fact, he's reserved far in advance.' The latter was a little hyperbole added for comic effect, and Thelma looked at him sharply. He went on. 'How do you feel about cats? I was told to keep mine out of sight when you were coming.'

'I'm not enthusiastic.

'We had all kinds of barn cats on the farm, and they adored my brother. He had a kind of magnetism, even then, that attracted cats and dogs. I was jealous I think. I pulled their tails and one of Bud's cats bit me. They were the only thing he and I ever fought about . . . After he was a doctor – and we kept in constant touch – cats were never mentioned.'

Qwilleran nodded sympathetically. 'But that was then, and this is now. You're living in a community where there are one-point-five cats for every person. We all have our likes and dislikes. Still, there are busybodies who are spreading the rumor that you're a "cat hater." Now is the time to make some gesture that will squelch the rumor. You might consult Dwight Somers. And who's your local attorney?' He knew, but he wanted to hear it from her.

Thelma brightened. 'Mavis Adams! First woman attorney I've ever had. She's a gem! She listens; she understands; she gives good advice; she solves problems.'

Qwilleran added, 'And she lives on Pleasant Street. It wouldn't hurt to discuss the matter with her. She founded the local chapter of an animal-rescue movement and is spearheading a revue to raise funds for it. Whatever amount is realized, the K Fund will match dollar-for-dollar.'

The hostess interrupted to say their table was ready, and they went into the conservatory. It was a many-windowed room with views on three sides.

Thelma said, 'Pop built one of these on the back of the farmhouse after he did well in potato chips. We called it a sun parlor.'

After they had ordered (roast beef sandwich for him, something patently healthful for her), he brought up the subject of Bud's letters. 'Do you still want an opinion as to their possible publication?'

'I do! I do! Janice is putting them in chronological order and then in letter files for your convenience. She's such a joy! – an efficient secretary, wonderful cook, and careful driver! Off the record, Qwill, I've set up a trust fund for her future financial needs. And now that we're living here, I hope she will make some friends. She goes over to the Campbell house to play with the kittens, and that's good for her.'

After lunch they walked down the hill to the creek, carrying some bread to feed to the ducks. They sat on a park bench facing the water, and immediately two mother ducks and their broods sailed toward them in perfect formation. Thelma was delighted with the performance, and after the bread was gone, she was reluctant to leave.

'It's so peaceful here,' she said. Then, after a long pause, she asked suddenly, 'Do you think I was right to start Thelma's Film Club?'

'It seems like a great idea to me, Thelma. And you say the memberships are selling well. Are there problems?'

'Only one. My nephew! He's not the man his father was. He wants to have Bingo at the club one night a week! I told him in no uncertain terms that I would not allow gambling in a club with my name on the marquee. He said, "It's only a game, Auntie." It irritates me when he calls me that! If it's not gambling, why is it outlawed in so many communities . . . and in places where it's considered legalized gambling, why are there so many restrictions and regulations?'

'You're quite right, Thelma, to limit a film club to films. There's a gambling casino in Bixby County, but Lockmaster and Moose Counties have never permitted it. Was that the end of it?'

'He said we're a private club and can do anything we want – even strip-dancing! – as long as it's undercover. I said, "I'll hear no more of this twaddle! Decide whether you want to work for me – or not!" So he backed down. He knows which side his bread is buttered on!'

'I'm glad to see you stick to your guns, Thelma.'

'I *always* stick to my guns.'

'When do you start showing films?'

'One week from tomorrow. Everything was going so well until the upsetting argument with my nephew.'

'Forget about Dickie Bird and what a bad boy he is,'

said Qwilleran. 'Do something constructive that will cancel out your negative feelings! Make a spectacular gesture that will win the admiration of the county.'

The rest of their conversation is best reported in Qwilleran's own words – in his personal journal:

Wednesday, April 23 – All during our nostalgia trip around the county and our pleasant luncheon at the Nutcracker Inn, I had been waiting for the right moment to pop the question (as Dwight phrased it). This might be it. I knew she appreciated my hospitality, but I didn't want to ask a favor in return. It would have the taint of *quid pro quo*.

Now she was disenchanted with her nephew and dispirited about the Film Club. I thought fast. The trick would be to boost her morale and solve the Kit Kat problem with one stroke. I said, 'I know the situation is disappointing, Thelma, but you must rise above it! Do something constructive that will benefit others as well as yourself!'

Thelma regarded me questioningly, and I went on. 'Restoring the old opera house is a boon to the whole county! Even people who aren't interested in old movies are curious to know what you've done with the building. And it so happens that we have plenty of affluent citizens who would pay to have a private look at the building if it would benefit a local charity. (Tax deductible, by the way.) They like to put on dinner jackets and long dresses and be treated like celebrities: valet parking, red carpet, press photographers, even TV cameras from Down Below, and publicity all over the state.'

I was on my soapbox, as Polly calls it. Thelma was mesmerized, if I do say so myself. She asked, 'Do you mean I should open the theatre for a charity preview? Did you have a charity in mind?'

I said, 'Mavis Adams is doing a commendable job of spearheading a new kind of animal-rescue effort and has been rehearsing an entertainment to raise funds. Civic leaders will pay two or three hundred dollars a ticket if it's presented in an environment like the Film Club, and for you to offer the premises would be a handsome gesture. Ask Mavis for details, and consult your P.R. man. I'm sure Dwight will applaud your suggestion.'

She said, 'I have an appointment with Mavis at the law office tomorrow. I'll mention it . . . It might be an interesting thing to do.' Mission accomplished! With no arm-twisting!

But I have a hunch that Dickie Bird is going to be more of a problem than his 'auntie' expects.

Seventeen

On Thursday morning three young men with high-tech cleaning equipment and Mrs Fulgrove with home-made metal polish arrived at the barn, and that meant removing the Siamese from the premises. They wouldn't bother the cleaning crew, but the crew would bother them. Qwilleran put them in the SUV along with their blue cushion, commode, water dish, and snack bowl, and off they went to Pleasant Street to help photograph hats.

Janice met Qwilleran and said, 'Bushy's upstairs; Thelma had an appointment with her attorney. Is there anything I can do for you? Coffee? Cold drink?'

'You might like to go out to the car and say hello to the Siamese.'

'They could come indoors, since Thelma isn't here.'

'No, thanks. They're happy where they are. They have all the comforts of home.'

Bushy was in the upstairs room called the Gallery of Hats, setting up. The two side walls had hats displayed on shelves. Others on pedestals were spaced in the middle of the room. Each hat had its own acrylic hat stand.

'Here's what we'll do,' he said. 'Move all the hats to one side of the room; then move them to the other side one-by-one as they're photographed. That way we won't shoot one hat twice.'

Qwilleran said, 'That reminds me of the story about the man who wanted some new trousers shortened three inches, and the tailor shortened one leg twice.'

'Funny, but I don't have time to laugh. Too much to do.' Bushy had set up one pedestal, as a stage for the hat to be photographed. Two floor-standing lights were placed to bounce light off walls and ceiling. The camera was placed on its tripod, ready to go. It would be Qwilleran's job to place a hat on the pedestal and rotate it this way and that until Bushy had the best angle. Then he would tell his assistant how to direct the handheld light to best advantage. 'Raise it . . . tilt it down . . . a little to the left . . . move it an inch.' The tricky ritual would be repeated three times for each hat.

The first two shots were interesting; after that Qwilleran entertained himself by inventing names for them: Heavenly Hash . . . Chef's Salad . . . Crème de

Chocolat. Despite his talent for description, he would find it impossible to do justice to creations like these. There were wisps of this and swirls of that, unexpected trims, touches of hand-painting or stitchery, defiant color contrasts, crowns and brims in mad shapes.

Halfway through, the photographer said, 'See if you can scare up some coffee, Qwill, and let's take a breather.'

'How do you want it?'

'Naked.'

'What do you think of the hats?'

'Well . . . they're different! Wonder what she paid for them?'

'Did you notice the hatboxes?'

Stacked in the corners of the room were two dozen round hatboxes covered in shiny alligator-print paper.

Qwilleran asked about them when he went downstairs for coffee.

'Thelma had them custom-made,' Janice said. 'She adores the alligator look. She has alligator shoes and handbags.'

'Did you go out to see the Siamese?'

'Yes, and I took them a little treat. I also put a couple of boxes of letters from Thelma's brother in the car. I went through them and put them in chronological order to make it easier for you.'

'I appreciate that.'

Upstairs he told Bushy, 'I'll look forward to seeing your prints. You always make everything look better than it is.'

'Did Thelma tell you I'm going to do a portrait of her? It'll be a companion to the one hanging in the lobby of the clinic.'

'You spoke highly of Dr Thurston, but I don't think you knew much about the son did you?'

'Only by reputation. My ex-wife was a native of Lockmaster, and she said he was a drifter. But he always seemed to have money.'

After his dubious experience with twenty-four hats, Qwilleran would have relished a Reuben sandwich and fries at Rennie's, but the Siamese had been confined long enough so he drove back to the barn. His passengers seemed to be peacefully aware of their destination until they entered the deep woods leading to the barnyard. Then a low rumble in Koko's innards became a growl. It was a familiar expression of disapproval. The cleaning crew had gone. There was something indoors that aroused Koko's resentment.

Leaving the cats in the car, Qwilleran let himself into the barn cautiously. There was the reassuring aroma of cleaning fluid and metal polish. And on the bar was a gift-wrapped package – also a scrawled note in the unique style of Mrs Fulgrove: 'A man brung this gift which he left no name.'

It was wrapped in alligator gift wrap with gauzy black ribbon, and a note from Thelma: 'With much thanks for everything; Dick is here and will drop this off at your barn.' The box contained a pair of glazed porcelain parrots in brilliant green with patches of red and yellow.

He put them on the mantel beak-to-beak, like Lolita and Carlotta gossiping in Thelma's aviary.

When the Siamese were brought into the barn and released from the carrying coop, Yum Yum emerged timidly as if she had never been there before, but Koko rushed forth, growling and looking in all directions.

Qwilleran slapped his forehead as the situation became clear. Dick Thackeray had delivered the gift. There was something about Thelma's nephew that Koko found repugnant, and he had sensed his presence before they even reached the barnyard. Likewise, after the champagne reception, Koko had entered the barn snarling – snarling at someone who had been there.

Qwilleran opened a can of smoked oysters, which he diced and spread on two plates.

He was led to wonder if Koko's unfriendly performances corroborated Thelma's outpourings on the park bench at Black Creek. And did they explain the cat's choice of books to push off the shelf?

There was always the possibility, of course, that Koko simply enjoyed dislodging a book and seeing it land on the floor with a *thlunk!* The fact that one was *Poor Richard's Almanac* and the other was *Richard Carvel* might be coincidental. Only one thing was sure. Koko had a passion for smoked oysters. He and Yum Yum retired to the blue cushion on the refrigerator and went to sleep.

Now Qwilleran went to the gazebo with a cheese sandwich and a thermos of coffee and the boxes of letters Janice had put in the van. The cordless phone was purposely left indoors.

Thelma's brother was indeed a good writer, but content was more important. The question was: Were they worthy of publication? They spanned thirty-odd years. Bud had married another graduate veterinarian, Dr Sally, and Pop had set them up in a clinic in Lockmaster. But their greatest joy, it seemed, was their son, Dickie Bird — all the more so because Sally would never be able to have another child. They were enthusiastic about their work. They believed in holistic medicine. Sally was taking a course in acupuncture. Their hobbies were music and hiking. Bud played the flute. Every Sunday they left Dickie Bird with his nanny, and they hiked along the rim of the Black Creek Gorge. Bud's descriptions of the gorge bordered on the poetic. They would sit on a large flat rock and eat energy bars and drink bottled water from their knapsacks.

Dickie Bird, as his parents called him privately, was a handsome boy with a genuine likable personality. He did very well in school, played a little tennis, and was popular with classmates, but he showed no interest in hiking. In high school he preferred the company of his own friends.

Bud wrote, 'Dick has a talent for living beyond his allowance, but we indulge him. He's our only son! And we know he's not into drugs or anything like that. The kids he runs with are all achievers, with plans for professional careers. Dick hasn't decided what he wants to do. He's old enough to drive now, and we're giving him a car for his birthday . . . Sis, do you remember when Pop gave us a movie palace for our birthday?'

Qwilleran's reading was interrupted by a high-decibel howl from the barn. He raced indoors and found Koko prancing in front of the answering machine. The message was an indignant complaint: 'Qwill! Where are you? It's seven o'clock! You were to be here at six!'

'Uh-oh! I'm in the doghouse!' he said to Koko.

The situation was that Polly was in Chicago, and Mildred was in Duluth, and Arch was grilling two porterhouse steaks for a bachelor supper on the deck. Qwilleran thought fast and phoned Wetherby, who lived a city block from the Rikers. It was a long shot, but luckily Wetherby was at home.

'Joe! Do me a favor!' he said with desperation in his voice. 'Run – don't walk – to the Rikers' condo and tell Arch you're there to eat my steak. No explanation! No apology! Just tell him I called from the jail.'

Qwilleran chuckled. He and Arch, in their lifetime of friendship, had survived many a gaffe, bluff, and tiff – with all systems intact.

Now the phone rang and – thinking it was Arch again – he let the machine pick up the message. It was Hixie Rice, calling from the news office.

Returning her call, Qwilleran listened to her exuberant

announcement. 'Qwill! We're getting the opera house for the revue! Next Tuesday! Tickets are going to be two hundred! Isn't that thrilling! I told Mavis I'd notify you. Also, Doug Bethune is printing the programs, so he needs to know the titles of the readings you're going to do.'

Hixie stopped for breath, and Qwilleran asked the unwise question: 'Is there anything I can do?'

'I could really use your input on the subject of the Grand March, Qwill, and the sooner the better. If you could hop up here to the office—'

'If you could hop down here to the barn,' he interrupted, 'I could offer you a drink.'

Hixie Rice was an attractive, spirited woman of unguessable age who was unlucky in love. Qwilleran had first met her Down Below and had followed her exploits like the segments of a soap opera. In the business world, though, her infectious enthusiasm and bright ideas made her a success even when her ideas failed. Qwilleran was always glad to see her.

She arrived at the barn in what Moose Countians would call 'two shakes of a lamb's tail.' 'Where are those adorable cats?' she asked, and they came out to greet her. Everyone liked Hixie.

'What will you have to drink?' Qwilleran asked.

'What are you having?'

'A Q cocktail.'

'I'll have a martini.'

When they settled into the 'seductive' sofas (Hixie's word for them), Qwilleran asked, 'How successful have you been in lining up prominent citizens for the finale?'

'Everyone's cooperating!' she said with her usual exuberance. 'How does this sound? Newspaper columnist, meteorologist, innkeeper, superintendent of schools, prize-winning woodcrafter, a medical doctor, director of the public library, food editor, two professors (retired), and . . . Her Honor, the mayor! The professors are the Cavendish sisters. Jennie is confined to a wheelchair, so she'll ride with two cats in her lap and Ruth will push.'

'Have the rhinestone harnesses been ordered?'

'They're on the way.'

'May I refresh your drink?'

She wriggled to get out of the deep-cushioned sofa. 'No thanks, but you mix a superb martini! What's your secret?'

'Fourteen to one.' Actually he had no dry vermouth, so it was fourteen to zero!

Later that evening, when he phoned Polly in Chicago, he told her about the rhinestone harnesses, the impressive lineup of prominent citizens, and the harmless herbal sedative that would keep the cats calm.

'Oh dear!' she said. 'It sounds like another of Hixie's bright ideas! I hope it all works.'

'Are your conferences progressing well?'

'We've brainstormed, that's all. We toss out whatever enters our heads. It's quite fun. The K Fund people are charming, and there's been much wining and dining. I'll be glad to get home to an egg salad sandwich. Happily,

I'll be leaving Saturday morning and arriving on the noon shuttle flight . . . And I'm bringing you something!'

'What?'

'Wait and see! . . . *A bientôt!*'

'*A bientôt*,' he mumbled. He objected to being on the dark side of a secret.

Eighteen

On Friday morning Qwilleran filed his copy earlier than usual, leading the managing editor to say, 'Is something wrong? Or are you a better person from eating all that broccoli?'

'I have other work to do, Junior! And don't you dare touch a single comma in my copy! After last week's proverb fiasco—'

'I know! I know!' Junior threw up both hands in defense.

The truth was that Qwilleran had an urgent desire to return to Thelma's letters from Bud. A familiar sensation in his upper lip was the forerunner of suspicion, corroborated by Koko's growling and spitting at someone or something that was not present. Qwilleran was convinced that it was Dick who was on what he called 'Koko's spit list.'

First there were errands to do, however, like mailing a letter to England and cashing a check for daily needs.

At the bank Qwilleran found himself in line behind Wetherby. He leaned forward and said quietly, 'Has WPKX started paying you for your services?'

The weatherman turned quickly. 'Hey! Qwill! That was the best steak I ever ate in my life! I'll understudy you any old time!!'

'Have you time for coffee at Lois's?'

'Next!' the teller said impatiently.

After their transactions were completed, the two men walked to Lois's the long way, in order to see what was happening to the opera house. The old stone building was looking noble once more. The boardings had been taken down. There were new doors. At one side of the entrance a carved wood plaque of tasteful size announced THELMA'S FILM CLUB with letters highlighted in gold. The parking lots on either side were freshly paved. And across the street a strip of storefronts was upgraded. Gone were the plumbing fixtures and printshop clutter. An ice-cream bar, antique shop, and gift gallery were moving in. In the center of the row the door leading to the small apartments upstairs was newly lettered: OPERA HOUSE TERRACE.

Wetherby said, 'They're not bad apartments. I visited someone there once. One-bedroom. There's a little upstairs porch all along the back, but good only for raising tomato plants.'

'Have you joined the club?' Qwilleran asked.

'Nah. I'm not into old movies. Did you?'

'Only so I can take guests once in a while. I hear that Thelma's nephew is managing it.'

'Lots a luck,' Wetherby said.

At Lois's they ordered coffee and whatever was freshly baked. It proved to be cinnamon sticky buns.

The implied sneer in Wetherby's last remark supported Qwilleran's growing disenchantment.

He said, 'Did I detect a note of cynicism in your remark about Dick Thackeray?'

'Well . . . you know . . . we were in school together all the way through twelfth grade. Us kids from the Village of Horseradish attended a consolidated school in East Lockmaster – a bunch of country bumpkins among all those rich dudes. I knew Dick when we were pitching pennies in the schoolyard. He always won. In high school I had to work hard to get a B; Dick got all A's. I acted in plays; he hung out with eggheads who were going to be scientists. My sport was track; theirs was playing cards – for money. I had to work my way through college; Dick thought college wasn't necessary; he went traveling. Never did settle down to a career. How long is he going to act as manager of his aunt's Film Club?'

'I see what you mean,' Qwilleran said.

Then they talked about the Kit Kat Revue; how the cats would get along backstage while waiting to go on . . .

what kind of music should be played for the Grand March ... what Jet Stream and Koko would think about rhinestone harnesses.

Wetherby said, 'Well, we'll get a few answers at the rehearsal Monday night.'

The Siamese were waiting anxiously at the barn, knowing their noontime snack was eleven minutes late. Qwilleran fed them and even read a passage from the *Wilson Quarterly* aloud – to make them drowsy. After they had crawled away to some secret nap-nook, Qwilleran took a large dish of ice cream to the gazebo, along with the second box of Thackeray letters.

Bud's letters continued infrequently as he grew older. Most of them recounted unusual cases he and Sally treated in their clinic – a veritable name-dropping of famous race-horses and the winners of dog shows. Once there had been a terrible barn fire, and Bud agonized with the owners. Occasionally Dick would arrive unexpectedly and stay for a week. His ingratiating smile and happy disposition always made him a welcome visitor. Sometimes he had a clever idea for a new business venture and they gladly lent him money, although experience had taught them that it would never be returned but that was all right. He was their only son. What better investment could they make? It was too bad he never wanted to go on a nature walk along the Black Creek Gorge.

Then Sally began to slow down, have bad days, stay home from the clinic. During this period investors offered to buy the clinic and relieve him of a burdensome responsibility. After all, he was in his late seventies. But Sally urged him to keep the clinic that had meant so much to him. Dick came and went. Then Sally just faded away. That was all he had the heart to say. He no longer walked along the gorge. But he was thankful that he had his challenging work – and the health to carry on.

That was the last letter in the box. What had happened to the final letter that Thelma called so beautiful? He phoned the Thackeray house, and Janice answered. Thelma was at the club, she said, working out details.

'I've read the two boxes of letters,' Qwilleran said, 'and the last one seems to be missing.'

'Oh! . . . That's right! She keeps it close by so she can read it. It's getting quite worn from all the folding and unfolding.'

'You should make a photocopy and preserve the original in some special way. Do you have a copier?'

'No, but I could have it done somewhere in town.'

'I have a copier. If you can find the letter, you could bring it over here, and the job could be done in . . . no time.' He congratulated himself for avoiding the Moose County cliché.

Soon the green coupé drove into the barnyard, and he took the cherished letter to his studio for copying while Janice talked to the Siamese and looked at titles on the bookshelf.

'This is a funny title,' she said when Qwilleran came down the ramp. She was looking at *How to Read a Book* by

Dr Mortimer Adler. 'If you can read a book on how-to-read-a-book,' she said, 'why do you need to read this book?'

'Some day I'll lend it to you, and you'll find out . . . I made two copies of the letter and will put one in the box with the others. You can have the other to save wear and tear on the original. Do you have time for a glass of fruit juice?'

He was glad she declined the invitation. He wanted to read Bud's last letter.

Dear Sis,

A miracle happened on this 20th of June – Sally's birthday. For almost a year, I haven't been able to face the beauties of our old hiking trail. Dick is here on one of his infrequent visits – his old room is always ready and waiting for him – but his presence has not succeeded in lightening my heavy heart since the loss of my dear Sally.

Then the miracle happened! The houndmaster at the Kennel Club invited me to go 'walking the hounds.' There are fifty foxhounds that are walked en masse along country roads every day. A kind of loving understanding exists between the master and the hounds. He speaks to them in a firm but gently musical voice. Mr Thomas is his name.

'Come on out now,' he said, and the pack of hounds left the kennel and headed for the road.

'Come this way now.' They followed him to the left.

My job was to bring up the rear and coax stragglers back to the group. Both Mr Thomas and I had whips – but only to crack the ground and get their attention.

There was hardly any traffic on that back road, but when a vehicle appeared, Mr Thomas would say, 'Come over here now,' and they would herd to the right or left. They could read his mind, I was sure. Once, a farmer stopped his truck and said, 'Purtiest thing I ever seen!'

And I was part of it. The countryside was beautiful. The air was fresh and uplifting. I walked with a springy step as the emotional burden of the past year began to disappear.

By the time I returned to the club, and Mr Thomas had said, 'Kennel up now' . . . I wanted to go walking the gorge once more! All the wonders of nature that I enjoyed with my dear Sally came rushing back with love instead of sorrow.

Dick is spending a couple of weeks here, and I even invited him to go along on Sunday. To my delight he agreed and said he would go into town for some hiking shoes.

Dear Sis – Be glad for me. I feel as if an angel dipped a wing over my troubled brow.

With love from Bud

P.S. Why don't you come for a visit? It's been so long! Exchanging snapshots isn't 'where it's at' – to quote Dickie Bird. Don't worry, Sis. I won't make you go hiking.

Slowly and thoughtfully Qwilleran placed the photo-copied letter back in the box. There was a tingling in the roots of his moustache that disturbed him.

He looked at his watch; it was not too late to phone his friend Kip MacDiarmid, editor of the *Lockmaster Ledger*.

'Qwill! Speak of the devil— We were talking about you at the Lit Club last night. They want to know when you're coming down to our meeting again.'

'As a guest? Or do I have to pay for my own dinner?'

'Put it on your expense account,' said the editor.

After the usual amount of banter Qwilleran said, 'I'll be in Lockmaster Monday. Would you be free for lunch? I want to discuss a book I'm thinking of writing, and it would help if you could copy some news clips for me.'

Arrangements were made.

By long experience Qwilleran knew that newspaper-men always know the story-behind-the-story, and it was more often true than false. He also had a ploy for uncover-ing buried facts and/or rumors. 'I'm writing a book,' he would say. Laymen and professionals were always willing – even eager – to talk to the purported author of a book that would never be written.

Nineteen

On Saturday morning Qwilleran drove downtown to buy a flowering plant to celebrate Polly's return from Chicago. He parked in the municipal lot and was walking toward the Main Street stores when the friendly toot-toot of a horn attracted his attention. Fran Brodie lowered her car window and beckoned. 'Have you heard the news?' she asked.

'Is it going to rain?' he asked, although he could tell by her expression that the news was not good.

'I think I'm losing my assistant – after all the time and training I invested in her. I even took her to California on the Thackeray job.'

'What's her reason?' Qwilleran asked.

'She's getting married and may move out of town,

197

where her fiancé is investigating a new job.'

That would be the Holmes girl and her Dr Watson, Qwilleran thought, and it was a legitimate reason, but Fran wanted only sympathy, so he consoled her.

'Amanda will have to spend more time in the studio and less at City Hall.'

'You try telling her that!' Fran replied sourly.

Qwilleran, instead of buying potted tulips, went to Amanda's studio. Lucinda was sitting at the consultation desk, and a young man lounged casually in one of the chairs for clients. But the radiant expression on both faces was not that of a designer-client relationship.

'Hi, Lucinda,' Quilleran said. 'I thought I would browse for a few minutes before picking Polly up at the airport.'

'Hi, Mr Q!' she said, waving a hand with a sparkler on the third finger. 'This is Blake Watson.'

'Hi, Mr Q,' he said, jumping to his feet.

Qwilleran said, 'If that ring means what I think it means, best wishes to you both. What are your plans?'

Lucinda said proudly, 'We'll be married in June, and then move to Minneapolis, if Blake takes the position that's been offered him.'

Blake said, 'They're impressed by my five years with Dr Thurston. That's how well known he was in the profession. But when he died and the clinic changed hands, they started cutting corners.'

'That often happens,' Qwilleran murmured. 'Lucky they didn't buy the Thackeray name.'

'Sure is! ... but you have to meet a plane, and I'm keeping you.'

When Qwilleran drove Polly home from the airport Saturday noon, he asked if she would like to stop for a little lunch at Onoosh's.

'Thanks, but I'd rather go home and collapse and see my Brutus and Catta.'

'I stopped in twice during the week, and they seemed to be in good spirits and amply fed. Your cat-sitter left a report on the kitchen table each morning and filled the automatic feeder for their dinner.'

'Yes, she's very conscientious and absolutely trustworthy. She goes to my church.' Polly glanced at the landscape. 'Everything looks dry. We need rain.'

'Were there any momentous decisions made about the bookstore?'

'Yes and no, but it's all strictly confidential. They don't want it known until the plans are final, and I don't want it known that I'm leaving the library at the end of the year.'

'Then tell me while we're driving,' he said. 'There are no spies in the backseat. I checked.'

Polly was too tired to appreciate the whimsy of his remarks.

'Well, they've definitely decided to build on the site of Eddington's old store. And the realty experts who visited Pickax said that Book Alley is really an alley, and the old store faced the back of the post office with its trucks and loading dock. So the new building should have its entrance on Walnut Street. I didn't tell them about the buried treasure. I didn't want to lose my credibility. You can tell them about that later on.'

As Qwilleran understood it, Eddington's grandfather was a blacksmith who moonlighted as a pirate and buried his loot under a tree in the backyard. After he died – or failed to come home – his wife discovered his secret and had the yard paved with cobblestones. She told the story to Eddington on her deathbed. Whether or not he believed it, he covered the cobblestones with asphalt and it would be one of the legends reported in Qwilleran's collection of *Short & Tall Tales*.

Qwilleran said, 'The thought of the Klingenschoen Foundation digging for pirate's treasure under the parking lot before building the bookstore strikes me as highly amusing. The question is: Whether it is better to dig and be disappointed – or not dig and be forever unsure.'

They rode in silence for a while, considering the options.

'I admit I had stage fright about brainstorming with the Klingenschoen think tank, but they were all relaxed and jolly, and it was fun.

'There were suggestions like . . . No food, no gifts, no greeting cards . . . A special-events room for book reviews, signings, and literary discussions, with guest speakers . . . Sponsorship of a Literary Club . . . Donation of a percentage of each sale to the Literacy Council . . . No videos . . . A room for large-print and recorded books . . . One wing of the store for preowned books, to be named the Eddington Smith Room . . . Children's programs without lollipops . . . Purchase of the vacant lots across from the entrance – to turn into a grassy park.'

'Did you broach your pet idea?' Qwilleran asked.

'Yes, I told them that in the nineteenth century, the stores on Main Street had living quarters on the second floor, and it was considered smart for a merchant to live over the store. That changed with the coming of the automobile and suburban living, and the upstairs rooms are now used for storage and offices. Today we have a shortage of downtown apartments for singles and young marrieds. Also, there are professionals living around the county who would appreciate a pied-à-terre downtown. And there are MCCC faculty members who come up here to teach two or three days a week and would prefer a studio apartment to a hotel room. And the idea of an apartment *over a bookstore* with a view of a grassy park would appeal to intellectuals . . . Well, Qwill, imagine my surprise when they applauded!'

'No wonder, Polly. It was good reasoning, and it came from a good-looking woman with a mesmerizing voice!'

She demurred modestly, and for a while they drove in the preoccupied silence that can be enjoyed by two close friends.

'What did you bring me from Chicago?' he asked.

'A Prokofiev opera on CD. I'm dying to hear it on the barn stereo.'

'We'll play it tomorrow – after brunch at Tipsy's.'

'It's in Russian, of course, based on a novel by Dostoevsky – all about scandal, intrigue, falsity, and greed.'

'Sounds just like Pickax,' he said.

Tipsy's Tavern was a roadhouse in a sprawling log cabin – with a yardful of hens and a menu of two dozen interesting egg dishes. Qwilleran ordered ham and eggs with home fries; Polly chose poached eggs on corn pancakes topped with melted cheddar and served with homemade apple chutney. She said it was good but they made the mistake of leaving the raisins whole. 'It's important for the raisins to lose their identity,' she said.

After that, they went to the barn to listen to the new recording. Qwilleran had only recently become interested in opera, and it was chiefly to please Polly and show off the barn's magnificent acoustics. The Siamese always joined the audience – more for togetherness than appreciation of music. The first soprano aria always had them covering their ears with their hind legs.

Before the music started, Qwilleran served glasses of pineapple juice on a Shaker-style wood tray.

'Where's your silver tray?' Polly asked.

'I haven't been able to find it since cleaning day. I left it out for Mrs Fulgrove to polish, and she has a habit of putting things away where they don't belong. I haven't had time to do a thorough search as yet.'

Polly said, 'I was unable to find a libretto in English. I have the scenario, though. It's in four acts.'

The action took place in the gambling casino of a spa, where men and women won and lost fortunes, borrowed money to pay debts, trusted no one, lied to support their addiction. An aged woman gambled away the fortune that her heirs were waiting to inherit.

Koko hated it! The first act had barely begun, when he raised an indignant howl and continued to scold the speakers until he was banished to the gazebo.

'He doesn't like Prokofiev,' Qwilleran explained. But he wondered, How could that cat sense the theme of an opera titled *The Gambler*?

Monday morning Qwilleran drove to Lockmaster to meet Kip MacDiarmid at Inglehart House, a restaurant operated by Bushy's ex-wife. Inglehart was a famous name in that town, and this was a historic mansion on the main thoroughfare. The conversation started in a predictable manner.

Qwilleran said, 'How's Moira? . . . Are you taking any trips? . . . Did you decide to get a new puppy? . . . What's new at the Lit Club? . . . We need rain, don't we?'

Kip said, 'The Lit Club enjoyed *Cool Koko's Almanac* . . . How's Bushy doing? I see his credit line. Moira wants me to ask if he ever remarried . . . Are you taking any trips? . . . How's Polly? . . . Now what's this book you have in mind?'

Qwilleran said, 'A bio of the Thackeray twins, born in Moose County about eight decades ago. Thelma has just returned after a successful career in California; you know about Thurston's animal clinic.'

'It was ahead of its time,' Kip explained. 'Moira used to take our pets there, and she said Dr Thurston was something special – not only his skills but also his caring attitude. The Thackeray Estate sold it to a consortium, and it's now the Whinny Hills Animal Clinic.'

'What I can't find out is the cause of Dr Thurston's death. That's why I'm here.'

'I've brought you copies of all the clips in the file. The rumormongers had a field day. They considered it suicide because he was depressed after the death of his wife. But it was officially ruled an accident. A recent rain – slippery rocks on the edge of the gorge – perhaps a momentary dizzy spell. He was getting on in years.'

'Who were his heirs?' Qwilleran asked.

'He left his house to the county for a horse museum, his liquid assets to his sister, and the clinic to his son, Dick.'

'What's Dick's line of work?'

'Good question. He's always pursued his business interests in other parts of the country, coming home to visit his parents at intervals . . . I might add that he was involved in a fracas a couple of years ago when he applied for a permit to operate a motorbike dirt-racing track. He had acquired some acreage in the western part of the county, near some posh condos. The neighbors rose up in arms. They virtually rioted at a meeting of the county commissioners. They bombarded the *Ledger* with angry letters to the editor, opposing the proposed venture on grounds of noise, dust, weekend traffic on quiet country roads, disturbance of the Sabbath peace, and lessening of property values.'

Qwilleran shook his head sympathetically. 'This must have been painful to Dr Thurston.'

'His clients and admirers considered it an outrage, and the scuttlebutt was that Dick acquired the acreage as payment of a gambling debt owed him. The doctor had never accepted the notion that Dick was a compulsive gambler, but – sub rosa – it was considered a fact.'

Quilleran felt a tingling in the roots of his moustache as he recalled Koko's tantrum during the Russian opera. 'What was the outcome?'

'Dick disappeared from the local scene, and the acreage was put up for sale. The consensus was that his father paid him to leave town. It must have been a crushing blow, so soon after the death of Dr Sally.'

'Dick's former schoolmates said he used to be very popular. Too bad he turned out to be a blot on the Thackeray escutcheon,' Qwilleran said.

'Yes, he made a few enemies in Lockmaster during the motorbike episode.' The editor lowered his voice. 'In fact, when the suicide rumor was ruled out, there were quite a few hints of patricide. Dick was so quick to sell his father's clinic that the accident on the gorge trail began to look fishy to many locals.

'Dick told the police that his father went out at day-break

as a matter of course – to avoid the crowds of Sunday hikers. He said he would be home by noon and they would go out for Sunday brunch at the Palomino Paddock. When the doc didn't return by three o'clock, Dick notified the police . . . It's all in these clippings I've brought you. The amateur sleuths even brought up the question of hiking shoes. Dick claimed he never went hiking; a local store claimed that he bought a pair of hiking shoes the day before his dad's accident . . . It would have been ludicrous if it weren't so tragic.'

On Monday evening, the shuttle flight bounced to a stop, and the passengers emerged, carrying briefcases or shopping bags. A husky gray-haired man carrying a duffel bag came down the ramp with quick glances to right and left.

Qwilleran stepped forward. 'Mr Simmons? Qwilleran's Limousine Service.'

The duffel bag was transferred to the other hand and the right hand shot out. 'You're the famous Qwill! I'm Mark Simmons.'

'Welcome to Moose County! Do you have other luggage?'

'One bag. Thelma told me to bring my tux.'

'What does the bag look like?'

'Blue nylon. Red stripe.'

'Hi, Mr Q!' the baggage handler said. 'Which one is yours?'

'Blue nylon. Red stripe. But I'll take anything that looks good.'

The visitor was filling his lungs. 'The air smells good. What do you do to it?'

'Secret formula. Don't breathe too deeply or you'll float away.'

As soon as they were in the SUV and headed for Pickax, the conversation started and never stopped.

'How d'you like our Thelma, Qwill?'

'She's a grand lady! But she's not yours! She's ours, and we let California have her for fifty-five years. You're not a native of the West Coast?'

'Sure ain't! I'm a Hoosier. Met a girl from L.A. when I was in the armed services and followed her out there. Perfect marriage. Two sons, one daughter – all married. Grandkids on the way. Can't complain. Had my good years. Widowed six years ago. Retired for five. Do a few security jobs. That's how I met Thelma.'

'I understand you've been a great help to her, Mark.'

'Call me Simmons. That's what I was in the Army and that's what I was on the police force. Only Thelma adds the Mister.'

'Thelma and *The New York Times*,' Qwilleran muttered.

'Thelma's a smart woman, but I don't see why – at her time of life – she should come here to help her nephew, a grown man . . . You've met him, Qwill. What do you think of him?'

'He smiles a lot.'

'Sure does! . . . What's that thing over there?' He pointed to a tall, weatherbeaten shack.

'A shaft house. It marks the site of an abandoned mine. There were ten mines here. When they closed, Moose County went into a three-decade depression.'

'Thelma told me about it. Her dad – she calls him Pop – was a poor potato farmer until he got into the potato chip business.'

Qwilleran glanced at his passenger, looking for a glimmer of tongue-in-cheek or twinkle-in-eye. There was none. The potato chip myth had reached the West Coast.

Qwilleran asked, 'Did Thelma tell you about my barn?'

'Sure did. I'm looking forward to seeing it.'

'Then I have a suggestion,' Qwilleran said. 'Since Thelma's spare room is occupied by her nephew while the Film Club is getting under way, she planned to put you up at a hotel, but there's a vacant apartment near my barn that you may as well use. It's only a few blocks from Pleasant Street, and she'll give you the keys to one of her vehicles, so you can come and go as you please.'

'Sounds good,' Simmons said. 'Better than being holed up with two females, five parrots, and a guy who smiles all the time. Much as I like Janice's cooking, I have to say that I've eaten enough of her waffles to sink a battleship. Have you met Janice?'

'Oh, yes. She's a nice young woman – very thoughtful and devoted to Thelma. She said she would come to the apartment and make up the bed, hang towels, and leave a little something in the refrigerator for you.'

'That sounds like Janice,' Simmons said.

At a certain point on Main Street Qwilleran pulled

to the curb. 'Look down that street. What does it look like?'

'Disneyland.'

'That's Pleasant Street, and Thelma has the third house on the left.'

At a traffic circle, Qwilleran turned into the driveway of a large fieldstone building. 'That was once a mansion filled with antiques, but it was gutted by fire . . . Arson, you'll be interested to know . . . Now it's a small theatre for live productions . . . The former carriage house at the rear had stalls for four carriages and servants' quarters upstairs. That's where you're going to bunk while you're here . . . I suggest we drop your luggage there and then drive through the woods to my barn and have a drink.'

'I may never return to California,' the guest said.

'How do you feel about cats? I have two Siamese.'

'Cats, dogs, hamsters, white mice! My kids had 'em all. Thelma hates cats!'

'I know. They were kept out of sight during the champagne reception here.'

They drove through the dense woods and emerged in a clearing, where the four-story octagonal barn loomed like a medieval castle.

'I don't believe it!' Simmons said.

'Wait till you see the interior!'

Qwilleran was accustomed to the gasps, gulps, and speechlessness of first-time visitors, but this Hoosier from Hollywood seemed stunned by the vast spaces, the balconies and ramps, the rafters four stories overhead, the large white cube in the middle of it all.

'How about a drink?' Qwilleran asked.

The guest came out of his trance long enough to say, 'A little bourbon and water.'

Twenty

Thelma's Mr Simmons was enjoying the barn so much – and the attentions of the Siamese – that he was reluctant to leave when Janice came to pick him up. They were going to dinner at the Grist Mill and Qwilleran was invited. He declined, saying he had to attend a very important meeting.

It was the dress rehearsal for the Kit Kat Revue, and it proved Qwilleran's contention that a cat trained to walk on a leash will walk where he wants to walk and not where he's told to walk. Wetherby's Jet Stream acted as if he had fleas and sat down center-stage to scratch. Nick Bamba's Nicodemus kept sniffing invisible spots on the floor and baring his fangs in an expression of disgust. It was decided that all cats would be carried or otherwise

211

conveyed. Apart from that, all went well. The creative dance club from the high school and the tumbling team rehearsed to get the feel of the stage – and the feel of their furry costumes with tails.

Bushy was there to project his slides of kittens on the backdrop. The idea was to show a different slide for each act. He had photographed them in all the kitten colonies on Pleasant Street: tiny creatures with large ears and floppy feet and comical markings. There was a mother cat suckling her brood, playing games with her soft paw, fondly carrying them around by the scruff of the neck.

Then there was a run-through of the grand finale. All cats had been brought to the opera house in carriers, and they would remain cooped up until it was time for them to go on – sequestered in the various dressing rooms and offices backstage. It was hoped that this would prevent squabbles.

Hixie said to the prominent citizens who awaited briefing, 'Until the finale, it will have been a program of lighthearted song and dance and humorous verse. Suddenly the mood changes. A recording of Elgar's "Pomp and Circumstance" fills the hall, signifying a solemn occasion, and the procession of prominent citizens begins – one by one – walking with dignity – carrying a beloved pet.'

Qwilleran said, 'Suppose there are whistles and shouts from the audience?'

'They'll be instructed to limit responses to polite applause,' Hixie said. 'When the last cat is off the stage, there will be whistles and shouts and a standing ovation.'

'What should we wear?' someone asked.

'Anything of neutral color – gray, tan, brown, black – whatever will show off your cat's coloring.'

'What about the harmless herbal sedative?'

'We have an envelope for each of you, containing a capsule that is to be broken open and the powder sprinkled on the cat's meal beforehand.'

Someone said, 'Do you have any extras? I could use one myself!'

The following evening, supporters of the Kit Kat Agenda would have a preview of the renovated opera house, forty-eight hours before Thelma's gala first night. It was a memory to boast about in years to come – for more reasons than one.

The red carpet was on the sidewalk. There was a canvas marquee at the entrance. A cordon of press photographers waited. And a flock of MCCC students in KIT KAT T-shirts would park cars, earning credits for community service.

It was a black-tie event, and patrons arrived in dinner jackets and long dresses, to be seated in comfortable swivel chairs at round cabaret tables. Then more students in KIT KAT T-shirts served chilled splits of champagne and hollow-stemmed plastic wine glasses.

When the lights dimmed, the master of ceremonies, Wetherby Goode, welcomed them in his irreverent style, then sat down at the piano and played 'Kitten on the Keys.' It was a finger-tickling number that had been

213

played by Moose County piano students for seventy-five years. Wetherby played it faster.

Then Hannah MacLeod sang Noel Coward's 'Chase Me, Charlie, Over the Garden Wall.' Qwilleran read T. S. Eliot's whimsical verses about Jellicle cats and such famous felines as Skimbleshanks and Bustopher Jones. The cat dancers danced and the cat tumblers tumbled. In between, the six-foot-eight Derek Cuttlebrink, Moose County's gift to country western, loped into the spotlight, strummed his guitar, and sang original lyrics, such as:

Kit Kat kittens have love to give,
Kit Kat kittens are fun!
A handful of fur, just learning to purr —
Two are better than one.

All the while, the audience was enchanted by the changing background of kittenlife.

Then the stage blacked out for a moment, and the sonorous chords of 'Pomp and Circumstance' filled the hall and a disembodied voice said, 'During the following presentation of cats marching to save kittens, please limit your response to polite applause.'

The solemn procession began. Each pair was announced by the 'voice.' Each pair moved slowly across the stage without acknowledging the polite applause.

'Her Honor, Mayor Amanda Goodwinter . . . and Quincy.'

'The WPKX meteorologist, Wetherby Goode . . . and Jet Stream.'

'Food editor for the *Moose County Something*, Mildred Riker . . . and Toulouse.'

'Prize-winning woodcrafter Douglas Bethune . . . and Winston Churchill.'

'Dr Diane Lanspeak . . . and Hypo.'

'Nutcracker Innkeeper, Nick Bamba . . . and Nicodemus.'

'Professors Jennie and Ruth Cavendish . . . with Pinky and Quinky, short for Propinquity and Equanimity.'

'High-school custodian for forty years, Pat O'Dell . . . with Wrigley.'

'Superintendent of schools, Lyle Compton . . . and Socrates.'

'Director of the public library, Polly Duncan . . . and Brutus.'

'And last but not least, columnist James Mackintosh Qwilleran . . . and Kao K'o Kung.'

The polite applause reached a climax. Murmurs of enjoyment became a roar of approval. Someone shouted, 'Cool Koko.'

The cat riding on Qwilleran's shoulder stared with alarm at the darkened hall. Then, blinded by stage lights, he sprang into the air, wrenching the leash from Qwilleran's grasp. He flew off the stage into the first row of tables. The shouts and screams only alarmed him more, and he went flying around the hall with leash trailing – jumping over heads, landing on backs and shoulders, while champagne bottles and glasses scattered.

'Close the doors!' Qwilleran yelled. Thwarted in his escape, Koko turned and scampered across more tables and patrons, until something stopped him abruptly.

'TREAT!' Qwilleran thundered, and the cat returned to the stage, pouncing on a few more heads and a few more shoulders.

By the time Qwilleran had grabbed the frantic animal, the other cats had gone home, and their rhinestone harnesses were on a table backstage. Koko's was added to the pile, and he was stuffed into his carrier – to wait while Qwilleran helped the others clean up.

Hixie, the MacLeods, and Mavis Adams were picking up empty bottles and plastic glasses. Fortunately, nothing had spilled or broken. Cabaret tables and chairs had simply to be restored to their orderly rows.

Hixie said, 'That Koko really knows how to bring down the house!'

Qwilleran grunted with irritation. 'His performance won't do any good for the adopt-a-kitten campaign.'

'Did you give him the sedative?'

'I sprinkled it on his food, as you instructed.'

Then he had a sudden hollow feeling. He tossed the carrier in the backseat and drove to the barn in a hurry. Leaving Koko in the car, he rushed indoors to look at the cats' plates under the kitchen table.

Both plates were licked clean. Had Koko eaten the wrong one? Where was Yum Yum? He found her on the hearth rug, lying flat-out on her side. He spoke her name, and she raised her head and gave him a glassy stare . . . It was all evident. Koko had sensed that something unacceptable had been added to his dish. He pushed Yum Yum aside and ate the contents of her plate and she consumed the harmless herbal sedative. She liked it!

In a few minutes Polly phoned from Indian Village.

'Qwill! What happened? Wasn't Koko sedated?'

'You won't believe this!' he said. 'The cats never change plates. Koko's is always on the right, and he knows right from left, but he detected a foreign substance. Somehow he convinced Yum Yum to change plates. She not only got the sedative but a larger serving of food than usual. She's bushed!!'

The first week of the Film Club would also become noted for the 'electrical storm of the century' in Moose County. According to the meteorologist, a weather front was stalled over Canada, gathering fury by the day. Bushy postponed the cruise for Thelma, Janice, and their guest; Qwilleran hunkered down in the snug safety of the barn; the Siamese were nervous.

Then there was a phone call from Simmons.

'Are you busy, Qwill? Thelma wants me to deliver something.' A few minutes later the green coupé pulled into the barnyard.

'Are you comfortable in the carriage house apartment?' Qwilleran asked.

'Very! I'll hate to leave.'

'Don't be in a hurry,' Qwilleran said. 'It's vacant for

the month of May. Be my guest . . . How about a little bourbon and water?'

'Won't hurt. And may help.' He handed over a plastic shopping bag.

Peering into it, Qwilleran said, 'I don't believe this. Where did she find it?'

'It's a long story,' his guest said.

After they settled into the deep-cushioned sofas, there was the usual talk about the weather. The big electrical storm was on the way. Koko's fur was standing on end as if electrified. He kept washing over his ear – with his left paw, not his right. Then he would tear up the ramp at ninety miles an hour – then race back down again. Yum Yum had already burrowed under the hearth rug.

'Let's hear the long story,' Qwilleran suggested casually.

'Well!' said his guest. 'Thelma went to the club in early morning, when Dick was not there – to see if everything was being done right. He had furnished his private office lavishly, she thought. Included was a small bar with several bottles of liquor. There were also two cut-glass decanters. She wondered if they were Waterford. There was a silver tray. She wondered if it was sterling. Turning it over, she found your name inscribed . . . She decided not to mention it to Dick. She would just take it. And here it is!'

Qwilleran thought, It figures! . . . The cleaning crew was here . . . I was helping Bushy shoot hats . . . Dick delivered a gift . . . he saw the tray Mrs Fulgrove had polished . . .

'Well! Thank you! What else can I say?'

Simmons said, 'You can agree with me that the guy's a kleptomaniac! Thelma's finally getting that idea. In fact, she went through Dick's desk, looking for a valuable object that disappeared from her house, but all she found was a handgun in the bottom drawer. She wondered if it was registered.'

'All very interesting, Simmons. What was the valuable object?'

'A wristwatch of Pop's that she'd had on her dressing table for forty years! It was a gold Rolex with winding stem.'

'May I refresh your drink?'

Simmons sipped in thoughtful silence for a while, as Yum Yum played with his shoelace. Then he said suddenly, 'Do you use a pocket tape recorder, Qwill?'

'All the time.'

'I've brought one for Thelma. A woman of her age and wealth and position should have one on her person at all times. She's had a couple of run-ins with Smiley and who knows what that four-flusher has up his sleeve. To tell the truth, Qwill, I'm worried about Thelma . . . She seems to think she put him in his place, but can he be trusted? He shows all the symptoms of a compulsive gambler. He could turn to crime to pay off gambling debts – or get wiped out if he defaults. Thelma won't accept the fact that he's a gambler, any more than she'll admit that her pop was a bootlegger. Why? Is it because she's so protective of her image?'

'You knew about the bootlegging?' Qwilleran asked.

'I know that this coastline was a major port of entry for contraband from Canada, which is more than you can say for potato chips.'

Qwilleran said, 'Denial seems to run in the family. I've read all her brother's letters, and he mentions Dick's financial troubles but never his gambling, although it's considered a fact among those who claim to know.'

'Ever since his father died, Smiley has been coming to California and buttering up his aunt.'

'Yow!' Koko howled with piercing intensity, and at the same moment blue-white lightning flashed in the many odd-shaped windows of the barn, followed immediately by the crack and rumble of thunder that reverberated in the vast interior. The wind howled. The rain lashed the walls of the barn.

Conversation was drowned out by the tumult above, and the visitor grasped an arm of the sofa and waited for the roof to cave in overhead.

Gradually the intervals between lightning flashes and thunderclaps widened, as the storm moved on to another target, and Qwilleran said, 'You have your mud slides and earthquakes. We have our northern hurricanes, and if you liked this, just wait and see what we do with snow!'

The day after the storm, Wetherby Goode said to his listeners on WPKX: 'It was fun while it lasted, wasn't it, folks? There's some flooding caused by overloaded storm sewers, but it was the good drenching rain that we hoped for. Now you can take a shower and water the geraniums without feeling guilty, and the weather will smile on the gala opening of Thelma's Film Club. All the first-nighters will be dressed up, and I'll be wearing my new cuff links . . .'

Twenty-one

On the opening night, Qwilleran and Polly were among those absent. He had explained to Thelma that it was more important to sell their seats to enthusiastic first-nighters. She understood.

Actually they were more interested in the following week's offering – the 1930 talkie release of Eugene O'Neill's prize-winning drama, *Anna Christie*. It was the film in which Garbo's throaty voice was heard on the silver screen for the first time, saying, *Give me viskey, baby, and don't be stingy.*

Qwilleran observed opening-night amenities, however, by sending Thelma a long telegram to the theatre and a dozen red roses to her home.

He and Polly dined at the Grist Mill – at a second

seating following one for early show-goers. Derek Cuttlebrink seated them at the table beneath the scythe. He said, 'The lobster curry's good tonight.'

Qwilleran said, 'Does that mean it's usually bad? Or did you sell too little at the first seating – and you're stuck with it?'

Derek smirked and said, 'For that remark you get a fly in your soup.'

Polly said, 'I hope the boss doesn't overhear this exchange of pleasantries.'

Elizabeth Hart, the owner, was heading for their table. 'Polly, so good to see you! I know you love curry. Try the Lobster Calcutta! . . . Qwill, thank you for sending Thelma to us! She's delivering the hats Sunday, because she's involved with her Film Club till then. We'll open the exhibit the following Saturday. A whole fleet of yachts will be coming over from Grand Island. The media will love it. And we're having a New York model here to model the hats and pose for photographs!'

Both Qwilleran and Polly ordered Lobster Calcutta and enjoyed it. Then he told her about finding the silver tray.

'Where was it?' she asked with concern.

'In a plastic shopping bag.'

'That's a good idea. Mrs Fulgrove knows what she's doing. It will keep the tray from tarnishing so fast. Every time you use metal polish on your tray, you know, it loses a minuscule bit of the silver surface.'

Then he told her about his pleasant visit with Thelma's

Mr Simmons – but not what they talked about. He said, 'His first name is Mark.'

'I'm very fond of that name,' she said. 'My father used to say that anyone named Matthew, Mark, Luke, or John has a built-in advantage over the Georges and Walters. His name was Orville.'

Qwilleran said, 'I've often thought I should write a column on the naming of offspring: Why parents give them the names they do . . . how many persons go through life with a name they don't like. My mother named me Merlin! One man I know narrowly escaped being named Melrose. And how about the fashions in names that change from generation to generation. No girl babies are named Thelma in the twenty-first century. Yet there was once a vogue for female names with "th" in the spelling: Martha, Bertha, Dorothy, Edith, Faith, Ethel, Samantha, Judith . . .'

Polly said, 'Sometimes, Qwill, you sound exactly like my father!'

The next day was a workday, and so Qwilleran took Polly home directly after dinner. By the time he arrived at the barn, Koko was doing his grasshopper routine, meaning a message was on the answering machine.

It was from Janice. 'Qwill, I need to talk to you. Important. Call me anytime before midnight.'

He phoned her immediately. 'Is something wrong, Janice?'

'Very sad!' she said in a sorrowful voice. 'A message

came for Mr Simmons while he was at the club. His daughter in California was in a car crash and is hospitalized in critical condition. He's flying home tomorrow.'

'What a shame!' Qwilleran said. 'Shall I drive him to the airport?'

'That would help. I'd drive him, but I have to be available for Thelma. There are problems at the club, you know, during its first week. So it's very kind of you, Qwill.'

'Not at all. It's the least I can do.'

This would be his last chance to talk with Thelma's confidant, adviser, and self-appointed watchdog.

Early Friday morning Qwilleran picked up the troubled father and asked, 'Any news from the hospital?'

'I can't get any information. What happened? Where did it happen? Whose fault was it? She's always been a careful driver. What's the nature of her injuries? I didn't sleep a wink last night. I have a thirty-two-year-old daughter with two kids – who is hospitalized two thousand miles away. I can't worry about an eighty-two-year-old woman with all the money in the world, who's going to leave it to a relative who's a nogoodnik.'

'Forget about Thelma,' Qwilleran said. 'I'll step in and do what needs to be done. But I'll need information from you.'

'For one thing, she's given me power of attorney in California, and I told her to name a local person. But so far nothing has been done. When she came here, full of family feeling and generosity, she made a new will, leaving everything to Smiley! A big mistake! It should be changed before it's too late. She admires you, and you could talk some sense into her head! She's a smart, successful, independent, opinionated woman, but she has this simpering sentimentality about her "dear Bud" who played the flute and loved animals and was so good to his son, giving him everything he wanted . . . and her "dear Pop" who invented a new kind of potato chip and was so good to his children. He left her his gold Rolex wristwatch, and she kept it wound for forty years. It has always been on her dressing table. It disappeared recently. Go figure.'

'One question, Simmons. Did you hear about the kidnapping of the parrots shortly after Thelma arrived?'

'No!' was the thundering reply. 'Why didn't she tell me?'

'She was afraid – or embarrassed. I wormed it out of her assistant. It happened on the Sunday of the big welcoming party. Two days before, she had been pictured with two parrots on the front page of the *Something*. But I say that had nothing to do with it. I say it was an inside job. Someone knew about her intense fondness for those birds. Someone knew the family would be out of the house – in fact, all of Pleasant Street was attending the party . . . with one exception. The O'Dells left early, and they saw a delivery van drive around behind the Thackeray house and leave a few minutes later.

'Someone knew that large, talkative birds require caging and covering. Someone knew about Thelma's fabulous jewelry collection, hidden on the premises. The ransom demand specified an instant payoff – or else! Dick made himself a hero by making the transaction and bringing the parrots back alive.'

'And the girls didn't suspect him?'

'If they did, Thelma chose to forget it . . . but there's more to the story. On that same night, two vans met on a country road in Bixby County, and large square containers were transferred from one to the other. The sheriff decided they must have been TV sets stolen in a recent burglary at a television store. Before leaving, the driver of the loaded van shot and killed the other. I maintain that the shooter was Dick, and he drove off with the ransom as well as the birds. No doubt he knows a fence who handles stolen jewelry.'

Simmons said, 'Someone's got to warn that woman!'

'It would be more logical for a longtime friend and security aide to break the news,' Qwilleran said. 'If you agree, I'll give you some more ammunition . . . When Bud Thackeray fell to his death in the Black Creek Gorge, it was ruled officially to be an accident. But there was a discrepancy between what Dick told the police and what Bud wrote in his last letter to Thelma. Dick, visiting his father, agreed to go hiking with him and would even buy some hiking boots. Yet, the newspaper clippings have Dick waiting for his father to come home from hiking, so they could go out to lunch.'

'If I wanted to be a devil's advocate, Qwill, I could say that the reluctant hiker changed his mind. But, from what I know of this particular devil, he has mud on his boots.'

* * *

The day after Simmons's sudden departure, two days after the opening of the Film Club, and three days after the great electrical storm, Bushy phoned Qwilleran's barn. 'I'm in your neighborhood. Want to hear the latest installment in the Bushland-Thackeray story?'

Qwilleran knew the photographer had sent Thelma glossy prints of her and the parrots.

He knew Bushy had further ingratiated himself by making a print of her brother's portrait – on matte paper suitable for framing.

He knew she had sat for her own portrait in Bushy's studio, after which she said, 'It's the best likeness I've ever had. He captured the way I *feel*!'

Now what?

When Bushy arrived, they went to the gazebo with a thermal coffeepot and a plate of shortbread from the Scottish Bakery.

Bushy said, 'There's nothing wrong with shortbread that couldn't be improved with chocolate frosting and chopped walnuts.'

'They'll never let you into Scotland again, mon! Are you still wowing the potato chip heiress, Bushy?'

'Well, she told me she thinks balding men are sexy. I call her Lady Thelma, and she calls me Mr Bushy. And yesterday she asked me to do a strange favor. She gave me a green card to the late-night show at the Film Club and asked me to do a little spying. That's my word for it. She wanted to know what kind of people attend and how they behave. She said everyone at the early show was appreciative and well mannered.'

'Did you go?'

'I told her I'd be tied up yesterday but I'd go tonight. She told me not to talk to anyone at the club . . . What d'you think, Qwill? Doesn't it sound like she suspects some kind of monkey business at the late show?'

'I believe the apartment dwellers across the street have complained about noise and rowdyism at three in the morning. I'll be curious to know what you find out . . . By the way, has she seen the prints of the hat shots?'

'Yeah, and she flipped over them!'

'Her nephew and Janice are transporting the hats up to Mooseville tomorrow, and I'm driving Thelma. So maybe I'll have something to report.'

The twenty-four hatboxes were wedged tightly into Thelma's van on Sunday afternoon. Thelma was as excited as a fond parent seeing her child play the lead in a high-school production of *My Fair Lady*. They took off with the van in the lead; Janice had driven up there before and knew the route. Once they were on Sandpit Road, it was straight going to Mooseville.

In an attempt to calm Thelma's nerves, Qwilleran tried to entertain her with legends of Mooseville: the Sand Giant who lives in the dune overlooking the town and can be heard to grumble when angered . . . and the mysterious fate of the *Jenny Lee*, a fishing boat owned by Bushy's ancestors . . . and—

'Why are those ditches filled with water?' she asked.

'Those are drainage ditches that keep the farmers' fields from being flooded after a heavy rain. You'll notice a lot of farm equipment on this road.'

A large tractor was lumbering ahead of them at twenty miles an hour.

'You learn to be patient when you drive through farming country, and you don't complain about mud on the road. This tractor won't be with us long; it's just transferring from one field to another.'

It was a two-lane country road, paved but muddy from the treads of farm equipment.

Qwilleran was following the Thackeray van, in front of which was the slow tractor.

Dick Thackeray, driving the van, was not patient. Several times he pulled into the southbound lane in an attempt to pass the slow-moving vehicle, but there was always a southbound vehicle that forced him back in line.

Qwilleran stopped talking and watched the maneuvering with apprehension. 'Don't try it, buddy,' he said under his breath. Dick tried it. He pulled out of line and accelerated. The tractor driver, from his high perch, waved him back. There was a pickup coming south. Its driver leaned on his horn. Dick kept on going – faster.

Thelma cried, *'What is that fool doing?'*

At the last minute, realizing he couldn't make it, Dick veered left onto the southbound shoulder. It was muddy. The van slid toward the ditch, then toppled over into the water.

'Oh my God!' Thelma screamed. 'My hats! . . . *Janice!*'

All traffic had stopped. Thelma was fumbling with her safety belt.'

'No! Stay here!' Qwilleran was calling 911 on the cell phone. The truck driver could be seen doing the same. Thelma was fumbling for the door handle, and he grabbed her left forearm so tightly that she cried out in pain.

The farmer had jumped down and was heading for the van, which was upside down and half submerged. The truck driver waved all approaching traffic to the north-bound lane – to keep the road open for emergency vehicles. In a minute or two their sirens could be heard; the First Responders . . . a sheriff's patrol . . . the Rescue Squad . . . two ambulances, one from each direction . . . another patrol car . . . a tow truck with a winch.

Qwilleran had released his grip, and Thelma covered her face with her hands and moaned, 'That fool! That fool!'

What could he say? How could he comfort her? He had seen the alligator-print boxes float away in the muddy ditch, then sink. He spoke her name, and there was no answer. Fearing she was in shock, he called to a deputy:

'She saw the accident. Family members are in the van. I'm worried. She's in her eighties.'

A medic came to check her vital signs.

'She's okay,' he reported to Qwilleran. 'She's angry that's all. Madder'n a wet hen!'

The accident victims were lifted from the wreck and put on stretchers, to be whisked by ambulance to the Pickax hospital.

Qwilleran said to Thelma, 'They both seemed to be conscious. I'll call the hospital after a while. Meanwhile I should make a few phone calls. Excuse me.' He stepped out of the car, taking the cell phone and a county phone book from the pocket in the door.

First he called Elizabeth Hart, who was shocked, then concerned about Thelma, then dismayed over the ruined plans.

He notified Thelma's physician, Diane Lanspeak, at home in Indian Village.

He also called Celia O'Dell, who had been a volunteer care-giver and knew exactly what to do and say. She said she would be standing by. She was waiting for them when they returned to Pleasant Street. She asked Thelma if she would like a cup of cocoa.

'All I want is to sit in my Pyramid for a while.'

Soon, Dr Diane phoned. She had called the hospital and learned that the two accident victims were being treated and released.

Qwilleran huffed into his moustache. He was not eager to face Thelma's fool nephew and mouth the usual polite claptrap, and he was glad when Celia said her husband would pick them up.

It had not been Qwilleran's idea of a pleasant Sunday afternoon in May.

And it was not over!

When he returned to the barn, the self-appointed monitor of the answering machine was going wild. It was mystifying how that cat could tell the difference between an important message and a nuisance call. Could he sense urgency in the tone of voice?

The first message was from Simmons: 'Sorry to miss your call. I've been baby-sitting with the grandkids. My daughter has a fractured pelvis. Painful, but could be worse. As soon as things straighten out, I'll read the riot act to Thelma – tell her what I learned from you about the kidnapping and her brother's so-called accident. She should dump that guy!'

Qwilleran thought, Wait till he hears about the hats!

The message from Bushy was his espionage report. 'The late-night film ended at midnight. Half the audience went home. The others went backstage for booze, slot machines and – believe it or not – a porno film on a smaller screen. It was that real sick stuff! How can I tell Thelma about this? She'll have a stroke! I checked vehicle tags in the parking lot. Mostly from Bixby County.'

Twenty-two

As someone who liked publicity, Thelma was getting more than her share. 'Thackeray' had become a buzzword among headline writers in Moose County. Her opening of the Film Club and her magnanimous loan of the opera house to an animal-rescue cause put her in the limelight, but not all the news was good.

On Monday the banner headline read: 24 WORKS OF ART DROWNED IN DITCH. Dick Thackeray Cited for Reckless Driving.

On Tuesday the news was better but less dramatic: LOST CHURCH FOUND IN FOREST. Thackerays Buried in Graveyard of Tiny Log Chapel.

There was no name-dropping on Wednesday: PUBLIC REST ROOMS SLATED FOR DOWNTOWN PICKAX. Merchants and

Shoppers Applaud Town Council's Decision.

On Thursday morning Bushy stopped at the barn on the way to cover an assignment for the paper. 'The newsroom is hot this morning. Thought you'd want to know. It ties in with the bad news I had to report to Thelma. If she didn't have a stroke then, she'll have one when she reads today's headline.'

Thursday's headline read: INDECENT EXPOSURE LANDS 3 IN JAIL. Members of Film Club Nabbed While Strip-Dancing in Parking Lot.

As soon as papers were delivered to the library, Polly phoned Qwilleran. 'That poor woman! My heart bleeds for her! But I can't think of anything we can do.'

He was silent.

'Qwill, did you hear what I said?'

'I'm thinking . . . Thelma's a trouper! She'll drink a lot of cocoa and sit in her Pyramid and the club will continue as if nothing had happened.'

Later, to confirm his prediction, he phoned the club and heard a recorded message:

'Seats for tonight's showing of *Anna Christie* featuring Garbo are sold out. If you want to make a reservation for future shows, press one. Next week's billing: *City Lights* (1931). Charlie Chaplin's last completely silent film.'

It wasn't until Friday, however, that Qwilleran's low blood pressure started to rise. His friends at the *Something* were always eager to tip him off. And in this case they knew he had a special interest in Thelma Thackeray.

First Bushy phoned from his van. 'One of the guys in

the lab was sent out to get a shot of the entrance of the Film Club. They say it's closed until further notice.'

Roger MacGillivray, a longtime friend, phoned Qwilleran on the way to the police station. 'There's been a shooting at the club,' he said.

And the managing editor phoned and said, 'Qwill, how fast can you get your copy in? We've got an early deadline. There's been a murder.'

The Friday headline read: MANAGER OF FILM CLUB SHOT DURING BURGLARY. Dick Thackeray's Body Found by Janitors. Safe Cracked.

Qwilleran was taken aback – not because of the murder; after all, Dick moved in questionable circles. What daunted him was Koko's behavior in the middle of the night – not howling . . . more like . . . crowing! It had been the kind of strident, affirmative communication that could now be interpreted as 'I told you so!' . . . That cat! At the time, when Qwilleran was wakened so rudely, he thought Koko had swallowed something unacceptable and he would upchuck in some unacceptable place. But now . . . the incident assumed new meaning.

Qwilleran sent Thelma flowers and a note of consolation, resisting the urge to say 'Good riddance!' When he phoned Simmons in California, the security man said, 'Well, that solves the security problem, doesn't it? Too bad she won't continue it and hire a manager . . . I wouldn't mind handling it myself. I'd enjoy working for her again.'

Then there was another call from Bushy. 'Well how

about it, Qwill? I feel sorry for Thelma. This really messes up her plans, doesn't it? I wish there was something I could do. But I don't want to step out of line.'

'How about taking her and Janice for a cruise Sunday afternoon. It's peaceful out on the lake. It might be therapeutic. Call Janice and sound her out. I think she'll agree.'

As for the author of the 'Qwill Pen,' he had never really wanted to write a biography of Bud and Sis. But 'The Last of the Thackerays' would make a fascinating legend for *Short & Tall Tales*. He would have to work fast if he wanted to interview her in depth; she was, after all, eighty-two.

He was not fast enough. In Monday's newspaper there was a news bulletin important enough to warrant a remake of the front page. A black-bordered box focused attention on the sad news: 'Thelma Thackeray, 82, died peacefully in her sleep early this morning, at her home on Pleasant Street. She recently returned from a fifty-five-year career in Hollywood, CA, to found Thelma's Film Club. She was the last of the Moose County Thackerays. Obituary on Wednesday.'

Qwilleran subdued his urge to phone Janice for details, knowing she would be busy with helpful neighbors. Burgess Campbell, as the Duke of Pleasant Street, would be supervising the arrangements. Mavis Adams was Thelma's attorney. Celia and Pat O'Dell would be enormously helpful.

He was surprised, therefore, when Janice called him. 'May I drive over there, Qwill? I need your advice.'

Within a few minutes the green coupé pulled into the barnyard, and he went out to meet her. Besides her usual shoulder bag she was carrying one of Thelma's capacious satchel-bags of soft leather. It was bulging as if it contained a watermelon. He refrained from commenting.

'Let's sit in the library,' he said.

The old books that covered one wall of the fireplace cube from top to bottom made a comforting atmosphere for confidences.

'So many books!' she said.

'That's only half of them. The rest are in my studio . . . Now, how can I help you, Janice?'

'I don't know whether I did the right thing.'

'What did you do?' he asked in a kindly voice, although he was bristling with curiosity. 'Would you like a little fruit juice? A glass of wine?'

'Well . . . yes . . . I think I'd like a glass of wine.'

The white Zinfandel relaxed her, but Qwilleran continued to bristle.

'Thelma's always an early riser, and I knocked on her door to see if she'd like a cup of tea. She was still under the covers, but I got a sick feeling when I saw a liquor bottle on the bedside table – the bourbon that we bought for Mr Simmons. Thelma's always had chronic pancreatitis and was supposed to avoid stress and alcohol—'

'She's had plenty of stress lately,' Qwilleran interrupted.

'Dr Diane put "acute pancreatitis" on the death certificate.'

They were both silent for a while, Qwilleran remembering how Thelma had said, 'I have to be a very good girl.'

Janice was fidgeting and glancing at Thelma's handbag on the desk. 'There's something I want to tell you, Qwill . . . about what we did Thursday night. Or Friday morning, really. Thelma said she wanted me to drive her to the club at about two-thirty A.M., and she told me to take a nap and set the alarm clock for two o'clock. When we got there, a few cars were still in the lot, and we parked at the curb until they were all gone except Dick's loaner. He wrecked his old van, you know.'

'I well remember!'

'She told me to stay in the car, and when she came out a few minutes later, she was smiling, and her big handbag was stuffed full of something. She said, "All's well that ends well." One thing I had learned was not to ask questions. She was quite calm all weekend, sitting in her Pyramid and taking care of the Amazons. And Bushy invited us for a cruise on Sunday afternoon – not a party, just a quiet time on the water. I thought that was very sweet of him, and Thelma said it was just what she needed. We came home and she retired early, and the rest is kind of a blur.'

'You've handled everything very well, Janice.'

'Yes, but after the doctor had been at the house, I looked in Thelma's handbag, although I felt I was doing something wrong. She was a very private person, you know . . . It was full of money! Bundles of currency! And the little handgun that Mr Simmons insisted on giving her for our cross-country trip. She wanted to give it back to him when he was here, but he wouldn't take it . . . So then I went looking for the pocket tape-recorder he brought her as a gift. It was in the top drawer of her dresser.'

'Had she used it?'

'Yes,' Janice said with a frightened stare.

'Did you listen to what was recorded?'

'Yes. And that's why I'm here – to ask you what to do with these things of Thelma's.'

'Before I can advise you,' Qwilleran said solemnly, 'I'd better hear the tape.'

'Why, Auntie! What are you doing here at this hour? You should be home, getting your beauty sleep – not that you need it! You're beautiful – for your age!'

'Wipe that oily smile off your face, Dickie Bird, and explain who gave you permission to turn Thelma's Film Club into a gambling casino and porno gallery. Next, you'll be renting rooms by the hour!'

'Why, Auntie—!'

'Where's the silver tray you used to have here?'

'I never had a silver tray.'

'You're a liar as well as a thief! How much of that money you're counting goes in the club account and how much into your pocket? You're fired! As of now! I want you off the premises in half an hour. And my guest room is no longer at your disposal! You'll find your belongings in a box on the back porch.'

'You've got me all wrong!'

'Then tell me what you did with a hundred thousand dollars' worth of jewels that you took from your kidnapping accomplice after killing him on a country road in Bixby. And tell me what happened to your muddy hiking boots that you wore when you pushed your father over the cliff? Your own father who loved you so much and gave you everything you wanted! You had the unmitigated callousness to go home and notify the police that he hadn't come home to lunch! He was my brother! And I'm the only one who cares! . . . You . . . are a monster!'

'You're cracking up, Auntie!'

'Then you came out to Hollywood and put on your loving-nephew act until I changed my will and made you my sole heir . . . Well, I'm going to change it again! And you're not getting a penny!'

'You selfish old woman! You're not going to live long enough to change your will—'

'And you're not going to live long enough to inherit!'

(Two gunshots.)

(Click.)

When the tape ended, Qwilleran said firmly, 'Show everything to Mavis Adams as soon as possible. She knows the law, and Thelma was her client.'

'Did I do right, Qwill?'

'Yes, but you don't need to tell anyone that you brought it over here. Show everything to Mavis ... and don't worry. May I freshen your drink?'

'No, thanks. This is a big load off my mind. Now I want to go home and ... maybe try sitting in Thelma's Pyramid.'

'One question, Janice. Did Thelma have a chance to sign her new will?'

'Yes. She'd been working on it with Mavis, and was due to sign it Saturday morning. Mavis brought it to the house. Thelma left everything to a foundation that will reestablish the Thackeray Clinic as a memorial to her dear Bud.'

There were two thumps in the kitchen, as Koko jumped down from the top of the refrigerator.

Qwilleran thought, He's been listening to this whole scenario! ... Did he recognize Dick's voice on the tape? NO! He's never met Smiley; he's just sensed his evil presence.

Koko stared pointedly at his empty plate under the kitchen table, and Qwilleran gave him a little something.

Qwilleran himself had a dish of ice cream. Then he sprawled in his big chair to think. He could imagine Simmons's reaction to the drama. The tape recorder had been an inspired idea.

When Thelma confronted her nephew and he said she wouldn't live long enough to change her will, she knew there was a gun in the desk drawer and she had told Simmons about it.

Did Thelma know all along that Dick was no good? It was too bad that Simmons had to leave so soon. Qwilleran would have enjoyed telling him of Koko's investigative exploits.

It was a curious fact that lawmen were the only ones who accepted Koko's peculiar talents. There had been Lieutenant Hames, Down Below, and there was Brodie, the Pickax police chief. Qwilleran had a hunch that Simmons would have been a third. Too late now.

Koko knew the man was thinking about him. The cat was sitting on a nearby lamp table, squeezing his eyes. He also rubbed his chin on the bottom edge of the lampshade. It was a gesture that seemed to give him a catly thrill. Knocking books off a shelf was another of Koko's quirks, although it sometimes appeared as if there might be a method in his madness.

In the last two or three weeks he had shown a fondness for books with 'Richard' in the title. And he had exhibited a sudden interest in Robert Louis Stevenson. In quick succession he had dislodged *A Child's Garden of Verses* and *Travels with a Donkey* and *Dr Jekyll and Mr Hyde*. Now, Qwilleran felt a prickling sensation on his upper lip. He thought, Could it be that Koko was looking for *Kidnapped*? It was the only Stevenson favorite not on the shelf. The notion, of course, was preposterous. And yet . . .

Qwilleran thought, If the kidnapping connection is preposterous, how about the catfit he staged when we played *The Gambler*? We thought it was Prokofiev's music he didn't like. More likely he was trying to tell us something about Thelma's nephew... Koko knows a skunk when he smells one!

'Yoww-ow-ow!' Koko declaimed impatiently and rubbed the lampshade once more.

It was then that Qwilleran noticed an envelope on the table addressed simply to 'Qwill.' It was large and square and ivory colored, and Qwilleran was not surprised to find the initials 'T.T.' embossed on the flap. Obviously, Janice had left it there.

Inside there was a sheet of blank white paper.

Dubiously and reluctantly and even furtively, Qwilleran removed the lampshade and passed the paper back and forth over the hot lamp bulbs.

Gradually the message materialized printed in large block letters: THANKS, DUCKY, FOR EVERYTHING.

And where had Koko gone? He was under the kitchen table staring at his empty plate – the one on the right.

Yum Yum sat huddled on her brisket, guarding her one-and-only treasure, her silver thimble.

The Cat who Blew the Whistle

Lilian Jackson Braun

Jim Qwilleran and his Siamese sleuths are back in another crime-busting adventure.

When the residents of Moose County, including the reclusive millionaire, Jim Qwilleran, board the old steam locomotive – the celebrated Engine No. 9 – on its inaugural journey, little do they know that this first trip will also be the last ...

By next morning, Qwill discovers that the affluent owner of Engine No. 9, Floyd Trevelyn, has disappeared, along with his glamorous secretary and millions of dollars belonging to Moose County investors.

While the search is on for the fugitive, Qwill stays in Pickax and probes another mystery – why has Koko developed a sudden interest in certain works of literature and started to steal black pens?

0 7472 4815 X

headline

The Cat Who Played Brahms

Lilian Jackson Braun

Is it just a case of summertime blues or a full-blown career crisis? Newspaper reporter Jim Qwilleran isn't sure, but he's hoping a few days in the country will help him sort out his life.

With cats Koko and Yum Yum for company, Qwilleran heads for a cabin owned by a long-time family friend, 'Aunt Fanny'. But from the moment he arrives, things turn strange. Eerie footsteps cross the roof at midnight. Local townsfolk become oddly secretive. And then, while fishing, Qwilleran hooks on to a murder mystery. Soon Qwilleran enters into a game of cat and mouse with the killer, while Koko develops a sudden and uncanny fondness for classical music . . .

Qwilleran – a prize-winning reporter with a nose for crime. Koko – a Siamese cat with extraordinary talents and a flair for mystery. Yum Yum – a loveable Siamese adored by her two male companions. The most unlikely, most unusual, most delightful team in detective fiction!

0 7472 5036 7

headline

The Cat Who Smelled a Rat

Lilian Jackson Braun

As autumn draws to a close in Moose County, four hundred miles north of everywhere, Qwilleran and the rest of Pickax City are awaiting the annual snow storm which marks the official start of winter. But this year the storm is particularly significant. After months without rain, brush fires are starting with alarming regularity and it is only a matter of time before one of them gets out of control.

But it is soon evident that the fires are following a pattern that defies any force of nature and when Edd's Editions, the much-loved bookstore, is destroyed in a clear case of arson, the inhabitants of Pickax are forced to accept that they are facing a very human enemy. Luckily for them all, it's not long before Qwilleran & Co begin to sniff out the rat responsible.

Qwilleran – a prize-winning reporter with a nose for crime. Koko – a Siamese cat with extraordinary talents and a flair for mystery. Yum Yum – a loveable Siamese adored by her two male companions. The most unlikely, most unusual, most delightful team in detective fiction!

0 7472 6505 4

headline